"By the time all that equipment clashes over the central Asian battlefield, the rocketing tempo of Peters's plot will captivate even the yellowest of bellies. . . ."

—ALA *Booklist*

"In a chilling followup to his hugely successful *Red Army*, Peters looks at a world 30 years in the future and sets a disturbing scenario. . . . Peters has outdone himself. . . ."

—*Muncie Star* (Indiana)

"THE WAR IN 2020 is an exciting, shoot-em-up war story. . . . The United States responds with its most technically sophisticated cavalry regiment, peopled by those colorful, three-dimensional military men whom Peters crafts so well."

—*Los Angeles Times*

"Relentlessly absorbing . . . harrowing . . . explosive. . . . Warn friend and family that once you begin reading, interruptions could prove fatal."

—*Flint Journal* (Michigan)

Books by Ralph Peters

Bravo Romeo
Red Army
The War in 2020

Published by POCKET BOOKS

Most Pocket Books are available at special quantity discounts for bulk purchases for sales promotions, premiums or fund raising. Special books or book excerpts can also be created to fit specific needs.

For details write the office of the Vice President of Special Markets, Pocket Books, 1230 Avenue of the Americas, New York, New York 10020.

RALPH PETERS

THE WAR IN 2020

POCKET STAR BOOKS

New York   London   Toronto   Sydney   Tokyo   Singapore

A Pocket Star Book published by
POCKET BOOKS, a division of Simon & Schuster Inc.
1230 Avenue of the Americas, New York, NY 10020

ISBN: 0-671-75172-7

First Pocket Books paperback printing January 1992

10 9 8 7 6 5 4 3 2 1

POCKET STAR BOOKS and colophon are registered trademarks of Simon & Schuster Inc.

Printed in the U.S.A.

One watches things that make one sick at heart.
This is the law: No gain without a loss,
and Heaven hurts fair women for sheer spite.

—*The Tale of Kieu*
from the Vietnamese

Prologue

In the year of our Lord 2005, the United States made a terrible mistake. In the course of yet another internal crisis in post-Mobutu Zaire, South Africa had seized extensive mineral-laden tracts in Shaba Province. Bound by half-forgotten treaties, ignorant of the details of the local situation, and anxious to convince a doubting world of our continued importance as a superpower, we deployed the XVIII Airborne Corps to Kinshasa. The operation proved awkward, and slow. The Army had been gutted during the euphoric reductions of the nineties, when standing ground forces had come to seem as anachronistic as they were extravagant. But we still had faith in ourselves.

The XVIII Airborne Corps limped onto a sick continent. Africa had been largely written off by the solvent nations of the world. Unable to feed its people, unable to pay its bills, and annoyingly incapable of governing itself decently, Africa had nothing more to offer than occasional troughs of minerals and dwindling animal herds that had come to seem far more valuable to the civilized world than the continent's emaciated millions. The continent was dying. First, the AIDS pandemic had taken the joy out of photo safaris, then, shortly after the turn of the century, a new plague had begun to stray out of the African bush.

Such considerations did not bind Americans. We believed we heard the slightly off-key call of duty, and we sent the best we had. Wheezing from the effort, our forces raised the flag in the heat of a country for which they were ill-equipped, ill-trained, and about which they were blithely *ill-informed. But none of this seemed to matter. The Americans had landed, and, really, the deployment hardly seemed more than a formality to the men who made the decisions.*

No one seriously believed the South Africans would fight.

PART I

The Journey

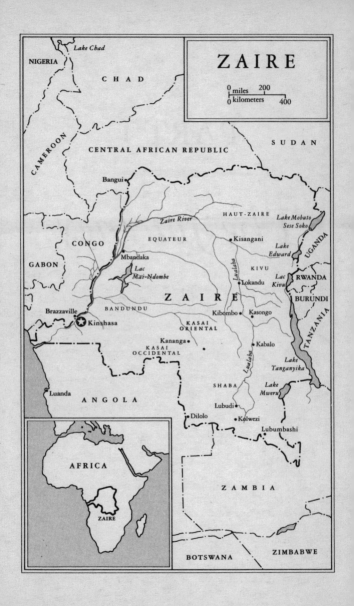

1

Africa
2005

YOU CAME IN OVER THE GRASSLANDS, WITH ANIMALS bolting then turning again and again beneath the sound and shadow of the metal birds. It was punishingly hot in your flight suit and helmet, and you already had a water debt, but at least the patrols were a break from the monotony of life at the bivouac site. You came in over the light brown sea of the grasslands, skimming over islands of twisted shrubs, and the distant flight controller's voice tinned sleepily in your earphones. Then the country began to rise. Just slightly. You could see the hills of mining waste from a long way out, and you hardly bothered to glance at the controls. You wanted to fly. You always wanted to fly. It was the only life in the languid days. But now, with the squadron's African home in sight, a duller side of you was anxious to get back down on the ground.

You patterned in around the tallest waste bank, and the metal roofs of the mining complex mirrored the high sun of southern Zaire. Shaba Province, alias Katanga. You cursed and turned your head slightly. The glare quit, leaving you a view of military tentage and perfect rows of helicopters at rest in the dappled shade of the camouflage nets. A red and white cavalry guidon stirred to life atop the only two-story building in the settlement, and the dust began to rise toward you. A hatless soldier in aviator sunglasses, his mouth and nose protected by an olive drab bandanna, raised his arms. Come to Papa. Africa disappeared in a brown storm.

You were home. Walking off the flight stiffness amid the familiar fixtures of a field site anywhere in the world: fuelers and lines, warning markers, portable guide lights, wind streamers, GP-medium tents with their sides rolled up to show neatly ranked cots with sleeping bags rolled or canoed, soldiers in T-shirts, dog tags hanging like macho jewelry. The torn brown envelopes of field rations. Texan heat. No war.

The unit had quickly settled into a normal field routine. Regular patrols flew south, inspecting the emptiness. There was an unmistakable feeling of disappointment among the men who had been primed for combat, but there was relief, as well. Soldiers cursed the weather, the godforsaken landscape, the insects and meandering snakes, the rations, and the brass who never knew what was going on and never got anything right. Some swore that the U.S. Army was on the wrong side again, that the Zaireans were worthless motherfuckers. The few books that had been tossed into rucksacks or kit bags for the trip were read, passed around, reread.

"Hey, George," a fellow captain called, passing down the lines of cots, "what the hell're you reading now?"

Taylor held up the cover of the paperback so his friend could see.

"That some kind of horror novel, like?"

"Not exactly," Taylor answered, lazy on his bunk.

"Heart of Darkness." The man laughed. "Sounds like one of my old girlfriends. You want a beer, George?"

"Got one."

The captain smiled goodnaturedly. "Captain George Taylor, troop commander. The guy who has everything." And he headed off toward the field canteen.

Taylor and his comrades spent their nonflying hours getting magnificent suntans and listening to the English-language South African radio station that broadcast the most powerful signal in the region and played the best music. The female disc jockeys with their fantasy-inspiring off-British accents never said a word about crisis or plague or their own troop deployments, but as the situation seemed to normalize, they began dedicating songs to the "lonely GIs up north." Everyone's favorite announcer was a woman named Marnie Whitewater, whom the troops quickly renamed Marnie Skullfucker. When there were no missions to fly and the sun made it too hot to remain under the canvas, Taylor loved to lie in a jerry-rigged hammock with a can of beer chilling a circle on his stomach muscles, browning his skin for the girls back home and listening to the teasing radio voice. He knew she had to be blonde. And morally unsalvageable.

There was no war. Only the sun, boredom, and bad food. Taylor's unit had not been stricken by Runciman's disease, and the reports that filtered down through the staff of mounting RD casualties closer in to Kolwezi or back in Kinshasa held little reality for the aviators in their isolated cocoon. It was all somebody else's nightmare, less important than speculating about how long it might be before they all went home. They argued about whether or not there had ever been elephants in this part of Africa, and bored young pilots broke flight discipline in their efforts to take snapshots of the lesser wildlife they encountered on patrol. Occasionally, Taylor would get a flash that these long, hot days were idyllic, paradise before the fall. But his inspirations never lasted long, and most of the time he simply felt weighed down by the empty, uncomfortable drudgery of it all.

Once, he flew over a village where corpses lay at random intervals in the dirt street, bloating in the sun. *Plague*. His hands jerked at the controls. But the effect was ultimately no more than that of watching a troubling film clip. He simply banked his helicopter away, rising into the clean blue sky.

The last morning seemed especially clear, and the air still had a freshness to it when they took off. The mission was as routine as could be. Patrol south along the Lualaba River trace toward Zambia. No wild-assed flying. The squadron commander had delivered a stern lecture to all of the pilots the day before, after a lieutenant had nearly crashed his Apache trying to get a photo of what he swore was a cheetah. So it was going to be a day of dull formation flying, with no reason to expect anything out of the ordinary. The squadron S-2 had even stopped delivering regular threat updates.

Taylor was in a down mood, and he was unusually snappish with his subordinates over the radio. He had received word that one of his classmates from Fort Rucker, a man who was almost a close friend, had died of Runciman's disease back at the 101st's main command post. The death was absurd, since Chuckie Moss had the least dangerous assignment imaginable—chauffeuring general officers around in the best-maintained helicopter in the division. Chuckie was recently married, a bit of a clown, and not yet thirty years old. For him to have died, when there had not even been any combat, seemed absurd and inadmissible.

Taylor's thoughts strayed in disorder. Remembering Chuckie on a wild weekend down in Panama City, Florida, his thoughts tumbled into bed with an old girlfriend. Joyce Whittaker. An absolute wild woman. He could remember Chuckie, beer in hand, laughing about the noise and declaring that old Joyce was a gal of considerably more energy than judgment. And he remembered Joyce's body glazed with sweat, her eyes closed, as the scrublands slipped away under the belly of his aircraft. The sunlight began to dazzle through his face shield, and he wriggled out of his survival vest in preparation for the impending heat.

They were barely ten minutes out of the field site when the radar on Taylor's bird milked out, its screen frothing with pale discolorations. Taylor assumed it was an equipment malfunction, since the new electronics on the A5 Apaches were finicky on the best of days, and the dust of the field site was hard on them.

"One-four, this is Niner-niner," Taylor called to the aircraft flying echelon right to his own. "My radar's crapping out. You've got sky watch."

"*This is One-four,*" a worried voice came through the headset. "I'm all milked out. What the hell's going on?"

Suddenly, the voice of an old chief warrant officer cut into the net from one of the trail birds:

"Goddamnit, we're being jammed."

Taylor realized instantly that the chief was right, and he felt stupid for missing the obvious, as though he had been half asleep. No one had expected hostile activity.

"All ponies, *all* ponies, open order. *Now*. Prepare for possible contact," Taylor commanded. Immediately, he could feel his troop's formation spread itself across the sky.

The radar screens remained useless. But no enemy appeared to the eye. Taylor wished he had a few scout aircraft out front, but the scout flights had been discontinued as unnecessary, since there was no real threat of hostile action.

"Sierra six-five, this is Mike niner-niner, over," Taylor called, trying to raise flight operations back at the field site.

Static.

"Si*err*a six-five, this is Mike niner-niner. *Flash traffic*. Over." Nothing. A low whining that might have been nothing more than engine bleed.

"Sierra—"

On the periphery of his field of vision, an intense flash replaced one of his helicopters in the sky. Lieutenant Rossi. In the wake of the flash, the distorted flying machine plummeted to earth as Taylor watched. The autorotation failed to work, and the ship dropped straight down and hit so hard that sections of the fuselage and subassemblies jumped away from the wreck, lofting back into the sky, as the frame disappeared in a cloud of fire.

Taylor's eyes dazzled, and the world seemed to crack into a mosaic. His voice continued to pursue a previous thought, "Sierra six-five . . ."

"Jesus Christ," a voice shouted over the troop's internal net. *"Jesus Christ."*

Taylor frantically scanned the horizon.

Nothing. Absolutely empty. Clear hot blue.

"All ponies. Take evasive action. Countermeasure suites *on."* The control panel reflected the anxious actions of his weapons officer, a new boy Taylor hardly knew. *"One-one,"* Taylor ordered, "break off and check the site for

survivors . . . break . . ." Taylor radioed the chief warrant officer in the trail bird. "One-three, what do you have back there? Somebody on our six?"

"Negative. Negative." The chief's voice was high-pitched with excitement. It was the first time in their year-long acquaintance that Taylor had heard the least emotion in the man's voice. "Niner-niner, that was a frontal hit. And there ain't no survivors. Rossi and Koch are dead meat, and we're going to need One-one if we get into a dogfight."

Taylor felt a surge of fury at this questioning of his authority. But, in a matter of seconds, he realized the chief was right.

He felt so helpless—there was no enemy to be seen, either in the air or on the ground.

"One-one, disregard previous instructions. Rejoin formation."

"Roger."

Apaches aren't supposed to crash like that, Taylor told himself. Apaches don't burn. Apaches don't break up. Apaches don't—

"Where the hell are they?" Taylor demanded of the microphone. "Does anybody see *any*thing?"

"Negative."

Negative, negative.

"One-four, can you see anything?"

"My eyes are fucked up."

"Somebody's got a goddamned laser out here. A *big* goddamned laser," the chief interrupted, his voice impassioned with the suddenness of the revelation. "That was a goddamned *laser* hit. I seen that shit out at White Sands."

Impossible. The South Africans did not have laser weaponry. Nobody had tactical lasers, except for a few specialized blinding devices. Nonlethal stuff. Killer lasers were for stationary space defense, strategic shit. No one had yet managed the power source miniaturization required to make the weapons tactically feasible.

Taylor felt lost in the big, empty sky. All he could think to do was to continue flying. Even though he felt very afraid, flight suit soaking with sweat and his skin rashed red and white. He wanted to turn and scoot for the safety of the field site. But that was not the way cavalrymen behaved.

He tried again to raise flight operations. "Sierra six-five, this is Mike niner-niner. Possible enemy contact, I say again—*possible enemy contact.*"

With no further warning, another of his aircraft flashed white and gold, then tumbled crazily out of the sky. This time, the Apache began to disintegrate while it was still in midair.

"*Down on the deck,*" he ordered his remaining helicopters. "Get right down on the goddamned grass." He hoped that he could hide his ships from the unseen enemy by flying absolute-minimum nap-of-the-earth. "Taking her down," he told his weapons officer. "Hold on."

He wanted to shoot back. To fire at something. He even had the urge to fire into the empty sky. Anything not to passively accept the fate of the two lost aircraft.

"*There they are,*" the old chief warrant officer called over the net. "*Two o'clock high.*"

When he looked up through the canopy, Taylor could barely make out the distant black specks on the horizon. His eyes hurt, tearing, reluctant to focus.

They were out of range. And they had already knocked down two of his birds.

He could feel his remaining crews waiting for his decision, the order that would decide all of their fates.

There were only two choices. Run . . . try to outrun them . . . or attack, closing the distance in the hope they could at least get off a few in-range shots.

"Sierra six-five, this is Mike niner-niner. *Confirmed enemy contact.* Two friendly ponies down. We are moving to attack."

He knew without doubt that his aircraft were outclassed. He had always had faith in the old Apache, with its reliable multipurpose missiles and its good old Gatling gun with the depleted uranium rounds. But he knew now that somebody had changed the rules, that he was little better off than if he had been mounted on a horse, with a saber and revolver.

"Chief," Taylor radioed, forgetting the call signs, "you

move wide to the right and fly cover. We're going straight for them. The evasion drills aren't worth shit. *Let's go, Bravo Troop.*" He watched the black dots growing unmistakably larger. "Let's get those bastards."

But there was already little left of Bravo Troop. Another flash of light punched his wingman into the baked earth. The rotors slashed at the scrub, catapulting the fuselage wildly into the sky, then slamming it down to earth.

The chief warrant officer ignored the orders Taylor had given him, climbing fast toward the enemy, head-on, firing off a missile at a still hopeless range, as though to frighten the enemy away by a display of ferocity.

Before Taylor's ship could climb into the sky, an unseen blow sent it spinning brokenly against the rotors, and, although Taylor could still feel his hands on the controls, his eyes saw only shimmering ivory. In the instant before the aircraft skidded into the brush, Taylor screamed at his weapons officer:

"Fire, goddamnit, fire."

He did not know whether the gunner could make out any targets, whether he could see at all, whether he was still alive. Taylor just knew that he did not want to die without hitting back, and the last thing he felt before the force of the crash knocked him unconscious was a fury as big as the sky itself.

No one had really expected the South Africans to fight. It had all appeared to be a matter of calculated risks, of posturing, blustering, of marching up and down. The wisdom in Washington was that the South Africans were just calling the world's bluff. Figuring that the Europeans had neither the will nor the forces to do much, and that the United States would not have the guts to send troops. Washington had confidently dispatched the XVIII Airborne Corps, certain that it was all just a matter of flexing muscles. The intel boys knew that the South Africans had an arrangement with Japan to put the latest generation of Japanese military equipment through its paces. But that was assumed to be merely a sales showcase. And the one Toshiba gunship that the U.S. technical intelligence community had gotten its hands on showed some interesting evolutionary features, but nothing that was likely to change the overall equation on the battlefield. In retrospect, it became obvious that the United States had been duped with a dummy model, stripped of its key systems. But no one had suspected anything before the intervention.

The South Africans had allowed the laborious shuttling in and out of Kinshasa required to deploy the barely mobile U.S. corps. And the U.S. Army had done its best, scrambling at the last moment to beef up the corps with troops from other units stationed throughout the country, juggling to avoid calling up Reserve units. The defense cuts and troop reductions of the nineties and the starvation budgets of the turn of the century had left even those formations at the highest readiness level short of everything from medics and linguists to ammunition and spare parts. The deployment was chaotic, with Air Force transports unable to fly, while the Air Force nonetheless insisted on deploying B-2 bombers to Kinshasa, even though no one could define a mission for them. The Navy sent two carrier battle groups, but neither jets nor missiles nor guns proved targetable against an enemy who lay dispersed and out of range in the heart of Africa. No one really expected a fight, of course, and everyone wanted to be on the scene. Military Intelligence threw up its hands. The collection systems worked, more or less. But there were no analysts capable of interpreting the data, since the Army had moved to maximum automation—and the automated systems were not programmed for so unexpected a contingency as a deployment to an African backwater. But the shortage of medical personnel trained for catastrophe soon proved the greatest deficiency.

With each passing day, the decision makers grew more convinced that the South Africans would never fight. It became a joke in Washington, if less so on the ground in Kinshasa, where confusion, shortages, and Murphy's Law kept attention focused on matters closer at hand. Still, even the corps command group reasoned that, had the South Africans wanted to put up a fight, their only chance would have been to strike while the U.S. was establishing its initial airhead—not after the entire corps was on the ground.

At first the South Africans had remained down in Shaba Province, noncommittal, while the United States threatened to deploy forward into the province itself. For a time the two sides simply postured, armies of observation, since no one on the U.S. side had quite figured out how to attack across half a continent where the road and rail network was either broken-down or nonexistent.

Slowly the XVIII Airborne Corps began to feel its way forward, attempting to threaten without actually forcing a confrontation at the tactical level. But there was an increasing sense of urgency now. For a new and terrible enemy had appeared.

By the time of the Zaire intervention, the AIDS epidemic was on the wane. Wide stretches of Africa had virtually been depopulated, since the effective vaccines were far too expensive for use on the indigenous populations. But the Western world felt safe, and even in Africa, the disease appeared to be sputtering out. Only Brazil continued to host an epidemic of crisis proportions, while the rest of South America appeared to have the situation reasonably under control. Few had paid serious attention to the reports of a new epidemic ravaging the surviving populations of backcountry Uganda and Tanzania, and even the World Health Organization at first thought they were simply seeing a virulent cholera outbreak. The difficulties in assessing the extent of the situation were compounded by the reluctance of image-conscious African nations to admit the extent of the problem in their hinterlands. The disease reached Mozambique. International health officials began to tally the losses in health-care workers and found that the rate of fatalities was unprecedented. Soon, much of East Africa seemed to be dying.

The rest of the world remained unmoved. International quarantines were imposed on the stricken nations. The epidemic remained just one more African problem.

In Uganda and Kenya the people called the disease Ashburn fever, because of the burnlike scars it left on the skin of those lucky enough to survive. But it soon acquired a civilized name, when Sir Phillip Runciman isolated the startlingly new virus in a laboratory in Mombasa. Runciman's disease managed to combine viral potency and effects with symptoms normally associated with bacterial infections. Initial signs did resemble cholera, with rapid depletion of bodily fluids through diarrhea and vomiting, but there was an accompanying assault on the nervous system that appeared completely new. The disease quickly passed into a stage where the skin withered and died in discolored patches, while, in the worst cases, the brain began to separate, causing extreme pain, and, in most cases, death. Victims fell into three broad categories— fatalities, which ran as high as eighty-five percent without treatment, survivors with permanent brain damage and various degrees of loss of control over basic bodily functions, and the lucky ones, who were merely disfigured.

The issue of Runciman's disease had come up during the hasty planning phases of the deployment to Zaire, as one of the many matters of concern to the Joint Chiefs of Staff. But there was a sense in the government of no time to lose; there were fears of yet another countercoup in Kinshasa, which might put a legitimate face on the South African occupation of Shaba. And the Department of State assured the President and the National Security Council that the ruling Sublime Democracy Party in Zaire had given guarantees that there was no evidence whatsoever of Runciman's disease along the middle or lower reaches of the Zaire—or Congo—River or in southern Zaire. There was certainly none in Shaba Province.

The U.S. ambassador to Zaire sent a supporting cable stressing that both the image and national interests of the United States were irrevocably at stake and that, although, frankly, there were some cases of Runciman's disease reported in the backcountry, the disease did not present an immediate threat to U.S. personnel, given sensible precautions.

The U.S. forces began their deployment.

The Department of State had worked out a special arrangement with the government of Zaire to "facilitate the efficient and nondestabilizing deployment of U.S. forces." Those U.S. forces were to remain confined to the general vicinity of the Kinshasa airport until they further deployed southeast to Shaba Province. A State Department spokesman told the press that the agreement was designed to prevent the appearance of some sort of American invasion of Zaire, of an unacceptable level of interference in the nation's internal affairs. But it did not take the arriving U.S. troops long to discover the real reason for the restriction.

The slums of Kinshasa were haunted with plague. The situation was so bad that, when ordered to dispose of the bodies of the victims of Runciman's disease, the Zairean military had mutinied. The back streets of the capital recalled the depths of the Middle Ages.

The U.S. Army command group on the ground immediately reported the situation. But the fundamental sense of mission, of commitment, did not waver. With a "can-do" attitude the XVIII Airborne Corps and the Air Force's Forward Command, Africa, instituted rigid quarantine procedures. Yet, exceptions had to be made. U.S. commanders and planners had to meet with their Zairean counterparts, U.S. and local air controllers had to work side by side, waste had to be disposed of beyond the confines of the airport, and senior officers had social responsibilities that could not be ignored without deeply offending local sensibilities.

By the time the U.S. Army began its wheezing deployment to the disputed area downcountry, it had become apparent that Runciman's disease—or RD, as the soldiers had quickly renamed it—was not strictly a disease of the African poor.

Still, operations seemed to go well enough. The Second Brigade of the 82nd Airborne Division conducted a flawless combat jump into the grasslands near Kolwezi, the heart of Shaba Province. They found the South Africans had abandoned the town, after setting it ablaze. Quickly, the paratroopers secured a sizable airhead. And the next wave of transports began to land. The South Africans made no move to interfere. They could not even be located. It appeared that they had backed down, evacuating the province.

The forward deployment of U.S. forces continued, having become little more than a strenuous logistics exercise. On the scene in Shaba, at corps headquarters in Kinshasa, and in Washington there was jubilation. It was decided that U.S. forces would remain on the scene just long enough to tidy things up and to make our unequivocable support of the present Zairean government clear to all interested parties.

Taylor cried out in pain as he regained consciousness. There was a hammering at the back of his skull that made it painful to breathe, painful to move, painful to keep still. His eyes felt as though he had been punched with pepper-coated fists, and his head felt too large for the flight helmet clamped around it. Then he realized that his back ached deeply, as well, commanding him not to move.

But he did move. Jumping madly at the thought that the aircraft must be on fire. He tore at the safety harness, screaming, hurling himself out of the cockpit in a panic, a frightened child. His pant leg caught on the frame, and he fell facedown, the force of his weight sending a shudder through the remnants of the airframe. He tore wildly at his leg, struggling to free himself, almost dragging the wreck behind him until the fabric of his flight suit gave way, freeing his calf to cut itself against the sharp metal. The world seemed to have no end of pain in store for him, and he curled into himself, whimpering, imagining that he was screaming, still waiting to die.

There was no fire. The tattered aircraft frame sat erectly in the churned grassland, its Gatling gun loose as a hang-nail and its snout nuzzled against a leathery dwarf of a tree. The tail section was missing, and the rotors looked like broken fingers. The multipurpose missiles were gone, perhaps fired off in the last moment, or stripped away as the machine skidded through the undergrowth. Taylor was so amazed that he was alive, unburned, and that his bird, at least, had held together the way it was supposed to, that it took him a long moment to remember the weapons officer.

None of it had been the way it was supposed to be. You were supposed to outfly and outfight the enemy. You were supposed to fly home in triumph. And if your heroics and sacrifice caused you to crash, the first thing you were to do was to think of your comrade. But Taylor had only been able to think of his own pain, his own fear, overwhelmed by a terror of burning alive.

The weapons officer sat slumped in his subcompartment. Not moving. As still as the inert fuselage.

A young warrant officer, hardly out of flight school. When asked why he had taken the most inexperienced man in the troop to be his gunner, Taylor always replied that it was his responsibility to train the man properly. But he also wanted someone who was malleable, who would do as he was told. Not some cranky old bastard who had seen a dozen troop commanders come and go.

Taylor hardly knew the man. As the troop commander, he always kept a bit of distance from the others, and the leadership technique was compounded by Taylor's essentially private nature. Now, dizzy and sick, with his eyes tricking out of focus, he looked up from the ground at the slumped figure in the aircraft, shocked at the summary of his failures.

This was not the way it was supposed to be. He had done nothing correctly, failing in everything. His troop lay squandered across the wastes, and the man for whom Taylor bore the most immediate responsibility had lain dead or unconscious or unable to move while his superior, the swaggering cavalry captain, had rescued himself without a thought for any other living thing. It was not the way it was supposed to be.

At the same time, Taylor could not suppress a physical joy, inexplicably akin to sex, at the knowledge that he was really alive, that he had *survived*.

He lifted himself up, half cripple, half crab, and began tugging and slapping the cockpit. The frame was bent, locking itself shut. Finally, Taylor had to smash it with a rock. All the while, his gunner's only movement was a slight shudder of the helmet and torso in response to the waves of energy Taylor's clumsiness sent through the machine.

"Ben?"

Nothing.

"Ben? Are you all right?"

The gunner did not respond. But Taylor's eyes had acquired enough focus to see that the man was still breathing, however faintly.

A few dark stains decorated the chest of the gunner's flight suit, and, as Taylor watched, a large fly settled near the gunner's name tag.

"Ben?" Taylor unfastened the man's oversize helmet, lifting it off, trying not to hurt him.

As the clam-shaped sides of the helmet cleared the gunner's temples, the man's head fell awkwardly to the side.

His neck was broken. So badly that he should have been dead. Yet, now, at last, he moaned.

"Oh, God," Taylor told him, unsure what to do or say. "Oh, God, I'm sorry. I didn't mean to hurt you. Oh, God."

The man's eyes didn't open. But he moaned again, and Taylor could not tell whether it was from sheer pain or in response to his voice.

"Ben? Can you hear me? Can you understand?" Taylor was weeping in shame, failure, frustration. "I can't get you out of there. Do you understand me? You've got to stay strapped in. I can't move you. Do you . . ."

Another fly settled on the gunner's face, strolling down a cheek to the dried blood painted under the man's nose. Taylor flicked at it, careful not to touch the head, not to do any more damage than he had already done. Looking at the caked blood, Taylor realized that they must have been sitting there for hours before he himself had come to.

Where were the rescue aircraft? The world was utterly silent.

The gunner made a sound that was more like that of a badly wounded animal than of a human being. Then without warning, he spoke one distinct word:

"Water."

The hopelessness of it all made Taylor begin to cry again. He could find no trace in himself now of the superpilot, the fearless cavalryman.

"Ben . . . for God's sake . . . you can't drink. I can't give you anything. You mustn't move your head."

The gunner moaned. There was still no evidence of genuine consciousness in the sound. The single word might have been an eruption out of a coma's dream.

19

"Please . . . water."

Periodically, throughout the afternoon and evening, the gunner would call for water, or mumble the word "drink." His eyes never opened. Taylor rigged a bit of shade for the man out of scraps, but there was no practical way to reduce the heat in the narrow cockpit. Taylor tried to fan his broken companion, but the effort was so obviously ineffectual it became ridiculous. Soon, he settled himself into the meager shade on the side of the wreck away from the sun, flare pistol ready to signal at the first sound of search helicopters. He tried to be stingy with the emergency water supply, but it was hard. He grew thirstier. Yet, invariably, after he allowed himself a taste of the sour wetness, the gunner would begin calling for water, as though he were watching as Taylor drank, accusing him of drinking his share too. Occasionally, Taylor would get up and chase the flies away from the injured man's face and hands. But they soon returned. The gunner's lips were already swollen and oozing.

In the night, the younger man's voice woke Taylor. The sound was a horrible rasp. But the man did not beg for a drink now. He spoke to a third person:

"Can't make me go off there. I won't do it. *No. I'm not . . . going off of there . . .*" Then he moaned back into his dream.

Taylor made one of his periodic attempts to bully the radio to life. But there was nothing. And the emergency transponder had gone astray somewhere in the course of the crash landing. He was afraid to light a fire, afraid that the wrong party might see it, afraid that it would attract animals rather than keep them at bay. He found it impossible to go back to sleep after the gunner's ravings had awakened him. All of his body seemed to hurt. But, far worse, he seemed to be thinking very clearly now. He realized that, although he wanted the gunner to survive, wanted it badly, he would unhesitatingly choose his own survival over that of the other man, if a choice had to be made. He had always imagined himself to be selfless, ready for sacrifice. But now it was very clear to him that he wanted, above all, to live, and that his own life was more important to him than was the life of any other man. His year of service in Colombia, during the drug-war deployment, had not truly tested him. Beyond occasional small-arms fire from the jungle or a hilltop, the greatest enemy had been boredom, and he had imagined himself to be fearless, a real stud. But the captain's bars on his shoulders, all of the words he had spoken in dozens of ceremonies, his cherished vision of himself . . . it was all a joke. In his moment of responsibility, he had failed, and there was no rationalizing it away. Even now, if he could have chosen to be in the warm, safe bed of any of a dozen girlfriends instead of here pretending to nurse the injured weapons officer, he would have made his decision unhesitatingly. Sitting afraid in the African night, under a painfully clear sky, he found that he had never known himself at all in his twenty-nine years. The man in the mirror had been a dressed-up doll.

A sharp new pain woke him from his doze, and, in the morning light, he could just make out the ants scouting over his body, feeding on his torn calf. He jumped up, slapping at himself in fresh terror. He danced wildly, smashing at the tiny creatures with his fists, scraping at his ankles and boots, tearing at the zipper lines of his flight suit as he felt the bites moving along his legs.

After stripping himself half-naked, he won his battle. Gasping and shaking, he went to check on the weapons officer.

The man's face was covered with ants. The eyes were open, their blinking the only sign of resistance against the swarm. The pupils never moved, staring straight ahead at the wrecked console. But they were unmistakably alive. Sentient.

"No," Taylor screamed. He tried to be gentle in his frenzy, scooping away the copper-colored ants. But he felt as maddened as if they were plundering his own face.

Despite his best efforts, the gunner's head shifted on its skewed axis, and the man moaned. Then the eyes moved, staring up at Taylor with perfect clarity from a face swollen so badly it was almost unrecognizable.

"It's no good, sir," the gunner whispered, his voice incredibly calm. "They're all over me. I can feel them." He paused, as though he were merely discussing a minor disappointment. "I was just afraid you were gone. I thought you were mad because I didn't fire."

Taylor carefully undid the zipper in the front of the man's flight suit. As he pulled it down, ants began to spill down the teeth onto the outer fabric. The cockpit floor, the man's boots were invisible under a coppery mass.

"Please give me something to drink."

Taylor could feel the ants working at his own ankles again.

"Just a drink."

"Ben . . . for God's sake . . . if I . . ."

"I know . . ." the gunner said. Tears were seeping out of his swollen eyes now. "It doesn't matter. I want to drink."

Taylor hastened to fetch the double canteen.

"Ben . . ."

The gunner closed his eyes. "Can't talk . . ." he said. He seemed to be clenching himself against an unimaginable pain.

As gently as he could, Taylor put the canteen to the man's lips. But the mouth was already dead. He carefully tipped the water as ants began crawling up over his own hands.

With a jerk, the gunner gagged. His head lolled forward, throat gurgling, unable to accept the water.

Taylor almost dropped the canteen. But the self-preservation instinct in him was still too strong. He pulled back, spilling only a little of the water. With ants chewing fire into his hands and forearms, he carefully screwed the cap tight. Then he drew his pistol and shot his weapons officer through the forehead.

The map was useless at first, since the landscape was all the same, and he simply followed the compass. North. Flying above the earth, it had been easy to find beauty in the rugged grasslands and bush, but now, on foot, the country was a monotonous nightmare of heat, thorns, vermin, and snakes. It took him a full day of steady, pained walking before the waste hills of the mining complex swelled up in the distance. Then his water ran out. Maddeningly, the waste hills refused to grow larger, and the bush clutched at him, as if determined to hold him back. His flight suit shredded away from his arms, and sweat burned down over his opened flesh. In panic, he fired his pistol at a rearing snake that appeared immediately in front of him. He began to shake, and to dream. In his lucid moments he was uncertain whether he was suffering from fear or dehydration. He forced himself to focus on his goal, to remain focused, and he refused to consider the possibility that he might finally reach his squadron's field site only to find it evacuated. He thought about water and about safe rest in a place where nature's wretchedness would not crawl over him as he slept.

As he finally approached the bivouac site in the twilight, he scanned desperately for signs of life. He had not seen a single helicopter in flight. No vehicles stirred the dust along the portage roads. Crazily, he walked faster, almost running, staggering, his damaged back stiff, as though the spine had been fused into a single piece.

Surely, they would not have left him behind.

Water.

Rest.

He trotted dizzily around the spur of waste that shielded the field site from view.

And he staggered as though punched hard in the chest. Then he sat down in the dirt, staring.

The support site had been turned into a blackened scrapyard. Wrecked helicopters and vehicles sat in jagged repose amid shredded tentage and camouflage netting.

They had not heard his broadcast warnings. Or they had not reacted in time. Or they had been caught out by the same technological imbalance that had swept his troop from the sky.

Eventually he picked himself up, dizzy, and wandered about the ruins of his army. Not everything had been destroyed. Vehicles, a field kitchen, miscellaneous field gear, even a precious water buffalo had simply been left behind. No bodies, though. In the American tradition, the survivors who had pulled out had taken their wounded and their dead. But precious little else. Atop the two-story administration building, a red and white cavalry pennant hung limply from its pole, forgotten.

Taylor realized that it must have been very bad. But he could not quite feel sympathy for them, or outrage. He simply felt sick, with all the self-focus illness brings. He drank water too quickly from the tap of the water buffalo, then let the liquid stream over his head. He could tell from the pain the coolness produced that he was badly sunburned. But it seemed so minor a problem that he wasted no further thought on it. He wanted to rest.

The African darkness fell with the swiftness of a heavy curtain released from above, and Taylor stumbled through the litter of the administrative building up onto the flat roof where the cavalry guidon hung. He hoped that no creatures would pester him there. He had degenerated into a childish terror of all small crawling things, even of flies. He felt as though he had been overloaded with nature's horrors, and he wanted only to be left in peace for a little while.

The sun woke him. He jerked up from the concrete bed of the roof. *Helicopters*. He heard helicopters. But, even as he struggled to his feet to search the sky, he realized that the sound was only the buzzing of flies.

His legs were very weak, and he had to go down the stairs carefully. He drank more water, tasting it now, sour and warm. Stacks of ration cartons had been knocked about by the kitchen trailer. But the thought of food sickened him. Still, the day seemed hopeful. He was alive. And he could take his choice from a number of vehicles in operative condition. He could take a truck if he wanted. Or a lighter utility vehicle. It struck him that he might just survive after all.

He moved slowly, but he tried to move methodically. He loaded a light, all-purpose truck with boxes of rations, with ten-gallon fuel cans, with water cans. He worked through the wreckage of the helicopters, searching out forgotten emergency kits. Ammunition, matches, first-aid kits, flare guns. It was possible to salvage something from even the worst wrecks. But he could not find a working radio. The late-model sets that had been left behind had been cleared, deprogrammed. Someone had been thinking about operations security.

There were civilian phone lines in the administrative

building, but they were dead. Still, he was able to lift a decent set of maps from the abandoned stock, some outdated, others with broad expanses where there was no detail, yet far better than the single local flight map disintegrating in his pocket. He made a plan. No point heading for Kolwezi without adequate knowledge of the combat situation. Better to head north, roughly along the Lualaba, as the backcountry roads and trails allowed. In the wreckage of the tents, he sifted through the burned duffel bags and kits. His own oversize aviator's bag had burned, but he found stray uniform pieces of the necessary sizes where the enlisted tents had stood. He could even have taken a supply of pornographic magazines, but he settled for loading a sleeping bag onto the truck.

He was ready to go. He still felt weak, but he was convinced that he was going to make it. He could almost feel a spark of his old fire, thinking: George Taylor versus Africa, round two. He folded the local map sheet and tucked it in by the gears. He had loaded himself down with pistols and knives like a cartoon cowboy. He started the engine. But a last glimpse of the abandoned cavalry banner on the roof stopped him.

Laboriously, he reclimbed the stairs. He grabbed the fabric in one hand and cut it free from the pole with a sheath knife, noticing with his first smile in days that some young soldier had inked into the fabric, in small block letters, the informal cavalryman's motto:

IF YOU AIN'T CAV, YOU AIN'T SHIT.

Taylor folded up the guidon and slipped it into one of his oversize uniform pockets. Moments later he had left the scene of defeat behind, on his way to conquer a continent.

His journey took four months. He had hoped to link up with U.S. forces at a corps support command site at Lubudi, but he found only a dump of pallets and blivets, repair tents, and a plundered medical support site, all abandoned by the U.S. military and now inhabited by local squatters. The native dead lay casually about the compound, victims of RD that no one else would touch, let alone bury. Taylor sped off, trying to bathe away any contagion in the rush of air moving over the vehicle, unwilling to risk the contact questions would have required.

He followed the river. His fellow Americans were somewhere to the west or northwest, but he had no way of knowing how far back the war had carried them. The river, with its necklace of remote, fetid towns, was his only hope. Bukama, too, was dying, but the remnants of government and a few Belgian missionaries were fighting back, burning the corpses. Taylor had smelled the stench miles before he reached the straggling edge of the town, but nothing in his experience had allowed him to identify it. At a ferry crossing, a Lebanese wanted to purchase anything Taylor would be willing to sell from the stock aboard the vehicle, but Taylor was determined to husband his riches, rationing himself on the long progress toward Kinshasa. In response to Taylor's pidgin questions about Americans, the Lebanese responded angrily in French overgrown with localisms, so that all Taylor could make out was that the Lebanese did not know where there were any Americans and did not care where there were any Americans. Beyond that, Taylor could only catch the word death, which came up repeatedly. Shortly thereafter, just as the landscape was going bad, Taylor's vehicle stopped in the middle of a dirt track. Nothing he could do would make it start again, and he had no choice but to abandon the riches the Lebanese had so badly wanted to buy.

He continued on foot, bartering for occasional rides on ancient trucks, on ferries and riverboats seeping with plague. He had diarrhea, but it passed over him in cycles, hitting him hard, then weakening, then punishing him again. Each new surge of pain teased him with the thought that he was coming down with Runciman's disease. But he never sickened beyond stomach cramps and the breakdown of his bowels as his belly filled with parasites. Far from his dreams of military glory, he killed his first enemy in a filthy café, shooting the bandit in the instant before he would have been shot himself, then shooting the bartender-accomplice a moment later, watching an old hunting rifle slip from the man's hands. One more trap for travelers in a dying land.

He traveled over a thousand winding miles to the great falls and the ghostly city of Kisangani, its population first thinned by AIDS, now slaughtered by Runciman's disease. There was no help for him there, but the whores desperately trying to make a living along the enfeebled trade route told him that, yes, there was a very big war.

"Kinshasa. No one talk."

Americans?

A gold-toothed smile.

South Africans?

The wasting prostitutes so wanted to please, yet Taylor was utterly unable to make them understand with his shreds of high-school French. For two years, he had sat inattentively, his only thoughts concerning the wiry blond girl who sat in front of him, dreaming over her grammar. Now, at an incalculable remove, the precious words would not come. A whore raised her arm toward him, its long bone wrapped thinly in burned cork.

There was no escaping any of it. The mails did not function, phones were a memory. All that was left were the basic essentials: grim food—unnameable, slithering through the bowels—the nightmare whores who imagined that the pockets of his tattered uniform held wealth, and the incredibly resilient traders, who worked their way along the rivers on unscheduled steamers. Taylor passed through mourning towns and through villages where no sign of human life remained. Survivors of Runciman's disease wandered the bush and jungles, waiting for another death, many begging, some gone mad. The most amazing thing to Taylor was the speed with which he learned not to see, not to care.

Fragmentary details of the war filtered up the great river lines, jumbled out of chronology. On a river bank, between skewers of smoked monkey and displays of bright cotton, a merchant told him that the Americans had made a great fire, but he could supply no further details. Great fire, great fire. It wasn't until he reached Kabalo that a world-band radio shocked him with an off-handed reminder that the United States had struck the South African government center of Pretoria with a small-yield nuclear weapon weeks before. A last surviving relief worker let Taylor look through the stack of outdated newspapers awaiting service in the water closet. Taylor hurried through them, in a mental panic. Uncomprehending, he slowed, and began again, sifting the reports into the order of the calendar.

The South African military had set a trap, launching a broad, coordinated attack on the U.S. forces in Shaba Province, on those deploying downcountry, and on those remaining in Kinshasa. The same morning that Taylor's troop had been blasted out of the sky, South African commandos and rebel forces from within the Zairean military had destroyed the sixteen unnecessarily deployed B-2 bombers on the ground back in the capital. The planes had cost the United States well over one billion dollars each. The South Africans destroyed them with hand grenades, satchel explosives, and small-arms ammunition that a private could have bought with a month's pay. In the fighting downcountry the South African military's Japanese-built gunships with on-board battle lasers and a revolutionary arsenal of combat electronics had introduced a qualitatively new dimension into warfare. In the nineties the U.S. had built-down in concert with the Soviets, and even as the military force shrank, the only new weapons introduced to keep pace with the times were enormously expensive Air Force and Navy systems that had never proved to be of any practical utility. The only program that worked, even though underfunded, was strategic space defense, while the only service that saw significant action in the wake of Operation Desert Shield was the bare-bones Army, committed to a series of antinarcotic interventions in South America. But even that action was hampered by the Air Force's cutbacks in airlift capability, made in order to continue to fund the more glamorous manned bomber program. While carrier battle groups paid port calls around the world and stealth bombers flew patrols over Nevada, infantrymen cut their way through the jungles of Latin America with machetes and fought bitterly and successfully against the better-armed bands of the drug billionaires. When the Army had been ordered to Zaire, its tactical equipment proved to be, at best, a generation behind that developed by the Japanese—much of which had been based on technology initially developed in the United States in support of strategic space defenses.

The XVIII Airborne Corps fought hard, but the South Africans never dropped the initiative. The Japanese battle electronics proved impenetrable to the U.S. systems, while the lack of well-trained intelligence analysts left the Military Intelligence elements with nothing but useless equipment. The South Africans, however, always seemed to know where the U.S. forces were located and what their weaknesses were. The Japanese suite of electronic countermeasures and countercountermeasures would keep the U.S. forces deaf and blind, then the Toshiba gunships would sweep in, followed by strikes employing more conventional aircraft and fuel-air explosives.

U.S. casualties mounted so quickly, with such apparent helplessness on the U.S. side, that the commander of the XVIII Airborne Corps, after long-range consultation with the President, requested a cease-fire.

The South Africans ignored him and continued their strikes on the U.S. columns attempting to make their way northward to an imagined safety.

Finally, the corps commander attempted to surrender all remaining U.S. Army elements in Shaba in order to prevent the further loss of life.

The South African response was to strike a fifty-mile-long U.S. Army column with improved napalm.

The President ordered the U.S.S. Reagan, the nation's newest ballistic missile submarine, to strike Pretoria from its station in the Indian Ocean.

Taylor finally raised the U.S. embassy in Kinshasa on shortwave from an upriver station, only to be told that his case did not rate special evacuation consideration, given the general conditions in the country. He would have to make his own way for another thousand miles down the Zaire River.

He rode on asthmatic steamers where the crew shoveled the dead over the side at oar's length, and whose captains continued to work the channels and currents only in the hope that the next river port would be the one where the epidemic had already burned itself out and passed on. On one dying boat Taylor opened the rickety latrine door to find a corpse resting over the open hole, pants down and pockets turned inside out. Another night, he had to sit awake through the darkness, pistol in hand, to ward off the sick who insisted on sharing the magic medicine that kept the white man alive. And it truly was as though he were possessed of some remarkable power, so easily did he pass among the dead and dying, untainted except by the smell of his own filth. He began to suspect that he had some natural immunity, and, by the time he reached Kinshasa, that belief, along with a ragged uniform, dog tags, a half-empty pistol, and a folded-up, sweat-stained red and white cavalry guidon, was all he possessed.

Kinshasa, his goal, his city of dreams, proved to be the worst part of the entire journey. He had expected to be welcomed back into the safe, civilized, white fold, to be whisked away at last from this dying country. But as he approached the U.S. embassy compound, a bearded shambles of a man, the Marine guards in protective suits lowered their weapons in his direction. *Stand back. Do not touch the gate.* Taylor's rage eventually drew a Marine officer from the chancellery, but he only closed to shouting distance. He declared that, if Taylor truly was a U.S. serviceman, he should make his way to the U.S. armed forces liaison office at the military airfield. If everything was in order he would be evacuated to the quarantine station in the Azores. Almost all of the surviving U.S. personnel were gone now, withdrawn under the cover of the cease-fire that was the only positive result of the strike on Pretoria.

Taylor, hating the man, nonetheless craved information. About the war, about his world, about comrades and country. But the Marine officer was anxious to break off the discussion and go back inside.

Upriver the disease had created an atmosphere of resignation, a sense that the epidemic was the will of the gods, that there was nowhere to hide. For all the wails and songs of mourning, the dying out in the bush had a quiet about it. But in Kinshasa's motley attempt at civilization, the plague seemed to further distort and corrupt. Penniless, Taylor made his way across the urban landscape on foot, newly afraid now that he had come so close to rescue, forcing himself to go on. None of the few vehicles in the streets would pause to give a stranger a lift, and they drove with their windows sealed despite the torrid heat. Men and women came out into the streets to die, fleeing the premature darkness of their hovels or the broken elegance of colonial mansions. On the Zairean skin, the marks of the disease showed purple-black on the newly dead, but ashen as acid burns on those fortunate enough to live. And, despite the ravages of the epidemic, a fierce life persisted in the city. Howling children robbed the dead and dying, inventing new games in the alleys, and silken masks had come into fashion for those disfigured by the disease. Upriver, women waiting to die in way stations had made desultory overtures, but here, in the capital, brightly veiled prostitutes called out musically, playfully, threateningly. Shanty barrooms and cafés still did a noisy trade, and passing by their human froth, Taylor was glad that he looked so poor that he was hardly worth killing. After all he had seen, it struck him as all too logical that he might be killed now, at the end of his long journey. He felt that he was cheating his fate with each corner safely passed.

His most persistent vision of Kinshasa remained the public coupling of a big man with a woman in a red silk mask. The two of them leaned up against a doorway in a garbage-strewn alley. With no change in rhythm, the man turned his head and eyed the passing stranger with the disinterested expression of a dog.

"Yes, sir," the old master sergeant had said to him, as he guided Taylor through the disinfectant showers at the Kinshasa airfield processing detachment, "you're looking a little the worse for wear. But we'll fix you up."

The hot jets of the shower felt as though they were barely reaching his skin through the accumulated filth. The master sergeant had placed all of Taylor's uniform remnants in a dangerous-waste container. He had wanted to dispose of the matted cavalry pennant, as well. But the sudden look in Taylor's face, perhaps touched with just a bit of jungle madness, perhaps a look like the one his face had worn in the instant before he killed the bandit and the bartender upriver, had persuaded the other man to provide Taylor a special bag and receipt form that promised the item would be sterilized and returned to him.

"I suppose it's one hell of a mess up-country," the master sergeant said in a voice loud enough to reach into the shower stall with Taylor.

Taylor found it too hard to talk just yet. But the NCO went on, perhaps sensing a need in the half-crazed officer who had just walked in out of the bush, or perhaps because he was the kind of NCO who simply liked to talk—about wars and women and life's infinite small annoyances. He seemed wonderfully familiar to Taylor, a cursing, grunting, eternally weary symbol of Home. Taylor wanted to respond with words of his own. But it was very hard. It was much easier just to let the disinfectant-laced water stream down over him.

"It's a hellhole, I'll tell you," the sergeant continued. "Captain, I was in Colombia, from ninety-seven to ninety-nine, and I deployed to Bolivia a couple of times. But I never seen a mess like this place. They ought to just give it back to the Indians."

"I . . . was in Colombia," Taylor said, testing his vocal cords.

"Yeah? With who? I was with the Seventh Infantry Division. You know, 'Too light to fight' and all. Jeez, what a clusterfuck."

"I was with the Sixty-fourth Aviation Brigade." Taylor's hands trembled helplessly as he struggled to manipulate the big bar of soap under the torrents of water.

"Oh, yeah. Them guys. Yeah. Maybe you gave me a lift sometime."

"I was flying gunships."

"You were lucky. I hate to tell you what it was like humping up them jungle mountains. Christ, how we used to curse you guys. If you don't mind me saying. The chopper jockeys would be lifting off again before our butts cleared the doors. Of course, that's nothing to what the Navy done when the shit hit the fan with the South Africans."

"What's that?"

"You didn't hear, sir? Yeah, well. I guess you were out

in the woods. As soon as the casualties started piling up—especially, the RD victims—that old carrier battle group that was sitting off the coast just unassed the area. Protecting and preserving the force, they called it. What it amounted to was that they weren't about to load any sick grunts onto their precious boats. But, I mean, what the hell? The only reason the Air Force is still flying us out is because of a presidential order. Ain't that a kick in the ass? Everybody was just ready to let Joe Snuffy die like a dog in a ditch. I guess they figured there weren't going to be any medals and promotions out of this one."

"You're kidding. How the hell did they expect us to evacuate?"

The master sergeant laughed, and the sound of it echoed through the concrete shelter. "The Air Force weenies . . . wanted us to book charter flights. They said it would be more cost effective. Of course, I guess they were a little gun-shy after losing twenty billion dollars worth of B-2s to a handful of cowboys. Like the Navy guys said, you got to protect and preserve the force."

Consciously steadying his hand, Taylor turned off the flow of water. As he stepped out of the narrow booth, rubbing himself hard with the towel, trying to wipe away the past four months in their entirety, the master sergeant looked him up and down and shook his head.

"Looks like you could use a good meal, Captain."

Taylor left for the Azores quarantine site on an evac run for those not yet ill with RD. Sitting in an ill-fitting special-issue uniform, with the freshly sterilized cavalry guidon in his breast pocket, he felt the greatest relief of his life as the shrieking Air Force plane lifted away from the African continent. He scanned old copies of *Stars and Stripes,* but even the relentlessly negative news articles could not fully suppress his elation.

In the poorly lit belly of the transport, he learned that the nuclear strike on Pretoria had been sufficient to force a South African withdrawal. The South Africans had overplayed their hand, after all. But the U.S. had lost far more than it gained. The world condemned the U.S. action. There was no sympathy, even from the nation's closest allies. Instead, the event gave furious impetus to the movement to eliminate all nuclear weapons. The Japanese used the strike as a pretext to launch a trade war of unprecedented scale. Over the decades, the Japanese had slowly forced the United States and even the European Union out of key markets, such as electronics and high-grade machine tools, and now they announced that they would no longer trade with any nation that continued to trade with the United States. It was, Tokyo said, a moral issue. The Japanese did allow that they would continue to sell *to* the United States, since a total embargo would cause excessive hardship for innocent people. . . .

The American government found itself helpless. There were no made-in-the-U.S.A. replacements for many of the items that made a neotechnological society function, and without Japanese spare parts, large sectors of the U.S. economy would have ground to a halt within weeks. Warfare suddenly had parameters that the military could not penetrate with radar-evading bombers or vast fleets. Even the military machine itself had come to rely on crucial components originally designed in the U.S.A. but improved and produced more efficiently in Japan.

The news media blustered about an economic Pearl Harbor, running their newspapers on state-of-the-art presses built in Yokohama, or broadcasting their commentaries over Japanese hardware to high-definition television sets made by Panasonic, Toshiba, and Hitachi. There seemed little hope for a second Battle of Midway in the near future. Certainly, even a strategic military response was out of the question, not only due to the debacle suffered by U.S. arms in Africa and the anti-U.S. sentiment prevailing worldwide, but also because the Japanese home islands' Space and Atmospheric Defense Complex—SAD-C—was far more sophisticated than were the partially deployed U.S. space defenses, which had both inspired and provided the initial technology for the Japanese effort.

The U.S. received the blame for everything, including the spread of Runciman's disease. Smug at America's humiliation, the European Union quickly forgot its initial support for the U.S. intervention. There was a sense that the Americans were finally getting what they deserved, and the Europeans congratulated themselves on having effectively dismantled the North Atlantic alliance back in the nineties. War, the Europeans declared, would no longer solve anything, and they pointed to their own miniaturized military establishments—barely large enough for a good parade—as cost effective in a world where the crippled giants of both East and West were equally condemned as failures. The fundamental thrust of Euro-diplomacy seemed to be to reach a market partition of the world with Japan and the less-powerful Pacific economies, even if appeasing the Japanese required significant concessions. After all, the Europeans rationalized, their home market would remain untouched by the agreements, and, at heart, the European Community had become almost as introspective as China.

The only thing for which the Europeans were not ready was Runciman's disease—and the crippling effect it had on the world economy, as well as on indigenous European production. Only the Japanese managed to initiate truly effective quarantine measures, sealing off the home islands but continuing their export trade through a vast clearing house on the island of Okinawa.

Taylor paged through the casualty lists, unwilling to look at them too closely yet. And he could not bring himself to study the accounts of lost engagements in detail. Even as he read, his resistance was growing. He had survived—and his country would emerge from all of this as surely as he had emerged from the jungle.

He finally tossed the dog-eared papers aside when one headline summed up the depressing jumble of reports:

THE END OF THE AMERICAN CENTURY

He remembered little of the Azores. Just the monotony of the tent city where every evacuee had to remain for ninety days, moving from one "sterile" subsection to another, and his surprise to find that he had been presumed dead and that he had been posthumously awarded the Distinguished Flying Cross on the strength of his last radio messages, which had been recorded by a U.S. Military Intelligence outfit. He remembered listening to the ranting of a fellow captain, a Military Intelligence officer named

Tucker Williams, who swore that he was going to live for sheer spite just so he could beat the service back into shape. Taylor half-listened to the man's tales of how Military Intelligence had corrupted itself in the quest for promotions—"We stressed the jobs that brought tangible rewards in peacetime, command, XO, operations officer, everything except the hard MI skills. And when the country needed us, we went to Africa with more commanders and XOs and S-3s than you could count, but without the analysts and collection managers and electronic warfare officers it takes to fight a war . . . and I swear to God I'm going to fix it, if I have to pistol whip my way up to the Chief of Staff . . ." Taylor was not certain what his own future would hold. He suspected he would remain in the military, although he was not sure now that he was the right man for it, in view of his battlefield failure. But he wanted, above all, a chance to prove himself, to get it right. To atone.

He did not worry about Runciman's disease, even when two other officers in his tent came down with it. He was convinced that he had some sort of natural resistance. If Africa had not cut him down, the Azores certainly were not going to get him. Then he briefly awoke to his own screams and abdominal pains of unimaginable ferocity. For the first few moments he managed to tell himself it was simply the multiple parasites for which the Army doctors were treating him. Then the truth bore down upon him, just before he lost consciousness.

Beyond the initial shock, he remembered virtually nothing of the disease. It was merely a long sleep from which he awoke with the face of a monster, where once the mirror had reflected an overgrown boy.

He was lucky, at least to the extent that his faculties were not impaired. The battery of tests given to all survivors revealed no deterioration in his mental capabilities whatsoever. Later the Army even offered him plastic surgery, as they did to every soldier who contracted RD in the line of duty. In the wake of the plague years, plastic surgeons developed fine techniques for repairing disease-damaged skin. The results were never perfect, but the work allowed you to sit in a restaurant without disturbing those around you.

Taylor never submitted to the treatment. In the years of our troubles he wore a lengthening personal history of medals and campaign ribbons on his chest. But when he was alone in front of the mirror, it was his face that was the true badge of his service, and of his failure on a clear morning in Africa.

2

Los Angeles
2008

FIRST LIEUTENANT HOWARD "MERRY" MEREDITH, child of privilege, stood among the dead. The medics had moved on, shrugging their shoulders, leaving him alone with the boy he had just killed. There were plenty of casualties, on both sides, although he did not yet know the exact number. Voices called out orders, as the Army began to put the street back in working order. But for Meredith the familiar commands and complaints were only background noise. Another helicopter thundered overhead, drawing its shadow over the scene, while a mounted loudspeaker instructed the local residents to remain indoors. The wash of air from the rotors picked over the loose fabric of the dead boy's clothing, as though sifting through his pockets. Well, there would be time for that too.

The color of blood was far softer than the tones of the boy's costume. The garish rejectionist uniform of the streets. Meredith would not even have worn those mock satins and gilt chains to a costume party. They were almost as foreign to him as the lush, loose prints worn by the Zairean women had been. He wanted no part of them.

And yet, they were a part of him. In a way that he could not understand, in a manner intellectually suspect, perhaps only learned, imagined, imposed. The dead boy's eyes appeared swollen and very white in their setting of black and deep maroon. Far from achieving any dignity in death, the boy looked like something out of an old, vulgar cartoon. The moronic minstrel who chanced upon a ghost.

No connection, Meredith insisted. It's bullshit.

It occurred to him that the light was very good. It was an off-season light, soft, yet very clear. The smoke of the firefight had withered away, and there was almost no smog in a city come to standstill. The slum was almost picturesque, when you discarded the baggage of your preconceptions. A poor neighborhood in some handsome southern place. Drowsing, in a very good light. It seemed unreasonable to Meredith that he could not see his way more clearly in a light of such quality.

Merry Meredith, child of privilege, born to confidence, handsome and markedly intelligent, fumbled to put his pistol back in its holster. He turned away from the boy he had killed and began to call out orders to his men. His voice had the brilliant confidence of an actor stepping back out onto the stage while his life crumbles behind the curtains.

He had come a long way from Ann Arbor, where the first serious prejudice he had encountered was that of his parents against his choice of a career. He always thought fondly of his parents, grateful to them for so much, sorry only that he had never managed to find the time to sit down with them as an adult and explain why his life's path had needed to diverge so markedly from theirs. Anyway, he had not possessed the words. So much of it was a matter of feelings, of intuitions.

The plague had swept through the ranks of the university's professors with a ferocity that seemed to seek revenge for finding the dormitories emptied of students. Whether the victim was liberal or conservative, a mathematician or Chaucerian scholar, Runciman's disease had shown a great appetite for knowledge. His father had been a historian whose lifework consisted of reinterpreting the history of the United States through the eyes of its minorities, while his sociologist mother had labored to explain the statistical problems of a black population from which her own background, education, and standard of living had kept her utterly separate, despite the color of her skin. The plague had called them in swiftly, as though starved for their expertise, before a son returning from the confusion of Zaire could take them in his arms one last time.

When he remembered his parents it was usually in terms of a golden, astonishingly untroubled childhood, or in the light of scenes where their exasperation, anger, and very best intentions struggled against his desire to go to West Point. He set his face in a near smile, recalling their well-meant reproaches: Where had they gone wrong? Where had they failed? How had they been so inept in the transmission of their values that a son of theirs would want to become a military officer? Had he declared himself a homosexual or perhaps even a drug addict, they would have felt far less a sense of parental inadequacy. They even reached the point where they were willing to let him stay home and go to Michigan. He could even continue to play football. . . .

Well, he had played football, on the first winning team West Point had fielded in a decade. And the child who had been forced to hide his toy soldiers from his parents the way other children hid only partially understood works of pornography became an officer in the United States Army. His parents had come up to the Point for his graduation, but his mother wept helplessly and his father's face bore the stoical look of a man whose son had just wed the town harlot.

Then his childhood ended. Two days before he graduated from the Military Intelligence Officer's Basic Course at Fort Huachuca, his orders were amended to send him to the XVIII Airborne Corps at Fort Bragg. He was to proceed directly, without home leave. Almost his entire class found themselves in the same boat, as the Army struggled to flesh out at least a few key units to full strength during the Zairean crisis. At Fort Bragg he underwent emergency in-processing, signed for his field gear, and loaded onto a transport aircraft to join his new unit, which had already deployed to Kinshasa.

He had been excited, and only occasionally did his stomach suffer a quick tinge of fear. He was going into combat. All of his training would be put to immediate use. A range of dramatic, if nebulous, opportunities seemed to open up before him.

But he did not see combat. Instead he remained in the grubby, diseased environs of Kinshasa, sitting behind a bank of intelligence work stations that glowed with multicolored electronic displays and did absolutely nothing to alter the outcome of the campaign.

But he learned. He learned the emptiness of the things he had been taught in school about war, and, above all, he seemed to learn the depth of his Americanness. Despite his rebelliousness, his parents had managed to imbue him with a residual belief that there *must* be some magic in his African heritage. Their casual iconography promised an untutored wisdom about life, a deeper, richer humanity, and a natural splendor beyond compromise, beyond the reach of the cold, pale refugees from the Northern Hemisphere.

Instead, he found plague. And a level of corruption, greed, and immorality that shocked his middle-class soul. He detected no evidence of spiritual grace or moral charity—no single hint of latent racial greatness. He resisted the African reality that confronted him, struggling against the evidence of his senses with an outraged ferocity, unwilling, even now, for his parents to have been *so* wrong in the dreams that had shaped their lives.

In the end, he had to recognize that he had more in common with a white private from backwoods Alabama than he had with the Zaireans. Culture, the immersion in television, video, automated games, music, advertising, textbooks, social habits, conveniences, breakfast foods, the triggers to personal embarrassment, the simple differentiation between the good deed and the bad, overpowered any real or imagined racial bonds. Instead of romance, he found squalor. In the end, the Africans did not want his brotherhood. They only wanted his money.

He wrote to his parents that, while war and disease limited his opportunity to really see the country, sunrise on the big river was very beautiful, and the vegetation was full of color.

Then, still unable to comprehend how things had gone

so wrong for *his* army, for *his* country, he loaded back onto another transport plane and went into quarantine in the Azores. By an accident of fate, Runciman's disease passed by his bunk. Things had gotten so bad in the quarantine camp that virtually everyone assumed they would die or at least suffer the corollary effects of the disease. The suicide rate among the waiting men and women soared. At one point, the last bulldozer broke down and details of still-healthy men had to dig burial pits by hand. They ran out of body bags. Then the decision was made to burn the corpses. Then came the order to disinter the earlier victims and burn them too. Terribly afraid, Meredith volunteered for the worst of the details. He told himself it was his duty. As his penance for sitting safely in Kinshasa while his classmates were dying downcountry.

Even though the smoke from the chemical-laden fires haunted his nostrils, burrowing into his lungs, his temperature never climbed, his bowels never exploded, and his skin never blotched with the special badges of the African campaign. It occurred to him that, perhaps, he was being saved for a special destiny, even though he tried to suppress the notion as unlucky.

On the island the living talked primarily of one thing— of going home, to a safe, healthy land. But Runciman's disease got off the plane ahead of them, and by the time Meredith stepped off the military transport at Dover, the plague had spread across the United States, just as it was sweeping impartially around the world. The schools and universities closed early on. Then the theaters and restaurants closed. Then the shops that sold nonessentials were shut. But the plague would not be appeased. The disease snaked out from the transportation hubs, uncoiling down the exit ramps of the interstates, tracing secondary routes to their intersections with county roads, then following unmarked lanes to the farms and ranches and mining patches. In the Midwest isolated towns crumpled and died on dusty sidewalks, along rural routes where the fields went wild. But the greatest impact by far was on the cities.

Public services were swiftly and severely stricken. No prophylactic measures tolerable in a free society seemed to work. Medical masks and gloves were of no greater utility than the beaks and pomanders of medieval plague doctors. The disease gobbled sanitation workers, policemen, transportation workers, repairmen . . . health workers. City residents began to wander the rural areas in their cars, looking for an untouched hamlet where a room might be had, spreading the plague until they ran out of gas, or until they died in a fever by the side of the road. Or until a property owner shot them as they approached. Towns and villages tried to close the roads that led to their limits. But it was no longer possible to live cut off from the rest of the world, when even your bread came from far away. And RD arrived in any case, even when the delivery trucks failed to show up.

The plague brought out the worst in men. From hucksters pitching expensive miracle cures, to television prophets who damned their contemporaries in terms of the Book of Revelations before demanding money to intercede with God on the viewers' behalf, from street criminals who thought nothing of breaking into the homes of the sick to steal and to murder the already dying, to doctors who refused to treat RD victims, men learned the measure of each other and of themselves. In the backcountry posses took to sealing off the houses of victims with an armed ring of men, then burning the structure to the ground along with all of its inhabitants, living or dead. In better-organized areas, schools and National Guard armories were converted into hospitals—but there was little that could be done beyond the intravenous replacement of lost fluids and simply waiting for the victims to live or die on their own. Then the sterile solutions began to run out, as the demand skyrocketed and the production facilities closed and the distribution network collapsed. Black-market fluid packs killed as many as they saved. Ambulance attendants were gunned down and their vehicles torched as rumors spread that they were a major source of contagion. Among those who recovered, some found that their families or lovers, landlords or neighbors, would not accept them back into the fold, and hobo camps of scarred survivors developed into semipermanent settlements beside the interstate and rail lines, while renegade colonies sprang up in the national parks, where the residents were somewhat less likely to be massacred in a midnight vigilante raid.

Yet, the will to civilization never disappeared entirely. There were always volunteers, men and women who against all common sense and personal instinct went to work manning the ambulances or lugging the mass-produced chemically lined body bags. Men whose lives had been spent behind desks and computers strained to load the mountains of accumulated garbage in the streets, while others served as police auxiliaries or truck drivers. When the state governors called out the National Guard, the Guard came—not every man or woman who had sworn the oath, but enough to deliver the essential food, to dig the burial pits, to patrol the most lawless of the city streets and country roads. There seemed to be no way to predict who would cower and try to flee, or who would risk his life to serve the common good. Neither religion nor race, nor age or income served to indicate the man or woman of courage. But they were always there, never quite as many as might be wanted, but always more than the logic of self-preservation alone would have allowed.

The plague hit hardest in the great coastal cities of California. In the boundless sprawl of Los Angeles, the haphazard infrastructure quickly went to pieces, and the desperate efforts of surviving officials and volunteers could not begin to put the situation back together. The gangs permanently embedded in East Los Angeles and in other enclaves of the underclass, whose grip had developed greater strength with each passing year, ruled their territories completely now, even deciding who would have access to the sparse supplies of food. And the plague brought opportunity. The gangs soon reached out, first rampaging through the more prosperous districts of Los Angeles, then embarking on expeditions to ravage small towns, settlements, or individual homes as far away as Utah. Along with their increase in membership and wealth over the decades, the gangs had also learned increasingly sophisticated methods of presenting themselves to the world. At a time when food suppliers were afraid to enter gang-controlled areas, aware that their loads would be pirated and their drivers beaten or killed—if the plague spared them—gang representatives appeared on public-access radio and television to accuse the government of purposefully spreading Runciman's disease in the ghettos and barrios, and of attempting to starve minority survivors. Even the commercial media made time for the gang stories, anxious to offer something other than reruns and official announcements. The gang members were colorful, provocative . . . entertaining.

An attempt to move the California National Guard into Los Angeles resulted in the deployment of understrength units with little or no training for such a mission. Assailed whenever they drove or marched down a street, whether to unload canned goods or to pick up the garbage, it was inevitable that the guardsmen would eventually open fire. This time, the media stories focused on the Guard's brutality and on their victims. The reporting proved so inflammatory that violence erupted in other cities across the nation, where the situation previously had been brought under control.

In Los Angeles, the power system failed and water service became erratic, with the available water contaminated. Bodies lay in the streets. Unable to enter vast areas of Los Angeles County, the thinned ranks of the police and the Guard struggled to protect those neighborhoods where the gangs did not have roots, leading to even more strident charges of racism, both from the now unprotected poor and from reporters who did all of their investigations by telephone, afraid to risk their lives on streets that the plague and the gangs had divided between them. Increasingly, the media relied on gang-supplied video material.

The Kingman massacre, in which a desert town was largely destroyed as its residents fought it out with far-better-armed gang members, forced the issue onto the President's desk. Against the advice of the most politically adept members of his cabinet, he declared a national state of emergency and ordered the United States Army into Los Angeles County.

The Army took only volunteers. Many of the men who stepped forward were victims of the disease who had survived and thus had nothing to fear from at least one of the enemies ravaging Los Angeles. As a result, the first units deployed often had the grimmest look of any the United States Army had ever fielded. But there were other volunteers as well, men who were willing to risk everything at the call of duty. Unit commanders were not always certain whether they should be ashamed of how many men refused to go or proud of the majority who quietly signed the release forms and earned their pay. It was an Army whose morale had been shattered by the African debacle— but which still discovered the strength within itself to face a mission that promised to be even more thankless.

Lieutenant Meredith found himself cradled in a relatively safe job at Fort Devens, Massachusetts, working on computer analysis models that attempted to explain the African debacle, and mourning the dreams of his parents. The worst of the plague seemed to have passed by the local area, and Meredith was slowly overcoming the nightmare of death and disfigurement that had followed him from Kinshasa to the Azores, intensifying even as the regularity of horror numbed the conscious mind. He had always been vain about his looks. Yet he put in the paperwork to join the special task force on duty in California. Terrified whenever he paused to think, he could not explain to his bewildered commander or to himself why he would choose so foolish a course of action. There was no logic in it, no sense. They could not even offer him an intelligence position of the sort for which he had been trained. There were, however, plenty of openings for substitute cavalry and infantry platoon leaders, who seemed to die as soon as they breathed the East Los Angeles air.

He found himself in charge of a ground cavalry platoon on escort duty east of the Interstate 710–210 line. He received no special training. There was no time. The platoon itself was operating at an average strength of sixty percent, and the troop commander under whom Meredith found himself looked as though he were barely up from his own sickbed, his face and hands gruesomely scarred by Runciman's disease. Although the man was rumored to be one of the few genuine heroes to emerge from the mess in Zaire, it took all of Meredith's self-control to reach out and accept the hand his superior offered in welcome.

Meredith entered no-man's-land. White residents feared

and did not trust him. The Hispanics attacked him with insults whose thrust was unmistakable despite the language barrier, pelting his utility vehicle with dead rodents and excrement. But the worst of his problems came with the black gang members and their hangers-on. Meredith found himself accused of levels of betrayal he had never realized might exist. Shots punctured his carryall and a firebomb barely missed him. Late one night he returned from a dismounted patrol to find a decaying corpse propped behind the steering wheel of his vehicle.

Thankfully, there was little time for soul-searching. There were always more convoys to be escorted than there were available cavalry platoons, more ambulances to be accompanied, more streets to be patrolled than the most rigorous schedules allowed. And there were soldiers for whom lieutenants needed to care.

Keeping the soldiers under control was one of the most difficult aspects of the mission. It was hard for young boys not to lose their tempers and respond with the loaded weapons they kept at the ready. Further, the gangs sought to corrupt the soldiers with money, women, and drugs— and not every soldier proved to be a saint. In his first three months in L.A., Meredith found it necessary to relieve one man in every five, including one bone-thin mountain boy overheard bragging that he had come to California to do him a little legal coon-hunting.

Slowly, the tide appeared to be turning. The plague began to signal an intent to move south for the winter, and the system of food distribution points, medical care, and quarantine sites took hold. There were more volunteers from the public at large now, usually men or women who had survived a bout with RD. The Army had established order in the city during daylight, and the nighttime situation was improving. The media were never censored, but they were required to have a reporter on the scene if they wanted to file a report from the martial law zone, and they were required to publicize the sources of any secondhand news footage they broadcast. The hearsay reports taken by telephone across a continent stopped, and the reporters who were gutsy enough to accompany the Army into the most troubled areas soon began to air and publish stories far less deferential to the gangs. Incidents and even small-scale firefights continued. But there was no doubt about who was winning. The reorganized National Guard even began to assume some of the Regular Army's responsibilities in the county.

The gangs grew desperate. The number of soldiers lost to snipers or assassination increased, and the gangs threatened to execute volunteer workers. There was a pitched battle when a coalition of gangs attempted to raid the internment camp for gang members that had been established at Fort Irwin, California. Four bloody hours of fighting, with the camp guards forced to defend themselves against external attack and an internal prisoner revolt, resulted in dozens of Army casualties—and hundreds of dead or wounded gang members. A heliborne response force had blocked the escape of the raiding party, and many of the gang members involved in the attack found themselves inside the camp with the prisoners they had intended to rescue. The raiders who attempted to escape fared even worse. Army patrols continued to find corpses in the desert for months.

Meredith grew confident. He still seemed to lead a charmed life, untouched by bullets or disease, and his training as a Military Intelligence officer proved to be a good background for the challenges his cavalry platoon faced on the streets of Los Angeles. He had even become something of a favorite with his former troop commander, who had been promoted to major and appointed acting commander of the squadron after the car-bombing death of the lieutenant colonel who had been in command. Major Taylor was a hard, taciturn man, who showed his partiality by giving those officers in whom he had the most faith the most challenging assignments. Meredith, who had just pinned on the silver bar of a first lieutenant, received more than his share, and he relished it, quietly growing vain.

Then the inevitable happened. Unexpectedly. There was nothing special about the feel of the day. Just another food convoy to be escorted into Zone Fourteen. Slow progress through the streets, taking care. Machine gunners standing at the ready in the beds of their carryalls. Watching.

But there was nothing to watch. Only the slow movements of the city struggling back to life. The novelty of a taco stand that had reopened, and the routine chatter on the operations net. Down streets that seemed asleep, turning into others where rudimentary commerce had resumed. Street punks hurling curses out of habit, bored by it all. Then a gutted street where Meredith could remember spending one very bad night. It had all grown routine.

Meredith's vehicle was positioned in the middle of the long convoy, where he could best exercise control. He could not even see the problem that had brought the convoy to a halt. The lead vehicles had already turned the corner up ahead.

"One-one, you need to talk to me," he said into the radio hand mike. "What's going on up there? Over."

He waited for a response for an annoyingly long time, then he ordered his driver to cut out of the convoy and work up to the head of the column. He could smell burning tires now.

As soon as he turned the corner he saw the smoldering barricade of junk. A crowd had begun to emerge from the stairwells and alleys, from storefronts and basements. Meredith immediately recognized a gang-sponsored "event" in process.

Meredith's driver hit the brakes. A body lay sprawled in their path. It was impossible to tell whether it was a plague victim or just some local drunk on bootleg liquor. But the carryall sat at an idle.

Meredith could see the head of the column now, and he could see why Sergeant Rosario had not answered his radio call. His vehicle was surrounded by the crowd.

"One-one, I've got a fix on you. Just hold on. Out." Meredith flipped to the operations net. "Delta four-five, this is Tango zero-eight. Over."

The ops net was ready. "This is Delta four-five. Go ahead, Zero-eight."

"Roger. We've got an event. Between checkpoints eighty-eight and sixty-three. Looks like a big one. Maybe two hundred cattle, unknown number of cowboys working the herd. No smoke-poles in evidence, but you can feel them out there. Over."

"Lima Charlie, Zero-eight. Dad's on the way. Just hang on."

Meredith calculated. If the choppers were busy with a higher priority mission, it would take a wheeled response . . . two to three minutes for the reaction force to mount up . . . at least a twenty-minute drive . . . it was going to be a long half hour.

In the distance, Meredith could see Sergeant Rosario's beefy chest rise above the crowd. The NCO was standing on the passenger seat of the roofless vehicle, trying to talk the mob down.

"I'm dismounting," Meredith told his driver. "Listen to the radio." He turned to the machine gunner and rifleman in the bed of the carryall. "Keep your eyes open, guys. And don't do anything stupid."

He slipped out of the vehicle and began to trot forward along the stalled line of trucks, hand on his pistol holster, more to keep it from flapping than out of any intent to draw his weapon. Restraint had pulled him through more bad situations than he could count. If you could put up with the taunts and the little humiliations, you could survive. The gangs usually did not want to take on any Army element in direct combat.

He could see that Sergeant Rosario held no weapon in his hands either. The technique was to appear confident but not overly threatening. It took good nerves. He tried to remember which of the privates were manning Rosario's vehicle today. He hoped that they could just control themselves. Panic would make a mess of everything.

Walters was driving, he remembered. And Walters was all right. He'd sit tight. And Jankowski was on the machine gun. Who was the other one? Meredith could not recall. The replacements came so fast. Few vehicle crews and fire teams could maintain personnel integrity for very long.

His heart pounded. The civilians huddled in the doorways or grouped on the sidewalk watched him coldly. This was definitely Indian country, and none of these people were likely to be the sort who did volunteer work for the Red Cross.

Faces sullen. Touched with death. Scars from RD, scars from fights. No way to tell who was armed in the crowd.

Meredith slowed to a walk. He did not want to appear nervous. And he was close enough to hear the voices now.

"You fucking spic," a black man in a small leather cap taunted Rosario, shouting loudly enough for the crowd to hear. "You got no business here. You don't need to come around here with no guns. All that food you got, all that shit belongs to the *people.*"

The crowd agreed. Noisily. Rosario tried to respond, calling out something about the food being on its way to the people, but his voice sounded unsure. Rosario was a good NCO, but Meredith could sense the wavering in his big torso now. Meredith began to feel the specialness of this crowd, this street, this air. He could not begin to put it into words, but a charged, fateful feeling quickened his skin.

Rosario made a mistake. In a desperate, peevish voice, the NCO yelled at the crowd:

"You're all breaking the law!"

Several of the men in the crowd began to laugh, and their laughter excited the laughter of others.

A lone voice called, "Fuck you," and, with no further warning, the sound of an automatic weapon, the yanking of a giant zipper, changed the laws of time and space.

Still on the edge of the crowd, Meredith's eyes telescoped in on Rosario. He could see the amazed look on the sergeant's face as the man felt the abrupt changes in his body. The automatic weapon was small in caliber, and Rosario stood upright for a long moment, bullish, unable to believe what was happening. The sound of the weapon came again. This time the sergeant toppled backward, disappearing behind the heads and shoulders of the crowd.

Weapons sounded up and down the canyon of the street. The crowd scattered. Meredith automatically took cover behind a dumpster at the mouth of an alley, pistol ready.

He could distinguish the clear sounds of Army weaponry amid the free-for-all. But he himself could identify no target at which to fire. Only running civilians, none with weapon in hand. Two boys raced down the alley, almost running into Meredith. But they were only interested in escape.

He decided to risk a look around the corner of his metal

shield. The crew of Rosario's vehicle would be in a fight for their lives. If they had not already been killed.

The crowd between Meredith and the lead carryall had largely dissolved. Perhaps a dozen people lay on the ground, either wounded or simply frightened, forearms protecting their heads. Beyond them, a civilian with a machine pistol stood on the hood of Rosario's vehicle, emptying his weapon into the bodies of its occupants.

Meredith dropped to his knees and steadied his pistol with both hands before firing. Still, he missed twice before his third bullet caught its target. The gunman collapsed backward, falling headfirst to the street.

A round ricocheted off the dumpster, loud as a cathedral bell. Meredith looked around. There was plenty of firing. But there were no targets.

He huddled close to the dumpster, scanning. A woman ran from behind a truck where she had been trapped by the gunfire. She raced blindly toward Meredith. Then she stopped, standing upright. Staring.

"Get down," Meredith shouted.

But she continued to stare at him. Then she bolted. In the opposite direction. Afraid of the man in the uniform. The residents here lived in a different world. She made it halfway across the street when she seemed to trip, spilling forward.

But there was nothing to trip over, and her blouse began to soak red as she lay motionless.

Meredith thought he had spotted the killer. He fired into a window frame. But the shadow was gone.

Several of the civilians who had thrown themselves to the ground tried to crawl to safety, going slowly, in small stretches, trying not to attract attention. But the air was sodden with bullets. Meredith understood. Even though autopsies might not find Army bullets in innocent bodies, the deaths would be laid at the Army's feet. The gang was interested only in running up the casualty figures, regardless of who the casualties might be.

Perhaps a minute had passed since the first bullets bit into Rosario's chest. Now Meredith heard the distinct sound of machine gun fire.

He looked around. And he jumped to his feet, waving his arms, running.

"No," he screamed. *"No. Stop it. Stop."*

His carryall was working its way forward, sweeping the area with its machine gun. Coming to his rescue.

"Cease fire."

There could be no clear target for a machine gun. More civilians would die.

The machine gun continued to kick in recoil as the vehicle pulled up to the lieutenant.

"You all right, sir?" the driver shouted.

"Stop it," Meredith screamed. *"Cease fire."*

But, as Meredith spoke, the machine gunner seemed to jump off of the carryall, as though the lieutenant had given him a ridiculous fright. A second later the boy lay open-eyed on the street, bleeding.

"Pull in between the trucks," Meredith ordered. He threw himself down beside the fallen machine gunner. "Hendricks, Hendricks, can you hear me?" He felt for the pulse in the boy's neck. But there was none. And the open eyes did not move.

Meredith scrambled toward his vehicle, firing wildly into the distance. There was still no enemy to be seen.

His pistol went empty, and he hurled himself over the back fender of the carryall, squeezing down between the machine gun mount and the radios. The driver and the rifleman had already dismounted and were firing from the far side of the vehicle, sandwiched between oversized delivery trucks. Shooting at phantoms.

Meredith grabbed the mike. *"All Tango stations, all Tango stations. Drill five, drill five. Watch for snipers."*

The drill would bring his other platoon vehicles up along the convoy, working both sides and establishing overwatch positions so that the trail squad could dismount and rescue as many of the truck drivers as possible.

The sound of weaponry continued to ring wildly along the street, accompanied by the breaking of glass and the complaint of metal struck by bullets.

Meredith flipped to the ops net. *"One-four, One-four— action, action.* Multiple friendly casualties at last named location. We've got sonsofbitches shooting us up from all the buildings."

The squadron net came to life. *"Battle stations, battle stations."* Meredith recognized Major Taylor's voice. It was a reassuring sound. There was no panic in that voice. It was absolutely in command, practiced and economical. Surely, things would be all right now.

A spray of automatic weapons fire ripped across the front of the carryall. At the edge of Meredith's field of vision, the driver suddenly threw his arms up into the air, as if trying to catch the bullets as they went by. Then the boy crumpled out in the open, torso sprawled in front of the vehicle.

Meredith launched himself over the side of the vehicle and lay flat in the street. He jammed a fresh clip into his pistol. His knee hurt badly, although he had no idea what he had done to it. He looked around for the rifleman.

The boy sat huddled under the mud flaps of a delivery truck, pressed against the big wheels, weeping. Meredith scrambled over to him and grabbed the boy by his field jacket. *"Get out of here.* Head back toward the other squads. Stay on the far side of the vehicles. *Go."*

The boy stared at Meredith in utter incomprehension, as though the lieutenant had begun speaking in a foreign language.

Meredith did not know what to do. No one had prepared him for this. Even at the worst of times in his earlier experience, he had been able to maintain control of the situation. But now nothing that he did seemed to make a difference. He low-crawled forward around the carryall, to where his driver lay. The man was dead. Punctured by a gratuitous number of rounds, as though one of the snipers had been using him for target practice. Meredith tried to drag the torso back behind the vehicle. But the action only brought a welter of bullets in response. Meredith threw himself back into the tiny safety zone behind the carryall and between the trucks.

He caught an infuriating mental glimpse of himself. Trapped. Cowering. While street punks made a fool of him. In his anger, he raised himself and fired several rounds in the approximate direction from which the last wave of bullets had come. But the action only made him feel more foolish and impotent.

When he looked around, the rifleman who had been weeping under the truck was gone. In the right direction, Meredith hoped. He already had enough of his men on his conscience.

The quality of his anger changed. The bluster disappeared, and he felt very cold. His fear, too, seemed to change, turning almost into a positive force, into an energy that could be directed by a strong will.

Without making a conscious decision, he began to maneuver. Forward. Working up the far side of the trucks, from tire to tire.

At the first truck cab, he reached up and yanked at the door.

Locked.

"For God's sake, get out of there. Come on," Meredith yelled.

A muffled voice from within the cab told Meredith very graphically what he could do with himself.

Meredith ran for the next truck. He could hear the sound of his own men firing to his rear now, coming up in support, making the drill work.

A flash of colored clothing. Weapon. *Weapon.* A boy with a machine pistol. His destination was the same as Meredith's—the cab of the truck. There was an instant's startled pause as the enemies took stock of each other.

Meredith saw his enemy with superb clarity, in unforgettable detail. A red, green, and black knitted beret. Flash jacket and jewelry. Dark satin pants. And a short, angular weapon, its muzzle climbing toward a target. Vivid, living, complex, intelligent eyes.

Meredith fired first. By an instant. He hit his target this time, and he kept on firing as the boy went down. His enemy's fire buried itself in a pair of tires, ripping them up, exploding them. The boy fell awkwardly, hitting the ground in a position that looked more painful than the gunshots could have been. Unsure of himself, Meredith huddled by a fender, breathing like an excited animal.

The huge, unmistakable sound of helicopters swelled over the broken city. The closer sound of his men working their way forward, seizing control of the street, began to dominate the scene. He could even hear them shouting now, calling out orders, employing the urban combat drills whose repetitive practice they so hated.

The firing and hubbub of voices from the front of the column dropped off distinctly. The gang members were going to ground.

Pistol extended before him, Meredith began to step toward the twisted, restless figure of the boy he had just shot. His opponent's automatic weapon lay safely out of reach now, but Meredith's trigger finger had molded to his pistol. He could not seem to get enough breath, and he felt his nostrils flaring.

He guessed the boy's age at somewhere between fifteen and eighteen. It was hard to tell through the grimacing that twisted the boy's features.

As Meredith approached, his opponent seemed to calm. The skin around his eyes relaxed slightly, and he stared up at the tall man in uniform who had just shattered the order of his body. At first Meredith did not think that the eyes were fully sentient. But they slowly focused. On the winner in the two-man contest.

The boy glared up into Meredith's face, breathing pink spittle. Then he narrowed his focus, locking his eyes on Meredith's own, holding them prisoner even as his chest heaved and his limbs seized up, then failed.

"Tool," he said to Meredith, in a voice of undamaged clarity. "You . . . think you're a *big* man . . ." His lips curled in disgust. "You're . . . nothing but a fucking tool."

Meredith lowered his pistol, ashamed of his fear, watching as the boy's chain-covered chest dueled with gravity. There were no words. Only the hard physical reality of asphalt, concrete, steel, broken glass.

Flesh and blood.

The boy's chest filled massively, as though he were readying himself to blow out the candles on a birthday cake. Then the air escaped, accompanied by a sound more animal than human. The lungs did not fill up again.

"Medic," Meredith screamed. *"Medic."*

The final tally was six soldiers dead and three wounded, five civilians dead and a dozen wounded, and four identifiable gang members killed in the firefight. The Army cordon-and-sweep operation rounded up another fourteen suspected gang members in building-to-building searches—a task the soldiers hated not only because of the danger of an ambush but also because they were as likely to discover rotting corpses as fugitives from the law. Few of the supposed gang members would survive. They would all go to the internment camp at Fort Irwin, to await a hearing. But the judicial calendar was hopelessly backlogged, and waves of disease broke over the crowded camp, preempting the rule of law.

That night Meredith went to see Major Taylor. The acting commander was never very hard to find. When he was not out on a mission, he literally lived in his office. Behind the desk, beside the national and unit flags, stood an old Army cot, with a sleeping bag rolled up tightly at one end. The closest the room came to disorder was the ever-present stack of books on the floor beside the cot. Whenever he had to see the commander, Meredith's eyes habitually went to the litter of books, curious as to what this hard, unusual man might read.

Meredith knocked on the door more briskly than usual, and at the command to enter, he marched firmly forward, relishing the ache in his banged-up knee, and stopped three paces in front of Taylor's desk. He came to attention, saluted, and said:

"Sir, First Lieutenant Meredith requests permission to speak with the squadron commander."

Taylor looked up from the computer over which he had been laboring, surprised at the formality of tone. For a few seconds, his eyes considered the artificially erect young man in front of his desk. Then he spoke, in a disappointingly casual tone:

"Relax for a minute, Merry. Let me work my way out of this program."

With no further acknowledgment of Meredith's presence, of the lieutenant's swollen intensity, Taylor turned back to his screen and keyboard.

Meredith moved to a solemn parade-rest position. But the stiffness of it only made him feel absurd now. He soon softened into a routine at-ease posture, eyes wandering.

He felt angry that Taylor had not automatically intuited the seriousness of his intent, that the commander had not paid him the proper attention.

Taylor's desk was unusually cluttered today. Meredith noticed that a stack of mail remained to be opened. The squadron S-3 had been evacuated, sick with RD, and the executive officer's position had gone unfilled for months. Meredith felt, in passing, that he might not have a right to take up any more of Taylor's time. As it was, the man slept little, and even the scars on his face could not hide the chronic black circles the major wore.

But the lieutenant was determined to have his moment. He had launched himself from hours of meditation, finally decisive. And he intended to stick to his decision.

Taylor fiddled with the computer for an unbearably long time. Meredith felt his shoulders decline as his posture deteriorated even further. He realized that he was very, very tired.

His eyes roamed, settling on the stack of books Taylor had gathered by his cot. Meredith was eternally amused by the changing titles. The only constants were the Spanish grammars and dictionaries. Tonight, Meredith could make out the titles of a work on urban planning, a text on the Black Death in Europe, *Huckleberry Finn,* the short novels of Joseph Conrad, and the latest copy of *Military Review*. Meredith was just trying to make out the title of a half-hidden book, when Taylor startled him.

"All right, Merry, what's up?" Taylor glanced back toward the computer. "You know, it must have all been a lot easier back in the old Army when all they had were typewriters. Then there was physical limit on how much nonsense the system could expect out of you."

Meredith stood before the man who seemed so much older than the few years separating them. And he found it very difficult to bring himself to speech, to articulate the decisive words he had so carefully prepared.

"This looks serious," Taylor said, and the lieutenant could not be sure whether or not there was a flavor of mockery in the voice.

"Sir, I request to be relieved and reassigned to conventional duties."

Taylor looked up at the younger man, eyes hunting over his face. It was always difficult for Meredith to read Taylor's expression under that badly mottled skin. He felt perspiration breaking out on his forehead and in the small of his back. The major was taking an unreasonably, an unconscionably long time in responding. Meredith had expected shock . . . perhaps anger, perhaps disappointment. But this silent consideration was as unexpected as it was intolerable.

When Taylor finally responded, he offered Meredith only a single word:

"Why?"

Meredith reached for the appropriate response. "Sir . . . I do not believe . . . that I'm suited for this job."

Taylor nodded slightly, but it was symbolic of thought, not agreement. Then he tensed and leaned forward slightly, like a big cat who had spotted something that just might be of interest.

"Don't beat around the bush, Merry. What you *mean* . . . is that you think you fucked up. And you're feeling sorry for yourself." He brought the tips of his fingers together. "All right then. Tell me what you think you should have done differently today."

Meredith had no ready answer for the question. Instead, he felt himself seethe, defiantly childish in his incapability. Was Taylor trying to humiliate him? He searched for a sharp, tough answer that would set this *acting* commander straight.

But it was hard. He had done everything by the drill. He had taken the actions prescribed for such circumstances. There had been no warning, no intelligence that so big an affair was in the wind. Try as he might, he could think of no practical way in which he might have changed the day's events. It would have required a quality of foresight no man could claim. He had done his best, playing his assigned role. The only other thing he might have done would have been to die with Rosario and the others, and, even in his fury, he recognized the senselessness of that.

And the boy dying in the street? His eyes, his words? What *was* this all about, anyway? Had his parents been right? Was he just an oversize boy playing a very dangerous game with living toy soldiers? He was too emotionally excited to answer himself rationally. He *wanted* to feel guilty. But he could not help detecting a tone of falsity in these attacks on his long-held convictions.

"Sir, I don't know. But I know I failed."

The fright mask of Taylor's face never changed expression.

"Bullshit. I'll be glad to let you know when you're fucking up, Lieutenant. In the meantime I need every officer I've got." Taylor breathed deeply, as if disgusted at Meredith's childishness, refusing to make any attempt to understand. "Request denied."

"Sir . . ." Meredith began, in a peevish fury. He did not know what he might say, but he sensed it was now utterly impossible for him to go on performing this mission. He *would* not go back into those streets. At least not in uniform.

"Lieutenant," Taylor cut him off, "it would be a wonderful thing if military service consisted of nothing but doing the right thing when the choices are easy, of kicking the shit out of some evil foreign sonsofbitches with horns and tails, then coming home to a big parade." Taylor's eyes burned into his subordinate's. "Unfortunately, it also consists of trying to figure out what the hell the right thing can possibly be when the orders are unclear, the mission stinks, and everybody's in a hopeless muddle. A soldier's duty . . ." Taylor intoned the last word in a voice of granite, "is to do an honest day's work in dishonest times . . . and to make the best out of the worst fucking mess imaginable. It means . . . believing in your heart that some things are more important than your personal devils . . . or even your personal beliefs. It means the willingness to give up . . . everything." Taylor sat back in his chair, never breaking eye contact. "And sometimes it just means lacing up your boots one more time when the whole world's going to shit. You got that, Lieutenant?"

"Yes, sir. I've got it," Meredith lied, feeling only confusion in his mind and heart.

"Then get out of here and get some sleep."

Meredith snapped to attention and saluted, hoping that this outward display of self-possession would hide his inner collapse. He did a crisp about-face and marched toward the door. He was no longer angry with Taylor. He simply hated him for his strength, his superiority.

"Oh, Lieutenant?" Taylor called, just as Meredith was about to step into the safety of the hall.

"Sir?"

"I heard that you killed a man today. First time, I believe?"

"Yes, sir."

Taylor considered the younger man across the emotional vastness in the room. "Did you . . . happen to notice the color of his skin?"

Meredith felt an explosion of fury within himself beside which his earlier anger had been inconsequential.

"*Sir*. I killed a *black* man, *sir*."

Taylor nodded. He looked at Meredith calmly, ignoring the rage, the disrespect in the lieutenant's tone of voice.

"Lieutenant, it is my personal belief . . . that self-pity has ruined more good men than all the bad women in history. Decide who the fuck you are by tomorrow . . . and, if you still want to transfer out, I'll expedite the orders. Carry on."

Meredith returned to his billet and beat his locker with his fists until the knuckles bled and he could not stand the pain any longer. He did not know if he had broken any of the bones in his fingers or hand, and he refused to care. In the brackish hours before dawn, he decided, with the firmness of stone, that he would take Taylor up on his offer first thing in the morning. Then he fell asleep, torn hands burning, to the distant music of helicopter patrols.

He woke to a knock on his door. It was a Hispanic lieutenant Meredith had never seen before. The new man looked embarrassed.

"Sorry to wake you up."

Meredith mumbled a response, straining to clear his head.

"I'm Manny Martinez," the new officer said, thrusting out his hand, "the new supply officer. You're Lieutenant Meredith, right?"

"Yeah."

"The operations center sent me down to get you. Lieutenant Barret's down sick, and Major Taylor wants you to pull his duty for him. I told him I could do it, but—"

Meredith looked at the new man as they shook hands. Earnest. He seemed very young, although Meredith recognized that they were, in fact, approximately the same age. The visitor spoke with an accent that declared, "I'm from Texas and I'm educated, by God," with no trace of a Spanish drawl.

"It's okay," Meredith said, recognizing that he could not be a party to any action that sent this unblooded officer out into the streets in his place.

"—the ops sergeant said it's just a routine convoy. Same route you had yesterday." The new lieutenant spoke nervously, infinitely unsure of himself. "I told them I'd be glad to do it."

"Take it easy, man. It's okay," Meredith said. "I just need to get some coffee."

3

Mexico
2016

"THEY CALL HIM *EL DIABLO*," THE SCOUT SAID, STILL
breathless from his climb. The arroyo in which the guerrillas hid their vehicles lay far below the mountain village.
"The country people say he has risen from the dead."

"What's he saying?" Captain Morita, the unit's Japanese
adviser, demanded. His Spanish was limited to a very few
words, and he showed little interest in learning more.
Everything had to be translated into English for him.

Colonel Ramon Vargas Morelos did not mind that so
much. He was very proud of his English, which he had
learned in the border towns where he had worked hard as
a drug runner in the days before he became a Hero of the
Revolution. And the Japanese officer's lack of Spanish
made him easier to control.

Vargas purposely delayed answering the Japanese. The
man's tone was too insistent, almost disrespectful. Vargas
was, after all, a colonel, and he took his time with the
translation, glancing arrogantly around the smoky brown
interior of the cantina. A litter of unmatched tables and
chairs. An old dog who scratched himself with the im-
precision of a rummy. Vargas stretched the moment,
examining everything in the room except the Japanese.
Disordered ranks of bottles behind the bar, a mirror split
diagonally by a frozen fork of lightning. Fading postcards

from Tucson and Pasadena, garish in the light of the storm lantern.

Finally, he turned to face Morita. "He says," Vargas began, "that the new gringo commander has brought a nickname with him. People call him 'The Devil.' " He did not bother to translate the matter of the American's supposed resurrection. It was one of those things that the Japanese officer would not understand, and Vargas had already suffered enough remarks about the backwardness of his countrymen.

Morita grunted. "That is hardly useful intelligence."

Vargas briefly turned his back on Morita and the scout and leaned onto the bar. "Hey, you fucking dog," he called to the bartender. "Bring me two fucking tequilas."

The bartender moved very quickly. Contented, Vargas rolled his torso around so that he faced the scout again, with his back and elbows resting on the long wooden counter.

"Go on, Luis," Vargas said. "Tell me about this devil who fucks his mother."

The scout was covered in sweat. The night was cool up in the desert mountains, but the climb up the trail to the broad, bowllike plateau where the village hid had drained the man's pores. That was good. It told Vargas that the man took his responsibilities seriously. Had he strolled into the cantina looking too easy and rested, Vargas would have shot him.

"There is a great fear of this one, my colonel," the scout continued. "The gringos brought him in from San Miguel de Allende. They say he was a bastard there. They say he has the face of a devil. He wears silver spurs, and he whistles an old Irish song. They say that no man who hears those spurs and the sound of his whistling will live long."

Vargas picked up one of the small glasses of tequila and gestured for the scout to help himself to the other. He had long since given up on offering drinks to the Japanese, who never accepted them.

"What does he say?" Captain Morita asked impatiently.

Vargas looked coldly at the Japanese, then made a sharp, dramatic gesture of downing his tequila.

"He says the American is a clown. He wears spurs. He whistles."

"He told you more than that," Morita said curtly. "What else did he say?"

"He said the American is one ugly cocksucker."

"What about his background? Did your man gain any information about the new commander's operational techniques? What kind of threat does he pose?"

Vargas laughed. Loudly. Then he wiped the back of his hand across his stubble. "Man, what kind of shit are you talking about? He don't pose no fucking threat." Vargas stuck his thumb in his gunbelt. It was made of soft black leather with a circular gold device on the clasp. "You know where I got this, Morita? I took this off an American *general*. Everybody said, 'Hey, Vargas, this guy's a tough customer. You better look out.' And you know what I fucking did? I cut his throat, man. Right in his own fucking house. Then I fucked his old lady. And then I fed her his eggs." Vargas spat on the plank floor.

"Ask your man," Morita said sternly, "whether he managed to collect any real information on this new commander."

Vargas gestured theatrically to the bartender. Two more. "You worry too much, man," he told the Japanese. But he turned his attention back to the scout. "Hey, what the fuck is this, Luis? You come in here with ghost stories. We don't need no stinking ghost stories. You tell me something serious about this dude."

The scout looked at him nervously. "This guy, my colonel, he don't play by the rules. He does crazy things. They say he's very different from the other gringos. He speaks good Spanish and carries himself like some kind of big *charro*." The scout paused, and Vargas could tell that the man was weighing his words carefully. "He brought his own people with him. He has this black guy who's pretty as a girl—"

"Maybe they fuck each other," Vargas said. The scout laughed with him. But not as richly as the man should have laughed. A question began to scratch at Vargas.

"Also, my colonel, he has a Mexican from north of the

border. That one, he don't speak Spanish worth shit, but he talks real fancy English."

"That's good," Vargas said definitely. "All Mexicans go soft up north."

"And there's an officer who speaks with an accent. They say he is a Jew. From Israel."

"Another loser," Vargas said. "Luis, this fucking devil don't sound so bad to me."

The scout laughed again. But the sound was noticeably sickly. It was the laugh of a nervous woman. Not of a revolutionary soldier.

"You know, Luis," Vargas said, moving close enough so that the scout could smell his breath and get the full sense of his presence, "I think there's something else. Something maybe you don't want to tell me. Now I don't know why you don't want to tell your colonel everything."

"My colonel . . ." the scout began.

Vargas slapped a big hand around the back of the scout's neck. He did it in such a way that the Japanese would simply think it a personal gesture. Happy, dumb Mexicans, always touching each other. But the scout understood the message clearly.

"Here," Vargas said. "You drink another tequila. Then you fucking talk to me, Luis."

The scout hastily threw the liquor into his mouth, ignoring the usual ceremony.

"My colonel," he said, with unmistakable nervousness in his voice, "they say he is the one who killed Hector Padilla over in Guanajuato."

Vargas froze for a long moment. Then he made a noise like a bad-tempered animal. "That's bullshit," he said. He pulled his hand off the back of the scout's neck, then held it in midair in a gesture that was half exclamation and half threat. "Hector was killed in an accident. In the mountains. Everybody knows that."

"My colonel," the scout said meekly, "I only tell you what the people say. They say that the accident was arranged. That El Diablo infiltrated men into Commandante Padilla's camp. That—"

"Luis," Vargas said coldly. "How long have we known each other?"

The scout counted the months. The months became a year, then two. "Since Zacatecas," he said. "Since the good days. Before the gringos came."

"That's right, my brother. And I know you well. I know, for instance, when you got something to tell me. Like now." Vargas swept the air with his hand. "All this shit about Hector Padilla. When we're not really talking about Hector at all." Vargas stared into the scout's inconstant eyes. "Are we?"

"No, my colonel."

"Then who *are* we talking about, Luis?"

The scout looked at Vargas with solemnity in the yellow light of the cantina. "About *you,* my colonel. They say this gringo has been sent to . . . take you."

Vargas laughed. But the laugh did not begin quickly enough, and it was preceded by an unexpected shadow of mortality that fell between the two men.

Vargas slapped the bar. Then he laughed again, spitting.

"What are you talking about?" the Japanese adviser demanded. "What's he saying?"

Vargas stopped laughing. He gestured for the scout to leave the cantina, and the man moved quickly, in obvious relief. Vargas shifted his broad-footed stance to face the tiny yellow man who sat so smugly behind his table. Vargas did not trust the Japanese. He never imagined that these people were aiding the revolution out of the goodness of their hearts. It was all about power. Everything was about power. The relationship between men and women, between men and other men. Between governments and countries. The Japanese were very hungry for power. Crazy for it. As crazy as an old man who had lost his head over a younger woman.

It was a shame that the Japanese weapons were so good. And so necessary.

"He just said," Vargas told his inquisitor, "that I got to kill me one more fucking gringo."

"There was more than that," Morita said coldly. "A great deal more. Under the terms of the agreement between my government and the People's Government of Iguala, you must provide me with all of the information I require to do my work."

Yes, Vargas thought. The great People's Government of Iguala. What was left of them. Hiding like rats down in the mountains of Oaxaca. The glory days were over. Thanks to the fucking gringos. Now it was a matter of survival. Of holding on to your own piece of dirt, your own little kingdom. They had come a long way since they had paraded down the boulevards of Mexico City under the banner of the revolution.

Vargas snorted. "Government of Iguala, government of Monterrey—it don't mean a fucking thing up here, man. You know what the government is, Morita?" Vargas drew out the ivory-handled automatic he had taken from the American general and slammed it down on the table in front of the Japanese. "That's the fucking government."

Vargas watched the Japanese closely. The man was obviously trying not to show fear, but the situation was getting to him. Morita was new to Mexico, to the food and water, to the simplicity of death. He was a replacement for an adviser lost months before. The system was breaking down. Vargas's men had received their late-model anti-aircraft missiles without readable instructions, without training. Vargas had suffered through a season of relative defenselessness against the American helicopters. He had only been able to stage small operations—raids, bombings, robberies. Then, finally, this impatient captain had made his way up through the mountains.

Now they were ready for the helicopters. Vargas thumped the bar. More tequila. When the bartender came within reach of Vargas's arm, he found himself yanked halfway across the bar.

"You're slow, old man."

The bartender paled. White as a gringo. It made Vargas smile. They were ready for the helicopters now. And they would be ready for this devil in spurs.

The gringos were always too soft. That was their problem. They never understood what a hard place Mexico had become. They were too respectful of death.

"Your agent," the Japanese said, "seemed unbalanced by the thought of this new American commander. In fact, he seemed afraid."

"Luis? Afraid? Of some fucking gringo?" Vargas shook

his head at the hilarity of the thought, even as he realized that it was true, and that some things were so obvious in life that you did not need to share the same language. "Morita, you don't know how we do things here. You don't know how Mexicans live, how we think. We're emotional people, man. Luis, he's just worn out from all that traveling. And he's excited to be back with his brothers. But he ain't afraid. That ain't even possible. He and I been fighting together since Zacatecas. I seen him kill half a dozen Monterrey government sonsofbitches with his bare hands." Vargas paused to let the effect of the exaggeration sink in. In truth, the only time he had seen Luis kill a man with his bare hands had been the time the scout strangled a prisoner.

"Perhaps," the Japanese said, "we should take increased defensive measures. Your sentinels, for instance. I've noticed that they do not have good fields of fire in all cases. The defense of your headquarters should be better organized."

Vargas hitched up his trousers, resetting the precious gunbelt he had taken from the American general. "Morita, you worry too much. I *know* this country. I been fighting now for six years. And I'm still here." In the background, out in the street, one of his men tuned in a radio to a station whose music combined the bright sound of horns with rhythms that made a man want to move his feet, preferably toward a woman. Someone laughed out in the darkness, and a second voice answered with a routine curse. "Anyway," Vargas said, "there ain't nobody coming up here, man. No fucking way. You need a four-wheeler to make it up that trail. And we'd hear anybody before we could even see them. And we'd see them long before they ever saw us. The only other way is to hump it right across the mountains. And, if the rattlesnakes don't get you, the sun will."

"They could always stage an air assault," Morita said.

"Yeah. But that's where you come in. With your fucking missiles. First, they got to find us. Then they got to make it through the missiles. Right? And, even if they landed the whole U.S. Army up here, we'd just shoot them down like dogs." Vargas looked at the other man with a superior smile. "Would *you* want to land a helicopter up here?"

"No," the Japanese admitted.

"So what are you worried about, man?" Vargas said, happier now that he had reassured himself. "Anyway, we're not going to be here much longer."

From somewhere outside of the cantina, a low throbbing sound became audible. The noise spoiled the gorgeous calm of the night.

Vargas cursed his way across the room. "I told those crazy sonsofbitches not to start up the generators anymore. We don't—"

He had reached the doorway of the cantina, where an old blanket hung at a slant. The noise was much louder now, and it no longer reminded him so much of the familiar throb of the generator.

"Jesus Christ," Vargas said. He turned back toward the Japanese in disbelief.

Morita's face mirrored exactly the way Vargas felt his own face must look.

"Helicopters," the Japanese said, half whispering.

Vargas drew his pistol and fired it into the darkness.

"Wake up, you sonsofbitches," he screamed, bursting out into the street. "The fucking gringos are coming."

Morita was already running down the dirt street toward the nearest air defense post.

The helicopters were thunderously loud now. It sounded as though there must be hundreds of them, swarming around the plateau, circling the mountaintops. Throughout the village, men began to fire their automatic weapons at phantoms.

Vargas dashed to the nearest cluster of gunmen. He slapped the first one he could reach across the back of the head.

"What are you firing at, you crazy sonofabitch? You can't see nothing."

"Gringos," the man answered.

"Save your fucking bullets. Wait till you see something. All of you—just get to your positions."

The men dispersed hastily, and Vargas trotted along in the wake of the Japanese adviser. Flares shot into the sky to illuminate the broad stretch of meadow between the village and the low western ridge. It was the only place where helicopters could safely put down. A machine gun tested its field of fire.

The helicopters could not be seen. They remained just outside of the cavern of flarelight, all mechanical bluster and grumbling. They seemed to come just so close, but no closer. Swirling around the nearby peaks. To Vargas, it seemed as though they were doing some sort of crazy war dance.

He came up to the first man-portable missile position just as the weapon's operator sent a projectile hurtling up into the sky with a flush of fire.

"Don't shoot," Morita screamed at the operator in English. He waved his hand-held radar in the brassy wash of the flares. "I told you not to shoot, you idiot. They're out of range."

The three men watched as the missile sizzled outward and upward. Then the light began to wobble. The missile self-destructed as it reached its maximum range without discovering a target.

"Put the launcher down," Morita commanded.

Even in the bad light it was evident to Vargas that the gunner had simply decided to pay no attention to the Japanese. The man could not understand Morita's English, in any case.

From the far end of the village, another missile burned up into the sky.

"Colonel Vargas," Morita said, in a voice that offered insufficient respect, "you must tell your men to stop firing. The helicopters are still out of range." The Japanese shouted to be heard over the surrounding throb and thunder, and his spittle pecked at Vargas's cheeks. "We can't afford to waste any more missiles."

Vargas was not yet ready to agree with the Japanese. Yes, the missiles had to be smuggled over an ever-lengthening route, finally coming by donkey up the mountain trail. And they truly were wonderful weapons, capable of putting the gringos in their place. But it was evident that Morita did not really understand the psychology of fighting. Vargas was ready to expend a few more of the precious missiles, as visibly as possible, to keep the gringos at a distance. He knew that the Americans had an inordinate fear of taking casualties, and even now, he thought he might just be able to warn them off. Then in the morning his force could begin moving to a new hiding place.

Suddenly, the helicopters seemed to lunge audibly toward the village.

"Fire," Vargas commanded the gunner. *"Fire."*

"I have to load this piece of shit first, my colonel. It's hard to do it in the dark."

"Morita," Vargas bellowed, ripping the apparatus from the hands of his revolutionary soldier. "Take this thing. You fire it."

"They're still out of range," Morita said in a strained voice that betrayed the extent of his frustration. "Helicopters always sound louder at night. And they're echoing from the canyons. There is nothing I can do until they come closer."

"What kind of shit is that?" Vargas demanded. "Maybe I should throw rocks at the gringos?"

Another surface-to-air missile sizzled up into the heavens from the far side of the village.

"It's a waste," Morita cried. "This is nothing but waste."

"You don't know shit," Vargas told the Japanese. "Why do you think the fucking gringos aren't already on the goddamned ground? They're afraid of the missiles, man."

It did, indeed, appear that the Americans were afraid of the Japanese weaponry. For hours, the helicopters swooped and teased toward the village. But they always kept a margin of safety. No balls, Vargas decided. In the end, you could always back the gringos down. They expected their machines to do everything for them. But they were scared shitless when you got in close with a knife.

Intermittently, one of Vargas's men would send a burst of automatic weapons fire toward the stars. But ultimately the senseless circling and feinting of the helicopters simply had a numbing effect. The ears could barely hear, the head ached. From the panic that had gripped everyone at the sound of the Americans' initial approach, the atmosphere had changed to one of near boredom, of forced wakefulness.

"Here," Morita offered Vargas the use of his long-distance night goggles. For a while Vargas watched the black mechanical insects pulsing across the horizon. But he had seen plenty of helicopters in his day.

"No balls," Vargas told the Japanese. "They're burning up fuel for nothing, man. They're afraid to come in and land." He spat. "Shit, you know what I'd do if I was a gringo? I'd just blow this whole mountaintop to hell. But the gringos got no balls. They don't want to hurt no innocent civilians." Vargas laughed. "Morita, there ain't no such thing as an innocent man."

The deepest shade of black began to wash out of the sky, and Vargas realized that he had grown cold standing out in the night air. The sweat of fear had cooled his clothing, and he was ready to call out to one of his men to fetch his coat from the cantina when the sound of the helicopters abruptly diminished.

Vargas still could not see the enemy without the assistance of Morita's technology. But the change in the noise level was unmistakable. The helicopters were leaving. Without accomplishing anything. They had not even had the guts to make one attempt to land their cargoes of troops.

"They're going," Morita said. His surprised voice was already audible at the level of normal speech.

Vargas smiled at the weakening darkness.

"No balls," he said.

He strutted back toward the cantina, resettling his gunbelt under his belly. One more time, the gringos had failed to take him. He felt a renewed sense of confidence—and something greater, as well. It was as if the revolution, with all its excesses, with all its failures, had been vindicated in his person. And it would go on being vindicated. He would live to fuck their daughters and piss on their graves.

The scout's ramblings, all the spooky nonsense, had briefly unsettled him. But it was all right now.

"We wasted too many missiles," the Japanese said.

Vargas had been only faintly conscious of the smaller man trailing beside him in the street. He wiped his hand across the grizzle of his chin, cleaning the night from his lips. He spit into the pale gray morning.

"It don't matter, Morita. You got to learn. Those missiles were the price of victory." He laughed out loud. "The gringos were probably shitting in their pants."

Vargas pushed through the draped blanket and entered the sweet dark warmth of the cantina.

"Hey," he shouted. "Let's have some fucking light in here."

"My colonel," a voice called from the shadows. It was Ramon, one of his captains. "I've been calling around to the outposts on the field telephone. Station number four doesn't answer."

Vargas grunted. Another deserter. He had watched his band dwindle from a full brigade in the Camacho Division of the North to the handful of half-organized survivors his will and their crimes had kept by his side. More and more, the men just disappeared into the mountains, or sneaked off to a woman in Guadalajara, or to a promise of amnesty.

The gringos were insidious. With their promises. But Vargas suspected that no amnesty would ever stretch to cover him.

A storm lantern sparked to life at the touch of a match. Through the gap in the doorway where the blanket did not reach, Vargas could see that it was already lighter outside than it was in the musty shadows of the barroom. It was a lean, half-blighted place.

"Hey, Morita," Vargas called. "Come on. We're celebrating." Vargas hammered on the bar. "Where's the fucking bartender? Hey, you bastard. Show some respect, before I have your eggs for breakfast."

"I don't want to drink," Morita said wearily. "It's time to sleep."

"First, we drink," Vargas insisted. He could feel the overtired village losing consciousness all around him. But he did not yet feel ready to lie down. There was still something chewing at him. Something he could not quite explain. He hammered the bar again. "Hey, you fucking dog of a bartender." Then he repeated himself to Morita. "First, we drink. Like two great big pricks. The biggest pricks in Mexico. Then maybe we go to sleep."

A ripple of explosions rattled the bottles on the shelf

behind the bar. Before the glass had finished chiming, a new, low-pitched rumble filled the morning. Vargas imagined that he felt the earth moving under his knees.

"What the fuck?" he said, in English, to Morita.

The Japanese looked blank.

A few weapons began to sound. Seconds later the morning had filled with the sounds of a pitched battle. The big rumbling sound grew louder with each instant, approaching the village, a tide of noise, as unrecognizable as it was powerful.

At first Vargas thought it was an earthquake. Then another series of explosions reawoke him to the immediacy of combat.

He ran for the doorway, drawing his pistol as he went. The thundering sound, utterly unfamiliar, seemed to engulf the entire mountaintop now.

He shoved the blanket aside to the sound of shots and shouts and wild howling. Stepping down into the street, he stared off toward the long meadow that began just past the last shacks of the village. And he stopped in amazement.

Cavalry. The gringo sonsofbitches were on horses. Ghosts from another century, galloping down from the western ridge where the trail came up from the valley. He just had time to see the full spectacle of the charge, as eerie as it was violent, before the first section of horsemen burst into the main street of the village, blocking his view of the rest of the action. The riders screamed like lunatics, firing their automatic weapons from the saddle.

"Machine guns," Vargas shouted. "Use the fucking machine guns."

But he knew it was already too late. He fired twice in the general direction of the horsemen, while beside him one of his men fell to a sniper's bullet.

The fucking gringos had used the noise of the helicopters to cover the approach of their goddamned horses. Right up the damned trail. And they had infiltrated snipers into the village. The machine guns had never had a chance to speak.

A fucking horse cavalry charge. Who would ever have thought of such a crazy idea?

Down the street, men in U.S. Army uniforms began to swing from their saddles, smashing and shooting their way into the buildings. Others rode onward, shrieking at the top of their lungs and laying down suppressive fire in their path.

Suddenly, Vargas knew exactly who had thought of such a crazy idea. He felt his shooting hand waver. The one of whom the scout had spoken. This fucking El Diablo.

Vargas could see the details of the riders' helmets and flak jackets in the pure mountain light. He could see their jouncing hand grenades and the drab cloth bandoliers. He could see their faces. And the flaring nostrils and huge eyes of the horses.

He ran back for the cover of the cantina, careening off Morita in his haste. Instantly, the Japanese threw up his hands at the morning and tumbled back through the blanketed doorway, exploding with blood.

The bullet had been intended for Vargas.

There were times when you were beaten. All you could do was survive to take your revenge another day.

With the enemy's horses pounding in the street behind him, Vargas raced through the front room of the cantina, sweeping chairs out of his way with a crazy hand. He pushed through the living quarters of the bartender and his family. A woman screamed in the body-scented dusk, and Vargas banged his knee against a jut of furniture.

Cursing, he ripped open the flimsy back door and was about to dash for the nearest animal shed when he saw that the gringos had already beaten him to it.

They were everywhere.

He jerked inside the cantina building just as a splash of bullets struck the nearby wall.

Behind his back, the bartender's wife shrieked and prayed, while her man cursed her and told her to shut up.

Annoyed at his helplessness, Vargas turned around and shot them both.

Back in the barroom, he hurriedly smashed out the storm lantern with the butt of his pistol. But it was already light enough for him to see Morita's wondering stare. The man's corpse continued to discharge blood over the splintering planks.

Outside the shooting dwindled. Vargas heard Anglo voices calling out commands in elementary Spanish. Orders to prisoners.

He crouched behind the bar. There was a broken-out window across the room, but he knew instinctively that it offered no safety. He considered surrendering. But his fear of punishment held him back. He had done things that he did not believe the gringos were ready to forgive.

With shaking fingers, he stripped off the precious gunbelt he had taken from the American general and stuffed it into a cabinet, hiding it behind dusty bottles of beer.

He was very much afraid. And he was aware of his fear. He had not believed that he, of all men, could ever be this afraid.

Now there was only the occasional snort of a horse, a testing hoof. The world had become an astonishingly quiet place. The silence was bigger in his ears than the sound of the helicopters had been.

He heard the faint jangle of spurs.

His shooting hand felt as wet as if he had dipped it in a bucket. He checked the slippery pistol, making sure that he had a round chambered.

The music of the spurs grew louder. He could hear booted footsteps.

Someone began to whistle.

It was morbid. Terrible. The melody was far too light and joyful. The notes cascaded through the morning, swooping like a small bird in flight. The tune was almost something to make a man dance.

The boots approached the cantina. Then everything stopped. No more metal tangle of spurs. No footsteps. The whistling, too, ceased abruptly.

Vargas hunkered lower. Unwilling to look, unwilling to risk being seen. He felt himself shaking. It was unthinkable that he might die here, in such dusty unimportance. He was not ready.

He realized that he was weeping. And praying. It had begun automatically, and he could not stop himself. *Mother of God . . .*

He heard the soft rustle of cloth, and he knew it was the blanket being drawn away from the doorframe. It was the perfect time to rise and fire. But he could not will himself to move.

The melody of the spurs began again. But the tempo was slower now, like the music at a funeral. Vargas followed each next footfall across the room. There was a heavier note as the intruder stepped over Morita's body. The spurs became unbelievably, unbearably loud.

Somewhere in the middle of the room, his opponent stopped.

Silence.

Vargas made himself ready. Hurriedly he crossed himself with the pistol in his hand. He seemed unable to fill his lungs with the breath he needed.

"Don't move, gringo," he shouted. But he could not move himself. He remained crouched in his hiding place, staring up from the canyon behind the bar, able to see only the blistered paint on the ceiling.

He clutched his gun, tightening his bowels. Imagining the other man somewhere out in the vast freedom of the room.

"I know your fucking rules, man," Vargas called out. "You can't kill me. I'm a prisoner of war, man."

Silence. It went on so long that dust seemed to settle and stale on a man's ears. Then a slow voice spoke in perfect Spanish.

"Throw your weapons over the bar. Then raise your hands. Keep the palms open and turned toward me. Get up slowly."

"All right, man," Vargas shouted, his voice hitting its highest pitch. He was already rising. He still held the gun in his hand, swinging it around toward the other man's voice. He squeezed the trigger too soon.

The last thing Vargas saw was the face of a devil.

PART II

The Russians

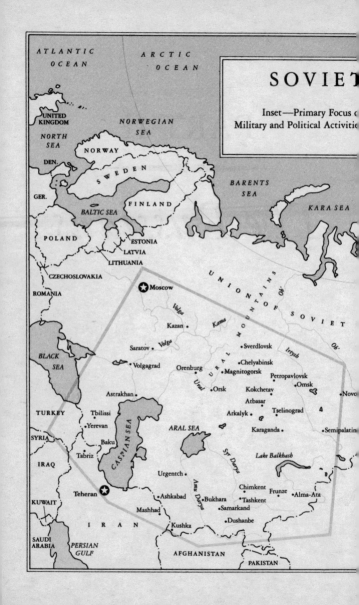

4

MOSCOW
2020

THE REAL VETERANS, THE WOMEN WHO HAD BEEN HERE so many times they had lost count, said it was nothing. Less of a bother than having a tooth pulled. But the slow cramping deep inside made Valya want to draw her knees as close to her chin as bones and sinews allowed. Yet she did not move. She felt as though all of the energy had been bled out of her, and the comforting movement of her knees remained a vision, a futile dream. Her legs lay still, extended. Dead things. Only her head had turned out of the corpselike position in which the assistants had left her. She faced the wall at the end of the ward, facing away from herself, away from her life, away from everything. Staring at chipped pipes and plaster that had not been painted or even scrubbed down for decades.

She focused casually on a spray of brown droplets that trailed along the gray wall. Old stains, the beads and speckles seemed to have grown into the surface, and it was impossible to tell now whether their substance was old blood or the residue of waste. The business had been hard on her before. But Valya did not remember it as being quite this hard. Yes, it had seemed like a punishment then too. But not such a blunt punishment. Windows painted over, discoloring the cold daylight. The iron of the bedstead. She was conscious of a sharp, metallic clattering and terse voices in the open ward. But her humiliating inability to move, the dead weight of sickness in her belly, seemed to insulate her from practical concerns. If they could not help her, she would settle for being left alone on this bed whose sheets had not been changed under the day's succession of women.

Behind the masking smell of disinfectant, a morbid odor brewed. Valya sensed that she knew its identity very well, but each time she almost named it, the label dissolved on her tongue, teasing her, prickling her ruined nerves. And her failure to find the word, to anchor reality with the hard specificity of language, left her somehow more alone than she had been in the emptiness of the previous moment. She thought of the lies she had needed to tell, another use of words, to escape from the routine of the school for a day. Wondering how much they knew or divined. Superiors sour with small authority. And the children with no color in their faces. The usage of definite and indefinite articles in the English language. . . .

No. She would not think of that now. Especially not of the children. Nor of Yuri. And where was he now? God, the war. How could there be a war? It was impossible to imagine. There was no sound of war. Only the sameness of the evening news. Yuri was fighting in a war. She knew it to be a fact. Yet, it held no meaningful reality for her. And it was unclean to think of Yuri now.

She wished she could clear her mind of all thought. To purge herself of present knowing like some mystic. But the harder she tried to empty her mind, the more insistently the images of her life tumbled out of their mental graves. Beds, lies, betrayals. The worst thieveries. And the feel of a new man's whiskers scrubbing her chin. The distinctiveness of the breath.

More than anything else, she hated the weakness. She hated any kind of weakness in herself, struggling against it. Only to grow weaker still, a greater fool. And now this dull physical weakness tethering her to this bed. And the faint, constant nausea.

Most of the other women in the ward remained silent. There was no desire to make new friends here, or to be known even by sight. Like a dirty train station, the clinic was a place through which to pass as quickly and anonymously as possible.

A girl became hysterical. Valya tried to keep her total focus on the plaster desert of the wall. But the voice, young and stupid with pain, would not relent. Valya thought that, if only she could find the strength to rise, she would slap the girl. Hard.

"First-timer," a woman's voice announced to anonymous neighbors. The remark was answered by cackling laughter and snickers.

Footsteps came down the ward.

An unwilling alertness in Valya isolated the sound. Heavy. Mannish. Cheap shoes on broken tile. Valya closed her eyes. She felt as though she would give anything she owned to lie undisturbed just a few minutes longer. Her best dress, the red perfect dress from America. The jacket from France that Naritsky had given her to wear to the party with the foreigners. The few precious shreds of her life. Take them.

"Patient!" The word was dreary from years of repetition. "Patient. Your time is up."

Reluctantly, Valya opened her eyes, turning her head slightly.

"Patient. Time to go."

"I . . . feel ill," Valya said, and, as she listened to herself, she despised the cowardice, the subservience in her voice. Yet she went on. "I need to lie here for a few more minutes. Please."

"This isn't your private apartment. Your time is up. And you're not bleeding."

Valya looked up at the shapeless creature beside the bed. Barely recognizable as a woman. The attendant's gray uniform smock looked as though it had been last washed long ago, in dirty dishwater, and her fallen bosom strained at a plastic button that did not match the others holding the cloth stretched over a lifetime of poor diet. When the attendant spoke, no anger animated her voice. There was no real emotion at all. Merely the unfeeling voice of duty, tired of repeating itself. The lack of emotion rendered the voice unassailable.

For a moment, Valya looked up into the woman's face,

trying to find her eyes. But there was no spirit in them. Bits of chipped glass in a mask of broken veins, divided by a drunkard's nose.

Will that be me? Valya thought in sudden terror. Is a creature like this waiting inside of me, just waiting to appear? The thought seemed worse than dying.

In a last, uncontrolled attempt at fending off the attendant, Valya shook her head.

The older woman's expression did not seem to alter, but, then, in the instant before the woman spoke, Valya realized that the face had, indeed, changed, hardening into a mask of professional armor, refusing to regard Valya as anything more than a number.

"The bed is needed. Get up."

Valya surprised herself with her ability to rise unassisted. She imagined a real, well-defined cavity inside herself, a place of vacancy and coldness, and the ability to bring her legs so easily together and then to force them over the side of the bed astonished her.

"I think I'm bleeding," Valya said.

"No, you're not," the attendant said. "I'd see it." But she let her eyes trail down below Valya's waist. A flicker of doubt. "Finish dressing and report to the desk."

The woman left. And even before Valya could draw on her litter of clothing, another young woman appeared. Guided impatiently by a thickset woman in uniform who might have been a sister to the one who had roused Valya.

The new girl was a colorless blonde, whose hair and complexion struck Valya as much less vivid than her own, possessed of less of the tones men wanted. Yet, some man had wanted her. As the girl approached the bed her eyes looked through Valya, fumbling with reality. Her skin was white to the point of translucence, as though she had lost far too much blood. Steered by the attendant, she collapsed onto the soiled bed just as Valya herself had recently done, without regard for Valya or anyone else on earth. She stared at the ceiling.

Valya steadied herself against the wall, drawing on a stocking. The attendant marched away. And the girl touched herself timidly, as if expecting to discover some terrible change. Then her lower lip began to flutter. At first Valya thought the girl would speak, perhaps asking for help. Instead, she simply began to cry, a lanky child smashed by an adult world.

Valya averted her eyes, refusing to make a gesture toward the girl. But as she looked away she found herself trapped by the gaze of a solid little woman dangling dark-haired calves over the edge of a bed. Somewhere in her thirties, the woman had coal-black hair and a bit of a mustache. Georgian, perhaps. Her face bore the scars of disease, but otherwise she looked as robust as if she'd merely been on an outing. She grinned at Valya as though she had only been in to have her temperature taken.

"If they can't take the consequences, they shouldn't be so quick to spread their legs," the woman said with a slight accent, nodding proudly to the sickened girl who had taken possession of Valya's bed. "They all want to have their fun, then they don't want to pay the price."

Valya broke away from the woman's stare and worked unsteadily down between the rows of beds toward the exit. But the harder she tried to avert her eyes, the more she seemed to see. She tried to force her eyes down to the floor, to simply scan her next steps, but the sight of old stains and splashes, chips and scuffs, only aggravated her feeling of hopelessness. Why couldn't they take a bucket of water to it? It certainly was not sanitary. Weak-legged, she suddenly saw her future with perfect clairvoyance. Another nondescript clinic. Another bed not quite dirty enough to force a change of sheets. Another . . .

What kind of a life was this?

Trailing her little bag of essentials, Valya stood in line before the desk. She breathed deeply, fighting the nausea, but the effort only poisoned her with bad air. She felt sweat prickling under her clothing, polishing her forehead. She thought that she would collapse at any moment, that she would be terribly sick. Then they would see. Then they would understand. . . .

But nothing occurred beyond the slow falling away of the queue ahead of her, until she stood before the clerk at the desk. The woman's hair was drawn back into a strict bun, and the skin stretched over her lean features with no hint of softness or resilience. She did not look up from her paperwork.

"Patient's name?"

"Babryshkina. Valentina Ivanovna."

"Difficulties?"

For an instant, Valya imagined herself telling this woman how sick she felt, how badly she needed to lie down just a little longer.

"No."

"Sign here, Comrade."

Valya bent down over the emptiness that seemed to grow larger in her with each new thought or action. She almost wished she would discover some terrible wetness on her legs that would make them let her rest a little while.

She signed the form.

"*And* here, Comrade. In two places."

Valya made no effort to read the forms. She signed where she had been told to sign, wanting now to be gone from the place.

Without a discernible gesture of completion, the woman behind the desk said, "Next."

Naritsky waited for her down the block, posing against his automobile. Even before she could distinguish the expression on his face, Valya knew that Naritsky was very pleased with himself. For waiting all the while. The thought of him sickened her now and, for a moment, she could not imagine how she had ever allowed him to touch her, to have her. But even at her most self-pitying, Valya could not tolerate such mental flaccidness for long. She had *enjoyed* her times with him. And the sex had been all right. Not as sheerly athletic as with Yuri. But far more imaginative. Naritsky was vulgar. And that part of her was vulgar too.

Yet, handsome though he was, it was not sex that had attracted her to Naritsky. She could do without sex. And she had not run out man-hunting the moment Yuri left for central Asia. But Naritsky had seemed like a chance, a last chance.

Once, Yuri had seemed like a chance too. To a young,

very foolish girl. And she had thought she was being so wise. An Army officer would always have a job. And Yuri was so bright, so much the ideal of what an Army officer should be. Everyone had predicted a great future for him. But this was not a country of great futures.

*Off*icers, Valya thought, in a split second of disgust. Lives as stiff as their uniforms. In a country falling apart, where everything had been falling apart for decades, where nothing ever quite worked, where no dream ever quite came true, Yuri had seemed so strong and safe and capable of providing a worthwhile life. But there was nothing to it. And behind the rough uniform cloth he had hidden a love that did not even respect itself. Yuri and his slobbering devotions. A love all weakness. When she needed him to be strong. Men were filth.

And what does that make me? Valya asked herself.

Naritsky. Smiling. By his late-model automobile. Not too flashy. Naritsky was too clever for that. Naritsky was clever in so many ways. But he had been an ass when it mattered.

A friend had put them in touch. There's this guy. Works with foreigners. Business. You know. Nothing illegal. Not really illegal. You know. Anyway, he's got friends. But he needs a good English interpreter. A few extra roubles. Odd hours. Supplement your income. And he can get the nicest things. Let me show you . . .

The nicest things. Men aren't really my vice, Valya decided. I'm the tart of nice things. When it all went to pieces, she had considered, for an instant, destroying all of the material goods Naritsky had given her. But the mood passed like an inkling of terror, forcibly suppressed. She knew that she did not have the strength to cut and tear and throw away the only primary colors in her gray world.

And Yuri? I'm not a good woman, Yuri. I lied. And when you had to choose, you chose your army. What did you expect?

Yet, she knew that she would never tell him a thing. And if he found out, she would deny. And, anyway, he would forgive her. Everything. Yuri was hopeless.

Thank God for that, she thought.

Well, she had failed. She had convinced herself that she

could control the situation with Naritsky. That she could use him. But now, wobbling out of a clinic on a lifeless October afternoon, there was no denying her failure. She had not controlled a thing. Naritsky had used her as his whore, paying her off in clothes and little toys that blinded her to everything else. And they were trifles to him.

She had considered turning him in. But there would have been no point in it. Naritsky had too many friends. And it would have been far cheaper for him to buy off the militia than it had been to buy her off. Minor consumer electronics. Or just the European condoms he refused to use.

She had actually imagined that Naritsky would marry her, that it would only take a divorce from Yuri. But Naritsky had never intended to marry anyone. Thank God she had not written to Yuri, hadn't really started anything.

She had been a fool.

Drunken, Naritsky had laughed in her face. "You're spoiled goods, my darling."

Later he had sought, lavishly, to make up for that single, killing, honest remark. But Valya had finally grasped the extent of her folly.

Now Naritsky preened against the side of his little blue car, jacket thrown open despite the cold air. A rich man in a country that grew poorer by the day. A country that, after a hundred years of promises, could not provide adequate birth control devices to its people. A country that still could not feed itself. All the promises. Like the promises a man made to a stupid mistress.

As Valya approached, Naritsky gestured toward her but did not really move. He had selected an expression of concern that made Valya want to shout, *"Liar, liar, liar."*

"Are you all right?" he asked.

Valya pulled her light stylish jacket closer against the chill, tucking in her scarf. She nodded. This was no place for a scene, no time for final decisions. And Naritsky seemed to sense something. He did not touch her but merely opened the car door. Automatically, she moved to get in.

Then she stopped.

"I need fresh air. I want to walk."

Naritsky looked at her, unsure.

For a moment, she imagined that he feared her. Some scandal. But he would be easily capable of managing that. She was the one with something to fear, with everything to lose.

"Valya," he said, in his warm, convincing voice. "You're in no condition to walk. You need to rest. Get in."

Unexpectedly, Valya lost her temper. "I'm *walk*ing. Do you understand?" Then she stopped, as surprised by her reserve of energy as by her loss of self-control.

"It's too far," Naritsky said, with an unaccustomed edge of uncertainty in his voice.

"I'll get a trolley."

"Please. You're not well. You need to rest."

He was already back in control of himself. It was as if he could see into her, know everything about her. While she could not look into him at all. And she had considered herself so wise, the master of men.

"Don't speak to me as though I were a child," she half shouted.

"Valya. Please."

"I want to walk. And don't follow me."

Naritsky backed away, palms open, as if he had been accused of an infraction of the criminal code. He opened his mouth, then chose not to speak.

Valya took a last, heartbroken, furious look at him, and turned away.

"I'll phone later," he called after her. "To see . . ."

She forced herself to think of sex with Naritsky, and with others. Making herself sicker now with the images, even though she recognized that it was all emotional and physical reaction, with no intellectual honesty in it. She thoughtlessly swore that she would never let another man slop his weight on top of her ever again, then she began to choke with laughter at her brazen dishonesty. And her physical illness returned, nearly dropping her against a wall lathered with torn posters: *The Future Belongs To Us!*

Lies, lies, lies. A world of lies. Promises broken before they could be fully articulated. She forced herself to move along, eager to be well out of Naritsky's sight.

The back streets through which her journey took her

seemed dismally gray and poor. All her life she had wanted to climb out of this plodding squalor. But there was nowhere to go. All of the good men were hopeless fools. And the bad men helped only themselves. Reformers came, but the reforms always failed or, still worse, worked halfway. Nothing ever worked more than halfway in this country. The reformers disappeared. But the reactions against the reforms, too, only worked halfway. As Valya walked along the broken pavement, the sickness in her made her feel as though she were slowly sinking, as though all her life she had been slowly sinking but had not noticed because everything around her was sinking as well.

She looked up at the balconies hung with wash, collecting the tiny particles of poison that haunted the Moscow air. She did not understand how others could tolerate it so easily, accepting the decayed communal apartments, where families shared one another's dirt and secrets, the struggle for poor food, and men who never gave a thought to their women except when they were aroused or drunk or both.

As she passed a butcher shop, Valya automatically glanced in the window. White-aproned attendants stood about slackly, crowned with undersize white hats. The display cases were empty. But the display shelves in the window were decorated with pictures of various meats and sausages, as though the passerby might be fooled into visions of abundance.

Even the sight of photographed food made Valya feel sicker. The nation of empty shops. Of empty wombs. She felt unreasonably cold.

Around the corner, a line had formed, but for once Valya had no interest in what had suddenly become available. Her only concern was to find the quickest way past the huddling women in their coats that smelled of storage. A few idle men had joined the line, as well, and they looked Valya up and down.

Valya laughed to herself. And if you could have seen me an hour ago? If you could have seen the bloody mess of me. Would you have wanted me then?

Probably. And then they would have complained about the waste left on them. They were all pigs.

Valya stumbled slightly and almost lost her direction. The nearest faces regarded her sullenly, as though she might attempt to push into the line. She heard the word *oranges*. And it was a remarkable thing to think of oranges appearing wondrously, magically now, in October, with the groves where oranges grew engulfed in war. Surely, these would be the last of the year. But she had no appetite for oranges now.

Perhaps Yuri was fighting amid the orange groves. What a pretty place that would be to have a war. Perhaps Yuri was happier with his tanks and guns and soldiers than he had ever been with her. In his letters he offered no details of his life, only maudlin reminiscences.

Valya tried to focus her eyes, her efforts. To decide where she was really going. She tried to think about trolleys and bus stops, routes and schedules. But she was uncertain of this street. Abruptly, she changed her direction.

Her thoughts would not come clear. All of the faces she passed appeared identical. Even their scars were identical. Horrible scars. She began to cross a bridge slumped over a drainage canal. She idly touched the old wrought-iron work, a rusted reminder of past centuries, cold under her fingers. Then she found herself gripping the oxidized spearheads, clinging to the bridge, struggling to remain on her feet. A wave of unexpected pain rippled up from her belly to her stomach and she began to spill a bit of saliva from the corner of her mouth. Now, too late, she felt a growing wetness at the top of her legs. It was a joke. Another punishment. Valya, the girl who was in control of everything. Closing her eyes, she gripped the railing still harder, praying not to fall to the pavement. But closing her eyes only made it worse.

She opened her eyes. And the pain suddenly receded. But the wetness was still there, quickly losing its warmth, sliming down over the inside of her thighs.

For a long moment, she could only stare into the filthy murk of the canal. Spotted with oil rainbows. So still. Necklaces of garbage on the banks. Islands of junk expelled from high windows. When leaves floated down, the water seemed to reach up and clutch them, anxious to coat them with its filth. The high walls of the apartment buildings lining both sides of the canal were flecked like old, sick skin.

She needed a toilet but had no idea where to look. It was a country that could not even receive its own waste properly. Suddenly Valya imagined that she would die before she found anyone or anything that would help her. Two grandmothers scuttled by, commenting sourly about public drunkenness and sparking Valya back to life, into a powerless, frozen rage.

She had dirtied herself. She had dirtied her entire life. And what if Yuri ever found out? She would lose even that. The bare minimum of safety.

She made herself walk. She went into the first open building she could find and tried to clean herself in the shadows of a basement stairwell. Her underpants were slopping with blood and a thick wetness, and her handkerchief was too small to cope with the problem. At first reluctantly, then resolutely, she pulled the silk scarf from around her neck. Another gift from Naritsky. And she began to clean her thighs, struggling not to lose her balance or to faint, no longer even caring if anyone saw her.

She leaned back against the wall, drinking in the dead air. She released the silken rag from her hand, and it fell heavily to the floor. As her eyes learned the darkness, she saw a row of dustbins, some with newspapers overflowing their collars. Determinedly, she tore off the cleanest-looking pages and bunched them, then held them against herself, trying to bring enough pressure to stop the bleeding. She was awash with sweat, and very cold.

She shoved hard at herself, trying to force away the ache as she stanched the flow of blood. How could men become so helpless over it? she thought. My God, what if they saw you like this? And she began to laugh again, dropping her head back against the cinder blocks, catching her hair.

She made her way back out into the gray day, walking out of any sense of time, until she came to a small, half-recognized park. She limped down a curling path to a bench and sat down hard, as though dropping from crutches. She stared up into the gray vacancy, aware that she was cold, yet oddly calm and very still. There was no need to shiver. That would have been far too bothersome, too violent. She lowered her eyes slightly, to the emaciated white trees. Going bald. Their last leaves shriveled, hanging on randomly. Her bones pressed down on the cold slats. She felt a bit of wetness, but sensed that the worst bleeding had stopped.

Lies.

Suddenly, she felt hungry, even though her stomach still sent contradictory signals of nausea. Perhaps, she thought, it was just the other emptiness. My body wants to be full again. Any way it can. Utterly confused at herself, Valya buried her face in her hands. And, at last, she began shaking with the cold.

A female voice intruded. Speaking in a foreign language. English. But with a very bad accent. Perhaps an American. Valya looked up.

She saw the woman's clothes first. Because they were so much more impressive than the woman herself, who merely looked big and well fed. But the richness of the cloth in the coat, the wasteful generosity of its cut, the deep leather gloss and stitching of the shoes, these were qualities beyond anything that Valya possessed. The woman wore a scarf in rich, subdued colors, and Valya realized in shame that she would not have had the sophistication to choose such a scarf, that she would have missed it with her child's eye, captivated by hot colors and too-bold patterns. In a glimpse Valya saw the extent of her ignorance of the world in which she had imagined herself, realizing that her failure was even greater than she had intuited.

The woman held a book, and she turned hastily through its pages with her plump pink fingers. It was an English-language book. The cover said, *A Guide to Moscow*. The woman muttered a few English words. *Oh, where is it now? Oh, wouldn't you know it?* She caught her lower lip in her teeth as she scanned the pages, not once looking at Valya.

And perhaps I am not worth looking at? Valya considered.

The woman mumbled, tearing at the pages. Her English was so unlike the clean, careful sentences Valya drilled into her students. The boys in their blazers, arms growing out of the sleeves. And the white-aproned girls. This foreign woman had a nasal, distinctly unattractive voice.

She was not pretty. But her skin and hair had a quality as rich as her clothing, the sum of a foreign life of luxury. Even after all that had happened, the Americans were very rich. Valya could not understand why any of them would want to come to Moscow. For a vacation in a graveyard.

Perhaps she was a diplomat's wife. Of course. With the war, there could not be tourists. Or perhaps her husband was a great businessman. Naritsky said that business never stopped. Not even for wars.

The big woman's face brightened. And she nodded positively to herself, like a horse about to neigh. She had found her page. And she began to speak.

It was an attempt at Russian. But it merely came out as gibberish. Valya could not understand a bit of it. But she obstinately refused to offer the woman a word of English.

The woman ceased reading and looked at Valya. Imploringly. The sudden confidence had disappeared again. But Valya would not meet the woman's eyes. It was hard enough to look at the soft, thick, flowing fabric of her winter coat, or to consider the fine soft shoes that Valya's own glued-together bits of vinyl and plastic sought pathetically to imitate. Valya was certain that this woman had never suffered, had never endured anything. That she had been able to gobble dependable little pills or use some comfortable device that kept her body out of hell and be damned to her soul. By accident of birth this woman had everything of which Valya dreamed. A life without want, without pain.

Let her suffer now. For this one moment.

The big woman tried again, more timidly, in a measured voice. And Valya could just make out the substance of it. Where was the nearest metro station?

Valya did not even try to answer. She merely stared up at the woman, meeting her eyes at last, in the profoundest hatred she had ever felt in her life. Her feelings toward the brusque attendant at the clinic, or toward Naritsky at the depth of her humiliation, toward other women who had stolen boyfriends or precious clothes, had never approached this intensity.

The foreign woman did not understand, of course. Or did not care. She simply gave up and wandered off in her plush confusion, wearing Valya's ambitions and dreams.

Valya's anger trailed after the woman, weakening with each of the foreigner's steps, finally disappearing with her. It simply took too much effort. Exhausted from the ferocity of her emotions, Valya slumped back emptily against the hard slats, her mind finally idle. Soon, she sensed, she would need to gather her strength and go on. But for one peaceful moment she sat vacantly.

A snap of wind crisped dead leaves around her ankles and calves, then a ragged handbill lofted against her skirt, caught, and fell back onto the pavement. Valya could just make out the faded headline:

VICTORY WILL BE OURS, COMRADES

5

near Omsk, western Siberia
1 November 2020

COLONEL GEORGE TAYLOR STOOD ERECTLY IN HIS Soviet greatcoat, waiting for a ride. He set his ruined face
against the cold and thought of enemies old and new, of
the crisis lurching toward them all, and of a nagging problem with spare parts. He reviewed a recent disagreement
with one of his subordinates, a general's son who had been
pressed upon him, and that somehow tricked him into
thinking about the woman he had left behind, about whom
he disagreed with himself. Unexpected, contradictory, and
so very welcome, she had a way of coming to mind whenever he failed to concentrate hard enough on the business
at hand.

He quickly mastered his thoughts and marched them on.
A part of him continued to suspect that the woman was
plain bad medicine, and he had far more important problems with which to grapple. The Soviet forces were taking
a godawful beating. And his own options were running
out.

He whistled as he stood in the cold, without really being
aware of his action. "Garry Owen," the old Irish reel that
another cavalryman had taken for the U.S. Army, many
years before. Taylor had begun the whistling business as
part of the carefully constructed persona he had employed
in Mexico, but afterward the habit proved impossible to

unlearn completely. It settled into a sometime quirk, another sort of scar to be worn through the years, something you tended to forget until a stranger's reaction called your attention back to it.

It was very cold. The autumn snows had not yet come, but the industrial wilderness in which the regiment under Taylor's command lay hidden had the sharp feel of winter, of cold rusting iron. It struck Taylor as the sort of place that could never hold any real warmth, although Merry Meredith insisted that this part of Western Siberia could be miserably hot in the summer. The site was a museum of inadequacy, with tens of square miles of derelict means: work halls with buckling roofs, broken gantries and skeletal cranes, crumbling smokestacks, and mazes of long-empty pipes. Inside the metal shells lay useless antique machines, numbering in the tens of thousands. The sheer vastness of the abandoned site was unsettling. But it was a perfect place to assemble a military force in secrecy.

Still, it was no place a man would choose to be of his own free will. The site was a graveyard, leaking old poisons. It offered no evidence of life beyond a few withered fringes of grass, brown and futile in the decaying afternoon light. The regimental surgeon and the medics were going to great lengths to create sterile islands, to monitor toxin levels, to hold death at arm's length until the regiment was committed to battle. And Taylor let them go, commending their efforts, even as he suspected that the prophylactic measures were no more determinate than incantations or crosses painted on doors. The Soviets had poisoned this landscape, just as they had poisoned their country. This was the land of the dead. The cold acid-sharp air was haunted by death. The catacombs of plants and warehouses in which his war machines lay waiting felt infectious. Not only with the chemical waste of generations, but with a sickness of spirit. The troops either whispered or spoke too loudly in the course of their duties. Of all the grim places his career had taken him, only a few had made Taylor so anxious to leave. Above all, the broken industrial complex had a feel of enmity, of resentment. Of jealousy toward the living.

Taylor laughed, startling the officers gathered loosely

around him. He was thinking that, after all, this landscape and he bore a certain resemblance to each other.

"You're in a good mood, sir," Major Martinez said, baffled. His voice wavered in the cold.

Taylor turned his jigsaw-puzzle face toward the supply officer, cutting a smile up into his cheeks. "Come on, Manny. The Russians are late, there's a nightmare of a war going on, we're stuck here in this . . . this Soviet Disneyland, and we're all trying to pretend we're not freezing our butts off. Why shouldn't I be in a good mood?"

Even as he finished speaking, the constructed smile collapsed. He was in the worst of spirits, worried about his mission and his men, at a point beyond shouting. But he knew enough about the devils in each of the officers who relied upon him in this bad hour to want to be strong for them, even if he could not always be strong for himself.

"Well, it certainly isn't Texas," Martinez answered, with an exaggerated shiver of his shoulders.

"Or Mexico," Merry Meredith offered. A coffee-skinned man so handsome that most men underestimated his ferocity. Toughest intelligence officer Taylor had ever met. Loyal to the end. And, no doubt, missing his bright, redheaded wife and his children.

"Or Los Angeles," Martinez shot back. They were teasing each other with the most wretched military memories they could bring to bear.

"Or Zaire," Lieutenant Colonel Heifetz said suddenly, with an awkward, well-intentioned smile. "Lucky Dave" Heifetz found it terribly difficult to deal with his fellow officers on anything but a professional level, and he had a reputation as the greatest of stoics, the man without emotion. But Taylor recognized the intent of the clumsy reference, the overwrought grin. Heifetz, too, felt the need to draw a little closer in the dying afternoon.

Taylor never spoke about Zaire. It was a rule that everyone tacitly recognized. Except Lucky Dave, whose social skills had begun to wither years before, in another country.

Taylor nodded to his hapless subordinate. Even now, after so long a time, it was the best he could do.

But Heifetz did not understand. He blundered on. His

Israeli accent grew more pronounced when he was ill at ease, and it was unusually heavy now.

"Yes, I think so," Heifetz said. "I believe that Zaire must have been the worst of climates. A very bad place."

Taylor shrugged, not quite meeting any man's eyes. "Up on the big river," he said. "It's a hard place up on the river. But the grasslands weren't so bad."

"Where the hell are the Russians?" Merry Meredith said quickly. Meredith had been with Taylor longer than any of them.

"I can't believe they're jerking us around like this," Manny Martinez said. Martinez had made a life's work out of leaving San Antonio behind. Yet his body still wanted the southern sun.

"I don't think they're jerking us around, Manny," Taylor said. "Something's wrong. You can feel it."

"Everything's wrong," Meredith said. He was the regimental S-2, the intelligence officer, responsible, according to the time-honored division of labor, for enemy, weather, and terrain. "The Soviet front's coming apart. It's gotten to the point where I don't know which problem area to look at first." He laughed slightly, bitterly. "Hell, I think one of the reasons I'm standing out here with you guys is that I just can't take it back in the bubble anymore. The combat information's just pouring in. And all of the news is bad."

Taylor glanced off into the vacant afternoon. Still no sign of the Russians. It was especially troubling, since, up until now, they had been careful to live up to every support commitment, despite the overwhelming problems they themselves faced.

"Why don't you all go in and have a cup of coffee," Taylor said. "Go ahead. I need a little time to think. Merry, you can get us a threat update."

Taylor knew that they all wanted to go back inside the vast work hall where the regimental headquarters had been established. It was not much warmer inside, but the difference was enough that your mind did not dwell constantly on the cold. Still, none of them moved. Nobody wanted to seem disloyal to the old man.

"Goddamnit, fellas," Taylor said, "if I tell you to go back inside, you go back inside. Do you understand me?"

Heifetz moved crisply for the battered tin door set into the huge double gates of the work hall. Heifetz always obeyed promptly, with no outward sign of approval or disapproval. Of them all, Taylor knew, Heifetz had the least interest in creature comforts. He would have moved as sharply had Taylor ordered him to march into a freezing swamp.

Martinez dropped his eyes, then went off at a lope, trailing a mixture of reluctance and childlike relief. Merry Meredith was the last to go.

"Bring you out a cup of coffee, sir?" Meredith asked.

"No. Thanks. I just want to admire the beauty of the Soviet landscape."

Meredith lingered, feet almost moving. "You have to feel sorry for them." Between their shared duty in Los Angeles and Mexico, Meredith had spent several years in a military educational program that taught officers a foreign language and thoroughly immersed them in the whys and wherefores of the country where that language was spoken. Meredith's language had been Russian, and Taylor knew the solidly middle-class black American had fallen a little in love with the object of his study.

"I suppose," Taylor said.

"I mean, look at this. As far as the eye can see. And it's worthless. Dead. The whole damned country's like this. Thirty years ago, this was still one of the most productive industrial complexes in the Soviet Union."

"You said that. In the briefing."

"I know," Meredith agreed. "Maybe I'm just trying to convince myself that it's true."

Taylor turned slightly away from the younger man. "Could have been us, Merry. Almost was. Oh, I know you're a sucker for Russian culture and all that. But, where you see Anton Chekhov, I see Joseph Stalin." Taylor paused for a moment, his mind filling with dozens of other names enchanted with beauty or ruin. "Just remember. They did this to themselves. And now we're here to pull their irons out of the fire. *If* we can bring it off. *If* the M-100s work as advertised. *If* some sonofabitch back in

Washington doesn't lose his nerve at the last minute. God-damnit, Merry. I haven't got time to feel sorry for them. I've got the only fully equipped heavy cavalry regiment in the United States Army—and possibly the only one we'll be able to afford to equip. And what's behind us, if we screw it up? A couple of tired-out armor outfits with gear that's thirty years old? God knows, the light infantry boys have their hands full down in Sao Paulo. And we'll have to garrison Mexico for another ten years." Taylor shook his head. "We're it, pal. And our butts are on the line because our little Soviet brothers spent a century turning what might have been the richest country on earth into a junkyard. And don't give me your speech about how they tried to reform. Too little, too late. They only stuck it halfway in. And they damn near bankrupted the Euro-peans in the process. You know the figures better than I do. All those big *perestroika* loans. Pissed away. And then, with what's-his-name gone, they couldn't even maintain the little bit of progress all those European investments had bought them." Taylor looked hard into Meredith's face, warning him against his own decency. "They've turned their country into one colossal cesspool, and we're here to dig them out with a teaspoon. And we'll do it, by God. If it's remotely possible. But don't ask me to love them."

Taylor stared out across the ruined industrial park. It seemed to go on forever. Black. Abandoned. He knew why he was here. He understood politics, economics, strat-egy. He even *wanted* to be here. Yet, the rational, dutiful officer in him suspected that it was all tied in with irrevo-cable folly.

"Go get yourself a cup of coffee, Merry," Taylor said.

"Sure you don't want a cup, sir?"

Taylor shook his head. "Just makes me piss."

The major turned to go, historically and ethnically all wrong in the gray Soviet greatcoat each officer wore as part of the deception plan. Then he hesitated, not yet reconciled.

"It's just," Meredith said, "that when I look at all this . . . I can't help seeing it in terms of all the dreams gone bad. Some of them really believed. In the possibility of a heaven on earth, in a planned utopia. In a better world. Back at the beginning, I think, there were real believers . . . and it all went so damned wrong."

Taylor shrugged.

"Could have been us," he repeated.

It was important, Taylor told himself, to remain objective. To avoid letting your emotions interfere in the least with your judgment. But it was very hard. He always hastened through the intelligence reports Meredith put in front of him, anxious to find any reference to the Japanese. He knew that the odds were very good that not one of the men under his command would come into contact with a single Japanese soldier during the entire campaign. The Japanese were too good at insulating themselves. Once, they had hidden behind the South Africans. This time they had concealed themselves behind the alliance that had slowly congealed against the continued Russian domination of the Soviet empire: ethnic-Asian Soviet rebels, Iranians, and Arab Islamic fundamentalists. No Japanese officer ever gave a direct command. Yet, the equipment was Japanese, the "contract advisers" who enabled the alliance to make military sense of itself, the trainers and repair personnel were all Japanese, and the ultimate goal was Japanese, as well. Dominance. Dominion. Domination. You could split hairs, play with words like a diplomat's clerk. But it all came down to the issue of the disposition of the world's richest supply of minerals, in a very hungry age.

He and his men had been sent to shore up a Soviet Union grown as frail as a diseased old man. To deny the Japanese yet another magnificent prize. But Taylor knew in his heart that he himself was sick. Cancered with the desire to strike back at the Japanese. To cause them a level of suffering and humiliation that paid back old debts with interest. He feared the day, the moment, when Merry Meredith would come to him with a report that a Japanese control site had been located in the regiment's area of operations. He was not sure he would be able to make a rational judgment, to prioritize his targets intelligently. He was afraid that he would turn out to be a mad animal, who merely walked like a man.

Taylor sought to be a good man. But even in this dead Siberian landscape of rusted metals he was still a young troop commander, flying up through the brief coolness of the African morning, cocksure and unwitting, on his way to see his command destroyed and his country humiliated. Even with his beginning gray hairs, his old scars, and his tiring body, he was still a boyish captain sailing the clear blue sky above those grasslands, waiting for the shock of the Japanese gunships. And he feared that Africa had ruined his soul as surely as it had ruined his skin. He wanted to be a good man. But he worried that he had become a killer in his heart, and a racist. A warrior to whom his opponents were no longer fully human. A smart, quick, cultured animal.

The first time his unit killed a Japanese military adviser in Mexico, Taylor had felt a level of exhilaration and self-righteousness that he knew could not be squared with any legitimate concept of human decency. And his satisfaction had not diminished with the further kills his unit chalked up. As a leader, his behavior, in word and deed, had always been impeccable. Yet, he wondered if he had not managed somehow to telegraph to his men that certain types of prisoners were not welcome. It was impossible to know, as difficult to master the past as it was to foretell the future.

His face worked into a tight-lipped smile he could not have explained to any man. Perhaps, he thought, I really am a devil.

Suddenly the roof of a nearby work hall exploded, shattering into the sky. But it was only a flock of birds lifting off. They briefly broke apart, then gathered into a black cloud and turned south. Toward the war.

Taylor kept his eyes on the bright green ribbon of light that marked the last twilight in the west. It was going to be very cold. He hoped the temperature would not affect the operation of his war machines. Every imaginable precaution had been taken. But the magnificent new killing machines had never before gone into battle, and there were many doubts. The M-100s were so complex that there was a seemingly infinite number of potential problems.

Behind us, nothing, Taylor reminded himself.

He heard the tinny door of the work hall open just beyond his field of vision, and he made an innocent game out of guessing which of his officers it might be. Possibly Meredith with a threat update. But he bet on Lucky Dave. He knew that Heifetz was going crazy with all the waiting. A dispossessed little man from the new diaspora, haunted with the soul of a Prussian staff officer. Above all, Heifetz could not bear the disorder he found in the Soviet Union. Capable of something very close to perfection in his own work, Lucky Dave found it very difficult to tolerate anything less in others.

"Colonel Taylor, sir?"

It was Heifetz.

"We finally reached the Russians. They say they're on their way."

Taylor nodded. Accepting the news.

"We cannot afford such a loss of time," Heifetz went on. "It is hardly responsible. It's only a matter of time before the enemy finds us. We have been too lucky."

Lucky David Heifetz. Lucky, lucky Dave. His family dead, his homeland destroyed. Lucky David Heifetz, wearing a foreign uniform because he had nowhere else to go, because soldiering was all that was left to him. Lucky David Heifetz, who would never have betrayed this bit of worry, of uncertainty, to anyone else in the regiment. Heifetz, who allowed himself no friends.

Taylor turned, making a slight opening in his world, as if lifting the flap of a tent. Heifetz carried out the functions of both executive officer and S-3 operations officer of the regiment, since the Romeo tables of organization and equipment had combined the two positions in a desperate attempt to save a few more spaces. It was too much to ask of any man, but Heifetz did as well as any human being might under such a burden. It told on him, though, and he looked years older than his actual age.

Of course, there were other causes for the man's worn look. Taylor pictured the young tank commander in a dusty pause on the road to Damascus, goggles lifted up onto the fore of his helmet, a handsome young Israeli, compensating with vitality for the physical stature he lacked. Taylor imagined him frozen in the moment before the word came down the radio net that Tel Aviv had been the target of multiple nuclear strikes. Tel Aviv, where a young officer's wife and child should have been safe.

It was all a long time ago now. Before the worldwide nuclear ban. The last Mideast war, launched by a fanatic coalition who saw their chance, with the United States beaten in Africa and seemingly helpless. It was a madman's war, begun by an alliance ultimately willing to trade Damascus for Tel Aviv in a war of extermination. Taylor had been so ill during the brief conflict that he had viewed the events at a passionless remove, and he had not recuperated sufficiently to take part in the evacuation of the surviving Israelis from a land poisoned by nuclear and chemical weapons.

Taylor curled one side of his mouth up into the jigsaw puzzle of his face. "Our Russian friends give any reason for their tardiness, David?"

The Israeli shook his head adamantly. "Nothing. A promise to explain. I spoke to Kozlov's alter ego—you know, the one who gestures all the time. Afraid to tell me anything. You know how they are. He claims that Kozlov will explain everything in person." Heifetz paused, considering. "All of them are frantic about something. I don't like it."

"Neither do I," Taylor said. "We haven't got a hell of a lot of margin on this one." He cocked an eyebrow. "Merry have anything new?"

"Just more of the same. From bad to worse. The question is which of their many crises the Soviets find so threatening at the moment. And why. At times, I find their logic difficult."

"You're thinking in purely military terms," Taylor said. "But for them . . . well, it's their country. It's the emotional triggers we've got to watch out for now."

Heifetz backed off slightly, as if Taylor had seriously admonished him. For a man who showed the world such a hard, uncompromising mask, Lucky Dave could be remarkably vulnerable. Of course, Taylor thought, out of all of us he's the one who really understands threatened homelands and emotional triggers. He's just fighting it.

"I was thinking, David," Taylor said. "You're a long way from home."

"Which home?" Heifetz asked, a bit of the twilight chill flavoring his voice.

"Israel, I suppose. Anyway, that's what I meant."

"I carry Israel with me. But the Army is my home."

Yes, Taylor thought. If not this army, then another. The eternal soldier.

"Anything new down in the squadrons?" Taylor asked, changing the subject.

Heifetz relaxed at the impersonal turn in the conversation.

"They're simply young soldiers. Fine young soldiers. Ready to fight, even though they're not entirely certain against whom, or even where. No change in systems readiness rates."

"You think we're ready?" It was the sort of question that might have been merely bantering. But Taylor let it be serious.

Heifetz looked at him soberly through the near darkness. "Half of the support base hasn't arrived. Fifteen percent of our crews aren't even range qualified. We've got half a dozen birds down for maintenance, three of them serious . . ." Suddenly, Heifetz smiled. It was a surprising, generous, confident smile. A gift to Taylor. "But we can fight," Heifetz said. "God willing, we're ready to fight."

Taylor smiled too. "Yeah, Dave. That's just about how I figure it. Now I guess it's up to the goddamned Russians."

Taylor was not about to succumb to Meredith's affection for things Russian. But neither did he wish to be too hard on his new allies. He was looking for a rational, functional middle ground. And the Russians had been very good at some things. Even as the fabric of their world was ripping apart, they had done a magnificent job on the deception plan, covering the secret—and hurried—deployment of the big heavy-cavalry regiment, first on the ships supposedly loaded with grain, then by rail across European Russia, the Volga, the Urals, and on into this industrial wasteland buried in a natural wasteland. And there had not been one single indication that the enemy had detected the operation. Even the fine Japanese strategic collection systems appeared to have been lulled to sleep. Meredith had joked that the Soviets were so good at deception because they had practiced self-deception for so long.

The work hall door opened again. This time the footsteps came almost at a run. It was Manny Martinez.

"They're on their way in, sir." He sounded almost out of breath. The cold was very hard on him. "Checkpoint Delta called in on the landline. I've got the sergeant major rounding up the staff and the liaison officers. Merry's going to hang on in the bubble for another minute or two. He's got something hot."

As the supply officer spoke, Taylor could begin to hear the vehicles. Now that the wait was almost over, he finally realized how cold it was. It would be a fine thing to get into one of the little range cars with the heater turned up. If nothing else, you could say that much for the Soviet vehicles: the heaters were kept in good repair.

Taylor had already gotten to know the Soviet range cars with unwelcome thoroughness. Given the volume of heavy equipment his regiment had needed to deploy in secret, it had been agreed with the Soviets that the U.S. forces would leave their light support vehicles behind, relying on Soviet trucks and range cars. It also made good sense in terms of operations security. And the Soviets had been very good about providing vehicles and drivers on request. But the system was cumbersome, with a built-in delay that took the accustomed crispness out of routine ops. The Soviets were reluctant to turn the vehicles over outright, however, pleading insupportable shortages.

Perhaps they were being honest. Every one of Merry's statistics indicated that the Soviets really were in a bad way. But Taylor also suspected it was their method of controlling the whereabouts of the Americans and of ensuring that the Americans did not prematurely compromise their own presence by joyriding around Western Siberia and Central Asia. Taylor had let it go, out of respect for the brilliance and efficiency with which the Soviets had designed and carried out the deception plan, and there had been no major problems. Until today.

He listened as the hum of the vehicles slowly increased in volume while they worked their way through the junk-yard maze with their lights blacked out. The pitch dropped abruptly. That would be the halt at the inner perimeter, where young boys from Arkansas or Pennsylvania in uncomfortable Soviet uniforms would carefully check the identities of the genuine article. Taylor imagined his boys, accustomed to their comfortable cavalry combat uniforms, cursing the antique wool tunics and trousers of their old adversaries.

The pitch of the vehicles climbed again, and Taylor could distinctly hear the shifting of gears. He felt like an old Indian scout, at the job too long. It was too easy to gauge the speed, to judge the range. One of the vehicles in the little convoy needed a tune-up. They were riding light, coming in nearly empty.

A small task force of officers slowly gathered around Taylor. The men who made a plan fit, who worked for the men who made the plan go. Taylor suspected it was going to be a long night's work with the Russians. Even if the news they brought turned out to be miraculously good. The time for contemplation was over. Mars was in the heavens.

Merry Meredith came up beside him. "Sir," he whispered, "it's bad. Jesus Christ, it's bad. They've lost control of it entirely."

Taylor hushed the younger man. "I know," he said.

The lead range car pulled up very close to the work hall, stopping just a few feet away from the group of American officers. Immediately a bundled figure jumped from the passenger's side and hastened toward the human shadows. Taylor recognized Colonel Viktor Kozlov by the silhouette of his permanently slumped shoulders. Kozlov was Taylor's intermediary with the Soviet front commander, General Ivanov.

Kozlov instinctively headed straight for Taylor. The Soviet had become something of a bad joke among the American officers, despite his obvious abilities. The man had spectacularly rotten teeth and breath as powerful as it was unforgettable. Taylor had already upbraided one of his staff captains for making fun of Kozlov. In a voice louder than customary, Taylor had lectured the embarrassed young officer on the Soviet's skills and contributions to the combined U.S.–Soviet effort. Now Taylor himself dreaded the Soviet officer's impending assault.

Kozlov threw a salute into the darkness, his gloved hand a night bird in flight. He came up very close to the object of his attention.

"Colonel Taylor, sir," the Soviet began, his voice infectiously distraught, "we have a great problem. The Kokchetav sector. A great problem. The enemy has broken through."

6

northwest of Kokchetav
northern Kazakhstan
1 November 2020
2200 hours

MAJOR BABRYSHKIN CAREFULLY FITTED THE LAST FRESH filter into his protective mask, listening to the sounds of disaster. Chugging, overloaded civilian cars and trucks struggled to work their way northward without turning on their lights, while the mass of bundled refugees on foot trudged along, unwilling to keep to the side of the road. Apart from an occasional staccato of curses, the ragged parade rarely wasted energy on words. Black against the deep blue of the night, the mob shed sounds uniquely its own: a vast rustling and plodding, the grumble and wheeze of the overburdened vehicles, and the special silence of fear. Thousands behind thousands, the heavily dressed men, women, and children moved on booted feet, slapping gloved hands, shifting parcels, nudged along by the frustrated drivers of automobiles or trucks commandeered from an abandoned state enterprise. Now and again, a dark form simply collapsed by the roadside, a faint disturbance in the night, almost imperceptible. Others broke away to beg the soldiers for food. But the majority kept marching, driven by the memory of death witnessed, closely avoided, rumored. Startling in the darkness, a driven animal would suddenly bleat or bray, sensing the mortal fear of its owner. Then the big silence would return, the huge silence of the Kazakh steppes, an emptiness that drank in the sounds of dozens of battles, a hundred engagements. Only the sputtering horizon acknowledged the ceaseless combat. It was a bigness that trivialized death.

The sharp metallic sounds of the shovels biting into cold soil and the mechanical grunting of engineer equipment marked the positions of Babryshkin's command, deployed on both sides of the endless dirt road that served as a highway, occupying a long reverse-slope position on a decline so slight it was almost imperceptible even in the daylight. You made do.

There wasn't enough food. Babryshkin had been forced to order his men not to hand out any more of their rations to the refugees—the exodus of ethnic Russian and other non-Asian citizens of the Socialist Republic of Kazakhstan. The last precious issues of rations were fuel for the fight now, the same as petrol, as important as the dwindling stocks of ammunition. Without food, the men could not bear the sleeplessness of battle, the heavy duty of digging into the freezing steppes, the energy-robbing chill of the autumn nights. Babryshkin himself hated to get too near the column of his homeless countrymen. He shrank inside at the need to march by their pleas for a bit of food, which, when ignored or denied, so often drew forth insults about an "overfed" army, or, more painful still, about that army's failure.

There wasn't enough food. Nor was there enough medicine. Doctors sought to tend the wounded, injured, or sick by the side of the road, attempting to adapt modern knowledge and techniques to the physical conditions of earlier centuries. There were not enough combat systems or soldiers left, and there was insufficient ammunition for those who remained. The communications did not work. There was never enough time. And there were no answers.

The retreat had gone on for well over a thousand kilometers, punctuated by repeated attempts to dig in and halt the enemy and by successive failures. Combat was a nightmare, a hammering confusion in which each side's systems slammed against each other until the surviving Soviet forces were, inevitably, forced back yet again. Short, sharp exchanges, often a matter of minutes, highlighted days or weeks of nervous skirmishing and endless repositionings. Actual battles were characterized by their brevity and destructiveness. Six weeks before, Babryshkin had begun as a combined-arms battalion commander. Now he commanded the remnants of his brigade, which, except for attachments such as engineers and air defense troops, now fielded a combat force smaller than the battalion Babryshkin had initially led into combat. Staff officers crewed tanks, and cooks found themselves behind machine guns. No one had even formally ordered Babryshkin to assume command of the crippled unit. He had simply been the senior combat-arms officer left alive.

He struggled to maintain control of his force, to continue to deliver some resistance to the enemy, however feeble, to delay the end, to cover the human rivers meandering northward, to cling to this soil made Russian by the armies of the czars so many centuries before.

The worst of it was the chemical attacks. Time and again, the enemy delivered massive chemical weapons strikes against the Soviets, forcing the soldiers to live in their suffocating protective suits and the masks that shriveled then lacerated the skin of the face and neck. No doubt, another chemical attack would hit them soon. There was never any warning now—the entire system seemed to have broken down—and he had not received any messages from corps for days, save one stray broadcast reminding all officers that losses had to be documented on the proper forms.

Babryshkin was glad for this bit of fresh night air, this slight respite between batterings and sudden chemical hells. He had even taken a few moments to scribble a note to Valya, although he had no idea when he might be able to mail it, or if the mails still functioned. According to the last information he had, there had been no attacks on population centers deep in the Russian heartland. The war, brutal though it was, was oddly mannered, localized in the Central Asian republics, the Caucasian republics, and the Kuban. That meant that Valya was safe.

Still, it was far too easy to picture her trudging along in

this mass, on legs not made for such labor. He had made his peace with his mental image of Valya now. He knew she had been unfaithful to him at least once in the past. She was foolish. And selfish. But he was a man, mature, perhaps matured beyond what was truly desirable now, and he was responsible for her. Lovely, unreliable Valya, his wife. In the wake of combat action after combat action, he had grown to appreciate his happiness, and it seemed to him that his life would be a very fine thing if only he might live to get on with it.

The cold air felt wonderful on his cut, chapped face, just cold enough to deaden the discomfort. He had allowed his men to strip off their protective suits to facilitate the process of digging positions. He knew it was unwise in a sense, since chemical rounds or bombs might descend upon them at any moment. But he knew they needed a rest, a chance to feel the living air again. Later, he would order them back into the old-fashioned rubberized suits. But it was increasingly a formality. Living and fighting in the costumes had pricked and torn them until they offered dozens of entry points to chemical agents. And there were no replacements.

Still, he reasoned, his men were far better off than the civilians. Chemical strikes against the unprotected refugee columns produced up to one hundred percent casualties. And there was nothing to be done.

He remembered the dead in Atbasar, thousands of blistered corpses in postures of torment, far worse than his teen-aged memories of the plague years in Gorky, when the river bobbed with dead. Those were hard years, for hard men. But the combination of old-fashioned blood and blister agents, followed by virtually redundant nerve-agent strikes, had created scenes he knew he would carry with him forever.

It was, after all, a racial war. The unthinkable had come to pass. Certainly, few Soviet citizens of his generation— if any—had taken seriously the threadbare ramblings about international and interracial solidarity to which the schools still subjected their charges. But neither had anyone quite expected the peoples of the Soviet Union to explode with such vast and consequential hatred.

Babryshkin wondered which of his many enemies he would fight next. In one engagement or another, as the shrinking brigade had been shunted between sectors, his men had encountered the Iranians, the armored forces of the Arab Islamic Legion, and the rebels, the latter's equipment and uniforms largely mirroring those of Babryshkin's force. He wondered if any of the officers opposing him were men with whom he had attended the combined tank school: Kazakhs, Uzbeks, Turkmen, Tadzhiks, Kirgiz. There had always been a shortage of officer cadets from the central Asian republics, and it told against the rebels now. Even after the military reforms that had allowed recruits from each fringe republic to serve in ethnically uniform units close to home, ethnic Russian or Ukrainian or other European Soviet officers had been required to fill out the command and staff positions. Most of them had been murdered or imprisoned by the mutineers at the start of the revolt, and consequently the rebel units suffered from a pronounced lack of qualified officers. Babryshkin had cut up rebel detachments again and again—only to suffer in turn when the invulnerable Japanese-built gunships returned, or when the Iranians or Islamic Legion forces bullied through with their Japanese-built combat vehicles, whose quality seemed to guarantee success no matter how inept the plan or its execution. The electronics brought to bear by the enemy prevented Babryshkin from communicating and fooled his target-acquisition systems, making a joke even of the Soviet Army's latest acquire-and-fire automatic tank fire control system. Soviet missiles and main gun rounds were drawn astray. And even when Babryshkin's men managed to land their fires dead-on, the enemy's prime fighting systems often seemed to be invulnerable.

He worried that his men would not be able to bear up much longer, that a point would come when the dwindling unit would simply dissolve. But, somehow, the men hung on. Probably, he realized, they felt many of the same emotions he himself felt. Desperation, a battered patriotism, and, above all, a furious hatred that could grow very cold without losing the least of its spiritual intensity. Babryshkin had never imagined himself as the sort of man who would develop a taste for killing, who would ache not only to kill his enemies but to kill them as painfully, as miserably as possible. Yet, he had unquestionably become such a man. The joy he felt when he saw an enemy vehicle explode was certainly different from, but matched in intensity, his best, early nights with Valya. After a time, after he had witnessed enough atrocities, the act of killing attained a sort of purity that would have been unimaginable to the man he once had been.

Babryshkin's brigade had been one of the ethnic Slav organizations garrisoned in Kazakhstan beside local "brother" units, each representing a distinct part of the regional population. Now the blood Russians made up these long columns of refugees, fleeing from the soil that had been their home for generations, that they had struggled to plough and make prosperous, fleeing from the wrath of people they had long imagined or pretended were their brothers in the Union of Soviet Socialist Republics.

Certainly, there had been problems before—the old enmity between the Armenians and Azerbaijanis, between dozens of other ethnic groups whose fates had brought them to the same watering trough. But the Soviet Union seemed to have worked beyond the time of troubles that followed the end of the Gorbachev period, the phases of reaction, counterreaction, and uneasy compromise. A period of somnolence, of dreary but thankfully unmenacing mediocrity seemed to have settled back down upon tundra and desert, steppe and marshland. The clumsy, ultimately unsuccessful repressions, the anarchic impulses, the unsatisfied needs, both spiritual and rawly physical, seemed to drowse off under the cobbled-together solution of dramatically increased federalism, with far more authority devolved upon the individual republics. Racial tensions sputtered now and again, but always settled back down into the prevailing lethargy.

Marx had been right, though. Economics were fundamental. And economics had ultimately exacerbated the smoldering ethnic tensions. As the Soviet Union had struggled to find herself, first under Gorbachev, then under the troika of decayed conservative nonentities who attempted to rule after the blunt end of the *Gorbachevshina,* the rest of the world rushed by in an explosive series of techno-logical revolutions. While in the Soviet Union, nothing ever seemed to quite work, no approach appeared to solve the ever-worsening problem of relative backwardness. With tremendous pain and effort, the Soviet Union took a step forward. The West took three or four. And Japan took five. Then the great Japanese-Islamic Axis had sur-faced in the wake of American retrenchment and Euro-pean neutrality. The combination of Japanese technology with Islamic natural resources and Islam's population base sparked a dynamism that inevitably attracted the impov-erished Asian and traditionally Islamic populations within the Central Asian and Azerbaijani republics of the USSR. The total inability of the state medical system and the central government in general to cope with the stresses of the plague years, and the resultant local famines, lit the fuse. In retrospect, it only seemed remarkable to Babrysh-kin that the bomb had taken such a long time to explode.

Now, as so often throughout history, the Russian people and their ethnic brethren stood alone against the Asian onslaught. Even the East Europeans, who had long since slipped their tether, looked on with a sense of amusement, almost a black joy, as the mighty Russians got their come-uppance. Thankfully, China slept. The Chinese were lost in another of their long cycles of introspection, occasion-ally raising an eyelid to check on the Japanese, then closing it again, content that their carefully delineated sphere of influence had not been annoyed. The developing—or hopelessly underdeveloped—world supported the right of the Central Asian republics to complete independence, lashing out at a bankrupt Soviet Union that had sent them neither goods nor weapons for a generation. The Russians stood alone, again, with a fatalistic sense of history re-peating itself. Mongols, Tartars, Turks, and now these steel horsemen out of the Asian darkness. Even the pos-sibility of a brisk nuclear response, such as the one that had saved the Americans in Africa, had been stolen away by a world too ready to take the Soviet Union at its word in the aftermath of the American blow against Pretoria and the suicidal exchanges in the Middle East that had taken only three days to gut a circle of nations. The Soviets had bellowed loudly, glad for one last chance to strut upon the world stage, insisting on complete nuclear disarmament. And, indeed, the nuclear arsenals had finally, foolishly been dismantled. Babryshkin's handful of tanks and infantry fighting vehicles were all that remained.

"Comrade Commander?" Two helmeted figures approached Babryshkin in the starlit darkness. He recognized Major Gurevich, the brigade's deputy commander for political affairs, by his voice. The position had been abolished back in the nineties, only to be revived again in the conservative retrenchment, with its archaic language and grim nostalgia. Babryshkin was not certain exactly what the political officer still believed in at this point, but he knew that it was not hard work. Gurevich's fitful attempts at making a contribution were far more self-important than helpful, but thankfully they did not take long to sputter out. None of the men would listen to the political officer anymore, and when Gurevich had complained to Babryshkin, the latter had brushed him off with the observation that the men were too busy for lectures and, besides, what was left to say? The men were fighting. There were no deserters. What did Gurevich expect? The political officer had answered that it was not enough to take the correct action, if it was taken for the wrong reasons. The men had to be made to see the theoretical imperative, the political propriety of their actions. But Gurevich had not pressed the issue further, and Babryshkin suspected that the man was simply lost, trying to find some point to his continued service with the unit, to his continued existence. With the collapse of the empire, Gurevich's world had begun to crumble, as well.

"Comrade Commander," the political officer said now, enunciating the antique title in his eternally officious voice, "I've brought the chief of signals. We're picking up a broadcast from headquarters."

Babryshkin turned directly to Lazarsky. He had not recognized the communications officer in the darkness, away from his bank of radios.

"What do they say? What's happening? I thought the secure nets were all being jammed off the air?"

"Comrade Commander," Lazarsky said, "the message is coming in code groups over the unencrypted net. I believe they're broadcasting from an airborne platform. They're repeating it over and over."

Babryshkin stared at the two silhouettes before him. "Well, for God's sake, what does it say?"

"We're to withdraw to the north," Gurevich cut in. "Immediately. It's a blanket message for all units and subunits that have been out of contact with their superior staffs. All units are to withdraw to a line just south of Petropavlovsk."

Babryshkin was stunned. That couldn't be right. "My God, that's over a hundred kilometers from here. At least." He shifted his eyes from one shadow to the other. "There must be some mistake."

"I checked the code groups myself," Gurevich said.

Lazarsky shrugged. "We've been out of contact. The war's been moving on without us."

The only thing Babryshkin could detect in the signal officer's voice was weariness, resignation. But he suspected that Gurevich, despite all of his political demagoguery, did not mind resuming the withdrawal in the least. Instinctively, Babryshkin glanced back at the human river flowing along the road.

The order was impossible. It would leave countless thousands of refugees undefended. In any case, the road was so completely blocked up that the brigade would have to move across country, at a creeping pace. It was a journey beyond the capability of much of the unit's battered equipment. Besides, he was not even certain all of the vehicles had sufficient fuel to cover the distance.

Babryshkin could not believe that anyone who really understood the situation would issue such an order.

"Can we reach headquarters?" Babryshkin demanded. "Can we talk back to whoever's broadcasting?"

Gurevich cut off the commo officer's response, saying, "We can only receive—and that's faint. As soon as we try to call anyone, we're jammed off the air. If we continue with these vain attempts, we risk revealing our position. Such actions are irresponsible. And an order is an order."

"But, damnit," Babryshkin said, raising his voice, waving his right hand toward the road, "what about *them?*"

"Orders . . ." Gurevich stuttered.

Babryshkin's anger continued to rise. It was a sharp, general anger, aimed not only at the fool who had issued such an order but at all of his comrades and countrymen who had brought things to such a pass.

"How do we know it isn't a ruse?" he said, his voice changing pitch with excitement, with bitter vigor. "If we can't call back to verify the order, how do we know it isn't a trick, some sort of imitative deception? It could be the enemy ordering us to pull back. How the hell do we know?"

"The code groups . . ." the political officer said, ". . . it was all in code."

"But, for God's sake, we haven't received new code books since . . . since when? Since we pulled out of Tselinograd. You think the bastards haven't captured any code books?"

"It's a possibility," Lazarsky said matter-of-factly. The debate was of no deep interest to him. His was a world of radios, of antennae and cables, of microwaves and relays.

Gurevich would not respond directly to the question. Instead, he simply said, "The situation . . . is clearly irregular. But we are not in a position to question authority."

Babryshkin felt the weight of command bearing down upon him. It was important, he knew, to think clearly, to avoid emotionalizing. But he did not want to believe that the Soviet forces had been thrown back all the way to Petropavlovsk, the last major city on the northern edge of Kazakhstan, bordering on Western Siberia—and astride the best east-west lines of communication. The very thought was an admission of defeat, and despite the experience of battlefield failures one after the other, Babryshkin was not ready to admit that he had been beaten. Down in his depths, he believed that the Soviet forces would somehow pull off a miracle, first stemming the enemy advance, then beginning to reverse it. He knew that such imaginings had far more to do with emotion than with any reason or logic. But, just as there were certain thoughts he refused to think about Valya, he could not accept any situation in which these grumbling, spiteful, terribly frightened refugees would simply be abandoned.

"Maxim Antonovich," Babryshkin said to the chief of signals, "try to raise headquarters. Just try it one more time." Then his voice subtly altered its target, not really a conscious change, speaking now to the political officer. "I can't just leave them. We can't just turn our backs and go. And this is a good position. We can fight from here."

Sensing a weakness in Babryshkin's voice, Gurevich attacked. "We need to bear in mind the larger picture. Surely higher headquarters has a plan. We cannot be blinded by local conditions. This is all part of a greater whole. After all, winning the war is ultimately more important than any number of . . . of . . ."

"Damnit, what do you think this war's *about?*" Babryshkin demanded. Again, he gestured toward the miserable parade staggering northward. "It's about *them,* for God's sake."

But, even as he spoke, he knew he was lying to himself. Guilty of subjectivism, emotionalism. He knew that the war was about greater things: minerals, gas, oil. The riches of Central Asia. And the far greater wealth of Western Siberia beyond.

"Comrade Commander," Gurevich said, slipping into the lecturing tone with which he was so comfortable, "the war . . . is about the integrity of the Soviet Union. About people, surely. But the state as a collective is greater than individual fates. No one wants to sacrifice a single precious life. But we must bear in mind the greater aim."

You bastard, Babryshkin thought. Walk over and look at them. Let them beg *you* for a few crackers. Then listen to them curse you. But they're not really cursing you, or me. They're cursing what we represent. The failure at the end of all the promises, at the end of all *their* sacrifices. *Go,* damn you. Join that parade for a few minutes.

"*I* am the commander," Babryshkin said, regaining control of his voice. "The decision rests with me. And I do not accept the validity of the message. I believe it to be an enemy ruse. We will stay in these positions and fight, until we receive a message that can be verified directing us to do otherwise. Or until the position becomes untenable or impractical. Or until I decide it's time to move. Let the decision be on my shoulders."

"Comrade Commander, you're tired. You're not thinking like a true Communist."

Babryshkin almost laughed out loud in his exasperation and weariness. Valya would have said the same thing as Gurevich, he knew. Only she would have put it into different words: You fool, you're throwing away your chances, *our* chances. You've got to learn to give them what they want.

Valya. He wondered what she was doing at that instant. In Moscow.

"No," Babryshkin said, digging himself in deeper, relishing it, "Comrade Major Political Officer Gurevich, the problem is that I *am* thinking like a true Communist. You see, the problem is that it's easy to *speak* like a Communist, and for a hundred years we've all spoken like good Communists. The problem . . . is with the way we've *acted*." Babryshkin found himself foolishly waving his protective mask, posturing on the steel soapbox of a tank fender. He caught a glimpse of the absurdity of it all. This was no time for debate. Anyway, Communism meant nothing, and had meant nothing for a generation. It was an empty form, like the rituals of the Byzantine court. At the end of the Gorbachev period, the vocabulary had been revived, to try to fill the frightening emptiness. But the words had no living content.

Babryshkin carefully stuffed the mask into its carrier. "You may try to reach higher headquarters, if you wish, Fyodor Semyonich. But I will not give the order to move until I receive a confirmation."

Suddenly, the southern horizon lit up with flashes far closer than either of them expected. The sound of battle was slow to follow across the steppes, but Babryshkin realized that the enemy had almost reached his outpost line. Perhaps the outposts were already engaged. Or the enemy had caught up with the tail of the refugee column.

The enemy's presence was almost a relief to Babryshkin. After all the waiting. And the false dilemmas of words. Now there was only one thing left to do: fight.

Even before the booming and pocking noises reached the refugees, the display of light quickened the column. Women screamed. A vehicle accelerated, and Babryshkin realized that a driver was attempting to plow right through the mass.

Babryshkin had learned the temper of the crowds over the weeks. Far from reaching safety, the panicked driver would be dragged from his vehicle and beaten to death.

"Let's go," Babryshkin shouted. "Everyone in position." He raced back to the command tank, a battered T-94. All of the combat vehicles had been dug into the steppe at right angles to the road. Only their weapons showed above the shorn earth. Babryshkin nearly stumbled as he leapt from the collar of soil onto the deck of his vehicle, and he reached out to steady himself on the dark line of the main gun. A moment later he sat, knees skinned, down in the hull. The basic T-94 design, introduced more than two decades earlier, consisted of a tank hull traditional in appearance, but instead of an old-fashioned turret there was merely an elevated gun mount. The tank commander, gunner, and driver all sat in a compartment in the forward hull, scanning through optics and sensors packed into the gun mount. The design allowed for a much smaller target signature, especially in hull defilade, but tank commanders always missed the visual command of the situation their perches up in the old-fashioned turrets had allowed. The situation was especially difficult now, since Babryshkin's electro-optics only worked erratically, and Babryshkin was sometimes forced to rely on an old-fashioned periscope. He had meant to swap vehicles, but the work required to remount the command communications sets into a standard tank involved extensive rewiring, and Babryshkin had always found more pressing matters to which to attend. Now he regretted his omission.

Even the acquire-and-fire system, which identified a target and automatically attacked it if the correct parameters were met, had broken down on the command tank. Babryshkin and his gunner were forced to identify targets and fire on them the way tankers had done it more than a generation before. Only a few of the complex acquire-and-fire systems still functioned correctly in the brigade, and Babryshkin had ordered that they be reprogrammed to attack the robot reconnaissance vehicles that always preceded the attacks of the best-equipped enemy forces, such as the Iranians or the Arab Legion. The Japanese-built robotic scouts could steer themselves across the terrain, extracting themselves from all but the worst terrain problems into which they might blunder and providing the enemy with a view of his opponent's positions that allowed him to direct his fires with deadly precision. The recon robotics had to be destroyed, even when it meant ignoring the enemy's actual combat vehicles. Babryshkin felt as though he were waging war with broken toys against technological giants.

"All stations," Babryshkin called into the radio mike, wrenching the set up to full power to cut through any local interference, "all stations, this is Volga. Anticipate chemical strike," he said, hoping he was wrong, that they would be spared that horror this time at least. He knew how the road teeming with refugees would look after the engagement if chemicals came into play. Stray rounds did enough damage. "Amur," he continued, "scan for the robot scouts. Lena, all acquire-and-fire systems that remain operational will fight on auto. All other stations, you have the authority to engage as targets are identified. Watch for Dnepr coming in. Don't shoot him up. Dnepr, can you hear me?" he called to the reconnaissance detachment on the outpost line. "What's out there?"

Babryshkin waited. The airwaves hissed and scratched. He did not know very much about the communications equipment in foreign armies, but he doubted that they were still using such old-fashioned radios. Except for the similarly equipped rebel forces, he never heard inadvertent enemy transmissions on his net. The confused, stray voices that occasionally appeared in his headset were almost invariably Russian.

"Volga, this is Dnepr," Senior Lieutenant Shabrin reported in. He was the only reconnaissance officer still alive in the brigade. "Looks like a rebel outfit. No Japanese equipment. No robotics. A mix of T-92s and 94s. Old BMP-5s. Possible forward detachment structure, feeling their way. The firing isn't directed at me. They're shooting up the vehicles in the refugee column."

Shabrin's voice betrayed more than the lieutenant might have hoped. Babryshkin could feel the boy struggling to control his emotions, to do his job as a recon officer. But the unmistakable tension in the voice conjured up images of the rebel forces savaging the helpless civilians.

Fury rose from under Babryshkin's weariness. Rebels. Men who still wore the same cut of uniform as his own, who had sworn the same oath. Who now believed that ethnic differences were sufficient reason to butcher the defenseless.

Babryshkin wanted to move forward, to attack the attackers. But he knew it would be a foolish move. He had no assets to squander on gallantry. In a running fight his men would divert themselves trying not to harm the refugees—while the rebels could devote their full attention to destroying Babryshkin's handful of vehicles. No, the correct action was to wait in the position his men had so laboriously prepared, to block out the suffering, to sacrifice some for the good of the many—was Gurevich right after all?—and to allow the enemy to close the last kilometers, hopefully without detecting his force, coming on until they became visible to the target acquisition systems, until they were silhouetted on the low rolling steppe. Be patient, Babryshkin told himself. Don't think too much.

"Volga, this is Dnepr. Looks like a reinforced battalion. Hard to tell for sure. I'm getting some obscuration from the column, and they're deploying on an oblique. Listen— I don't think they're just taking random shots as they roll along. They seem to be going after the refugees with a purpose. It's hard to see, but I think there are some infantry vehicles in among them already."

Again, Babryshkin could feel the terrible strain in the tired voice from the outpost line. But he could not indulge Shabrin, any more than he could indulge himself.

"Keep your transmissions brief, Dnepr," Babryshkin radioed. "Just send factual data. Out."

He stared into his optics. The horizon dazzled with golden explosions and streams of light. He knew the central Asian rebel units very well. Ill-disciplined, apt to run out of control. That's right, he told himself as coldly as he could, that's right, you bastards. Shoot up your ammunition. Shoot it all up. And I'll be waiting for you.

Still the flashes that kept lifting the skirt of the darkness would not give him any peace. The display insisted that he acknowledge the level of human suffering it implied, and he could not suppress the mental images, no matter how hard he might try. He toyed with the idea of moving out in a broad turning maneuver, taking the unsuspecting rebels in the flank.

No, he told himself. Don't let your emotions take control. You have to wait.

"Dnepr," he called, "this is Volga. I need hard locations. Where are they now?" He realized how difficult the task of pinpointing the enemy was in the steppes, in the dead of night. Even laser-ranging equipment helped only so much—and Shabrin had been forbidden its use, so as not to reveal his position to the enemy's laser detectors. Now Babryshkin was asking a frantic boy to define the exact location of enemy vehicles in a fantastic environment of darkness and fire, while the enemy continued to move.

"How far out are they now?" he demanded. "Over."

"Under ten kilometers from your location," Shabrin responded. Good boy, Babryshkin said under his breath, good boy. Hold yourself together. "I've got them within top-attack missile range from your location," Shabrin continued. But now Babryshkin detected a dangerous wavering in the lieutenant's voice. And, inevitably, the breakdown followed. "It looks like they're driving right through the refugees, running over them . . . we've got to . . . to . . ."

"Dnepr, get yourself under control. *Now,* damnit." Babryshkin was afraid that the boy would do something rash, perhaps attacking with his handful of reconnaissance vehicles, compromising everything. It was critical to be patient, to wait, to spring the trap at the right moment. Even if he were to open up with his limited supply of top-attack missiles, it would only warn the bulk of the enemy force that there was trouble ahead. And he wanted to get them all, to destroy every last vehicle, every last rebel. He gave no thought to taking prisoners. His unit had not taken any since the war began, and neither, as far as he knew, had the enemy.

". . . *they're just killing them all,*" Shabrin reported, almost weeping. "It's a massacre . . ."

"Dnepr, this is Volga. You are to withdraw from your position at once and rejoin the main body. Move carefully. Do not let them see you. *Do you understand me?* Over."

"Understood." But the voice that spoke the single word bore a dangerous weight of emotion.

"Move *now,*" Babryshkin said. "You'll get your chance to deal with those bastards. If you fire a single round, you'll just be warning them. *Now get moving.* Out."

Babryshkin dropped his eyes away from the cowl of his optics. He snorted, sourly amused. One officer wanted him to retreat a hundred kilometers, and five minutes later another one expected him to launch a hasty attack. While he himself was hoping that he could just get off the first rounds in the coming exchange, to hit first and very hard. Still, he was glad he was not in Shabrin's position. He was not certain he would even be able to muster as much self-discipline as had the lieutenant.

"All stations," Babryshkin spit into the mike, "change to combat instructions. Enemy force approximately battalion in size." He hesitated for a moment. "They're rebels. No robotic vehicles in evidence. Automatic systems will be placed on fire-lock. No one opens fire until I give the order. I want to make damned sure we get as many of them as possible." He paused, worried about the length of his transmission, even though he knew that modern direction-finding equipment could locate a broadcast station in a split second, if any intercept systems happened to be in the area. "After Dnepr comes in, no vehicle is to move," he continued. "*Any* vehicle in movement will be fired upon." He said it forcefully, trying to sound as ruthless as possible to his subordinates. Considering that the rebel equipment was so similar to their own, a running battle would soon degenerate into hopeless confusion and fratricide. The only real difference between his equipment and that of the rebels, he consoled himself, was that theirs was apt to be in even worse condition. The central Asians were terrible at maintenance, and Babryshkin expected to have an advantage in functional automatic systems. We can win this one, he thought. "All stations acknowledge in sequence," he concluded.

One by one, the platoon-sized companies and company-sized battalions reported in. As he listened to the litany of call signs, Babryshkin peered out through his optics. He could not help but translate the spectacle of light in the middle distance into terms of human suffering, the destruction of his people, his tribe. Without fully understanding himself, he felt an urge not only to drive forward and kill the other men in uniform, but to continue southward, to kill their wives and children, responding to them in kind, pushing to its inevitable resolution this war between the children of Marx and Lenin.

Bogged down in their sport with the refugee column, the rebels were slow to advance. Babryshkin's men sat at the ready for hours, watching as the dazzling lines of unleashed weaponry simmered down into the steadier glow of the burning refugee vehicles. Babryshkin could sense the nerves prickling in each of his men. He could feel their torment through the steel walls of the vehicles, through the earthen battlements. They existed in a volatile no-man's-land between exhaustion and rage, aching to act, to do *some*thing, even if it proved to be a fatal gesture. They did not think about dying because they no longer thought about living. They hardly existed. But the enemy . . . the enemy existed more palpably than the frozen earth or the mottled steel hulls of the war machines. The enemy had become the center of the universe.

In the middle of the night, in the hours beyond the clear recognition of time, a furious banging started up on the exterior of Babryshkin's tank. The first thump was so startling in the stillness that Babryshkin thought they had been fired upon and hit. But the force of the blows was on a more human scale. Someone was hammering at the tank with an unidentifiable object, trying to get them to open up.

Cautiously, Babryshkin ordered the crew to sit tight. Then he swiftly flipped open the commander's hatch, pistol in hand.

By starlight, Babryshkin could see the posterior of a man's form kneeling on the steel deck. Then the man stopped his banging and turned toward Babryshkin, slowly, stiffly. He was sobbing.

The battle noises in the distance had faded to random small-arms fire now, and the stretch of road flowing between the wings of Babryshkin's unit was deserted.

The man was old. He panted, out of breath. When Babryshkin scanned him with his pocket lamp, he saw white hair, blue worker's coveralls, a forehead smeared with blood.

The old man searched for Babryshkin's face in the darkness, hunting for the soldier's eyes.

"Cowards," he shouted, weeping. "Cowards, cowards, cowards."

Babryshkin drowsed, reaching his physical limit. In an hour, the horizon would begin to pale, yet the rebel force remained out of direct fire range. They had clearly taken their time with the refugee column. Sated, Babryshkin told himself. A man can only take so much blood. They're drunk with it. Again, he considered launching a sweeping surprise attack, and, again, he suppressed the urge. Stick to the plan, stick to the plan. His heavy eyes settled over visions of earlier years. As a new lieutenant, he had had the hilariously bad luck to be assigned to Kushka, the notorious base at the southern extreme of Turkmenistan. His professors of military science had been embarrassed for him. Kushka was, after all, an assignment where officers were sent as punishment. Junior lieutenant and fresh graduate Babryshkin had been a top student, and he had no black marks on his disciplinary record. Yet, what could you do? The system needed a junior lieutenant at Kushka, where the summer temperatures soared above fifty degrees celsius and poisonous snakes seemed to crowd as densely as Moscow subway passengers at peak hour. Meaning to console the boy, the professors could not help laughing.

Really, an assignment to Kushka was the stuff of which jokes were made—so long as you were not the assignee.

Kushka had been every bit as miserable as had been foretold, added to which the indigenous population was hostile to ethnic Russians—unless you had hard currency to spend or military goods to sell on the black market. But he had learned. How false so many of the teachings had been, how naive he had been himself. The locals felt far more kinship with their smuggling partners across the Afghan border in Toragundi, or with the not-so-distant Iranians. Even then, the lieutenant with the thin blond mustache had known that a change in borders, in formal allegiances, was inevitable. He had even told himself, "Let them have the godforsaken place." Yet, he had naturally hoped that the upheaval would not come when he was on duty, that it might somehow be delayed until it was no longer an immediate concern of his. Let the deluge wait until tomorrow, he thought sarcastically, sitting in his tank almost a decade later. It was the national attitude—may the disasters wait until someone else is on shift, until other shoulders bear the responsibility. He was ashamed of himself now. But there was nothing to be done.

Except to wait for the enemy. And to fight.

A sudden crackling in his earphones startled him out of an unwilling doze.

"Volga, this is Amur. Can you hear me?"

"I'm listening," Babryshkin said.

"I've got movement out to my front. Auto picked them up. I've got my main gun on fire-lock. But it wants to cut loose. Multiple targets. They're so bunched up I can't get visual separation on the screen. Over."

Good. That was how he wanted them. All shot out. Crowding. Unwary. Hungover with death and blood.

"How many?" Babryshkin demanded. "Give me a rough idea." He stared hard into the wasteland of his optics, but the enemy was still out of sight. He wished his on-board electronics were not broken. He wished he had had the determination and energy to transfer his command setup to a tank in better all-around condition.

"This is Amur. Looks like at least thirty heavies. Maybe

more. They're moving like a pack of drunks. Nose to ass-hole. All jammed up."

"All right. Range?"

"Lead vehicles at seventy-five hundred."

Closer than Babryshkin had expected. "All stations, all stations. Anticipate engagement at five thousand meters." He wanted them in close. Theoretically, he could begin engaging now, with both missiles and the swift, oversize guns. But he made up his mind to risk the further wait. The hull defilade positions were good. If the enemy was not very, very alert, they would detect nothing before they reached the deadly five-kilometer line. Once they were that close, none of them would get away. *If* his unit got off the first shots.

"This is Amur. I've got them under seven thousand. They're moving fast. It looks like their higher bit them on the ass."

"No sign of a combat deployment?" Babryshkin asked nervously.

"No. They just look like a mob."

Babryshkin pushed his brows hard against the optics, aching to see with his own eyes. But the darkness, the range, and the long, long reverse slope prevented him from locating the longed-for tanks and infantry fighting vehicles.

"This is Amur. Six thousand meters. They don't even have flank guards out. No forward security."

It was too ideal. For a moment the thought flashed through Babryshkin's mind that it might be a trap.

No. He knew the rebels. He had gone to school with them, served with them, lived with them. And he knew that they had grown overconfident now.

Probably, he thought, the enemy had intercepted the directive to pull back to the north. Gurevich was likely correct—the message was genuine. And now this rebel unit, glutted by a night of murder, had been ordered to get moving, to make up for lost time, to initiate a pursuit of the Soviet forces who were supposed to be pulling back.

Babryshkin grinned. The enemy had finally made a mistake. They had counted too heavily on the Russian tendency to obey orders, no matter what. They had forgotten that there would always be exceptions.

Now the bastards were going to pay for it.

"Volga, this is Amur. Fifty-five hundred meters. Like shooting pigeons."

"All stations, this is Volga. Hold your fire. Keep those autosystems locked up. Let them come all the way in." Yes, there it was. He could just see the first slight movement in his telescoping optics. The manual system was inadequate to fire effectively at this range. Still he knew that he would fire. Wasting ammunition. He would allow himself that one indulgence. While the tank commanders who had better performed their maintenance or who had had better luck would gain the kills.

"Fifty-two hundred."

Babryshkin felt the tension gripping his men. Everyone wanted to feel the big guns going off. To destroy the other men rolling so clumsily, so unsuspectingly toward them.

"Fifty-one hundred meters."

At the Malinovsky Higher Tank Academy, Babryshkin had been assigned a Tadzhik study partner, along with orders to ensure that the central Asian passed the course, no matter what it took. The Tadzhik had clearly understood the system, and he had done as little work as possible. Babryshkin wrote papers for him and put together presentations, while the Tadzhik passed exams by cheating wildly. Anyway, there was a harder grading system for ethnic Europeans. Babryshkin had hated the system, hating the duplicity and dishonor of it all, the injustice. . . .

Now he was glad the system had been the way it was. He only hoped his Tadzhik study partner was commanding the approaching detachment.

"Five thousand meters."

"Fire," Babryshkin called into the mike. "Free autosystems. All others, engage at will." But his men heard nothing beyond the first word. They knew what to do. The huge, thumping sounds of the high-velocity guns penetrated the steel walls of his tank, the padding of his headset.

Explosions filled the lens of his optics. He tried to count the stricken targets in the distance. But they were bunched too closely. One tiny inferno blazed into the next. His headset buzzed with the mixture of elation and complaint he had come to know so well over the past weeks. It was the special sound of men at war now that they fought in separate machines, unable to look at, to touch, to smell each other, reassuring themselves that they were not alone. Babryshkin had come to the conclusion that, even if the radio were not required for communications on the modern battlefield, it would be psychologically necessary so that men locked in combat could reach out to one another. Tell me that my brothers are with me.

"Don, this is Volga," he called to the fire support commander. "Fire deep illumination *now*." He could not hear the response of the combination guns, which were deployed well behind the zigzag of tanks and infantry fighting vehicles, but the sky above and just behind the enemy vehicles soon glared with a false dawn as the parachute flares ignited and began to drift.

The brassy light was just enough to allow Babryshkin to distinguish individual targets. Perhaps two-dozen enemy vehicles were already burning, but, to their credit, the rebels were attempting to organize themselves into battle order. Some of the enemy tanks returned fire, but none of Babryshkin's subunit commanders had reported any losses yet, and the enemy fire had a desperate, unaimed feel to it. For an instant, Babryshkin pictured the chaos, the terror, and the flashes of heroism in the enemy ranks. In that quick sensing, the rebels almost became human again.

"Gunner," Babryshkin called. "Target . . . forty-seven-hundred . . . the guide tank on the far left."

"I see him."

"Fix?"

"It's a long way."

"Goddamnit, have you got him in your sights?"

"Got him."

"Fire."

The hull shivered with the only partially cushioned recoil. And Babryshkin counted the seconds.

The enemy tank kept moving. There was no explosion. They had fired right past him.

"Range," Babryshkin called out in fury, "forty-five hundred . . ."

"Comrade Commander, he's too far out."

"Do as you're told, damn you . . . range, forty-four-fifty."

Suddenly, the enemy tank disappeared in a splash of fire. Someone else had made the kill.

For a moment, Babryshkin said nothing. He did not even scan for another target. The gunner was right. He knew it. It was foolish to waste the ammunition. God only knew when there would be any more of it. Better to let the tanks whose automatic acquire-and-fire systems were still operational do the killing. It was far more efficient.

It was only the matter of *wanting* to kill, to destroy. The feeling went far beyond the desire simply to contribute to the victory. It was far more intense, more personal than that, and Babryshkin could not help experiencing a feeling of disappointment, even of failure, as his brigade annihilated the enemy spread out across the steppes. He listened to the slow, cyclic fire of the autosystems as they moved from target to target. The sound was almost hypnotic, with each loud report followed seconds later by the appearance of another distant bonfire.

He had not seen a single enemy vehicle putting out cyclic fire. Probably, he realized, they had not had a single operational automatic system. In a way, the war was even harder on the overbred machines than it was on their human masters.

A good thing, though, Babryshkin considered, that they were only rebels. He knew his tattered unit would not put up nearly so good a showing against the Arabs or the Iranians, with their magnificent Japanese war machines.

"All stations," he called, "this is Volga. Don't waste ammunition. All manual systems cease fire. Autosystems . . . finish them off. Out."

When he looked very hard through his optics, he could still spot the occasional frantic movement as a rebel vehicle tried to get clear. But the autosystems soon gunned down the last of them. The expanse of steppe looked as it might have looked almost a millennium before, dotted with the campfires of the Mongols.

Babryshkin waited for the familiar feeling of elation to come over him. But it was very slow in coming this time. At first, he wrote it off as due to his weariness. Yet, the adrenaline charge had always been enough to overcome any level of exhaustion.

They had destroyed the enemy force in its entirety. Without losing a single vehicle of their own. It was a significant achievement. They had gained time, saved lives. But Babryshkin felt as he might have after making love to a woman who repulsed him.

He surveyed the torchlit steppe. The sky had begun to pale. There would be a new day, with new enemies. It had been the rebels' turn to misjudge, to take the wrong step. But next time? And the time after that? No one's luck lasted forever.

Well, Babryshkin told himself, we'll just take our bloodbaths one at a time, thanks.

The vehicle fires had already begun to burn out. Babryshkin smiled, as at the taste of bad liquor shared among friends. If nothing else, he considered, Soviet-built tanks were perfectly capable of destroying each other.

The morning light revealed a sea of frost around the battle-warm islands where Babryshkin's tanks were entrenched. He decided to spare Shabrin, the reconnaissance officer, this round of horrors, and he led the security party forward himself: a smattering of infantry fighting vehicles, followed by empty utility trucks to salvage any useful supplies and load up any wounded survivors from the segment of refugees the rebels had attacked. The ambulances remained behind, already filled with military casualties from several days of fighting. A single platoon of tanks moved off to the flank, guarding the searchers, while the remainder of the brigade prepared for movement to the north.

When they closed sufficiently to make sure that every single enemy vehicle had been hit, Babryshkin ordered the tanks to cease their forward movement. Every liter of fuel was critical now.

The infantry fighting vehicles made trails through the frost. It would be even easier to track them now, easier still to find them when the snows came. If they survived that long.

The motorized rifle troops rode with their deck hatches open, making a sport of hunting down any surviving rebels.

136

Only the enemy soldiers who appeared very seriously wounded went ignored. They weren't worth a bullet, and it gave the motorized riflemen more satisfaction to think of them dying slowly, unattended. Babryshkin made no effort to stop the small massacre, even though he had been taught that such actions were criminal and subject to severe penalties. He sensed that such niceties no longer mattered now. This was a different kind of war.

When the snorting war machines finally reached the point of collision between the rebel armor and the refugees, Babryshkin received still another lesson in the varieties of combat experience. He had truly believed that he had seen the worst of the worst, that nothing else would shock him or even move him very deeply, but the sight of the calculated butchery along the dirt track taught him differently. Even the victims of the massive chemical attacks farther south had been impersonally chosen, struck coldly by systems that stood at a distance—aircraft, missiles, or long-range artillery. But many of the bodies along the road had been killed by men who stood before them, close enough to sense them as human beings, to hear the varieties of fear in their voices.

The women had received the worst treatment. The men had merely been killed. But the corpses of the women, either naked or with winter coats and skirts bunched about their waists or pushed over their heads, looked particularly pained, especially cold. All around them the litter of their belongings rustled in the random stirrings of the air. Vehicles had been looted and burned, suitcases emptied beside the corpses of their owners. One of the women, especially vain, had attempted to carry her perfumes with her to safety, and the voluptuous scent from the smashed bottles jarred Babryshkin as he walked between the stench of cordite and the odor of torn bowels. The perfume reminded him of Valya, who always wore too much.

In his wonder at the spectacle of so much very personal death, it took Babryshkin a long time to realize that some of the scattered bodies still had life in them. The silence was deceptive. No one screamed. And you had to listen very closely to hear the rasp of injured lungs or the sobbing beyond hope or fear or any sense at all. The silence of it all frightened him in a way that the prospect of battle had never done.

Then the first scream came. From the mouth of a hemorrhaging girl, who thought that the Soviet soldier bending to help her was simply another rebel back for a bit more fun. Shrieking and slapping at the senior sergeant, she resisted his efforts to cover her and lift her in his arms. Finally the sergeant backed off, giving up. Other casualties were anxious for help. The fate of a single individual had become almost irrelevant, in any case. They left the child in the middle of the roadway, sobbing and clutching a headless doll.

7

Omsk, Soviet Front Headquarters
2 November 2020
0600 hours

VIKTOR KOZLOV'S TEETH ACHED. HE WANTED TO SHOW the American officers, with their fine, strong, white teeth, how effectively a Soviet officer could perform in a critical situation. But he had to struggle to remain clearheaded. Each exchange he translated for General Ivanov, each small detail, had to be conveyed exactly to the impatient Americans. Yet, as he spoke Kozlov imagined he could feel his bad teeth shifting in his gums, and intermittent streaks of pain tightened the skin around his eyes. The combined staff meeting had dragged on through the night, under tremendous pressure, as the front dissolved more thoroughly with each incoming intelligence report. Kozlov felt bleary, hungover from the lack of sleep. He had made the mistake of eating iced salmon and caviar from the buffet table that had been erected and adorned with edible treasures to impress the Americans—and the cold had bitten into his sick gums. He had told himself that he needed food, that fuel was necessary for the body to continue under stress, without sleep. But he recognized now that it had been greed, jealousy, even malice that had made him select the specialties that had grown so hopelessly rare and expensive, even for a Soviet lieutenant colonel. The Americans had munched casually, uncaring, unaware of the effort that had gone into the provision of such a wealth of food. Many of them left their little plates half full of the snacks, in obvious distaste. It was difficult, very difficult to like the Americans. With their bright animal teeth.

He looked at the American colonel with the horrendously scarred face and the black major who made such a show of speaking Russian. Kozlov was certain that the black officer had been sent simply to insult the Soviets. In the U.S. Army nowadays, the Russian language was only worthy of the attentions of blacks. And the remarkable fluency with which the black major spoke only made it worse. Kozlov wondered how much the man could pick out from the hidden meanings skulking behind General Ivanov's admissions and omissions. No, Kozlov decided, he would never be able to like the Americans. He almost suspected that they had picked out officers with the very best teeth to send on this expedition. To offer one more small lesson in humiliation to their Soviet—their *Russian*—hosts.

"General Ivanov assures you," Kozlov translated to the colonel with the nightmare face, "that you will have no problems in such ways with our air defense forces. In the time of your movement to contact, these forces will be under the strictest of orders not to fire unless attacked. There will be absolute safety for you."

Kozlov's teeth felt brittle against his spongy gums, and the slow miserable aching between the jolts of lightninglike pain made him want to drink enough hard liquor to numb himself. But he could not and would not do such a thing, and all he could do was attempt to lull himself with the imagined relief. He wondered if these rich, hard-toothed Americans had some sort of dental officer with them, and if there might be some way to receive treatment without suffering too much humiliation.

He quickly dismissed the notion. Any amount of pain was better than further admissions of inadequacy in front of the Americans. The situation was bad enough. It was shameful that his country had come to such a pass, to require the help of the old enemy, to be reduced to the quality of an international beggar-state. No, it was better to lose all of your teeth than to admit even the slightest additional failure.

"It's of the utmost importance," the American colonel, this famous Colonel Taylor, replied. "There's no way our target acquisition programs can distinguish between your systems and the rebel systems. To our sensors, they're identical. Obviously, it's not a problem with the Arabs or the Iranians. The Japanese gear is easy to spot. But with Soviet-built systems, we can only rely on geography to tell friend from foe. We'll need the very latest information you have before we lift off—and in the air, if we can work it out. We just don't want to hit your boys by mistake."

Kozlov listened as the black major translated for Taylor. It was the exact opposite of the way dual translations should work, but Taylor and General Ivanov had agreed on the backward arrangement between them. He watched the general's face as he listened to the translation, wondering how much the man's expressions gave away to the Americans. The whole situation was made even more difficult by General Ivanov's constant stream of lies. Kozlov knew that the Americans, with their magical systems, knew a great deal more about the situation than they let on. And General Ivanov's deluge of untruths and half-truths was simply embarrassing, even when they were told with the best of intentions. The need to translate those words, to pass on those lies directly to these Americans who knew them for what they were, made him want to grind his teeth. But that was out of the question.

At the very least, Kozlov knew, it would be impossible to reach all of the Soviet air defense elements. Communications were erratic, almost impossible, and the Soviet forces east of the Urals were in such disarray, so fragmented across the enormous, gashed front, that no one knew their strength any longer. The Soviets could not even use their own space intelligence systems to locate friendly forces because the Japanese-built weaponry of the enemy had destroyed them at the start of hostilities. The Soviet forces were reduced to striking wild blows in the dark, unaware of the precise locations of the enemy, unaware even of the current friendly situation at any given time, and all they knew for certain now was that the enemy had almost reached the border between Kazakhstan and western Siberia in a breakthrough between Atbasar and Tselinograd, and that only tattered remnants of the Soviet 17th Army stood in their way in a frantically arranged defense just south of Petropavlovsk. The enemy forces had moved methodically over the last weeks, advancing and consolidating, then advancing again. But now the situation had gone utterly out of control. The intelligence briefing offered to the Americans had stated the enemy situation as clearly as possible. But Kozlov had been able to tell by the facial expression of the black major—a man who for some reason was addressed as "Mary"—that the Americans knew far more than the hapless Russian briefer. Kozlov wished he could get just one look inside the American regiment's field intelligence center. Not to spy—he was past that. Just to find out what in the name of God was really going on out there on the Central Asian steppes.

Everyone knew that it was bad, of course. But there was such a tradition of lies, of glossing over all but the most evident failures, that Kozlov's countrymen could not quite bring themselves to admit to foreigners—even to allies in a desperate hour—how dismal the situation had become. General Ivanov was perfectly willing to admit there had been a breakthrough. But the desperate request for an American commitment to battle a full week ahead of schedule was excused as necessary only to guarantee the success of a planned Soviet counterattack. While the general knew very well that the closest the Soviet forces could come to a counterattack would be to hurl empty shell casings in the direction of the enemy. Ivanov, in fact, considered two real possibilities. First, the Americans, with their secret wonder machines, might actually achieve some degree of success. In which case, the Soviet defenses would be shifted southward, creating a larger buffer south of the border of Western Siberia and, in a sense, constituting something that almost qualified as a counterattack in a very liberal interpretation of the term. More likely, the American commitment would simply buy some time to sort out the incredible mess out there on the steppes. Moscow, of course, hoped that the shock of the American presence might bring about a cease-fire. But that was a desperate hope. General Ivanov had long since stopped speaking to Kozlov or any of the staff about victory. Now they all simply fought on from day to day, struggling just to gain a clearer picture of the situation. For weeks, they had lived and worked in a mist. It was only with the Americans that General Ivanov still spoke as though he really commanded a wartime front, with all its units and support, when, in fact, the battlefield had collapsed into anarchy.

Kozlov poked at the rotted husk of a molar with his tongue. He had to admit that the Americans were very cooperative. As soon as General Ivanov had formally passed on the request for immediate assistance as approved by Moscow, the American colonel had excused himself to contact his superiors. The request had, of course, been transmitted from government to government, and Kozlov had watched anxiously as the American staff officers simply unpacked a gray suitcase lined with electronics and began a direct keyboard dialogue with Washington. Without the extension of an antenna or need of an external power source. The Americans conducted themselves nonchalantly in regard to the technology, as though the device were no more consequential than a cigarette lighter. Yet, a calculated display could not have slapped the watching Soviets across the face more sharply with the evidence of their technological inferiority. Kozlov felt as though he had been living in a country where time stood still.

The American colonel had not attempted to make any excuses in order to avoid entering battle early. Nor had he attempted to bargain to better his own position. He had simply spoken electronically to his superiors, his dreadful face impassive, and, within fifteen minutes, he had returned to General Ivanov with the words:

"Washington says go."

And the frantic planning had begun, with more American staff members hustled in from their hideaway in the industrial center. Now, in the heavy morning hours, the sealed planning facility stank of Soviet tobacco and unwashed bodies. Everyone, even the smooth-complected Americans, wore a weary, grimed look, and they spoke more slowly, in shorter constructions. The two staffs, awkwardly asymmetrical in design, struggled to work out the countless small details of a combined operation, pencils, pens, markers, and keyboards chiseling away at concepts as they sought to sculpt a viable plan that would bring the U.S. force to the battlefield in thirty-six hours. Technically, enough translators were available. But it soon became evident that the language skills were not sufficiently acute. Repeatedly, Kozlov himself had been called to help settle a point of misunderstanding in operational terminology or graphics, and he worried that he, too, might make a critical mistake. The Americans from the southern part of the United States were especially difficult to understand, while the easiest, curiously, was the Israeli mercenary operations officer—who spoke in English that was self-consciously precise.

Kozlov had studied the Americans for much of his career as a GRU intelligence officer. Even when he had labored beside line officers in the new Frunze Academy program for the Soviet Army's chosen, he had done his best to stay current with the status of U.S. military adventurism in Latin America. He sought to understand the nature of the United States and to grasp why its military was different from his own. He had shared the delight of his fellow lieutenants years before, when the United States had undergone its African humiliation. Of course, none of his peers had been able to read the portents any better than Kozlov. They had not, as the English poet had written, really understood for whom the bell tolled. Now the world had turned upside down. But Kozlov found that at least the American military character as he had imagined it remained a constant. These officers bending over maps and portable computers, though various in detail, seemed so typical as a group: aggressive to the point of thoughtlessness, undaunted by sudden changes, impatient with details, superficially open but in fact quite closed as people, poor theorists but instinctive fighters with a gutter edge, argumentative even with superiors and unperturbed by responsibilities that a Soviet officer would take pains to avoid. These were men so accustomed to a wealth of possessions, both military and personal, that they were blind to the small sacrifices and special efforts of others. The matter of the buffet table was a perfect example. Despite the urgent demands of the hour, the Soviet command had gone to outrageous lengths to provide the best possible foods for the American officers. Even the most embittered, calloused Soviet officers had paused in shock at the bounty spread over the tables at the end of the planning cell. The buffet was, of course, meant to impress the Americans. But it was also intended sincerely to convey the depth and self-sacrifice of Russian hospitality. To the Americans, however, the food hardly appeared worth eating. For hours, it went ignored, while the Soviet officers eyed it incredulously. Only when General Ivanov personally led the American colonel to the table—verbally dragging the man—had a few of the Americans broken loose from their maps and electronics to nibble a bit of this and that.

Kozlov had felt the humiliation and outright pain of each Soviet officer in the room as they waited until enough of the Americans had picked over the food to make it barely acceptable for them to help themselves. With guilty faces, the Soviet staff officers had sneaked toward the delicacies. For some of the junior officers, Kozlov suspected, it was the first opportunity in their lives—and perhaps their last— to sample some of these famous Russian specialties. As the early morning hours dragged on Kozlov had almost reached out to strike a young captain he noticed picking over the food an American had abandoned on a stray plate.

Yes, Kozlov decided again, in many ways the Americans were to be admired. Even envied. But they were impossible to like.

Colonel Taylor struck him as something of a stereotype of the American combat leader. Despite the eccentric details of the man's biography. This man appeared heartless, expressionless, businesslike to the point of cruelty. Even the man's scarred face was warlike, giving him the appearance of some tribal chief painted to frighten his enemies. Kozlov remained forever on edge in Taylor's presence, always expecting the man to lash out suddenly, unreasonably, to criticize his translations as too slow or somehow incorrect, or to call him a liar to his face. Normally, Kozlov was the most self-possessed of officers, successful, full of boundless promise, comfortable in the presence of generals and high officials. But this man Taylor had the power to keep him off balance with a casual glance. This tall, scarred man from a child's nightmare. In his no-nonsense fashion, the American colonel was unfailingly polite, even considerate. Yet Kozlov always felt on the verge of making a fool of himself.

Kozlov was familiar with the secret file on Taylor. Born in April 1976. U.S. Military Academy, class of 1997. Light athletics, a fine runner. An especially good horseman. Academically sound. A veteran of the African debacle who had made a near-legendary journey through the back-country of Zaire. He had survived a bout with Runciman's disease with no apparent mental impairment but with heavy scarring that he refused to have treated. Kozlov paused in his mental review, ambushed by the image of his own young wife and child dying without decent care, without medicine, their fevered eyes full of blame. Then the image was gone, leaving only a residue of pain far harsher than the ache of his teeth.

Taylor was a bachelor. He had apparently been a bit wild as a young lieutenant, before the deployment to Zaire. But the facial scars had brought his amorous adventures to a sharp conclusion.

Kozlov rushed forward through the man's history. There was, of course, the little tart who worked for the Unified Intelligence Agency. A woman who had slept with every-one in Washington except the Soviet embassy staff. But that was a very recent development, and despite the gossip and laughter about the affair back in Washington, Kozlov doubted that anything would come of the matter. He could not imagine even the most slatternly of women sharing more than a few clumsy hours of Taylor's life. Even then, they would need to turn out the lights.

But, if Taylor's career as a lover had been cut short, he had certainly developed an impressive reputation as a soldier. Increasingly austere personal habits. Nonsmoker, light drinker. Obsessed with physical exercise, though not an outdoorsman by nature. Neither hunted nor fished, although he was reportedly fond of mountain hiking. Quietly intellectual behind his hard public personality. Professionally very well-read for an American. Liked to read classic American novels in private, especially Mark Twain,

Melville, Hemingway, and Robert Stone. A penciled note in the biographical file had pointed out that all of Taylor's favorite books were about men who were outsiders. He had gained a master's degree in electronics and information theory—even though his personal interests lay elsewhere. He had survived each new wave of the personnel cutbacks that had so hollowed out the U.S. military. During the plague years, he had commanded first a cavalry troop, then a squadron in Los Angeles, where he had simultaneously enhanced his reputation as a soldier, taught himself Spanish, and completed a critique of the U.S. intervention in Zaire so merciless it nearly resulted in his dismissal. Instead, the ultimate outcome had been an accelerated promotion. American military personnel policies were completely unfathomable.

Taylor had then been instrumental in the U.S. Army's reorganization, when the colors of the old cavalry regiments were resurrected to identify the new, streamlined units replacing the heavier, almost immovable divisions and corps. An expert in the field of heavy forces and emerging military technology, Taylor had nonetheless been sent to command a light task force in Mexico as the United States attempted to halt the multisided war on its southern border. Arriving in the wake of the Tampico massacre, Taylor had exploited the newly imposed press controls to keep reporters out of his area of operations, first in San Miguel de Allende, then, upon his further promotion, in the Guadalajara region. This part of the file had been defaced with question marks where GRU analysts had tried to figure out the paradox of the man's success. He broke rules, always doing the unexpected, and gained a reputation as a savage mountain fighter. His subordinates employed techniques ranging from helicopter descents to old-fashioned cavalry patrols, eradicating rebel groups one after the other, many of whom were little more than bandits, while others were Japanese-funded patriotic forces. Almost invariably, he was very well received by the local population, who should have been supporting the insurgents. None of the Soviet analysts could sort out the dialectical equations.

This killer who read good books, this scarred man who

was a perfect robot of a soldier, had returned to the United States to assume command of the newly reformed and re-equipped Seventh Cavalry Regiment (Heavy) at Fort Riley, Kansas. The unit was built around a new series of weapons systems the details of which were still unclear to Soviet intelligence, even as the Americans planned their mission on the same maps as Kozlov's comrades-in-arms. Taylor had been in command only nine months, much of which actually had been spent in Washington, testifying before various committees, when the Soviet Union had secretly asked the United States for its assistance in the face of a growing threat of a war for national survival.

And why were these men here after all? Why had the United States responded positively? Kozlov was certain their purpose was not to selflessly assist the people of the Soviet Union. Nor did they particularly covet the mineral wealth of Western Siberia for themselves, since they had largely purged the Japanese presence from Latin America—and the new finds there were adequate to American needs. He did not even believe the American motivation was vengeance, either against the eternally recalcitrant and bloody-minded Iranians or even against the Japanese, whose long shadow lay so obviously over the Islamic executors of their imperialist plans. In the end, Kozlov suspected, his country had simply become a proving ground for a new generation of American weapons, nothing more.

His teeth ached so badly he wanted to claw them out of his gums. When would it end? When would any of it end?

To hell with the Americans, he decided. He didn't give a damn why they were here. As long as their weapons worked.

Major Manuel Xavier Martinez stood beside Taylor at the corner of the ravaged buffet table, picking at a few leftovers to take the place of a combat ration breakfast and working through yet another set of interoperability problems. The two men spoke in Spanish for the sake of privacy and, despite his weariness, the supply officer could not help finding the situation bizarrely amusing. He routinely addressed Taylor as *"Jefe,"* but this was only an inside joke. In fact, Taylor's Spanish was more grammatically correct, cleaner, and more exact, than was his own. Martinez's blood was Mexican-American, but his primary language—the tongue of his education and elective affinities—was the English of an erudite and educated man. His Spanish was the barrio dialect of his youth in San Antonio, fine for bullshitting on a street corner, but inadequate for expressing sophisticated logistical concepts. As they spoke Martinez punctuated his Spanish with far more English-language military terminology than his utterly Anglo-Saxon commander found necessary.

"I still see two areas where we can really get screwed, sir," Martinez said. "And I'm only talking about the log business." He glanced across the smoke-fogged room to the portable workstation where Merry Meredith stared wearily at the incoming intelligence information. "I wouldn't want to be in Merry's shoes."

"Merry can handle it," Taylor said.

"Yeah. I know that, *Jefe*. But it's not just that they're a lying bunch of bastards. It's the way they treat him. That lieutenant colonel with the rotten teeth. Christ, he acts like an Alabama sheriff from back in the nineteen fifties." Martinez shook his head. "And you know it breaks Merry's heart. He's so into that Russian culture shit."

"Merry's been through worse. You're just lucky they think you're a Georgian or an Armenian."

"I still can't get a straight answer out of them," Martinez said. "It's worse than Mexico."

"Mexico was the bush leagues," Taylor said.

"All the more reason why I wish these guys would play it straight."

"They can't," Taylor said, with surprising patience in his voice. The man's calm never ceased to impress Martinez. "They can't tell us the truth about the overall situation because they just don't know it themselves. Listen to them, Manny. They're lost. And they're scared. And they're trying to put the best face on it they can. Their world's coming apart. But they're willing to give us what they've got."

"The problem is finding out *what* they've got," Martinez said. He took a drink of flat mineral water to wash the last bits of cracker from his throat. "Anyway, the first issue

I've got to look at is fuel. We've got enough of our own to run the mission. But the M-100s will be nearly empty at the end of it. First squadron is going to be running on fumes, judging by the arrow Lucky Dave just drew for them. That means depending on Soviet fuel. Our own complement won't be full-up for another five, six days, depending on the Soviet rail system."

"So what's the Martinez solution?" Taylor asked, face impassive, a graven death mask to which Martinez was only now becoming accustomed, after so many years of working together.

Martinez smiled. "I'm that predictable?"

Taylor nodded. A ghost of amusement on the dead lips.

"Well," Martinez said, "the Sovs have one type of fuel that's almost as good as JP-10. And their boy says he can provide it. Of course, their fuel's polluted as often as not. We'll have to test each last bladder and blivet. But, if we can corner them into delivering the fuel on time, I suggest we run this mission on their fuel and conserve our own." Without burdening Taylor with unnecessary details, he quickly reviewed the other advantages of such an option. Their own fuel reserves were already uploaded on the big wing-in-ground fuelers, and it would save transfer and upload time. They would preserve their independence of action.

"You're sure their fuel won't have us falling out of the sky?"

"No," Martinez said, even as he thought the problem through one last time, "no, we can quality control it. As long as we get the pure stuff, the composition is just fine. Anyway, I'm not worried about the engines. Battle-site calibration's another issue."

"All right. Go ahead. You said there were two problem areas."

"Yeah, *Jefe*. You and Lucky Dave may have to get in on this one. These guys are just congenital centralizers. My counterpart wants to stash all of the supplies in one big site. At the far end, where we finish up the mission. He says the general wants it that way, that, otherwise, they can't guarantee support site protection. Logic doesn't make a dent in these guys. And decentralized ops just give them the willies." Martinez shook his head. "We come at everything from different angles. They're worried about guarding the stuff on the ground. You know. 'Who goes there?' and all that. While I'm worried about missiles and airstrikes. Christ, the way they want to heap everything up in one big pile, it would only take one lucky shot to put us out of business."

For the first time, Taylor's face showed concern. The scarred brows bunched. "I thought we were clear on that. We agreed that each squadron had to have its own discrete dispersal area. Heifetz has them on the graphics."

"But Lucky Dave's talking apples, and they're talking oranges. They don't automatically assume that each squadron should have its own self-contained *support* site."

Martinez caught the electric flash in Taylor's eyes. The old man had missed the potential problem, as had everyone else. Martinez was sorry he had not been able to resolve the conflict himself, because he knew Taylor well enough to realize that the old man would beat himself up unmercifully for not having spotted the potential disconnect earlier. Martinez had never met another man, another soldier, who was so hard on himself. Not even Merry Meredith or Lucky Dave Heifetz, the other members of the Seventh Cavalry staff's self-flagellation society.

Martinez's life had not been full of heroes. He had been lucky enough not to look up to the street-corner cowboys back in San Antonio, boy-men as his absent father had been, and his adolescence and young adulthood had been spent in a struggle to be better than the rest, to show everyone that the kid from the barrio could shut them down. Getting higher grades, speaking better English. His ROTC scholarship to Texas A&M had not only paid the bills, but it had proved that he was every bit as *American* as any of the Anglos. He refused to be categorized as anything less, to let any man define him in any way that might diminish his singularity. When he went home to visit his mother, he refused to speak Spanish with her, even refused to eat the Mexican food she was so anxious to cook for him. And as a captain he had put down his entire savings to buy her a solid, middle-class house in a suburb in northwest San Antonio, one whose payments would bind his salary for years to come. It was an enormous step, a triumph for him. Yet his unsuccessful, increasingly worried attempts to call home, to speak with the prematurely aged woman, soon brought him back to earth. He finally tracked her down at his aunt's number. And his mother wept, claiming she loved the house and she was as proud of him as any mother could ever be. It was only that the new house was so big, so empty, and so far from all that she knew. The neighbors did not understand Spanish. So she had taken to staying with her sister back in the barrio. Where she felt at home. Now the house stood empty, except on the rare occasions when he went back on leave. It was a monument to the personal limits, to the failure, of the young man without heroes.

And then there was Taylor. Martinez did not like to use the word *hero*. But, had he chosen to apply it to any man, his first choice would have been this unusual colonel who stood between him and the desolation of the buffet table.

Taylor of Mexico, intuitively grasping the situation and its requirements so much better than the Quartermaster captain who shared the indigenous bloodlines. The civilian academics and specialized advisers attached to the Army had lectured Taylor on the nutritional requirements of the populace and on the infrastructural deficiencies associated with chronic underdevelopment. And Taylor had kicked them out of his sector, in defiance of Army policy. He understood the need to satisfy minimum dietary requirements, but, above all, he understood the need for *theater*. Wearing preposterous silver spurs, Taylor was always the first man out of the helicopter. He traced canyon rims on a magnificent black stallion and walked upright where other men crawled. Martinez knew what it was to be afraid, and he did not believe that any sane man could be truly fearless. But Taylor certainly disguised his fear better than the rest—driving his utility vehicle, alone, into towns where the representatives of the U.S.-backed Monterrey provisional government hung from the utility poles with key body parts conspicuously absent. Exploiting the dramatic ugliness of his face to maximum effect and living on tortillas and beans so that he could ostentatiously give his rations to widows and orphans, Taylor transcended all of the Anglo rules of behavior to achieve the grand level of gesture demanded by a tormented Mexico. His peers called him a hot dog, a show-off, a nut, and a dirty sonofabitch—as they struggled to emulate his success. Taylor, who seemed able to project himself with equal ease into the mindset of a Mexican peasant or a Los Angeles gang member. Taylor, who masked his intelligence and command of language behind the terse, requisitely profane speech his subordinates imagined a commander must employ. Major Manuel Xavier Martinez did not believe in heroes. But he was not certain he could ever be such a man as Colonel George Taylor.

"Manny," Taylor said to the supply officer, "it's a good thing I've got you to keep me from fucking this whole thing up. I should have made the goddamned Russians clarify exactly what they understood by force dispersion." The colonel was angrily intense, but the sharpness was directed solely against himself. "When our boys come back in from the mission, I want to be damned sure they come in on top of all the fuel, bullets, beans, and Band-aids they need. The standard drill."

"Standard drill," Martinez agreed, anxious to please this man, to serve him well, yet, at the same time, ashamed that he would have to ask for further help. "I'm afraid you're going to have to take it up with Ivanov himself, *Jefe*. He's driving the train, and my counterpart's afraid to throw any switches on his own. He thinks I'm nuts for wanting to scatter our log sites all over creation and even crazier for questioning what a general wants."

Taylor nodded. "All right, Manny. Let's grab Dave and Merry and have another powwow with our little Russian brothers."

Martinez smiled. "I guess that means we have to let that sorry bugger Kozlov breathe on us again." He looked down at a smeared cracker he had lifted off his plate. The sight of it was so dismal, laden with a rough gray paste, that he held it in midair, unable to bring it the rest of the way to his mouth.

He felt Taylor staring at him. The intensity of the colonel's gaze seemed to freeze the supply officer's hand in midair, the trick of a sorcerer. Instantly, Martinez's eyes were drawn to Taylor's, and he saw absolute seriousness in the depths of the other man's stare.

"Eat it," Taylor said quietly, the tone of his Spanish as dry and ungiving as a high mountain desert. "And then smile."

Major Howard "Merry" Meredith had almost forgotten what it was like to be judged by the color of his skin. Although the Russians were not blatantly impolite, they barely masked their distaste in dealing with him. He was the sole member of Taylor's primary staff who spoke Russian, yet his opposite number obviously preferred dealing with Meredith's white subordinate through a translator.

Merry Meredith could take it. He had been through far, far worse experiences in his life. Yet he could not help being saddened. He had long been warned about Russian racism . . . but he had believed that *he* would be the exception. In deference to Pushkin. Only he of all these Americans had read the Russian classics. He knew the titles and even the dates of Repin's paintings, just as he believed he alone of the Americans grasped the iron inevitabilities that had brought this people to such tragedy. He even knew the names and ingredients of the array of *zakuski*, the bounty of snacks, which the hosts obviously had gone to great lengths to produce. Yet the Russians offered him only uneasy glances as he approached the buffet table, as though the color of his skin might dirty the food.

Racial discrimination was something that had found no entry into his sheltered college-town youth, and West Point had constructed its own barriers against such prejudice. The Army itself had been so starved for talent that a man's racial, ethnic, or social background truly made no difference. It was only a bit later that he had finally been forced to look in the mirror.

And now, years after that terrible day in Los Angeles, he found himself trying to work beside a Soviet colonel who regarded him as only a marginally higher form of animal. His counterpart lectured him on the intricacies of the enemy forces and the battlefield situation in so elementary a fashion that Meredith had to continually call up the example and image of Colonel Taylor to refrain from verbally launching into the paunchy *polkovnik,* if not physically assaulting him. The worst of it was that the Soviet clearly knew far less about the enemy and even the Soviets' own condition than did Meredith, and what little the colonel knew was out of date. Thanks to the constant intelligence updates he received in his earpiece and on the screen of his portable computer, Meredith knew that the battlefield situation was growing more desperate by the hour. Yet Colonel Baranov seemed interested only in demonstrating his personal—his racial—superiority.

Meredith was grateful to see Manny Martinez break away from his one-on-one with Taylor and head toward the worktable that had been set up as an intelligence planning cell.

Manny wore an inexplicably grand smile on his face, which hardly seemed to track with the prevailing atmosphere of physical and mental exhaustion.

"Excuse me, sir," Manny said to the potbellied Soviet colonel, who looked for all the world like the leader of an oompah band, his pointer waving like a baton. Then he turned to Meredith. "Merry, the old man wants you to listen in on a little powwow. Can you break away for a minute?"

Meredith felt like a schoolboy suddenly authorized to play hooky. He quickly made his excuses in Russian to the colonel, leaving his subordinate to suffer on in the name of the United States Army.

Squeezing between the tables, Meredith found that Manny's grin was contagious.

"What the hell are you smiling about, you silly bastard?" Meredith asked his friend.

Manny's smile opened even wider. "It's the food. You've got to try it."

"I have," Meredith said, puzzled. Although he intellectually understood the effort that had gone into the preparation of the buffet and the relative quality of the provisions, he could not believe that Manny really enjoyed the *zakuski.* His efforts to persuade other officers to eat had failed embarrassingly. "Come on, you're shitting me."

"Not me, brother. It's great food. Just ask the old man."

Meredith decided that it was all just a joke he'd missed,

after all, and he let it go. Brushing past the last workstation, he caught the edge of an overlay on the rough wool of his trousers and tipped a number of markers onto the floor.

"Some quarterback you must've been," Manny said.

Meredith and his friend hastily retrieved the fallen tools from amid the wasteland of computer printouts on the floor, apologizing to the bleary-looking captain whose work they had upset. When they arose, Colonel Taylor was standing before them, along with General Ivanov, Kozlov, and another Soviet whom Meredith recognized as Manny's counterpart. In a moment, Lucky Dave Heifetz marched up, along with the Soviet chief of operations.

Careful not to call attention to his maneuvering, Meredith shifted along the backfield so that he was not in the direct line of Kozlov's breath. The Soviet was a reasonably handsome man—until he opened his mouth, revealing broken, rotted teeth, the sight of which made a man wince.

The Russian's breath was easily the most powerful offensive weapon in the Soviet arsenal. Meredith felt sorry for Kozlov, since it was evident that he really was a first-rate officer, determined to do his damndest to make things work. But Meredith did not feel sufficiently sorry for him to stand too close.

As it was, the room stank and the air felt dead, heavily motionless. The fabric of the stiff old-fashioned Soviet uniforms worn by all had grown rougher still with dried sweat. Meredith was not certain his stomach could take Kozlov's halitosis at this time of the morning, without sleep, and with the Russians' rich, bad food clumped in his belly.

Taylor drew them all toward the map that lined the wall of the chamber, glancing toward Meredith to ensure that the intelligence officer was prepared to translate.

"It seems," Taylor began, "that our haste has accidentally created some minor confusion for our Soviet allies . . ."

The translation was not difficult. Meredith knew precisely the tone Taylor wanted to strike, and it was exactly the right one. Whether dealing with street punks or Mexican bandits, with senators or Soviet generals, Taylor's ability to find not only the correct voice, but even the specific tone that best exploited his opposite number's preconceptions, never failed to impress Meredith.

What did the Soviets think of Taylor himself? Meredith wondered. Meredith had noted that few of the Soviet officers bore noticeable RD scarring. He knew that the Soviet Union had suffered a far higher percentage of plague casualties than had his own nation, but it appeared as though there were some code that prevented badly scarred survivors from attaining high rank. Meredith wondered if it was merely the old Russian military obsession with appearances at work in yet another form.

He tried to view Taylor afresh, as these strangers might see him. It was difficult to be objective, having worked with the man for so many years and feeling such a deep, if inarticulate affection for him. Even in the United States of 2020, Taylor was far more apt to be the object of prejudice, even of primitive fear, than a well-dressed, unscarred, full-fledged member of the establishment who just happened to wear skin the color of milk chocolate. Meredith wondered if the Russians would judge this man, too, solely by his appearance.

". . . and we want to resolve all problems in an atmosphere of openness and good faith," Meredith translated.

Army General Ivanov listened to the easy flow of the black American's Russian, wondering where he had learned to speak the language so well. The Americans were full of surprises. And some of them were pleasant surprises—they were so willing, so confident, so quick. But other surprises were more difficult to digest. Such as this business about the dispersion of the support sites. The Americans' speech was very polite. But behind the courtesy they were adamant. Ivanov had already noticed the pattern. The Americans would give in on inconsequential points, but insist on having their own way in the more significant matters.

Ivanov was physically tired, and he was weary of arguing. All right, let them do what they wanted. And the Soviet Army would do what it wanted with its own forces. Let the Americans have their try. Ivanov would have liked to believe, to have faith, but he had experienced too much failure over too long a time. He doubted that a single regiment of these mystery-shrouded American wonder weapons would be enough to make a decisive difference. But he would be grateful for whatever they achieved. The situation was desperate, and he was haunted by the vision of going down in history as one of those Russian military commanders whose names were synonymous with disaster.

But who could say how much longer there would even be a Russian history? Look at the depth to which they had already sunk. Begging for help from the Americans. . . .

Well, they, too, were living on borrowed time. Ivanov believed that the age of the white race was past, that the future belonged to the masses of Asia, and that the best one could hope for would be to hold back the tide a little longer.

Ivanov looked from American face to American face. How awkward they looked in their Soviet uniforms. This brutal-looking colonel—the man had to be some kind of monster inside as well as outside, or he would have availed himself of the fine American cosmetic surgery. And the one who looked like a Georgian playboy. Then there was the Israeli—Ivanov knew his type, the constipated sort who never smiled, never took a drink. You always had to watch the Jews. The Germans had not been able to manage them, nor had the Arabs, with their nuclear weapons and nerve gas. But the Jews had not been so smart after all—they had backed the American horse, when they should have bet on the Japanese. Then there was this black major who spoke such fine Russian. Ivanov believed that this American staff had been consciously selected, man by man, to convince the Russians of the internal solidarity of the American people, much as the staged photos of his youth had attempted to do with Soviet society, posing smiling Estonians and Ukrainians with Azerbaijanis and Tadzhiks. But the Americans were not fooling anyone, and Ivanov wondered how such a staff would fare in combat.

It had all been so different once, when he had been a young officer. Even a junior lieutenant had commanded respect. Then that man Gorbachev had come, with his reforms, his promises. And he had begun chipping away at the military. And ambitious men within the military had helped him. Ivanov himself had been convinced of the need for *perestroika,* caught up in the delusions of the times. So few of the promises had come true. People simply lost their respect, their fear. They wanted to live like West Europeans, like Americans. They did not understand the role of the Soviet Union, of Russia, in the world. They thought only of themselves. Then, as the country began to come apart, more sensible men had finally taken over. But it was too late. Ivanov was familiar with the theories—the inevitability of the decline of an economic model that had outlived its utility, the price of decades of overspending on defense, the oppressiveness of the system that stifled possibilities of growth . . .

Lies, lies, lies. Gorbachev and his cronies had betrayed the trust, they had given victory away. In the end, gutting the military had saved no one. The economy did not magically spring to life. Instead, conditions had become worse and worse. Shooting would have been too good for the men who had ruined the greatest country on earth.

Once the system had been spoiled, nothing else had worked, either. It was like trying to squeeze toothpaste back into the tube. *Democracy.* The word was barely worth laughing at. The Soviet Union had needed *strength*. In its place, the people had received promises, inequity, betrayal.

The decades during which Ivanov had gained his rank had been little more than a chronicle of decline, of insurgencies, of riots, of half-measures. His life had been squandered in a long twilight.

And now it had come to this. Civil war, invasion, collapse. And these Americans, who had come out of spite, for revenge.

As he settled the last details with these arrogant, overly confident men masquerading in the uniform that had clothed his life and dreams, Ivanov felt a tragic sense of loss toward his country's past, like a man in the worst of marriages remembering the girl he should have wed.

The staff meeting was breaking up. The Americans would go and finish their final preparations. Then they would enter the war. With their miraculous new weapons whose details they would not discuss even now.

Well, good luck to them. Ivanov hoped they would kill many of his country's enemies. Certainly, if confidence alone could kill, the Americans would do very well, indeed.

Perhaps they had very great secrets, even greater than Soviet intelligence suspected. But, alone among the Soviets and Americans in the room, General Ivanov also knew a secret. It was a terrible secret, one which the Soviet hierarchy had kept from everyone below Ivanov's rank, so as not to further demoralize the war effort. Not even poor Kozlov knew. But, Ivanov suspected, the Americans were soon going to find out.

8

Washington, D.C.

"Perhaps . . ." Bouquette said, "we should slip off somewhere for a drink after all this. I do think we owe ourselves a break."

Daisy looked up from her notes. Clifton Bouquette stood above her, a bit too close. Her eyes scanned up the weave of his slacks, then along the silken breeding certificate of his tie. In these frantic days, when everyone else's shirt looked as though it had been worn hours too long, Bouquette's starched collar glowed with perfect whiteness. He was the sort of man who was born with a perfect knot in his tie, and now, at an age when other men had begun to soften toward incapability, when faces grew ashen with care, Bouquette stood easily, with a sportsman's elasticity, and his skin showed only the handsome damage of countless weekends spent sailing. When she first arrived in Washington, Daisy had been anxious to look up to, to believe in, men such as Clifton Reynard Bouquette, and the readiness of such a man to overlook his wife in order to spend even a few of his sought-after hours with a plain, if bright, young analyst had made her feel as though dreams—serious, grown-up dreams—really did come true in this city. She had felt that way for the first half-dozen affairs. Then it had all become routine, and the men with so many names had not needed to offer quite so many excuses for their absences, their inabilities, their growing inattention. She told herself that she was their equal, using them as sharply as they elected to use her, and she could not understand the feeling of desolation that had grown up around her professional success. Daisy Fitzgerald was a woman who could understand the course of nations, who could brilliantly intuit the march of events. But, she realized, she had never managed to understand men. Why, indeed, did a man such as Clifton Reynard Bouquette, deputy director of the Unified Intelligence Agency, wealthy in so many ways, married to a forbiddingly attractive woman not much older than Daisy, want to risk even the slightest embarrassment to sleep with a woman whose hair was never quite right and whose skin still broke out under stress or when she ate any of half of the good edible things in the world, a woman whose plain features had driven her to achievement? She remembered a workmate's laughing comment to the effect that Cliff Bouquette would crawl between the hind legs of anything female and breathing.

"I can't, Cliff," she said. "I've got too much work."

Bouquette inched closer, the nap of his trousers almost brushing her. She could smell him. It was a smell she remembered.

"Oh, come on, Daze. Can't keep going without a little break."

"Really . . ."

"Things will sort themselves out." Bouquette smiled beautifully. "After all, we don't want to get stale. Need to keep our perspective."

"I've got to get back to the office after this." The soft wool of his trousers. And the remembered feel of him. The taste. The things he liked to do. And the urgency he had always felt to leave when he was done.

She could feel a slight change in him. As though he had already invested too much time and effort in her tonight, as though, by her refusal, she were treating him with an inconceivable lack of gratitude.

"Well," he said, in a subtly changed voice, still carefully low, so that the secret service men would not overhear, "just a quick drink on the way back then. For old time's sake. All right?"

"Cliff, please," Daisy said, "I've got to look over my notes—"

"You know that stuff inside out."

"—and I'm seeing someone."

Bouquette backed away slightly. He smiled and shook his head. "Oh, Daze . . . Daze . . . we're two of a kind, you and I. And you know it. We'll have our little flings with others, but we'll always—"

"You have no right—" she said angrily. It was the first time she had ever raised her voice to him when they were both fully clothed, and it shocked him even more deeply than she had surprised herself. He backed up still farther, then instantly came very close to her, bending down as if to discuss something in her notes.

"For God's sake," he whispered, "keep your voice down. Do you know where we *are?"*

Nerves, she told herself, it's all nerves. I need sleep. Control yourself, control yourself.

"I know *exactly* where we are," she said. "Now *stop it."*

For a moment that she promised herself she would treasure, Daisy saw a shadow of fear, of self-doubt, of age pass over Bouquette's face. Then he recomposed his features into the sculpted mask the world knew so well.

"We'll see," he said, smiling indulgently now, as though he pitied her foolishness. And he abruptly turned away. A few seconds later he was across the room, discussing the President's schedule with the secretary.

She stared briefly at his back, aching to see an imperfection in the lines of his body, any sign of the tyranny of the calendar. She already had her first gray hairs. Just a few of them, but, it seemed to her, at far too young an age. Bouquette would never gray—his hair was of a blondness that would simply mellow. He was a man who knew the names of wines and waiters, who affected to like nothing so much as a beer drunk from a bottle. He preened over his sports injuries and worked very hard to impress when he made love, seeking to convince his partner that he was still coursing with boyish energy. He had boyish names, too, for the things he wanted her to do for him, and she had done each thing even when it hurt her, unable to explain to herself why she could not say no to actions that would leave her uncomfortable for days. And the more a thing hurt her, it seemed, the more controlled he would be in it, drawing it out. Where her pain excited another man to lose control, to stream wildly inside of her, it only seemed to strengthen Bouquette. He savored the sexual borderland between misery and the passionate cry. Then, suddenly, he would begin to curse, to growl obscenely, and with a powerful thrust into her vagina or anus, he would finish. Anxious to leave, ready with an excuse as to why, after hours of mingled limbs and sweat and whispers full of praise, he had to disappear into the night or afternoon. Yet, she had valued him as a lover. Because he had known so many things about her desires. As a matter of course. In the physical sense, he had been a far better lover than the man for whom she told herself she was waiting.

There were, she suspected, few things that made a woman such as her more uncomfortable than being loved by an honest man.

And what kind of a woman was she? She tried to concentrate on the scribbled notes that updated her computer printout. But she could not help thinking of the unexpected man, the unreasonable, embarrassing man who had suddenly turned up in her life like a blemish found on the skin upon waking. What kind of a woman was she? The kind who lashed a sincere—hopelessly sincere—lover with her past, telling him needlessly much about what she had done with others, speaking in the name of honesty, making him suffer for the unforgivable crime of loving her when all of those other better, smarter, richer, far handsomer men had simply used her body as a place to empty themselves. The only time she had not been able to hurt him consciously had been in her bed. Over a dinner table, over a drink, she had been able to savage him with her confessions, instinctively aware that he could take all of this hurt and survive. But as his clumsy hands searched over her body, as he pushed himself into her with a laughable attempt to resurrect some long-forgotten finesse, as he held her with a ferocity that made her gasp, holding her as though she might slip away from him forever even as he stabbed himself urgently inside her, she sensed a weakness that could not tolerate the slightest mocking, the least teasing word. She was the kind of woman who shut her eyes tightly in the struggle not to weep as he continued to hold her—desperately—after he had drained into her, reluctant even to let her rise to go to the bathroom.

A plain girl with bad skin and bad judgment, who could foretell history, but not her own heart. Falling in something that might almost be love with a man whose face was something out of the shadows of an old horror film, a man too naive to lie, even to a woman such as she. She remembered him standing in her kitchen that last morning. She had known more about the situation into which he was being sent than he had, important things that he was forbidden to know, but which a lover of quality, of decent heart, could not have helped telling him. To warn him. But she had been unable to speak, and he had stood clumsily in the gray light, the wreck of his face curiously boyish, almost weak above the tie into which he had never learned to work a confident knot. "I love you . . ." he had said. Not in the splendid darkness, which teased out so many lies, which excused the most ill-considered choice of words, but in the flat gray sober light, with rain tapping at the windows above the sink. In an unkempt kitchen in suburban Virginia, he had waited for a response. And, when she did not reply, he repeated himself: "I love you." As if testing his voice to see if it had really said such a thing. Eyes pretending to drowse, she kept her silence, legs cold where the bathrobe would not grip. Feeling slovenly, sluttish in a way that had little to do with her sex, a matter of hangovers worn on the skin and untidy hair. He stared at her in hopeless fear, and she recognized that nothing in his life, no matter how terrible or physically punishing, had cost quite the same sort of effort as those tentative words. "I . . . don't . . ." she said finally, in a voice too drab for his moment, "George, I just don't know . . . what I feel right now." Her heart pounded, and she felt with painful intensity that, yes, at least for that instant, she did love this man, that she loved him with the same ferocity with which he had clutched her to him in the darkness. But she could not say the words. She felt as though her speech would damn her beyond all hope of redemption. No god was sufficiently forgiving to tolerate those words from her mouth. And the moment collapsed into the inconsequence of a teaspoon chiming the porcelain sides of a cup, the stuck lid of a jam jar, and terrycloth slipping from a bruised thigh. At most, she managed to convey to him that she would make an effort to keep her knees together until she saw him again. And she watched him go, a plain girl who had done so much more to hold a life's history of uncaring men, saying good-bye to the one good man who had happened to her.

The door to the briefing room opened. John Miller, a staff aide, stepped halfway into the waiting room.

"Mr. Bouquette, the President's ready for you."

Bouquette marched across the room to retrieve his briefcase from its place beside Daisy's thicker, heavier attaché case. Grasping it confidently, he turned:

"Is the President ready for Daisy, Miller? Or does he want to see me alone first?"

The aide considered it for a fraction of a second, while all the politics and intricacies of his job raced through his mental computer.

"She can come in too. Just remember, the President's tired. It's been a long day."

Bouquette nodded. "For all of us."

Daisy hastened to fit her notes back into her attaché case, feeling clumsy against Bouquette's polished manner. She had only recently reached the level where she personally briefed the President and the National Security Council, and she remained in awe of this holiest of realms, despite the years she had spent learning how very, very mortal and fallible the men were who governed the nation.

At first, the familiar faces were a blur. The room was slightly overheated, the air surprisingly stale. She hastily put down her attaché case, then stood awkwardly, trying to look both alert and at ease. Inevitably, her eyes were drawn to the black man in the navy pin-striped suit.

President Waters had loosened his tie. Normally, he was every bit as fastidious as Bouquette, and Daisy read the opened collar as a sign that the man had truly grown weary. President Waters had been elected in 2016, on a platform that focused on domestic renewal and on bridging the gap between the increasingly polarized elements in American society. Even after the disastrous trade war with the Japanese, as well as the long sequence of military humiliations and hard-won successes, even after Runciman's disease had cut a broad path across the continent, the United States remained a relatively wealthy country in an impoverished world. Yet the decades had more and more turned its society into a solvent majority and a number of marginalized subsectors whose members had fallen ever farther behind contemporary demands for an educated, highly skilled work force and the need for cultural integration to facilitate competitiveness. Then the United States had given sanctuary to the Israelis who had survived the final Mideast war, and although the Israelis settled largely in "homelands" located in the least promising areas of the Far West, they soon constituted a powerful force in postepidemic America, where the shortage of skilled, dedicated workers had grown critical. The resulting explosion of anti-Israeli sentiment from minority groups that had isolated themselves ever more drastically from the mainstream manifested itself in demonstrations, confrontation, and, ultimately, in bloodshed. The candidacy of Jonathan Waters in 2016 succeeded on the premise that all Americans *could* live together—and succeed together. He promised education, urban renewal, and opportunity, and he was a handsome, magnetic man, who spoke in the rhetoric of Yale rather than the Baptist Church. A campaign-season joke called him the white-man's black and the black-man's white . . . and he felt like the right man for the times to a bare majority of the citizens of his country. He defeated an opponent who was a foreign policy expert, but who had few domestic solutions with which to inspire a troubled nation. Yet, the first term of President Waters had been shadowed by a wide range of international issues, while his domestic solutions remained promising—but the stuff of generational rather than overnight change. As Cliff Bouquette was fond of putting it, "The poor bugger's *to*tally lost in all this, and he's about to be equally the loser at the polls." Everyone believed that Jonathan Waters was a genuinely good man. But a series of nationwide surveys indicated that he had lost his image as a leader.

The President looked first at Bouquette, then at Daisy, before settling his noticeably bloodshot gaze back on the tanned, perfect man at Daisy's side.

"Good evening, Cliff," the President said, "and to you, Miss Fitzgerald. I hope you've brought me some good news."

President Waters wanted a cheeseburger. It seemed unreasonable to him that so trivial a desire could haunt a man in an hour of grave discussions and fateful decisions. But, he told himself, the body could go only so long without fuel. Countless shots of coffee and some scraps of doughnut, even cut with the spice of adrenaline and nerves, could carry a man only so far. And now, faced with the prospect of Clifton Reynard Bouquette, whom he could not abide, and his sidekick, who was as nerve-rackingly intense as she was genuinely good at her work, the President wished he could just put everything on hold for fifteen minutes of quiet. Spent alone. With a Coke and the sort of monumental, dripping cheeseburger that his wife went to great lengths to deny him, in the interests of the presidential health.

But there was no time. And, the President reflected, you could hide behind a cheeseburger for only so long, in any case. Then you would have to return to this obstreperous, all too violent world, where the very best of intentions seemed to have no power at all.

He had dreamed of going down in history as the President who taught his people to join hands, to understand one another, and to go forward together. He wanted to be the President who spoke for the poor, the ill-educated, the badly nourished, the men and women whom the streets had educated to make the worst possible choices, and he wanted to speak for them in a voice that did not threaten, but that softened life's harshness—for all Americans. His vision had been of a great returning home—by all those socially or economically crippled citizens who lived as exiles in the land of their birthright. He valued, above all, kindness—generosity in spirit and in fact—and peace. But the world demanded a man with the strength to order other men to kill, to ruin, and to die. In his gestures and words President Waters took great pains to remain firm, strong, commanding. But, in his heart, he wondered if he was a man of sufficient stature for the hour. He had even taken to praying, in private, for the first time since the age of fifteen, when he had watched his father die unattended in a hospital hallway.

He smiled slightly, wearily, dutifully, greeting Bouquette and his assistant. Bouquette looked so damnably pleased with himself. Waters had first met the Bouquettes of the world at Yale, and he had been forced to recognize their genuine importance, their utility. But, even though he suspected it might be owing to sheer jealousy on his part, he had never learned to like them—even as he had laboriously taught himself to imitate their dress, their choice of words, their confidence. . . .

His smile grew genuine for a moment, as he considered the reaction he would get if he asked Bouquette to run along and fetch him a cheeseburger.

Bouquette was already bent over the audiovisual console, feeding in the domino-sized ticket that held the classified briefing aids. Momentarily, the monitor sets perched above and behind the conference table flickered to life.

"Just a second, Cliff," the President said. "I've got some critical business to attend to before you begin." He turned his attention to Miller, the lowest-ranking man in the room. "John, would you mind sending down to the kitchen for some sandwiches? I suspect we're going to be here for a while. Call it a working dinner."

Miller stood up. Ready to go and do his president's bidding. "The usual for you, Mr. President?"

Waters nodded. The usual. A small chef's salad, crowned with a few shreds of tuna packed in water and, just to be daring, some tidbits of low-cholesterol cheese. No dressing. Two pieces of whole wheat bread. And grapefruit juice.

"Oh, and John," the President said, "remind the chef that there is . . . no urgent necessity for my wife to hear about our doughnut orgy at lunchtime." He laughed slightly, and the members of the National Security Council were careful to laugh with him. Just enough.

Miller disappeared. Bouquette stood erectly, portentously. God only knew what new disasters the man held ready on his tongue. The turbulent, seemingly unpredictable course of military operations baffled Waters. By comparison, the world of post–Chicago School economics, in which he specialized, seemed simple, orderly. Like most American males of his generation, President Waters had never served in the military, and for the first time in his life, he regretted the omission. He knew the generals and admirals tried to simplify things for him. But so much of it simply did not seem logical. The dynamics did not correspond directly to the laws of physics. The very vocabulary was arcane and forbidding.

Commander-in-Chief. During his presidential campaign, the title had simply been another term among many. Now he wished in his heart that he might pass off this responsibility to another, better-prepared man.

Well, perhaps the election would see to that. Waters did not expect to win this time around. Only his wife and a handful of men and women who had welded their careers hopelessly to his still spoke of reelection with even hollow confidence. Certainly, there was a part of him that wanted to remain in office, to complete the real work so barely begun. But he had no special desire to sit for one unnecessary moment in this chair of blood. If he could have, he would have created a dual presidency—one for the master of distant wars and interventions, another for the builder of a better nation. But there was only one presidency, and despite the natural, indescribably powerful urge to hold on to the office, to its delicious power, Waters had made himself one promise: He would in no way attempt to exploit the present situation to electoral advantage. To the best of his abilities, he would make the decisions that were correct for the United States.

Waters sat back in his chair, tugging at the already loosened collar that felt so inexplicably confining today.

"All right, Cliff. Let's hear what you have to say."

Bouquette nodded. "Mr. President, we have a great deal to cover tonight. We've trimmed it down to the minimum—"

Just get going, Waters thought. Speak of the things that matter.

"—but that still leaves a lot of ground to cover. I'll lead off with the counterintelligence update, then Miss Fitzgerald will cover the events on the ground in the Soviet Union." Bouquette looked directly into the President's eyes, a veteran of many briefings. "First, you may already have seen the story in today's *New York Times.*" At the intonation of *"New York Times,"* the monitors instantaneously exhibited the inside-page story about which Bouquette would speak. The headline read: WHERE IS THE SEVENTH CAVALRY?

"No, I haven't seen it," the President said. He turned to the chairman of the Joint Chiefs of Staff to see how alarmed he should be. But the general's face remained noncommittal.

"Well," Bouquette continued, "the good news is that there's no evident suspicion as to the real location of our forces at this time. The planted stories about secret training in northern Canada seem to be holding. But the *Times*'s piece doesn't read well. They're a bit too interested."

"Any reaction from the Japanese?" the chairman of the Joint Chiefs asked.

Bouquette shook his head. Businesslike. "Nothing we've picked up as of yet. They've got their hands full. And they seem relatively confident that we've got our own hands full south of the border."

"What got the *Times* interested?" the secretary of state asked.

"Let me handle that one, Cliff," the secretary of defense said. But he did not speak directly to the secretary of state. Instead, he addressed the President. "Sir, we've been tracking this one. We didn't consider it of sufficient importance to bother you with it, but since Cliff's brought it up, I might as well give you the background myself. As you know, we constructed the Seventh Cavalry—which is a 'heavy' unit—and the Tenth and Eleventh cavalries—

which are 'light' units of the sort we used to call Military Intelligence—as very special organizations. We carefully sought to fill those units with unmarried men. Of course, that's not always possible, especially with officers and senior NCOs. But we tried to avoid the private-with-six-kids syndrome. We wanted to be able to deploy these units on short notice, with as little bother as possible. We went through the personnel files carefully. We designed spouse support and education programs. Above all, these are basically volunteer units—very few soldiers come down on orders without first requesting to join. We wanted to kill the old commissary-PX grapevine, where you could learn more about a unit's activities in the checkout line than in the ops office. And we think we've done a pretty good job. We even made it policy not to tell the majority of the officers and men their destination until they're wheels-up— and we do not permit personal communications from the combat zone. So, all in all, we've been successful." The sec-def paused, leaning back as though to take a deep breath. "But this sonofabitch from the *Times* has been phoning up the Building, prying. He smells something. And you know why? Because some little girl in Manhattan, Kansas, wants to know where her boyfriend is. She claims she's engaged to a corporal in the Seventh Cavalry, and she wants to know what we've done with him." The sec-def smiled, waving his chin at the absurdity of it all. "So, in a way, we're better off with this sudden speedup in the commitment of our force. From an operations security standpoint. We've had a hell of a run of bad luck. But nothing lasts forever."

For a moment, President Waters was filled with a terrifying vision of how very, very fragile everything was. He had never considered that the success or failure of a military mission in the middle of Asia might depend on a lonely, angry girl in Kansas.

"As a nation," the President said, "we've never been very good at secrecy. And, in many ways, it's been a blessing to us. But, all things considered, I think we might want to keep our current activities quiet just a while longer. Bill," he said to the chairman of the Joint Chiefs, a great bear of a man, "why don't we just get that soldier to write his girl a letter saying he's fine and that he'll be home soon. Make her happy."

"And make her keep quiet," Bouquette said anxiously. His briefing had been taken away from him too quickly, and he wanted to get back into the game. "We could even get it postmarked from somewhere up in the Canadian wilderness. Let our friend from the *New York Times* dust off his snowshoes."

"We can do that, Mr. President," the chairman said. "But I think we have to be prepared for further inquiries from the media, now that the *Times* has made an issue of it. I'm just afraid that somebody's going to put two and two together. The situation in the Soviet Union is front page and lead story, every day."

President Waters was uncertain how to respond. He wanted these men to provide him with assurance, not with additional worries. "Well," he said, "we'll just hope our luck holds a little longer. Now let's move on. Cliff, what's next?"

"Staying with counterintelligence, Mr. President . . . the Soviets continue to be exceedingly cooperative. As you know, we have key elements of the Tenth Cavalry, the intel boys, on the ground in Moscow and elsewhere, supporting the combat commitment of the Seventh. And the Soviets have brought us in on almost everything—joint technical exploitation, interrogations, sharing of information. We're learning a great deal about their system, how it works and so forth. I must say, they've surprised us a few times. Their country may be in a sorry state, but they're still devilishly good at certain kinds of intelligence work. Bad at others, though. Their battlefield intelligence system is in the process of breaking down completely. At the strategic level, we've got a better picture of their tactical and operational situations than they do. In a few moments, Miss Fitzgerald will cover those developments for you. But, the good news is that the Soviets do not appear to be running a serious, comprehensive operation against us. We do know that General Ivanov, their senior man in central Asia and western Siberia, has orders to police up the wreckage of one of our M-100s, if possible. But that's to be expected. They tell some little lies to save face, but all in all, they're playing it remarkably straight with us. Or at least they appear to be." Bouquette looked around the table.

"They're desperate," the chairman of the Joint Chiefs of Staff said. "But I still don't think we should trust them too far. Once they get back on their feet, they'll be back at our throats."

"*If* they get back on their feet," the secretary of state said. "They've been struggling to do just that for over a generation. You're talking about a broken, ruined country, hanging on for dear life."

"Between nations," the national security adviser said, "trust is merely a matter of shared interests. If the Soviets are currently behaving toward us in a trustworthy manner, then it's because it's to their advantage to do so. When such conduct ceases to be advantageous, I can assure you that it will stop." The national security adviser rarely spoke, but when he did it was in a sharp, lucid, tutorial voice. He was the architect behind the President's foreign policy views, and Waters had come to depend on him to an uncomfortable extent. "Today, the United States shares the Soviet Union's interest in keeping the Japanese out of Siberia. Tomorrow, the Soviets may begin asking themselves why they allowed us *in*to Siberia. For I remind you, gentlemen, that our assistance to the Soviet state is not intended to preserve that state for its own sake, but, rather, to maintain a regional balance of power. And . . . we are not there to help the Soviets achieve victory, but to prevent a Soviet defeat. The opening of Siberia to the world economy is inevitable. We just have to ensure that the United States has equal, or, ideally, preferred access to Siberian resources, and that the Japanese access is on the most restrictive, disadvantageous terms possible. We need to remain honest with ourselves, to keep our goals clear. Our fundamental purpose is not to aid the Soviets, but to deny the Japanese."

"The little buggers still ought to be grateful," the chairman of the Joint Chiefs said.

"Mr. President, if I may . . ." Bouquette said.

"Go ahead, Cliff."

"There *is* one area of concern with the Soviets, one

matter—and we're not sure of its relative importance—in which they don't appear to be telling us everything they know. Now, this is all rather nebulous . . . but we've picked up a reference in high-level Soviet military traffic to something called a Scrambler. Now, in the context of the message, it appeared that this Scrambler was some kind of Japanese operation or system. At any rate, the Soviets seemed very, very worried about it."

"Why don't we just ask them what the hell it is?" the chairman of the Joint Chiefs asked.

Bouquette spread his hands out at waist level, as though holding an invisible beachball. "If we did, we'd have to tell them we were reading their communications on the most secure system they've got. We can't afford to do that. For a number of reasons. As you all realize."

"Well," the chairman continued, "with the only fully modernized outfit in the United States Army about to enter combat, I'd like to know exactly what we might be getting into."

"Oh, I think we're all right. At least for the present," Bouquette went on. "I want to show you the text of an intercept we took off the Japanese earlier today. Intriguing coincidence. They were having trouble with their system, and we got some good take. By dumb luck. They didn't realize how badly the signal was bleeding, and with computer enhancement and advanced decryption, we got about an hour and a half's worth of traffic." Bouquette looked confidently about the room, setting the rhythm at last. "Now, this was General Noburu Kabata's private line back to Tokyo. You all recall that General Kabata is the senior Japanese officer on the ground out there. His command post is in Baku. Supposedly, of course, he's just a contract employee working for the Islamic Union. But that's merely a nicety. In fact, Kabata is running the whole show. Well, we found out that he's not entirely pleased with his Arab and Iranian charges—to say nothing of the rebel forces in Soviet Central Asia. But, then, you know the Japanese. They hate disorder. And Kabata's got a disorderly crew on his hands. But look at this . . ." He pointed to the nearest monitor. A bright yellow text showed on a black background:

TokGenSta/ExtDiv: Tokuru wants to know what you've decided
on the other matter.

JaCom/CentAs: I have no need of it at present. Everything is going
well, and, in my personal opinion, the Scrambler
is needlessly provocative.

TokGenSta/ExtDiv: But Tokuru wants to be certain that the Scrambler is ready. Should it be needed.

JaCom/CentAs: Of course, it's ready. But we will not need it.

"Now, gentlemen," Bouquette said, "the first station is
the voice of the Japanese General Staff's External Division
in Tokyo. The respondent from the Japanese Command
in Central Asia—something of a misnomer, since the actual location is Baku, on the western shore of the Caspian
Sea—is none other than General Kabata himself."

"That's all well and good, Cliff," the secretary of defense
said, "but what does it tell us? That's raw intelligence, not
finished product."

Bouquette shrugged. "Unfortunately, it's all we've got.
Of course, we've made this Scrambler a top collection
priority. But, at least this intercept seems to indicate that
whatever it is, it's not an immediate concern."

President Waters was not convinced. Here was yet another unexpected element in a situation the complexity of
which he already found unnerving. He looked to the chairman of the Joint Chiefs for reassurance yet again. The
chairman had a tough old-soldier quality that had acquired
new appeal for Waters as of late. But the chairman was
already speaking.

"Now, goddamnit, you intel guys had better find out
just what's going on over there. We can't play guessing
games when the nation's premier military formation is
about to go into battle. You assured us that, and I quote,
'We have the most complete picture of the battlefield of
any army in history.' " The chairman tapped his pen on
the tabletop.

"And we do," Bouquette said. "This is only one single
element. When the Seventh Cavalry enters combat, their

on-board computers will even know how much fuel the enemy has in his tanks—"

"Mr. President?" the communications officer spoke up from the bank of consoles at the back of the room. "I've got Colonel Taylor, the Seventh Cavalry commander, coming in. He's back from his meeting with the Soviets. You said you wanted to talk to him when he returned, sir."

Taylor? Oh, yes, President Waters remembered, the colonel with the Halloween face. He had forgotten exactly what it was he wanted to talk to the man about. More reassurances. Are you ready? Really? You aren't going to let me down, are you? Waters could not explain it in so many words, but, in their brief exchanges, he had found this fright-mask colonel, with his blunt answers, far more reassuring than any of the Bouquettes of the world.

"Mr. President," the chairman of the Joint Chiefs said, leaning confidentially toward him, as though Taylor's face had already appeared on the monitors, as though the distant man were already listening in, "I don't think we should mention this Scrambler business to Colonel Taylor. Until we have a little more information. He's got enough on his mind."

President Waters spent the moment in which he should have been thinking in a state of blankness. Then he nodded his assent. Surely, the generals of the world knew what was best for the colonels of the world.

"All right," he said. "Put Colonel Taylor through."

Taylor did not want to talk to the President. Nor did he want to speak to the chairman of the Joint Chiefs of Staff, as much as he liked the old man. He did not want any communications now with anyone who might interfere with the operations plan that was rapidly being developed into an operations order for the commitment of his regiment. Besides, he was very tired. He had not yet taken his "wide-awakes," the pills that would keep a man alert and capable of fighting without sleep for up to five days without permanently damaging his health. He had hoped to steal a few hours of sleep before popping his pills, so that he would be in the best possible condition and have the longest possible stretch of combat capability in front of him. Now he sat wearily in the communications bubble in the bowels of an old Soviet warehouse, waiting.

Just let me fight, damnit, Taylor thought. There's nothing more to be done.

Sleep was out of the question now. By the time this nonsense was finished, it would be time to start the final command and staff meeting with the officers and key NCOs of the regiment. Then there would be countless last-minute things to do before the first M-100 lifted off.

"Colonel Taylor," he heard the voice in his earpiece. "I'm about to put you through to the President."

The central monitor in the communications panel fuzzed, then a superbly clear picture filled the screen. The President of the United States, looking slightly disheveled, elbows on a massive table.

The poor bastard looks tired, Taylor thought. Then he tried to perk himself up. His past exchanges with the President had taught him to be prepared for the most unexpected questions, and it was difficult not to be impatient with the President's naiveté. For Christ's sake, Taylor told himself, the man's the President of the United States. Don't forget it.

"Good morning, Mr. President."

For a moment, the President looked confused. Then he brightened and said, "Good evening, Colonel Taylor. I almost forgot our time difference. How is everything?"

"Fine, Mr. President."

"Everything's all right with the Soviets?"

"As good as we have any right to expect, sir."

"And your planning session? That went well, I take it?"

"Just fine, Mr. President."

"And you've got a good plan, then?"

Here it comes, Taylor thought.

"Yes, sir. I believe we have the best possible plan under the circumstances."

The President paused, considering.

"You're going to attack the enemy?"

"Yes, Mr. President."

"And you're happy with the plan?"

Something in the man's tone of voice, or in his weariness

of manner, suddenly painted the situation for Taylor. The President of the United States was not trying to interfere. He was simply asking for reassurance. The obviousness of it, as well as the unexpected quality, startled Taylor.

"Mr. President, no plan is ever perfect. And every plan begins to change the moment men start to implement it. But I harbor no doubts—none—about the plan we've just hammered out with the Soviets. As the combat commander on the ground, I would not want to change one single detail."

Taylor heard a laugh from the other end, but the sound was disembodied. The President's face remained earnest, worn beyond laughter. Then Taylor heard the unmistakable voice of the chairman of the Joint Chiefs of Staff in the background.

"Mr. President, Colonel Taylor's telling you not to fiddle around with his plan. We'll give him a lesson in manners once we get him back in-country, but for now I think we better do what he says." The chairman laughed again, almost a snort. "I know Colonel Taylor, and he's apt to just ignore us, anyway. Isn't that right, George?"

Thank you, Taylor thought, fully aware of the risk the chairman had just taken on his behalf, and of the cover he had provided. I owe you one.

"Well, I'm not certain I like the thought of being ignored," the President said seriously, but without malice. "However, I have no intention of interfering with the colonel's plan. I think I know my limitations."

If I live, Taylor thought, until election day, I just might vote for the poor bastard, after all.

"Colonel Taylor," the President said, "I'm just trying to understand what's going on. I'm *not* a soldier, and I seem to spend a great deal of time being confused by all this. For instance, these wonder machines of yours, these miracle weapons. No one has ever managed to explain to me in plain English just exactly what they're all about, how they work. Could you take the time to do that?"

How, Taylor wondered, could you tell your president that you did not have time, that you had everything *but* time?

"You mean the M-100s, Mr. President?"

"Yes, all that gadgetry the taxpayers bought you. What's it going to do for them?"

Taylor took a deep breath, searching for a starting point. "Mr. President, the first thing you notice about the M-100 is that it's probably the *ugliest* weapons system ever built." Taylor heard a background voice ordering that an illustration of the M-100 be called up. "The troops call it the flying frog. But, when you fly it, when you learn to fight out of it, it becomes very beautiful. It's squat, with a big belly to hold all the equipment and the fire team of dragoons—mounted infantrymen—in the back. It has tilt rotors mounted on stubby wings. It doesn't look like it could possibly get off the ground. But it *does* fly, Mr. President, and it flies very fast for a ship of its kind—or slow, when you want it to. Its electronics make it almost invisible to the enemy. He might see it with the naked eye, but our countermeasures suite—the electronics that attack his electronics and confuse him—is so versatile, so fast, and works on so many levels, that one of his systems might see nothing but empty sky, while another sees thousands of images. His guided munitions will see dummy aircraft projected around the real one. But our target acquisition system— the gear we use to find *him*—has 'work-through' technology. Unless the Japanese have come up with a surprise, we should be able to look right through their electronic defenses.

"You see," Taylor continued, choosing his words from the professional history of a military generation, "we rarely fight with our own eyes anymore. It's a competition of electronics, attempting to delude each other on multiple levels, thousands of times in a single second. The Japanese taught us a lot, the hard way. But we think we've got them this time. Anyway, the revolution in the miniaturization of power components gives us a range of up to fourteen hundred nautical miles, one way, depending on our combat load. That's good for a bulky system that's really still more of a helicopter than anything else. But the best part of all is the primary weapons system itself. The Japanese surprised us with laser weaponry back in Africa. And they're still using it. But on-board lasers have more problems than were apparent back in Zaire. We didn't realize how de-

180

pendent the Japanese were on recharging their systems, for instance. They were closely tethered to their support system and they could only fight short, sharp engagements. We took a different technological tack.

"Our main weapon is a 'gun' that fires electromagnetically accelerated projectiles. Just think of them as special bullets that use electromagnetic energy instead of gunpowder. These projectiles travel very, very fast, and when they strike their target, they hit with such force that they either shatter it or, at least, shatter everything inside it by concussion. There are several kinds of projectiles—the fire-control computer selects the right type automatically. One type is solid and can penetrate virtually anything. Another has two layers, the first of which detonates against the outside, igniting anything that will burn, while the hard inner core proceeds on through any known armor. The shock wave alone kills any enemy soldiers inside a vehicle, while rendering the vehicle itself useless. A tremendous advantage is that one M-100 can locate and destroy several hundred targets on a single mission. After that, the 'gun' needs to be recalibrated back at its support base, but it's still far more versatile, lethal, and survivable than the Japanese laser gunships."

"And the pilot's . . . just basically along for the ride?" the President said. "The M-100 . . . does everything automatically?"

"It can do a great deal automatically. But the vehicle commander—the pilot—and his copilot/gunner still make the broad decisions. And the desperate ones that a machine still cannot think through. Ideally, you go in firing fully automatic, because the computers can identify and attack multiple targets in a matter of seconds. And the computer gets intelligence input directly from national-level systems. But it's still the man who decides what to do when the chips are down. For instance, the computer never decides when to land and employ the dragoons. It's a smart horse. But, in the end, it's still a horse."

Despite Taylor's best efforts, the President still looked slightly baffled. Then Waters spoke:

"Well, Colonel Taylor, while you've been filling me in, I've been watching some graphics your boss called up for me. Very impressive. Very impressive, indeed." His distant eyes seemed to search very hard for Taylor's. "Tell me, is it really going to work? In combat?"

"I hope so, Mr. President."

"And . . . you have enough . . . of these systems?"

Enough for what? You never had enough.

"Mr. President, I've got what my country could give, and we're going to do the best we can with it. I'm confident that we have sufficient combat power to accomplish the mission as foreseen by our current op-plan. Besides, there's more to the regiment than just the M-100s. First, we have fine soldiers: superb, well-trained soldiers who are ready to believe in the job you sent them to do, even if they don't fully understand it. Without them, the M-100 is just an expensive pile of nuts and bolts." Taylor paused, as the mental images of countless men with whom he had served marched by—not just the soldiers of the Seventh, but faces remembered from half a dozen trials, as well as from the endless drudgery of peacetime garrisons. "Mr. President, I've got other equipment, as well. Magnificent electronic warfare gear . . . a battalion of heavy air-defense lasers to protect us while we're on the ground . . . wing-in-ground transporters that can haul my essentials in a single lift. And the Tenth Cav is giving me tremendous intelligence, electronic attack and deception support. But, in the end, it's going to come down to those soldiers down in the squadrons and troops. Are they tough enough? Are they sufficiently well-trained? Will they have the wherewithal to hold on longer than their adversaries? I think the answer is yes."

President Waters felt greater confidence than ever in this man with the ruined face and the firm voice. As a politician, he recognized that he had been a bit taken in by his own desire to believe that all would go well, coupled with the infectious persuasiveness of this colonel in the odd foreign uniform. He had been listening to exactly the sort of speech he wanted to hear, a speech in which the spoken words themselves were far less important than the manner in which they were spoken. Yet, this recognition of his own weakness did little to dilute the new confidence he felt. That, too, would slip away. But, for the moment, he felt that things might not go so badly after all.

He wondered if he should tell this hard-eyed colonel about the Scrambler business, to warn him, just in case there was something to it. But the chairman of the Joint Chiefs of Staff had recommended against bringing up the matter. And, surely, these military people knew among themselves what was best for their own.

Still, the Scrambler business nagged at him. The instincts that had led him to the White House said, "Tell him. Right now."

The briefing room door opened, and John Miller poked his head inside.

"Excuse me. Mr. President, if we could clear the monitors for a moment, the sandwiches are here. And your salad."

President Waters nodded. But he held up his finger to the communications officer. Wait.

The President stared into the central monitor, where Colonel George Taylor's discolored face waited impassively, larger than life-size.

"Colonel Taylor," the President said, "we're going to blank the system out for just a moment. But I'd like you to stand by. We have an intelligence briefing coming up, and I'd like you to listen in. To ensure that we all have exactly the same picture of what's going on."

Waters thought that his logic sounded pretty good. But, in his heart, he knew that the intelligence update was only a pretext. He simply was not quite ready to release this man who had so much confidence to share.

When the monitor came back to life, Taylor saw the President with a forkful of lettuce in his right hand. The man looked surprised, and Taylor figured that the sudden reappearance of his face was not particularly good for anyone's appetite. The monitor system was superb—state of the art—and keyed to respond to certain registered voices, giving the effect of brisk, clean editing. But it had not been programmed to beautify its subjects.

"Colonel Taylor," the President said. "You're back with

us. Good. We're just about to begin the intelligence update. It will probably mean more to you than to me." The
President's eyes strayed from contact with the monitor,
hunting more deeply into the briefing room. "Miss Fitzgerald?" he said.

Before Taylor could prepare himself, the monitor filled
with a shot of Daisy, showing her from mid-thigh upward.
For an instant it seemed as though their eyes made contact,
then Taylor realized, thankfully, that it was merely an
illusion. His face would no longer be on the monitor now.
Only the intelligence briefer and the visual supports.

He relaxed slightly. *Daisy*. He had tried so hard not to
think of her. There was too much to resolve, too much to
fear—and he had far more important matters with which
to occupy his mind. But, watching her now, as she went
through the formalities of opening her portion of the briefing, he was struck by how weary she, too, looked, and by
how much, and how helplessly, he loved her.

A map of the south-central Soviet Union replaced Daisy
on the screen, while her voice oriented the President to
the location of cities, mountains, and seas. She swiftly
recapitulated the most significant developments, speaking
in terms far simpler than those she had used when briefing
Taylor on the developing situation in her office in the old
CIA building in Langley, now property of the Unified
Intelligence Agency that had been formed to eradicate
interagency rivalry and parochialism in the wake of the
African disaster and the unforeseen dimensions of the
trade war with the Japanese. Taylor smiled to himself. He
remembered how her hair had been pinned up, as though
in haste, and the visible smudge on the corner of her oversize glasses. She had not reacted to the sight of him with
any special distaste. She had hardly reacted at all. He had
been merely another obligation in the course of a frantic
day. And he remembered the first remotely personal thing
she had said to him, an hour into the briefing that had
been scheduled to take up thirty minutes of her time:

"Well," she had said, looking at him through those
formidable glasses, "you certainly do your homework,
Colonel. But I don't think you really understand the background of all this."

She was behind in her work. Far behind. And what she believed he needed to understand was not really classified, not of immediate importance. Perhaps they could put it off until another time?

Taylor had stared at her for a long, long moment, mustering his courage. Professionally, she was fierce, merciless. Yet, he imagined that he sensed something else about her too. Something he could not quite explain to himself. In the end, his voice shook as he offered her the sort of invitation he had not spoken in many years.

"Maybe . . . we could talk about it over dinner?"

She simply stared at him. And he felt himself shrinking inside. A foolish, foolish man. To imagine that even this plain girl with the loose strands of hair wandering down over her ears would, of her own volition, face him across a dinner table. Then, without warning, without giving him time to prepare himself for the shock, she said:

"Yes."

He was so surprised that he merely fumbled for words. Until she came to his aid:

"You might as well come over to my place. It's far more private than a restaurant. We can talk shop." She considered for a moment. "I'm not much of a cook, I'm afraid."

"It doesn't matter."

She made a frumpy, disapproving face, as though he did not fully realize the risk he was taking.

"Pasta all right?" she asked.

"Terrific."

"This is," she said, "strictly business, of course."

"Of course."

He had spent the rest of the day tormenting himself. It had not mattered to him before that his one decent suit did not fit very well. Neither did he know what sort of tie was in fashion. He had always accepted that these more polished men who hastened down the corridors and sidewalks of the District were a different breed, that he would never look like them, that he was meant to appear in his uniform. But he could not go to dinner in uniform. Instead of stopping by the office of an acquaintance in the Pentagon as planned, he went downtown and bought himself a new shirt and tie, relying on the salesman's recommendations.

Only when he was dressing in his hotel room, did he realize that the shirt would not do without being pressed. And there was no time to use the valet service. He settled for the bright new tie on an old shirt that had made the trip to Washington without too many wrinkles, and as he fumbled with the knot in the bathroom mirror, it occurred to him that this probably *was* strictly business on her part and that she had probably invited him to her home because she was ashamed to be seen with him in public. The thought made him sit down on the closed lid of the commode, tie slack around his collar. He considered phoning her and canceling. But the thought of another evening alone in his room with his portable computer seemed impossible to bear.

He appeared at her door with flowers and a bottle of wine. To his relief, she smiled, and hurried to put the flowers in water. She glanced at the wine, then quietly put it aside, calling out to him, "Please. Sit down. Anywhere. I'll just be a minute." And he sat down, uncomfortable in his suit, admiring the surroundings of this woman's life, not because they were especially beautiful or aesthetically appealing, but simply because the ability to sit in the intimacy of a woman's rooms, the object of her attentions on any level, was a forgotten pleasure. He could not sit for long, though. The spicy smell and the noises from the kitchen made him move, and he examined the prints on her walls without really seeing them, glanced over the titles of her books without really registering them, waiting for the moment when she would come back through the doorframe.

He had not had the courage to kiss her that first night, nor even to ask her if he might see her again. He had tortured himself through the night and morning until he finally found the strength to dial her number at work. She wasn't in. He did not have the firmness to leave a message, convinced she would not return the call. Later, he tried again—and reached her.

"Listen . . . I thought that perhaps . . . we could have dinner again?"

The distant, disembodied voice replied quickly:

"I'm sorry, I've got something on for tonight."

That was it, then.

"Well . . . thanks for last night. I really enjoyed it."

Good-bye.

"Wait," she said. "Could you make it tomorrow night instead? I know a place over in Alexandria . . ."

Later, when he began to learn of her reputation, the effect upon him was brutal. For all his age and ordeals, he was little more than a schoolboy emotionally. The sexual escapades of his youth were enshrined in his memory, but the following years of loneliness had brought with them a sort of second virginity, and the thought that the woman he loved, whom he had even imagined he might marry, could be the butt of other men's jokes, little more than a creature they used and discarded, burned horribly in him. But he could not, would not, give her up. He tried to reason with himself. These were modern times. Everybody slept around. Anyway, what did it matter? In what way did it diminish her as a person, or lover, if she had shared her bed with others? Could you physically feel their leavings on her skin? Could you taste them? Did it really change anything about her when you were with her? How did the past matter, anyway? What mattered, after all, was the present—not who you had been, but who you had become. And who was he to criticize her? A wreck of a man? A fool, with the face of a devil? What right did he have?

Yet, the thought of her past would not let him be. He held her tightly, fearing she would be gone, but also trying somehow to make her his property and his alone, to make all of the ghosts disappear. In the darkness he would torment himself with the images of his beloved with other men, and he wondered, too, how he could possibly compare with those other men, the well-dressed, handsome men who knew from birth how to do everything correctly. Into whose arms would she tumble when he was gone?

He remembered the morning when they had said good-bye. The look of her, unpolished, askew, not quite awake, and the rich long-night smell in the air around her and on his hands. She seemed more beautiful to him in that slow gray light, in her spotted robe, than any woman he had ever seen. He did not want to leave her, did not want to go to some distant land to fulfill the long-held purpose of his life. He only wanted to sit and drink one more cup of coffee with her, to capture indelibly in his memory the wayward confusion of her hair and the disarray of the tabletop on which she rested her hand. But there had been no more time. Only one last moment wrenched from duty, the time needed to say, "I love you." And she did not really reply. He ached to hear those words from her. In a sense, that was why he had spoken them. But she only waited, pretending she was still more asleep than in fact she was. He had repeated himself, trying to bully the words out of her. But she only mumbled a few half-promises, and he left her like that: an indescribably beautiful plain woman in a soiled bathrobe, slumped by a littered kitchen table. He went out into a drizzling rain, telling himself that the words did not matter. She had filled so much of his emptiness with color and beauty that the words did not matter at all.

Now Taylor sat in a secure bubble in a tin cavern in the wastes of Siberia, listening from half a world away to the words of the woman he loved. She spoke in her brisk, assured, professional voice, the bit of low raspiness that was so erotic under other circumstances merely masculine now. Nothing in her tone, or her demeanor, gave the slightest hint that she knew he was listening, that she had watched him while he had been unaware. He was glad he had not known she was in the room while he had been speaking with the President. Somehow, he was certain, he would have collapsed into folly and incapability in the knowledge of her presence.

But she was stronger. She was every bit as serious as her subject, as her voice intoned over the succession of maps, films, and photos on the monitor. Taylor listened, fighting to pay attention.

". . . The last pause in ground operations by the enemy seems to have had a more complex purpose, however. During the lull, the opposing coalition moved all of the Soviet rebel forces up to the front—forces that are still nominally Soviet and that are native to the region, in a broad sense. Such a move accomplishes two things. First, it allows indigenous 'liberating' forces to lead the attack northward out of Kazakhstan and across the border into western Siberia, and second, it bleeds the rebel forces white, ensuring that, when the smoke clears, the Iranians and the Islamic Union will clearly be militarily preeminent and that, thus, there will be less of a likelihood of any effective indigenous reaction against foreign exploitation of the mineral wealth of both Kazakhstan and Siberia. The Iranians and the Islamic Union will effectively control the key territories east of the Urals—and the Japanese will exercise a significant measure of control over them, in turn, since their military power would collapse without continued Japanese assistance. There is strong evidence, for instance, to support the theory that every military system exported by Japan has a sleeper virus buried in its electronics, which, if triggered, destroys the utility of the system. No matter what nominal government might be in place east of the Urals, the Japanese would be the de facto masters of northern Asia."

The monitor filled with Daisy's image. Intense, determined, her personal vulnerability was hidden behind the set of her chin and the armor of those oversize glasses. But she looked so tired. Taylor wished he could fold her in his arms. Just for a moment.

Had she forgotten him? Already?

"Unless we stop them, of course," a voice said. The secretary of defense. Another lawyer who had not spent a single day of his life in uniform. Taylor had to give the man credit, though. He had acquired a surprising grasp of his responsibilities. Unlike the secretary's old friend, the President himself.

"Yes, sir," Daisy said.

"And what chance do you think we have of stopping them, Miss Fitzgerald?" the secretary asked. "I'd just like your view."

Daisy was, again, the subject of the monitor's attention. Taylor was genuinely curious as to what she would say in response. A smart, smart woman.

"Mr. Secretary," she began, "I can't give you numerical odds or any kind of probability statement. There are too many variables. I can only offer you an analyst's . . . hunch. Not very scientific, I'm afraid."

"Please. Go on."

So far away, captured by electronics and delivered to him, Daisy's eyes were nonetheless alive, wonderfully, fiercely alive.

"First," she continued, "I am convinced that our presence is going to come as a shock to the Japanese. There are no indications at this point that they have the least suspicion we've got forces on the ground. And that alone will give them pause. On the other hand, they may feel compelled to teach us a lesson in Central Asia, to pay us back for recent defeats elsewhere. They're still smarting from their reverses in Latin America. The performance of U.S. arms will be an important factor, of course. If our military systems perform according to specifications, the war will suddenly become much more expensive for the Japanese, both literally and figuratively. In that sense . . . the chances for a negotiated settlement would increase dramatically. If we perform well enough on the battlefield."

The President interrupted. "Miss Fitzgerald, you haven't said anything about actually *winning.*"

Daisy looked into herself for a moment. Yes, Taylor thought. What about winning?

"Mr. President," Daisy said, "an outright victory would exist only at the extreme range of possibility. No matter how well the Seventh Cavalry and its supporting elements might perform, the numbers don't work out. A single regiment . . . can't win a war."

Oh, Daisy, Daisy, Taylor thought. That's your problem. You don't understand faith. The ability to believe against the numbers, against the facts, against science and learned men. He believed that he had suddenly learned something very important about her, and he wished he could tell her. That she lacked only faith. That the world *could* be hers, if only she believed.

"In any case," Daisy went on, "we have to ask ourselves to what extent an outright victory would prove advantageous to the interests of the United States. Certainly, if the enemy wins, we lose access to key resources, while failing to deny those resources to the enemy—specifically, to the Japanese. Further, we lose influence. And prestige.

And, of indirect concern, the Islamic Union, the Iranians, and especially the rebels will continue their practice of massacring ethnic Slavs. Not a desirable outcome overall. However, should *we* 'win' outright, we might only be setting the Soviet Union up for continued problems—for which we would suddenly share responsibility. The Soviet empire simply cannot hold together in its present state. Further, a victorious Soviet Union would be less susceptible to our influence. We want to enhance their dependence on us in key spheres. And the spectacle of a U.S. ally undertaking bloody retaliations and repressions in postrebellion Central Asia would not present a desirable picture to other clients of the United States. Fundamentally, a compromise agreement ending hostilities on terms economically advantageous to the United States would be the optimum solution."

"Miss Fitzgerald," the chairman of the Joint Chiefs of Staff said, in a voice of barely controlled anger, "your logic is very impressive. But let me tell you something both I and that colonel off in Siberia have had to learn the hard way. Victory is *always* advantageous. You can sort the rest of that shit out later."

"Well," the President said quickly, filling Taylor's monitor screen again, "we seem to have a divergence of views." Waters looked down at the ruins of his salad, mouth twisted up as though something had not tasted quite right. He raised his left eyebrow. "Colonel Taylor? Are you still with us?"

"Yes, sir," Taylor said immediately, snapping back to the present.

"Well, tell me. What do you think about this discussion?"

"Mr. President, my soldiers . . . don't picture themselves as fighting—or dying—for clever compromise agreements. They don't understand any of that. But they do understand the difference between victory and defeat, and from their position the difference is pretty clear-cut."

"Does that mean . . . you think we can *win?*"

Taylor made a face. "I honestly don't know. I just know that an unknown number of fine young soldiers are going to die tomorrow thinking that we can win. No, 'thinking'

191

is the wrong word. *Believing* that we're going to win. Because I told them so. And they believed me."

The President pondered the little islands of lettuce shreds in his bowl. "Well . . . " he said, "I hope they're right. Thank you Colonel. I won't hold you up any longer. I'm sure you have plenty to do." The President looked out over the miles, searching for Taylor's eyes. "And good luck. To all of you."

Taylor panicked. He had wanted so badly to end this nonsense, to return to his troops. But now the thought that he might never see Daisy again and that they had ended on a note of enmity, however indirect, paralyzed him.

Just a glimpse. Somehow, some impossible how, a word.

The monitor left the President. But it did not go dead. Instead, the heavy, almost swollen-looking face of the chairman of the Joint Chiefs appeared.

"George," he said, "just one last thing. When the hell are you going to get out of that Commie uniform? You look like hell."

Taylor knew he was supposed to smile. But he could not.

"Just before we lift off, sir," he said.

"Well, give them hell, George. And God bless."

"Thank you, sir."

And the screen went blank.

Daisy.

Daisy felt as though everyone in the room must have realized how distraught she had become. She had struggled to overcome her emotions, forcing herself to brief in a voice that was even more dispassionate than usual. But the words, as she spoke them, seemed to come out just short of her intentions, and she felt as though she could not quite manage her thoughts.

It was *his* fault. She had watched him on the monitor during his conversation with the President, aware that he could not see her, that he had no reason to be aware of her presence. And, listening to him, to his raw, direct voice that would never compete with the Bouquettes of the world, she had wanted to get down on her knees and beg the President to call it all off. The fate of the Soviet Union, the disposition of far-off minerals, could never be as important as this one decent man, with his antique notions about duty. As she talked in her turn, adorning the classified imagery on the monitors with professional terminology and icy judgment, she had felt as though she were condemning him, sending him to a certain death. The logic of politics and power, once so evident to her, now seemed like so much nonsense. It was only about people, after all. About men. And women. Who had found someone they just might love. Only to see them go, in the name of highsounding foolishness. It was about George Taylor, with his pathetic face and his determination to do the right thing at any cost for a country whose citizens would shudder to look at him.

Was she punishing herself? Was it only a travesty of love? How on earth could she imagine for a moment that she loved that man? She had needed to turn off the lights and close her eyes, as well.

She liked him best when he held her, with her back small against his chest, and his strong arm cradling her breasts. Taylor, in his dress suit bought carelessly from some post-exchange rack, giving him the look of the world's most serious appliance salesman. The clown who brought a bottle of dessert wine for dinner.

How could she feel so much at the sight of such a man?

When he answered the President in those blunt, sensible words that made a mockery out of her analysis, her career, her fine education, she had only wanted to tell him that she was sorry, that she hadn't really meant it, that it was only that her thoughts and words would not come out clearly tonight.

He was not coming back. She knew it.

A demon inside her wanted to call out to him, right in front of the President and all of the old identical men who served him, to tell Taylor that, yes, she loved him, and she had loved him already on that last morning, but she had not had the strength, or the common sense, to tell him.

Then Taylor was gone, the communications link broken, and she was left with the blank monitors, and with Clifton Reynard Bouquette by her side.

The President was smiling, shaking his head. He glanced around the big table and tugged wearily at his tie.

"Well, gentlemen," he said happily, "I suspect that this colonel of ours is going to strike genuine fear into the hearts of the enemy." He bobbed his head slightly, in amusement. "God knows, just looking at him scares the hell out of me."

Everyone laughed. Except Daisy. Beside her, Bouquette laughed loudest of all. Then he leaned in close to her, whispering:

"You're not going to make a fool of yourself, are you?"

9

northern Kazakhstan
2 November 2020

THE NURSING MOTHER CROUCHED AGAINST THE MAIN gun housing of Babryshkin's tank, her small, emaciated face barely visible under the oversize winter hat. Her layers of scarves, sweaters, and coat appeared to weigh far more than she could possibly weigh herself, and the infant was barely perceptible amid the disorder of felt and wool and worn-out fur. A small leg kicked back, the way a weaning pup pushes out at space, trying to bury itself closer to its bitch, and the tiny mother renewed her grip. Babryshkin sensed that the woman was very young, and that she might have been rather attractive under other circumstances, but now her cheeks were chafed until they looked like the dry skin of an old woman, and her sunken eyes lacked focus. Now and then she spoke quietly to her other child, a boy of perhaps four years, who clung to her coat with vacant eyes. When Babryshkin had lifted the boy onto the tank, lice flurried up from his cap like spanked dust. But the boy seemed unaware of the pests. He simply assumed his place beside his mother and stared out across the frost-bitten steppes. The only sign he gave of normalcy was the avidity with which he devoured the stale crackers Babryshkin had put into his small hand.

Babryshkin had found the woman and her children at the rear of the truncated refugee column just as his tanks caught up with the plodding survivors. The boy had been unable to walk, and the half-starved mother was struggling to carry both her infant and her son, accomplishing little more than dragging the boy a few paces at a time. No one offered to help her. The refugees trailing the column felt the breath of the enemy a bit too strongly on their backs, and each had his or her own personal misery. The world had gotten beyond charity.

At the scene of the massacre, Babryshkin had abandoned his resolve to maintain full combat readiness at all costs. Instead of growing harder, he found that his strength of purpose had peaked, and that his will was now on a steeply descending curve. He had ordered the survivors of the bloody ordeal loaded onto his vehicles, and his column had quickly taken on a ragged, undisciplined look. There was a pervasive sense, almost as strong as an odor, that little more could be done. The ammunition was virtually gone. The fuel hardly sufficed to continue the retreat. Against the political officer's protests, Babryshkin had continued to load the sick and disabled onto his tanks, personnel carriers, and trucks throughout the morning's progress. If he could no longer defend them, he could at least carry them.

The turretless tanks had proved to have an unforeseen advantage under such conditions. Since only the narrow main gun housing rose above the flat deck, there was room for a greater load of human cargo than the older tanks could bear. Besides the young woman and her two children, an old man, two bent grandmothers, and a sick teen-aged girl cluttered the vehicle, hanging on to whatever bits of metal their gloved or rag-wrapped hands could grasp. The weather had turned very cold, and the air felt ready with early snow, but each of the passengers was glad for this opportunity to ride exposed to the wind. The alternative was to die by the side of the road.

Not everyone could, or would, be helped. They had come upon a grandmother, sitting off to the side of the road on a battered plastic suitcase, resting her bearded cheeks on her fists. Babryshkin had ordered his vehicle out of the line to pick her up, and he jumped off the fender to help her climb on board. But she hardly found Babryshkin worth a glance, and her expression showed that she did not relish being disturbed by such a fool.

"Little mother," Babryshkin said to her, "you can't stay here."

She briefly raised her eyes, then lowered them back to the vacant steppe.

"Far enough," she mumbled. "This is far enough."

There was no time to argue. And there were too many others who wanted to be saved. Babryshkin remounted his tank, shouting at the driver to work his way back into the formation. Behind him, the shrunken black figure sat on imperturbably, balled fists pressed up against her cheekbones.

The column's progress took them past blackened intervals of military vehicles that had been caught by enemy air strikes, by undamaged war machines that had run out of fuel and been abandoned, and past still more whose mechanisms had simply been overtaxed: the vehicular equivalents of starvation, stroke, or heart attack victims. Government vans and private cars, city buses and rusted motorbikes, farm tractors drawing carts, a carnival of wastage covered the dirt road cut through the steppes. Bodies lay here and there, dead of exposure, or hunger, perhaps of disease, or the victims of murderers who killed those who wandered too far from the mass in the darkness—looking for food, or money, or anything that might increase the killer's chance of survival, however slightly. A collection of ravaged tents marked the site where someone had attempted to establish an aid station. All pride was gone. The proud were dead. As Babryshkin's tanks grunted by, men and women simply continued to squat by the side of the road, emptying shriveled bowels, many of them obviously sick. Here and there, a husband jealously stood guard over his wife, but, overall, there was only a sense of collapse, of the absence of law or reason.

The cold air narrowed Babryshkin's eyes as he leaned out of the commander's hatch. The nursing mother reminded him of Valya, although his wife was not yet a mother and had told him frankly that she did not wish to become one. "Why saddle ourselves?" she had said. Babryshkin suspected that few men who really knew her would classify Valya as a genuinely good woman. She was selfish and dishonest. Yet, she was his wife. He loved her, and, now, he craved her. He felt that, if only he could speak to her now, he might share some of his newfound wisdom with her—how important it was to be satisfied with what one had, to be grateful for the chance to live in peace, to love each other. He had not found new words with which to reach her, yet, somehow, his fresh conviction would persuade her. How lucky they had been just to be able to lie down together in a warm bed, without the slightest thought of death. To lie down in each other's arms with the sure knowledge that morning would come with nothing more unpleasant than the need to rise a bit before the body was ready and to go work. He realized that, before witnessing the spectacle of all this helplessness, failure, and cheap mortality, he had never grasped the spectacular beauty of his life. Cares that once had seemed immense were nothing now. He had been surrounded by beauty, bathed in it, and he had been blind.

A desperate man tried to climb onto the tank ahead of Babryshkin's while the vehicle was still in motion. Unpracticed, the refugee immediately snared himself between the big roadwheels and the grinding track. The conscious watched helplessly as the machine devoured the man's legs below the knee, slamming him to the ground, then twisting him over and over before the vehicle could be halted.

The man lay openmouthed and open-eyed in the gravel. He did not scream or cry, but propped himself up on his elbows, amazed. Two soldiers jumped from the vehicle, yanking off their belts to serve as tourniquets. The soldiers had seen plenty of wounds, and they were not shy. They felt quickly along the bloody rags of the man's trousers, searching for something firm amid the gore and riven bone. But the man simply eased back off his elbows, still silent and wide-eyed, utterly disbelieving. And he died. The soldiers dragged him a little way off the road, although it made no difference, then hurried back to their tank, wiping their hands on their coveralls, with Babryshkin screaming at them to hurry, since they were holding up the column.

Now and again, some of the refugees had to be forced

off of the vehicles, usually because their pleas for food, when denied, turned aggressive. At other times, they were caught trying to steal—anything, from food or a protective mask to the nonsensical. One man even tried to choke a vehicle commander, without the least evident cause. He was a terribly strong man, perhaps a bit mad, and he had to be shot to prevent him from strangling the vehicle commander to death.

Once, a pair of Soviet gunships flew down over the endless kilometers of detritus, and Babryshkin waved excitedly, delighted at this sign that they were not completely alone, that they had not been entirely forgotten. He attempted to establish radio contact with the aircraft, but could not find the right frequency. The ugly machines circled twice around the march unit, then flew off at a dogleg, inscrutable.

The young mother had finished nursing, and Babryshkin felt it was allowable to look at her again. He wondered where her husband might be. Perhaps in some other military unit, fighting elsewhere along the front. Perhaps dead. But, if he was alive, Babryshkin sensed the intensity with which he must be worrying about his family now, wondering where they were, if they were safe.

Babryshkin leaned back toward the woman, who was clutching her infant in one arm, while simultaneously cradling her son and holding on to the gun housing with the other. He felt the need to say something to her, to reach out somehow, to reassure her.

He brought his face as close to hers as possible and could not tell whether he saw fear or simply emptiness in her eyes.

"Someday," he shouted above the roar of the engine, "someday all of this will seem like a bad dream, a story to tell your grandchildren."

The woman was slow to respond. Then Babryshkin imagined that he saw the ghost of a smile pass briefly over her lips.

He reached down into his hatch, to where his map case hung, and he drew out the tattered packet containing his last cigarettes. One of his sergeants had stripped them from the corpse of a rebel officer. He crouched to light one against the cold breeze, then held it out as though to insert it between the woman's lips.

Again, she seemed unable to respond at first. Finally, she shook her head, slightly, slowly, as though the machinery in her neck wanted oil. "No. Thank you."

The old man seated just behind her on the deck looked hungrily at the cigarette. Disappointed at the failure of his gesture, Babryshkin passed the smoke into the old man's quivering hand.

By the side of the road, a man and a woman struggled to drive along two sheep who had balked at the grumble from the armored vehicles. Babryshkin was amazed that the animals had not yet been butchered and eaten. Lucky sheep, he thought.

The dull, constant static in his headset sparked to life.

"This is Angara." Babryshkin recognized the anxious voice of the air defense platoon leader. "We have aircraft approaching from the south."

"Enemy?"

"No identification reading. Assume hostiles."

"*All* stations, *all* stations," Babryshkin called. "*Air alert.* Disperse off the roadway. *Air alert.*"

At his command, his driver turned the steel monster off to the left, scattering the two sheep. Their owners ran after them, openmouthed. Soon, Babryshkin thought, they would have other, greater worries.

"*Don protective masks,*" Babryshkin shouted into the headset mike. "*Seal all vehicles.*" He tugged hastily at the carrier of his mask. The refugees mounted on the vehicle's deck looked at him with fear, their faces vividly alive. He imagined that they were accusing him, as he pulled the mask over his head, temporarily hiding from their sight.

There was no alternative. There was no point in dying out of sheer sympathy.

The unclean mask stank in his nostrils. Looking around him, he could see his vehicles churning off into the steppe, spreading out to offer as difficult a target area as possible.

No more time. He could see the dark specks of the enemy planes, popping up before entering their attack profile. They were aiming straight for the column.

There was nothing else to be done. The surviving air defense gunners had no more missiles. All they could do was to open up with their last belts of automatic weapons ammunition, which was as useless as trying to shoot down the sky itself.

All around, hatch covers slammed shut, leaving bewildered refugees stranded on the vehicle decks. Some of the civilians leapt to the ground, running off into the fields with their last reserves of strength, imagining that there might be someplace to hide, or that they might have time to distance themselves from the military targets. Babryshkin caught a glimpse of a struggle in the back of one of the infantry fighting vehicles as soldiers fought to clear away enough of the refugees to close the troop hatches. A burly civilian grabbed a soldier's mask, and shots rang out.

No time.

Without making a conscious decision, Babryshkin grabbed the woman's little boy, tearing him away from her. He forced the child wildly down into the belly of the tank. Then he pulled at the woman.

She began to resist, not understanding. Swatting and staring in horror at the creature in the bug-eyed mask.

Babryshkin launched himself out of the hatch as the planes grew larger on the horizon. He slapped the woman on the side of the head, then lifted her and the infant away from the gun housing.

The planes were hurtling down into the attack, clearly recognizable as fighter-bombers now.

"Come *on*," Babryshkin bellowed through the voice filter of the mask. He manhandled the woman over to the hatch and shoved her down inside, as though he were stuffing rags into a pipe. The other refugees watched in terror, struggling to hold on to the lurching vehicle as the driver maneuvered out into the steppe.

No room. No time.

Babryshkin kicked the woman's back downward with the flat of his boots, dropping in on top of her, kicking her out of the way. She tumbled to the floor of the vehicle's interior, attempting to wrap herself protectively around her infant. Babryshkin could hear the little boy screaming, even over the engine roar and through the seal of the protective mask.

He slammed the hatch cover down behind him, fumbling to seal it. The last thing he heard before shutting the compartment was the huge scream of the jets.

"Overpressure on," he shrieked into the intercom, aching to be heard through the muffle of his mask's voice-mitter. He slapped at the panel of switches in front of him.

One more time, just one more time. He prayed that the vehicle's overpressure system would function. He didn't care what would come afterward, that was too far away. He only wanted to survive this immediate threat. He knew the filters were worn, and the vehicle had taken a terrible beating. Death could come in an instant. Irresistible.

He felt a shudder through the metal walls. Then another. Bombs.

Perhaps it would be a purely conventional attack, without chemical weaponry.

But he doubted it. The chemical strikes had become too commonplace. The enemy had become addicted to them, having grasped the marvelous economy of such weapons.

He tried to look out through his optics. But it was difficult with the mask on. The tank lurched over rough ground, and the bouncing horizon filled with smoke and dust.

The first test would be whether the woman and her children lived. If they survived, the overpressure system was still functional.

The boy continued to scream. But that was a good sign. Nerve gas victims did not scream. They just died.

Radio call. Hard to hear, hard to hear.

"This is Kama."

"I'm listening," Babryshkin said, dispensing with call signs, trying to keep everything as simple as possible with the mask on.

"This is Kama. Chemical strike, chemical strike." Kama was the last surviving chemical reconnaissance vehicle in the shrunken unit.

"What kind of agent?" Babryshkin demanded of the radio, already envisioning the scene that would await him when he unsealed his hatch. Nothing helped, there was nothing you could do.

"No reading yet. My remote's out. I just read hot."

"Acknowledged."

"This is Angara," the air defender jumped in. "They're leaving. Looks like just one pass."

The voice sounded too clear.

"Do you have your goddamned mask on?" Babryshkin demanded.

"No . . . no, we were engaging the enemy. We've got a good seal on the vehicles, and—"

"Get your mask on, you stupid bastard. I don't want any unnecessary casualties. *Do you hear me?"*

No answer. His nerves were going. He had stepped on the other man's transmission. They had merely canceled each other out. He was forgetting the most basic things. He needed to rest.

"All stations," Babryshkin said, enunciating slowly and carefully. "Report in order of your call signs."

This was the test. How many more call signs would have disappeared?

The overpressure system had worked. The woman and her children were still breathing on the floor of the crew compartment. The boy screamed without stopping, making up for his earlier silence. Babryshkin was about to command the woman to shut the brat up, when the skewed angle of the boy's arm caught his eye, evident even through the camouflage of his winter coat.

Nothing to be done. At least the boy was alive. Arms could be set. The woman looked up at Babryshkin, her eyes near madness. Her forehead was bleeding. She had protected her infant in the fall, not herself. A good mother. Hardly more than a child herself.

He listened as his subordinates reported in. The voices were businesslike, if weary and a bit slurred. Everything was reduced to a matter of routine.

The reporting sequence broke. Another crew gone.

Babryshkin spoke into the intercom, ordering his driver to turn back toward the road. Then he ordered the radio reporting to resume at the next sequence number.

Unexpectedly, his vehicle jerked to a halt. The engine was still running, however, and Babryshkin did not understand what was happening.

"Wait," he told the radio net. Then he switched to the intercom. "Why in the hell did you stop? I told you to get back on the road."

The driver mumbled something, unintelligible through the protective mask.

"I asked you why the hell we've stopped, goddamnit," Babryshkin barked.

"I can't . . ." the driver said in a flat voice.

"What do you mean, you can't? Are you crazy?"

"I can't," the driver repeated. "I'd have to drive over them."

"What in the hell are you talking about?" Babryshkin demanded, putting the eye piece of his protective mask as close to his optics as he could.

The driver did not need to answer. Where there had been a plodding army of humanity a few minutes before, there was only a litter of dark, fallen shapes. No hysteria, no struggling, no shivering movements of the wounded, not the least evidence of suffering. Only stillness, except where scattered military vehicles continued their slow, aimless maneuvers, like riderless horses on an antique battlefield.

The only thing that still held the power to shock Babryshkin was the ease with which death came. The casual quickness. Whether to the man whose legs had so unexpectedly been gobbled by a tank, or to this stilled multitude. No allowance for struggle, for passion, for heroism. There was barely time for cowardice.

They said that the new nerve gases were humane weapons. They killed their victims so swiftly. And, within minutes, they dissipated back into the atmosphere, grown completely harmless.

Babryshkin radioed to the chemical defense officer. "Do you have a definite reading at this time?"

"This is Kama. Superfast nerve, type Sh-M. It's already gone. I've unmasked myself."

Babryshkin shook his head at the universe. Then he tugged at his mask, feeling the sudden wetness as the rubber lifted away from his skin. He shook the mask out, then tucked it methodically into its carrier.

"Hold in place," he ordered his driver. "I'm going to dismount." But first he reentered the radio net. "All stations. All clear, all clear." He paused for just a moment, searching for the right words. When he could not find them, he simply said, "Clean off your vehicles." Then he unlocked his hatch and climbed out.

He was lucky. There wasn't so much dirty work. All of his passengers had tumbled from the maneuvering tank in their struggles with death, save for the old man, who still lay coddled against the rear of the gun housing, burned-out cigarette stub in his hand. Babryshkin got him under the armpits and rolled him off the side of the tank.

There was nothing you could do. He stood up, drinking in the cold, harmless air. As far as he could see, nothing remained alive in the roadway. Worse than the plague, he thought. Far worse. No act of God.

Something white caught his eye in the middle distance. At first, he was baffled. Then he recognized the carcasses of the two sheep that had been driven from God knew where.

Pointless.

Suddenly, a scream slashed out at the world, piercing, even over the idle of the big tank engine. Babryshkin looked around.

The woman whose life he had saved was standing up in the commander's hatch, screaming at the panorama with a ferocity that hurt in the listener's throat.

Well, at least she's got a voice to scream with, Babryshkin thought, glad even of this much evidence of life.

10

Moscow
2 November 2020

RYDER SAT IN THE SPARSELY FURNISHED OFFICE OUT-side of the interrogation block, drinking gray coffee and waiting for his Soviet counterpart to return. Although he had drunk no alcohol the night before, he felt hungover. The captain billeted in the next hotel room had been hammering one of the Russian bar girls all night, with an energy that was as impressive as it was annoying. For hours, Ryder had lain awake as his neighbor's bed thumped against the wall. Now and then, the captain's partner would call out in a language Ryder did not understand, but whose message was unmistakable, and Ryder's thoughts would return to his wife, Jennifer, who refused to be called Jenny, and who had always been so silent in the bedroom. Ryder suspected that his old friend had been right when he declared that Ryder was biologically programmed to end up with the wrong women, but Ryder felt no malice toward his wife. Lying there in the Moscow night, he simply missed her, without understanding exactly why. The one affair in which he had indulged since his divorce the year before had been premature and unmemorable, and had not made the least impression on the lingering image of his wife. Ryder hoped she was happy now, with her new husband who promised to be all that he had failed to be.

Finally, Ryder had given up trying to sleep. Propping

himself up, he drew his field computer from the shoulder holster slung over the bedpost. The tiny machine lit up at the electronically recognizable touch of Ryder's fingers, unable to spring to life under any other hand, unable to share its secrets with anyone else. It was almost as if the machine was relieved at his touch, as though it, too, had been made restless by the lions in the next room. Ryder called up a program he had been working on in Meiji, the Japanese military-industrial computer language, and he strummed through its odd music until he came to the problem that had been annoying him for days. Then the sexual thunder exploded again.

The problem between Ryder and his wife had not been physical disappointment. If anything, he had shown the greater appetite and resourcefulness, and he had never tired of her. But Jennifer had married him as a very promising graduate student in one of the elite new government-funded programs, not as a soldier. Ryder had been specializing in computer science and Japanese, along with a variety of specialized Japanese computer languages. It was a program open only to the brightest, and although it called for four years of military service after graduation, the long-term prospects were fantastic. American industry was screaming for employees with such qualifications, and Jennifer had married that particular future, while Ryder had been delighted to marry such a smart, beautiful, loving girl. Her parents had died in the plague years, she was alone, and he imagined that he would fill a terrible need in her life.

The problems had begun in the Army. Although Ryder's specialty pay as a warrant officer interrogator put his income above that of the average line major, Jennifer could not accustom herself to what she perceived as their low financial and social status. Her behavior was not the behavior of the physically enthusiastic college girl he had married. In private, then, later, in public, when she was drunk, she took to calling him Pretty Boy. She said that she should have married a man, someone who knew how to get ahead in the world, and not a child.

Ryder had actually looked in the mirror one night when Jennifer did not come home, wondering at his face, trying to understand *how* a man looked and what it meant. He had never cared much about his appearance. But the girls back home in Hancock, Nebraska, had cared, as had the wonderful, sun-washed girls of Stanford University a bit later on. There had always been girls, to the envy of his friends, who could not believe he would not take advantage of every last opportunity, who were utterly baffled by his inclination to treat girls and, later, women as people. "You're nuts," his old friend told him. "You're crazy. You treat them too good. If you just learn to treat them like shit, they spend their lives on their knees with their mouths open. Jeff, I swear, you're biologically programmed to end up with the wrong . . ."

He wanted to be a good man, to behave responsibly and decently toward women and toward other men. And the more Jennifer complained and threatened, the more attractive his military service became to him. On his own, he would never have dreamed of joining the Army. But the financial support for his attendance at the university had allowed him to study hard at a good school, instead of working his way through a mediocre one. He had initially regarded his term of required military service as an obligation to be fulfilled, nothing more. But he found the work satisfied him, filling him with a sense of worth he knew he would never find in Jennifer's dreamworld of corporations and credit cards. So he betrayed her, her trust, her faith. When he told her he intended to remain in the Army, she paled. Then she began to scream, cursing him with a vividness for which her relatively demure conduct in the bedroom had not prepared him. She swept her arm across the nearest countertop, hurling glass, wood and cork, dried flowers, and magazines across the room. Then she left, without real argument and without a coat.

She returned the next day but did not speak to him. Yet, their lives slowly seemed to normalize. Just before he went out on maneuvers, she even slept with him again. She seemed to be trying. Then, in the middle of the war games, he had the opportunity to return to main post for a few hours, and he phoned her, asking her to meet him in the cafeteria. She did. And she told him she was leaving him, just as he was biting into a slice of pizza.

Well, Ryder told himself, Moscow was an easy enough city in which to become depressed. The hotel rooms were never quite clean, the food was difficult to get down, and the daily ride to and from the fabled faded building that housed KGB headquarters led through dishwater gray streets where no one ever smiled. Not much to smile about, of course. From what little Ryder had seen of their lives, these people lived under conditions an American would find absolutely intolerable. On top of that, the war was going very badly for them.

Ryder felt sorry for the Russians. He was sorry that any man or woman had to live in so gray a world, and he yearned to make a professional contribution to the joint U.S.–Soviet effort, to somehow make things better. But, thus far, the joint interrogation sessions, although revealing as to Soviet capabilities, had produced little of value concerning the enemy.

Ryder took another sip of the thin, bitter coffee to clear his head and glanced again at the subject file. He had almost memorized the data. The case was a windfall, a miracle of good luck—but it promised to be tough going, perhaps the most important and difficult interrogation in which he had ever been involved. The subject was potentially very lucrative, but there would be layers of defenses. And time was critical. The Soviets were collapsing, and Ryder had just learned that morning, at the prebreakfast U.S. staff meeting, that the Seventh Cavalry, who were out in the thick of things beyond the Urals, were going to be committed early. None of the officers of the Tenth Cavalry, all military intelligence specialists, had been happy to hear that. Men had mumbled through their hangovers, still wearing the smell of women with whom they were not supposed to be fraternizing. The speedup in events meant that carefully plotted work schedules had to be discarded and that the officers, got up in a poor imitation of businessman's dress, would have to wake up properly and scramble to get some results with their well-meaning but hopelessly bureaucratic Soviet counterparts.

Ryder knew he had been lucky in at least one regard. Nick Savitsky, his counterpart interrogator, seemed to be completely open, and he was relatively flexible for a Soviet, anxious to learn about the American methods. Of course, much of that was simply the desire to gain information for the KGB files—but Ryder was doing the same for the U.S. It was the nature of the business.

Ryder was worried about Savitsky today, however. The subject they were going to work on had the potential of opening up the enemy's entire infrastructure. But you had to go delicately, patiently. Savitsky, like the other Soviets Ryder had encountered, did not always seem to understand that. They were given to excesses that sometimes ruined a subject's ability to respond. A Soviet interrogation, no matter how sophisticated, always had an air of violence about it, and there was a tendency to mishandle a subject severely, without really thinking through the consequences. He had already seen Savitsky in one fit of vengeful fury.

The door opened, and Savitsky came in, smiling, ill-shaven.

"Good morning, Jeff," he said, pronouncing the name as "Cheff." He dropped into a chair just opposite Ryder. "And how are things?"

Usually, the two men worked in English, which Savitsky spoke reasonably well. For highly technical exchanges, they switched to Japanese, but Savitsky was less comfortable in that language than was Ryder.

"Horrasho," Ryder replied, using one of his half-dozen words of Russian. He had been told that the word meant "very good." It was a very popular word with the officers of the Tenth Cavalry, who liked to pronounce it "whoreshow," and regularly applied it to the nightly follies in the hotel bar.

"Today will be a big day," Savitsky said, helping himself to the coffee, "an important day." Ryder had learned that the coffee was put there each morning especially for him, and its presence was a treat for Savitsky, who never made a move toward the interrogation chamber until they had finished each last sip. Ryder had also noted that Savitsky would quietly wrap the used grounds in newspaper and slip them into his briefcase.

Ryder watched for a moment as the Russian thickened his coffee with teaspoon after teaspoon of sugar.

"Nick," he said, trying to sound nonchalant, "I had an idea last night about how to approach this case. I think I've got an angle—"

"Don't worry, don't worry," Savitsky interrupted. "Today—everything is the Russian way. I will show you something. A thing you have not seen." Savitsky smiled, either at the thought of the interrogation or at the piercing warmth of the coffee. "You will like it, I know." The Russian cradled his chipped cup in red hands, and nodded his head happily. "You *must* trust me."

Oh, shit, Ryder thought.

But Nick was in high spirits. "I have learned so much from you, my friend. You Americans . . . you Americans . . . always with such technology perfection. But today, *I* am showing *you* something splendid. Something I know you have not seen." The Russian laughed slightly into the steam from his cup. "All of your American comrades will have a great interest."

Ryder let it go for the moment. He did not want to do anything to spoil the cooperation between the two of them. But neither did he wish to waste a subject of such incredible possibilities. He decided to wait, at least until things threatened to get out of hand. If nothing else, he was anxious just to see the subject. Until now, the Soviets had played this one close to the chest.

Nick drained the last of his coffee, his facial expression moving from near ecstasy to regret.

"Everything is very good," he told Ryder. "Now we will go to work."

Ryder followed the Soviet through the cramped maze of hallways and security barriers that was slowly becoming familiar. Corridors as decayed and dank as an inner-city school after hours, stinking of disinfectant and age. Standard locking systems, not all of which worked the first time Savitsky tried them. Sometimes the vault doors were simply propped open, or minded by an inside guard. Framed photographs on the walls showed mostly unimportant men, since the years of infighting had stripped the walls of the readily recognizable faces. Bad air, poor light. An old woman mopping the floor with formidable slowness.

The last security door slammed shut behind the two men.

They followed a short hallway that was cluttered with electronics in various stages of disassembly, then turned into a small room that resembled the inside of a recording studio's control booth. The walls and counters were covered with racks of artificial-intelligence terminals, direct-function computers, environmental controls, recording and autotranslating devices—the tools of the contemporary interrogator's trade. Only these were all a bit nicked or chipped. There was a smell of old burned-out wires, and not all of the monitor lights worked. Much of the equipment was a generation out of date, while the most modern gear was of European or even U.S. manufacture. The Soviets had specialized in the areas of electronic translation, inferential patterning, and specialized software, and one of Ryder's superiors had compared them to brilliant tacticians who were forced to rely on foreign weaponry.

A long glass window covered most of one wall. To anyone out in the interrogation chamber, the window appeared to be a mirror, but from Ryder's position in the musty booth he could look out on the shadowy forms of the "application room." The design was a holdover from the old days, and the room remained so dark that he could not yet see the subject. He waited impatiently for Savitsky to turn up the lighting.

"The subject is already wired into our system," Savitsky said, as he touched over the control panel in the bad light. "We'll double-check, as you Americans like to say. But you will see. Everything is fine. Today, everyone is anxious to see how our performance will be." Savitsky turned his shadowy face toward Ryder. "Today, for the first time, I have received a direct call from the Kremlin. There is very much interest."

"I hope they're not too impatient," Ryder said. "This could take time."

Savitsky laughed slightly. It was a friendly laugh, that of a confident man. "But that is the surprise," he said. "Soon you will see. A very big surprise for our American friends."

Ryder did not know how to respond. This was so important. If any sort of foolishness were allowed to destroy the utility of the subject, an enormous opportunity would go to waste.

Turn up the damned lights, Ryder thought. Let me *see*.

As if responding to Ryder's thoughts, Savitsky flipped a row of switches. Beyond the big window, spotlights came up to scour an electronic operating room with a sterile white glare. Despite the complicated disorder of the interrogation chamber, with its cascades of wires that connected one clutter of electronics to the next, Ryder focused immediately on the subject.

"Christ," he said to Savitsky, in honest surprise. "I expected . . ."

Savitsky laughed. "Amazing, isn't it?"

"Smaller than I thought, for one thing. Much smaller."

Savitsky stood with his arms folded across his chest in satisfaction. "Remarkable, I think. You know, such . . . inconspicuity—is that what you say?"

"Inconspicuousness."

"Yes. Inconspicuousness. How easily overlooked. It was only pure luck that a specialist was on the scene."

Ryder shook his head. It really was amazing.

"Well, my friend," Savitsky said, "shall we go out and have a closer look?"

Ryder followed the Soviet out of the control booth, almost stepping on the man's heels in his excitement. His sole interest now was the subject, and he almost tripped over a coil of wires.

Savitsky made straight for the central operating table, and he hovered over the subject for a moment, waiting for Ryder to come up beside him. Ryder remained so astonished that he felt almost as though he were out of breath. It truly was amazing. Unless the Soviets had made some sort of mistake, unless this wasn't the great brain after all.

But all of Ryder's professional instincts told him that this was the genuine article, that there had been no mistake, and that the Japanese were still the best at some things, no matter how broadly U.S. technology had struggled to come back. The electronic intelligence brain that processed and stored all of the data necessary to command

and control vast stretches of the front fit into a solid black brick little larger than a man's wallet.

"My God," Ryder said. "I thought . . . it would be at least the size of a suitcase."

"Yes," Savitsky agreed. "It's frightening. Had you been able to combine the power of every supercomputer in the world at the turn of the century, the power would not have approached . . . such a power as resides in this device."

Ryder possessed access to the latest classified research in the States, as well as to intelligence files on foreign developments. But no one had anticipated that the process of miniaturization had gone *this* far. The Japanese had pulled off another surprise, and it worried Ryder. What else might they have in store?

"It was really pure luck," Savitsky stressed, as though he still could not quite believe it himself. "Perhaps the only luck we have had in this war. Not only did we not shoot down the enemy, our systems did not even detect him. The enemy command ship experienced the simplest of mechanical malfunctions. Imagine, my friend. One of the most sophisticated tactical-operational airborne command centers in the Japanese inventory . . . dropping from the sky because a bolt came loose or a washer disintegrated. Such wonderful luck. Had the aircraft experienced an electronic problem, the brain would have destroyed itself to prevent capture. Computer suicide."

"There may still be active self-destruct mechanisms built into it," Ryder said, in warning.

Savitsky shrugged. "Of course it is possible. But the electronic cradle in which we have placed the subject is a good mimic. How would an American say it? 'Reflexively imitative.' The cradle continues to assure the subject that it is a part of the system for which it was designed. No matter what happens."

"And . . ." Ryder began carefully, "what's going to happen, Nick?"

Nick smiled. "You'll see."

Ryder stared down at the tiny brain. How on earth were the Soviets going to attack this problem? They were good.

But Ryder had yet to see them manage anything at the level of sophistication required to overcome the powerful counterintrusion mechanisms such a system would possess.

"You know," Ryder said, "I feel almost solemn. Maybe 'humbled' would be a better way to say it. To stand in the presence of an intelligence so great." He put his hands in his pockets, as if to prevent himself from reaching out just to touch the device one time, the way a man might feel compelled to touch a masterpiece of art. "I don't know. I didn't get much sleep last night. But . . . I could swear it knows we're here. That it senses us."

Savitsky just continued to smile. "Oh," he said brightly. "It *will* know we're here. In a manner of speaking."

"Nick," Ryder said, choosing his words carefully, "I don't want to blow this. I mean, we can't afford to . . . make any mistakes. There is . . . a primary computer system . . . of which you may not be aware. It's in the United States, in Colorado. We could connect it to this. It's possible, I'd just need approval, and—"

Savitsky's smile withered slightly, like a flower at the first light hint of frost. "Perhaps that will be necessary," he said. "Later. But I think you will see . . . that we are not so incapable." Then his smile returned. "Come," he said. "Let's get to work."

The Soviet turned with an air of decision, heading back for the control booth. It was difficult for Ryder to leave the proximity of the brain. He wished he could simply slip it into his pocket and take it away. To where it would be safe. From foolishness.

"Come on," Savitsky called. "I want to show you something, Jeff."

Ryder moved heavily now, the sleepless night returning to haunt him after the flare of excitement he had just experienced. He stepped over electronic switching boxes and loose jacks, more of the weapons of the modern interrogator. In a moment, he was back beside the Soviet in the control booth.

"Take a look at this," Savitsky said.

Ryder glanced after Savitsky's directing hand. Nothing much. An antique-looking device of the sort that was used to measure cardiac waves or earthquakes. A crude high-resolution screen of a type no longer used in the United States. Manual controls. Knobs.

"That looks interesting," Ryder lied. "What is it?"

Savitsky waited before answering. He looked into Ryder's eyes in the weak light, and Ryder could sense a new, weighty sobriety in the man.

"It's a pain machine."

"What?"

"A pain machine." Upon repetition, the Soviet's tone had lost its heaviness, becoming almost nonchalant. But Ryder sensed that the man was still serious. As serious as possible. "You're the first outsider to be let in on this . . . development." Savitsky smiled slowly, as if his facial muscles had become very cold. "It's a mark of honor."

Ryder did not understand. "What does it do, exactly?"

Ryder sensed the faintest air of maliciousness about the Soviet now. It was his turn, after a host of casual humiliations at the gold-plated hands of the Americans. "It occurred to us some years ago, that . . . interesting possibilities might come into existence, as artificial intelligence systems and their corollaries became more sophisticated. That, to say it in simple words, these devices would develop more and more of a resembling—is that the right word?"

"Resemblance?"

"Yes. More of a resemblance to the human animal. Consequently, they might also develop the same sort of vulnerabilities as the human being. It occurred to us that there must be *some* way in which a computer could be made to feel pain." Savitsky considered his words for a moment. "The electronic equivalent of pain, to be most exact."

Ryder slowly moved his hands together in front of his hips, interlacing the fingers, tapping his thumbs. Waiting for information. The concept was utterly foreign to him. He looked at Savitsky.

"Of course," the Soviet continued, "it's not 'true' physical pain, as you and I would know it. Just as the computer does not perceive the physical environment as we see it. I am speaking of *simulated* pain, for a simulated mind."

Savitsky examined his American counterpart's reaction. A small, hard smile tightened his lips. "And it works."

The gloomy control booth, with its odor of charred wires, had taken on an eerie atmosphere for Ryder. The Soviet was talking about an entirely new dimension of thought in a field where Ryder considered himself competent, and very well-informed. On one hand, Savitsky's speech sounded as silly as a tale about witches and ghouls, while, on the other, the man's voice carried an unmistakable message of veracity, of confidence. Ryder tried to think through at least the immediate ramifications, but his mind kept jumbling with questions of possibility.

"Your . . . approach," Ryder said. "It can't destroy the subject, can it?"

Savitsky's voice was merely businesslike. "We haven't had that problem with the latest variant of our system. As you can imagine, my friend, there has been some trial and error. We found that machines can no more tolerate unlimited amounts of pain than can the human animal. And, you might say, some machines have weaker hearts than others. Just like men."

"Have you ever tried it on so sophisticated a system?"

Savitsky looked at him in surprise. "Of course not. We don't *possess* such a system."

Of course not. Foolish question. "Nick, I'm honestly . . . concerned. I don't want to waste this opportunity."

The Soviet began to lose his patience. "And what, then, is the American solution? What is your alternative? Weeks of trial and error? The cautious stripping of logic layer after logic layer, like peeling an onion that has no end? My country doesn't have weeks. We . . . may not have days." The anger went out of Savitsky's voice, and he looked away from Ryder, staring off through the two-way mirror, perhaps staring at a battlefield thousands of kilometers away. "There is no time," he said.

No, Ryder thought. Savitsky was right. There was no time. He remembered the morning briefing. The Seventh Cavalry about to be committed to battle. A world in collapse. And he had been thinking like a bureaucrat.

"You're right," Ryder told the Soviet. "Let's see what you can do."

The two men worked briskly, side by side, readying the banks of interrogation support computers. The system was operating on Meiji. In less than a second, the machines could ask more questions than had all of the human interrogators in preautomation history, and they could make their inquiries with a precision denied to human speech.

Savitsky adjusted the lighting out in the interrogation chamber so that the harshest spots shone down directly on the subject. The electronic jungle that filled the room receded into an artificial night out of which peered dozens of tiny colored eyes.

"Ready?" Savitsky asked.

Ryder nodded in agreement.

The process would begin with logical queries on the most elementary level, trying to get the subject to agree to propositions on the order of two plus two equals four. The complexity was not important. The point was to compromise the subject's isolation, to get a hook in, to induce interaction. The first stage was normally the most difficult. Working in through the security barriers and buffers, it could take weeks to get a military computer to concur with the most basic propositions. But, once you broke them down, the data came pouring out.

"Query bank on. Autobuffers active."

In front of them the green lines on the "pain" monitor flowed smoothly, ready to register the subject's reaction.

Looking at Savitsky's profile, Ryder was surprised to see jewels of sweat shining on the man's upper lip. The Soviet was nervous, after all.

Savitsky twisted a dial that might have been salvaged from an antique television set of the sort Ryder remembered from his grandmother's living room, where the device had delivered the world to a child snowed in on the Nebraska prairie.

The lines jumped on the response meter. The bright movement was startling in the darkness, and Ryder reacted as though he himself had received a slight shock.

The language flow reader registered a negative response. Savitsky quickly turned the "pain" back down, and the green lines settled, trembling for just a moment, then resuming their smooth, flat flow.

"Well," Savitsky said. "Now we try again."

He gave the dial a sharp turn.

The green lines fractured into jagged ridges and valleys, straining toward the borders of the monitor. But the interrogation support computers continued to report negative interaction.

Perspiration gleamed on Savitsky's forehead. He turned the control back to its zero position, and said, "You know, when I was beginning my training, so many years ago, everything started with the theory of interrogating humans. I had not yet specialized in automation. That came later. Anyway, they told us that the breakdowns often came very suddenly, that it was important not to feel despair. You might think, oh, I am never going to break this subject. But you had only to persist. Because, in the end, everyone broke." The Soviet stared out through the window, to where the miniature electronic brain lay still under the spotlights. "It will be interesting to see if the same holds true for machines."

Ryder followed his counterpart's stare. Certainly, there had been no visible change in the subject. Just a small, obviously inanimate black rectangle that looked as though it had been hewn from slate. Yet, he imagined that something about it had altered.

You need a good night's sleep tonight, he told himself.

"I'm going to break this bastard," Savitsky said, his voice full of renewed energy. It was unmistakably the energy of anger.

The Soviet twisted the dial again, jacking up the intensity well beyond the previous level. Whatever the machine was doing, Ryder only hoped that it would not destroy the captive treasure for nothing. In the name of some arcane mumbo jumbo.

The green lines on the monitor went wild. There was, of course, no sign of movement, no physical reaction from the subject. But Ryder suddenly felt something unacceptable in the atmosphere, a change that he could not put into words but that felt distinctly unpleasant and intense.

The unexpected flashing of the language flow reader, where an interrogation's results were reported, made Ryder jump.

The screen merely read, "Unintelligible response."

But that was where it started. It was the beginning of interaction, a sign of life.

"Jesus Christ," Ryder said. "You're getting something, Nick."

Beside him, the Soviet was breathing as heavily as if he had been delivering blows to a victim's head. He stared at Ryder as though he barely recognized him. Then he seemed to wake, and he turned the system's power down once again. The green lines calmed, but never quite regained their earlier straightness. They appeared to be shivering.

"I wonder," Savitsky said, "if our computers could understand the nature of a scream."

He twisted the dial again, sharply. With a grunting noise that was almost a growl, he wrenched it all the way around, focusing on the captured computer brain out on the interrogation table with something that resembled hatred. He kept his hand tightly fixed to the control, as though he might be able to force just a bit more power out of it that way.

The green lines on the "pain" register rebounded off the upper and lower limits of the screen.

It could not be true. Ryder refused to let himself believe it. It was only the result of too little sleep and bad nerves, of allowing oneself to become too emotional. It was crazy. But he could not help feeling that *something* was suffering.

Tonight, he promised himself, he wouldn't be such a stick-in-the-mud. He needed a few beers. To relax. To sleep.

Machines, Ryder told himself, do not feel pain. This is absurd.

Savitsky turned the dial down as though he were going to give the captured computer a respite, then, without warning, he quickly turned the intensity up to the maximum degree again.

Ryder felt an unexpected urge to reach out and halt the work of the other man's hand. Until he could get a grip on himself, sort things out.

You silly bastard, he told himself. It's just a machine.

And machines don't suffer.

Savitsky ignored him now. The Soviet was spitting out a litany of Russian words that could only be obscenities. He had bent himself over the control panel in an attitude of such tension and fury that Ryder expected the man to lash out with his fists.

The monitor registered a craze of green lines.

There is pain in these rooms, Ryder thought. He tried to catch himself, to tell himself yet again that machines do not feel pain, but as he watched the tiny captive brain he imagined he was watching a grimacing, sweating, agonizing thing.

He lifted his hand toward Savitsky, whose face had become almost unrecognizable.

Suddenly, the entire bank of computers whirled to life. The eruption of corollary light from monitors and flow screens indicated that the machines were working frantically, pushed nearly to their capacity. The control booth dazzled with light issuing from all angles in staccato bursts.

Savitsky remained bent over the dial, covering it with hands like claws.

The main language flow reader began to flash, announcing a message from another world. Then the flow of characters began, in the peculiar language of top-end Japanese computers, repeating the same simple message over and over again:

"Please. Stop."

The data take was so voluminous that it quickly overloaded several of the Soviet storage reservoirs, and it kept coming, a deluge of information. But the two interrogators gave no sign of elation. They simply sat in the control booth without speaking to each other, without even acknowledging the other's presence. Each man was trapped in his own private weariness, his own confusion. Soon, linkages between data banks would need to be established, and superiors would need to be informed. The vast military bureaucracies would need to be moved to take advantage of the incredible range of opportunities that now presented themselves. But neither man was quite ready to start.

Finally, Ryder forced himself to climb out of the theoretical swamp through which he had been slopping, to consider the practical applications. There was a possibility of literally taking the enemy's war away from them. Their artillery could be directed to fire automatically on their own positions, their aircraft could be directed to attack their own troops. An entirely false intelligence picture could be painted for the enemy commander, lulling him to sleep until it was too late. The possible variations were endless. And there was only one catch: someone would have to sit down at a fully operative Japanese command console—the higher the level, the better—to infiltrate their network.

Ryder was confident. Nothing seemed impossible anymore. He felt his energy returning, compounding. He began to think about the best way to present the information to his superiors, to help them see the full possibilities, to get things going.

"Nick," he said. When Savitsky did not respond, Ryder touched the man's knee. "Nick, we've got to get moving."

The Soviet snorted. He looked exhausted, as if he had not slept for days, for years. He had given everything he had, and now he sat drained, his tunic sweat-soaked.

There would be a thousand problems, Ryder realized. But he was confident that each could be solved.

Savitsky blinked as though something was bothering his eyes, then he looked away. His limbs, his hands appeared lifeless.

"Yes," he said.

Looking at his weary companion, Ryder suddenly had a sense of things far greater than any single man, of things beyond words, of worlds in motion and the power of history. The hour of the Americans had come.

11

Baku
the Provisional Islamic Republic
of Azerbaijan
2 November 2020

GENERAL NOBURU KABATA SIPPED HIS SCOTCH, MARveling at his unhappiness. Professionally, he had every reason to be pleased. The offensive continued to make splendid progress. The Soviets were all but finished east of the Urals, and they were in serious trouble between the Urals and the Caucasus. None of the problems within the friendly forces appeared insurmountable, and there was no apparent reason why all of the military goals of the operation should not be fulfilled. This was a time for joy or, at least, for satisfaction. For, even though his status was nominally that of a contract adviser to the Islamic Union and the government of Iran, this was his operation, the highlight of his career, and a triumph for Japanese policy. Yet, here he was drinking Scotch on an empty stomach, in the morning.

His father would not have approved. His father, who had pushed his eldest son to become a master of the golf club, rather than of the sword, as had been the family tradition. In Japan, he remembered his father saying, there was nothing more important than the ability to play a good round of golf—even for a general. And he remembered the vacation on which he had accompanied his father, so very many years before, to the golf courses of Pebble Beach, in California. He remembered the perfect greens along the stony, splashing coast, the remarkable private homes set among the cypresses, and his father's quiet comment that someday these careless, irresponsible Americans would be their servants.

His father had loved Scotch. He had trained himself to appreciate it, just as he later conditioned his son to the gentleman's drink of choice. So much was handed down. The tradition of bespoke suits from H. Huntsman & Sons of 11 Saville Row, the preference for the links of Scotland, the family military tradition that was older than the game of golf or the patent of any tailor shop. He knew his father would have been very proud of his military record, graced with achievements of a sort denied the older generation. But the elder general would not have approved of the consumption of alcohol in the morning, on duty.

Noburu consoled himself with the thought that he never lost control with alcohol. The drink was merely to better his temper in the face of yet another frustrating meeting with the foreign generals who commanded the armies executing his plan. Shemin, the Iraqi-born commander of the Islamic Union's forces, was a sharp politician, occasionally helpful in mediating disputes with the Iranians. But he was no soldier. Merely a strongman's brother, on whose shoulders his family had sewn epaulets. Shemin would have been far more at home plotting a coup than in planning a battle. On the positive side, Shemin usually accepted Noburu's plans and carefully worded orders, even when he did not quite understand them. But, on his bad days, Shemin struck Noburu as a typical Arab—illogical, apt to become fixated on the wrong thing at the wrong time, dishonest, subject to emotional outbursts, and very difficult to control when he was not in the right mood.

Tanjani, the Iranian commander, was worse. As fanatical as he was inept, he liked nothing better than to rear like a snake and spit poisonous accusations at Noburu. Nothing was ever good enough for the Iranian, who did not even begin to understand the physical principles that made the weapons that Japan had put into his hands function. The Iranian grasped only what was immediately visible to him and seemed to have no sense at all of the incredibly complex levels of warfare carried out in the electromagnetic spectrum. Of course, the others hardly understood the business themselves. Even Biryan, the commander of the Central Asian forces in revolt against the Soviet yoke, had only a nebulous understanding of the invisible battlefields flowing around the physical combat on the ground. Biryan was the most professional of the three subordinate commanders, the best schooled in military affairs. But he was also the most relentlessly savage, a man who could never drink his fill of blood. Noburu hated dealing with them, and their meetings always left him feeling soiled.

He took a sip from his glass, feeling the diluted liquid soak bitterly over his tongue, leaving a taste of acid and smoke. Then he shifted his eyes to the shoulders of his aide, who sat at the commander's private workstation, sifting through incoming reports for those that might require Noburu's personal review. The aide could be trusted to eliminate all but the essential. He had an unerring eye for the material his commander needed. Akiro was a fine officer from a very good family, and Noburu had no doubt that the younger man, too, would be a general one day. But Noburu had not selected the man for either his bloodlines or his professional abilities. There were other young officers possessed of greater talents and technical skills than Akiro. Noburu had chosen Akiro as his aide because the younger man was a perfect conformist.

If ever Noburu wondered what his own superiors or peers would think about a given matter, he had only to ask Akiro's view. Akiro was the perfect product of the system, convinced of its rightness, of its perfection. Of course, Noburu realized, he, too, had once been much like that, believing, if not in the perfection of the system, at least in its ultimate perfectibility. Now, on the verge of triumph, Noburu felt himself laden with doubts, almost physically bowed, as though each doubt were a brick piled upon his shoulders. He finished his Scotch, draining the last bit of sour water, and put the glass down. He would not have another.

Perhaps, he told himself, it was only the business about the Americans. An overreaction, almost a superstitious response to the shock of his success. His senior intelligence officer's report that unprecedented communications had been detected between Washington and Moscow nagged at him. Tokyo was not concerned. There was little the Americans could do, even if they did elect to intervene. The United States was far away, and the American forces remained tied down in Latin America—and if Tokyo had its way, they would be tied down there forever. The United States had retreated into its determination to maintain hegemony in its own hemisphere, and the rest of the world had received scant attention of late. In any case, what did the Americans owe the Soviets? It was not merely a military equation—Tokyo did not believe that the United States could muster the financial wherewithal to intervene. And, militarily, no one believed that the United States could compete with Japanese technology—an impossible task. No, the United States had been taught a good lesson, as Noburu knew firsthand from his experience as a young lieutenant colonel in Africa. They would not be anxious for another such humiliation. Primitive exchanges in the Brazilian backcountry were one thing; a full-scale confrontation with Japanese heavy weaponry was an entirely different matter. Even if the U.S. had not honored its treaty commitments and had hidden away a cache of nuclear weapons, none of their delivery systems could penetrate Japan's strategic defense shield, and any tactical employment on the field of battle could be parried militarily and exploited politically. At most, the Americans could send the Soviets an Air Force contingent—which Noburu's forces would simply knock out of the sky.

He had firsthand experience at knocking Americans out of the sky. He knew how very easily it could be done. Yet, beyond the strictures of logic, his instincts had perked up at the mention of the communications link between Washington and Moscow, and he wished the intelligence service would find a way to break into the system and decipher what the Soviets and Americans were discussing. For now, there was only the information that such a link existed, and that shred of information tantalized Noburu. Perhaps, he thought, it was only his fear that the dreams would come again. It was difficult enough with these Arabs and Iranians and the squalid minor peoples of Central Asia. He was not certain that he could bear the return of those dreams and still exercise sound judgment.

He thought again of the impending meeting, wondering how he could ever bring such men to their senses. Noburu certainly did not consider himself a softhearted man. His worldview was one of duty intermingled with existential—and physical—pain. But he could not reconcile himself to the way these savages made war. Personally, quietly, he was proud of the fact that he had not needed to employ the Scramblers to accomplish his mission. To Noburu, such weapons were inhuman beyond the tolerance of the most hardened warrior, and he was not pleased that his nation had gone to such lengths to develop them. Noburu pictured himself as an old-fashioned military man, a man of honor. And he saw no honor whatsoever in weapons such as the Scramblers. He had carefully concealed them from the men who were technically his employers and theoretically his allies. Once Shemin, Tanjani, and Biryan were aware of the existence of such devices, they would hound Tokyo until the Scramblers were employed. And then warfare would reach a level of degradation that Noburu did not care to contemplate.

Perhaps it was age, he told himself. Perhaps he was going soft after all. But he worried that Japan had made a terrible mistake in backing the forces its weaponry presently supported. He suspected that all of this was merely about greed, about needless overreaching. The Soviets had been perfectly willing to sell off the riches of Siberia on reasonable terms. But Tokyo was obsessed with control. There was vanity at play, as well. Noburu could recognize it because he had come to recognize it first in himself: the unwillingness to depend on the mercies of others. The need to be the master. Now Noburu found himself waging war beside men he could not regard as any better than savages.

They had begun the chemical attacks without consulting him. There had been no real military necessity involved. The Japanese weaponry was sweeping the Soviets out of the way. But Noburu had not been prepared for the depth of hatred his allies felt against the Soviets, against the "infidels." Noburu had urgently reported the attacks on populated areas and refugee columns to Tokyo, even as he shouted into every available means of communications with his allies, furiously attempting to bring a halt to the attacks. He had, of course, expected Tokyo to back him up, to support his threats to terminate Japanese support for the offensive.

To his surprise, Tokyo was unconcerned. The chemical attacks were a local matter. If the inhabitants wanted to murder each other with their own tools, it was of no concern to the General Staff. Noburu was admonished to stop disrupting friendly relations with Japan's allies and to simply ensure that military operations did not reach beyond the agreed-upon boundaries of the theater of military operations, to guarantee that Soviet home cities beyond the Volga were not attacked and that the conduct of the war did not violate its limited aims. Noburu was well-versed in the theory of modern limited wars. He had helped develop it. Now it seemed to him that all of his fine theoretical constructs had been the work of a precocious child, too immature to realize the basic truth that warfare involved human beings.

Noburu obeyed orders. His lifetime had been devoted to obeying orders. But for the first time, he had begun to feel that the job in which he found himself was greater than the abilities of the man who filled it.

It was *not* merely softness of heart, he insisted to himself. Despite the legal niceties of the Japanese role, they would be blamed for the atrocities of their allies. Again, the world would view Japan as a ruthless, merciless nation. Noburu was proud of his people, and the thought of being judged on the same level as these barbarians sickened him. He knew that many of his peers valued toughness of spirit, stoicism in the face of all suffering, above all other military virtues. But, to Noburu, the tradition of the soldier was that of defending the weak, of seeking the true path and right action.

I've grown soft, he thought. He touched the expensive wool of his sleeve. I've lived too well, too richly. How can

I be right and Tokyo wrong? Aren't my very thoughts disloyal? Isn't the greatness of Japan everything?

Greatness. Power. Was it too easy to confuse the two concepts? And what was greatness without honor? The greatness of a barbarian.

He thought again of the Americans, almost wistfully this time. What a greatness theirs had been! A confused, exuberant, self-tormenting, slovenly, self-righteous, brilliant greatness . . . faltering ultimately into sloth, decadence, and folly. The Japanese people, humiliated by the kindness of their enemies, had had no choice but to humiliate those enemies in turn.

Suddenly, the illogic of his position struck him. Weren't the central Asians, the Iranians, and the Arabs right after all? What good did mercy do? The safest thing was always the complete massacre, the sowing of the ground with salt.

Enough. His duty now was to finish the mission entrusted to him. Afterward, it would be equally his duty to resign in protest. Not publicly, but quietly, stating his reasons only to those at the heights of power. Even though he knew in advance it would do no good.

We are a bloody people, he told himself.

The gods were laughing, of course. He had considered himself safe from the threatened moral dilemma as the offensive rolled northward, with the Scramblers remaining unused at a succession of closely guarded airfields. Then his allies had begun supplementing Japanese technology with their chemical attacks. No, Noboru realized, the ancients were correct. A man could not avoid his fate.

Noboru remembered the joy of his first combat mission. It seemed at once long ago and only yesterday. Riding along with the South Africans as a technical adviser on the new gunships. B Squadron, he remembered, Natal Light Horse. They had lifted off from their hide positions near Lubumbashi, rising into the perfect morning light, one squadron among many dispersed from southern Zaire down into the Zambian copper belt, erupting suddenly in a coordinated attack on the witless Americans. His squadron had been the first to make contact, and he had been at the controls himself, correcting the inept mistakes of a young lieutenant. They had easily swept the Americans from the sky. He remembered the pathetic attempts at evasive maneuvers, then the Americans' hopeless aerial charge. It had been a wonderful feeling, the richest of all elations, to watch the old American Apache helicopters flash and fall to earth. It had not occurred to him until years afterward that there had been living, thinking, feeling men in those ambushed machines. He had known only the joy of success in battle, something so elementary it could not be civilized out of a man. Never before and never afterward had he been so proud to be Japanese.

But he had carried those dead American pilots with him, unknowingly. They had waited deep inside of him as he garnered new ranks and fresh honors. Then, unexpectedly, unreasonably, their ghosts had begun to appear to him. His dreams were not the dreams of amorous regret that visited the sleep of healthy men. Nor were they the dreams of a true soldier. They were the dreams of a coward. His gunship sailed the morning sky, the blue, vast African sky, again. But this time he was the hunted. He could see the faces of the Americans behind the windscreens of their gunships, far too closely. They were the faces of dead men. Flying around him, mocking him, teasing him. Drawing out his agony until they grew tired of the game and decided to finish him off, laughing, howling for revenge.

"Sir," Akiro called suddenly, in his startling military bark. "This is interesting."

Noburu shook off his demons. He rose and crossed the room to where his aide sat intently before the screen of the commander's workstation. There was no trace of the Scotch in his walk. All that remained of the drink was a sharpness in his stomach. I'm growing old, Noburu thought.

"What is it?"

"Have a look at this imagery, sir. It's the Soviet industrial complex outside the city of Omsk."

Noburu considered the crisp picture on the screen. Like all of his contemporaries, he had learned to read imagery from space-based collectors at a glance. He saw rows of industrial halls and warehouses, with the active heat sources indicating a very low level of activity. Everything looked antique, monuments to decline. He could detect nothing of evident military importance.

"You'll have to explain it to me," Noburu said. "I see nothing."

"Yes," Akiro said. "In a sense, that's the point." He gave the terminal a sharp verbal command, and the industrial landscape faded, then reappeared. Noburu noted the earlier date in the legend of the new picture. In this previously harvested imagery, the buildings were cold, unused.

"This image was recorded just before the start of the offensive," Akiro said. "You see, sir? No activity. The industrial park had fallen into complete disuse. Then, yesterday, as our forces approached the border of western Siberia, we scanned the area again." He gave another quick command. The first image reappeared. "And this is what we found. Suddenly, there are heat sources in the derelict buildings. But there are no signs of renewed production. Only these muffled heat sources. They were so faint that we barely picked them up. This image has been greatly intensified."

"Have we X-rayed the site?" Noburu asked.

Akiro smiled. After another brief command, an X-ray image appeared.

Now there was nothing in evidence except the skeletons of unused machinery, vacant production lines. Emptiness.

Noburu got the point. Someone was going to great lengths to use very sophisticated technical camouflage means to hide whatever was dispersed throughout the mammoth complex.

He and Akiro understood each other.

"If the weather had not taken such a cold turn, we could have missed it entirely," Akiro said. "As it was, the imagery analyst almost passed over it."

"How large a force does intelligence believe is in there?"

"It is, of course, difficult to say. The camouflage techniques are remarkably good—this must be the very best equipment the Soviets possess. In any case, intelligence believes it would be easy to hide an entire armored division in there. Perhaps more."

Noburu reviewed the geography in his head. The force

could be employed to defend Omsk. But, given the lengths to which the Soviets had gone to hide it, the formation would more likely be used as a counterattack force, probably on the Petropavlovsk front.

"Well," Noburu said, "even a fresh division won't make much of a difference. It would take at least an army-level formation to begin to shore up their lines around Petropavlovsk. And, given the backwardness of their military technology, even a full Soviet army could not sustain a deep attack against us now."

"We could, of course, simply catch them as they attempt to deploy," Akiro said.

Noburu waved his hand. "No. There's no point in taking chances. How current was that image?"

"We just scanned the area during the night."

Noburu thought for a moment, reexamining the details of the battle map he held in his memory. "Even if they moved immediately, they could not influence the battle in less than forty-eight hours. The distance is too great. I'll tell Yameshima to hit them tomorrow. There's no point in disrupting today's schedule. But tomorrow we'll take care of whatever the Soviets have hidden in there." He stared at the screen a moment longer. "Really, quite a remarkable effort. It almost seems unfair that none of them will ever reach the battlefield."

"The weapons are no good," General Ali Tanjani told Noburu in English, which was the only language all of the commanders shared in common. "They are breaking."

Noburu looked at the man, trying not to reveal the slightest hint of his disdain. He shifted his glance from the Iranian to General Shemin of the Islamic Union, then to General Biryan, late of the Soviet Indigenous Forces, Central Asia, and now the senior military man in the Free Islamic Republic of Kazakhstan. To Noburu, they looked like a gang of thieves. Finally, Noburu met the eyes of Colonel Piet Kloete, another "contract employee," who was the staff man responsible for the stable of South African pilots who flew the most sophisticated intermediate-range Japanese systems. Noburu shared many of the South African's views, not least of which was disgust at the illogic and ineptitude of these men to whom they were nominally subordinate. Yet, ultimately, Kloete had the limitations of the mercenary, just as his nation had those same limitations on a grander level.

"My dear General Tanjani," Noburu began, choosing his words carefully, "warriors who fight as boldly as yours are very hard on the machinery of war. Your successes have taken many of these land systems well over two thousand kilometers in less than a month. Under such circumstances, careful maintenance procedures are very important. It would be of the greatest help if your soldiers would follow the prescribed methods."

Tanjani would not budge. "It is not the task of the soldiers of the Islamic Republic of Iran to work as rude mechanicals. It is the task of the Japanese to guarantee that all machines operate."

Noburu wondered how on earth Tokyo would deal with men such as this in the future, when the Tanjanis had no more pressing needs for Japanese military support. The unconsidered arrogance involved in driving the Soviets—the Russians—from the heart of Asia was becoming ever more clear to him. As suppliers of resources, the economically starved Soviets were bound to be more dependable than the half-savages with whom Tokyo had determined to replace them.

Noburu was especially irritated with Tanjani today because Noburu's in-house intelligence sources had informed him of the Iranians' loss of one of the latest-variant command aircraft. Tanjani had not said a word about it, which told Noburu that the unexplained accident had been indisguisably the fault of the Iranians. The loss was potentially an important intelligence compromise—although, fortunately, the computer system was utterly unbreakable. The revelation of new aircraft composites to the enemy was nonetheless a sufficiently serious matter to outrage Noburu, but he had learned the hard way that it never paid to directly confront the Iranians with their failures. He would simply have to wait, exercising all of his self-control, until the day came when Tanjani decided to mention the loss—if such a day ever came.

"General Tanjani, I assure you that all maintenance

workers are doing their best to maintain the systems. But basic measures taken by the operators are essential. Otherwise, too many systems break down unnecessarily, and the maintenance system becomes overloaded. We have discussed this before."

Tanjani smiled cynically. "If the great industrial power of Japan can do no better than this, perhaps our confidence has been misplaced."

Noburu wanted to shout at the man. Those systems have carried your incompetent mob farther and faster than any force in history. You have crushed one of the fabled armies of the world. But, when hundreds of vehicles develop major problems simply because no one bothered to maintain proper lubrication levels or to change dust filters, you cannot expect to parade around in them indefinitely. The yen costs resulting from inept—or nonexistent—operator maintenance were astronomical.

"We must," Noburu said in a controlled voice, "all work together. We must cooperate. There are no more systems in the rear depots to instantly replace those lost unnecessarily. At present, I'm told that there are more tanks in the forward repair yards at Karaganda and Atbasar than there are on the front lines."

"Your system of maintenance is very slow," Tanjani said.

"Our system of maintenance," Noburu replied, "is overwhelmed. If only the truly avoidable maintenance problems could be prevented by your operators, you would find our system very effective."

"The problem," Tanjani said, "is that the tanks are no good. You have sold us second-rate goods."

"General Tanjani," Noburu said, trying to smile, to reach back toward friendliness, "consider your successes. Whenever our tanks have been deployed against the Soviets, you have not lost a single significant engagement. Consider how few of the tanks in our repair yards are actually combat casualties. Not one in twenty."

"Our success," Tanjani said, "is the will of God. Everything is the will of God."

"The will of God," General Shemin agreed, awakening from his daydreams at the explosively powerful words.

Biryan, the ex-Soviet, moved about uncomfortably in his seat, mumbling something that might be taken for agreement. Noburu knew that Biryan had been sufficiently well-trained by his former masters to understand that poor maintenance was not necessarily a direct reflection of the divine will. The maintenance problems in Biryan's rebel units were as much the result of combat stress on the decrepit systems with which the central Soviet government had equipped the regionally homogenous formations as they were of incompetence—although there was still plenty of that to be found.

Perhaps, Noburu thought bitterly, Allah could be persuaded to do a bit of preventive maintenance, or to do some overnight repair work.

"This . . . is a very important issue," General Biryan said carefully, catching Noburu off-guard. "The combat strength of the great forces of Iran must be maintained. My troops alone cannot finish the task before us."

Noburu pitied the man, who seemed to have no real understanding of the fate planned for the rebel forces. Noburu knew that, for all of the problems under discussion, Tanjani's Iranians had the strength to make a far larger frontline contribution, as did the forces of the Islamic Union on the southwestern front. But it had been agreed that the rebels should be sacrificed to the maximum feasible extent now that success seemed imminent. It was vital that those with nationalist tendencies in the liberated regions have no significant military strength of their own on which to fall back. This very expensive war was not being waged to cater to the intoxicated visions of Kazakh or Turkmen nationalists.

"God will provide," General Shemin offered. The chosen tone suggested that Shemin might take on his occasional role as mediator. "But I think that we are under an obligation to help our Japanese friends when they tell us that they are in need. Just as they have been helpful to us. Now is not the time for such disagreements between friends. Surely, my brother," he said to Tanjani, "we will help the Japanese. We must consider their requests about this matter of maintenance."

Tanjani sensed that he was in the minority on this issue.

Yet, Noburu well knew, nothing was predictable. At times, Shemin would side rabidly with Tanjani. And, despite any verbal concessions, Noburu suspected that little would change as regarded maintenance. The conditions in Shemin's Islamic Union formations were only marginally better than those in the Iranian forces. It was astonishing that they had done so much, come so far. A tribute, Noburu thought, to the technical mastery of his homeland. The war-making systems were simple to operate and really very simple to maintain. It had taken negligence bordering on the ingenious to run them into the ground.

But the margin was thinner now than it had been at any time during the campaign. It was a good thing that the Soviets were so disorganized, so psychologically distressed. Noburu thought again of the incredible ratio of maintenance losses. At present, there were almost five combat systems awaiting repair for every one on the front lines. Even the most skillfully designed high-technology systems did not have the simplicity of a bow and arrow.

Noburu's mind drifted back to the imagery of the possible Soviet counterattack force in the industrial park outside of Omsk. Really, a negligible matter in the great scheme of things. But he would have to deal with it. The Iranian and rebel forces were so depleted, so worn, that the sudden introduction of an organized counterattack force might prove capable of causing at least local panic. He decided not to rely on Yameshima and his Iranian Air Force charges to do the job. Kloete's South Africans could fly this one. It was not a time to take chances. And the South Africans needed to earn their keep.

An orderly delivered fresh tea and a plate of biscuits, catering to Noburu's guests. Noburu himself would have much preferred another Scotch, but he deferentially took the required thimble glass of tea. He watched as Tanjani dropped cube after cube of sugar into the orange liquid.

"And now," Noburu said, bracing himself against the impending storm, "there is another matter I would like to discuss with you. Among friends." He glanced toward the workstation, where his aide sat monitoring the flow of information, temporarily suppressing anything that might not be appropriate for the eyes of Noburu's guests. Noburu knew that Akiro would disapprove of his next tack. Perhaps the aide would even report the matter to the General Staff. Personal loyalty was not all that it once had been. But Noburu was determined to go ahead with the business. "This matter of the employment of chemical weapons against mass targets . . . specifically, against noncombatants . . . I know we have spoken of this before." He looked at Tanjani. "But the battlefield situation has continued to develop in our favor, and I'm certain that we all can agree that there is no longer the least justification for such attacks. We are on the edge of victory. I do not think our cause is furthered by attacks that can only turn world opinion against us."

Noburu noted that Akiro had stopped fiddling with the computer. The aide was listening attentively, aware that his commander was speaking in violation of the directive from Tokyo.

To Noburu's relief, Tanjani showed no immediate excitement. He continued to sip his sugar-laden tea. There was a moment of near silence, the clinking of metal and glass. Then Tanjani said wearily, "World opinion? Why are we to concern ourselves with the opinion of the world? Especially as we are still speaking largely of the opinion of the Western world, are we not?" He put down his tea glass, readying himself to speak at greater length. "For more than forty years, my country has laughed in the face of world opinion, and today we are the victors. World opinion? What does it matter? Dust in the wind. The American devil is impotent. He is a caged Satan." He laughed in tepid amusement, as at a good joke heard once too often. "And the Europeans care only for their economic welfare. They may weep, but they will still line up to buy our oil." Tanjani's eyes came to rest on Noburu's beautifully cut uniform. "They have become our tailors, our purveyors of sweets. Nothing more. And the Soviets . . . cannot effectively retaliate. Even if they had threatening weapons, they would not attack our home countries—they are too anxious not to draw our attacks down upon their main cities. They are degenerate cowards, who deserve to be destroyed. God is great, and his sword smites the infidel. He places fear in their hearts."

"But is it necessary to strike the refugee columns?"

"It costs Japan nothing," Tanjani replied haughtily. "These are *our* weapons. And, you see, they are more dependable than your machines."

"But such actions," Noburu said, "simply cause the enemy to retaliate with chemical weapons of his own. Your forces have taken needless chemical casualties."

"God is great," Tanjani said. "The soldiers of Iran welcome the opportunity to die the death of the martyr."

Biryan, the rebel commander, leaned forward abruptly. It was a strikingly violent gesture that betrayed anger that could no longer be contained. He inadvertently knocked over his tea glass, but made no move to right it.

"The Russian and his brethren *must* be destroyed," he said. His face had grown pale. "They are all demons, the worst of infidels. *My* people have lived under the Russian yoke for more than a century. We know the Russian. He is an animal, a dog. And he must be beaten like a dog, destroyed like a mad dog. Not only the men, but their women and children—they are the source of the greatest evil in this world. They are a plague on the earth. There is no suffering too great for them."

Noburu glanced at Shemin but saw instantly that he would get no help from the man this time. Shemin was a survivor of struggles both military and political, and he picked his fights carefully. Born in Baghdad, he had begun learning his lessons as a lieutenant, back in 1990, leading a tank platoon into Kuwait.

Biryan's intensity had genuinely shocked Noburu, who still could not believe that this man had lately served beside the men he now wished to annihilate, that he had lived among the women and children whom he so ardently wished to butcher.

When will it be *our* turn? Noburu wondered.

Tanjani was smiling, clearly feeling himself the master of his Japanese counterpart. Yes, Noburu told himself, I'm just another infidel to them. Not fully human. It is only that I am temporarily useful. How on earth did we ever allow ourselves to make a compact with men such as these?

"My brother," Tanjani said to Noburu, "it brings . . .

surprise to the righteous to hear you take the side of the infidel. Especially, when you refuse to employ all of your own weapons on our behalf."

Noburu wondered how much surprise his face betrayed. Hopefully, the years of discipline were standing him in good stead now.

Was Tanjani merely fishing? Did he really know?

"General Tanjani . . ." Noburu said, ". . . the government of Japan is supporting you to the full extent of our treaties. You have received all specified aid."

"And yet," Tanjani said, "friends do not conceal their wealth from their true friends."

"I don't understand," Noburu lied.

Tanjani sat back in his chair, thoughtful, teasing. Then he lifted his eyebrows at the amusing trend of his thoughts. "Perhaps . . . if *all* of the Japanese weapons came to the support of the true cause . . . perhaps then there would be little need of these chemical weapons that are such trouble to you."

No, Noburu thought. Far better the chemicals.

"My friend," Noburu said, "you must tell me the details of your concern. Exactly which weapons are you speaking of? Perhaps I am too ill-informed."

Tanjani looked at him hard. "And what is at the base in Bukhara? What is so great a secret there? Why are my men not trusted to guard their Japanese brothers?"

He doesn't know, Noburu decided, relieved. He's only guessing. He's caught wind of something. But he doesn't know the details.

"The base at Bukhara," Noburu said, regaining his self-assurance, "is a very sophisticated technical support site. You know the terms of our agreements. There are some electronic matters . . . industrial secrets . . . which were developed at great expense to the people of Japan. Today, in a world still hungry for the tightening supplies of oil, Iran has no need of such things. You are very rich. By the grace of God. But, for Japan, these technical matters are our 'oil,' our only wealth. There is nothing at the Bukhara site other than electronics—to be used in your support, as necessary." The last part was true, Noburu told himself. If the whole story came out, he had not actually lied. There *was* nothing at Bukhara but electronics. The Scramblers were really nothing more than another arrangement of conductors.

Noburu sized up the others. Tanjani had played his card—neither Shemin nor Biryan had known anything about the matter. They were, however, rapidly becoming interested.

Noburu could not imagine worse allies. What did they have to offer Japan other than trouble, threats, complaints, endless discontents? He wondered if Japan were not unconsciously replacing the United States in yet another sphere.

"My dear General Tanjani," Noburu said, "may I offer you a visit to the Bukhara site? You are welcome to inspect everything. You will see for yourself. There is nothing at Bukhara other than aircraft, maintenance facilities—and electronics. General Yameshima could arrange such a visit immediately."

It was Tanjani's turn to be caught off-guard. Noburu knew that the Iranian could easily walk through the facility and even sit behind the controls of the aircraft without realizing their purpose.

"Perhaps . . ." Tanjani said, ". . . when there is more time. Yes. Perhaps this is a very good idea. But Bukhara is far from the front. A commander's place is with his troops."

Noburu knew that Tanjani would not return immediately to the front from the combined headquarters at Baku. First, the Iranian would stop off in Meshed, in the safety of northern Iran, where he would spend the night in the company of a woman who was distinctly not his wife. But the war would go on without him.

"Yes," Shemin said, rising, "we should all be with our troops. And the road is long." He smiled. "Even when we journey in the fine aircraft our Japanese brothers have provided."

Noburu rose and bowed formally to the other men. Tanjani made a great show of hugging and kissing the prim Japanese, mussing Noburu's uniform. Shemin followed with a token embrace that took better account of Noburu's customs, while Biryan, the rebel, shook hands like a Westerner.

A strange world, Noburu thought.

Amid the formalities of departure, Noburu mentioned to Kloete, who had silently listened to the verbal maneuvering, that the South African pilots would soon have a mission, and that he should keep himself readily available. The tall blond man gave a terse, if polite acknowledgment.

There is not one among them whom I can trust, Noburu thought.

Then they were gone. Akiro did not move to update his superior at once, sensing that Noburu required a breathing space after the ordeal of the meeting.

Noburu moved to help himself to another Scotch. But, bottle in hand, he stopped himself. What was the point? Even such controlled drinking suddenly struck him as unmanly under the circumstances. He was, surely, stronger than this.

He punished himself, disallowing this one comfort. At least for now. But the meeting had, as always, exhausted him. It was like trying to wage war with armies composed of wicked delinquent children.

Grateful for the fresh quiet, Noburu crossed the big room and opened the drape, conscious that his aide was watching him, squinting at the intensity of the sunlight. Until recently, the suite had belonged to a high-ranking Soviet officer. Now the last Soviet reoccupation forces were gone from Azerbaijan, and there was only scattered guerilla resistance in Armenia and Georgia, as the rebels and the forces of the Islamic Union pushed northward as far as the Kalmuck steppe. In the east, the Soviets had been expelled from Tadzhikistan, from Kirghizistan, Uzbekistan, and Turkistan. And they were almost gone from the vast expanse of Kazakhstan. Everywhere, the Soviets were on the run. Noburu mused that, if the Soviets regretted any single thing at this juncture, it must be their too-successful crusade to ban nuclear weapons. They had overestimated by far their ability to maintain a conventional hegemony on the Eurasian land mass. Now they were being dissected.

Of course, the technology still existed to construct nuclear weapons anew. But the Soviets were out of time. All they could do, he thought mockingly, was to ring up the poor Americans for help.

Well, it would all go well. Despite the sort of men Japan had chosen as allies. Everything would be fine. It was really a great day for Japan.

Beyond the oversize window, the cluttered hillside fell away to the density of Baku and the golden-blue sea beyond. A long way from home, he thought. In the southern sunlight, the autumn day still held the sort of warmth that felt so good on an old man's back. And the city lay in a midday swoon. It was a handsome, peaceful vista, where not long before all of the non-Moslem Soviet residents had been massacred in the streets by the maddened Azerbaijanis.

How had the Russians been so blind, for so long? Or had they merely been obstinate? Had they seen the inevitable and simply put it out of mind, dreaming away the danger in the slumber of their long decay?

Nightmare sleep. You woke, and there was your brother with a knife.

"Tell me," Noburu said suddenly, turning away from the panorama of green and white, of brown, blue, and gold, "what do you make of these contacts between the Soviets and the Americans, Akiro?" He wanted to hear the voice of Tokyo, of his own people, explaining it all to him one more time.

The aide gave a verbal command that froze the flow of data on the monitor. "The Americans?" he said, surprised. Clearly, his thoughts had been elsewhere.

"Yes. The Americans," Noburu said. "What could they possibly offer the Soviets?"

"Sympathy?" Akiro said with a tight smile, dismissing the issue. "The Americans have given up. All they want is to be left alone in their bankrupt hemisphere. And to sell a few third-rate goods here and there. To those who cannot afford ours."

"It's well known that the Americans have been working hard to catch up militarily. And their strategic defense system is very good."

"They'll never catch up," Akiro said in a tone of finality that was almost rude. "They're racially degenerate. The Americans are nothing but mongrel dogs."

Noburu smiled, listening to his aide speak for the General Staff and the man in the Tokyo street. "But, Akiro, mongrel dogs are sometimes very intelligent. And strong."

"America is the refuse heap of the world," the aide replied, reciting from half a dozen Japanese bestsellers. "Their minorities merely drag them down. In the years of the pestilence, they even had to order their own military into their cities. And the military could barely meet the challenge. For all of their 'catching up,' they still cannot completely control the situation in Latin America. In Mexico alone, they'll still be tied down for a generation. The Americans are finished." Akiro made a hard face, the visage of a warrior from a classical Japanese print. "Perhaps they can take in a few Soviet refugees, as they took in the Israelis."

Noburu, an officer of legendary self-control, crossed the room and broke his promise to himself. He poured himself a Scotch, without measuring.

"It simply occurs to me," Noburu said quietly, "that Japan underestimated the Americans once before." And he let the bitter liquor fill his mouth.

12

Omsk
2 November 2020

TAYLOR STARED AT THE FACE ON THE OVERSIZE BRIEFING screen, searching the features for any trace of vulnerability. Marks of weakness, marks of woe, he told himself, the words singing briefly through his memory. He had become a careful observer of men's faces, and he was convinced that you could tell a great deal about your enemy from his appearance. The primitive cultures in which the belief prevailed that photographs stole away the soul were, in Taylor's view, closer to the truth than Western man realized. There, captive within the boundaries of the big screen, was his enemy, unable to resist this silent interrogation. And Taylor already sensed weakness in the features, although he still could not pin down the precise physical clue. The mouth was trim and strong, the skin smooth. The foreign contours of the eyes made it difficult for Taylor to see into them. The hair was dark and impressively youthful. No, he could not point to the perceived vulnerability as he might point to a spot on the map. But it was there. He was sure of it.

"All right, Merry," he told his intelligence officer. "You can go on."

Meredith briefly scanned the rows of waiting officers, then settled his gaze back on the colonel.

"This," he repeated, "is General Noboru Kabata, the

senior Japanese officer in the theater of operations." His words echoed in the cold gloom of the warehouse. "Kabata is a senior Japanese Defense Forces general officer, with broad experience both in field positions and in staff jobs related to defense industry. If you look at the ribbons on his chest—just there," Meredith gestured with his laser pointer, "in the third row—that sand-and-green ribbon indicates that he served with the Japanese advisory contingent in South Africa, during our . . . expedition."

Taylor almost interrupted Meredith a second time, anxious to ask for specific details. But he caught himself. He would wait until the S-2 finished his pitch. He did not want to risk revealing a sign of his weakness in front of his subordinates. Africa was far from their concerns at the moment.

"Kabata has always been involved with heavy forces and cutting edge technology," Meredith continued. "He's not only aviation-qualified, but he was reportedly a test pilot for a while. When he was younger, of course. Speaks excellent English, which he perfected as an exchange student at the British staff college at Camberly, class of 2001. Reputation as an Anglophile. Even flies to London to have his suits tailored. Kabata's *not* in the military because he needs a job. His family's wealthy, although they took a beating when we nationalized all of the Japanese-owned real estate in the United States. Their holdings were rather extensive. Anyway, the guy's from a powerful old family, with a long military tradition." Meredith paused for a moment, chewing the air. "But not everything tracks. His wife's a professor of linguistics, and they have two children, a son and a daughter. The daughter works in publishing. Son's a chemical engineer. And that's what doesn't follow. This family has been military since Christ was a corporal, and Kabata's had a career that's been highly successful by any standards. Yet, he reportedly discouraged his son from becoming an officer."

We're alike in that, Taylor thought. If I had a son, he would never be a soldier.

"Other than Africa," Meredith went on, "the highlights of his professional career include a voluntary tour on the United Nations' team that assessed damage and helped supervise the evacuation of the last Israelis to the United States. He was one of the few inspectors willing to enter the dead zone around Tel Aviv and the nuclear wastelands surrounding Damascus, Latakia, and the other sites targeted by Israeli retaliatory strikes."

"Merry," Lieutenant Colonel David Heifetz, the regiment's operations officer, interrupted. "I met him, you know. In Israel. It was only the briefest of meetings. He was on a committee of the UN that was sent to receipt for our weapons. Before we could get on the planes. He did not seem at all a bad man to me. Very much a decent sort of man. I felt . . . well, you know, he is a soldier. As we are all soldiers. And I felt that he understood what I was experiencing. Watching and counting as my men turned over their arms. It was a very bad day for me, and I felt that he did not want it to be any worse. That's all. I wish I could remember more. But other things were important to me then."

"Dave," Taylor said coldly, before Meredith could resume, "if he's such a great guy, why is he dumping nerve gas on refugee columns?"

Heifetz looked down the row of chairs toward Taylor, his face set even more earnestly than usual.

"I don't know," he said, voice tinged with genuine regret. "I cannot answer that question."

Taylor switched his attention back to Meredith. "All right, Merry. Tell us more about this . . . man."

Merry shrugged. "He's the sort of officer who seems to do everything well. Even writes. His reports on collateral damage from the Middle East were repeatedly cited at the International Conference on the Immediate Elimination of Nuclear Weapons the Soviets sponsored in New Delhi. That was," Merry said, "perhaps the last time Soviet and Japanese interests coincided. Over the past few years, he's been a key player in the Japanese program to equip and train the Islamic Iranian Armed Forces and the military arm of the Islamic Union. This operation is the culmination of his work. Yet, there are persistent rumors in the military attaché community in Tokyo of problems between him and the General Staff."

"What kind of problems?" Taylor asked sharply.

"Unknown. And the reports may be unsubstantiated. Other than that, we don't have much on him. Drinks Scotch, in moderation. Loves to play golf. But so does anybody who's anybody in Japan. Whenever he's in London, he goes to the theater."

"Whore around?"

Merry shook his head. "Nothing the Brits thought worth mentioning."

"Merry," Taylor said, careful to maintain a tone of relative nonchalance, "did you happen to pick up anything else about his service in Africa? Was he . . . an active participant?"

"Sir, I don't know. All we have on that is the ribbon on his chest. He could have received that for sitting in Capetown."

"Or . . . for any number of things."

"Yes, sir."

It didn't matter, Taylor told himself. He had the man now. General Noboru Kabata. Who flew around the world to dress up in another man's heritage. Whose preferred drink was Scotch. Who encouraged his son to break with tradition in a land where tradition still mattered. "Reputation as an Anglophile," as Merry put it. But the chosen mask was unimportant. Taylor recognized the type. If not an Anglophile, then a Francophile, or Germanophile. It did not matter. Anything to get out from under the burden pressing down on him since birth. Anything, in order to be anyone other than the man he had been condemned to be.

I can beat him, Taylor insisted to himself, hoping it was true.

He looked at Meredith, who was waiting for any further questions. The assembled officers shifted and rustled, and Taylor knew that they were cold and anxious to return to their own subordinates, to solve the inevitable last-minute problems. And the briefing had only begun. Well, he would not waste too much of their time.

"You know, Merry," Taylor began. The small noises ceased as the collected officers leaned to hear the commander's words. "There's just one thing I can't for the life of me understand. It nags at me. I know the Japanese have a reputation as being hard sonsofbitches. But I just don't get the chemicals. What's the point? What is it in this bastard that makes him do such a thing? With his god-damned English suits and his golf clubs."

Merry touched a control and the big screen went blank. At once, there seemed to be a greater silence in the room, a visual silence.

"Perhaps," the intelligence officer said, "it's another object lesson. Maybe the Japanese are making a point about absolute dominance."

Taylor considered it. He himself could not come up with a better answer. But it did not ring true for him. With all of the capabilities of Japanese technology, the chemicals were merely a crude display of barbarism. It was hard to imagine a payoff commensurate with the growing level of international revulsion.

"Colonel Taylor, sir," Heifetz said, "suppose that it is not the Japanese. Suppose that the Arabs and the Iranians are using the chemical weapons on their own. Perhaps this man cannot control them. They are, you know, unpredictable, unreasonable. And they have used such weapons before."

Taylor turned to consider Heifetz, turning his thoughts as well. That certainly would be one possible answer. He looked at this homeless soldier, who had lost so much. Heifetz's face sought to project a toughness beyond emotion: detachment, strength. And, to most men, Heifetz's efforts were successful. But, looking at the graying Israeli, Taylor saw only a man who had lost his family, his nation, his past, and his future. Of course Lucky Dave would blame it on the Arabs. He could not help himself. But, even if there was some logic to it, Taylor could not accept the proposition. There was simply no way the Japanese would have allowed their surrogates to run so far out of control so early in the game. The Japanese were not that stupid.

David Heifetz had all but lost his sense of wonder. Only the inconstancy of time still held the occasional power to make him marvel at life's possibilities, even if, for him, those possibilities lay buried in bygone years, in a country passed into history. The creation of calendars and clocks seemed to him a desperate, frightened attempt to make time behave, to disguise the unreasonable, unpredictable accelerations and periods of slow drift, the instants of wild inarticulate revelation, and the eternities of dusty routine. At times, he struck himself as the most cowardly sort imaginable, hiding from time's unmanageable currents on his little military island, forcing his slowly deteriorating body through the rituals of schedules so abundant in any army, bound by the excuse of duty to retreat at the approach of his black early morning dreams, to shock himself awake, to bind himself tightly into polished boots, and to plunge into the endless, numbing work that made an army go. And time would seem to grow docile as he deadened himself with late nights at the office, evaluating, planning, writing, correcting, laboring over range schedules, training ammunition allocations, school quotas, exercise plans and orders, SOPs, post police responsibilities, efficiency reports, natural disaster evacuation plans, mobilization plans, countless briefings, inspection programs—he was only sorry that there was not more, that the moment would inevitably come when he would have to extinguish the last light in the building and lock the door behind him, to return to his nearly bare quarters and the utter vacancy that passed for his personal life. He rarely neglected the ceremonies and self-denials required of a Jew, in hope that there might finally be some comfort there, but the words and gestures, each strict abstinence, remained futile. His God was no longer the remarkably human God of Israel, but a fierce, malevolent, relentless, and unforgiving God, not a God for the suffering, but a God from whom suffering flowed, a God who laughed at agony, then set his face in stone. His God was the primitive deity of the savage barely elevated from the beast, of dark ancient armies marching to burn the cities of light and hope, to massacre their inhabitants, to scour away all life.

Then time would swallow him up into one of its unseen cataracts, and in the artificially measured brevity of a second he would relive the past with gorgeous intensity, not merely remembering, but inhabiting it all again, *there*. Mira by an olive tree, seated with her arms around her knees, smiling up at the warm blue sky with her eyes closed. And he could feel it all with her, the air still and pungent with thyme. The sun. He could feel the warmth deepening in her cheeks, as though there were no difference between them at all. The spilled dregs of wine, the spoiling ruins of a picnic on a stony hillside overlooking their rich, ripe world. *How can it be so beautiful?* she said, without opening her eyes, and he knew exactly what she meant. These were the words he felt but could not form. Their world was so beautiful that physical sight was almost inconsequential. *How can it be so beautiful, David?* He closed his eyes too. Settling for the coursing of flies and the distant sounds of automobiles on a road that sacred feet had marked with blood. In that instant of memory, there was also time to remember the feel of a cotton skirt under his hand, and the warmth beneath the cloth, and the intoxicating feel as he moved the cloth higher to let the sun touch more of her.

How can it be so beautiful, David?

The startling sight of bloodstains at the small of her back as the two of them rose to return, finally, to the car. During their lovemaking, a sharp rock had been cutting into her spine, through her sweat-soaked cotton blouse. But it had not mattered, and he understood that too. He said nothing, but simply put his hand on the stain, as if his touch might heal her.

In the same instant, he watched as his brown-eyed son ran through their apartment, his face a masculine interpretation of his mother's beauty. Dovik. Perhaps his failures had begun there. In his memory, there were only the times when he had been too busy for the boy, when he had bellowed at Mira that the noise was intolerable, when he had offered the boy only obtuse adult excuses for his unwillingness to take the child's requests seriously. Brown eyes, a striped shirt, and turned-up jeans. *Mira, for God's sake, could you please . . .*

Mira, the lawyer who had been working for laughable wages in an organization engaged in defending Palestinian rights. When an impatient warrior charged into her unready life. Who could ever say why humans loved?

Mira, who had made him human, formidable in her

beauty, but whose kisses spoke urgency at unexpected times. Looking back, it was almost as if she had known that they had little time, as if she had sensed all that was coming. He could not think her name without voicing it inwardly as a cry, as if calling out to her disappearing back across a growing distance. *Mira*.

He had been sitting loose-legged on the turret of his tank, drained by a successful battle, when the single code word came down over the radio net, irrevocable, reaching out to a spent tank company commander in the Bekka Valley, to infantrymen on the Jordan, to pilots guiding on the great canal.

Armageddon.

There had been no immediate details, and he had been able to hope as he continued to fight. But, already, a part of him had known. When the order came to maneuver all vehicles into the most complete available defilade, to remove antennas, to cover all sights and seal the hatches, he had known with certainty. There would be no more warm flesh under shifting cloth.

He had failed. He had failed to defend his family, his nation. But that was only his most obvious guilt. In retrospect, he knew his failure had been far greater. He had never been the man he should have been, that Mira and his son had deserved. He had never been a man at all. Merely a selfish shell in the armor of a uniform.

How can it be so beautiful?

He had read that epileptics experience a rare elation on the verge of a seizure, that their worst sufferings were preceded by a fleeting joy that some described as approaching holiness. And that was what time did to David Heifetz. In an unguarded instant, his memory filled with the fullness of his life with Mira, with blue seas and orange groves and a passionate woman's smell, only to kill her again and again and again. And he was convinced that each time she died anew in his memory, she suffered again. Time was far from a straight line. Mira was always vulnerable, her agony was endless. His God was the merciless god of eternal simultaneity.

Armageddon.

In his wallet, Lieutenant Colonel David Heifetz, of the

United States Army, had buried a trimmed-down snapshot of his wife and child. He was constantly aware of its presence, and he knew each shadow and tone, he knew the exact thoughts behind the four eyes considering the camera, the faint weariness of the boy at the end of a long afternoon, Mira's needless anxiety about dinner, the history behind her necklace, and the slight blemish that had temporarily made her beauty human.

He had not looked at the photograph for seven years.

"Lucky Dave looks tired," Merry Meredith whispered. He had just plopped back down in the field chair beside Manny Martinez, his closest friend. He felt drained by the intelligence briefing he had just delivered, troubled by its inadequacies, yet relieved, as always, that it was over. He did not fear Taylor. He only feared failing the old man. Now he sat, loose, and grateful that the honor of briefing had passed on to Heifetz. Meredith watched the S-3 as the man punched in the codes that filled the briefing screen with the exact map coverage he wanted. It seemed to Meredith that Heifetz was a bit off his usual crisp precision. Nothing the average observer would necessarily notice. But just the sort of thing an intelligence officer who had earned his spurs in the Los Angeles operation would pick up. A minor human failing, perhaps the beginning of a vulnerability. "He really looks tired," Meredith repeated.

"Oh, man," Martinez said in a low tone of dismissal, "Lucky Dave always looks tired. The guy was born tired. He eats that shit up."

"Yeah," Meredith said. "I know. But there's something off. He almost looks sick."

"Lucky Dave?" Martinez said. "Lucky Dave never gets sick."

"Look at him. He's as white as if he'd just seen a ghost."

The two men looked at the operations officer. A compactly built man, with graying hair and shoulders a bit too big for the rest of his bodily proportions. Heifetz was about to begin his briefing.

"I just wonder if he feels okay," Meredith whispered to his friend.

"Come on," Martinez answered. "Old Lucky Dave doesn't *feel* anything. The guy's made of stone."

Heifetz surveyed the collection of officers before him, giving himself a last moment to catch his mental breath before he began sentencing them with his words. His instructions would send them to their particular fates, and he sensed that few of them really grasped the seriousness of the actions they would take in the coming hours. There was so much lightheartedness and swagger left in the Americans. No sense of how very dark a thing fate was. For many of the junior officers, this was a great adventure. And even those who were afraid feared the wrong things. These were men . . . who did not understand how much a man could ultimately lose.

But it was better so. Best to go into battle with a lightness of spirit, so long as it did not manifest itself in sloppiness. Best to go with a good heart into the darkness. With confidence that shone like polished armor. He remembered that feeling.

Perhaps a better god hovered over these bright-faced Americans sitting so uncomfortably in their Soviet greatcoats in the cold. After all their nation had suffered in recent years, the Americans still struck Heifetz as innocents. And perhaps they would be spared the sight of the black-winged god, whose jaws had slimed with the gore of Israel.

All of them except Taylor. Taylor had seen the burning eyes, smelled the poisoned breath. Taylor knew.

Taylor had insisted on this last face-to-face meeting with his subordinates. The purpose of the orders brief was to ensure that each man clearly understood his role, that there would be no *avoidable* confusion added to that which would be unavoidable. Technically, the briefing could have been conducted electronically, with all of the officers comfortably seated in their environmentally controlled fighting systems and mobile-support shelters. But Taylor had insisted on gathering his officers together in this sour, freezing cavern, unable to risk the comfort of an unmasked heat source that might be detected by enemy reconnaissance systems, but unwilling to forgo a last opportunity for each man to see his commander and his comrades in the flesh. Taylor knew. Even more important than the clarity of each last coordination measure was the basic need felt by men in danger to know that their brothers were truly beside them.

Heifetz knew about his nickname. He understood the soldierly black humor behind it and felt no resentment. And he knew that, in at least one sense, he truly was a lucky man. There were few men under whom he could have served without reservation, without resentment. Serving under Taylor was . . . like serving under a better, wiser, far more decent version of himself. There was only one fundamental difference between them. Taylor's sufferings had made him a better man. Heifetz would never have claimed the same for himself.

"Good afternoon, Colonel Taylor, gentlemen," Heifetz began. "I should almost say 'Good evening.' But we will go quickly now." Heifetz scanned the earnest faces. "Everyone has a hard copy of the order? Yes? Good. The flow copies and all of the supporting data are being loaded into your on-board control systems at this time. Each of you will run a standard up-load check immediately upon the termination of this meeting."

Heifetz touched a button on his remote control, and a bright map filled the briefing screen, covering the area of the Soviet Union from Novosibirsk in the northeast to Dushanbe in the southeast, then west as far as Yerevan and back north to Perm. A second button filled the map with colored symbols and lines, green denoting the positions of the enemy, red for the Soviets, and a tiny spot of blue marking the assembly area of the Seventh Cavalry. The little blue island was separated from the green enemy sea by only a thin, broken reef of red symbols.

"As the S-2 briefed you," Heifetz continued, "the Soviet front east of the Urals is in a state of virtual collapse. Our mission . . . is to attack the enemy in depth, with the immediate intent of destroying or dramatically disrupting key elements of his forces so that the Soviets are allowed time to reestablish an integrated defense. Beyond that, it is the overarching intent of the President of the United

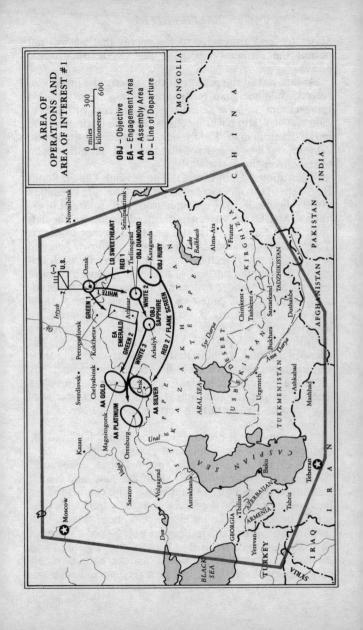

States to send a message to the enemy that we will not permit the dismemberment of the USSR by external powers."

Heifetz waved the remote at the screen. The image dissolved, then the map reappeared with a more detailed representation of the actual operational area of the Seventh Cavalry, still covering almost half the territory of the initial situation map. The friendly and enemy positions still showed, but now blue arrows and control measures began to trace over the battlefield.

"Execution," Heifetz said. "The Seventh United States Regiment of Cavalry crosses its line of departure beginning at 2400 hours, local. First Squadron, with fourteen operational M-100s of sixteen authorized, leads on the left flank. First Squadron has the greatest distance to cover. You will deploy along axis Red-one, as shown here, in route south to Objective Ruby in the vicinity of Karaganda. During the passage of lines, all Soviet air defense systems will be under orders not to engage unless specifically attacked. Of course, we know that some of them may not get the word, so, on a practical level it means we will risk going with only our passive defense up until we cross the line of departure. There is no point in giving our enemies advance warning that something is coming their way. In any case, your scout drones will be immediately preceded by unmanned light cavalry jammers from the Tenth Cav forward detachment. In-depth electronic warfare support—we're talking very deep—has been laid on by the Air Force."

"Don't hold your breath," someone mumbled from the audience. There was a splash of gloomy laughter.

"Knock off the bullshit," Taylor said in annoyance. "This is war. We're all on the same side now, and I don't want to hear any more of that crap." The colonel looked back over the rows of officers, a fierce parent. Then he settled back down into his chair. "Go ahead, Dave."

"First Squadron does not engage unless fired upon prior to reaching Objective Ruby. I know you're going to be looking for a fight," Heifetz said, "and there will be plenty of stray targets out there. But your target-acquisition systems are initially going to pick up mostly junk that belongs to the rebel forces. And there may even be roving pockets of Soviets out there who have been cut off. We can't sort them out, since their equipment is essentially identical— and, anyway, we're after the Japanese-built gear. Which brings us back to Ruby and Karaganda. As Merry briefed you, there are two principal targets in the objective area." The screen narrowed its focus all the way down to the area under discussion. "First, the most critical target—the Japanese maintenance facilities and the forward marshaling yards. I think that is what the old American Army called a 'target-rich environment.' There are over a thousand of the latest Japanese fighting systems on the ground at Karaganda, awaiting greater or lesser repairs. The volume . . . is irreplaceable. Further, the maintenance facility itself is a critical node. The Iranians—and the Arabs—are breaking their gear like toys. And if the Japanese can't repair the stuff, it's useless. I know what you are thinking: you want to kill shooters. But the maintenance facility is your primary target.

"Your secondary target at Ruby is the assembly and reconstitution area for the III Iranian Corps. They've pulled off-line to reorganize while the rebels carry the fighting northward. And they've grown overconfident. The sin of pride. The Iranians are just sitting there. You've seen the imagery. Barely an attempt at camouflage, no meaningful dispersion. They are so sure that the Soviets cannot touch them any longer."

Heifetz switched back to the midsize operations map. "Anticipated time on station vicinity Ruby is twenty minutes for either target area. Dismounted operations are not planned, except for the local protection of disabled systems. All right. Following action at Ruby, First Squadron continues along axis Red-two, with the mission of screening the left flank of the regiment. You have a long flight ahead of you, so you must not become distracted by insignificant targets of opportunity. You're on picket duty in case the Japanese have a surprise up their sleeves and get some sort of interceptors up into the air fast. You will be the first element across the line of departure, and the last to close. You will come in to Assembly Area Silver here, near Orsk. The S-4 will have fuelers waiting for you, and you'll need them. Axis Red stretches the capabilities of the M-100 to the maximum. Finally, some very good news," Heifetz began, telling the closest thing he could manage to a joke, but without the slightest trace of a smile. "I will be flying just off-echelon from First Squadron to help the regimental commander control the flank defense effort. I will not, of course, be interfering with the command of the squadron, but I will be there to keep you all company."

The officers of First Squadron, gathered behind their commander, groaned theatrically. It was all right. Heifetz was glad they could still make a joke of things.

"Any questions, First Squadron?"

Lieutenant Colonel Tercus, the squadron commander, shook his head.

"It's just a long goddamned way," Tercus said. "But we've got good horses."

"Any chance of getting those two down systems back up before you lift off?" Taylor asked the squadron commander.

"Doesn't look good. The motor officer's working on one of them right now. That's a straightforward hydraulics problem, but we're missing a part."

Taylor looked at Martinez.

"Shortage item, sir," the supply officer said. "We're authorized three on PLL, but we've already used them. It's turning out to be another bug they haven't gotten out of the system. We're trying to get an emergency issue from the States, but I can't even promise you the manufacturer's got spares. They may have to strip them from the new birds coming off the line."

"How about the birds that are down in the other squadrons, Manny?" Taylor asked. "It's your call. If the regimental motor officer has one he doesn't think he can fix by mission time, let's cannibalize it. We need every possible system up in the air."

"What we might as well do, then," Martinez said, "is cannibalize Bravo one-four right in First Squadron. She's never going to be back up in time for the mission. Software problem. That way we can keep the can-job under control within one squadron."

"How bad is Bravo one-four," Taylor asked, "really?"

Martinez looked at him earnestly. "Sir, she's not going to be back up in time for this war. The software problem's bad. It's depot-level maintenance."

Taylor turned to Tercus, the First Squadron commander. "Bud," he said, "I'm going to do a job on you. Sorry." Then he turned back to Martinez. "Manny, I want you to write off Bravo one-four. Combat loss. Then strip it for every damned part you're short. Get every bird up that you can in all three squadrons."

"Yes, sir."

"Dave?" Taylor shifted his attention back to the operations officer. "Go ahead. Give us what you got."

Heifetz cleared his throat. "Second Squadron," he began, "you will deploy along axis White-one to an initial target concentration vicinity of Objective Diamond, near Tselinograd. The Iranians and the rebels have cluster-fucked themselves around in there. They're probably massing for the big push into western Siberia, to the northwest of the Kokchetav sector. A successful attack on Diamond takes the pressure off the seam between the two Soviet armies just to the north and turns the tables by splitting the enemy's front in two. Gut the forces near Tselinograd, and the breakthrough area to the northwest starts to look extremely vulnerable."

Heifetz traced along the continuation of Second Squadron's route. "Following a thirty-minute action on a broad front at Diamond, Second Squadron continues the attack along axis White-two to Objective Sapphire, engaging significant targets of opportunity en route. Sapphire wraps around Arkalyk—here—where the Japanese have another forward maintenance site with extensive yards. Your mission here is identical to First Squadron's primary at Ruby. Take out the maintenance site itself, then the yards. Clear? Good. Second Squadron then continues along axis White-three, prepared to turn to the assistance of First Squadron to the south, on the regiment's left flank—should an emergency situation arise. Second Squadron will not, however, seek dogfights. No white-scarf nonsense, gentlemen. Remember, First Squadron cannot come in until you close, and they'll be flying on fumes. Your assembly area is here, at Platinum, in the Orenburg region, where you will be positioned to spearhead a follow-on attack to the southwest, if one is ordered. Colonel Taylor will fly off-echelon from Second Squadron, in control of the main battle. Any questions, Second Squadron?"

There were no questions. Those officers who had not been directly involved in planning the operations had nonetheless had the opportunity to read over the op order.

"All right," Heifetz said. "That brings us to Third Squadron. Thirteen operational M-100s out of a complement of sixteen."

"I'll have two more birds up by H-hour," Lieutenant Colonel Reno, the Third Squadron's commander, announced. The swagger and peevishness in his voice sought to telegraph that he was a *commander,* while Heifetz was merely a higher form of staff flunky. "Don't worry about Third Squadron."

Heifetz did not believe the man. Of all the squadron commanders, Heifetz had the least faith in Reno's being where he was supposed to be, doing what he was supposed to do, when he was supposed to be doing it. But Reno was the son of a retired four-star general, and even Taylor had had no say in the man's assignment to the Seventh Cavalry. Taylor and Heifetz had been careful to assign Third Squadron the least demanding mission.

"Third Squadron," Heifetz continued, ignoring Reno's tone, "deploys along axis Green-one only upon receiving confirmation that First and Second squadrons have both crossed their LDs. Third Squadron's mission is simply the destruction of enemy forces along the corridor formed by Engagement Area Emerald. Now the Soviets have friendly forces cut off and scattered all along Green-one, so you're on weapons-hold until Emerald. Then you're on your own. Emerald stretches roughly from Kokchetav to Atbasar. Your navigational aids will automatically key when you hit the initial boundary. Within the engagement area, any military system is fair game. Your mission is extensive destruction of enemy follow-on and supporting forces in the rear of the breakthrough sector. The single specified target is here, at Atbasar. The headquarters of the I Iranian Corps is set into an excavation site just outside of town. The coordinates have been programmed in for Charlie Troop, and for Bravo, as a backup. The S-2 suspects this site doubles as a Japanese forward command-and-control site, so make sure you clean it out thoroughly. Upon exiting Emerald, you follow Green-two directly to Assembly Area Gold in the industrial park outside of Magnitogorsk, where you will prepare to accept a follow-on mission. Any questions?"

None.

"Fire support," Heifetz continued. "The regiment's dual-purpose artillery battalion will be employed in its air defense mode. The mobile operations envisioned by the plan will be too swiftly paced for heavy-artillery accompaniment. Thus, we have decided to move the regimental artillery directly to the follow-on assembly areas, by routes to the rear of the areas of contact. One battery will deploy to each site—Platinum, Silver, and Gold. You will be prepared to intercept any hostiles on the tail of our squadrons as they close."

Heifetz did a quick mental review. Had he forgotten anything?

No. He went into his closing. "Nonspecified coordination measures per SOP. Quartering parties are authorized to depart for the follow-on assembly areas at end-evening-nautical-twilight. Keep to the approved routes so you don't have some trigger-happy Soviets shooting at you. Artillery follows at EENT plus one. Scouts up at LD minus ninety minutes. Sir," he addressed Taylor, "are there any questions?"

"No. Good job, Dave."

"Then I will be followed by the electronic-warfare liaison officer from the Tenth Cav."

Heifetz rested the remote device on the field podium and moved for his seat, passing a tall, very lean young man on his way. The younger man took up a position just to the side of the briefing screen and began to discuss the intricacies of maneuvering jammers and conducting electronic deception assaults, of electronic tides, digital leeching and ruse dialogues with enemy radars, of ambient energy and frequency deconfliction.

Back in his cold metal chair at Taylor's side, Heifetz had no difficulty imagining the new briefer in a different battle dress, describing the employment techniques for a new type of arrow or sling.

Manny Martinez missed laughter. In peacetime exercises, even during the Mexican deployment, he had always been able to deliver his support briefings with a touch of humor. It was a tradition in any unit commanded by Taylor that the S-4 briefed last. And Martinez had always managed to brighten even the bad days with smiles and small jokes, with banter that made fun of himself or the world. But the humor was gone now, and he shifted uncomfortably in his seat, awaiting his turn to speak as he might await his turn in the dentist's chair. Nothing he had experienced had ever been this serious, and he felt only the weight of his problems—growing problems—within the support and maintenance system, doubt about his personal adequacy, and the deepening worry that he would let down Taylor and all of the other men who depended on him.

He war-gamed possible realignments and shortcuts that might better accomplish the ever greater number of required repairs, that might more efficiently move the regiment's extensive support infrastructure to the new assembly areas, that might begin to ready the maintenance crews for the still-not-quite-imaginable challenges they would face in the aftermath of combat. Martinez had always had a light, clever way with solutions to support problems, the ability to see the obvious answers hidden by the camouflage of regulations and routine, and he had been vain about his talents. Now he saw only the possibility of failure on a dozen fronts.

He half-listened through the series of other briefers, as the chemical officer reported on the latest strikes and the types of agents employed, and as the regimental surgeon warned of typhus among the refugees and lectured the warriors yet again on the uses and abuses of the stimulant pills they had been issued and on the limitations of the fear suppressants given to the dragoons and other junior enlisted soldiers—tablets the troops nicknamed suicide pills because they were convinced, despite all assurances to the contrary, that they impaired a man's judgment. If the pills were so hot, the soldiers asked, how come the officers didn't have to take them?

Martinez listened, wishing the briefings could go on forever, suspending them all on the edge of war, on the verge of action, forgiving them their impending duty. Despite the kidney-penetrating chill in the warehouse, he felt himself sweating.

It never occurred to him to be afraid for his life. He was only afraid of failure.

Then it was time. A startling voice said:

"I will be followed by the S-4."

It was time.

"Manny?" Taylor said, turning his discolored face down the row of chairs.

Martinez sprang to his feet, surprised to find his body as ready and buoyant as ever.

"Good afternoon, sir, gentlemen . . ." he began, ". . . as of 1600 local all combat systems have been fully fueled and their weapons suites calibrated and loaded. From the logistics and maintenance standpoint, there is nothing to interfere with the immediate mission, although there is still some question as to how many M-100s we'll actually get across the LD. Assuming the parts swap-out allows First Squadron to get Zero-eight up, that leaves us with a present strength of forty-five operational systems of fifty assigned. There *is* a possibility that we'll be able to get one more of Third Squadron's birds up by lift-off time, but I can't guarantee it."

"Now, damn it, Martinez," Lieutenant Colonel Reno cut in, "you and the motor officer told me you'd have all three of my down birds back up."

It was a lie. Martinez knew it, and he knew that Reno knew it. Reno, the general's son.

"Sir," Martinez said, "I told you we'd do our best. But—"

"That's the damned trouble with this army," Reno said, "you can't count on—"

Reno, who, as Martinez knew, had joked that, "That little spic's going to find out that logistics means more than stealing car parts in some back alley."

"Colonel Reno," Taylor entered the exchange in his stark, commanding voice, "I agree it's worth a fight to get every damned machine in the air that we possibly can. But I'm personally convinced that regimental maintenance is doing a good job for all of us. No, a *great* job. As the Seventh Cavalry commander I'm about to go into battle with a ninety-five percent ready rate. I'll tell you frankly, that's better than I expected. *I'm* going to cross that LD confidently tonight—and I think everybody else who's going along on the mission can feel the same way." There was a quality about Taylor's presence that seemed ready to leap into an audience, like one of the big cats. At times like these, Martinez realized, it was not Taylor's relatively subdued words that invoked discipline, but the ferocity of his silences, the intensity of the pauses between the mannered sentences, expressing exactly what his language masked. "Anyway," Taylor went on, "I'd cross that line of departure tonight if I had to walk south throwing stones at the enemy. So I'm not sure we should complain about having forty-five of the most powerful combat systems ever built ready for action." Taylor took his eyes off of Reno. "Manny, I'm one hell of a lot more concerned about the problem with the calibrators. What's going on there?"

After being so firmly defended by the old man, Martinez felt doubly bad about the problem he now had to address.

"Sir," Martinez said, "as you know, the regiment's authorized four calibrators for the electromagnetic gun system on the M-100s. Due to deficiencies, the first issue was recalled in July, but so far we've only received two of the A2-variant replacements. We deployed with both of those. Now one of them has gone down. The motor officer's been working on it personally, and we've got an emergency requisition in to the States. But it looks like we may only have a single calibrator to rotate between the squadrons at the follow-on assembly areas."

"And there's no way the recalibration can be done manually?" Taylor asked.

"No, sir. The system's far too complex. It's not just a matter of sights and a gun tube like in the old days—we've got to reset the control electronics, and it takes the recalibration computer to do that."

"All right. Assuming we'll have only one calibrator. How long until we can have the entire regiment ready for a follow-on mission?"

"That depends," Martinez began. He was about to say "on the number of losses we take," but thought better of it. It seemed like bad luck. "There are a number of variables. We have to factor in the distances between the assembly areas. We can re-cal a bird in fifteen minutes. But there's mounting time too. My best guess would be between thirty and thirty-six hours. With most of that being displacement time between sites."

"Shit," Taylor said. "I don't want to be down that long. Based on range firings, what's the maximum number of targets a system can engage before degradation becomes noticeable—and at what point is that gun nothing more than an expensive noisemaker?"

Martinez thought. He knew that range firing was not as stressful as combat. But Taylor knew that too.

"Sir, technically speaking, degradation begins with the first round downrange. But it only becomes pronounced after the expulsion of approximately three hundred to four hundred projectiles. Every system is a little bit different. They almost seem to have personalities. The best birds might still be hitting at a fifty percent kill rate out to six hundred rounds. But you can't count on it."

Taylor turned in his chair to address the assembly. "I'm sure most of you feel fat, dumb, and happy with those numbers. Sounds like a lot of killing power. But my gut feeling is that we're going to go through ammo at a far higher rate than either the contractors or Fort Leavenworth figured." Taylor nodded to himself. "Best system in the world. But even if it works exactly as advertised, gentlemen, those neat little war games back at the Combined Arms Center don't factor in the redundant kills, the inexplicable misses, the confusion, and the just plain fucked-up nature of combat. We've got a big mission, spread out over a geographically vast area. And I do not expect that it will be our only mission. So, what it means to me, is that systems commanders have to closely monitor their automatic acquisition systems to make sure we're getting the kind of kills we want—and that we're not all killing the same range car a couple of dozen times. You can use technology, you can even believe in it—but, in the end, you can't trust it." Taylor stared out coldly from under his ravaged brow. "Keep your eyes open out there. And *think*."

Taylor's last word had the ring of metal, and it hung in the frozen air.

Settling back into a more relaxed posture, he continued: "All right. The operational calibrator goes first to Second Squadron at Platinum, then to First at Silver, finally to Third Squadron at Gold, unless the evolving mission dictates otherwise. You have anything else that's not covered in your annex, Manny?"

"No, sir. Nothing for the group as a whole. The intent remains to be clear of this place by sunrise, but the work to get the M-100s back on-line is keeping us from uploading the maintenance shop." Martinez lifted his shoulders. "But that's my problem."

"Don't be afraid to crack the whip. There's a good chance the Japanese strategic systems will pick us up as we break out of our hide positions, and I don't want to leave any courtesy targets back here on the ground. As soon as you can manage, Manny, I want you and your log animals and all of the motor officer's grease monkeys out of here. Move in even smaller increments, if you have to. But get them out of here. We're going to need you at the new sites."

"Yes, sir," Martinez said. But he did not know if he could pull it off. There was still so much to do. There was no end to the work, no clear-cut point at which you could say, well, that's all done, now we can pack up our tools and be on our merry way. You fixed one problem, and turned around to find a pair of nervous lieutenants waiting to tell you about two more.

Be strong, man, Martinez told himself. Be hard. Like the old man. *El Diablo*.

This is the real thing, this is the real thing.

As he left his briefing position at the front of the assembly, Martinez suddenly laughed inside, remembering, with the blackest of humor, what Taylor had once told him.

"You can always tell when combat's coming your way," the old man had said. "Everything starts going wrong."

Taylor had said that to him in a cantina in an ugly little Mexican mountain town called Bonita. And Martinez had laughed, thinking that *that* was combat, chasing bandits in fatigue uniforms through the desert mountains. He had laughed happily, drinking a thin, sharp margarita, certain that he had everything under control, that he would always have everything under control. And Taylor had smiled his dead man's smile, with his spurred boots up on the table.

Taylor had known. He had known far more than a young quartermaster captain had imagined there was to know.

The real thing.

Taylor stood in front of his officers. He knew all of their names, even of the newest and most junior man. But that was not the same as knowing the men themselves. In his audience there were varying degrees of anxiety and bravado, of ignorance and enthusiasm. Even now, combat was not merely a tournament of machines, but the result of the countless unanticipated decisions made by a human collective. It had been his responsibility to prepare this group of men for war. He had not had them long, and he knew he had not prepared them adequately. But he also knew that there was never sufficient time for this, and that no man was ever fully prepared.

He knew that many of them, especially the younger ones, expected him to make a speech. If it were a film, there would surely be a speech. But he suspected that no amount of oratory on his part would be quite as valuable to them as time spent with their own subordinates, explaining, correcting, assuring. His purpose in bringing them together had been accomplished. They were reassured that they were not alone, neglected, forgotten. Each man was part of a greater work. And the briefing had dragged on long enough to content even the hungriest of them, to make every man anxious to rise from his seat and immerse himself in doing.

Manny was nervous, but that was all right. Taylor had faith in him. And in Meredith, who was frustrated by his inability to count each last hair on the enemy's heads. In Heifetz, whose bravery was born of despair. In the lieutenant in the back row who had embarrassed Taylor one night at the officer's club by apologizing profusely because his parents had seen to it that he had the best available cosmetic surgery to cover up his scars from Runciman's disease. He said he didn't want Taylor to think he wasn't a real man. And Taylor had been startled into silence.

He trusted Tercus to lead his squadron with vigor and dash, so he had assigned Lucky Dave to ensure that Tercus did not grow too dashing or vigorous. He even had faith in Reno to do his best when the chips were down, with his father's demanding ghost at his shoulder. He had faith in the grinning young troopers with their tough-guy tattoos, in the mechanics and ammunition handlers. He had great faith that the majority of the men before him would find more in themselves than they had ever expected.

But he did not have faith in himself to speak well to them now. He had read too many books in his lifetime, and he feared that the words he would say would come from long-digested pages and not from his head and heart, that his words would ring false.

Better to say nothing at all.

He would have liked to tell them about the worn red and white pennant he carried folded small in his pocket. To tell them how he had taken it from a rooftop where it had been forgotten in the African wastes, and how he had carried it with him across the miles, through the years. He would have liked to draw it out and show them, the way a man might show his children or grandchildren. Here. This is what I am.

But he knew he did not have the words for that either. Or to tell them that he had waited a long time for this day, dreaming of it, when he knew in his intellect that no sane, decent man should wish for anything but peace.

He touched the Soviet greatcoat he still wore, feeling

through the heavy material to the place where he had nestled the old cavalry guidon. It was still there, he reassured himself.

He did not draw it out. Instead, he began to unbutton the greatcoat, looking out at the rows of officers similarly dressed.

"Let's get out of these godforsaken rags," he told them, "and get to work."

13

Moscow
2 November 2020

"You don't have to *do* anything," her friend told Valya. "Just talk to them, have a drink or two. Come for the fun of it."

Valya told herself she could not go. There were countless reasons to decline the invitation. Since her visit to the clinic, she had resolved to behave as a wife should, to think only of Yuri, struggling to imagine that their lives together would improve. And she still had not recovered fully from the minor operation. The work had been carelessly done, and she still bled intermittently and often felt tired and weak. Standing in front of her students all day, forcing them to repeat in English, "I am pleased to meet you," took all of the energy she had. She barely cooked for herself, yet the table in the combination living and dining room was covered with neglected plates and cups. When she came home at the end of the day, she was even conscious that the tiny apartment had begun to smell unpleasantly, nursing a dreary odor of clotted broth and clothing left unlaundered. But she could not bring herself to raise her hand to work in earnest. In lieu of a proper cleanup, she halfheartedly shifted a few items about the room. At first Naritsky had phoned her again and again, but, slowly, he wearied of her unwillingness to give him an audience. She told herself that she must write to Yuri, while, night after night, she sat on the old green sofa, wrapped in a blanket, half-watching the television with its unkempt mixture of patriotic and sentimental programming punctuated by oddly fractured news reports from the war. She grasped that things were going very badly, and that Yuri might be in terrible danger. Yet, the recognition was merely intellectual. The small images had no real power to move her. No bombs fell in her street, and except for even greater shortages than usual in the shops, the war could not yet touch her. Absent, Yuri, too, was only an abstraction. She sat on the broken couch, staring at the livid rug hung to hide the disrepair of the opposite wall, while a songstress with mounds of chemical-soaked hair complained of the sorrows of love. Write to Yuri, she thought, I must write to Yuri. Yet, she did not write, and in her most lucid moments, she knew that she did not love the man to whom she had bound herself and that she simply feared being found out.

"I can't go, Tanya," she told her friend. "I really can't."

Tanya grimaced. She glanced instinctively at the random uncleanliness of the nearby tabletop, then forced her eyes back to her friend. But Valya was only faintly embarrassed. Things mattered less these days.

"You can't just sit here like a cabbage," Tanya said. "What in the world's gotten into you?"

"I've been thinking of Yuri," Valya half-lied. "I've treated him so badly. I haven't even written."

"Yuri can take care of himself," Tanya said. "You're being foolish. What's he done for you? What's so special about your life?" Tanya scanned the feckless clutter of the room. "They think they're so important. All puffed up in their uniforms. And look what a mess they've gotten us into. I always told you not to get involved with a soldier."

This was not true. When they had begun going out together, Tanya had praised Yuri boundlessly, stressing the security of being an officer's wife, the dwindling but still considerable privileges, and even admiring Yuri's looks. Once, a two-room apartment in Moscow had seemed like a very great thing. Now the same living space felt like a prison to Valya.

"You were better off with what's-his-name," Tanya continued. *"He* at least had money. *And* he didn't mind spending it."

"Please," Valya said. "I don't want to talk about it. You don't know."

"Valya. For God's sake. You have to pull yourself together. I mean, look at this place. It's so unlike you."

But Valya knew that it was not really unlike her at all. She suspected that this was a truer reflection of her nature than imported perfume and careful makeup. But she also knew that she would, indeed, go with Tanya to the hotel. She only needed to delay the admission a little longer, not for Tanya's sake, but for her own.

"I haven't been well," Valya said.

"Oh, don't be a baby."

"I really should write to Yuri. For all I know, he's out there fighting or something."

"Don't be silly. Yuri's clever enough to take care of himself. Don't you believe all that talk about 'duty' and 'officer-this and officer-that.' Men love to talk." Tanya paused momentarily, as if she had to catch her breath at the thought of how many lies men had told her. Then she purged her expression of all mercy. "I'll bet he doesn't even think about you. He's probably sleeping with some nurse or with one of the local tramps. Those Siberian girls have no morals."

"Not Yuri," Valya said vehemently, certain of this one thing. "Yuri's not that way." It might have been better, she thought, if he *had* been that way.

Tanya laughed, a loud burlesque snort. "You just don't understand men, my dear. They're *all* that way. You can't judge a man by the way he acts at home."

"Not Yuri," Valya repeated flatly.

Tanya sighed. "Well, time will tell. But why talk about Yuri? I came to talk about *you.* Valya, you simply *must* come out tonight. It's too good an opportunity to miss."

Valya tried to wrap herself in an aura of innocence, as though it were a second blanket. "I just don't think I can," she said. Then she glanced off toward the television. A man with silver hair called for a new era of self-sacrifice. A new spirit in the people was going to win the war. For a surplus moment of their lives the two women faced the television wearing the identical sober expressions that had allowed them to drift through hundreds of official meetings without hearing a word.

"What are they like?" Valya asked quietly, without looking at her friend. "I'm just curious."

"Well, *first* of all," Tanya said, "they know how to treat a woman properly. They're all rich, of course." Tanya thought for a moment. "Naturally, they're just the same as any other men *that* way. They just want to get your skirt up around your waist. But . . . well, if I can't be honest with you, who can I be honest with? At least they don't grunt once and roll off you."

"Tanya."

"Oh, don't act like the little innocent. I'm just saying I've never been so . . . so . . ." Tanya finally blushed at her own thoughts. In the moment of truth she could not overcome the force of the behavioral code. What you did was not of so much importance. But you had to be guarded in what you said. "They must study it at school or something," she giggled, as though a decade had been wiped away and they were both teenaged girls again.

The moment of silliness passed, and Tanya primped the line of her skirt. "But that's not why I came. I just thought you wouldn't want to miss a chance to talk to them. To practice your English. You know. You might learn some new expressions, the latest slang."

Valya looked down at the floor. That, too, badly needed cleaning. "I wouldn't know what to say to them," she told her friend. But she was already rehearsing verbal gambits in her mind.

"Oh, they'll take care of that. They really *are* friendly. Just like in the old Western movies. All scrubbed and clean and smiling all the time. And they don't act like stupid little bullies. Really, they're just the opposite of Russian men."

"But . . . I've heard they're very uncultured."

Tanya closed her eyes in an expression of disgust. "Well, if you want to go to an art museum, you can always go by yourself. *I* think the Americans are *won*derful." To emphasize her point, she squeezed out a few words of her best English, far weaker than Valya's drilled speech. *"To* *have fun,"* Tanya said. *"Always to have fun. Darling, it is very nice."*

"I don't think I'd like them," Valya said, already imagining dull-witted American smiles, solid shoes, and lives of unforgivable material well-being.

"That's silly. First meet them, then make up your mind. I've already told Jim about you. He and his friends would love to meet you."

"Jeem," Valya said disdainfully. "It sounds like a name from a film. It's a foolish name."

Tanya shrugged in sudden weariness, as though Valya's slovenly malaise had grown contagious. Then she looked at her watch.

"It's getting late," she said. "I promised Jim I'd meet him."

Valya felt a rush of fear. Fear of being left behind, in these sour rooms, in her soured life. Who knew what possibilities might exist with the Americans? And a drink or two would do no harm. Perhaps there would even be something good to eat at the hotel. She felt herself blossoming back to life, after the long dead weeks. Surely, there would be marvelous food, gathered up just for the foreigners. Seductive, not-quite-focused visions began to crowd her mind.

"You're right," Valya said suddenly. "I need to get out. For some fresh air. I'll sleep better."

Tanya brightened again, and Valya wondered whether her old schoolmate had begged her to go along out of antique devotion, out of the need for further help in communicating with these rich men from abroad, or as some sort of procuress. But it did not matter.

"How long are they staying in Moscow?" Valya asked, letting the coverlet slip from her shoulders. In the background, the television displayed a map of far-off battles.

"A long time, I think," Tanya said. "Jim says he doesn't know for sure. They're on business. It's some kind of trade delegation. But don't worry. They're not boring, not at all the way you'd picture American businessmen. They're all friends, and they're always telling stories about when they were in the Army together."

It suddenly struck Valya as odd that a trade delegation

would be in Moscow for an extended stay while the country was desperately at war. But she quickly shrugged it off. A thousand articles, programs, lectures had assured her that the Americans even made money off of plagues and famines, while Naritsky had already demonstrated to her how easily money could be made off of war. Perhaps that was why they were here now, to sell the tools of death. Valya found it no cause for serious concern.

"I'll have to wash up. And fix my hair."

"That's right," Tanya said happily. "And make sure you wash really well. They're very particular about it." She wrinkled her nose. "While you're getting dressed, I'll just clean up some of this mess."

Valya hastened into her tiny bedroom and began rummaging through a pile of neglected clothing. What was clean enough to wear? She had to be cautious with colors—she had been looking very pale.

China clacked in the next room, and she just heard Tanya's musing voice:

"You're such a bad girl, Valya."

Ryder sat at the bar. Alone. Drinking bottled beer that tasted as though it had gone stale in a can. He had not intended to stay so long. There was plenty of work waiting for him up in his room. Yet, it had been a very difficult day, troubling in ways that refused to be neatly labeled and put away. *Machines don't feel pain.* And a world of new possibilities. He had explained it all as clearly as he could to his superiors, and they, too, had grown excited. Opportunities like this, the detachment commander had said, only come once. Yet, Ryder worried that they did not really understand. He longed for them to come up with a plan instantly, to exploit this new dimension of the battlefield without hesitation.

He laughed to himself, playing with his half empty glass. *So that this machine will not have suffered in vain.* He had carefully played that aspect of the business down, stressing instead the enemy's near-miraculous vulnerabilities. And now it was up to *them* to make it all go, to forge the plan that sent the men to realize the possibilities. He knew he could not do that himself. But neither could he let go of the project. He sensed that his role had not yet been played out.

He sipped the warming beer. Never much of a drinker. Absurd, he told himself. The entire thing. Absurd. But the word he felt and could not bring to bear was "haunting."

The entire world was haunted now. The hotel bar. Constructed in some bygone fit of hope, it was intended to be elegant but managed to achieve only a worn biliousness. Velvet seats with their contact surfaces rubbed white by countless rumps; brass plating crazed and chipped. Only the mirror had a genuinely antique feel, thanks to the years of cigarette smoke that had given it a deep gray tint. It was in that mirror, just above the palisade of bottles, that he first met the woman's stare, and now it was the memory of that stare, held a moment too long, that kept him fixed to the barstool.

He had been ready to leave, despite the passing admonishments of his fellow officers to join the party. Ready to accept the loneliness that was not really all that bad when you made yourself think about it logically. Ready to go back to the small overheated room with its grumping noises of too much liquid in an old man's throat. There was always work, and work could justify any sacrifice.

Then her eyes caught him. Almost too strong for so delicate a face, he knew they were brown even though he could not begin to see their color through the smoky twilight of the bar. She had been watching him in the mirror, and the first thought that struck him was how bluntly out of place she was. Squeezed into a booth between two loud officers in ill-fitting sport jackets. It was finally the big sweep of a forearm that broke the reflected stare between them.

She seemed to be with a paunchy lieutenant colonel, whom Ryder knew as professionally incapable, politically adept, and delighted to be in a foreign country with a pocket full of money and without his wife. Ryder knew everyone at the table: officers for whom he had little respect. He even knew the other Russian woman by sight, even though he rarely strayed into the bar. Tallish, with a helmet of metallic-looking black hair. Charter member of the Bar-girl's International.

He knew everyone—except this fine-featured girl with honey colors strained down through the tangles of her hair. She sat silently, her face almost somber, while the increasingly drunken party spun its web around her. Neither the laughter nor the strangers with whom she sat seemed to touch her. She looked like a princess who had too little to eat, and he remembered a fellow warrant officer's snicker that "Most of them would do anything you could dream up for a good meal." Ryder felt a proprietary sense of loss that such a woman should be wasted on her present company.

Her face dropped back into the shadows, and Ryder could see only that she was smiling now, speaking words he could not hear.

He looked down at his beer. But he could see even more of her now, in his memory. Below the snapshot of face and hair a long white neck led down to bared collarbones and lace trim on a dress cut in a style that had been popular in the States some years before. A red dress, as if she were making a broad joke out of it all. He shook his head, telling himself that this one was genuinely beautiful, even though he knew it was not true. Somehow, her features fell just short of legitimate beauty. But, alone of the women in the crowded bar, this one had the power to jar him, to shake the hell out of his tenuous grip on the night.

There was nothing to be done about it, of course. The officers surrounding her distinctly outranked him. But, even had she been sitting alone, he would not have had the nerve to approach her. He had a fistful of excuses. Despite the detachment's general disregard for the rules, they were not supposed to be fraternizing with the locals. Besides, any of the girls could be KGB. And venereal disease was rumored to be epidemic in the city. Anyway, he had nothing to offer her. He could be gone at any moment. And he had far too much work to do. He had to hold himself in readiness.

He had never been much good at coming on to women. His friends could never understand him. Christ, an old friend had said to him, if I had your looks, my dick would be worn down to a nub. The women with whom he had swapped bits of life had almost invariably initiated things, like Jennifer waiting for him in the hallway outside of the computer science classroom. In one of her better moods, on one of their better days, she had told him, you just don't realize what a doll you are. Then she had divorced him.

Now there was no one at his side, and nothing in front of him but the dregs of a beer and another Moscow night of listening to the asthmatic plumbing and the escapades of his neighbors. So he sat a little longer, indulging himself in a fantasy about this woman with whom he knew he would never exchange a single word, imagining a life for her, the steps that had forced her to squander herself on the blustering drunks at her table.

He pictured her standing in line to buy rags of meat. The lines in the streets had grown so long that they seemed almost to meet themselves, to join until there was no beginning and no end, waiting for the opening of some rumored shop that did not even exist. Driving together through the streets, his Soviet counterpart had been unconcerned.

"The people of Russia," Savitsky said, "have always waited."

The wrong woman, Ryder thought, and the wrong country too.

He was just about to force himself away from the bar and his reverie, when the lieutenant colonel, who had the woman boxed in, noisily excused himself and weaved off toward the men's room. Ryder instinctively glanced at the spot in the mirror where his eyes had caught her stare, and he saw that she, too, was excusing herself now. He suddenly felt sick to his stomach, thinking that she was about to follow the lieutenant colonel, realizing that he was headed not to the men's room but up the hotel's back stairs.

The woman surprised him. She did not follow the man to whom Ryder's imagination had condemned her. Instead, she boldly met his eyes in the mirror once again and marched straight toward the bar.

He lost the courage of his fantasies now. He broke the stare and huddled closer to his empty glass.

He sensed her coming up beside him. He stared nervously at the bartender's paunch as the man lolled it over a sink. Sergey, the hard-currency-holder's friend.

A hand, unmistakably feminine, touched lightly at his shoulder.

"This seat is occupied?" the woman asked. He did not have to look back into the mirror, or to turn. He knew it was her. He knew her voice with a certainty built on concrete and steel, even though he had heard only a faint, half-imagined laugh across a crowded room.

"No," he stammered, turning at last. "Please. Please, sit down."

KGB. Of course. She had to be. Otherwise, there was no reasonable explanation for it.

"How do you do?" she asked, and it was only then that he realized that she was speaking to him in English. Her voice was careful, the intonation studiedly flat, as though she were not quite sure of the words. But, as he looked at her closely for the first time he could not imagine why she should ever be afraid of anything.

Often, when you came close to Russian women, their skin proved unexpectedly bad, or the sudden foulness of their teeth shocked you. But this woman had a clear, perfect complexion. Pale, though. Almost as though she had been a little ill. Her teeth were small and even, behind lips that were, perhaps, just slightly too heavy. The close smell of her was just rich enough to tease him.

"I'm fine," he said automatically. "How are you?"

The woman sat down beside him, her body flowing in smooth elastic lines beneath her dress. Too thin a fabric for the Moscow autumn, washed almost to nothing. She, too, appeared too frail for the world in which she lived. But this was a country where even the beauties did not eat terribly well.

"I am very well tonight, thank you," the woman said. "Do you have a cigarette?"

"I don't smoke," Ryder said, instantly regretting that he did not.

The woman's eyes took on an uncertain look.

"Wait," Ryder said. "Hang on a minute." He reluctantly turned his face away from her, as if afraid she might disappear at this momentary inattention. "Sergey?" he called down the bar.

The bartender, who professed that he really loved Americans, that he loved Americans best of any of his distinguished customers, and why weren't there more Americans? moved down behind his barricade of polished wood.

"Please, mister?"

"A pack of cigarettes," Ryder told him, adding "Marlboros," at the sudden recollection that he had seen that one Western brand passing above the counter.

"This is not necessary from you," the woman said, her words devoid of conviction.

"No trouble," Ryder said, drawing dollars from his wallet. "By the way, my name's Jeff."

The woman looked at him. Dark brown eyes only enriched by the dark circles beneath them. Eyes, Ryder thought lightheartedly, that men would die for.

"I am Valentina," the woman pronounced slowly. "But I am called Valya. It is my shortened name, you see."

"Valya," Ryder repeated. "That's a very nice name." He was conscious of the inanity of his words. But he could not think of anything clever, and he feared a silence that might drive her away.

The bartender delivered the cigarettes.

"Marlboros all right?" Ryder asked the woman.

"Oh, yes. Very good." The woman seemed slightly nervous, although Ryder could not imagine how anyone so attractive, so graced by God, could be nervous in such a situation. He could not even believe that she was here. How could the men of this country have allowed her to slip through their grasp?

He thought again that she must be KGB. But he did not want to believe it.

She looked a bit hardened up close. But, in a way he could not explain, this slight defect only made her more attractive. He guessed that she was in her late twenties, approximately his age.

Striking, he thought. Not beautiful. Striking.

He fumbled to open the pack of cigarettes for her, unfamiliar with the task. Finally, relieved, he extended the open pack toward her, then he lit the cigarette for her, using the action as an excuse to close slightly on her, to get the near sense of her, to smell the mixture of womanly body and discount-shop perfume.

"Thank you," she said. "You are very kind, Jeff." She, too, pronounced it "Cheff." A word she had not practiced.

"You speak English very well."

"I am a teacher. Of the children. I think that children are very wonderful. I am their teacher for the English language, which I love. It is very interesting."

Ryder struggled to find something to say, desperately afraid that she would abandon him at each next moment. He drained the very last of his beer.

"Can I get you a drink? What are you drinking?"

"That is very nice. But it is not necessary. I will have a Pepsi-Cola, with whiskey, please."

Ryder ordered. And another beer.

His language account went bankrupt again. The woman puffed at her cigarette, then tilted her head back in a display of her long white throat and thick, tumbling hair. She wore a schoolgirl's heart pendant that showed bright as blood against her skin. She blew out the smoke, and the action seemed oddly exotic to Ryder, something out of a very old film. No attractive woman in the States would be caught dead with a cigarette in her mouth anymore.

"You're a very lovely woman, Valya," he said, unable to think of anything else and afraid that this was far too much.

She smiled. "What a nice thing that is to say to me. Thank you very much."

"Do you live in Moscow?"

"Oh, yes. I am a Moscow girl. I was born in Moscow."

"It's a very interesting city," Ryder said.

The woman wrinkled her face slightly. "I think it is not so interesting. It cannot be so interesting for you. I think America is very interesting."

"Have you ever been to America?"

She shook her head, making it into a gesture of theatrical sorrow. "It is not easy, you know. Also, America is very expensive. But I think you laugh at us in Moscow. We are very poor. Not like life in America."

"I hope someday you can visit the United States."

The woman's eyes brightened. "Oh, yes. I would like that. To see America. There is everything in America."

The woman seemed to have a talent for saying things that left him blank in response. And he ached to go on talking with her.

Their drinks arrived, and Ryder sent more dollars into the bartender's hand.

The woman tasted the drink, then shook her head sharply, bitten by the taste.

"He puts in very much whiskey. I must not drink so much. Tonight I forgot to have dinner."

"Would you rather have something else to drink?" Ryder asked hurriedly.

"*No*. Oh, no," the woman answered quickly, alarmed at the suggestion. "This has made me happy. Thank you."

He had the urge to ask her to join him in the dining room. He had not eaten, either. And the service hours had been extended for the well-paying Americans. He was no longer so concerned that she might be KGB. Somehow, he could not imagine that this woman of all women was some sort of undercover agent.

And yet, he thought.

He put off asking her. Not because he feared being compromised so much as because he was afraid she would say no, that his offer would force them to separate all the sooner.

"Do you know many Americans?" he asked.

"No," she said, then added hurriedly, "I do not come often to hotels such as this. Tonight, you see, I have only come to keep company with my girlfriend. She has invited me."

Ryder sensed that her girlfriend's character was not the stuff of which good recommendations were made. But. He refused to think badly of the woman sitting beside him. She had asked him for nothing. And he knew that few of the women in the bar were actually hookers. The Americans were a feature attraction in a glum season. And who knew what this woman had gone through in her life? All at once it struck him that he and all of his peers were far too quick to judge.

His silence bothered the woman, who offered an additional line to keep things going. "I think Americans are very friendly."

Ryder nodded. Then he smiled. Yes. Indeed. Every American in the room would be glad to be friendly toward this woman.

In a moment of near panic, followed by deep relief, he saw the beery lieutenant colonel return to his table. Ryder was sure the man would head right for the bar when he noticed that he had been deserted, coming to take the woman back. But the big man just tottered for a moment, then sat down hard, reaching for his waiting glass.

"Americans are pretty friendly people," he agreed, as if he had given it a great deal of thought. "Most of the time."

"But you are sitting alone. That is not very friendly."

"I'm not alone," Ryder smiled. "You're here."

A shadow of annoyance passed over her face, and Ryder realized with the insight of a long-term language student that his response had spoiled the sequence of verbs and nouns she had planned ahead in her mind.

"You should not sit alone," she said adamantly.

"I had a long day. Hard work."

"And what is your work, Jeff?"

"I work with computers."

She thought for a moment. "That is very interesting. But I could not do it. The mathematics are very difficult for me."

"Math's only part of it," Ryder said. But he wanted to steer the conversation well away from his work. If she was KGB, she was not going to get anything out of him.

"Listen, Valya," he said boldly. "I haven't eaten yet. Would you join me for dinner? You said you haven't eaten."

He had taken his cowardice by surprise, pushing the words out. But the last breath of speech brought with it a collapse into fear. She would leave him now.

"That would be very nice," she said quickly. Her response came so fast that he almost missed it in his anxiety.

He still could not believe that she had come to him, that she was still sitting beside him. "I think I would like that very much," she continued. "To dine together."

"Great," Ryder said, aware, somewhere down under his exuberance, that he was suddenly willing to risk far more with this woman than he had ever intended.

Valya struggled not to eat too quickly. She wanted to appear well-mannered, elegant. But it was difficult to offer sensible responses to the American's words. The food was simply too good, too bountiful. Even Naritsky, with all of his black market connections, had not been able to obtain meat of such quality. Valya had never tasted anything like it, and each bite—carefully, agonizedly restrained—left her in a fermenting mix of gratitude and anger. The quality of this meal, served to foreigners in her own city, was humiliating to one who had never been allowed to experience this world. She trimmed the beef into ladylike bits, wanting all the while to pick it up with her hands and devour it like a bad child. She believed that she had never known how hungry she really was until the waiter placed this meal before her.

"The food is very good," she told the American. "Thank you very much."

The American nodded. "Glad you like it. God, I wish I could serve you up a real American steak. Something right out of the Kansas City stockyards. You'd be knocked out."

His words seemed to imply that American beef would be much better than this. But such a thing was unimaginable to Valya. She had never tasted meat of this quality, had not even supposed that it might exist. Now this American seemed to think it was not very good at all. He picked at his food. It made her angry.

Perhaps he was just a braggart. Like so many of them. Not just Americans. Men in general. And yet. This one truly did not seem that way. So quiet. Anxious to please.

Imprisoned by the boors to whom Tanya had introduced her, Valya had spent a long time watching him in the mirror before he noticed her. He was very handsome, in an immature American sort of way, and at first she thought he was sitting alone out of arrogance. But his gestures were too unsure, and when their eyes finally met, his face showed nothing of the wolflike traces she would have expected to encounter in so handsome a man, had he been a Russian.

Perhaps he was truly a good man, decent and generous.

Then why should he speak badly about the best meal she had ever had?

"This is very good," she insisted, her voice polite but definite.

He seemed to sense that he had made a wrong move.

"Yeah, this certainly isn't bad. They're doing their best. Would you like some more potatoes? I can't eat them all."

"No," Valya lied. "This is very much food. Thank you." She wanted to close her eyes and listen to the splendid melody the dinner sent singing through her body. She took another forkful of the vegetables in their thick sauce, careful not to spill anything on her dress. She felt as though she would give anything she had, as though she would even steal, for just one more meal like this.

She had watched him sitting at the bar, and she had made up her mind. The swine with whom Tanya had thrown in her lot were so obviously after only one thing that she knew there was no future with them. They offered no real possibilities. But the handsome, boyish one at the bar. Perhaps he had something to offer. He was young enough to be unattached, to have more future to him than past. She decided he was worth an effort. If nothing else, she wouldn't end the evening being pawed by a middle-aged drunk.

"How about some more wine?" he asked her, with the bottle already raised in his hand.

"Oh, yes. Please. You see it is very good, the Russian wine. It derives from the Crimea."

She saw a slight frown of disagreement cross his face, evidence of further dissatisfaction. What on earth was wrong with this man? What did he want? What did he expect?

She decided that he was simply trying to impress her. Perhaps not in such a bad way. He was still so much a boy. And he wanted her to think he was a man.

Valya warned herself again to slow down, to stop eating like a stray dog. As a penalty for her bad behavior she forced herself to put down her knife and fork for a moment, to talk to the American.

"Jeff. You are such a nice man. I think you are married, yes?"

She watched his face closely. It did not change in a bad way. There was no sudden embarrassment. No stupid furtiveness. Just a barely visible stiffening, a look of pain in the eyes.

"No," he said slowly. "No, I'm not married. I was. But not now."

"Oh. I am sorry. Your wife is dead?"

He smiled slightly, and the pain was gone. "No. Nothing that dramatic. We just weren't right for each other. We're divorced."

The woman was probably some faithless American slut, Valya decided. A bitch who had so much she could discard husbands without a care. In America, every woman had her own private automobile.

"You have children?"

"No," he said. "No, I guess we were lucky that way." Then he changed his tone, leaning in toward her. "But what about you? I can't believe you're not married."

Valya finished chewing and looked at him with her most serious face.

"My husband was killed," she lied. "On the first day of the war."

He retreated into his chair. Sitting up very properly.

"Valya, I'm sorry . . ."

"I do not wish to talk about it," she said. "Tonight is the first night when I am not at home. My friend thought that I must come out."

"All right," he said. "I just . . ."

"It is not important. Tell me about your wife," Valya said, although she did not want to hear about the woman at all. "I think she must be a very bad woman." Then she slipped another piece of beef into her mouth, convinced that he would talk for a while.

"Jennifer?" the American said. "No, Jennifer's not a bad woman. She just sees the world differently than I do."

He smiled. "There's a joke in America that everyone is authorized one trial marriage. I guess that was mine."

Valya swallowed hurriedly. "Then you will marry again, Jeff?"

"I don't know. Maybe. If the right woman comes along. I don't think about it."

"Perhaps you still love this woman?"

The American thought for a moment. "No. I'm pretty much over her, I think. I mean, I'll always remember the good times we had. And I think I kept on loving her a long time after she stopped loving me. But it's all over now."

"I think you must find a very good woman."

The American smiled. He had a wonderful boy's smile. "Or hope that she finds me." He poured more wine, leaving her glass a bit too full.

Without the least warning, Valya felt her stomach cramp. The pain was brutal and very sharp. She stopped chewing, and her eyes opened wide. Then the pain receded, leaving her shocked and numb in the torso, with sweat jeweling on her forehead. Her right hand clutched the tablecloth.

She forced herself to continue chewing.

"Are you all right?" the American asked.

Valya nodded. "I am fine. There is no problem." She reached for the overfilled wine glass. "I think it is hot in here."

Just as she lifted the glass, a second blade of pain ripped through her belly. She moaned slightly, absolutely helpless. The first shock had opened her eyes. Now she had to close them. She swallowed, miserable. Cursing to herself as bitterly and horribly as she had ever done.

"Valya?"

She felt cold sweat on her forehead and temples. Then another bigger, sharper pain cut through her, and she realized that everything was coming apart.

"Please. You will excuse me." She had to hurry, she could not worry about correct stress and pronunciation now. She got up, unsteady, ready to weep, hoping only that she would not embarrass herself too badly. She reached for her purse with a blind hand, but felt only the confusion of the tablecloth and the hard line of her chair.

There was no time. She marched herself quickly across the room, with the desperate, stiff dignity that teeters on the edge of shame, heading for the nearest waiter, to whom she could speak in her own language.

The waiter coldly gave her directions, not interested in being polite to her now that she had separated from her foreigner.

She walked swiftly, growing dizzy and faint, trying to find the way. She sensed that she did not have the spare seconds a wrong turn might cost.

Shadowy hall, buckled carpet. Blistered paint on an old, huge door. She charged inside, past the thick, middle-aged woman who sat guarding a pile of towels and a little plate of coins. As she flashed by, Valya saw quick changes pass over the woman's face. First disapproval, then the forced, begrudged smile that hoped for a tip, then anger.

Valya rushed toward the first stall. Anxious to get down on her knees, yet not quite sure what to do first. In the background, behind an invisible membrane that separated her from the rest of the world, Valya could hear the attendant cursing her. The woman had followed her, and a part of Valya sensed her hovering over her as she shouted insults. But it was all too distant for real concern. There was only the immediacy of sickness, terrible sickness. The burning in her stomach and the strain in her throat existed outside of time.

Then everything grew slow and rancid. The attendant had given up on her and returned to her perch, muttering. Valya sat down on the cracked tile, unable to care now what happened to her precious dress. With all available energy, she reached up to release a gush of fresh water to cleanse her world. Then she sat back down hard.

The physical sickness decayed, leaving her with a different sort of discomfort. Thinking over her folly. She had eaten like an animal. The food had been too rich, too much. It was heartbreakingly good food, and, even now, in the acidic wake of her sickness, she could only hope that there would be more such food in her life.

She breathed deeply. Several times. Finally, she stood up. Her legs felt unsteady at first. But it was evident that the sickness was not serious. Sheer gluttony. Like a child gobbling down sweets.

She lifted her skirt to fix her hose. And the legs that had seemed so long and lovely to her in the mirrors of her life now seemed to have grown too thin. Her wrists showed too much bone. In a world, in the very city, where there was such hidden bounty, Valya caught a glimpse of her body, of her life, wasting.

She approached the attendant, who was sitting sullenly at her post.

"Please," she said, all the while trying to iron her dress with the flat of her hand. "Please give me a towel. I left my purse outside. I was sick."

The woman, mighty in her authority, looked Valya up and down with disapproval.

"The towels," she said, "are fifty kopecks."

"I know," Valya begged. "I understand. But please. I have to clean myself. I can't go back out there. I have to wash."

The attendant laid a hairy wrist across her stack of towels and looked up at Valya with a lifetime's accumulated hatred.

"Fifty kopecks," she said.

Surrendering, Valya stripped off her watch. The marvelous Japanese watch that Naritsky had given her on his return from one of his business trips. For being good, he had said. Naritsky the pig.

She tossed the watch at the woman's swollen waist. It caught, then slipped as the woman grabbed for it, settling in the well of skirt between her legs.

Valya took her towel.

She washed hurriedly. She tried to rinse out her mouth, to fix her hair as best she could. In the mirror, she appeared very pale. But not so very bad, she told herself. She simply felt acid and empty. With the sickness hardly ten minutes behind her, she could already feel her hunger returning. She told herself she would sit down calmly, smile, and pretend nothing had happened. Even if the American had been put off, she would at least finish her meal. She would have that, if nothing else.

She breathed deeply one last time. By the door, the

attendant was struggling to close the watchband over her thick wrist. Valya launched herself back toward the dining room.

To her immense relief, the American was still sitting at the table, and he brightened unmistakably when he caught sight of her. She straightened her back and slowed her step, feeling a surge of confidence that everything just might be all right after all.

Then she noticed that the food was gone. The table had been cleared, and all that remained was the wine. And the half-empty packet of cigarettes she had ravaged in her nervousness.

The lovely, heartbreakingly lovely food was gone. Valya continued her march toward the table, struggling to smile, to assure her American that everything was all right. He stood up clumsily and hastened to draw back her chair for her, and she sat down like a mechanical doll. She stared in disbelief at the white desert of the tabletop. The beautiful food was gone. Her belly felt emptier than it had ever felt in her life.

She began to cry. Helplessly. She did not even have the strength left to be angry with herself. She simply sat and wept quietly into her hands, overcome by her weakness and certain that her life would never be fine again.

"Valya," the American said in his flat, flinty voice, "what's the matter? Can I do anything for you?"

Take me away. Please. Take me away to your America and I'll do anything for you. Anything. Anything you want.

"No," Valya told him, mastering her sobs. "No, please. It has no meaning."

His jaw no longer worked properly and it was hard to push out the words through his swollen lips. He stared up at his tormentor through the pounded meat around his eyes. The light was poor to begin with, and the beating he had taken made it almost impossible to focus in on the KGB major who paced in and out of the shadows, circling the chair where Babryshkin sat with his hands bound tightly behind him. The man was a huge thing, a monster in uniform, a devil.

"Never," Babryshkin repeated, struggling to enunciate,

determined not to yield his last dignity. "I . . . never had such contacts."

The great shadow swooped in on him again. A big fist rushed out of the darkness and slammed into the side of his head.

The chair almost tumbled over. Dizzy, Babryshkin struggled to retain an upright position. He could not understand any of this. It was madness.

"When," the KGB major shouted, "did you first make contact with the faction of traitors? We're not trying to establish your guilt. We know you're guilty. We just want to know the timing." He slapped the back of Babryshkin's head in passing. This time, it wasn't a real blow. Just a bit of punctuation for the words. "How long have you been collaborating with them?"

Damn you, Babryshkin thought, hating. Damn you.

"Comrade major," he began firmly.

An open hand slapped his burst lips.

"I'm not your comrade, traitor."

"I am *not* a traitor. I fought for over a thousand kilometers . . ."

Babryshkin waited for the blow, tensing. But this time it failed to arrive. It was so unpredictable. It was amazing how they established control over you.

"You mean you *retreated* for a thousand kilometers."

"We were ordered to retreat."

The KGB officer snorted. "Yes. And when those orders finally came, you personally chose to disobey them. Shamelessly. When your tanks were needed to reestablish the defense, you purposely delayed their withdrawal. In collaboration with the enemy. The evidence is conclusive. And you've already admitted disobeying the order yourself."

"What could I do?" Babryshkin cried, unable to control himself. He could hear that his words, so clear in his mind, slurred almost unintelligibly as they left his mouth. He tasted fresh blood from his lips, and shreds of meat brushed against his remaining teeth as he spoke. "We couldn't just leave them all. Our own people. They were being massacred. I couldn't leave them."

The major slowed his pacing. The desk lay between him

and Babryshkin now, and the major walked with folded arms. Babryshkin was grateful for even this brief, perhaps unintended, pause in the beating.

"There are times," the major said firmly, "when it is important to consider the greater good. Your superiors recognized that. But you willfully chose to disobey, thereby endangering our defense. What if everyone chose to disobey? And, in any case, you can't hide behind the People. You feel nothing for the People. You purposely delayed, looking for the opportunity to surrender your force to the enemy."

"That's a lie."

The major paused in his journey around the cement-walled office. "The truth," he said, "doesn't have to be shouted. Liars shout."

"It's a lie," Babryshkin repeated, a new tone of resignation in his voice. He shook his head, and it felt as though he were turning a great, miserable weight on his shoulders. "It's . . . a lie. We fought. We kept on fighting. We never stopped fighting."

"You fought just enough to make a good pretense. Then you willfully exposed your subordinates to a chemical attack in a preplanned strike zone where you had gathered as many innocent civilians as possible."

Babryshkin closed his eyes. "That's madness," he said, almost whispering, unable to believe how this man in a clean uniform, who obviously had been nowhere near the direct-fire war, could so twist the truth.

"The only madness," the KGB officer said, "is to lie to the People."

Shots sounded from outside. The shots came intermittently, and they were always exclusively from Soviet weapons. Babryshkin realized what was happening. But he could not believe, even now, that it might happen to him.

"So," the KGB major said after a deep breath. "I want you to tell me when you first established clandestine contacts with the cadre of traitors in your garrison . . ."

Babryshkin's mind searched through the scenes of the past weeks. A newsreel, eccentrically edited, played at a desperate speed. The first night the indigenous garrison stationed side by side with his own had almost overrun the barracks and motor parks of Babryshkin's unit. Men fought in the dark with pocket knives and their fists against rifles. All of the uniforms were the same in the dark. The fires spread. Then came the armored drive into the heart of the city to try to rescue the local headquarters staff, only to find them butchered. The repeated attempts to organize a defense were always too late. The enemy was forever on your flank or behind you. He remembered the terrible enemy gunships, and the wounded lost in the swirling confusion, the murdered civilians whose numbers would never be figured exactly now. He recalled the sudden death of the last refugees, and the bone-thin woman with her louse-ridden offspring in his tank. Valor, incompetence, and death. Fear and bad decisions. Desperation. It was all there. Everything except treason.

He had finally brought his shrunken unit into the hastily established Soviet lines south of Petropavlovsk, pulling in under the last daylight, radioing frantically so his battered vehicles would not be targeted by mistake. And then they were behind friendly lines, marching to the rear to rearm, perhaps to be reorganized, still willing to turn back and fight when needed. But the column had been halted at a KGB control point several kilometers to the rear of the network of defensive positions. Who was the commander? Where was the political officer? Where was the staff? Before Babryshkin could make any sense out of the situation, he and his officers had been gathered together and disarmed, while his vehicles continued to the rear under the supervision of KGB officers who did not even know how to give the correct commands.

No sooner had the vehicles departed with great plumes of dust than the assembled officers were bound, blindfolded, and gagged. Several officers, including Babryshkin, protested angrily, until a KGB lieutenant colonel drew his pistol and shot one recalcitrant captain through the head. The action so shocked the men, who had believed that they had finally reached some brief, relative safety, that they behaved like sheep for the rest of the journey to the interrogation center. Made to jump off the backs of trucks still blindfolded and with their wrists bound together, officers who had survived twelve or fifteen hundred kilometers of combat broke arms and legs. Their blindfolds were finally removed to achieve a calculated effect: they were marched into the courtyard of a rural school complex and the first sight that met them was a disordered mound of corpses—all Soviet officers—that had grown up against a wall. Those who had broken limbs in exiting the trucks were forced to drag themselves, unaided, past the spectacle.

Everyone understood its implication.

Babryshkin had heard that one of the rules of interrogation was to keep everyone separated. But there were not enough rooms in the building. They were herded en masse into a stinking classroom, already crowded with earlier arrivals. The windows had been hastily boarded shut, and no provision, not even a bucket, had been made for the waste of frightened men.

At times, the officers were not even kept separate during their interrogations. Babryshkin's first taste of the questioning began when he was thrust into a room where his political officer was already seated. The political officer's eyes were unbalanced, and he recoiled from the sight of Babryshkin as if from the devil himself.

"It was him," the political officer cried. "It was all his doing. I told him to obey the order. I *told* him. And he refused. I told him and he refused. It was his fault. He even carried a woman on his tank for his personal pleasure."

"And why didn't you take command yourself?" the interrogator asked quietly.

"I couldn't," the political officer answered, terrified. "They were all with him. I tried to do my duty. But they were all in it together."

"He's a liar," Babryshkin said quickly, breaking his resolve not to speak out until he better understood what was happening. "I take full responsibility for the actions of my officers. The actions of my unit were the results of my decisions and mine alone."

The interrogator struck him across the face with a calloused hand that wore a big ring. "No one asked you anything. Prisoners are only to speak when they are asked a question."

"They were all in it together," the political officer repeated.

But the interrogator's focus had shifted. "So . . . a commander who even carries a woman with him for his pleasure. It must be a fine war."

"That's nonsense," Babryshkin stated coldly. "The woman was a refugee. With a baby and a little boy. She was at the end of her strength. She would have died."

The interrogator raised an eyebrow, folding his arms. "And you decided to rescue her out of the goodness of your heart? But why this woman, out of so many? What was special about her? Was she an agent too? Or was she merely pretty?"

Babryshkin thought of the dreadfully emaciated woman, remembering her screams when she emerged to see the devastation of the chemical attack. Well, at least she was safe now, deposited at a refugee collection point with her starving infant and the louse-ridden, broken-armed boy. And, as he thought of her, he found that her ravaged face grew indistinct, becoming Valya's fine, clear, lovely features. Valya. He wondered if he would ever see her again. And, for a moment, she had more reality for him than any of the surrounding madness.

"No," Babryshkin said flatly. "She wasn't pretty."

"Then she was an agent? A contact you were to meet and evacuate?"

Babryshkin laughed out loud at the folly of such a thought.

The KGB officer did not need any underlings to do his dirty work for him. He landed a square blow on Babryshkin's mouth that knocked in his front teeth. Unlike in films, where men fought forever without really harming one another, this man's fists did real damage each time they landed. First on the mouth, then on the side of the head, on the ear, beside an eye. In a flash of confusion, the chair toppled over, and Babryshkin found himself lying sideways on the floor. The major kicked him in the mouth. Then in the stomach. It was at that point that Babryshkin realized that he was, indeed, going to die, and he resolved at least to die as well as possible.

Through blood-clouded eyes he looked up at the cringing political officer. And he smiled slightly through his broken lips, almost pitying the weaker man in the knowledge that they would soon be together on the growing heap out in the courtyard, that nothing would save either one of them. The system had gone mad. It had begun eating itself like a demented animal.

Another kick left Babryshkin unconscious for an indefinite period, and when he awoke, he was alone with his interrogator. They were all wrong, Babryshkin decided. There *is* a God. And this is what he looks like.

Babryshkin had been set upright on his chair, and his hands had been rebound behind its straight back so that he could not slump and fall. The questions began again, insane, twisted questions, beginning with the truth and butchering it beyond all logic, making out of it a sinister new calculus that was so perverse it was almost irresistible.

When did you first think of betraying the Soviet Union? Who were your earliest coconspirators? What did you hope to accomplish? Did you act out of ideology or for material gain? How long have you been plotting? With how many foreigners did you have contact? What are your current orders?

There was never any attempt to establish guilt or innocence. Guilt was assumed. Babryshkin had heard stories about such things happening back in the old days, in the darkest years of the twentieth century. But he had never expected to encounter such a thing in his own lifetime.

He sought to tell his tale honestly, in an unadorned, believable manner. He tried to clarify the simple logic of his actions, to explain to this starched creature from the rear area what combat was like, how it forced men to act. But his words only met with more blows. Sometimes the KGB major would hear him out before attacking him. At other times he would squeeze his swollen, ring-speckled fingers into a fist and bring it down hard at the first words out of Babryshkin's mouth.

Babryshkin tried to maintain his focus. He set himself the goal of ensuring that no blame passed to any of his subordinates, of establishing that each action had been the result of his personal decision. But it became harder and harder to form the words. And the intermittent shooting outside tripped his thoughts. As the questions were repeated to him again and again, he found it ever more difficult to focus. And the interrogator exaggerated the smallest grammatical inconsistencies in his story.

When the beating was at its worst, he tried to close his mind to it, to think only of the thing he loved the most in the world. He had long thought that it was his military service, but he knew now, with utter mental clarity, that it was Valya. Not even his mother, who had died in the plague years, had meant so much to him. Dying was terribly frightening. And yet . . . he knew it was really nothing. There had been so much death. But it seemed needlessly cruel, unbearable, that he would die without ever seeing his wife again.

He was grateful that the questions posed to him were all of a military nature. The KGB major never once asked about his family or about his nonmilitary friends. Babryshkin guessed that those questions were for more leisurely peacetime interrogations. Now there was only the war. And he was glad. It would be all right to die. He would have preferred to die in combat, being of some use. But the manner of dying had come to seem increasingly a matter of accident. Perhaps, really, one death was as good as another. As long as Valya wasn't dragged into it, as long as nothing hurt her. He even knew—and remembered without malice—that she had been unfaithful to him once. Perhaps she was being unfaithful to him now. But it did not matter. She was such a special girl. And because he believed that she had been unfaithful that time out of spite, only to hurt him, it had not hurt so much. It was not as if she had really loved another. And he knew he had broken many promises, that he had failed her again and again. It was a country, an age, of broken promises. And he suspected that Valya was far, far more helpless than she realized.

He made a deal with God. Not with the brief, small god whose fist hammered him over and over again, but with the other God who might be out there after all, who *should* be out there. He would die willingly, so long as Valya was not harmed. So long as he became only another corpse and the affair ended at that. He thought of Valya: the smell of sex and lilacs, a woman always ready with a little lie, imagining herself to be so strong, and he filled with pity for her. He could not leave her much else. If only he could leave her safe from all of this.

He could not keep his thoughts under control any longer. Under the torrent of blows, Valya became the refugee woman, gaunt with beginning death. Everyone was dying. It was a dying world. Chaos. A woman shrieked across the death-covered steppes. All who were not dead were dying. To the music of a scream.

Babryshkin came to again. He raised his head, feeling as though his skull had grown huge and he were a small creature within it. Only one eye would open now. But he noticed that other men had joined his interrogator in the room.

Uniforms. Weapons. His soldiers. They had come to rescue him. He would see Valya again after all. And they would walk across the river and up into the Lenin Hills, through the university gardens. And gray, sad Moscow would look beautiful in the sunlight. *Valya.* She was very close to him now.

He saw his interrogator bend over the desk, then right himself and hand a piece of paper to one of the soldiers.

"Enemy of the People," the officer said. "To be shot."

Ryder lay guarding one of the woman's small breasts with his right hand. His head reached high up on the pillow so that the tumult of her hair would not tease his nose and mouth. He did not bother to close his eyes. This darkness was not meant for sleeping, and he held the stranger firmly, bedeviled by the warmth and the buttery smell of her, by the musk they had spilled on the bedding, by her remarkable fragility. She filled his palm, then fell away with the rhythm of her breathing. He tried to concentrate, to burn the reality of her flesh into his mind so that he might keep her with him after she had gone. Yet, his mind strayed. He could not begin to tell why the presence of this foreign woman in his bed should conjure up so many memories.

Consciously considered, the immediacy of their two bodies seemed to be everything of importance. But he lay in the mild damp of their bed remembering prairies and the sparse, anxious pleasures of being young in a small town long bypassed by the interstate. Laughing girls gathered in a convenience store parking lot, and the bitter combat of high school sports, briefly glorifying towns that had lost their way in every other sphere of endeavor. Clumsy, greedy kisses, starving kisses that ground on until suddenly, unreasonably, a nervous girl risked love. The acquired words would never do. No place on earth was lonelier or vaster than Nebraska on an October night.

Sometimes the girls pretended they did not know what you were doing, while others knew it all startlingly well. And the only things that ever changed were the new television shows or the shape of a new model car, and they didn't really change at all. Ryder could not understand why a Russian woman in a dowdy hotel room, so far from his home, should have the power to alert his nostrils to the dust of gone Saturday nights, or to fill his open eyes with the common failures of his kind.

He remembered a girl who told him in a voice all bravery and truth that she would, that she could love only him forever. She, too, lay beside him now, hardly an arm's length away, as he recalled the whiteness of her legs in a car parked late, far from town, far from the world. Only a moment before, he had clumsily worked himself into her body as she clutched and cried, afraid to help him, afraid not to let him, because she loved him and only him and only ever him, and her naked legs were so white under the luminous cloud-light, and her eyes were wet and dark, staring away, as she rested her head on the flat of the car seat. Children, he thought, smiling at the temperate agony of such a loss, only children. And he remembered that prairie voice: "Only you . . . only you . . ." He recalled dark hair and the cold wind off the plains. The wind tried to batter its way inside the car, to punish them. He recalled her sharp recoil as her child's hand accidentally touched him. He remembered her perfectly, acutely. Her good-family bravery and quiet. Then her worry over telltale marks on her dress, or in her eyes. But he could not recall her name.

The slender, different woman with him now moaned one foreign word in her sleep and stirred slightly. Calling him back to the vividness of their much more recent and far less innocent collision. No, he thought, that's too hard a judgment. Her very attempts at sophistication made her seem laughably innocent. In his room, in the wake of the first kisses, the coming to terms without words, she had done a pathetically inept striptease, making faces from a badly done film, closing her eyes in a cartoon of abandon, all the while taking obvious care not to damage any article of her clothing. In the poor light, she seemed more desperate than brazen, thin and cold in her briefs. He had taken her into his arms as much to end the embarrassment as to express his desire.

But, held against him, she came to life. In the physical acts that rampaged before sex itself, she was shameless, almost fierce. Where he might have gone slowly, gently, she hurried, despising his easiness. She seemed anxious to get through her repertoire of acquired knacks, almost masculine in her unspoken conviction that nothing short of sexual finality really mattered. Making love, she had little sense of him, as though he were a device for her to use. She bit hard and dug her strong, thin fingers into the small of his back until it hurt him so badly he had to knock her hands away. She moved herself quickly, unwilling to listen to his rhythms. It was not a challenge, as it might have been with an American girl. Rather, it seemed like a colossal hunger, driven by the fear that she might receive too little. She was a hard, bad lover. There was no luxury in pressing against her. Just the hardness of bone bruising on bone, the brief, deceptive glory and collapse. Warm, spent breathing, a shifting of hips that made them separate again. Then the feel of holding her back and rump against him, a woman so undernourished her body might have been a child's.

A sudden eruption of noise down the hall startled him. An American voice cursed harshly, and a sharp woman's voice stabbed back in a foreign language. Gently, Ryder smoothed his hand away from the woman's breast and laid it over her ear.

She was a hard, bad lover. And, sobered, he sensed that she wanted things from him that had nothing to do with his individuality. But it did not matter. In this wilderness of sheets, he was her protector. Charged to shield her from all pain.

The cursing faded off down the hall, and Ryder pitied those who had to fight in such a way. He felt peaceful, and even the bizarre scenes from the computer interrogation center had softened. He did not think of the war. The war would return soon enough. For these few hours, he simply wanted to hold this stranger and let these scraps of companionship cover him.

The woman rustled against him, realigning her bottom. His body responded and he trailed his hand down over her hair to the hard collarbones, pausing briefly at the humble softness of her breasts, then crossing the prairie of her stomach until his fingers caught at damp tangles. He slid a finger into the wetness left over from their earlier lovemaking, and the woman began to turn toward him, locking his hand in place with the swell of her thighs. In the pale darkness, he could see that her eyes were wide open. She reached her mouth up for a kiss, stale from cigarettes and sleep. She laughed slightly, and he did not know why. Then she reached for him as she freed his captive hand.

Valya had long lain awake, pretending to be asleep, trying to take the measure of this latest man to whom she had given herself. She was anxious for him to make love to her again, not at all for the act itself, but for the reassurance that she really did attract him, that there was, after all, a chance that she might have her way.

She was certain that he did not understand her. He seemed so sure of himself, taking everything for granted. He smiled too much, and everything about him seemed too young, despite their like ages. Making love, he began with a gentleness she found disconcerting. She had come to expect far brusquer treatment from her lovers. Trying to move him, she soon got lost in the act itself, and let him follow as he chose. But she worried when she could not make him finish. He seemed to want to linger over the act, making it last as long as possible, instead of simply letting go. It was a very different business, and she was not certain she would be able to get used to it. There seemed to be so little real feeling, so little passion or abandon to the American.

The worst part, however, was not his physical indifference to her efforts. Far more annoying was the sense that she had not reached him on a personal level. She scolded herself bitterly: What can you expect when you jump into bed with a foreigner like some tramp? She felt her anger growing against this man who seemed so annoyingly content to hold her in his arms. She doubted that he had ever felt any kind of physical deprivation. And whom was she trying to fool? American women were all whores, and he could have any he wanted. In fine clothes. Rich women. Perhaps, she thought savagely, she should count herself lucky that he had deigned to take her into his bed. She doubted that he had ever known real loneliness, the kind that was bigger than any single cause that could be put into words, the kind that made you into such a fool. The Americans were spoiled and insensitive, she decided. Every last one of them.

Suddenly, a vicious-sounding man's voice began to shout in another room. Or perhaps it was in the hallway, she could not tell for certain. But the sound frightened her. Then a woman's voice replied in Russian. Demanding money. Dollars. The unmistakable evidence of the company into which she had fallen chilled Valya.

Inexplicably, the American laid his hand over her ear. Why wouldn't he want her to hear what was going on? Perhaps, she thought, because the bastard didn't want her to demand money from him.

She wanted to curl up like a child. Alone. She did not know whether she was truly ashamed or merely disappointed by the situation in which she found herself. But she knew she was unhappy.

She nudged herself at the American, impatient for him either to make love to her or to go to sleep. If he went to sleep, she could eat the cookies he had left in an opened pack on the night table. If nothing else, she told herself, she should at least have a belly full of cookies for her night's work.

The American began to graze his hand down over the front of her body. He moved so that she could feel exactly what he wanted. Then she felt him working a finger inside of her.

All right then, she thought.

She turned to face the American, to open herself to him. She touched him, feeling the leftover slickness. At least he found her desirable. Worth a second time. She had been afraid that he thought she was too thin, that he had already lost interest in her.

Perhaps there was hope. Perhaps something good would finally happen. Perhaps . . .

Unprovoked, she suddenly thought of Yuri. Her husband. And she laughed at her utter inability to ever really enjoy anything without spoiling it for herself. The American pushed a second finger into her, and she canted a leg to accept him. She groaned, keying up to him now.

Well, she hoped Yuri was all right, anyway. With his beloved soldiers. They could keep him. She did not want to see him hurt. She simply did not want to see him at all.

She tasted the American, feeling the roughness of his beard stubble, letting her body react on its own. But she could not get her husband out of her mind. She began to grow angry, furious, flailing her hips against the American. *Why* did it all have to be such a mess?

You don't understand, she cried out in her native language, unsure now whether she was addressing the husband who had deserted her or this stranger who was taking her body away. *You don't understand, you just don't understand. . . .*

PART III

The Trial

14

November 2020
night 2–3

DOWN THE HILL FROM THE SUBURBAN HOME WHERE
George Taylor passed his childhood lay an orchard. Lost
between some dead farmer's dreams and a developer's
vision, the untended trees had gone wild. When you
walked down from the careful plots of television-
neighborhood houses, through the no-man's-land of
cleared fields yet unbuilt, the paved road turned to gravel,
then to red dirt. The last sewerage connection guarded the
edge of civilization like an undersized cement and steel
pillbox. Birds rose at your footsteps, and, in the summer,
dull snakes sunned themselves in the dust. The tangled
orchard encompassed a ravine that was perfect for rock
fights (no rocks above a certain generally acknowledged
size, and no aiming above the waist).

This little wilderness was unkempt, as are the very young
and the very old. The trees were very old, and the denimed
warriors who ran howling between them were very young.
George Taylor was the youngest of the tribe, and one of
the wildest, driven by his fear that his fears might be discovered by his older companions. Looking back with the
genius of an adult, he could only shake his head at the
terrified recklessness he had tried to pass off as a bravery
he had never, ever felt.

When George Taylor was very young, the oldest member of the band with whom he explored the world was a strong, loud boy named Charlie Winters. One of Taylor's first clear memories was of being together with other males drafted by Charlie for a special expedition down to the orchard. Armed with sticks, the file of boys passed out of the brightness of the morning into the golden-green twilight of the grove. Charlie went first, searching through the brambles and tramped paths for the way he had gone the afternoon before. Amid the gnarled branches with their spotted, unworthy fruit, Charlie had discovered a perfect apple. But there were problems: the treasure dangled from a forbiddingly high branch and, still worse, no climber could retrieve it, since it grew very close to the gray pulp of a wasps' nest.

Each of the boys came from homes where select apples lay disregarded in decorative baskets. Candy was by far the preferred sustenance of the tribe. But the apple in the orchard was a jewel, not least because Charlie claimed it to be such. The chief had spoken, and the wild fruit took on something of the mystery of lost worlds, dangling in the wild grove where there was just enough sense of danger to thrill a boy's heart.

Charlie had devised a plan. At his command, they would all throw rocks at once, knocking the apple off the branch. It was a good combat plan, brutal and direct, save for a single hitch: one boy would need to position himself immediately beneath the branch, in order to catch the fruit and make off with it before the surprised wasps could strike.

The leader looked around for volunteers.

Not one of the bold band stepped forward.

"Come on," Charlie said. "It'll be easy. We can do it."

All eyes rose to the high branch and its treasure. The wasps' nest swelled with a terrible splendor, and the lazy local activity of its guardians began to seem far more menacing than any of the boys had previously realized.

"Georgie," Charlie said. "You're the smallest. The wasps'll have more trouble spotting you. And you can run fast."

The last claim was a lie. He always came in last in the sudden races with the older, longer-legged boys.

Taylor did not answer. He simply looked up at the hideous sack of the wasps' nest. Afraid.

"Ain't afraid, are you?" Charlie demanded.

"No," Taylor replied. He wanted to run away. To go home and immerse himself in some other game. But he feared being called a baby. Or a puss.

"Well, prove it. *I* think you're chicken."

"Yeah," a third voice joined in, "Georgie Taylor's a chicken." The attack came from a gray, indefinite boy whose name Taylor would forget over the years.

"I'm *not* chicken," Taylor said. "*You're* more chicken than I am." And he forged his way down through the briars and thirsty brush.

He positioned himself as directly below the apple as he could, staring up to keep his bearings. It was very hard. The sun dazzled down through the leaves, blackening the boughs and making him faintly dizzy.

"You ready?" Charlie called.

"I guess so," Taylor said. But he was not ready. He would never be ready. He was indescribably afraid.

"Get ready," Charlie commanded. "Everybody, on three."

The boys clutched their rocks. Taylor shifted nervously, trying to see the apple clearly up in the tangle of brilliance and blackness.

"One . . . two . . . *three.*"

Everything happened with unmanageable speed. Shouts, and the whistle of projectiles. A blurred disturbance in the world above his head. Cries of alarm as far too much came falling: a spent stone clipped his shoulder and the apple fell just beyond his grasp. Beside it, the cardboard waste of the wasps' nest landed with a thud.

He reached for the apple. But it was no good. The wasps were already at him. He ran. The world exploded with disorder. He swung his arms, howling at the living fires on his skin. A wasp flew at his mouth.

Everyone else was gone. He ran through the wilderness alone, scrambling through a world of relentless terror that would not stop hurting him. He raced through thorns and sumac, batting his paws at the wasps, at the air. Crying, screaming, he clawed his way up the dirt bank of the ravine and burst from the poisonous gloom, imagining that the wasps would have to quit now that he had escaped their domain and regained the freedom of the clear blue day.

But the remarkable pains would not stop. The creatures droned, plunged, pelted him. Far ahead, nearly back to the world of paved streets and perfect houses, he saw his comrades in full retreat.

Charlie slowed briefly to yell, "Come on, Georgie."

The older boy was laughing.

Seated in the cockpit of his war machine, leading his grown-up warriors into battle, Taylor found himself wondering to what extent he was still the boy standing under a wasps' nest, while other, distant figures threw the stones.

Things had already begun to go wrong. The United States Air Force had been scheduled to fly a strategic jamming mission along the old prerebellion Soviet-Iranian border, wiping out enemy communications over tens of thousands of square kilometers. But the ultrasophisticated, savagely expensive WHITE LIGHT aircraft remained hangar-bound, grounded by severe weather at their home base in Montana. Taylor's regiment and the electronic warfare support elements from the Tenth Cavalry would be able to isolate the operational battlefield with the jamming gear available in-theater, but the enemy would retain his strategic and high-end operational communications capability. An important, if not absolutely vital, part of the surprise blow would not be delivered.

Locally, a lieutenant in the Third Squadron had disobeyed the order to lift off with his automatic systems in control. Hotdogging for his crew, he had attempted a manual lift-off in the darkness and had flown his M-100 into mercifully inert power lines. Thanks to the safety features built into the M-100, the lieutenant and his entire crew had survived the crash with only some heavy bruising, some missing teeth, and one broken arm. But the regiment had been robbed of another precious system before the battle had even begun. Controlling his temper over the incident, unwilling to exchange the image of control for the brief pleasure of public anger, Taylor nonetheless promised himself that the lieutenant would soon have the opportunity to seek a new line of work, if he and his regimental commander both survived the war.

Things had already begun to go wrong. But they were not yet sufficiently fouled-up to rattle Taylor. One of the very few truths that his long years of service had taught him was that military operations were simply fucked-up by their very nature. The selective maps and decisive arrows that made everything appear so obvious and easy in the history books and manuals were invariably instances of radical cosmetic surgery on the truth. Behind those implacable graphics lay scenes of indescribable confusion, misunderstanding, accidents (both terrible and felicitous), and the jumbled capabilities, failures, fears, and valor of countless individuals. Warfare was chaos, and the primary mission of the commander was to impose at least marginally more order on that chaos than did his opponent. The reason that military discipline would always be necessary was not simply to ensure that the majority of men in uniform would fight when ordered—that was only a small part of it. Discipline was necessary because every military establishment existed constantly on the edge of disaster, from the humbler inevitabilities of crushed fingers in the peacetime motor pool to the grand disasters of war.

Taylor would not receive the promised support of his nation's air force, and he had lost one of his war machines to the antics of a uniformed child. But his regiment was largely in the air—forty-six M-100s had lifted off, thanks to the last-minute achievements of Manny Martinez and the regimental and squadron motor officers. The electronic warfare birds from the Tenth Cav were on station. And there was still no sign that the enemy had discovered the American presence. In less than ten minutes, the First Squadron would cross its line of departure, followed quickly by the Second Squadron, then by the Third. So far, the untried war machines seemed to be working just fine, and their electronic suites enriched and thickened the darkness through which they would pass to strike their enemies. No recall order had arrived from the nervous men in Washington, and soon the Seventh United States

Regiment of Cavalry would have slipped its last tether. Somewhere behind a welter of new enemies, the old enemy waited.

Overall, Colonel George Taylor considered himself a very lucky man.

"Take the wheel, Flapper," Taylor told his copilot, Chief Warrant Officer Five Elvis "Flapper" Krebs. Since Zaire, Taylor had always chosen his personal crew from the oldest, toughest, and sourest men available. "I'm going back to the operations center."

"Got it," Krebs said in an offhanded southern voice that implied that Taylor's presence was superfluous. Like Taylor, Krebs had served long enough to remember the old days when the U.S. Army still held Cobra gunships in its inventory. The two men had grown up on the Apache, but they could remember the look of the Cobra's deadly panatela fuselage in flight. They had seen enormous changes in the technology of war, and the coming hours would either inaugurate yet another new stage, or mortally embarrass their nation.

"Send you up a cup of coffee, Chief?" Taylor offered as he finished unstrapping himself from his padded seat in the center of a display of electronic riches.

"Naw," Krebs said. "I'm about as wired as I need to be." The studied casualness of the man's tone always brought Taylor to the edge of laughter. Krebs was overdue for retirement—he had been extended to assist in the formation of the Army's first regiment of M-100s, having served for years in the developmental process and as a test pilot. To Taylor, he was one of the last of a vanishing breed, the crusty, mean-mouthed, generous-spirited old warrants who made the Army fly. Their shared experiences laid down a bridge between Taylor and Krebs that few other men in the regiment would dare attempt to cross. Bad times that added up to a life well-spent.

As a young warrant, Krebs had seen his first combat in Panama, in December of eighty-nine. There was a story that he had overflown the barracks of a holdout Panamanian Defense Force unit, dropping homemade leaflets that read: "Merry Fucking Christmas." Not long afterward, the Army had sent him to Saudi Arabia during the great deployment of 1990. Old Flapper had been through it all.

Taylor squeezed his shoulders through the short passageway that led back into the command and control center. Where the standard M-100s had a compartment for a light squad of dragoons equipped for dismounted fighting, the command-variant ships had been outfitted with a chamber crammed with the latest miniaturized communications and information-processing systems. The compartment was environmentally controlled and stabilized. Entering it, you were treated to a spectacle of colored lights from nine monitor screens of various sizes displaying everything from real-time images of the battlefield relayed from space reconnaissance systems to graphic depictions, in glowing colors, of the war in the electromagnetic spectrum. It always reminded Taylor of a magic cave where the invisible world became palpable. You could *see* the ferocious demons that hid in the air, invisible to the naked eye, or you could call up distant lands of wonder. Even the first-level secrets of life and death became available here, in the displays of enemy systems targeted, of friendly systems lost, of available ammunition and deadly energy sources. The commander, with his skeletal staff, could use radar imagery to erase darkness, clouds, or fog, allowing him a god's-eye view that penetrated the witch's sabbath of the battlefield. The commander could monitor the sectors in which his subordinates fought with greater ease than a civilian could watch television. Changes in angle, in levels of magnification, in enhanced color contrasts, and the visual evocation of waves of energy, it was all there lurking under a button or a switch. The voice of God had its source here too. Alternative-use laser systems allowed instantaneous encrypted communications with similarly equipped stations anywhere in the world, and huge volumes of data could be entered into or transmitted from the M-100's standard on-board computers in the middle of combat.

It was a marvelous machine. The on-board and external integrated target-acquisition systems were so capable and versatile that, during training flights, playful crews used them to track small game on the prairie from a distance of dozens of kilometers. The miniaturized "brains" were so powerful and so crammed with both military and general knowledge that they could be ordered to fuse data from all available reconnaissance systems in order to search for any parameter of target—such as the pinpoint location of each blue 2015 Ford on the highways of North America in which two adult occupants were riding and the fuel tanks were less than half full. The microsecond sort capabilities were so powerful that none of the experts in the regiment had been able to enter a problem which could stump the system. You could charge the target-acquisition system to locate distant plantations of yellow roses—or every enemy combat vehicle with a bent right front fender. The system was so swift that human beings simply could not handle the target volume without extensive automated support, and the M-100 was designed to fight on full automatic, relying on its human masters for key decisions, for overall guidance, for setting or revising priorities, and for defining operational parameters. Every on-board system could be employed under manual control, if necessary, but such a reduction in the system's overall capabilities would only be accepted, according to the draft doctrine, in the most exceptional circumstances. Technically, this most potent air-land warfare machine ever built had the capability to carry on the fight indefinitely even after its human crew had perished. Taylor once overheard a young pilot joke that the M-100 made every pilot a general. What the pilot had meant was that the M-100 let every man who sat at its controls play God without getting his hands dirty.

Taylor was willing to admit that he himself could not fully imagine all the implications this untried system might have for the battlefield. But he was certain of one thing: despite the technological wonders under the modern warrior's hand, that hand would manage to grow very dirty indeed.

Merry Meredith had just finished praying when Taylor squeezed into the operations center. Neither the assistant S-3 captain nor the two NCOs who shared the crowded chamber with Meredith had realized that the intelligence officer was praying, since Meredith did not join his hands together or kneel or close his eyes. Meredith's prayers were simply moments of silence aimed in the general direction of God, along with a few unspoken pleas. Just let me get through this. Let me see Maureen again. Let me hold her. Let me get through this. Please. And that was it.

Meredith was not a religious man. But, following repeated experiences in Los Angeles and Mexico, he had come to accept this particular form of cowardice in himself. In times of peace, he would never have dreamed of wasting a Sunday morning in church. But, on the edge of battle, God invariably loomed large.

"What's up, Merry?" Taylor asked, holding on to an overhead brace with one hand. His shoulder holster stood away from his uniform, and the reddish light from the control banks and monitors made the colonel's scarred face appear to be on fire.

"We're looking good, sir," Meredith said. "The bad guys are still just sitting there, fat, dumb, and happy." He tapped at a button. "Look at this. It's the target array at Objective Ruby. If the M-100s just work at fifty percent of capacity . . ."

"Still no indication that the enemy have picked us up?" Taylor asked.

Meredith understood the wonder in Taylor's voice. It was hard to believe that the regiment had made it this far. From Kansas to the edge of hell. Their luck only needed to hold a little longer now.

"Not a sign, sir. No increase in comms. No enhanced air defense readiness. No interceptors up. No ground force dispersal. It's almost too good to be true."

Taylor wiped his hand across his jaw, his lips. "I'm concerned about Manny. The Japs *must*'ve picked us up coming out of the industrial park. He needs to get his ass out of there."

Meredith smiled. "Manny's a big boy. He'll be out of there on schedule. Anyway, there isn't even the slightest indication that the enemy has detected anything. We're in better shape than I could've hoped, sir."

As he spoke to reassure his mentor, Meredith recalled the unsettling exchange he had undergone just a few hours before. There had been a lull in the communications traffic on one of the top-secret multiuse feeds, and a friend of his back in Washington had taken advantage of it to call him to the receiver.

"Merry, good buddy," his friend had said in a noticeably hushed voice, as though some third party might disapprove, "listen, you've got to watch your six out there."

"What are you talking about?" Meredith asked, unsure whether his friend was simply telling him to take care of himself personally or trying to communicate something larger.

"Just keep your eyes open. There's something funny going on. The puzzle's still missing some pieces."

"What kind of pieces? Intel?"

"I don't know exactly. You know how it is. You just get wind of things. The big boys over here have a secret. We've got this new priority intelligence requirement. It came out of nowhere. And suddenly it's number one on the charts. Something about a *Scrambler.*"

Meredith thought for a moment. "Doesn't mean shit to me. What's a Scrambler?"

"Maybe some kind of crypto stuff. I don't know. *They* don't know. That's the whole point. The boys two levels above me are jumping through their asses trying to figure it out."

"Nothing else?" Merry asked. "No context?" He did not much care for the appearance of sudden mysteries when the bullets were about to start flying.

"Listen, Merry. I got to go. I'm not supposed to be using this feed. You take care. Out."

And the voice was gone.

Now Meredith looked across the magic firelight of the electronics to where Taylor stood. He wondered if he should bother the old man with something so nebulous. Impulsively, he decided against sharing the scrap of information. It was insufficient to really mean anything to the old man. And Taylor certainly did not need any unnecessary worries at this point. Meredith mentally cataloged the scrambler business with his file of other unresolved intelligence concerns.

But he felt uneasy. Taylor was staring at him, and the old man's eyes always gave Meredith the uncanny feeling that Taylor could see right into him. He had felt that way ever since the night in Los Angeles when he had almost given up. Now Taylor's gaze made him feel uncomfortable, somehow inadequate.

Meredith tapped a button on his console, moving onto safer ground. A nearby monitor filled with multicolored lines: a hallucinatory spiderweb.

"Have a look at this, sir," he said to Taylor. "That's their command communications infrastructure in our area of operations. Just wait until the aero-jammers from the Tenth Cav hit them. They won't even be able to call out for a pizza."

Taylor smiled, showing a flash of teeth in his devil's face. To a stranger, the scarred mask would have appeared menacing, but Meredith could tell that Taylor was in good spirits. Confident. Ready. Meredith had never known any rational man to be as calm on the verge of contact as Taylor. The cold man turned briefly to the pair of NCOs who staffed the support consoles, exchanging mandatory pleasantries and bullshitting about the bad coffee, bolstering them so they would not think too much of death. Then he turned to Captain Parker, the assistant S-3, who was standing in for Heifetz while the S-3 rode herd on the First Squadron. Captain Parker was fairly new to the regiment, and very new to Taylor.

"How do we look on the ops side?" Taylor asked.

The captain stood up formally. "On time and on-line, sir."

"Sit down, sit down," Taylor said, slightly embarrassed by the display. "First Squadron ready to cross its line of departure?"

No sooner had Taylor spoken than the regimental command net came to life:

"This is Whisky five-five. Sweetheart. I say again: Sweetheart. Over."

That was it. First Squadron was in Indian country.

The United States was at war.

Taylor slipped on a headset. "This is Sierra five-five. Lima Charlie your transmission, Whisky. Over."

"This is Whisky. Red-one, in route to Emerald. 'Garry Owen.' Over."

317

The ordeal had begun. Meredith knew that they all shared the same worries: would the deception gear work? Would they make it all the way to the first series of objectives without being detected? Without the need to fight an unwanted engagement?

Surprise was everything.

"This is Sierra," Taylor said. "Turning on the noise. Good luck. Out." He turned to Meredith. "Tell the Tenth Cav to turn on the jamming."

Meredith punched his way down a row of buttons, then began to speak into his headset in a measured voice. A part of him was still listening to Taylor, however, watching the old man from the corners of his eyes. Whenever Taylor was physically present, Meredith felt invincible. The old man had the magic, the nameless something that you could never learn from leadership manuals alone.

The command net came to life again.

"This is Bravo five-five. Sweetheart now. Over."

The old man smiled his we-got-these-suckers smile. "This is Sierra five-five—"

"Hotel nine Lima seven-four," Meredith said into his headset, calling the commander of the Tenth Cavalry's electronic skirmish line. "This is Charlie six Sierra two-zero—"

"Roger last transmission," Taylor told his mike.

"—Waterfall. I say again, Waterfall," Meredith enunciated clearly, calmly, wanting to shout. "Acknowledge, over."

A third net came to life, answered by one of the NCOs.

"—White one to Diamond—"

"—Roger, Sierra. Waterfall now."

"This is Tango five-five. Sweetheart. Sweetheart. Over."

"Roger, Tango. Break. Bravo, report—"

Meredith felt both ferociously excited and wonderfully relaxed. Listening to the babble of the multiple sets, watching the monitors flash and the counters running numerics, he was at home. In the brilliant chaos of a tactical headquarters at war.

"Colonel Taylor, sir?" Meredith said in the first communications lull. "Got a second to look at this?"

Taylor bent down toward the visual display. Countless red and yellow points of light had been superimposed on a map of Soviet Central Asia.

"Tenth Cav's already kicking ass," Meredith said. "The red dots indicate communications centers the heavy jammers have already leeched and physically destroyed. If those stations want to talk, they're going to have to wait until morning and send smoke signals." Meredith made a gesture toward the screen. "The yellow dots are the well-shielded comms nodes or those at our range margins. We can't actually destroy those, but they won't be able to communicate as long as Tenth Cav stays in the air."

"Good," Taylor said coldly. "Good. Let those bastards feel what it's like to be on the receiving end."

In a manner for which he could not account, Meredith suddenly saw the display through Taylor's eyes. And he knew that the old man was looking beyond the Iranian or Arab or rebel soldiers who suddenly found themselves powerless to share their knowledge with one another, looking behind them to the Japanese. Out there. Somewhere.

Taylor glanced at a screen mounted on the upper rack. It displayed the progress of the regiment's individual squadrons. Coursing down their axes of advance toward their initial objectives. Holding their fire. Moving with good discipline. A smaller symbol trailing Second Squadron showed the position of the command M-100 in which they were working and its two escort ships, which also functioned as the commander's hip pocket reserve.

The command net spoke again, demanding Taylor's attention. "This is Whisky five-five. Over."

"Sierra five-five. Go."

"This is Whisky. You wouldn't believe the target arrays I'm passing up. The buggers must all be asleep. You sure you don't want us to take them out?"

"Negative," Taylor said. "Negative. Stick to the plan, Whisky. Save your bullets for the big one. Over."

"It breaks my heart."

"Weapons tight until Ruby," Taylor said. "Out."

Meredith understood this too: the difficulty of passing by your enemy without doing him harm. Especially now. With everyone aching to open up. To make the first kill.

To see if the megabuck wonders in which they were flying actually worked.

Noburu awoke unexpectedly. His bedding had clotted with sweat. He sensed that turbulent, unusual dreams had done this to him, but as his eyes opened, the delicate narratives of sleep fled from his consciousness, and he could not recall a single detail of the night visions that had broken his accustomed pattern of rest. Yet, even as he could not remember the substance of his dreams, he recognized with absolute clarity what was really worrying him. Although he sensed that his dreams had been of things far away, of lost things, he grasped that the swelling tumor of reality underlying all of this was the matter of the unusual activity in the industrial park outside of Omsk. He still had no idea what was going on there, but all of his soldier's instincts were excited. As if, in sleep, the shadow warrior within him had come to point the way. Noburu believed in the richness of the spirit as surely as he believed in superfast computers. And he knew that his spirit warrior would not let him return to sleep until this matter of the mystery site had been addressed.

Noburu waved his hand at the bedside light and a cool glow surrounded him. He reached for the internal staff phone and keyed it with his fingerprints.

"Sir," a sharp, almost barking voice responded from the below-ground operations center.

"Who is the ranking officer present?"

"Sir. Colonel Takahara. *Sir."*

"I will speak with him."

A moment later, Takahara's voice came over the speaker with a syllable of report only a little less violent than the voice of the junior watch officer.

Noburu felt himself shying from the purpose of the call, as though it were somehow too personal a matter to discuss.

"Quiet night?" he began.

"Sir," Takahara responded. "According to the last reports we received, the Iranian and rebel breakthrough at Kokchetav is meeting only negligible resistance. No change to the situation in the Kuban. We're having more

difficulty than usual reaching our forward stations in northern Kazakhstan—but I've already sent a runner to wake the chief of communications. I expect to have the problem corrected shortly."

"How long have the communications been down?" Noburu asked, annoyed.

"Half an hour, sir."

Half an hour. Not unprecedented. But Noburu was unusually on edge. Hung-over with dreams.

"What's the weather like in central Asia?"

There was a pause. Noburu could visualize Takahara straining to see the weather charts, or perhaps frantically querying the nearest workstation.

"Storm front moving in"—the voice came back. "It's already snowing heavily at Karaganda, sir."

"The famous Russian winter," Noburu mused. "Well, perhaps the communications problem is merely due to atmospherics."

"Yes, sir. Or a combination of factors. Some of the headquarters may be using the cover of darkness to relocate in order to keep pace with the breakthrough."

The explanation sounded rational enough. But something was gnawing at Noburu, something not yet clear enough to be put into words. "Takahara," he said, "if the chief of communications cannot solve the problem, I want to be awakened."

"Sir."

"Modern armies . . . without communications . . ."

"Sir. The problem will be corrected. *Sir."*

"Anything else to report?"

Takahara considered for a moment. "Nothing of significance, sir. Colonel Noguchi called in for final clearance for his readiness drill."

Air Force Colonel Noguchi. In charge of the Scramblers. The man was a terrible nuisance, staging one readiness test after another, flying dry missions. Aching to unleash the horrible, horrible toys with which Tokyo had entrusted him. Noburu understood, of course. You could not give a military man a weapon without inciting in him a desire to use it. Just to see.

But Noburu was determined that he would finish this

business without resort to Noguchi and the monstrous devices. Let the colonel fly his heart out behind friendly lines. Noburu was not going to give him the chance to make history.

I'm too old for this, Noburu thought. He had always been told that the heart hardened with age, but if this was so, then he was a freak. As a young man, he had not understood concepts such as mercy, humanity, or even simple decency. He had loved the idea of war, and he had loved its reality, as well. But now his youthful folly haunted him. He had been a very good officer. And he was still a very good officer. Only it was much harder now. He knew he was responsible for every crude bullet that tore human flesh out there on those distant battlefields. Even the side for which the victim fought mattered less now. All men, he had reluctantly, painfully realized, truly were brothers, and he had misspent his life in a manner that could never be forgiven.

It was too late now. All he could do was to try to dress it all in a few rags of decency.

Colonel Noguchi was an excellent officer. Exactly the sort Tokyo sought out for promotion these days: a heartless technical master. Starving for accomplishment, for glory. Noburu had decided that such men needed to be saved from themselves. And the world needed to be saved, as well.

Noburu thought briefly of his enemies. Surely they hated him. Even if they did not know the least bit about him, they hated him. They hated him even if he had no name, no face for them. They hated him. And rightly so. Yet, they would never know how much he had spared them.

My fate is written, Noburu thought, even if I cannot yet read it. I will play my role. And I still hold the power. Noguchi can fly his readiness test. And he can dream.

"Are you still there, Takahara?"

"*Sir.*"

"Review Colonel Noguchi's flight plan. I don't want his systems anywhere near the combat zone."

"Yes, sir. Shall I order the test delayed?"

"No. No, not unless it's otherwise necessary. Just review

the flight plans. As long as they're sensible, the drill can go ahead."

"Yes, sir."

"And, Takahara? I just wanted to be certain that the mission to strike the target in the vicinity of Omsk is proceeding on schedule."

Silence on the other end. Although Takahara was a very capable officer, the Omsk strike would not be foremost in his mind. It was only a minor detail in the management of a vast battlefield. Noburu pictured his subordinate hurrying through the automated target folders, growing angry at himself and the dark-circled night staff around him. Takahara was particularly abrasive, and he had been selected for the night watch because he had the temperament to keep everyone awake and full of nervous energy. Now Takahara would behave like a beast toward his subordinates for the rest of the night, embarrassed at this perfectly reasonable lapse in knowledge. Noburu was sorry for the junior officers on duty. But there was nothing to be done.

"Sir"—Takahara's voice returned. "Mission Three-four-one is in the final stages of physical preparation. Take-off is scheduled within . . . let me see . . . ex*cuse* me, sir. The mission is already in the air."

Embarrassment at his error filled Takahara's voice with a wonder that promised quite an ordeal for the night crew.

"Who is the mission commander?"

Takahara had already armed himself against that question. *"Sir.* Air Captain Andreas Zeederberg of the South African Defense Force."

"Contract employee Andreas Zeederberg," Noburu corrected the man automatically. Then he was sorry. This was already a phone call Takahara would take too much to heart and long remember, even though Noburu intended the man no harm. He remembered his father's admonition of years before, that a commander had to handle words as though they were sharp knives, for the least careless word could make a very deep wound.

"Sir," Takahara said, the obedient word filled with harnessed rage, "the aircraft will be—"

"That's enough. Really. I only wanted to be certain that

the mission would be executed on schedule. I want to be sure that the target is destroyed. By dawn."

"Sir."

"That's all. Good night." And Noburu touched the device to turn it off.

Perhaps, of course, it was all merely a dream. A few Russians trying desperately to keep warm in the ruins of their economy. Perhaps those heat signatures at Omsk were nothing at all, and he was only growing old and eccentric. But Noburu would have gambled a great deal that his instincts were right. At any rate, the new day would bring an answer. He reclined on the sleeping cushions, trying to gather some warmth from the sweat-brined bedclothes. He considered calling an orderly to bring him fresh linen. Then he decided not to bother. There was a part of him that did not really want to go back to sleep, afraid of what dreams might come to him next. The worst was always the one about the Americans in Africa. He did not think he could bear that one right now.

Manny Martinez liked working with his hands. Increasingly, his work kept him behind a desk, and he liked that too—in a sense, it was the white-collar job to which he had aspired as a scholarship student at Texas A&M. But, whenever he sat too long over paperwork, he heard the mocking street-corner voices from his youth in San Antonio: "Hey, man. You call that work? Come on, man. That ain't no fucking work." So, just as he enjoyed skinning his knuckles on the vintage Corvette he was restoring back home, he welcomed the occasional opportunity to get a bit of grease under his fingernails working on military equipment. Doing real work. Even when the conditions were as bad as they were now.

"Just hold it up there a little longer," the motor warrant told him. "I almost got her, sir."

Martinez pushed up with his cramped hands, feeling the bite of the cold in his fingers, in his toes, along his motionless legs. He lay on his back, twisted awkwardly to make room for the warrant and his mechanic assistant in the narrow access breech at the back of the M-100's engine compartment.

"No problem, Chief," Martinez told the warrant. "Take as long as you need." He tried to sound manly and cheerful. But the dull ache down through his forearms made him silently wish the chief would get on with it. It was very cold.

"Give me that other insert," the warrant told the mechanic, gesturing back across Martinez's body. The mechanic scrambled backward and began rooting about in a toolbox. It was difficult to see using only the low-light-level lanterns. *"That* one, goddamnit."

More crawling and sorting in the semidarkness.

"You want me to have Nellis take over for you, sir?" the warrant asked Martinez.

"Just do what you have to do, Chief. I'm all right," Martinez lied.

It hurt. But it was a good hurt. The tired ache that said, yes, I'm doing my part too. See? I'm pulling with you.

A voice from outside the compartment called loudly:

"Hey, you guys. Major Martinez in there with you?"

"Yeah, he's here," the warrant officer bellowed before Martinez could answer for himself. "What you want with him?"

"Colonel Taylor's on the comms link. He wants to talk to Major Martinez."

"Chief," Martinez said, "I've got to go." He was at once relieved that he would no longer have to brace the heavy panel and ashamed that he was so relieved.

"Yeah, I guess you better go, sir. *You. Nellis.* Get in here and take over for the major."

A bony knee poked into Martinez's waist. "Excuse me, sir," a very young voice said, following which the speaker rammed an elbow into the side of Martinez's head, just where the jaw touches the ear.

Martinez almost barked at the mechanic. But he knew the blows were unintentional. Tired men working in a cold, cramped space.

"Get your hands under it," Martinez said, waiting until he felt the boy's fingers looking for a space beside his. "You got it now?"

"Yes, sir."

"All right. I'm letting go. It's heavy."

"Got it, sir."

Martinez carefully withdrew his hands. The panel sagged slightly, but the boy caught the weight and pushed it back upward.

"Jeez," he said. "It's heavy."

"Shut up and hold it," the motor warrant told him. As Martinez eased back out of the compartment, the warrant said, "Thanks for the help, sir," in a halfhearted voice that sounded to Martinez like a form of verbal urination. Martinez knew that, as soon as he was out of earshot, the warrant would be complaining to the young mechanic about "real" officers. But it didn't matter.

Outside of the M-100, the work hall was as black as the depths of a tomb. Martinez turned on his hooded flashlight and followed its red trail across the metal and concrete litter of the floor. He could feel the cold burning right up through the soles of his boots. It was a miserable place, and he would be glad to see the last of it.

Outside, the snow was falling heavily now, and the earth was sufficiently luminous for him to switch off the flashlight. The snow crunched underfoot and burst wet against his eyes and cheeks, swirling and settling, drifting across the wasteland. Martinez headed for the dark, solid outline of the last wing-in-ground transport. All of the others were gone, en route to the follow-on assembly areas, and this last machine was ready to lift out of the snow-clad ruins as soon as they had taken care of the last repairs. There was one last salvageable M-100, the one Martinez had been laboring over personally half of the night.

One of the crewmen had been on the lookout. He opened the forward door at Martinez's approach. Behind the man's silhouette, the blue-lit interior promised warmth, and Martinez felt greedy for a little comfort now. It was a long damned way from Texas, he told himself.

He hauled himself up into the transport, dusting off the snow. Wasting no time, the guard sealed the door behind the supply officer and the lights came up automatically, dazzling Martinez.

"Over here, sir," an NCO called, offering Martinez a headset. "Want a cup of coffee, maybe?"

Coffee. As the regimental S-4, there were only three

essentials he had to provide to make the Army go: ammunition, fuel, and coffee. All the rest—rations, bandages, spare parts—were relatively minor concerns, especially to the NCOs. It was the one crucial vulnerability that no enemy of the United States had ever identified: take away the Army's coffee and its morale would plummet, with battle-hardened NCOs lurching groggy-eyed toward suicide.

"Sounds great," Martinez said. "Let me just talk to the old man." He pulled off his cap and adjusted the headset. "What the hell's my call sign again?" he asked himself out loud, scanning the cheat sheet the comms NCO had affixed to the interior of the fuselage. He found the alphanumeric, shaking his head at the ease with which it had slipped his mind.

"Sierra five-five, this is Sierra seven-three. Over."

All around him, the logistics and liaison nets crackled. He was just about to transmit again, when Taylor's miniaturized voice told him:

"Wait, Seven-three."

The old man was working another net. Martinez imagined how it must be at the moment for Taylor and Meredith: the amphetamine excitement of working the command and control system as the regiment neared combat. Then the thrill and danger of combat itself. Martinez both envied his comrades the excitement and shamed himself with the thought of their greater risks and responsibilities. He knew how essential a properly functioning support system was, before, during, and, especially, immediately after combat. But he could not help feeling that the others were doing the real work.

In the background, he heard a squadron S-4 reporting his subunit's fuel account status over the voice link. The report could have been handled more efficiently through the digital circuit. But Martinez understood that the other man was experiencing the same feeling of inadequacy as he was feeling himself. The desire to *do* something, to make a personal contribution. It was hard not to be out there within the sound of the guns.

"Sierra seven-three, this is Sierra five-five. Over."

Taylor. The sudden voice in his headset startled Martinez, just as an NCO put a gorgeously hot mug of coffee into his hands. Martinez caught the mug and wrapped both palms around its nearly scalding warmth, then keyed the mike with his voice:

"Sierra seven-three. Over."

"Status report. Over."

"Support operation on schedule," Martinez said. "All of the fuelers and the carryalls are under way. I've only got one WIG and one Mike-100 left here with me. Over."

There was a brief silence that Martinez did not quite understand, then Taylor's voice returned. Martinez could hear the exasperation hiding behind the studiedly calm inflection.

"You mean you're still at the initial site? Over."

"Roger. I've just got a skeleton crew of mechanics with me. We're still working on three-eight. Chief Malloy thinks we can get her back up."

Another pause. Then: "What's your estimated time of departure?"

"As soon as we get three-eight back up. We're all ready to go, except for that. I've got the operational calibrator on the WIG with me. I'll oversee its displacement. We're in good shape. When the squadrons close on their follow-on sites, we'll be waiting for them. Over."

"Manny," Taylor's voice came earnestly over the secure net, "don't fuck around. I know you're trying to do the right thing. But, if you can't get three-eight back up, just blow it in place. I want every last trace of an American presence out of there by dawn. We've got to keep the bad guys guessing. And I don't want to do anything to compromise the Russian security plan. Those guys have done a good job. Besides, some goddamned Jap space system might have picked us up moving out of there. You need to get moving. Over."

"Roger. We're almost done." Martinez knew in his heart that they could get three-eight into good enough shape to follow the WIG under its own power. He intended to bring Taylor the M-100 as a prize, to show that the support troops, too, could do their part. "See you at Platinum. Over."

"Don't wait too long to get out of there," Taylor's voice

warned him. The tone of admonition was softer, almost fatherly now. "Blow that bird if you can't get her up. And good luck. Out."

Martinez tugged off the headset, then put the cup of warm liquid to his chapped lips. It was odd. You were supposedly conditioned to do your duty to the country, to the Army. But he could not help feeling that his most important duty was to Taylor. He did not want to let the old man down.

Sipping the coffee, steeling himself to go back out into the cold darkness that lay between midnight and the sensible hours, he thought of a brilliant spring day in Mexico. They had been over in the Orientale on a special mission, and everything had gone well. No blood spilled. Just a dirty white flag and rebels throwing their weapons out into the street. After the last of their quarry had been gathered in, Taylor turned to Meredith and Martinez and said, "What the hell. Let's go for a ride, boys." And they had ridden up through the first pale green to where the rocks began, with Martinez struggling to stay on his horse. They followed an ancient, barely discernible trail up to a high canyon, where there was a well and a ruined shack. They tied the horses in the shade and climbed on foot to the nearest peak. And an odd thing happened. No one said a word. They just sat down in the sharp air and stared out over a brown world jeweled here and there with greenery, and the clear blue sky felt as soothing as a mother's hand. Taylor seemed to have forgotten all about his companions. His devil's face pointed off into the distance.

It was as if he had commanded the two younger men to hold their peace, to simply accept the world as it was. And Martinez's eyes opened. Nothing ever looked as beautiful to him again as that bare, thirsty landscape. The world was unspeakably beautiful when you finally shut your mouth and sat down and let yourself see. Time grew inconstant, as irregular as the breezes that whisked around the mountaintop and disappeared. When Martinez glanced at Taylor, the older man's eyes were closed, and he looked uncharacteristically peaceful. Even the scars on his face did not seem so pronounced, as if they had softened into his skin, tired of chastening his life. It was as if Taylor belonged on that peak, the way the broken stones belonged. A white scorpion scuffled its way through the rocks as Martinez watched peacefully, knowing it was not going to hurt them. There was no reason to hurt anyone or anything that day. Everything belonged just as it was. While the high cool air carried off the last of the sweat that made your shirt so heavy.

Then it was time to go. In order to make it back down to the village while there was still enough light. Taylor just stood up without a word and they all stumbled down to the horses, belatedly sharing a canteen of sour water. Martinez had hoped that there would be more days like that. But a week later, they were involved in a dirty little bloodbath, and after that there were other things to think about.

15

3 November 2020
early morning hours

"RUBY MINUS TEN MINUTES," THE COPILOT SAID.

"Roger," Heifetz responded. "Combat systems check." He glanced down at the control panel. "Weapons suite?"

"Green."

"Target acquisition suite?"

"Green."

"Active countermeasures suite?"

"Green."

"Go to environments check."

"Roger," the copilot said.

Throughout the regiment, Heifetz knew, other combat crews were running through the same drill. Making sure. One last time.

The environments check took them through the range of visual "environments" in which they could choose to fight. The forward windscreens also served as monitors. The first test simply allowed the crew to look out through the transparent composite material the way a man looked through a window. Outside, the night raced with snow, the big flakes hurrying toward the aircraft at a dizzying speed.

"Better and better," the copilot remarked. The storm meant that even old-fashioned visually aimed systems on the ground would have added difficulty spotting their attackers.

"Go to radar digital," Heifetz said.

The copilot touched his panel, and the night and the rushing snow disappeared. The big windscreens filled with a sharp image of the terrain over which they were flying, as though it were the middle of a perfectly clear day.

"Ruby minus eight minutes," the copilot said.

Heifetz briefly admired the perfection of the radar image before him. The view had the hyperreality of an especially good photograph, except that this picture moved with the aircraft, following the barren plains gone white under the snow and the sudden gashes and hills of waste that marked the open pit mines scarring the landscape. Then he said:

"Go to enhanced thermal."

The copilot obliged. The windows refilled, this time with heat sources highlighted over a backdrop of radar imagery.

"Target sort," Heifetz directed.

Immediately, each of the heat sources that the on-board computer had identified as a military target showed red. Hundreds of targets, near and far, filled the screen, as though the display had developed a case of measles. Below each target, numbers showed in shifting colors selected by the computer to contrast with the landscape. These were the attack priorities assigned by the computer. As the M-100 moved across the landscape, the numbers shifted, as new potential targets were acquired and others fell behind.

"Jesus," the copilot said. "Just look at that."

Heifetz grunted. It was as close as he would allow himself to come to admitting that he was impressed.

"Makes you just want to cut loose," the copilot said. "Blow the hell out of them."

"At Ruby."

"Ruby minus seven," the copilot reported.

"Go to composite," Heifetz said.

The next image to fill the screen resembled the "daytime" digital image, with targets added as points of light. This was a computer-built image exploiting all on-board systems plus input from space systems and a programmed memory base. In an environment soaked with electronic interference, or where radar countermeasures buffeted a single system, the computer reasoned around the interference, filling in any gaps in real-time information from other sources. The result was a constantly clear pure-light image of the battlefield. Further, if a particular target held special interest for the crew, they had only to point at it with a flight glove and the magnified image and all pertinent information appeared on a monitor mounted just below the windscreen.

"Ruby minus six," the copilot said. "Initial targets on radar horizon."

"Roger," Heifetz said. Then he entered the command net, calling Lieutenant Colonel Tercus, the First Squadron's commander, with whom he was tagging along.

"Whisky five-five, this is Sierra one-three. Over."

"Whisky five-five, over," Tercus responded. Even over the comms net, the squadron commander managed to sound dashing, flamboyant. Tercus stretched the regulations when it came to the length of his hair, and he wore a cavalryman's heavy mustache that would have been permitted on no other officer. Tercus was simply one of those unusual men in the Army who managed to make their own rules with baffling ease. Tercus seemed to be the eternal cavalryman, and he was always ready for a fight. In the past his valor had always outdistanced his occasional foolishness, but Taylor was taking no chances today—and so he had sent Heifetz along to make sure Tercus did not gallop out of control. "Superb officer," Taylor had remarked to Heifetz, "as long as you keep him in his sandbox."

"This is Sierra one-three. I've been off your internal. Status report. Over."

"Roger," Tercus responded. "All green, all go. Ruby minus five. Going to active countermeasures at minus three. Jeez, Dave. You been watching the target array? Unbelievable."

"Roger. Active countermeasures at minus three. Weapons free at minus one."

"Lima Charlie. And another great day for killing Indians. Over."

"One-three out," Heifetz said. He turned to his copilot. "Maintain composite."

"Composite lock. Alpha Troop diverging from main body."

"Roger. Stay with them." Alpha Troop had been assigned the mission of striking the Japanese-Iranian repair and marshaling yards at Karaganda, while the remainder of the squadron went after the headquarters and assembly areas of the III Iranian Corps. Heifetz had elected to maneuver along with Alpha Troop, since the squadron commander would remain with the main body of his unit. Heifetz could assist in controlling the action—and he could add additional firepower for Alpha Troop's big task.

"Ruby minus three."

"Activate jammers." For all his self-discipline, Heifetz could not help raising his voice. He felt the old familiar excitement taking possession of him.

"Jammers hot," the copilot said. "Full active countermeasures to auto-control."

There was no change in the sharp image that filled the M-100's windscreen. But Heifetz imagined that he could feel the electronic flood coursing out over the landscape. The simple stealth capabilities and passive spoofers had hidden the systems on their approach to the objective area. Now the attack electronics would overwhelm any known radar or acquisition systems. Enemy operators might see nothing but fuzz on their monitors, or they might register thousands of mock images amid which the First Squadron's birds would be hidden. The jammers even had the capability to overload and physically destroy certain types of enemy collectors. The latest technology allowed powerful jamming signals to "embrace" enemy communications, piggybacking on them until they arrived at and burned out the receiving-end electronics. It was a war of invisible fires, waged in microseconds.

"Ruby minus two," the copilot said. "That's Karaganda up ahead, on the far horizon."

"Sierra five-five, this is Sierra one-three, over," Heifetz called Taylor.

The old man had been off the radio set for a few minutes, but now his voice responded immediately.

"This is Five-five. Go ahead, One-three. Over."

"Objective area visual now. All systems green. Jammers active. No friendly losses en route."

"Good job, One-three. Give 'em hell."

Heifetz almost terminated the communication. Taylor's voice had seemed to carry a tone of finality and haste, of no more time to spend on words. Spread over a breadth of a thousand nautical miles, the regiment was moving to battle, shifting its support base, entering the unknown. Taylor had a thousand worries.

But the colonel was not quite finished speaking to Heifetz. Just before the operations officer could acknowledge and sign off, Taylor's voice returned:

"Good luck, Dave."

The tone of the small mechanical voice in his headset somehow managed to convey a depth of unashamed, honest emotion of which Heifetz would not have been capable. The three syllables reached into him, making human contact, telling Heifetz that he mattered, that he should have a future, not merely a past. That at least one man in the world cared for him. That he, too, mattered on a personal level.

Damn him, Heifetz said to himself, meaning just the opposite, as he fought down a wave of emotion.

"And good luck to you," Heifetz said. His voice sounded stilted and insufficient to him. Suddenly, he wished that he had made the effort to sit down and speak honestly to Taylor at least once, to explain everything, about Mira, about his son, about the loss of beauty, the loss of the best part of himself along with his family and his country. Just once, they should have spoken of such things. Taylor would have understood. Why had he been so proud? Why couldn't men reach out to one another?

"Ruby minus one minute," the copilot said.

"Unlock weapons suite."

"Shooters to full green."

No sooner had the copilot touched the forward controls than Heifetz felt a slight pulsing in the M-100. The high-velocity gun had already found its priority targets. The feel under Heifetz's rump was of blood pulsing from an artery. The stabilization system on the M-100 was superb, but the force of the supergun was such that it could not all be absorbed. Slowly, after hundreds of shots, it would lose accuracy and need to be recalibrated.

But that was in the future. Right now, the gun was automatically attacking distant targets that remained well beyond the reach of the human eye.

The visual display blinked here and there where targets had already been stricken. Dozens of successful strikes registered simply from the fires of the company with which Heifetz was riding.

"Ruby now, Ruby now," the copilot cried. *"Look at that. The sonofabitching thing works."*

Heifetz glanced down at the master kill tally that registered how many effective strikes the squadron had managed. Barely a minute into the action, the number—constantly increasing—was approaching two hundred kills. His own system had taken out fourteen, no, fifteen—*sixteen* enemy systems.

Lieutenant Colonel Tercus's voice came ringing over the command net, rallying all the members of his squadron, yelling down the centuries:

"Charge, you bastards, charge!"

One of his subordinates answered with a Rebel yell.

The elation was unmistakable. Almost uncontrollable. Even Heifetz wanted to leap from his seat.

He recalled something an Israeli general officer had told him many years before. When he had been young. And invincible.

"Only the soldier who has fought his way back from defeat," General Lan had confided, "really understands the joy of victory."

The counter showed that the brilliant machine in which Heifetz was galloping through the sky had already destroyed thirty-seven high-priority enemy combat systems.

Make that thirty-eight.

For the first time in years, David Heifetz found himself grinning like a child.

Senior Technical Sergeant Ali Toorani was very disappointed in the machine the Japanese had given him. They had fooled him, and the thought of his gullibility filled him

with anger. The Japanese had been alternately falsely polite and unforgivably superior at the training school on the
outskirts of Teheran, but he had been told that they would
give the Faithful infallible weapons, weapons far more
perfect than those of the devils in the north and to the
west. He had believed, and he had struggled to learn, while
the Japanese had been inhuman in their expectations of
how much a man could study.

He had been proud of his mastery of the radar system,
and he had possessed great faith in his abilities and in the
machine. He had learned how to read all of the data, to
comprehend what the displays foretold. He had acquired
great skill. And he had even attempted to perform the
maintenance tasks the Japanese demanded, although such
menial labors were far below the station of a senior technical sergeant. Usually, he performed the maintenance
when no one was around to see him. And the methods
seemed to work. Even when the other machines broke
down, his continued to function. He had done great things
with his radar machine in this war.

But, in the end, the Japanese devils had lied like all of
the other devils before them. Even when you humbled
yourself to work like the lowest of laborers to care for the
machine, it failed you.

Ali looked at the screen in despair and rising anger. The
night had been quiet. There were no Russian airplanes or
helicopters in the sky. There had been fewer and fewer of
them over the past weeks, and now the skies belonged
entirely to his own kind.

But, without warning, the screen set into his console had
washed with light. According to the Japanese instructors,
such an aberration was impossible. Now the treacherous
screen registered thousands of elusive images, each one of
which purported to be an enemy aircraft of some sort.
Such a thing was impossible. No sky could ever be so
crowded. Anyway, the Russians had few aircraft left. The
machine was simply lying.

Ali stood up in disgust and turned away from the useless
piece of devilry. He stepped through the gangway into the
next cell, where his friends Hassan and Nafik were also
working the late shift.

"God is great," Ali said, greeting his friends. "My machine doesn't work tonight."

"Truly, God is great," Hassan responded. "You can see that our Japanese machines do not work properly, either. The headphones merely make a painful noise."

"The Japanese are devils," Nafik muttered.

Captain Murawa's day was long and bitter, and his sleep was deep and hard. Until now his life had given him no cause to question the wisdom of his superiors. To be Japanese was to feel oneself part of the dominant political and economic power on earth, and to be a Japanese officer was to be part of a military whose abilities—if not actual forces—whose technological might, had humbled the great powers of the previous century. First, the United States, a flabby, self-indulgent giant, had received its lesson in Africa, where Japanese technology had savaged the ignorant Americans. And now it was the turn of the Russians, who had yet to put up any resistance worthy of the name. Yes, to be a Japanese officer, especially one of the new elite of electronic engineering officers, was a very fine thing. The entire world respected you.

It was a terrible feeling for Murawa to suddenly discover doubt in himself.

He hated the Iranians. He hated their indolence and filth, their inability to deal with reality as he knew it and their assumption that all things were theirs by due. Their criminal neglect of expensive military equipment was bad enough, what with their passive resistance to the accomplishment of basic maintenance chores, the neglect of a desert people to perform a task as fundamental as changing sand and dust filters, and their reluctance even to check fluid levels. But their social behavior was far worse. Murawa's image of the Iranians was of spoiled, bloodthirsty children. When their expensive toys broke—invariably through their own fault—the children threw temper tantrums, blaming the toymaker's deceit and bad faith—or lack of skill, an accusation Murawa found especially cutting and unjustified. The Japanese equipment that had been provided to the Iranians was the best in the world—the most effective and most reliable. Easy to operate and maintain, it required willful misuse to degrade its performance. It was, in fact, so simple to operate most of the combat systems that even the Iranians had been able to employ them effectively in combat.

The colossal repair effort had long since overrun its estimated costs. For want of a bit of lubrication or simple cleaning, major automotive and electronic assemblies were destroyed. Outrageously expensive components required complete replacement rather than the anticipated repairs. And the Iranians merely jeered: *You have sold us goods of poor quality. You have broken your promise. You have broken faith.* Murawa was sick of hearing it, and he did not know how much longer he would be able to control his temper. His military and civilian-contract repair crews were exhausted. And the effect of seeing their hard work result only in less and less care on the part of the Iranians and ever greater numbers of fine Japanese systems showing up ruined in the Karaganda repair yard—some for the second or third time—well, it was very bad for morale. Instead of being rewarded, their labor only turned them into fools.

Today, a barbarous crew of Iranians had turned in a kinetic-energy tank whose prime mechanisms had been hopelessly fouled by dirt. The vehicle would have been merely one out of hundreds—but the savages had played a trick. Struggling to contain their laughter, they had loitered in the reception and diagnostic motor pool. No one paid much attention, assuming they were simply typical badly disciplined Iranian troops, loath to return to duty. But, when a Japanese technician began climbing into their tank, they stopped laughing and watched with rapt attention. Only when the technician clambered madly out of the vehicle, screaming at a volume that tore the throat, did the Iranians resume their gaiety. They laughed like delighted children.

The Iranians had released a poisonous snake inside the crew compartment. Now a critical member of Murawa's team lay in the sickbay, delirious and possibly dying. And all the Iranians had offered in leaving was the comment that:

"God is great."

Murawa had wanted to shout at them, "If your god is so great, let *him* fix your damned tank." But it would have been unacceptable. Un-Japanese.

The incident had released a torrent of doubts that he had long been suppressing. He doubted that the wise, high men who led Japan truly understood all of this. He doubted that the Iranians would ever be faithful allies to anyone. Hadn't the Americans learned the hard way, almost half a century before? The Iranians were all too convinced of their own bizarre superiority. The world owed them everything. They understood neither contractual relations nor civilized friendship. What elusive concept of honor they had was little more than vanity soaked in blood. They could not even tell the truth about simple matters, as though honest speech were biologically impossible for them. Why on earth had Tokyo backed them? What would happen when the Iranians and the rest of the Islamic world turned again? Murawa could not believe that he was the only person to see the truth.

He wished he were home in Kyoto. At least for one night. Murawa felt lucky to have been born in that most precious, most Japanese of cities, so unlike Tokyo with its compromises with Western degeneracy. There was nothing more beautiful than the gardens of Kyoto in the autumn. Unless it was the Kyoto girls, with their peculiar, disarming combination of delicacy and young strength. Certainly, they were unlike the gruesome women of Central Asia in their dirty, eerie costumes, with their gibbering voices. Those with plague scars—obviously untreated in this primitive environment—were only grimmer than the rest by a matter of degree. There was no romance in Central Asia for Murawa. Only ugly deserts interrupted with excavation scars and cities erected madly in the middle of nowhere, choking with half-dead industries whose principal product seemed to be bad air. It was like taking an unpleasant journey back through a number of bygone centuries, collecting the worst features of each as you went along. Central Asia made Murawa feel sick in spirit, and he was grateful for each new day that his body did not sicken, as well.

Apparently, it was not only the Iranians who were a

problem. At the maintenance councils back at headquarters, Murawa had spoken with fellow officers who served with the Arab Islamic Union forces. Their tales made it plain that there was little to choose between their charges and Murawa's.

Despite unprecedented successes, the front was beginning to bog down. There was no military reason not to press on now. The Russians were clearly beaten. But each new local breakthrough proved harder to support and sustain logistically. The Iranians and the Arabs had gone through so many combat systems that they had too little left for the final blow. Their leaders barked that Japan was obliged to replace their losses. But even Murawa, a mere captain, knew that the additional systems did not exist. Japanese industry had gone all out to provide the vast forces already deployed. And, even if additional systems had been available, it would have been impossible to transport them all from Japan to the depths of Central Asia overnight. The prewar buildup had taken years.

The Iranians refused to understand. Murawa worked his crews until the men literally could no longer function without sleep. He sought desperately to do his duty, to return enough combat systems to the fighting forces to flesh out the skeletal units pointed northward. And all he heard were complaints that had increasingly begun to sound like threats.

Now all he wanted to do was sleep. It had been a hard day, a bad day. Sleep was his only respite and reward.

The explosions woke him.

Murawa had been dreaming of red leaves and old temple bells. Until suddenly the bells began to ring with a ferocity that hurled him out of his repose. He spent a long moment sitting with his hands clapped over his ears in a state of thorough disorientation.

The noise was of bells loud as thunder. Louder than thunder. The walls and floor wobbled, as though the earth had gotten drunk. *Earthquake,* he thought. Then a nearby explosion shattered all of the glass remaining in the window of his room and an orange-rose light illuminated the spartan quarters.

My God, he realized, *we're under attack.*

He grabbed wildly for his trousers. He was accustomed to seeing the mechanical results of combat. But he had never felt its immediate effects before. Once, he had seen an old Russian jet knocked out of the sky at some distance. But nothing like this.

The huge noise of the bells would not stop. It hurt his ears badly, making his head throb. The noise was so great that it had physical force. The big sound of explosions made sense to him. But not the bells.

The sound of human shouting was puny, barely audible, amid the crazy concert of the bells.

He pulled on his boots over bare feet and ran out of his room, stumbling down the dark corridor toward the entrance of the barracks building. The Iranian military policeman on guard duty huddled in the corner of the foyer, chanting out loud.

"What's going on?" Murawa demanded in Japanese. But he was not really addressing the cowering Iranian. He hurried out past the blown-in door, tramping over glass and grit.

Outside, heavy snowflakes sailed down from the dark heavens. The white carpet on the ground lay in total incongruity with the array of bonfires spread across the near horizon.

The motor park. His repair yards.

He watched, stunned, as a heavy tank flashed silver-white-gold as if it had been electrified, then jerked backward like a kicked dog. Nearby, another vehicle seemed to crouch into the earth, a beaten animal—until it jumped up and began to blaze.

With each new flash, the enormous bell sound rolled across the landscape.

The bells. His tanks. His precious vehicles. His treasures.

What in-the-name-of-God was going on? What kind of weapons were the Russians using? Where had they come from?

Another huge tolling noise throbbed through his skull, and he briefly considered that the Iranians might have turned on them. But that was impossible. It was premature. And the Iranians could never have managed anything like this.

He pointed himself toward the communications center, feet unsure in the snow. He brushed against an Iranian soldier whose eyes were mad with fear, and it occurred to Murawa belatedly that he had come out unarmed. The realization made him feel even more helpless, although a sidearm was unlikely to be very effective against whatever was out there playing God in the darkness.

He ran along the accustomed route—the shortest way— without thinking about the need for cover. The air around him hissed. At the periphery of his field of vision, dark figures moved through the shadows or silhouetted briefly against a local inferno. He was still far too excited to seriously analyze the situation. His immediate ambition was limited to reaching the communications center. Someone there might have answers. And there were communications means. Other Japanese officers and NCOs. The comms center called him both as a place of duty and of refuge.

He almost made it. He was running the last gauntlet, slipping across the open space between the devastated motor parks and the administration area, when a force like a hot ocean wave lifted him from the earth and hurled him back down. The action happened with irresistible speed, yet, within it, there was time to sense his complete loss of orientation as the shock wave rolled him over in the air exactly as a child tumbles when caught unexpectedly by the sea. For an instant gravity disappeared, and time stretched out long enough for him to feel astonishment then elemental fear before the sky slammed him back against the earth. In the last bad sliver of time, he thrust out a hand to protect himself. It hit the ground ahead of his body, at a bad angle, and his arm snapped like a dry biscuit.

He lay on the earth, sucking for air. He felt wetness under his shoulder blades. He raised his head like a crippled horse attempting to rise. He felt impossibly heavy.

He tried to right himself, but it simply did not work. He almost rolled up onto one knee, but he found that his right arm would not cooperate. When he realized that the dangling object at the end of his limb was his own hand, a wave of nausea passed over him. There was blood all over his uniform, all over his flesh. He could not decide where it had originated. The world seemed extraordinarily intense, yet unclear at the same time.

He dropped the broken limb, hiding it from himself. The snow turned to rain.

He collapsed, falling flat on his back. Cold rain struck his face. He could see that it was still snowing up in the heavens. A white, swirling storm. The stars were falling out of the sky. He felt the cold wetness creeping in through his clothing, chilling his spine, his legs, even as the exposed front portion of his body caught the warmth of the spreading fires. He lay between waking and dreaming, admiring the gales above his head and blinking as the snow turned to rain in its descent and struck him about the eyes.

He waited for the pain, wondering why it would not come.

"I'm all right," he told himself. "I'm all right."

The sound of the bells had stopped. In fact, the world was utterly silent. Yet the flashes continued. The pink wall of firelight climbed so high into the heavens that it seemed to arch over the spot where Murawa lay.

What was wrong? Why couldn't he get up? Why was everything so quiet?

The sky's on fire, he thought.

What was happening?

The fuel dump, he decided lucidly. They've hit the fuel dump. The Iranians had been allowed to manage it themselves, and expecting no further threats from the Russians, they had been careless, neglecting to build earthen revetments or even to disperse the stocks.

It's all burning, he thought resignedly. But why couldn't he get up? It seemed to him that he had almost made it to his feet at his first attempt. But now his muscles would not pay attention to him.

It crossed his mind that they would have to send him home now. Back to Kyoto.

Where was the pain?

Gathering all of his will and physical strength, Murawa hoisted himself up on his good elbow.

Everything was on fire. It was the end of the world. There should have been snow. Or mud. But dust had come up from somewhere. Clouds and cyclones of dust, flamboyantly beautiful. The burning world softened and changed colors through the silken clouds.

He began to choke.

The world had slowed down, as if it were giving him time to catch up. As he watched, a tracked troop carrier near the perimeter of the repair yard rose into the sky, shaking itself apart. He could feel the earth trembling beneath his buttocks.

Ever so slowly, dark metal segments fell back to earth, rebounding slightly before coming to rest.

He was choking. Coughing. But he could not hear himself coughing, and it frightened him.

Yet, it was all very beautiful in the silence. With the universe on fire.

Where was the pain?

He saw a dark figure running, chased by fire. The man was running and dancing ecstatically at the same time, flailing his arms, turning about, dropping to his knees. Then Murawa's eyes focused, and he saw that the man was burning, and that there was no dance.

Murawa collapsed back into the mud created by his own wastes. He wished he had not forgotten his pistol, because he wanted to be dead before the fire reached him.

Lieutenant Colonel John Reno's squadron had nearly completed its sweep along Engagement Area Emerald. Charlie Troop was finishing up the turkey shoot outside of Atbasar, and Alpha and Bravo had reformed into an aerial skirmish line that stretched for thirty nautical miles from flank to flank. His squadron alone had accounted for the destruction of, at latest count, two thousand four hundred and fifty-six enemy combat vehicles or prime support rigs, and they had not lost a single M-100. Reno had read his military history, and it seemed to him that his squadron's attack constituted one of the most lopsided victories on record. His father might have made it to four-star general, but the old bugger had never had such a victory to his credit. It was a glorious day.

There were only two real problems, in Reno's view. First, the regiment's other two squadrons had performed equally well. First Squadron even had a higher kill tally, although it was unfair to count them equally, since First Squadron had been able to run up the numbers by completing the destruction of all the vehicles massed and awaiting repair at the Karaganda yards. Still, there were ways of presenting yourself that made it clear to the media that your accomplishment had actually been the greater. The second problem, however, was considerably more formidable.

Taylor. Reno despised the sonofabitch. Neither did Taylor go to very much trouble to disguise his distaste for John Anthony Reno.

Reno understood why, of course. Taylor was a misfit. A misfit who just happened to have a string of lucky breaks. A misfit who surrounded himself with other misfits. That good-for-nothing kike Heifetz. So superior. After the Jews had gotten their asses kicked into the sea by the ragheads, for God's sake. It was positively unhealthy, the way Heifetz lived all alone in a bare apartment. With no apparent interest in women. And then there was Taylor's kiss-ass black boy, flaunting his red-haired wife in front of everybody all the time. They were like that, though. Always had to marry a white woman to prove they'd made it. Reno grinned, imagining the couple's embraces. Meredith's wife was an exceptionally attractive woman, and it was unfathomable why she would have thrown herself away on that colored ape. What on earth could she see in him? Of course, the worst of them all was that Martinez. A little wetback sand nigger. With a college degree. Fancied himself quite the playboy too. Worthless as a supply officer. No sense of priorities. Wouldn't dream of helping out a brother officer when there was a little problem with the books. Of course, they always went for the jobs like that. So they wouldn't have to mix it up out in the fighting. Why, Martinez was probably fast asleep somewhere, warm and safe. While better men were out doing his fighting for him. No, Taylor was as despicable as he was selfish. Surrounding himself with oddballs. Taylor's staff was a downright embarrassment to the Army. Christ, even the

Russians had picked up on it. Whereas your Russian got along just fine with a man like John Reno. Not that the Russians were anything to write home about.

And what was Taylor going to do? Well, Reno was certain, the sorry old bastard was not about to give credit where credit was due. No, if anything, he'd penalize John Reno just for having the good fortune to be born a general's son, for having a presentable wife from a good old Philadelphia family, for being all of the things that George Taylor could never be. Why, on his mother's side, Reno could trace his military ancestors back to the prerevolutionary frontier militia.

And that was the whole point. Taylor did not understand anything like that. Tradition. Honor. In another age, in a less confused army, Taylor would have been lucky to make sergeant.

And his face. You couldn't even introduce him to anyone. Then there was the rumor about the little tramp back in D.C.

Well, Reno was an insider. And he knew that Taylor had just about peaked. Oh, if this operation continued to go well, he might make brigadier general. But that was really about it. Taylor just didn't look the part of a very senior officer. And he certainly didn't act it. No, Taylor had made too many enemies over the years.

The fact of the matter was simply that the Army did not need characters like that. It continued to amaze Reno that Taylor had made it as far as this.

He had heard it repeated that George Taylor was the type of officer who was always ready to take on the dirty jobs. That hardly surprised Reno, since Taylor struck him as a dirty man.

He let his fantasies run for a moment. The best thing that could happen, of course, would be for Taylor to become a combat casualty. Not necessarily a fatality—since that might turn him into a hero. Just incapacitated. That would mean that Reno, as the senior squadron commander, would take over as acting commander of the regiment on the field of battle. Now *that* would be an opportunity.

"Saber six, this is Lancer," his internal comms net interrupted him. Reno made it a practice to assign colorful names to the stations within his own net, although it was forbidden by regulation. You had to add a bit of dash to things, if you were going to compete with show-offs like Tercus over in First Squadron.

"This is Saber six, over."

"We've got one," the other station said. "Looks perfect. Isolated. No nearby combat reserves. It's ours for the picking. Over."

"Roger. Report approximate size."

"Looks like eight box-bodied vans backed into a cluster. With a few dozen utility vehicles scattered about. No shooters."

Reno thought for a moment. The site sounded just about perfect. Safe. Manageable. They could do it quickly. Get it over with. Taylor wouldn't even know about it until it was too late to do anything about it.

"This is Saber six," Reno said. "Transmit grids to my navigational aids. Take out the support vehicles, just to be on the safe side, then have the dragoons secure everything. I'm on my way. Break. Second Saber, this is Saber six. Take over the squadron. I'm going to help Lancer capture an enemy headquarters site. Out."

Taylor was a fool, Reno thought as he strolled through the picturesque, carefully spotlit wreckage of the enemy field headquarters. It was really a very minor facility. But you wouldn't be able to tell that from the photographs.

"Sir, if you could just move a little bit to your left. There. I'm getting too much backlighting," Reno's staff photographer said. The enlisted man raised his camera to his eye.

"Well, move your goddamned lights," Reno said irritably. Taylor had scratched the idea of any dismounted operations except in emergency situations. But this was, of course, simply a matter of seizing the initiative. Taking advantage of the opportunity to capture an enemy headquarters. No one could challenge him on that. And the press would love it.

Reno stepped over an Iranian body. He waved his hand at the photographer.

"No. Too gory. Wait until we get outside and we'll take a few shots with the prisoners."

The media would be desperate for photos. The Pentagon would try to fob off "strategic" imagery that meant little to the unpracticed eye. The press would be only too grateful for on-the-ground human interest pictures, complete with the tale of a daring raid on an enemy headquarters.

Reno descended the ladder from a ruined van and stepped out into the darkness.

"Where the hell are the prisoners?"

"Over here, sir." A flashlight clicked on, lighting the way.

Reno turned to his photographer. "You're sure you've got the right goddamned film in?"

"Yes, sir. No problem, sir. The pictures are going to be great."

Reno's boot caught something heavy and slightly giving and he almost fell face forward in the snow and mud. He slammed his boot down into the object to steady himself.

"What the hell's this?" he demanded angrily.

"Sir," a voice came out of the darkness. "That's one of the friendly casualties. When we were dismounting, the Iranians—"

"Get him the hell out of here," Reno snapped. "You," he told the photographer. "No more pictures until all of the casualties have been cleared away. Understand?"

"Yes, sir."

Reno's dismounted cavalrymen scrambled to clear their fallen comrades from the scene, while the photographer arranged his battery-powered spotlights. In a few minutes, the photo session was able to resume.

Reno stood proudly in the cones of light, jauntily training an automatic rifle on a group of Iranian officers and men whose hands reached up to catch the falling snow.

It was a great day to be an American, Reno thought.

Air Captain Andreas Zeederberg of the South African Defense Force was in a bad mood. His deep penetration squadron had been only fitfully employed during the offensive, and now, promised a high priority mission, he found himself leading his aircraft against a rust heap.

"Old Noburu's got an itch," his superior had told him, "and we've got to scratch it."

There were not even any verified military targets in the Omsk industrial complex. But, what the Japanese wanted, the Japanese got. Zeederberg liked to fly, and he liked to fight. But he was getting a bit weary of Japanese imperiousness. And now there was a damned outbreak of Runciman's disease back at base. The squadron's energies would have been better spent in displacing their entire operation to a new, uninfected site. Instead, they were wasting mission time bombing big pieces of junk into smaller pieces of junk.

Zeederberg smiled, despite himself. He pictured some poor old sod of a night watchman in the Omsk yards when the enhanced conventional explosives started going off. Wake up, Ivan. There's a nice little cossack.

In a way, you had to pity the Russians. Although they had certainly made a cock up out of their country, Zeederberg would have felt more at home fighting on their side against the Iranian brown boys. Still, you took your shilling and did what you were told.

Old Jappers with a touch of nerves. And everything going so well. They wanted the Omsk site leveled. Completely.

What's the hurry? Looking at the overhead photos, Zeederberg had figured that, if only they were patient, the place would fall apart on its own.

Suddenly, the aircraft leapt up into the darkness, then dropped again, bouncing his stomach toward his throat.

"Sorry about that, sir," his copilot said. "We're entering a bit of broken country. Nasty bit of desert. I can take her up, if you like. Two hundred meters ought to more than do it."

"No. No, continue to fly nap-of-the-earth. We will regard this as a training flight. We shall make it have value."

Zeederberg snapped on his clear-image monitor, inspecting the digitally reconstructed landscape. Barren. Utterly worthless country.

His copilot glanced over at him. "Makes the Kalahari look like the Garden of Eden," he said.

It occurred to Zeederberg that men would fight over anything.

"We'll hit a sort of low veld to the north, sir," the copilot continued.

The navigator's voice came through the headset, unexpectedly nervous and alive. "I've lost Big Sister. I think we're being jammed."

"What are you talking about?" Zeederberg demanded. He hurriedly tried his communications set.

White noise.

"Any hostiles near our flight path?"

"Nothing registers," the weapons officer responded. "Looks like clear flying."

Probably the damned Iranians, Zeederberg decided. Jamming indiscriminately. "Keep your eyes open," he told the commanders of the eight other aircraft in his squadron, using a burst of superhigh power. "Minimize transmissions. Move directly for the target area. If we lose contact, each aircraft is responsible for carrying out the attack plan on its own."

The other aircraft acknowledged. It was a bit difficult to hear, but they possessed the best communications gear the Japanese had to give, and they were flying in a comparatively tight formation. The messages could just get through. But communicating with a distant headquarters was out of the question. The jammers, whomever they belonged to, were very powerful.

Zeederberg felt wide awake now, despite the heaviness of the predawn hour. The jamming had gotten his attention. The on-board systems read the interference as broadband—not specifically aimed at his flight. But you could never be too careful.

The mission was growing a bit more interesting than he had expected.

"Let's go with full countermeasures suites on," he told his copilot. "I want to isolate the target area as soon as we're within jamming range. And then let's do another target readout. See if they've got the digital sat links jammed too."

The copilot selected a low-horizon visual readout of the

target area from a triangulation of Japanese reconnaissance satellites. The seam-frequency links still operated perfectly, making it clear that the hostile jamming was directed primarily at ground-force emitters.

At first glance, the imagery of the industrial park looked as dreary and uninteresting as it had the afternoon before, when Zeederberg had carried out his mission planning. Warehouses, gangways, mills, derelict fuel tanks.

"Wait," Zeederberg said. He punched a button to halt the flow of the imagery, sitting up as though he had just spotted a fine game bird. "Well, I'll be damned."

He stared at the imagery of the wing-in-ground tactical transport, trying to place it by type. The craft certainly was not of Soviet manufacture. He knew he had seen this type of WIG before, in some journal or systems recognition refresher training. But he could not quite put a designation to it.

"Ever seen one of those?" he asked his copilot.

"No, sir. I don't believe I have."

"And there's only one of them."

"That's all I can see."

"What the hell, though?" He had almost missed the ship. It was well camouflaged, with the sort of attenuated webbing that spread itself out from hidden pockets along the upper fuselage. The kind the Americans had pioneered.

"Christ almighty," Zeederberg said quietly. "That's American. It's bloody American."

There was a dead silence between the two men in the forward cockpit. Then the navigator offered his view through the intercom:

"Perhaps the Russians have decided to buy American."

Zeederberg was hurriedly calculating the time-distance factors remaining between his aircraft and their weapons release point.

"Well," he said slowly, figuring all the while, "they're about to find it a damned poor investment."

16

3 November 2020

DAISY STARED WEARILY AT HER FACE IN THE WASHROOM mirror, glad that Taylor could not see her now. Her unwashed hair was gathered back into a knot, exposing the full extent of the deterioration of her complexion. She always broke out when she was overtired and under stress. Washing her face had helped her regain her alertness, but it had certainly done nothing for her looks. Hurriedly, she tried to apply a bit of makeup. She had never been very good at it.

Everyone back in the situation room was jubilant. The President, who had campaigned on a platform that barely acknowledged the existence of the military, was like a child who had discovered a wonderful new toy. He had no end of questions now, and the assorted members of the Joint Chiefs of Staff crowded one another out of the way to answer them. Bouquette was in his glory. The intelligence picture had apparently been dead-on, and the initial reports and imagery from the combat zone made it clear that the operation was already a resounding success, even though the U.S. force was still fighting its way across the expanses of Central Asia. There was not a single report of an American combat loss at this point, and the chairman of the Joint Chiefs kept returning to the intelligence workstation every few minutes to verify what he had just been told, unable to believe the extent of his good fortune. The chairman had repeatedly shaken Bouquette's hand, congratulating him on the intelligence preparation of the battlefield.

"Now that's the way intel's supposed to work," the chairman had said, smiling his old country-boy smile.

Bouquette, recently returned from a shower and a meal, his clean shirt a model of the purity of cotton, had drawn Daisy off to the side. Forgetting what a mess she looked, she had imagined that Bouquette was going to suggest some private victory party a bit later on. But he had only said:

"For God's sake, Daze, not a word about this Scrambler business. They're as happy as kids in a candy store. They've completely forgotten about it, and there's no point in causing the Agency any needless embarrassment."

For all of their trying, the assembled intelligence powers of the United States had been unable to come up with a single additional scrap of information about the Scramblers.

"It could still be important," Daisy said. "We still don't know."

Bouquette raised his voice. Slightly. Careful not to draw unwanted attention to their conversation.

"Not a word, Daze. Regard that as an order." He shook his head. "Don't be such an old maid, for God's sake. Everything's coming up roses."

And he turned his attention back to one of the National Security Council staffers, a female naval officer with a tight little ass squeezed into a tight little uniform. Perhaps, Daisy thought resentfully, the two of them could go sailing together.

The President had decided that he absolutely had to talk to Taylor in the middle of the battle, to congratulate him. Taylor's voice, in turn, made it clear that he definitely had more pressing matters to which to attend, but the President had been oblivious to the soldier's impatience. The thanks of a grateful nation . . .

Daisy had to leave the room. She hurried down the hallway, past the guards, to the ladies' room. The tears were already burning out of her eyes as she shoved her way in through the door.

They were all such fools, she told herself, inexplicably unable to be happy. She sat down in a stall and wept.

Something terrible within her, a hateful beast lurking inside her heart, insisted that all the celebrating in the situation room was unforgivably premature.

Noburu stared at the image on the oversize central screen, trying hard to maintain an impassive facial expression. All around him, staff officers shouted into receivers, called the latest shred of information across the room, or angrily demanded silence so that they could hear. Noburu had never seen his headquarters in such a state. Neither was he accustomed to the sort of picture that now taunted him from the main monitor.

It was a catastrophe. He was looking at a space relay image of the yards at Karaganda. The devastation was remarkable, and as he watched, secondary explosions continued to startle the eye. He had already reviewed the imagery from Tselinograd and Arkalyk, from the Kokchetav sector and Atbasar. Everywhere, the picture was the same. And no one knew exactly what had happened. There was no enemy to be found.

The first report of the debacle had come by an embarrassingly roundabout path. An enterprising lieutenant at Karaganda, unable to reach higher headquarters by any of the routine means, had gone to a local phone and called his old office in Tokyo with the initial report of an attack. Amazingly, the old-fashioned telephone call had gotten through where the latest communications means had failed, and the next thing Noburu knew he was being awakened by a call from the General Staff, asking him what on earth was going on in his theater of war.

It was a catastrophe, the extent of which was not yet clear to anyone. Especially to the poor Russians. Oh, they had pulled off a surprise all right. They had caught their tormentors sleeping—quite literally. The Russians had made a fight of it after all. But the poor fools had no idea what they had brought upon themselves.

He knew there would be another call from Tokyo. And he knew exactly what the voice on the other end would say.

I did not want this, Noburu told himself. God knows, I did not want this.

If only he could have foreseen it somehow. Prevented all this. He closed his eyes. The dream warrior had known, had tried to warn him. But he had grown too sophisticated to pay attention to such omens.

The spirit had known. But Noburu had not listened. And now it was too late. For everyone.

"Takahara," he barked, wounded beyond civility.

"Sir."

"Still nothing?"

Takahara was a cruel man. And, like all cruel men, embarrassment before a superior left him with the look of a frightened child.

"Sir. We still cannot find the enemy. We're trying . . . everything."

"Not good enough. Find them, Takahara. No matter what it takes."

It was time to be cruel now. In the hope that somehow he might still compensate, might prevent the unforgivable horror he knew was coming.

"Sir." Takahara looked terrified.

"And I want to talk to the commander of that bombing mission to the Omsk site."

Takahara flinched. *"Sir.* We have temporarily lost contact with mission Three-four-one."

"When? Do you mean they've been shot down? Why didn't you tell me?"

"Sir. We have no indication that the mission has been . . . lost. We simply have had no contact with them for some time. The interference in the electromagnetic spectrum has reached an unprecedented level . . ."

Noburu turned away. His anger was too great to allow him to look at the other man. It was more than anger. Fury.

Omsk. Why had he failed to trust his instincts? He had known that something was terribly wrong the minute Akiro

356

had pointed out the heat source anomaly in the abandoned warehouses. Why had he waited to hit them?

No one had suspected that the Russians still possessed such a capability to strike back. Japanese intelligence had missed it entirely. And why had the Russians waited so long to employ these new means of destruction? Why hadn't they employed these superweapons—whatever they were—immediately? When it might still have made a difference?

It was too late now. All the Russians had done was to call down a vengeance upon themselves that would be the one thing future historians remembered about this war. The one thing with which his name might be associated in the history books.

It would have been better for the Russians if Japanese intelligence had detected their preparations. The Russian deception effort had been too skillful for their own good.

The shadow warrior had known all along. And now he was laughing.

"Takahara."

But there was no need to shout. When he turned, Noburu found that the colonel had never left his side.

"Sir."

"Assuming those aircraft have not been shot down . . . or have not for any reason aborted . . . when will the bombing mission reach Omsk?"

Takahara glanced over at the row of digital clocks on the side wall, where the staff officers could instantly compare the world's crucial time zones.

"Momentarily," Takahara said.

"Go out and track him down," Taylor snapped. "You tell Tango five-five I want to speak with him personally. *Now.* Out."

Taylor drew off his headset, ruined face betraying disgust. Meredith had been in the midst of a detailed coordination call with the Tenth Cav, whose jammers had no more time on station, when the rising irritation in Taylor's voice caught his attention. He finished up his business and turned to the old man.

"Reno again?"

Taylor nodded. "The bastard's down on the ground. God knows what he's up to. His comms NCO doesn't know of any problems. But I wish the sonofabitch would follow orders."

Meredith understood Taylor's frustration. Reno would have to do something colossally foolish before he could be disciplined—and even then the general's son would get off lightly.

"Don't let it get to you, sir," Meredith said. "Come on. We ought to be popping champagne corks. It's a great day. A historic day."

"Merry," Taylor said, looking at the intelligence officer in earnest, "it's not over yet. This is when it gets dangerous. With everybody patting themselves on the back and trying to calculate how long it's going to be until they can get back home and give mama a squeeze. It only takes a single mistake . . ."

It was one of the rare occasions when Meredith disagreed with Taylor. The old man worried too much sometimes. The system had worked even better than expected. They had virtually destroyed the enemy's ability to carry on the war in sector and not a single friendly loss had been recorded. The mission was entering its final stage and they were about to turn into the last leg of the flight that would take them to their follow-on assembly areas. It was a time for Taylor to feel vindicated, avenged. The man's entire adult life had been pointed toward this day. And now he was being a spoilsport.

Meredith decided to shut up. He was feeling good, and if Taylor chose to squander the moment, it was up to him. Turning back to monitor the intel feeds, Meredith smiled to himself and played at phrasing the lines he would one day inflict on his grandchildren:

"I was with Taylor in Central Asia. Yes, sir. Me and Colonel George Taylor and the Seventh Cavalry. I was his right-hand man, you know. Why, during the battle Taylor and I were no farther apart than we are, boys. His face looked as though it had been painted up for war, just like a tribal chief. But he was a good-hearted man, really. Oh,

you wouldn't call him cheerful. But he was always good to me. He and I went way back, of course. Why, we were thick as thieves . . ."

"What the hell are you so tickled about?" Taylor demanded. But when Meredith looked around to answer, he saw that the old man was only bemused by the intelligence officer's behavior. A faint, halfhearted smile had crept over Taylor's mouth.

"Nothing, really," Meredith said. "I was just thinking, sir."

"Maureen?"

"No," Meredith said honestly, picturing his wife with her china skin and autumn hair for the first time in hours. "No, I'm saving her for later."

Taylor turned businesslike again. "Let's give Manny a call and update him on the situation. Knowing him, he's probably feeling guilty as hell at missing the battle."

Meredith asked one of the NCOs to pass him the earphones for the logistics net. He glanced at the list of call signs on the wall, then spoke evenly into the microphone:

"Sierra seven-three, this is Sierra one-zero. Over." He used his S-2 suffix.

Nothing.

"Probably smoking and joking," Taylor said. "Use my call sign. That'll get their attention."

"Sierra seven-three, this is Sierra five-five, over."

The two men waited, smiling, for Manny's anxious voice.

Taylor shook his head, almost laughing. "You remember that time in Mexico, when—"

Meredith began frantically throwing switches. He had not been paying sufficient attention. Now he recognized the tones he was getting in the headset.

"What's wrong?" Taylor asked.

Meredith ignored him for a moment. He wanted to be sure. He called up a graphic depiction of the state of the electromagnetic spectrum to the north of their present position, roughly where Manny should be. Somewhere between Omsk and the follow-on assembly areas.

"Merry, what the hell's the matter?"

Meredith looked up from the console. "Heavy jamming up north. Not from our side. The parameters are all wrong. The bastards might have slipped something by us."

He commanded the ship's master computer to do a sort: identify any hostile changes in the sector to the north.

Instantaneously, the screen flashed a digital image indicating enemy aircraft flying on a northerly axis. The computer had been doing its duty perfectly. It had been programmed to alert to enemy aircraft on a convergent course with the combat squadrons of the Seventh Cavalry. The computer had known of the presence of these enemy aircraft in the sky since they had taken off. But no one had told it to report enemy aircraft *passing* the regiment. Responding precisely to the demands of its human masters, the computer had not found the penetrating enemy flight of sufficient interest to merit a warning alert.

"Bandits," Meredith said.

"Project their route," Taylor told him, his voice heavy.

Meredith had the computer extrapolate from the enemy's past and present course.

The line of attack passed directly through Omsk.

Zeederberg was frantic. He had been trying for over an hour to reach any higher station. Without success. He wanted to report his discovery of the American transport. And to make absolutely certain that his superiors still wanted him to deliver his ordnance.

He looked at the image on the target monitor for the hundredth time. One single American-built wing-in-ground. What the hell did it mean? At the same time, he worried that the target would lift off before he was within range.

The sky began to pale. The on-board computers had regulated the flight perfectly. The bombs would land at dawn.

They were standoff, guided weapons, loaded with the most powerful compacted conventional explosives available, a new generation in destructive power, with a force equivalent to the yield of tactical nuclear weapons. These would be followed by the latest variety of fuel-air explosives, which would burn anything left by the bombs. The nine aircraft under his command had more than enough power to flatten the extensive industrial site.

"How long?" Zeederberg demanded from the navigator. He had asked this question so often that it needed no further elaboration. The navigator knew exactly what Zeederberg meant.

"Eleven minutes until weapons release."

Beneath the aircraft, the snow-covered wastes were becoming faintly visible to the naked eye.

"I'm going to try calling higher one more time," Zeederberg told his copilot.

"I *told* him," Taylor said. His voice had an unmistakable tone of pain in it which Meredith had never heard before. "I *told* him to get the hell out of there."

Everyone in the cabin had gathered around Meredith's bank of intelligence monitors. One showed the unchanging image of the wing-in-ground sitting placidly on the ground at Omsk, while others tracked the progress of the enemy aircraft.

They had tried everything. Relaying to Martinez. Alerting the Soviet air defenses. But the Japanese-built penetration bombers were jamming everything in their path. Exactly as Taylor's force had done and was still doing.

Taylor grabbed the hand mike for the command set, trying again. "Sierra seven-three, this is Sierra five-five. *Flash traffic.* I say again: *flash traffic.* Over."

Only the sound of the tormented sky.

"Sierra seven-three," Taylor began again, "if you are monitoring my transmission, you *must* get out of there *now. Evacuate now.* Enemy aircraft are heading your way. You only have minutes left. Over."

"Come *on*, Manny," Meredith said out loud. "For God's sake. Think of your goddamned Corvette. Think of the goddamned senoritas, would you? *Get out of there.*"

The enemy aircraft inexorably approached the red line that defined their estimated standoff bombing range.

"*Manny,* for Christ's sake," Meredith shouted at the sky, "get out of there." Tears gathered in his eyes.

Taylor slammed his fist down on the console. But the image of the transport craft at Omsk would not move.

Taylor took up the mike again.

"Manny," he said, dispensing with call signs for the first time in anyone's memory. "Manny, please listen to me. Get out of there *now*. Leave everything. Nothing matters. Just get on board that ugly sonofabitch and get out of there."

The console began to beep, signaling that the enemy aircraft were within standoff range of Omsk.

Zeederberg took a deep breath. Every attempt to reach higher headquarters had failed. And the rule was clear. When you lost contact, you continued your mission. No matter what.

In the target monitor he could actually make out magnified human figures in the first light of dawn.

"We're in the box," the navigator told him through the headset.

Zeederberg shrugged. "Releasing ordnance," he said.

"Releasing ordnance," a disembodied voice echoed.

Manny Martinez was in the best of spirits. From the last reports he had received over the log net a few hours earlier, the fight was going beautifully. Wouldn't even be much repair work. It sounded like a battle men would bullshit about for years to come. Over many a beer.

"Hurry up," he called. "It's time we un-assed this place." But he said it in an indulgent voice. His men were weary. They had finally gotten the last M-100 repaired. It could be flown to the follow-on assembly area under its own power. A present for the old man.

And he would not even be late. They could make up the lost time en route.

The new day was dawning with unexpected clarity. The storm had passed to the southwest, and the night's snowfall had given the tormented landscape an almost bearable appearance. Good day for flying, after all, he thought.

He breathed deeply, enjoying the cold, clean air, using it to rouse himself from the stupor to which the lack of sleep had brought him.

Behind him, the mechanics were rolling the repaired M-100 out of its shelter.

The old man's going to be proud, he thought. Then he strolled toward the transport to treat himself to one last cup of coffee.

17

3 November 2020

"AMERICANS," TAKAHARA REPEATED.

Noboru sat down. His eyelids fluttered several times in a broken rhythm. It was a small nervous tic he had developed over the years. The uncontrollable blinking only manifested itself for a few moments at a time, and only when Noboru was under extraordinary stress.

"That's impossible," he said.

"Sir," Takahara began, "you can listen to them yourself. The station is broadcasting in the clear. Apparently there is a defect in the encryption system of which the sender is unaware. Everything is in English. *American* English."

"It could be a deception," Noboru said.

Takahara pondered the idea for a moment. "It would seem that anything is possible today. But the intelligence specialists are convinced that the transmissions are genuine."

"Intelligence . . ." Noboru said, "does not have a very high standing at the moment. Does Tokyo know?"

"Sir. I personally delayed the transmission of the news until you could hear it first yourself."

"We must be certain."

"Intelligence believes—"

"We must be absolutely certain. We cannot afford another error. We have already paid far too high a price."

Americans, Noburu thought. He could no longer speak the word without conjuring the dead faces from his nightmares. What on earth were the Americans doing here? They had no love for the Russians. How could it be? How could it be?

Everything is a cycle, Noburu mused. We never learn. Misunderstanding the Americans seemed to be a Japanese national sport.

But how could it be? With the Americans still struggling to hold on to their own hemisphere, where Japanese-sponsored irregular and low-intensity operations had kept them tied down for over a decade. Japanese analysts preached that the United States had accepted its failure in the military-technological competition with Japan, that the Americans had neither the skills nor the funds to continue the contest on a global scale.

Noburu saw his personal aide, Akiro, making his way purposefully through the unaccustomed confusion of the operations center. What was it that Akiro had said just the day before? That the Americans were finished?

Now it would fall to him to finish them.

"Track them," Noburu told Takahara. "Identify who they are, what weapons they're using. We need targetable data."

"Yes, sir."

Only yesterday, he had been flying triumphantly above the African bush. Surprising the Americans. Vanquishing them. Today they had surprised him. But it wasn't finished yet. Noburu knew only too well what was going to happen. It had been written by more powerful hands than his.

The dream warrior had known this too. In his contest with the dream Americans, with their dead and terrible faces.

"Sir," Akiro addressed him. Noburu could see that the young man had been badly jarred by all this. Unaccustomed to the taste of defeat. Even temporary defeat.

"Yes?"

"Sir. Tokyo. On the satellite link. General Tsuji wishes to speak with you."

Noburu had known that the call would come. It was inevitable. And he knew what the caller would command him to do.

"I will take the call in my private office," Noburu said.

"Sir," Akiro and Takahara responded in near unison.

"Oh, and Takahara. Contact Noguchi. His readiness test is canceled. Instead, he is to hold his unit at the highest state of combat alert." Noburu hated to speak the words. But it was no less than his duty. And he would always do his duty. "But he is to take no further action until he hears from me personally."

Takahara acknowledged the instruction and turned to its execution. But Akiro seemed to shrink ever so slightly. As Noburu's aide, the younger man was privileged to know the highly classified capabilities of Noguchi's aircraft awaiting a mission at the airfield in Bukhara on the far side of Central Asia. The uncertainty around Akiro's mouth made it clear that he was not nearly as hardened as the uncompromising words that passed so easily between his lips pretended. Yes, words were one thing . . .

"Stay here," Noburu told his aide. "I can find my office on my own. Sit here in my chair and pay attention to all that goes on around you today. This is war, Akiro."

Noburu marched through the half-chaos of his operations center, proceeding down the hall past the room where the master computer soldiered in silence. He stopped at the private elevator that had once served a Soviet general. The guard slammed his heels against the wall as he came to attention.

Noburu used the few seconds remaining to him to muster his arguments. But he found them fatally weakened by the events of the early morning hours. Why had the Americans—if they truly were Americans—interfered? He knew in his heart he would never convince old Tsuji to behave humanely. But just as it was his duty as a soldier to follow orders, it was his duty as a human being to make one last effort to break the chain of events.

His office was cool and very clean. Its austerity and silence normally soothed him, but today the empty suite felt like a tomb.

He sat down at his desk and picked up the special phone.

"This is General Noburu Kabata."

"Hold for General Tsuji," a voice told him.

He waited dutifully, imagining the magic beams that sliced through the heavens to allow him to speak privately with another man so far away. The technology, in its essence, was generations old. Yet, at times, such things still filled Noburu with a sense of wonder. It still amazed him that metal machines could carry men through the sky.

I'm a bad Japanese, he thought. I don't know how to take things for granted.

"Noburu?" the acid voice startled him.

"General Tsuji."

"I cannot be certain of the view from your perspective, Noburu. However, from Tokyo, it appears that you are presiding over the greatest defeat suffered by Japanese arms in seventy-five years."

"It's bad," Noburu agreed. Ready to take his medicine.

"It's far worse than 'bad,'" Tsuji said, loading his voice with spite. "It's a disaster."

"Yes."

"I would personally relieve you, Noburu. But I can't. To take you out of there now would be an embarrassment to Japan. A *further* embarrassment. An admission of failure."

"I will resign," Noburu said.

"You will do nothing of the kind. Nor will you do anything . . . foolish. This is the twenty-first century. And your guts aren't worth staining a carpet. All you can do now is to try to turn things around. Have you got a plan?"

"Not yet," Noburu said. "We're still gathering information."

"You know what I mean, Noburu. You know exactly what I mean. Have you formulated a plan for the commitment of Three-one-three-one?"

Three-one-three-one was Tokyo's code name for Noguchi's command. Everyone else simply referred to them as Scramblers. But Tsuji was a stickler for the details of military procedure.

"No."

There was silence on the other end. Noburu understood it to be a calculated silence. Tsuji showing his contempt.

"Why?"

"General Tsuji . . . I continue to believe that the employment of . . . Three-one-three-one . . . would be a mistake. We will never be forgiven."

Tsuji laughed scornfully. "What? For*given*? By whom? You must be going mad, Noburu."

Yes, Noburu thought, perhaps. "The Scramblers are criminal weapons," he said. "We, of all people—"

"Noburu, listen to me. Your personal ruminations are of no interest to me. Or to anyone else. You have one mission, and one only: to win a war. For Japan. And can you honestly tell me, after what we have all seen this morning, that you are in a position to guarantee victory without the employment of Three-one-three-one?"

"No."

"Then get to work."

"General Tsuji?"

"What?"

"My intelligence department believes they have broken into the communications network of the attackers."

"*Well.* So you haven't been entirely asleep. Have you positively identified the units involved? Do you have any idea of the type of weapons? It's incredible to think that the Russians could have pulled all this off."

"The intelligence department doesn't think it's Russians."

Tsuji laughed. "Who then? Creatures from space, perhaps?"

"Americans."

"*What?*"

"Americans," Noburu repeated.

"That's insane. Who's your senior intelligence officer?"

"I believe it to be true," Noburu said. And it was not a lie. He did not need any further intelligence confirmation. He knew it to be the Americans. He had always known it. He simply had not been able to admit it to himself. Everything was so plain. It was ordained.

"Noburu, if you actually have evidence . . . if you're not dreaming this up . . ."

"It's true," Noburu said. "We're still working out the details. But the Americans are involved."

There was another silence on the Tokyo end. But this time it was not calculated and carefully controlled.

"Then get them," Tsuji said suddenly. "Destroy them. Use Three-one-three-one."

"General Tsuji, we have to think—"

"That's an order, Noburu. Introduce your Americans to the future of warfare."

"We're going to get them," Taylor said with forced calm. "Merry, start running the interception azimuths. Stay with them."

"Yes, sir."

"We're going to get those bastards," Taylor told the ops center staff. His voice was carefully controlled in volume, if not in tone. He had just watched the destruction of the Omsk site on the monitor. The way a civilian might watch a live television report from a riot or revolution—gripped by the images, but helpless to exert the least influence upon the situation. One moment, the wing-in-ground transport had been lying like a drowsing beast in the clear dawn. Then the screen smeared with the powdery swirls that sheathed the hearts of the bomb blasts. Next came the firestorm. There would be no survivors.

"We'll have to start turning," Merry Meredith said. "Right now."

"Flapper?" Taylor called forward through the intercom, "you listening up there?"

"Roger," the copilot said.

"Merry's going to plug in the new grids."

"Roger."

"Merry," Taylor said. "You and the boys guide us into a good ambush position. Cue the escort ships to follow us. I'm going forward to talk to the chief."

Taylor carefully put his headset back in its holder and squeezed out through the hatch that separated the ops cell from the small central corridor. He paused for a moment in the narrow, sterile passageway, closing his eyes, fighting to master his emotions. It was not as easy as it once had been. He remembered Manny Martinez as a bright, innocent lieutenant in Los Angeles, as a struggling horseman in Mexico. The boy had become a man in the years Taylor had known him, yet, he remained young and laughably earnest in Taylor's recollection. Why on earth hadn't the boy listened? He was normally such a fine, dutiful officer. Why, this time of all times . . . ?

Taylor rubbed at his armpit where the shoulder holster chafed. He knew that the flight of nine Mitsubishi aircraft was not a sufficiently lucrative target to cause a regimental commander to turn back in the middle of a battle. Objectively speaking. The action was unforgivably personal, and militarily unnecessary. He was needed elsewhere. He had to oversee the move into the new assembly areas, the rearming and re-fitting process . . . well, the rearming would be problematical. The last functional calibration device for the M-100s' main armament had been on the transport back at Omsk with Manny. They would have to fight on with the weapons systems in whatever condition they were in at the end of this day's combat. Taylor had already programmed the master computer to restrict further targets regiment-wide, attacking only the most valuable. But they would need to take stock, to see what remained in terms of immediate combat capability. It was always this way, somehow. You built the finest war machines in the history of military operations. Then you failed to supply an adequate number of the small tools that enabled them to carry on the fight. It was an imperfect world. He would do his best with what he had. And who could say? The day's combat had been so successful that everything just might grind to a halt. You could never be certain. Perhaps Merry was right. And maybe their luck would hold a little longer.

He had an impossible number of tasks to fulfill. There would be little rest, and the wide-awake pills ultimately carried a price in deteriorating judgment, in a collapsing body. The pills merely delayed the mind and body's failure but could not prevent it.

He knew that a better officer would never have turned to take revenge on nine aircraft that had already disposed of their ordnance.

But there were some things a man could not leave undone.

Taylor worked his way into the cockpit, dropping himself into his seat. He motioned to his copilot to remove the three-quarter flight helmet the old warrant officer wore in his dual role as copilot and weapons officer.

"Flapper, you've been working with these birds since they were scribbles on a blueprint. Tell me honestly—will we be wasting our time going after those fast movers?"

Chief Krebs made the face of a careful old farmer at an auction.

"Can't say for sure. Nobody ever figured on M-100s getting in a dogfight with zoomies. That's blue-suiter work. I mean, helicopters, sure. Knock 'em out of the sky all the day and night."

"But?"

The old warrant officer smiled slightly, revealing teeth stained by a lifetime of coffee and God only knew what else. "Well, I don't see a damned reason why it *can't* be done. If we get a good angle of intercept. The guns are fast enough. And we've got plenty of range. The computer don't care what you tell it to kill. And these babies are pretty well built. They'll take a hell of a shaking. Superb aeroelastics. No, boss, I'd say, so long as we can get a good vector . . . I mean, no forward hemisphere stuff . . . those Mitsubishis have a very low radar cross-section head-on. And they're fast. No, if we can just sneak in on them between, say, nine and ten o'clock, we just might take them down."

"I can mark you down as a believer?" Taylor asked.

Krebs shrugged. "What the hell. Anyhow, I'm anxious to see what these babies can really do." The old warrant grinned, a savvy farmer who had just made the bargain he wanted. "If nothing else, it's going to give them Air Force hot dogs something to think about."

Taylor settled his hand briefly on Krebs's shoulder. The old man was nothing but gristle, bone, and spite, as sparse as the hill country from which a spark of ambition had led him decades before. Then Taylor went back into the operations cell.

"We'll have to go max speed," Captain Parker, the assistant S-3, warned him. "Our biggest problem's going to be fuel."

"Can we make it?" Taylor asked.

"Barely. We'll have to divert into the nearest assembly area."

"First Squadron's site?"

"Yes, sir. We'll be running on empty after the interception. We'll have to stop off at Lieutenant Colonel Tercus's gas station at AA Silver."

"Silver. That's the one by Orsk, right?"

"Yes, sir."

Taylor nodded. All right. "Anyway, I like the sound of it. Omsk to Orsk. Sounds clean."

"Actually," Merry Meredith interrupted, "the assembly area's offset from the city. It's near a little hamlet called Malenky-Bolshoy Rog."

"Whatever," Taylor said. "Lucky Dave and I are going to need to talk, anyway, and he's riding with Tercus." Taylor straightened as fully as he could in the low-ceilinged compartment. "Now, let's get the bastards who got Manny."

Captain Jack Sturgis of Bravo Troop, First Squadron, Seventh United States Cavalry, felt a level of exhilaration he had not known since his high school basketball team won the game that took them to the state semifinals. He had been in combat. And not only had he done everything right—he had not even been afraid. Not really. Not once things got going. Basically, in Sturgis's newly acquired view, combat was a lot like sports. You got caught up in it, forgetting everything: the risk of personal injury, even the people watching you. Something inside of you took over. It was an incredible thing. He had read novels in which the heroes always felt sad and kind of empty after a battle. But he felt full of life, bursting with it. He had seen combat. And he had come through it just fine.

His troop had its major engagement well behind it. Now they were simply flying picket duty over empty expanses, keeping an eye on the regiment's left flank and steadily making their way toward their follow-on assembly area. They had flown out from under the snow, and the sky was clear at the southernmost edge of the regiment's deployment. Everything was perfect.

"Two-two, this is Two-seven," his wingman called. "So where's this place again? Over."

"This is Two-two. Orsk. *Orsk,* for God's sake. And don't get lazy on me. We're going to be flying back into the snow when we turn northwest."

"Think they'll cut us loose, if things quiet down? I'd really like to meet a couple of Russians before we go home."

Sturgis knew exactly what the lieutenant meant. He wanted to meet a few Russian *women.* Just to check them out. Sturgis had nothing against the idea himself. But he felt he had to maintain a mature face before his subordinate.

"Just keep your mind on the mission. Anyway, Orsk isn't exactly Las Vegas, near as I can tell. And you know the old man. He'll give you a medal before he'll give you a break. Over."

"We kicked some ass, though. Didn't we?"

"This is Two-two. Save the bullshitting for when we're on the ground. Maintain basic radio discipline."

Captain Jack Sturgis, former member of an Ohio State semifinalist basketball team and presently a United States Army officer, meant well. He wanted to get it right, and he had no way of knowing that the encryption device on his troop internal net had already failed over an hour before. His set could still receive and decode incoming encrypted messages, but, whenever he broadcast, his words were clear for all the world to hear. The state of encryption devices had become so advanced that none of the design engineers working the "total system" concept for the M-100 had considered building in a simple warning mechanism to indicate such a failure.

The engineers were not bad engineers, and the system's design was a remarkably good one, overall. The M-100 had proved itself in battle. But it was a very, very complex machine, of the sort that legitimately needed years of field trials before reaching maturity. The United States had not had the years to spare and, all in all, we were remarkably lucky with the performance of the M-100, although Captain Jack Sturgis might not have agreed, had he known what was waiting for him.

"Orsk," Noburu said.

"Sir," Colonel Noguchi barked through the earpiece, "I can have my aircraft off the ground in a quarter of an hour. We can complete the mission planning while airborne."

"That's fine," Noburu said. "The intelligence department will pass you the frequency tracks on which the Americans are broadcasting. You will have to pay close attention. We still cannot detect them with radar or with any other means. Their deception suites are far more advanced than any of us would have believed of the Americans. It may be hard to get a precise fix on them until they are actually on the ground."

"It doesn't matter," Noguchi said. "The Scramblers are area weapons. If they are within a one hundred nautical mile radius of Orsk, the Americans will be stricken."

Noburu wondered what the current population was of the city of Orsk. No. Better not to know, he decided.

"Noguchi?" he asked in genuine curiosity, "how do you *feel?"*

The colonel was taken aback by the question, which he frankly did not understand.

"Sir," he responded, after a wondering pause, "my spirits are excellent. And my health is very good. You have no cause for worry."

"Of course not," Noburu said.

Lieutenant Colonel Reno knew that everything was going to be all right. He had monitored Taylor's message on the command net as Taylor turned over control of the regiment to Heifetz so that Taylor himself could fly off on a personal glory hunt. No matter what he himself did, Reno knew, there could be no serious threat from Taylor now. The old bastard wasn't so sly after all. He had compromised himself. Any subordinate with half a brain would have no difficulty portraying Taylor's action in an unfavorable light. By stretching it a little bit, you could even make the case that Taylor had deserted his post.

"Bronco, this is Saber six," Reno told the microphone.

"Bronco, over."

"Have you gotten that damned problem fixed, Bronco?" From his command M-100, Taylor had electronically imposed limits on the range of targets the regiment's systems were free to attack. Taylor claimed he wanted to preserve a combat-ready force, now that the last functional calibrator had been lost.

But Reno was no fool. The regiment had been so successful—unimaginably successful—in destroying the enemy's ability to wage technologically competent warfare in the zone of attack that Reno suspected there might not be another battle. At the very least, things would settle down into a stalemate, with both sides materially exhausted and incapable. The likeliest scenario, from Reno's point of view, was that the politicians would get involved and there would be a negotiated settlement. Which meant that today might be the only chance a man got to prove his abilities.

"This is Bronco. The problem's fixed. We're ready to resume contact. Over."

"Good work. Now let's start running up those numbers again."

It had required some effort to override the restriction Taylor's master computer had imposed on his M-100s. But the weapons were free again now. In fact, they could attack a wider range of targets now than they had been permitted at the beginning of the day's hunt. Reno saw nothing wrong with spending a few extra rounds on the odd truck or range car. The important thing, at this point, was to run up Third Squadron's number of kills. And, given that the other two squadrons were under strict limits from here on out, Reno figured his score was likely to come out the highest, after all.

A good officer had to take the initiative.

"Are we going to make it?" Taylor asked.

The set of Flapper Krebs's face was unmistakably tense beneath the incomplete helmet.

"It's going to be close," the warrant officer said. "Damn close. The sonsofbitches have picked up speed. They must be scared as hell about something."

Taylor glanced at the man with concern. Then he got on the intercom.

"Merry, do you have any indication whatsoever that those bandits have picked us up?"

"No, sir."

"It looks like they're running scared. They're heading south fast."

"Might just be nerves," Meredith said. "Scary sky out there. They picked up speed, but there's been absolutely no deviation in their course. They're coming down the slot straight as an arrow."

"Roger. Parker," he said, addressing the assistant S-3, "how do we look on angle of intercept?"

"I know the chief wants to take them from behind," the captain said, "but the best we're going to do is about a nine-o'clock angle of attack. Maybe even a little more forward than that. If we try to get too fancy, we're going to lose them. They're just moving too fast."

Taylor looked over at Krebs, whose hands remained perfectly steady on the controls, ready to override the computer if it became necessary.

"What do you think, Flapper?"

Krebs shrugged. "Give it a shot."

"Merry?" Taylor asked, working the intercom again, "are the target parameters locked in?"

"Roger. Nine Mitsubishi 4000s. Alteration to program accepted."

"Flapper?"

"I got it. Weapons systems green."

"Okay," Taylor said. "Let's do a temporary delete on everything else. Keep all sensors focused on those bastards."

"Roger."

"Range?"

"Two hundred miles and closing."

"Colonel?" Krebs said to Taylor, "I can't promise you this is going to work. But I can guarantee you it's going to be quick. We're only going to get one chance."

"Roger. Parker, do a double check on our escort birds. Make sure their computers are on exactly the same sheet of music."

"Roger."

"One chance," the old warrant repeated.

Zeederberg was anxious to get back down on the ground. He had been out of contact with higher headquarters for hours, and the level of electronic interference in the atmosphere was utterly without precedent in his experience. Something was wrong. Even his on-board systems were starting to deteriorate, as though the electromagnetic siege was beginning to beat down the walls of his aircraft. He could no longer communicate even with the other birds flying in formation with his own, and the sophisticated navigational aids employed for evasive flying were behaving erratically. The formation had been reduced to flying higher off the ground than Zeederberg would have liked, and all they could do was to maintain visual contact with each other and head south at the top speed their fuel reserves would allow.

They had destroyed the target. Mission accomplished. The standoff bombs had proven accurate, as always, and what the bombs had not flattened, the fuel-air explosives burned or suffocated. Zeederberg hoped it had been worth it. The only confirmed enemy target he had been able to register had been that single American-built wing-in-ground transport. Perhaps there had been other equipment hidden in the maze of old plants and warehouses. Undoubtedly, the Japanese knew what they were doing. But during the mission brief, no one had warned them to expect a density of electronic interference so thick it seemed to physically buffet the aircraft. Something was terribly wrong.

Zeederberg felt unaccustomed streaks of sweat trailing down his back, chilling the inside of his flight suit. It was nerve-racking flying. This is what it must have been like in the old days, he thought. Before the computers took over.

"Sky watch report?" Zeederberg begged through the intercom. He half expected the intercom to go out too.

"All clear," a tiny voice responded. "Plenty of interference. But the sky looks as clean as can be."

It was like a visit to the dentist, Zeederberg told himself.

You just had to remember that it was all going to be over before you knew it.

He promised himself that as soon as he got home to South Africa he was going to pack up Marieke and the kids, go off to the beach for a holiday, lie in the sun, and laugh about all this.

"Forty miles and closing," Meredith's voice rang through the headphones.

"Roger."

"They're coming too fast," Krebs said. "We're going to have to engage at max range and take our chances."

"All right," Taylor said. "Weapons systems to full automatic."

"Thirty-five miles."

"Bad angle," the assistant S-3 cried.

"Fuck it," Krebs said. "You pays your money and you takes your chance."

Taylor's eyes were fixed to the monitor.

"Here they come," he said.

"Hold on," Krebs shouted.

The M-100 jerked its snout up into the air like a crazy carnival ride designed to sicken even the heartiest child. The main gun began to pulse.

"Jesus Christ."

The M-100 seemed to slam against one wall of sky, then another, twisting to bring its gun to bear on the racing targets. Taylor had never experienced anything like it.

"Hold on."

Taylor tried to watch the monitor, but the M-100 was pulling too hard. The machine's crazy acrobatics tossed him about in his safety harness as though he were a weightless doll. He did not think the machine would hold together. The system had not been designed for the bizarre and sudden angles of aerial combat with fixed-wing aircraft.

Going to crash, he thought. *We're going to break up*.

He strained to reach the emergency panel. But the rearing craft threw him back hard against his seat.

The main gun continued to pulse throughout the mechanical storm.

Taylor tried again to reach the emergency toggles.

"Flapper," he shouted. *"Help me."*

There was no answer. Taylor could not even twist his head around to see if his copilot was all right.

The M-100 went into a hard turn, slamming Taylor's head back.

The main gun blasted the empty sky.

Suddenly, the M-100 leveled out and began to fly as smoothly as if nothing had occurred.

Taylor's neck hurt, and he felt dizzy to the point of nausea. But beside him the old chief warrant officer was already on the radio, checking in with the two escort ships. Krebs's voice was as calm as could be. It took a damned old warrant, Taylor decided, to fake that kind of coolness.

The entire action had taken only seconds. One bad curve on the roller coaster.

Taylor looked at the target monitor. The screen was empty.

"Merry," he called angrily. "Merry, goddamnit, we lost them. The sonsofbitches got away."

"Calm down there, Colonel," Krebs told him. "Ain't nobody got away. Look at your kill counters."

"Chief's right," Merry said through the intercom. "We got them. Every last one. Look."

Meredith relayed a series of ground images to the monitors in the forward cabin. Taylor insisted on going through the images twice. Counting.

Yes. They had gotten them all. Or, rather, the M-100s had. Nine unmistakable wrecks lay strewn across the wasteland, with components burning here and there.

The staffers back in the ops cell were hooting with glee. Taylor could hear them through the intercom, and he imagined them all doing a little war dance in the cramped cubicle. But his own feelings had not settled yet. It had all been over so quickly. It made him feel old, a little lost. For all his education and experience, this was not war as he imagined he knew it. It was all so quick, so utterly impersonal. Taylor felt as though he were being left behind.

The battle staff continued their noisy celebration. Captain Parker, the assistant S-3, even overcame his fear of the old, severe veteran.

"Colonel Taylor, sir," the captain called forward, his voice full of childlike exuberance, "you think the Air Force will give us combat wings for that one?"

"Fat fucking chance," Krebs interrupted. His voice had the delectably exaggerated sourness that seemed to come naturally to warrant officers when they were very proud of something they and their comrades had done. "Those goddamned Air Force weenies are going to be in Congress tomorrow, lobbying to take these babies away from us." The M-100 program had taken the best years of Krebs's life and now his face glowed with the sort of pride a man might take in the spectacular success of his child. "No," he assured them all, "they'll be crying fit to flood the Potomac." He patted the side panel of the cockpit the way one of his gray-suited ancestors must have patted the flank of a horse. "They're going to tell you these babies are too good for dumb grunts like us."

"Merry," Taylor said, "I want you to call up our Russian friends. Get Kozlov. Or, better yet, go straight to old Ivanov. Ask them . . . ask them if they would please send a detail out to the staging area. See if there's anything . . . see if . . . damn it, you know what I mean."

The bodies. Anything identifiable. To bury in their native soil.

"Yes, sir," Meredith said.

"Parker?"

"Yes, sir?" the assistant S-3 replied.

"What's your first name?"

"Horace, sir."

"No. I mean, what do people call you?"

"Hank."

"Okay, Hank. While Merry's calling our Russian brethren, you can start reprogramming our route. Just get us to the AA Silver as quickly as possible. Head straight for Orsk."

"Do you think they're lying?" General Ivanov asked.

"No, sir," Kozlov said. "The picture's still a bit muddy—

we've got so many gaps in our coverage—but it's evident that the Iranians think they've just been struck by the wrath of God. Their communications discipline has fallen apart completely, and they're cursing the Japanese for all they're worth." Kozlov touched a dead tooth with his tongue. "It almost sounds as though the Japanese are going to have a mutiny on their hands. If they can't manage to pull things back together in short order."

"And the Japanese themselves?"

"Harder to tell."

General Ivanov paced across the room. He stopped in front of a wall that bore cheaply framed prints of the heroes of Russia's bygone wars with Islam in the Caucasus and Central Asia. Suvorov, Yermolov, Paskevich, and half a dozen others. Kozlov could feel a deep sadness in the general as his illustrious predecessors confronted him with his failures from a remove of two centuries.

"Incredible," Ivanov said, turning back to Kozlov. "Simply incredible. Even if the Americans are exaggerating the numbers twice over. It's virtually unthinkable."

"It provides us with a real opportunity," Kozlov said.

Ivanov lowered his eyebrows. The expression on the general's face did not make sense to Kozlov under the circumstances.

"I mean, in order to mount local counterattacks, sir," Kozlov continued. "To stabilize the lines. And then—well, who knows? If the Americans have really—"

"Stop talking nonsense, Kozlov."

A diseased tooth telegraphed a message of startling pain throughout Kozlov's jaw.

"There are things of which you know nothing," General Ivanov said bluntly. "The situation is more complex than you imagine. I want you to get the staff moving. Draw up hasty plans that specify the maximum troop dispersion that the integrity of the defense will permit. And don't waste a minute. Send out preliminary orders immediately."

"But . . . we promised the Americans that we'd support them, that we would attack . . ."

"The situation does not permit it."

"But—"

The Americans were having a splendid day, covering

themselves in glory. Their only setback appeared to be a minor air strike on the tail end of their support establishment out at the industrial complex. But, for Kozlov, things were going from bad to worse. There were rumors of extraordinary KGB activities in Moscow, including a wave of arrests without precedent since the long period of turmoil in the wake of the Gorbachev era. The security services had already run out of control in the rear of the combat zone, executing "traitors," while the front collapsed into ever greater chaos. Now, on top of everything else, it appeared that there was a significant secret about which he knew nothing. He had served with Ivanov since their days together in Baku, in the reoccupation army, and it stunned him to be so little trusted. He realized that the secret must be a very important one indeed.

His teeth ached unmercifully. He worried that he would have to have them removed. All of them.

"Comrade General," Kozlov began again, "can you please tell me what's going on? How can I direct the staff? How can I plan effectively when I don't know what's happening?"

Ivanov had turned away again, positioning himself before the lithograph of Suvorov's old greyhound face. "Simply do as you're told, Viktor Sergeyevich. Disperse our forces to the maximum extent compatible with the maintenance of the defense and unit integrity."

What defense? The little islands of half-frozen units stranded on the steppes, unsure of which way to point their empty weapons? And what unit integrity? The fantasies of the wall charts in headquarters where the latest information was three battles old? The true unit designators of regiments and divisions that had been slaughtered, forgotten by everyone but God and a few obscure staff officers?

The lessons of Russian history were clear to Kozlov. When the heavens were collapsing overhead, the only thing left to do was to counterattack. With bayonets. With stones and fists, if necessary. The Americans had shown them the way. And now it appeared that it was all for nothing.

"There is little time," Ivanov said, with despair suddenly evident in his voice.

"Yes, sir," Kozlov responded. He turned to leave and carry out the general's order.

"Viktor Sergeyevich?" Ivanov called out after his subordinate. The practiced severity of his voice relented slightly, reminding Kozlov of better days when they had served together under clear blue skies. "Don't be too impatient with me. You'll understand soon enough. Too soon, perhaps." The general moved wearily toward the plush chair behind his oversize desk. But he did not sit down. Instead, he braced himself with an old man's hand on the back of the chair and stared past the younger officer.

"You see, it's like a game," Ivanov said, "in which we are now merely interested spectators. First, the Japanese underestimated the Americans. And now the Americans are terribly underestimating the Japanese."

18

3 November 2020

SCRAMBLED EGGS. PALE, OVERCOOKED, THEN LEFT SITting too long on a serving tray, they were by no means the finest scrambled eggs Ryder had ever encountered. Liberally dusted with salt and pepper, they tasted of little more than pepper and salt. Further tormented with several hearty splats of the Louisiana Hot Sauce one of Ryder's fellow warrant officers carried with him everywhere in the world, the eggs finally took on a hint of flavor reminiscent of the dehydrated atrocities served up on maneuvers. The portion was meager, the texture resilient, and Ryder had to remove a short black hair from the margarine-colored clump. These were, at best, imperfect scrambled eggs. But Ryder was wordlessly grateful for them, just as he was grateful for the woman.

Breakfast in the threadbare Moscow hotel was always unpredictable in its details. The detachment of staff personnel from the Tenth Cavalry, waiting grumpily in their civilian clothes, received whatever happened to be available on that particular day in the capital of all the Russias. There was always bread—occasionally stale—or a bit of pastry dripping with weary cream. Sometimes cheese appeared, or even carefully apportioned slivers of ham. On days when the inadequacies of the system decided to assert themselves, the yawning waiters presented formless, nameless, sickness-scented constructions few of the Americans were brave enough or sufficiently hungry to eat.

Once, shredded cardboard fish in gelatin had been lurking in wait for the early risers—the waiters had been uncharacteristically animated, insisting that the fish was a great delicacy. The sole saving grace of the meal was the scalding gray coffee, which, blessedly, never seemed to run out.

And so, presented with this sudden gift of scrambled eggs, delivered straight from heaven with only the briefest of layovers in the Russian countryside, Ryder felt as though his life had accelerated into a realm of fresh possibilities, as though Christmas had come unexpectedly early along with this withered mound of cholesterol.

The woman was primarily responsible for this bloom of optimism, of course. The eggs were merely a gracious answer to the real physical appetite his night with Valya had excited in him. He could not remember the last time he had been this hungry, and despite the little sleep he had managed, he did everything with alacrity, whether spreading the slightly rancid butter on his bread, drinking the burning coffee, or thinking about the future.

He would see her again. In the sweat-stale morning she had jarred him by bolting from the bed, jabbering in Russian. He had finally reached the stout fortress walls of real sleep, and the first moments of waking had an aura of madness about them. Torn away from him, the girl spit words into the darkness as she noisily tried to find her way. The brain behind his forehead had gone to lead. He turned on the bedside lamp and saw Valya wrestling her slip down over her head and shoulders. It looked as if a white silken animal were attacking her. The instant froze in his memory—the still visible breasts suggesting themselves from the thin chest, the flat white belly, and the trove of low hair glinting like sprung copper wires. Patches of glaze topped her thighs. Then the white cloth fell down like a curtain, and the eyes of a smart animal took his measure.

"I'm late," she told him, speaking English.

"What?"

"I'm late. It's terrible. I must go."

"What? Go where? What's the matter?"

With an unbroken series of movements, she scooped up her stockings, turned about, and dropped her bottom on the side of the bed, then leaned back and kissed him over her shoulder. It was the kind of noisy, quick kiss offered a child. She leaned forward and began working her panty hose over her toes.

"But I have told you. I am a schoolteacher. I must go to the class."

"Valya," he said, trying the name in the light. "Valya . . ." He reached out toward her, capturing the paucity of a breast in his hand.

She offered him a little moan, half sex and half impatience.

"But you must understand," she said, going about the merciless business of dressing as she spoke, "even if I want to stay, I must go. For the children."

He trailed his hand downward from the breast he had kissed raw, tracing her frailness beneath the fabric.

"Valya . . . I'm glad about what happened last night."

She looked at him quizzically, panty hose stalled below her knees.

"I mean," he went on, "I'm glad you stayed. That you stayed with me."

"Oh, yes," she said. "Everything is nice." And she bounced to her feet to draw the hose over her slender thighs. Her slip rose on the back of her hands, and he wanted terribly to pull her back down, to lift the fabric a little higher still and to plunge back inside her, without the least further preparation. He felt as though he wanted her more fiercely now than he had at any time during the night, when he had only to turn her to him and briefly warn her with his hand.

"Can I see you again?" he asked carefully. "Will you have dinner with me again tonight?"

She looked at him as though he had surprised her utterly. Then she smiled:

"Tonight? You wish for us to have dinner *again?*"

"Yes. If you don't have other plans."

"No, no. No, I think this is a very good idea . . . Jeff." She threw herself back down on the bed, kissing him again, first on his morning-dead mouth, then along the flat field of muscle between shoulder and breast. "You are so wonderful," she said quickly. "I thought you do not want to see me anymore."

Before he could get a grip on her, before his body could insist that she delay her departure, she slipped away from him again, stepping into her red dress. Ryder did not know much about Russian classroom customs, but he was pretty sure she was going to go home and change rather than confront the system in that particular outfit.

"Tonight," she said gaily. "And at what hour?"

Work crowded back into his mind. He knew there would be a tremendous amount to do. In the wake of the breakthrough with the Japanese computer system. He would be a focal point of the exploration effort. The timing was terrible.

"Around eight?" he said, reaching for a compromise between duty and desire. Standing there on the verge of leaving, the woman looked as vulnerably beautiful to him as any woman had ever appeared. With her face that wanted washing for yesterday's makeup and her rebellious hair. "But wait for me, if I'm not there exactly at eight. Please. I might be running late. On business."

"Oh, yes," she half sang. "I will wait for you. We will have dinner with one another. And we will talk."

"Yes," he said. "We have a lot to talk about."

Then she was gone, in the wake of a blown kiss and the slam of an ill-mounted door. Her footsteps died away in the early gloom of the corridor.

While showering, he had been stricken by a sudden fear. He hurried, towel-wrapped, back into the bedroom. Frantically, he rifled through his wallet, then checked his other valuables.

His watch and the holstered computer were still in place. No money was missing. His credit cards lay neatly ranked in their leather nest.

He stood by the nightstand, dripping, ashamed of himself for suspecting her. Then the remembrance of her excited him so powerfully that he had a hard time tucking himself into his shorts.

He went down to breakfast with a gigantic emptiness in his belly, ready to eat every slice of brown bread on the table. And to his wonderment, the waiter laid a plate of scrambled eggs before him.

He sat across from Dicker Sienkiewicz, the granddaddy

of the staff warrants. When the question involved the order of battle of foreign armies, Dicker could beat most computers to the answer. And he had phenomenal connections. He seemed to have a personal line to every other veteran who had survived the series of reductions-in-force that had devastated the United States Army back in the nineteen nineties. He was also, in Ryder's view, a good man. Bald-headed and requisitely grumpy, he would nurse a beer or two in the bar with the other warrants, but then he would go back to his room, alone, to continue the day's work. Ryder felt he was a kindred spirit, despite the gap in their ages, and he trusted the old man.

When the waiters faded beyond hearing distance, Dicker leaned across the table toward Ryder.

"Heard the news, Jeff?"

Ryder looked at the other two warrants who shared the table, then back toward Dicker, shaking his head. He forked up another load of scrambled eggs.

Dicker leaned even closer, whispering. "The attack went in last night. I have it from a good source that the Seventh's kicking butt." The older warrant smiled slightly, but proudly. *His* Army was back in the field and doing its duty.

"That's *great,*" Ryder said, reaching for another piece of bread.

Dicker nodded. "You know, I've got an old buddy down with the Seventh. Flies for old man Taylor himself. Flapper Krebs. I wonder what the hell he's doing right now?"

One of the other warrants, whose age fell between that of Ryder and the bald-headed veteran, said, "Yeah, I know Krebs. All dried-up and used up. Kind of like you, Dicker."

The older warrant reddened right up through the desert of his scalp. The other warrants loved to tease him, since he never failed to rise to the bait.

"Chief Krebs," he said angrily, "could chew you up and spit you out. Why, I remember back in Africa—"

His tormentor made a face of mock curiosity. "What the hell were you doing in Africa, Dicker? Vacation or something?"

The teasing inspired the old warrant to begin a lengthy defense of the achievements of a long career. Ryder waited politely, if impatiently, until he could get a word in, then asked quickly:

"Dicker, you going to eat those eggs?"

"Well, fuck me dead," Ryder's third tablemate said, looking up from the wreckage of his breakfast.

Ryder looked in the indicated direction. Colonel Williams, the commander of the Tenth Cavalry, had entered the dining room. It was the first time during the deployment that Ryder had seen the colonel, who spent his time out at the field sites, directing the actions of his electronic warfare squadrons. It was apparent that something important was going down, since Colonel Williams had marched right in wearing his field gear over a worn-looking camouflage uniform. His boots marked his progress with traces of mud. The colonel looked impatient.

Lieutenant Colonel Manzetti, the senior officer in the staff detachment billeted in the hotel, erupted from his table, dropping his napkin on the floor as he hurried toward the regimental commander. Manzetti chewed and swallowed as he maneuvered through the tables. The lieutenant colonel was a holdover from the days before Colonel Williams had been given the command with the mission of clearing out the deadwood and the homesteaders, and Manzetti's haste to intercept Williams reminded Ryder of the movement of a frightened animal.

The two officers nearly collided. Colonel Williams stood with his hands on his hips, braced off his web belt. Manzetti sculpted excuses with his hands. It was impossible to hear what they were discussing, but the situation did not appear to be promising.

"Wonder what's up?" Ryder said to his tablemates. He lifted the last forkful of scrambled eggs to his lips, catching the woman's scent off his hand, despite his shower.

Tonight, he promised himself.

As the warrants watched in collective horror Manzetti suddenly pointed toward their table. Without an instant's delay Colonel Williams headed their way, leaving the lieutenant colonel behind with a devastated expression on his face. Williams looked angry.

"Oh, shit," Dicker muttered.

A warning bell sounded in Ryder's head, and the stew of eggs began to weigh heavily in his stomach.

"This can't be good news," said the warrant who had been tormenting Dicker. Each of the warrants carefully avoided looking at the approaching colonel, making a careful show of breakfasting.

Ryder already knew this had something to do with him. The cracking of the Japanese computer system had been too important an achievement to leave unexploited. Due to the special classification of his work, even Ryder's tablemates did not know exactly what had occurred the day before. But Ryder knew beyond any doubt that Colonel Williams had digested the information.

The colonel stopped just short of their table. Towering above them. Tucker Williams was a veteran of every shooting match in which the United States had been involved since the Zaire intervention. He was notoriously zealous and uncompromising, and when he was angry, the outlines of his RD scars showed through his cheeks and forehead, despite the artistry of the Army's plastic surgeons. He was said to be an old pal of Colonel George Taylor, the Army's number one living legend, and the scuttlebutt had it that one thing Williams and Taylor unmistakably held in common was that dozens of comfortable, satisfied midcareer officers had resigned rather than go to work for either man.

Williams's face looked smooth and unscarred now. He no longer appeared angry, and Ryder felt partially relieved.

All of the warrant officers stood up in the colonel's presence, although Dicker Sienkiewicz rose slowly, asserting his bone-deep warrant-officership.

"Chief Ryder?" Williams asked, briefly scanning their faces before his eyes settled on the right man. The colonel had not yet had sufficient time in command to thoroughly learn all of their faces, and there were no name tags on the warrants' ill-fitting civilian suits and sport jackets. "I need to talk to you." He glanced at the other warrants. "The rest of you guys just get on with your breakfast. Chief," he told Ryder, "you come with me."

There was no secure area within the hotel, and the colonel simply headed for a barren table a bit removed from the breakfast crowd, waving away concerned waiters as though they were of less consequence than flies. Ryder followed the big man across the room like a guilty convict awaiting his sentence. He could hardly believe the change in himself. Normally, he was as dutiful as an officer could be. He lived for his work. Since the divorce. And here he was, in the midst of the real thing at last, perhaps even a key player, and he could not help thinking fearfully of a woman he had met only the evening before. A foreign, unexplained, officially disapproved woman.

"Take a seat, Chief," the colonel said. He sat down heavily across from Ryder, slapping his field cap down on the tabletop. He did not bother to remove his carrying harness or the stained field jacket.

Williams looked at Ryder with the penetrating, don't-dare-try-to-bullshit-me eyes the Army had taught the young warrant to associate with leaders who got things done.

"Sounds like you broke the bank, Chief," Williams said. "Congratulations."

Ryder nodded his thanks, unsure of himself.

The colonel glanced around the big room one more time, making sure that no waiters would descend on them.

"What a cluster-fuck," the colonel said in disgust. "I can see I'm going to have to clean up this sideshow. Christ, I never saw such a bunch of hungover pussy-hounds. It's amazing you've gotten anything accomplished at all."

Ryder looked down at the tablecloth.

"Chief," the colonel said, "I'm going to get you out of this and give you a chance to do some real work. Not that what you've already done isn't top-notch. But it's just the beginning. You've opened up a world of new possibilities for us. Goddamnit, are you listening to me?"

Ryder stiffened, shocked by the colonel's apparent ability to see inside him.

"Yes, sir. I'm listening."

"Well, we've got a hell of a show going on downcountry. And it's far from over, if an old soldier's instincts are worth a damn. I've been up all night, working on a very special contingency plan with my field staff. Thanks to you. Son, do you realize that the President of the United States has already been briefed on your . . . achievement yesterday?"

Ryder had not known.

"That's right," Williams continued. "The goddamned President himself. And we've been busting our asses to come up with a con-plan to exploit what you've given us. Now we're just lacking one piece." The colonel looked at Ryder.

"What's that, sir?"

"You. We need you downcountry. And I'll tell you honestly—if we implement this plan, it might be dangerous as hell." The colonel laughed happily. "But you'll be in good hands. You'll be working under an old friend of mine. He and I go back to a tent in the Azores. Now, he doesn't know shit about all this yet. He's a little busy at the moment. But I know old George Taylor well enough to know what I can sell him and what I can't. And he'll buy this one, all right. He'll see the beauty of the thing." The colonel smiled, recollecting. "Anyway, we're going to put you to work. Lot of details to iron out. With any luck, we may never have to execute this plan. But, by God, we're going to be ready."

"Sir . . . if you're talking about actually entering the Japanese control system, we're going to need some support from the Russians. They've got the—"

"Taken care of." The colonel waved his hand. "I wasn't born yesterday, Chief. You'll have everything you need before you link up with old Georgie Taylor." Williams looked around in resurgent annoyance. "Chief, you just go on up and pack your things. Meet me in the lobby in half an hour. I'm going to have a cup of coffee and take a good shit. Then we'll get on the road and I'll fill you in on what's really happening. There's a bird waiting to take us both downrange."

"Half an hour?" Ryder asked meekly.

"Clock's ticking, Chief."

"We . . . won't be coming back here, sir?"

The colonel surveyed the room in disgust. "Not if I can help it. So don't leave anything behind, Mr. Ryder."

Shut into the arthritic elevator, Ryder closed his eyes and dropped his head and shoulders back against the wall, tapping his skull against the cheap paneling. The device rattled and rose, its motion stirring up a smell of ammonia and stale cigarettes. He was ashamed. He could think only of the woman, and thinking of her made him feel sick.

Ryder made a last stop at Dicker Sienkiewicz's room. The old man was gathering papers and paraphernalia into his briefcase, arming himself for another day's routine.

"So what did the old man want?" he asked Ryder.

"I got to go. Downcountry."

The older man stopped packing his briefcase and looked at his younger comrade.

"What the hell's the matter, kid?"

"I just got to go. Special project. Downcountry. Listen, I need your help. Please, Dicker." Ryder pulled out a sealed white envelope. "There's this girl—this woman—I've met . . ."

"The blondie? From last night? In the bar?"

"Yeah. That's the one. Listen, she's okay. She's really okay."

The older man smiled. "So I'm convinced. And not a bad looker."

"She's not just another . . . she's really all right. I promised I'd meet her tonight. At eight. For dinner. Christ, I don't want her to think I just . . ."

"So you want me to give her that?" Dicker said pointing to the letter in Ryder's hand.

"Please. It's important. It's just a note. I tried to explain."

"I'll see that she gets it."

"You'll recognize her okay?"

Dicker smiled. "Do bears crap in the woods? I still remember women I seen on the subway thirty years ago."

"Listen, I got to go. The old man's waiting."

"All right. Don't worry about a thing, kid. You just take care of yourself. And good luck with whatever the hell you're up to."

"Same to you. See you, Dicker."

"See you."

* * *

393

Chief Warrant Officer Five Stanley "Dicker" Sienkiewicz watched the boy go down the hall, then shut the door.
The kid was clearly rattled. Big things in the wind. The
old warrant felt a little left out, neglected. Once, he would
have been considered indispensable when things got serious. But there was a new generation coming up. Educated. And so fast off the mark.

You don't know when you got it good, Dicker told himself. At your age you just ought to be grateful for a warm
bunk at night. Let those young studs go out and freeze
their asses off.

He sat down on the side of the bed, staring at the burn-
spotted carpet. He tapped Ryder's letter against his free
wrist, thinking of other things. Then he roused himself
slightly and considered the envelope. He turned it over.
Ryder had scrawled a name on it: Vallia.

Dicker shook his head. He remembered her, all right.
A good-looker. But trouble, if he ever saw trouble walk
in on two legs. He was no puritan. But he knew that the
women who bobbed up in Moscow hotel bars were not
notable for their trustworthiness or general moral merit.

The kid was too young to have his head screwed on
straight. And Dicker knew that the boy had had a bad
time with his divorce. Odd how that went. Some men went
hog wild. Others turned inside. Or made bad decisions.

Dicker genuinely liked Ryder. He did not want to betray
his trust. But there was plenty more pussy where that one
had come from, and Dicker had no wish to see the boy
get himself in a fix over some little Russian tramp.

With a sigh, the old warrant tore the envelope in half,
then into quarters, dropping the shreds in the nearest
wastepaper basket.

The snowflakes fell like countless paper shreds. At first
it had seemed as though the squadron had flown beyond
the reach of the snowstorm, but as they skimmed above
the wastelands, following the long arc of their assigned
route, they gradually turned to the northwest and met the
snow again. Heifetz had come forward from his ops cell,
which mirrored the setup in Taylor's command M-100. He
had just had an exasperating exchange with Reno up in

the Third Squadron, and coming atop the cascade of events and emotions of the past hours, it had temporarily drained him. He took a break and squeezed up behind the pilots' positions. He did not sit down. Back in the ops cell, his world was of reality at a remove, registered through monitors and digital displays. Up here, where the copilot had cleared the windscreens of technical displays, he could remind himself of the world as the eye was meant to see it: cold, white, rushing toward him.

Immediately after Heifetz's exchange with Reno, Taylor had resumed command of the regiment. One of Taylor's two escort birds was having problems—evidently the result of the stress the system had undergone when engaging the enemy's jets—and Taylor was attempting to nurse the failing system along. But that particular difficulty had not stopped Taylor from flexing his authority over the regiment through the magical command and control mechanisms that the new century had deposited in the hands of its soldiers. All of the greater matters appeared to be in order now, with the three squadrons cruising toward their follow-on assembly areas, bristling with electronic armament as they burrowed into the sky.

Taylor had made short work of the enemy aircraft that had hit the old support site at Omsk, and Heifetz hoped that the action had offered Taylor a bit of the primeval absolution men felt upon killing in turn the enemy who had killed their kind. That old indestructible joy in blood that you would never scrub out of the human character.

Heifetz knew that Taylor would take Martinez's death hard. Taylor would feel responsible for every soldier he lost, and he would be furious when he caught up with the reports of Reno's unnecessary casualties during the squadron commander's unauthorized glory raid. But there was an inevitable difference in the intensity of feelings in the wake of the death of a half-familiar face or rostered name and the loss of a man with whom you had lived, struggled, and shared raw strips of your life.

Martinez had been a decent boy. Outwardly a bit of a joker, unable to settle his heart on any individual girl at an age when most officers were married with children. To Heifetz, a connoisseur in the matter, Martinez had seemed a bit haunted by his background. Capable, always surprisingly capable. And dutiful. With his sports car waiting for him late at night outside the headquarters building, the treasured machine facing the light-gilt office windows like an ignored sweetheart. Heifetz was sorry now for the exchanges that had been too peremptory, for the times he had passed by the younger officer's table in the mess hall. For his own ceaseless self-absorption.

But Reno, in his rude selfishness, had been more than a little right. "For Christ's sake," Reno had complained across the empty sky, "we've just hit the jackpot, and you're worrying about pennies."

For once, Heifetz did not think the turn of phrase had been a conscious ethnic slur on Reno's part. Which made it doubly painful to accept the accuracy of the observation. He was, Heifetz recognized, indeed the kind of man who allowed himself to become obsessed with life's small change: the perfect staff officer.

Yes, they had hit the jackpot. As painful as the combat losses had been, they had been brilliantly minor in relation to the devastation the regiment had spread across the vast front. Quite literally, all of the equations of the battlefield would have to be calculated anew. It was a triumph of the sort that sent the amateur historian reaching back for fabled names.

And yet, Heifetz thought wistfully, it was a death knell too. For the older generation of soldiers. For men such as David Heifetz. When he was a young man, he had gone to war mounted in his steel chariot. He and his gunner had selected the target, found the range, fired . . . and now the new rules reduced his kind to pushers of buttons, throwers of switches. He had always maintained that man would forever remain the central focus of combat. Now he was no longer so self-righteously certain.

He was certain of so little, really.

"Everything okay, sir?" the copilot asked back over his shoulder, unaccustomed to finding Heifetz astray.

"Yes," Heifetz said. "I am only looking at the snow."

"Going to make it a hell of a lot harder to hide these babies in the assembly area," the copilot said. "Pisser, ain't it? When they designed the automatic camouflage systems, they never did think about snow, did they?"

"We'll manage," Heifetz said. He really did not want to talk.

"Yes, sir," the copilot said quickly, afraid he had gone a step too far with the coldhearted warrior at his shoulder. "We'll work it out."

Heifetz looked at the streaming snow. There was so little of which he could be certain now. He had entered the battle with an almost religious zeal, with a peculiar kind of joy burning in him. As the enemy's casualties mounted he had felt *avenged*. He knew that the Iranian or rebel tank crews concussed or sliced or burned to death were not the same men he had faced years before on the road to Damascus. The Iranians, of course, were not even Arabs. But they shared the same primitive guilt. The religion, the view of the world, the moral and spiritual proximity. Yes, he was a prejudiced man. And where was the man without prejudice? Where was the fabled good man? In this world, where having a different word for God meant a death sentence, where a different shading in the skin reduced you to the status of an animal? Where was the justice, Lord?

He knew. He knew exactly where the source of goodness flowed. And it shamed him with an inexpressible thoroughness. All these years, he had lived the life of the zealot in his chosen desert, insisting that he was denying himself everything for Mira, for his son. To avenge them.

Today, as the kill counters boosted the American score with dizzying speed, he had had his revenge. And that was the problem. It had been, unmistakably, *his* revenge. It had nothing to do with Mira or the boy, really.

Mira had lived on the side of forgiveness, of atonement, even for the sins of strangers. He knew that had she been able to speak to him after her death by force and fire and the man-made light of God she would have spoken softly. *She* had never asked him to turn his back on the world. He had done it of his own volition, because it satisfied a need in him. He remembered her in light the color of lemons, her temples dark with sweat, as she labored over bundled reports in her office. Mira, the lawyer who worked for a laborer's wage, to atone for her country's sins. The rights of Palestinians. And if the brethren of those whom she struggled to shield had brought about her death, she would have forgiven them too. She was a being of unlimited forgiveness. She had never ceased forgiving him.

All of the self-righteous rituals, the self-denials, had been sins against her. He knew what she wanted. She wanted him to live. To go on. But he had defied her, nourishing his delicious guilt, forever ripping the scabs off the sores in his spirit. It had been for himself, all of it. The fortress of sacrifice in which he hid from life. And the killings, the killings, the killings.

Mira had never asked for that. Not for any of it. Mira had never asked for anything but love. And he had conditioned the boy to ask for even less.

Impulsively, he pulled his wallet from a hind pocket of his uniform. His fingers probed behind an identification card and a driver's license, reaching into the darkness where the photograph had lain hidden for so long. The ancient wallet began to tear at the unaccustomed stress on its seams.

The wrinkling and discoloration of the photograph disappeared in a moment's recognition. Mira. The boy. The sort of smile a good heart musters at the end of a long, hot afternoon. He had thought he remembered each detail of the photo, each nuance of light. But he had been wrong. He had forgotten how beautiful Mira had been. He had forgotten the boy's smallness, the mild unwillingness to look at the camera or the man behind it. He had forgotten so much.

Forgive me, he said. And he began to tear the photograph into tiny flakes, starting with an upper corner and going methodically about the business, ensuring that no man would get an inkling of the nature of the waste as the aircraft was groomed in the wake of battle.

The copilot looked back over his shoulder at Heifetz. For a moment it seemed as though he were about to speak. Then he thought better of it and turned his attention back to the controls.

* * *

Colonel Noguchi sat behind the controls of his aircraft. He felt ready, fierce, vindicated. They had needed him after all. Old Noburu, with his womanly niceties, had been swept aside by the course of events. It was time for new men to enter the field. It was time for the new machines.

The Americans had blundered. He, too, had been surprised to learn who his new enemies were. But it did not matter. In fact, it was better. The Americans had not learned their lesson. Now he would teach it to them with unforgettable clarity.

Some young American officer had given the game away. Blabbering naively on the airwaves. Telling everything. The city: Orsk. The name of the assembly area: Silver. Even revealing his personal feelings. It was unthinkable to Noguchi that an officer would betray his emotions to his subordinates.

Direction-finding based upon intercepts was, of course, far more difficult than it had been in decades past, thanks to ultra-agile communications means and spoofer technology. But, for every technological development in the science of warfare, there was ultimately a counterdevelopment. The Japanese arsenal had been just adequate to track down the Americans.

Once the intercepts had revealed the general orientation of the American unit, intelligence had been able to steer advanced radars and space-based collectors to the enemy's vicinity. The new American systems proved to be very, very good. Unexpectedly good. Even the most advanced radars could not detect them from the front or sides. But the rear hemisphere of the aircraft proved more vulnerable. The returns were weak—but readable, once you knew what you were looking for.

Now the enemy's location was constantly updated by relay, and Noguchi was able to follow the Americans quietly as he led his flight of aircraft in pursuit. He would have liked to see one of the new enemy systems with his own eyes, out of professional curiosity. But he certainly was not going to get that close. Noguchi believed that he had conquered his innate fears of battle, that he had turned himself into a model warrior. But once the Scrambler drones were released from the standoff position, he had every intention of leaving the area as swiftly as his aircraft could fly.

"This is Five-five Echo." A young voice. Earnest. Frightened. *"I've got to put her down. The control system's breaking down."*

"Roger," Taylor answered calmly, struggling to conceal the depth of his concern from the pilot of the troubled escort ship. "Just go in easy. We'll fly cover until you're on the ground. *Break.* Five-five Mike, you cover from noon to six o'clock. We'll take six to midnight, over."

"Roger."

"This is Echo. I've got a ville coming up in front of me."

"Stay away from the built-up area," Taylor ordered.

"I can't control this thing."

"Easy now. Easy."

"We're going down." The escort pilot's voice was stripped down to a level of raw fear that Taylor had heard no more than a dozen times in his career. The first time had been on a clear morning in Africa, and the voice had been his own.

"Easy," was all he could say. "Try to keep her under control."

"—going down—"

The station dropped from the net.

"Merry. Hank. Get a clear image of the site. Get a good fix on him." Taylor switched hurriedly to the regimental command net. "Sierra one-three, this is Sierra five-five. Over."

For a nervous moment, the answer failed to come. Then Heifetz's voice responded:

"Sierra five-five, this is Sierra three-one. Over."

"You've got the wheel again. I've got a bird down. Over."

Even now, Taylor could not help feeling a twinge of injured vanity. The sole M-100 that had gone down, for any reason, had been one of his two escort ships. Although the escort ships were responsible for his safety, he was also, unmistakably, responsible for theirs as well. And the loss was clearly his fault. For going after the enemy fast movers. He had asked too much of the M-100s.

"The one that was having trouble?" Heifetz asked.

"Roger. Not sure what happened. We're putting down to evacuate the crew."

"Anything further?"

"Just keep everybody moving toward the assembly areas," Taylor said. "Looks like I'm going to be coming in a little late. Over."

"Roger. See you at Silver," Heifetz said.

"See you at Silver. Out."

Good old Lucky Dave, Taylor thought. Thank God for him.

The assistant S-3 had locked the image of the downed craft on the central ops monitor. It looked like the bird had gone in hard. There was a noticeable crumpling in the fuselage, and shards of metal were strewn across the snow. But the main compartment of the M-100 had held together.

"Five-five Echo, this is Sierra five-five. Over." Taylor gripped the edge of the console, anxious for a response, for a single word to let him know that the crew had survived.

Nothing.

"Oh, shit," Meredith said. "Company."

The officers crowded around the monitor, edging out the nearest NCO. The standoff image showed the wreck about two kilometers outside of a ruined settlement. Small dark shapes had already begun moving toward the downed M-100 from the fringe of buildings.

"What do you think, Merry?"

"Personnel carriers. Old models. Soviet production."

"Any chance they're friendlies?"

"Nope," Meredith said immediately. "Not down here. Those are bad guys."

As if they had overheard the conversation, the personnel carriers began to send streaks of light toward the crash site.

"*Chief,*" Taylor called forward through the intercom, "*can you take them out?*"

"Too close for the big gun," Krebs answered. "We'll have to go in on them with the Gat. Going manual. Hold on, everybody."

401

"Five-five Mike," Taylor called to the other escort M-100. "You've got the sky. We're going in—"

A sudden swoop of the aircraft tossed him backward against the opposite control panel.

The wrong voice answered Taylor's call. It was the downed pilot. Still alive after all.

"This is Five-five Echo. Can anybody hear me? Can you hear me? We're taking fire. We're taking hostile fire. I've got some banged-up troopers in the back. We're taking fire."

"Mike, wait," Taylor told the net. "We hear you, Echo. Hang on. We're on the way."

In response, the M-100 turned hard, unbalancing both Taylor and Meredith this time.

"Come *on*," Hank Parker said to the monitor, as if cheering on a football team in a game's desperate moment.

"I'm going forward," Taylor said, and he pushed quickly through the hatchway that led toward the cockpit, bruising himself as the aircraft dropped and rolled.

By the time Taylor dropped into his pilot's seat, Krebs had already opened up with the Gatling gun. It was the first time all day they had used the lighter, close-fighting weapon.

"I've got the flight controls," Taylor told Krebs. "Just take care of the gunnery."

"Roger." The old warrant officer unleashed another burst of fire. "Good old weapon, the Gat. Almost left them off these babies. Damned glad we didn't."

Down in the snowy wastes, two enemy vehicles were burning. The others began to reverse their courses, heading back for the cover of the blasted village. Taylor manhandled the M-100 around so that Krebs could engage a third armored vehicle. Then he turned the aircraft hard toward the downed bird.

"Echo, this is Sierra," Taylor called. "Still with me?"

"Roger," a frantic voice cried in the headset. *"I've got casualties. I've got casualties."*

"Take it easy. We're coming."

"My ship's all fucked," the voice complained, its tone slightly unreal. *"We'll never get her off the ground."*

Taylor, having had the privilege of an overhead view of the wreckage, was startled that the pilot had given even a moment's thought to attempting to get airborne again. Battle reactions were never fully rational, never truly predictable.

"No problem, Echo," Taylor said. He passed manual control of the aircraft back to Krebs so that he could concentrate on calming the downed pilot, steering him toward rational behavior. "No problem. You've done just fine. Just take it easy. We're coming down to get you out of there. *Break*. Five-five Mike, you watching the sky for us?"

"Roger. All clear."

"Okay. Have your copilot keep an eye on the ground, just in case our little friends try another rush from the village. *Break*. Echo, can you get your crew and the dragoons out of the aircraft? If so, rig your ship to blow."

"I can't," the voice came back, nearly hysterical.

"What's the problem?"

"My legs, my legs."

"What's the matter with your legs?"

"I think they're broken."

Taylor fought with all his might against flickering visions from an earlier time, of earlier wrecks, in a land that had never seen snow.

"Can your copilot get things going?"

Silence. Then:

"He's dead."

Taylor closed his eyes. Then he spoke in a beautifully controlled voice:

"Echo, this is Sierra. Just take it easy. We'll have you out of there before you know it. Try to think as clearly as you can. Now tell me. Is anybody fully capable in the dismount compartment?"

"I don't know," the pilot answered. His voice had calmed a little, and the tone was almost rational. "The intercom's out, and I can't move. *Oh, my God. We've got a fire. We've got a fire.*"

"Flapper, get us the hell down there," Taylor barked.

The injured pilot had lost all control of himself now. *"Oh, God,"* he pleaded to the radio, *"please don't let me burn. Please don't let me burn."*

"Just hold on," Taylor said, trying to remain controlled himself. "We're almost there."

"Please . . . please . . ."

"What about your fire suppression system?" Taylor demanded. "Can you operate it manually?"

"I can't move. Can't. Please. Oh, God, I don't want to burn. Don't let me burn."

As it descended the M-100 turned so that Taylor could see the wreck again. It was very close now. And there was, indeed, a fire. In the forward fuselage, where the pilot's exit hatch was located.

Then Taylor saw one hopeful sign. At the rear of the downed M-100, a soldier was on his feet. He had already lain two of his comrades in the snow, and he was headed back inside the burning aircraft.

Taylor's ship settled, and he lost sight of everything in the white-out of blown snow.

"Echo," Taylor called. "We're on the ground. We're coming to get you."

"—burning—" The voice of an agonized child.

The M-100 had not yet made its peace with the ground, but Taylor leapt from his seat, scrambling back toward the exterior hatch.

"Stay with the bird," he ordered Krebs.

Taylor's shoulder holster snagged briefly on a metal projection. He tore it loose and bent to wrestle with the dual levers that secured the hatch. The covering popped outward and slid to the side with a pneumatic hiss.

A rush of cold air struck Taylor's face. He dropped into the snow and it fluffed well above his ankles. The noise of the M-100 was overpowering on the outside, but he nonetheless began to shout at the dark form lugging bodies through the snow a football field away.

"Move them further off. Get them further away."

The distant soldier did not respond. Unhearing in the wind and the big cloud of engine noise. Meredith came up on Taylor's left, followed by one of the NCOs from the ops center. Together, the three men ran stumbling through the snow, the NCO carrying an automatic rifle at the ready and glancing from side to side.

A billow of fire rose from the central fuselage of the downed craft.

"Jesus Christ," Taylor swore.

The NCO slipped in the snow at his side, then recovered. Up ahead, the soldier involved in rescuing his comrades paid them no attention whatsoever. He drew another body from the burning machine.

Taylor ran as hard as his lungs and the snow would allow. Even though he had left the comms net far behind, he still imagined that he could hear the pleas of the trapped pilot.

From somewhere off to the right, behind the veil of the snowstorm, weapons began to sound—hard flat reports against the whine of the M-100 waiting behind Taylor's back. Small arms. The enemy were coming dismounted this time. There would be no obvious targets for the escort bird flying cover.

Meredith was quick, with a quarterback's agility, and he reached the rear of the downed bird ahead of the others. He was shouting at the soldier, even as he tried to help the man with his human burden.

More firing.

Taylor and the NCO came up beside Meredith and the rescuer. On the verge of speech, Taylor was silenced by the sight of the boy's face. Bruised and swollen, the expression was nonetheless strikingly clear. The boy was in shock. He was dragging his comrades out of the wreck automatically, conditioned to the task. But he had no real consciousness of anything around him.

"Sarge, you come with me," Taylor ordered. "Merry, this mess is yours."

Taylor dodged a severed block of metal and ran up around the M-100's stubby wing and flank rotor, howling wind at his back. He leapt at the pilot's hatch, grabbing the recessed handle despite the nearby flames.

"*Fuck*," he shouted, recoiling and shaking his scorched hand.

The door was locked from the inside.

The NCO passed him, heading straight for the cockpit. Standing on the tips of his toes, the man could just look inside.

"Is he all right?" Taylor shouted.

"Can't see. Goddamned smoke."

"We'll have to smash in the windscreen."

The NCO looked at the fragile assault rifle in his hands. "No way," he said matter-of-factly.

A burst of fire reached the M-100 and danced along its armored side, ricocheting.

"Fuck it," Taylor shouted. "Just see if you can pick out where the shooting's coming from. I'll try to get to the engineer kit."

He doubled back to the rear of the wreck. Somehow, Merry had convinced the dazed soldier to drag his comrades to a spot more distant from the flames and smoke—and closer to Taylor's ship.

Merry's coffee-colored cheeks had grimed with smoke. He came up to speak to Taylor, but with hardly a glance, Taylor pushed past him, darting up the ramp into the smoke-filled dismount compartment built into the rear of the M-100.

His lungs began to fill up immediately, and he could not see. He knew the ammunition was all stowed in specially sealed subcompartments, but he had no idea how much longer the linings would resist the heat.

He stumbled along an inner wall, tapping over the irregular surface with a blistered hand. He was searching for the compartment where the pioneer tools were stowed—shovels and pickaxes for digging in. It was hard to judge the distance and layout in the smoke.

He almost collapsed in a faint. Instead, the near-swoon shocked him with adrenaline, and he hurriedly stumbled back out into the fresh, biting air.

The cold scorched his lungs. He bent over, hands on his knees, choking. His breath would not come. He realized he had come within an instant of going down with smoke inhalation. Probably dying.

The world swirled as if he had drunk too much. He fought to steady himself, to master his breathing. More shots rang out through the storm. Were they closer now?

He straightened, gulping at the cold. He tried to remember the exact distance to the compartment where the manual specified the stowage of the squad's pioneer tools. He had helped write the damned thing, but now it was a struggle to remember. Left wall, wasn't it? Third panel, upper row.

"You all right, sir?" Meredith called. His voice sounded flat and weak against the noise of flames, wind, distant engines, and pocking gunfire. The younger man came up and put a hand on Taylor's shoulder.

"No time," Taylor said, knocking the hand away. "Just get the wounded on board. *Go.*"

Taylor plunged back into the smoke.

The acridity drew tears from his eyes and he had to shut them. He held his breath. Feeling his way like a blind diver, all he could sense was heat.

Suddenly the latch was under his hand, hot and firm. He yanked it, breaking open fresh blisters. The gear had shaken loose in the crash, and a falling shovel nearly struck his head. Just in time, he caught it by the handle.

There was no more time. He felt the dizziness welling up. Coming over him the way a blanket came down over a child. It would have been the easiest thing in the world to surrender to it.

Taylor stumbled back out into the snow, falling to his knees and dry-retching. His eyes burned and he could barely see through the forced tears. He dropped his head and shoulders into the snow, trying to cleanse himself of the smoke and heat. When he tried to rise, he stumbled.

On the horizon he could just make out Merry carrying a body over his shoulder.

Taylor forced himself to his feet. He rounded the side of the wreck at a dizzy trot, hugging the shovel to him. Mercifully, the fire seemed to be spreading very slowly; the resistant materials in the M-100's composition were doing their job.

The NCO had his back to Taylor, assault rifle held up in the position of a man who wished he had a target at which to fire. As Taylor came up beside him the NCO jumped backward, as if he had seen a great snake.

The man crumpled, still holding fast to his weapon as the snow all around him splashed scarlet.

He was dead. Lying open-eyed and open-mouthed in the storm. More bullets nicked at the wreck, rustling the air above the crackle of the flames.

Still dazed from all the smoke he had drunk, Taylor wrenched the rifle from the NCO's hands and raised it to send a warning burst out into the whiteness. But the weapon clicked emptily.

Taylor slapped the man's body, searching the pockets for additional magazines. The man had been working with his battle harness stowed for comfort, and he had come outside without it. Now there was no more ammunition to be found.

Taylor discarded the rifle and drew the pistol from his shoulder holster. There were no targets, but he fired anyway, two shots, as a warning. Then he shoved the pistol back into its leather pocket and picked up the shovel again. Slipping in the snow and mud, he ran at the cockpit, swinging the tool with all his might.

It only bounced off the transparent armor of the windscreen.

He smashed at the barrier again. And again. Then he drove the blade as hard as he could into the synthetic material.

It was useless. The windscreens had been built to resist heavy machine gun fire. His efforts were ridiculous.

But you had to try, you had to try.

A single round punched the nose of the aircraft beside Taylor's head. He dropped to his knees, discarding the shovel and drawing his pistol again. What the hell, he thought furiously. If it's got to end here, so be it. But it's going to cost the sonsofbitches.

A burst of fire erupted just behind him. But his old warrior's ear recognized the sound as coming from a friendly weapon. The sharp, whistling signature of his own kind. Then he glimpsed Meredith coming up low along the side of the wreck, automatic rifle in his hands.

The younger man was short of breath when he got to Taylor's position. "Come on, sir," he begged. "We've got to get out of here."

"The pilot," Taylor said adamantly.

"For God's *sake,* sir. He's gone. The smoke would have got him by now. The goddamned windscreens are black."

Yes. The smoke. Better smoke than fire. The smoke would even have been welcome, in a way.

A sudden volley played an ashcan symphony on the side of the wreck.

"Let's get the hell out of here," Meredith said.

Yes, Taylor realized. Meredith was right. There was no more point to it. It had become an empty gesture. And it was only results that mattered.

They would all be waiting for him. He knew that Krebs would never lift off without him. Even if it meant that everyone on board perished. And he did not want to be responsible for any more unnecessary deaths.

A part of him still could not leave the site.

Meredith fired two shots out into the blowing whiteness, then followed them with a third.

"Come on, you bastards," he screamed.

Meredith. With his wife and a golden future waiting for him.

"All right," Taylor said with sudden decisiveness. He reached for the dead NCO and ripped off the man's microchip dog tag. "Let's give them another couple of rounds, then run like hell."

"You got it," Meredith said.

The two of them rose slightly and fired into the storm, wielding a rifle and a pistol hardly bigger than a man's hand against the menace of a continent.

"Move," Taylor commanded.

The two men ran sliding through the sodden snow that ringed the heat of the wreck. Meredith was well in the lead by the time they rounded the aft end of the downed M-100. He turned and raised his rifle again, covering Taylor.

"Goddamnit, just run," Taylor shouted.

They took off on a straight line for the dark outline of the command ship. The big rotors churned the sky in readiness. The underlying rumble of the engine promised salvation.

Krebs had seen them coming. He had increased the power to the upended rotors and soon the noise was so loud that Taylor could no longer hear the rounds chasing him. Up ahead, the M-100 began to buck like an anxious horse. Then Krebs steadied it again.

Taylor ran as hard as he could. I don't want to get shot

in the goddamned back, he thought. Not in the goddamned back.

The M-100 grew bigger and bigger, filling up Taylor's entire horizon.

His lungs ached.

"Come *on*," Meredith screamed at him.

He hated to leave the bodies. There was enough guilt already. Enough for a long, long lifetime.

Not in the back, he prayed, running the last few yards.

He felt Meredith's arms dragging him up into the hatch.

Krebs began lifting off before Meredith and Taylor could finish closing the hatch behind them. The ground faded away before their eyes. The universe swirled white. Then the hatch cover slammed back into place.

The two men dropped exhaustedly onto their buttocks, cramped in the tiny gangway. They looked at each other wordlessly, each man assuring himself that the other had not been touched by the send-off bullets. They were both covered with grime and with the blood of other men, and Meredith's eyebrows and close-cropped hair bore a fringe of snow that made him look as though he had been gotten up for an old man's part in a high school play. As Taylor watched, the S-2 wiped at the melting snow with a hand that left a bloody smear in its wake.

Taylor flexed his burned paw. Not too bad. Slap on a little ointment.

The M-100 climbed into the sky.

Taylor dropped his head back against the inner wall of the passageway, breathing deeply in an effort to purge his lungs of smoke and gas.

"Aw, shit," he said.

They had to gain sufficient standoff distance before they could use the main armament to destroy the remainder of the wreck. The Gatling gun would never have penetrated the composite armor. While they were gaining altitude, Meredith gave Taylor the rest of the bad news. Of the soldiers carried out of the rear compartment, only the shocked boy and one evident concussion case were alive. The remainder of the light squad of dragoons had died, victims either of the impact or of smoke inhalation. The command M-100 bore a cargo of corpses down in its compact storage hold.

"Goddamnit, Merry," Taylor said, "the ship shouldn't have gone down that hard. Just not supposed to. And the fire suppressant system's a worthless piece of shit."

Meredith patted an inner panel of the aircraft with exaggerated affection. "We still don't know exactly what happened, sir. Could've been a computer malfunction. Anything. Overall, these babies have been pretty good to us today."

The two men felt a quick pulse under the deck as Krebs delivered a high-velocity round that would shatter the wreck back on the ground beyond recognition.

"Anyway, Merry," Taylor said, "thanks." He gestured with a blistered hand. "For back there."

Meredith looked embarrassed.

The two men sat just a few moments longer, drained, and heavy now with the knowledge that they both had to get back to work as though nothing had occurred. So much depended on them.

"I wonder how Lucky Dave's doing," Meredith mused. He glanced at his watch. "First Squadron ought to be on the ground at Silver by now."

Noguchi trembled. He had never doubted his personal bravery, certain that he was somehow superior to average men with their average emotions. He had, until this hour, envisioned himself as a warrior with a marble heart, armored in a will of steel. But now, as he counted down the seconds before unleashing his weapons, his flying gloves clotted to his palms and his lower lip ticked as he counted to himself without realizing it. He fixed his eyes straight on, although the shield of his flight helmet would have prevented any of the crew members from seeing the uncertainty in them. He could not bear the thought that other men might scent the least fear in him.

It was the weapons themselves that frightened him. The glorious kamikaze pilots of yesteryear had been faced with so clean a proposition: to die splendidly and suddenly for the emperor, for Japan. Dying held little terror for Noguchi, who envisioned it as the door to an uncomplicated nothingness. What frightened him was the condition in which he might have to live, if anything went wrong with the Scramblers.

The counter stripped away the seconds.

They had almost reached the optimal release point for the drones.

And if something went wrong? If the Scramblers activated prematurely? If he was unable to turn his aircraft out of the Scramblers' reach with sufficient speed? If the effective range of the Scramblers proved even greater than projected? If ground control brought his aircraft back on the automatic flight controls, with a terrible cargo? There were so many ifs. The Scramblers had never even had a real field trial—it would have been impossible. And the experiments on animals could not be regarded as conclusive.

The thought that the Scramblers might touch back at him, might caress him, their appointed master, with their power, left him physically unsteady and incapable of rigorous thought.

He glanced again at the monitor. Within half an hour of touching down, the Americans' automatic camouflage systems had done a surprisingly good job of hiding the aircraft—even though it was evident that the mechanical measures had not been designed with the anomalies of a snow-covered landscape in mind. Of course, the Scramblers would affect everything over a huge area—but it was reassuring to know that the prime target was exactly where the transmissions had promised it would be.

"Sir?" A sudden cry turned Noguchi's head. The voice was that of the copilot beside him, squeezed up the scale of fear.

"What is it?" Noguchi asked savagely.

The man's eyes were impossibly wide with fear.

"It's time, it's time."

Panic razored through Noguchi. But when he turned back to the instrumentation panel, he saw that there were still several seconds left. His copilot had lost control. Unforgivably. Like a woman or a child.

"Shut up, you fool," Noguchi told him. But he did not look back at the man. He remained afraid that his face might reflect too much of the weakness revealed on his subordinate's features.

Noguchi struggled to steady himself. But the mental images challenged him again, attacking his last self-discipline with visions of the condition in which a faulty application of the Scramblers might leave him.

No. No, he could not bear to live like that.

A thousand times better to die.

He locked his eyes on the digital counter, finger poised on the sensor control that would release the drones.

Seven.

All my life

Six.

I have been

Five.

aimed like an arrow

Four.

toward

Three.

this

Two.

moment.

One.

"*Banzai,*" Noguchi screamed, tearing his throat.

He touched the release sensor.

"*Banzai,*" he screamed again.

"*Banzai,*" his crew echoed through the intercom.

He took personal control of the aircraft and banked as hard as he could.

"*Clean release,*" he heard in his helmet's tiny speakers.

One by one, the other aircraft in his flight reported in. Clean release, clean release.

Noguchi found his course and ordered all of the aircraft under his command to accelerate to the maximum. Behind them, the undersized drones sped quietly toward a place called Silver.

"Roger," Heifetz reported over the command net. "Everybody's tucked in. Assembly Areas Gold and Platinum report fully secure status. We have no systems losses. The Tango element took five KIA and eleven WIA during ground contact with an Iranian headquarters site, but I think you might want to get the details straight from him."

Taylor's voice returned. He sounded unusually raspy and stressed to Heifetz. "Everything okay at your site?"

"Basically. There was a small site-management problem. Part of Silver was already occupied by Soviet support troops. There's no coordination. Their system's gone to hell. One unit opened fire on us before we got it all sorted out."

"Casualties?"

"No. We were lucky. Now we have what they used to call 'peaceful coexistence.' "

"Christ," Taylor said. "That's all we need. Gunfights with the Russians."

"It's all right now. Tercus is putting his boys into good hide positions. He's very impressive."

"All right. We should be at your location in approximately forty minutes," Taylor said. "I've got a probable heavy concussion casualty on board and another soldier in ambulatory shock. We'll need medical support when we come in."

"Roger. We'll be waiting. Over."

"Five-five out."

Heifetz laid down the hand mike. Such a good day, he thought. It was bewildering how such a good day could be formed of so much death. A Jericho of steel, he said to himself, thinking of the Japanese-built war machine that had tumbled into ruin across the morning.

It was enough for him. He had already made up his mind. He simply did not know how he was going to break the news to Taylor.

He would finish the campaign. Then he would resign. He had squandered so much of his life in confusion, in self-deception, in the deep dishonor of the honorable man of mistaken purpose. He had been a good soldier, of course. In all of the outward respects. Now it was time to stop before he became a bad one.

He was going to go home. To the new home his fellow refugees were building in the Israeli settlements in the American West. Turning yet another desert into a garden. He did not know exactly what he would do, or for what he might be qualified after so many years in arms. But he knew with iron certainty that he would manage. He was not afraid of a little dirt under his fingernails, if it came to that. And he did not need much.

For an instant he regretted the years of salaries he had donated to the American-Israeli relief fund. Then he dismissed the consideration, ashamed of himself. It was better this way. To start clean. Without the false security that too much money insinuated into a man's soul.

Perhaps there would even be a woman. He recognized now that Mira had never asked for his celibacy. No, he had wronged her that way too. She had been so much better than that. She would have wanted him to love again, to the meager extent of his abilities.

All of his adult life had been spent doing the wrong thing, for the wrong reasons. He only hoped there was still time to put it right. He was going to allow himself to live again. And, this time, it truly would be for Mira. He would turn his face back toward the light.

Heifetz picked up the helmet that he always wore in the field to set the right example for his subordinates.

"I'm going outside to take a piss," he told his ops crew.

The cold was beautifully clean, and he thought of Taylor. It would be good to see him at the end of such a day. Taylor was his closest semblance of a friend. He did not yet have the words to explain to Taylor about resigning, but that could wait. Taylor had to concentrate on other things now, and Heifetz was determined to help him as best he could. There were plenty of problems waiting to be resolved, especially with the loss of the last functioning weapons calibrator back at Omsk. But, somehow, he and Taylor would find solutions. Heifetz pictured himself beside Taylor, leaning over a map, shaping destiny with a marker pen. The two men did not even need words to understand each other.

Heifetz tramped through the snow toward an undernourished-looking stand of trees. The white trunks and branches looked feminine and tubercular. It struck him that this country was poor in so many ways.

His musings were interrupted by the sight of a startled young captain who had been squatting in a little snow-

415

smoothed hollow. The captain had twisted over to clean himself above a display of steaming shit.

The younger man straightened at the sight of Heifetz, discarding the smudged paper from his hand and grabbing for his distended coveralls.

Heifetz could not help smiling. Life went on, after all.

"At ease," Heifetz commanded. "Continue with your mission, captain."

The young officer stammered something unintelligible, and Heifetz turned to urinate against the slender tilt of a tree trunk.

A more distant voice called Heifetz by his rank and last name. There was no escape, not even for a moment. Heifetz glanced back toward his M-100 and saw one of the staff NCOs trotting bareheaded toward the little grove. Have to tell them to keep their damned helmets on when they come outside, Heifetz thought. Like children. After combat, the natural tendency was to overrelax. To drop your guard and decline into slovenliness.

Heifetz shook himself vigorously, then tucked the cold-tightened bit of flesh back into his uniform. Too long unused for its higher purpose, he teased himself.

The NCO hurried toward him, hopping through the snow.

"Lieutenant Colonel Heifetz, sir. Lieutenant Colonel Reno's on the net. He says he's got to talk to you personally."

Heifetz nodded in weary acquiescence. Then he turned to the ambushed captain, who was hurriedly doing up his uniform.

"You know what the biggest problem is with the U.S. Army?" Heifetz asked. The captain had the sort of wholesome, handsome features Heifetz had come to associate with a peculiarly American invulnerability to intellect. After a moment's rumination, the captain resettled the web belt around his athlete's waist and said nervously, "No, sir."

"We talk too much," Heifetz said. But he could see from the captain's features that the triteness of the observation had disappointed the younger man, who apparently had expected a revelation of far deeper profundity.

"We talk too much," Heifetz repeated. He smiled gently and turned back toward his place of duty.

Captain Jack Sturgis couldn't believe it. He had actually seen Lucky Dave Heifetz smile. He wondered if he would ever be able to convince his friends of what he had seen.

He began to reconstruct the tale in his head. He immediately discarded the bit about his physical situation during the incident. Then he reconsidered, and modified his role into the more manly one of fellow-pisser-on-nearby-tree. How exactly had Heifetz put it? About the Army's biggest problem? Pretty dumb, really. Nothing much to it. Sturgis poked at Heifetz's words for some hidden meaning: "We talk too much." Did he mean, like, too much talk and not enough action? Or just too much talk, period?

Goddamn, though. There he was, with Lucky Dave Heifetz. The man who had *never* been known to crack a smile, the cradle-to-grave soldier. And the old bugger comes through with this big toothy grin.

He wished he had a witness. Then he recalled the more personal details of the encounter and decided that he was glad there had been no witness, after all.

Maybe Heifetz had just been laughing at him?

Naw. Old Lucky Dave had seen plenty of guys taking a dump before. No, it probably meant that things had gone really well. That they had really torn the enemy a new asshole.

Yeah. Now that could be tied into the tale very nicely. "Even old Lucky Dave was happy. Should've seen it, guys. *Smil*ing. Bigtime."

Lucky Dave Heifetz, the terror of the regiment. The guy who was reported never to have felt a single human emotion in his life.

Sturgis had been disconcerted by the unexpected appearance of a second party during his evacuation procedures—and Lucky Dave, of all people. All things considered, however, he figured it was worth it. For the tale he would have to tell. And for the reassurance Heifetz's good mood had given him.

417

They had met the enemy—and knocked their dicks in the mud.

He had been worried, of course. He had never been in combat before, and he had read lots of war novels and seen plenty of movies and heard how tough it all was from the veterans. They said you never knew who was going to break down and turn out to be a pussy.

Well, now he knew. He was no pussy. He had what it took, proven in battle. As he trudged back toward the camouflaged position of his M-100, Jack Sturgis luxuriated in visions of a great military career. Someday he might even be as famous as the old man, Colonel Taylor. Or even more famous. He had no intentions of becoming disfigured, however. He didn't want to *look* like Taylor. Sturgis cast himself in a far more romantic light, and no vision of success was complete without a complementary vision of well-disposed women.

Sturgis took a deep breath. It was a wonderful thing to be a soldier. To be a real combat leader.

A snowflake caught at the corner of the young man's eye. He paused to wipe it away, touching a gloved hand to his shying eyelash.

And Captain Jack Sturgis jerked perfectly upright, gripped by a pain the intensity of which no human animal had ever before experienced.

19

3 November 2020

"Sierra five-five, this is Saber six. Sierra five-five, this is Saber six . . ."

Taylor knew immediately that something was seriously wrong when he heard Reno's voice on the command net. The general's son was always careful to maintain a studied coolness over any open communications means, except when he was verbally destroying one of his subordinates, or in combat, when his voice screamed for medals, awards, citations. Now Reno's voice strained with emotion and he had done something which he never had done before. He had used the call sign "Saber six" on Taylor's net.

Taylor knew that Reno affected the call sign on his squadron's internal comms, but the man was always careful to use his proper call sign on the regimental command net, both because Taylor made it plain that he disapproved of unauthorized nonsense and because "Saber six" was a timeworn cavalry handle reserved for regimental commanders—not for the subordinate lieutenant colonels who commanded squadrons.

"Tango five-five, this is Sierra five-five. Over."

"This is Saber—I mean, Tango five-five. I can't contact *any*body at AA Silver. I was on the horn with the One-three, and he just cut out in midsentence. I've tried calling Whisky five-five, but I don't even get anything breaking up. *Nothing*. Is something going on down there? *What's going on?*"

"Tango, this is Sierra. Wait. Sierra one-three," Taylor called Heifetz, "this is Sierra five-five. Over."

Taylor waited. Around him, he could feel the tension in Meredith and Parker, as well as the concern of the surviving staff NCO. The crowded cabin stank with sweat and dried blood, and at the very back the shock case sat dully beside the bunk they had jerry-rigged for the soldier with the concussion.

Nothing.

Taylor knew that something was wrong. This was not a single comms malfunction. It was funny how you knew. The instinct you developed over the years of living in the proximity of death.

"Sierra one-three," Taylor tried again, "this is Sierra five-five. I cannot hear your station. If you are monitoring my transmission, meet me on the strat link, over."

He knew that something was wrong. Yet, he struggled against knowing it. He turned to the special satellite communications link that was normally reserved for conversations with the nation's highest authorities.

Meredith was already keying the system. Then they all waited again, while in the background Reno pleaded for attention and answers over the regimental command net.

They waited for five minutes. But there was nothing. The heavens were dead.

Finally, Taylor turned back to the command net, determined to make one last attempt.

"*Any* Whisky station, *any* Whisky station," he called First Squadron, his words reaching out toward Assembly Area Silver, "this is Sierra five-five. How do you hear this station, over?"

Nothing.

Suddenly, the comms set fuzzed to life. But it was only Reno with another plea for information. The man was badly shaken.

Taylor ignored him. He turned to Meredith.

"How long until we reach Silver?"

Meredith glanced at the panel. "Fifteen minutes. Do you want to divert until we find out what's going on, sir? We might just be able to make the northeast edge of AA Platinum before we run out of fuel."

Everyone looked at Taylor. There was a heaviness in the cabin's air that sobered each man like the sight of a dirt-encrusted skull.

"No," Taylor said. "We're going in. We're going to find out what the hell's going on."

Taylor called ahead to Second Squadron at Platinum, just outside of Orenburg. The squadron commander had been monitoring the traffic on the net, digesting it and maintaining radio discipline.

"If you lose contact with me," Taylor said, "you are to assume command of the regiment." Everyone knew that Reno was the senior squadron commander by date of rank. But Reno was in no condition to lead the regiment at the moment. If he ever had been.

Reno did not contest the message that had been sent openly for all command net subscribers to hear.

Well, Taylor thought, I've still got Second and Third squadrons. If worse comes to worst.

"Contact the escort element," Taylor told the assistant S-3. "Tell them we're going in ready to fight."

Meredith did not believe in ghosts. Even as a child, the dark had held no power over him, and the demonic tales each generation felt compelled to recast and retell simply bored him. The only witchery of interest had been the spell of the eighth-grade blonde with whom he shared his first date. Guaranteed a safety net of their mutual friends, she agreed to go with him to see a film that had captured the attention of young America for a split second. Their friends were noisy, probingly teasing, and, finally, unmistakably separate in the gloom as popcorn smells meandered above the tang of cleaning solution. When the seating lights died and the screen began to redefine the universe, a vault door shut over the mundane cares of homework and team tryouts. Actors labored to convince him of scarlet, improbable horrors, but their exaggerated agonies were nothing compared to the doubt he felt in the long minutes before his classmate took his hand. Unlearned, she gripped him with athletic ferocity as a once-human beast rampaged across a film set. He remembered feeling mature and very strong then, with his unwavering eyes and unquestioned command of the fingers another child had anxiously intertwined with his. These dressed-up unexamined fears were of too primitive an order to move him, and he grew older in a world where hauntings always turned out to be headlights reflecting off a window, and "supernatural" was merely a word from which ill-dressed hucksters tried to wring a profit. His devils had always lurked elsewhere, beyond the reach of vampire, astrologer, or special-effects wizard, and the last time the hackles on the back of his neck had alerted had been under the torment of a woman's fingernails, before love settled in and the woman became his wife.

The last time. But now his wife was half a world away, and the ghostly white snow fields unnerved him with their stillness. Translated through the monitor screen, the imagery of Assembly Area Silver had an unmistakable quiet about it that frightened him with its wrongness. It was eerie, unnatural. It occurred to him for the first time that silence could have a look about it, an intrusion across sensory boundaries that jarred the working order of his mind. The silent display of M-100s, partially camouflaged and dispersed over a grove-dotted steppe, was somehow so insistently incorrect that he could feel his body responding even as his mind struggled to process the information into harmless answers.

First Squadron was *supposed* to be quiet, lying still in hide positions. The goal was to blend into the landscape, to avoid offering any signs of life to searching enemy sensors. To play dead. Even beyond that—to become invisible. The problem was that the M-100s burrowed so neatly into the snow fields had achieved the desired effect too well.

No unit was ever completely silent. No unit was ever so disciplined that it could avoid twitching a human muscle or two for the practiced eye to spot. Perfection in camouflage and deception operations was a matter of degree.

But the First Squadron site had a special, unbearable silence about it. It had begun with the refusal of every last oral communications channel to respond to Taylor's queries. They all had assumed that First Squadron had been hit and hit badly by an enemy strike. Then Meredith tried a computer-to-computer query.

Each computer in First Squadron responded promptly when contacted. Data passed through the heavens instantly and exactly. The machines continued their electronic march through the endless battlefields of integers. It was only their human masters that made no reply.

The first imagery Meredith called up had filled them with a sense of relief. Yes. There they were, all right. Carefully dispersed M-100s. There was not a single indicator of battle damage. The snow drifted across the site with blinding purity, and when you looked carefully, the concealed contours of the M-100s on the ground betrayed no trace of destruction. The squadron looked exactly as it was supposed to look, and it occurred to Meredith that the whole business just might be a bizarre communications anomaly.

It was only the *feel* that was all wrong.

"Run a systems check on our environmental seals," Taylor ordered.

"You figure chemicals, sir?" Meredith asked.

"Could be. I don't know. Christ," Taylor said quietly, "I've seen week-old corpses that didn't look that dead."

"Nerve agent strike?"

Taylor bent closer to the imagery, narrowing his eyes, obviously straining to achieve a greater intensity of vision. "That's what I'd have to bet, if I were betting. But it doesn't make any goddamned sense. Even if a strike had caught some of the birds with their hatches open, others would have been sealed. If only because of the cold. And the automatic seals and the overpressure systems would have kicked in." He backed away from the monitor, touching his eyes with thumb and forefinger, weary. The palm and back of his hand had been wrapped in gauze that already showed dirt. "It just doesn't make any sense, Merry. If it was nerve gas, or any kind of chemicals, *some-*body would have survived. The autosensors would have alerted, and we would have had more flash traffic calls coming in than the system could've handled." He shook his head very slowly, then touched the edge of the gauzed hand to his hairline. "It just doesn't make any sense."

"Looks like a ghost town," Hank Parker said. The clumsy, too-colorful image annoyed Meredith, and he almost made a dismissive comment. Then he realized, with a chill that ran along his arms, legs, and spine, that the assistant S-3's comment bothered him so much not because it was naive but because it was precisely correct. There was no town in the imagery, and Meredith did not believe in ghosts, but the feel that rose from the monitor like cold air was exactly the feel of a ghost town—of a no-nonsense, technologically affluent military kind.

"Flapper," Taylor called through the intercom, "get us down there as fast as you can. Get a fix on the S-3's bird and put down right on its ass."

"Roger."

"Sir?" Meredith said, suddenly forgetting his personal alarm and remembering his duty, "are you sure you want to put down? If there's something down there we don't know about . . . I mean, the regiment needs you. We could direct one of the other squadrons to send in a recon party, do it right . . ."

"I don't want to wait," Taylor said.

"Neither do I," Meredith said truthfully. "But we've got to think about the big picture. We've got to—"

"Be quiet, Merry. My mind's made up." There was a tautness in the voice that Meredith had never before suffered.

Something was terribly, inexplicably wrong. Each man in the cabin knew it, but none of them could bring it out in words.

"*What's that?*" Taylor demanded, stabbing a finger at the monitor. As the M-100 approached the heart of the site, the on-board sensors picked up greater and greater detail.

Meredith squinted and saw only a black speck. He touched the selector pencil to the screen and the lens telescoped down.

It was a body. A man's body. Where before there had been only the disguised outlines of machinery and the insistent silence.

"*He's moving,*" Parker said.

They all bent down over the monitor, each man's stale breath sour in the nostrils of his comrades.

Yes. It was unmistakable. It was definitely a man, in uniform, and he was moving. He was lying on his back, making jerking, seemingly random gestures at the sky.

"What in the name of Christ?" Taylor whispered.

The unintelligent, wasted movement of the man's limbs came erratically. But he was unmistakably alive, although the snow was beginning to bury him. The man's movements reminded Meredith of something, but he could not quite place it.

"Get us down on the ground, goddamnit," Taylor roared.

It seemed to Meredith that Taylor had just realized what was going on. But the old man seemed to have no intention of sharing his knowledge.

"Yes, sir," Krebs's voice came back through the intercom, just a second late. The old warrant officer's voice seemed to tremble, astonishing Meredith, who had grown used to Krebs's theatrical toughness.

The sensors on the M-100 were very efficient, and although they were still several kilometers from the thrashing soldier's location, Meredith could already begin to make out the exact contours of the body, even the more pronounced facial features. He almost thought he recognized the man.

Suddenly, he realized what the man's unfocused pawings reminded him of: a newborn infant.

"Get a grip on yourself, Merry," Taylor said gently.

Meredith shook his head and wiped his eyes. He could not bring himself to look at Heifetz again. Or at any of the others.

"I'm going to be sick," he said.

"That's all right," Taylor told him. The old man's voice labored to steady him. "Just go outside. It's all right to be sick."

Meredith did not move. The smell of human waste hung thickly in the ops cell of Heifetz's M-100. Meredith closed his eyes. He did not want to see any more. But, behind his eyelids, the image of the last several minutes grew even grimmer.

"I'm going to be sick," Meredith said again. He could feel the tears searching down over his cheeks for a streambed, seeking out the lowest hollows and contours of flesh.

Taylor took him firmly by the arm.

"Don't let it beat you," he said. "I'm going to need you, Merry."

"I can't," Meredith said, "I just can't," although he had no clear idea of what it was he could not do.

"It's all right."

"My God."

"I know."

"Oh . . . my God," Meredith said. He felt another wave of nausea. But it was not quite strong enough to set him in motion.

"Let's go outside for a minute," Taylor said. "We'll both go." He spoke as though he were addressing a good child in a bad hour. Meredith could not understand it. Not any of it. And he could not begin to understand how Taylor could be so calm.

Unwillingly, Meredith looked around again. It was a little better now. When they had lugged the young captain's snow-dusted body into the shelter of Heifetz's M-100, they had found Lucky Dave and the crew spilled over the floor like drunkards, eyes without focus, limbs twitching like the bodies of beheaded snakes, mouths drooling. The smell of shit had soaked out through their uniforms, and they made unprovoked noises that seemed to come from a delirium beyond words. Taylor had immediately put Meredith to work, untangling the men's limbs, repositioning them onto their bellies so they would not choke on their spittle.

"What *is* it?" Meredith had demanded. It took all of his willpower to assist Taylor in repositioning the stricken soldiers. It was especially difficult with Heifetz. "What is it?"

"I'll tell you later," Taylor had said patiently. "Just help me now."

Meredith had set his hands upon his fellow officers and the crew NCOs with the combination of trepidation and overresolute firmness he might have employed with plague victims. Yet, these men were unmarked by evident disease. The warmth of their skin seemed normal. Nor were there any signs of wounds, except where one NCO had tumbled forward, breaking his nose. The man snorted blood like an ineptly shot animal as they laid him down properly.

Then Meredith needed to stand, as the nausea grew stronger. He saw Lucky Dave's eyes, and for a moment he thought they were staring at him. But it was only a trick of angles and light. There was no recognizable human expression on Heifetz's face. Only an unintelligent confusion of muscles.

"Let's go outside," Taylor repeated. He held Meredith firmly by the upper arm, and he steered him as carefully as possible over the closely aligned bodies.

The bloody-nosed NCO began to grunt loudly and rhythmically. Meredith recoiled, as if a corpse had bitten him. But Taylor had him in a close grip. He directed the younger man toward the rear hatch.

"Watch your step, Merry," he said.

The clean, cold air cued the sickness in Meredith's stomach. He stumbled down onto the snow-covered earth and began to retch. Taylor loosened his grip slightly, but never quite relinquished control of Meredith's arm.

When he was done, Meredith scooped up a handful of clean snow and wiped his mouth. He chewed into the cold whiteness. The regimental surgeon had counseled the men not to use snow to make drinking water, since the regional pollution had reached catastrophic extremes. But Meredith instinctively knew that anything was cleaner than the waste remaining in his mouth.

"It's all right," Taylor said.

Meredith began to cry hard. He shook his head. He knew that something was terribly, horribly wrong. None of his experiences offered a frame of reference for this. He could not understand what his eyes were seeing. He only knew that it was hideous beyond anything in his experience, without having any conscious understanding of why.

"What *happ*ened?" he asked, begging for knowledge.

"Quietly," Taylor said. "Speak quietly."

Meredith looked at the colonel. The cold made the old man's scars stand out lividly. But the sight of Taylor's ruined face was nothing beside the inexplicable condition of the men inside the M-100.

"Why?"

"Just speak quietly."

"Why? For God's sake, what's the matter with Lucky Dave? Is he going to be all right?"

"Merry, get a grip on yourself. We have work to do."

"What's going *on?"* Meredith demanded, his voice almost a child's.

"You have to keep your voice down. They might hear you. Let's not make it any worse for them."

Meredith looked at Taylor in shock. It had never occurred to him that the ruptured behavior of the men they had found might include consciousness of the speech of others. It was too incongruous. The men had obviously lost their minds. Their eyes didn't even focus. They were shitting and pissing all over themselves.

"Listen to me," Taylor said quietly. The snow was beginning to decorate his shoulders. "I think they hear us. I think they hear every word. They just can't respond."

Meredith stared at the devastated face in front of him, not really seeing it.

"Listen to me carefully, Merry," Taylor began. "Ten years ago, when you were off studying your Russian, I was involved in some unusual programs. Between L.A. and our little jaunt down to Mexico. We were working like mad, trying to come up with alternative technologies for a military response to the Japanese. The M-100s are one result of all that. But there were a lot of other projects that didn't make it all the way to production. For a variety of reasons." He shook Meredith by the arm. "Are you all right? Are you listening to me?"

Meredith nodded, with the acid aftertaste of vomit and snow in his mouth.

"We tried everything we could think of," Taylor said. He shook his head at the memory, loosening snow from his helmet. "Some of the ideas were just plain crazy. Nonsensical. Things that couldn't possibly have worked. Or that needed too much development lead time. But there was one thing . . ."

Meredith was listening now. Hungry for any information that would explain events that his mind could not process. But Taylor kept him waiting for a moment. The colonel stared off across the whitened steppes, past the waiting M-100 that had brought them to this place, past another ship half-buried in the snow, to a faraway, indefinite point that only Taylor's eyes could pick out.

"It was out at Dugway. You had to have every clearance in the world just to hear the project's code name. Some of the whiz kids out at Livermore had come up with a totally new approach. And we looked into it. We brought them out to Utah, to the most isolated testing area we had, to see what they could do. They didn't care much for the social environment, of course. But once we turned them loose, they made amazing progress." Taylor paused, still staring out through space and time. "They came up with a weapon that worked, all right. Christ almighty, we could've finished the Japs within a year. As soon as we could've gotten the weapons into the field. But we just could not bring ourselves to do it, Merry. I mean, I think I hate the Japanese. I suspect I hate them in a way that is irrational and morally inexcusable. But not one of us . . . not *one* of the people that had a say wanted to go through with it. We decided that the weapons were simply too inhumane. That their use would have been unforgivable." Taylor looked down at the snow gathering around their boots and smiled softly. "I thought we were doing the right thing. The scientists were disappointed as hell, of course. You know, the worst soldier I've ever known has a more highly developed sense of morality than the average scientist. Anyway, I really thought we were doing the right thing. I guess I was just being weak." He shook his head. "It looks like the Japanese have made fools of us again."

"But . . . what *was* it?" Meredith asked. "The weapon?"

Taylor raised his eyebrows at the question as though further details really were not so pertinent. "It was a radio-wave weapon," he said matter-of-factly. "Complex stuff to design, but simple enough in concept. You take radio waves apart and rebuild them to a formula that achieves a desired effect in the human brain. You broadcast, and the mind receives. It's a little like music. You listen to a song with a good beat, and you tap your foot. A ballad makes you sentimental. Really, sound waves have been manipulating us for a long, long time. Well, the boys from Livermore had been screwing around with jamming techniques for years. Same principle. They started off small. Learning how to cause pain. The next step was to focus the pain. And so on. You could cause death relatively easily. But that was too crude for men of science. They went beyond the clean kill. And we developed . . . well, compositions, you might say, that could do precisely focused damage to the human mind." Taylor looked at Meredith. "Think back to your military science classes, Merry. And tell me: is it preferable to kill your enemy outright or to incapacitate him, to wound him badly?"

"To wound him," Meredith said automatically.

"And why?"

"Because . . . a dead soldier . . . is just a dead soldier. But a wounded soldier puts stress on the enemy's infrastructure. He has to receive first aid. Then he has to be evacuated. He requires care. A dead soldier makes no immediate demands on the system, but a wounded man exerts a rearward pull. Enough wounded men can paralyze—"

"Exactly. And that's it, Merry."

"But . . . how long until it wears off? When are they going to be all right?"

Taylor strengthened his grip on Merry's arm. "Merry, it *doesn't* wear off. Christ, if it did, we would have fielded it in a heartbeat. The effects are irreversible. It's a terror weapon too, you see."

Meredith felt sick again. With a deeper, emptier, spiritually dreary sickness.

"But . . . you said they might be able to understand us?"

Taylor nodded. "It makes no difference to recovery. In fact, that's the worst part, Merry. You see, if the Japanese are using approximately the same formula we came up with, Lucky . . . Colonel Heifetz and the others have not suffered any loss in intelligence, or in basic cognitive recognition. What the weapon does is simply to destroy the victim's control over his voluntary muscles. There's some collateral deterioration on the involuntary side, as well, but basically you can focus the damage. See, that's the beauty of the weapon—the victims remain fully intelligent human beings, even though they are physically utterly incapable of controlling their basic bodily functions. They cannot even tell their eyes where to look. But they still process what their eyes happen to see. That way, by presenting your enemy with a mature, living intelligence, you rob him of the excuse to lighten his load with conscience-free euthanasia—you're not killing a *thing*. You'd be killing a thinking, feeling human being who lost the use of his body in the service of his country." Taylor snorted. "Beautiful, isn't it?"

Meredith did not understand how Taylor could speak so calmly.

"Merry. You need to pull yourself together now. We need to help them as best we can. And then we've got to get back into the fight."

Meredith stared at the scarred, scarred man as though he were crazy. What on earth was he talking about? Help them? How? And what would be the point of getting back into any fighting now? If this was all that was waiting at the end of it.

"Count your blessings," Taylor told him. "If that escort bird hadn't gone down . . . well, that's war, Merry. Some die, and others live. Luck of the draw."

"I *can't*," Meredith said. Again, he had no clear idea as to what it was he could not do. But he felt panic seizing him. "I just can't function. *I give up*."

Taylor's hand came up like lightning. He slapped Meredith so hard across the face that the younger man reeled and almost fell. Dazed, he could taste blood in his mouth. It was a far better taste than the vomit and snow had left behind.

Taylor caught him with both hands this time. The grip was noticeably weaker under the bandaged paw. He held Meredith upright, pinning the younger man's arms flat against his sides.

"Merry. *Please*."

Meredith tried to bond himself to reality. But this was a world out of horrific medieval paintings.

"Merry, I *need* you now," Taylor said. "You're a very brave man, and you've proved it time and again. I need you to be brave now. Because, if you can't handle this, think of the effect it's going to have on the others."

"All right," Meredith said slowly, emptily. The slap had jarred him, and he was still unsure of everything, but in a different way.

"Merry," Taylor begged, "we can't give up. You don't see it, but I do. They're all going to want to give up now, and we can't let them. It's up to us."

Meredith did not understand what Taylor was talking about. *Who* was going to give up? And to give up what?

"We won't give up," Meredith said flatly.

"That's right. We're not going to give up. Now listen to me." Taylor's voice took on the cold, clear tone it always had when he needed to give complex instructions under pressure. "I want you to go back to our ship. You go back there and get on the horn. Call Manny—" Taylor caught himself. For a moment, the two men looked at each other with eyes that met yet shared nothing. Then Taylor regrouped: "Call the assistant S-4. He'll be at the support site in Gold. Tell him to off-load every available wing-inground except the fuelers and get them down here to Silver. And I want the regimental surgeon on board, with every immediately available physician's assistant and medic. Call the assistant S-4 first. It's going to take him the longest. Then call Second Squadron over at Platinum. They're the closest. Tell the commander I want his scouts down here double-quick. Use the top-end secure. Explain that we have casualties. The scouts need to search each troop's local assembly area, just in case anybody else is lying out in the snow like that captain."

"Captain Sturgis," Meredith offered. He had known the officer slightly. An overgrown kid with a habit of bringing his sex life a little too close to the flagpole.

"Yes," Taylor said. "Sturgis. Anyway, get going. Get them moving. And prepare yourself, Merry. Please. I know you're with me. You just have to hang tough. Because we're going to have panic from here to Washington."

"All right," Meredith said. And, for the first time, there was a glimmer of capability in his voice. He realized that he was going to make it. He would do his duty. He just needed a little more time. "Anything else, sir?"

Behind the scars and grime on Taylor's face, Meredith imagined that he saw a look of defenseless gratitude. A very brief revelation of the weakness Taylor felt himself.

"No," the colonel said. "You just get that much done. Then stay on the net to take care of any necessary damage control. I don't think the enemy have picked up on the other squadrons, or they would've hit them too. It's going to be all right, Merry."

"Yes, sir."

Taylor finally let go of Meredith's arm, and turned back toward Heifetz's M-100.

Captain Horace "Hank" Parker had been through an interesting day. While he had deployed to Mexico, the assignment had come too late in the intervention for him to see any real combat, and today marked the loss of his battlefield virginity. He had done his best, sensing that it was somehow inadequate—especially in the presence of Colonel Taylor, a man he held in awe. He could not help being jealous of the easy camaraderie between the S-2 and the commander, and he had felt very much like an outsider at first. He knew very well that Taylor would have preferred to have Heifetz himself on board, instead of his far less experienced assistant.

Still, he had done his best, always doubting himself a little, but somehow avoiding major errors. A few hours into the battle he had relaxed, experiencing the odd sense that modern combat was almost identical to playing games in an amusement arcade in a shopping mall. All screens and images and numbers. You racked up the most points on the board, and you won. It had been surprisingly difficult to picture a real flesh-and-blood enemy out there.

Then that intangible enemy had reached out and hit the old staging area at Omsk. People he knew personally had died, and the game had turned out to be real after all. Then things had begun to move with such speed that it all blurred. There was the ambush of the enemy planes, after which Taylor surprised him by asking his first name, then calling him Hank—that had been better than receiving a medal, coming in the lonesome hour it did. Then Meredith had dismissively ordered him to stay with the comms sets while he and one of the NCOs followed Taylor out to try to rescue the crew of the downed M-100. He had obeyed faithfully, as the noise of gunfire reached into the controlled environment of the ops cell, frightened by his helplessness to influence events, waiting. Then the NCO had failed to return, and the casualties found a place in the cramped compartment, and death seemed to be sneaking closer and closer. The arcade game stakes were rising uncontrollably.

And now this. Waiting again. In an atmosphere of death. Afraid and uncertain, with Colonel Taylor and Meredith gone off into the silence. What was happening out there?

Parker waited in the ops cell with Meredith's shop NCO, who was also an ops backup in the austere modern Army. Both men hated the ominous quiet, and they agreed on it out loud. But they could not bring themselves to say much else.

They sat. Waiting. Imagining.

What was going on?

Without warning, the strategic communications receiver came to life.

Parker scrambled to put on the headset, then his fingers reached clumsily for the unfamiliar controls. Usually, Meredith or Taylor worked this set. Before he had begun to master the situation, the call came again.

"Yes," Parker answered hastily, "this is Sierra."

"Hold for the President," the voice said.

A moment later, a voice Parker knew only from television broadcasts came through the earpieces.

"Colonel Taylor?" the smooth, instantly recognizable voice began, "Colonel Taylor, one of your subordinate commanders has just contacted us with an emergency message. Lieutenant Colonel Reno claims—"

"Uh, sir?" Parker interrupted, instantly regretting both that Taylor was not immediately at hand to rescue him and that, in the last election, he had voted for the other candidate. Somehow, he suspected that the President would be able to tell about the miscast ballot. "Sir, this isn't Colonel Taylor. I'm just . . . like an assistant. Colonel Taylor's outside."

"Oh," the President said. "Excuse me."

Indeterminate noises followed from the distant station. Like miniature moving men hurriedly cleaning out a dollhouse. A new voice came up on the net:

"Soldier, this is General Oates. I want you to go find Colonel Taylor, wherever he is. The President of the United States wants to talk to him."

"Yes, sir," Parker said. He moved very, very quickly. Not bothering to search for his helmet, he launched himself out through the rear hatch and nearly collided with Meredith.

"Whoa," Meredith said. "Where're you going?"

"Major Meredith, sir? Where's Colonel Taylor? The President wants to talk to him."

Meredith seemed to take the news with reprehensible calm. He was well-dusted with snow, as though he had been standing outside for a long time. For a moment Parker did not even think Meredith had understood him correctly, and he opened his mouth to repeat his message.

Meredith beat him to it. "The colonel's over there. In the ops bird." He pushed past Parker into the waiting M-100.

Parker plunged through the blowing snow. He high-stepped and slapped his way through the cold, imagining vaguely that one wrong move would bring far worse punishments down upon his head than anything battle might devise. He wished he were a faster runner, and he wished he were not such a fool.

He rounded the back end of Lieutenant Colonel Heifetz's M-100 and hauled himself up through the open hatch without a pause. He was about to howl his news at Taylor when the scene inside the ops cabin froze the words on his lips.

Heifetz's personal crew—men Parker worked with every day and knew as well as shared duty allowed—lay ranked along the narrow floor. It was immediately apparent that they were all alive, and it was equally apparent that something was revoltingly wrong, although the details of the scene made no real sense to Parker. He had seen the image of the soldier sprawled in the snow, fooling his limbs at the sky, but he had assumed that the disjointed movements were the result of pain, of a wound. Now Parker was confronted with a cabin full of squirming bodies, each man making similarly inept movements without pattern or warning. There was a strong foul smell, and the nearest man made mewling noises that made Parker want to back right out of the hatch and get away.

But the sight at the end of the cabin held him. Colonel Taylor sat upon the floor, cradling Heifetz's head in his lap. Taylor was whispering softly to the S-3, the way Parker whispered to his twin daughters when they were sick. The colonel smoothed his unbandaged hand back over Heifetz's thinning hair, repeating the gesture again and again.

Parker did not know what to do. Then he remembered in panic: the President.

"Colonel Taylor, sir," he said too loudly. "Sir, the President is on the line. The President wants to talk to you."

Taylor looked up briefly. The fright-mask face was very calm, almost expressionless.

"Tell him I'm busy."

PART IV

The Journey's End

20

3 November 2020

DAISY LISTENED. SHE WANTED TO SPEAK, BUT COULD find no words. She wanted to act, but there was nothing to be done. Everything had gotten out of control. They had failed. *She* had failed. All of the careful intelligence analysis had turned out to be a joke. And the Japanese had kept the punchline hidden until it was too late. Now it was all over, and the only thing she could do was to listen.

"Mr. President, it's time to throw in the towel," the secretary of state said. He was a dignified old man who consciously cheapened his speech whenever he spoke to Waters, employing catchphrases and slang otherwise foreign to his tongue. "We gave it our best shot, and we missed. Now it's time to cut our losses. I'm certain we can negotiate a safe withdrawal for the remainder of our forces in the Soviet Union."

Daisy looked appraisingly at the President. The smooth, photogenic face had gone haggard, and the man looked far older than his years. She knew that the President suffered from high-blood pressure, and it troubled her. The Vice President was an intellectual nonentity who had only been placed on the ticket because he was a white southerner from an established political family—the perfect counterbalance for Jonathan Waters, who was black, northern, and passionately liberal. The election ploy had succeeded at the polls, but Daisy dreaded the thought of a sudden incapacitation of Waters. For all his ignorance of international affairs and military matters, Daisy could not suppress the instinctive feeling that the President's judgment was sound, while that of the men who served him was increasingly suspect. The Vice President was, perhaps, the most hopeless of the lot. Even now, with the nation's armed forces in combat overseas, Vice President Maddox was plodding on with the original itinerary of a tour of environmentally threatened sites on the West Coast. He would not even be back in the District until early the next morning.

Daisy certainly did not agree with all of the President's decisions. But she was convinced that his incorrect decisions were made with the best intentions, while the motives of his closest advisers were too often shaped by self-interest or parochialism. Watching the man age before her eyes, Daisy hoped he would take the measures that had become so evidently necessary as quickly as possible, then rest.

The President slumped back in his chair. He seemed smaller than he had appeared to Daisy in the past. His suit rumpled around him like a refugee's blanket.

"And the Pentagon's position?" Waters asked, turning to the chairman of the Joint Chiefs of Staff. "Give it to me straight."

The general leaned in over the table. He looked tormented. The secretary of defense had collapsed from exhaustion during a hasty early morning trip to the Building, and the chairman had been temporarily left adrift to define the military's position. He was a big, barrel-chested man, and his heavy face had the look of thick rubber that had lost its elasticity. His eyes were shrunken and dark, surrounded by a discoloration as mottled as camouflage paint.

"Mr. President," he began carefully, "we would do well to remember that the balance sheet isn't completely in the red. If you look at the raw numbers, for instance, the Japanese and their proxies have suffered a grave defeat at the hands of the United States Army. We've lost a squadron. They've lost their most potent field forces, the key combat equipment out of several corps. If the Japanese hadn't had an ace up their sleeve, we'd be sitting here having a victory celebration. Our forces performed brilliantly. Unfortunately, the intelligence services missed a vital piece of information—"

Daisy felt Bouquette bristle at her side. But it was true. It was all too true. The intelligence system had let them all down. And she already knew that they would not suffer so much as a single broken career for it. She knew Washington. Since she was a woman, her job was particularly safe.

"—and we got caught with our pants down. Our boys . . . did their best. They did a damned fine job."

"But?" the President said.

"Mr. President," the chairman said, looking at Waters with a face stripped of professional vanity, "I believe we should salvage what we can. It's not over. We can carry on the fight another day. But this round . . . Mr. President, this one's gone to the Japanese."

President Waters nodded. He made a church of his touched-together fingertips.

"And what does it cost us?" he asked. "If we just pull out?"

The secretary of state cleared his throat. "Mr. President . . . naturally, the Japanese will expect some concessions. I don't see it impacting on the Western Hemisphere . . . but, the Siberia question . . . of course, that's ultimately going to be resolved between the Soviets and the Japanese anyway."

Waters swiveled a few degrees in his chair, turning to stare down the table to where Bouquette and Daisy sat in the first row of seats beyond the table.

"Cliff," the President said to Bouquette, "is it the Agency's view that the Japanese will make repeated use of the Scramblers if we don't cut a deal?"

Bouquette rose. "Mr. President, there's no question about it. If they employed them once, they'll do it again. If we provoke them. We suspect that they've already delivered an ultimatum to the Soviets."

"And you now concur with the assessment of Colonel . . . uh, Taylor . . . that these are some kind of radio weapons?"

Bouquette pawed one of his fine English shoes at the carpet. "Yes, Mr. President. Radio-*wave* weapons, actually. Yes, it now appears that Colonel Taylor's initial assessment was correct. Of course, he had the advantage of being on the scene, while we had to work with second-hand information."

"And these are weapons that could have been introduced into the U.S. arsenal a decade ago?"

"We can still build them," the chairman interrupted. "We could field new prototypes in six months."

"I don't *want* to build them," the President said. There was an unmistakable note of anger in his voice. "If we had them, I would not order their use. Even now." Waters slumped again, then smiled wearily. "Perhaps, after the election, you'll be able to take up the matter with my successor." He turned back to Bouquette. "Do we have any idea whether the Japanese have other tricks up their sleeve? Do they have any more secret weapons?"

Bouquette glanced down at his hand-sewn shoes. Then he took a breath that was clearly audible to Daisy. "Mr. President, we have no further information in that regard. But we cannot rule out the possibility."

Waters nodded his head in acknowledgment. The movement was rhythmic and slight, the equivalent of mumbling to himself. It was the gesture of an old man.

The President looked around the room.

"Does anybody have a different opinion? Another view? Is it the general consensus that we should run up the white flag?"

"Mr. President," the chairman said quickly, "I wouldn't put it in quite those terms."

Waters turned to face the general. It was clear to Daisy that the President was having a very hard time controlling his anger. Despite his exhaustion.

"Then what terms would you put it in? What do you think the American people are going to call it? Do you think the man in the street's going to fish up some fancy term—what do you call it?—a strategic correction or something like that?" Waters looked around the room with harder eyes than Daisy had credited him with possessing. "I want you to be absolutely clear about this, gentlemen. I am *not* talking or thinking about the election. Let me say it outright. I've lost already, and there is nothing anyone in this room can do about it. No, what concerns me now is that we have made some very bad decisions. *I* have made bad decisions. We sent our fighting men to die—for nothing, it seems. We have squandered our nation's international prestige yet again—Christ, what were you telling me earlier?" he asked the secretary of state. "The Japanese, along with two dozen 'nonaligned' nations, have already introduced a resolution in the UN condemning us for interfering in the sovereign affairs of third-party states. The Japanese already have diplomats standing up in the General Assembly and blaming *us* for triggering the use of these Scramblers. They're making fools of us all, with record speed. While we sit here with our thumbs up our backsides. Gentlemen," Waters said slowly, "I am an angry man." He smirked. "But don't worry. I know exactly who to blame. I'm just sorry I was so damned smug." His smirk deepened, forcing painful-looking cuts into the skin around his mouth. "Maybe America wasn't ready for a black president, after all."

No one dared speak. Daisy felt sorry for Waters. He was, she sensed, genuinely a good man. Carrying too much baggage, and with too little experience. They had all failed him.

They had failed George Taylor too. *She* had failed him unforgivably. But she would make it up to him. She imagined how he must be feeling now. With his life's dreams lying in ruins in a foreign land. But at least he was alive, and as yet untouched by the unspeakable weaponry that had hidden behind so innocuous a word. He was alive, and if there was no more foolishness, he would be coming home to her. Of everyone in the overheated conference room, she was the only one with cause for joy.

I could be good for him, she thought. I really could. He'll need me now.

"Before I make a final decision," President Waters said, "I want to consult with our Soviet allies one more time."

"Mr. President," the secretary of state said impatiently, "their position's clear. While we lost—what was it—a squadron? A few hundred men? The Soviets still haven't begun to total their losses. An entire city—what was it, Bouquette?"

"Orsk."

"Yes, Orsk. And dozens of surrounding towns. Hundreds of settlements. Why, the Soviets are overwhelmed. They have no idea how to cope with the casualties. We're talking numbers in the hundreds of thousands. And what if the Japanese use these weapons again? Mr. President, you heard the Soviet ambassador yourself. 'Immediate negotiations for an armistice.' The Soviets have already thrown in the towel."

President Waters narrowed his eyes. "Have the Soviets established direct contact with Tokyo on this?"

"Not yet."

"So they still have not taken any unilateral action? They're still waiting for our response?"

"Mr. President, it's merely a diplomatic courtesy. They expect us to join them in the discussions—we can still lend a certain weight, of course."

"But the Soviets still have not 'thrown in the towel,' technically speaking?"

"Well, not formally, of course. But, in spirit . . ."

"Then don't contradict me," Waters said. "I want to speak with the Soviet president. One on one. I want to hear his views from his lips."

"Sir, the Soviets have made it clear they're going to call it quits," the secretary of state said. His voice carried the tone of a teacher sorely disappointed with his pupil. "We stand to lose leverage if we—"

Waters turned on the secretary of state with a look so merciless that the distinguished old man broke off in midsentence.

"You can give up your efforts to educate me," Waters said. "Write me off as another black dropout. Just get President Chernikov on the line—no, first get me Colonel Taylor. I want to talk to that man one more time."

"Mr. President," the chairman of the Joint Chiefs said carefully, "Colonel Taylor's in no position to give you an objective view of the situation. You heard what his subordinate, Lieutenant Colonel Reno, said about him. And you heard the man yourself. All Colonel Taylor wants to do is to hit back at what hurt him. He's reacting emotionally. He has absolutely no grip of the new geopolitical realities involved here."

Waters looked at the chairman. To her surprise, Daisy saw a genuine smile spread across the President's face.

"Well," Waters said, "I guess that makes two of us. Anyway, I'd be a damned fool not to hear out the one man who's got the balls to tell me when he's busy." Waters snapped his head around to look at Daisy. "Do excuse my language, Miss Fitzgerald. Just pretend you weren't listening."

The American was crazy. General Ivanov could not believe what he had heard. The memory of the American colonel's scarred face was troubling enough—now it appeared that the man's mind was deformed as well.

A raid.

A raid into the enemy's operational-strategic rear.

A raid on the enemy's main command and control center.

A raid on the enemy's *computer* system, of all things.

It was a madman's notion, in an hour when the world was coming apart.

The long day had begun so well. With American successes that promised to decisively alter the correlation of forces. American successes so great they both frightened Ivanov and made him envious, even though the Americans were on his country's side this time.

Of course, he and a select group of Soviets had known there would be a Japanese reply. They had even had an inkling of the form the Japanese response would take. But they had not understood the dimensions of the loss they would suffer, otherwise they would not have involved themselves with the Americans in the first place. They had attempted to call the Japanese bluff.

Then the world had ended for every Soviet citizen living within a zone of tens of thousands of square kilometers. A military transport had landed at Orsk to find its entire population reduced to infantile helplessness. It was worse than the chemical attacks. Worse, in its way, than the plague years had been. The Japanese had won. And, no matter how cruel and theoretically inadmissable their methods had been, their victory could not be denied. All that remained was to salvage as much of the motherland as possible. And that was up to Moscow, where there was already turbulence enough with the attempted coup in the Kremlin.

As nearly as Ivanov could sort it out from the incoming reports, the struggle was between the state security apparatus, which wanted to continue the war at all costs, and a faction of generals intent on salvaging what was left of the motherland. Ivanov had not been asked to support his comrades in Moscow, and he wondered why. He was ready. Oh, there were so many secrets. Thank God, the Americans seemed to have missed the revolt in its entirety.

Meanwhile, Ivanov waited in his headquarters for word that the Japanese terror weapons had descended from the heavens at yet another location, perhaps devouring an entire army this time. Perhaps they would come for a worn-out Soviet general who was no longer a threat to anyone.

Ivanov wondered exactly how the weapons worked. Was their effect instantaneous, or would a man who recognized what he was dealing with have time to put a pistol to his head?

"Viktor Sergeyevich," Ivanov said to Kozlov, "you realize the sensitivity of your role?"

"Yes, sir."

"The Americans have asked for an officer with firsthand knowledge of Baku, to help with their contingency planning. So help them. Answer their questions. And pay attention. Your real mission is to ensure that this American colonel takes no unilateral action. We cannot afford further provocations. Moscow is preparing a negotiating position."

"It's over, then?" Kozlov asked.

Ivanov nodded, unable to meet Kozlov's eyes. All these years, all the hard work and dreams, only to come to this. "Yes, Viktor Sergeyevich. We will continue to defend ourselves locally. But it's over."

"And there is nothing to be done?"

Ivanov shook his head. "How can we respond to something like this? The Japanese have made it very clear that the strike on the Orsk region was merely a warning."

"And the Americans have no technological counter-measure?"

Ivanov rose wearily and paced across his office. He stopped in front of the portrait of Suvorov with its faulty color tones. "If they do, they're keeping it a secret." He shrugged. "Moscow believes the Americans are as helpless as we are. Oh, there's some nonsense about attacking Japanese computers . . . But, really . . . with such weapons at the enemy's disposal . . . What is to be done?" Ivanov looked fully into Kozlov's stare for the first time, and saw the reflection of his desolation. "Nothing," Ivanov answered himself. "Nothing."

"Yet, Colonel Taylor is planning a raid? He plans to continue the fight?"

"We suspect it's all on his own initiative. As far as we know, Washington has approved nothing." He turned his back on the picture of the dead hero. "Watch him, Viktor. Watch him closely."

"Yes, sir."

"Answer his questions. Keep me informed."

"And he wants to raid *Baku?* The Japanese head-quarters?"

Ivanov smiled wistfully. "Yes. The Japanese headquarters. Of course, you and I remember when it was otherwise."

"Exactly so."

Ivanov turned from the picture of the old czarist warrior and stared across the office. "I always had a soft spot for Baku, you know. Oh, not for the Azeris. They were simply animals. But I loved the warmth. I truly did. It was still good when you and I served there together, Viktor Sergeyevich. But it was better still, far better, when I was stationed there as a young captain. With the reoccupation troops." The tiniest of smiles slipped onto the general's face. "Old Baku. It's changed hands so many times over the centuries. The Persians. Then us. And the Persians again. And so on. Even the British were there for the blink of an eye." Ivanov shook his head in wonder. "Who knows? Perhaps it will change hands again one day. It's all part of the ebb and flow that foreigners never really comprehend. Oh, things look bad enough for us at the moment. But they've looked bad before. Mongols, Tartars, Turks, Persians, Poles, Lithuanians, Germans. And all the forgotten names of the forgotten people who crossed the soil of Russia only to disappear into the pages of unread history books. Perhaps Great Russia must become a smaller Russia for a time. So that she can become a Great Russia once again." Ivanov looked down at the worn Caucasian carpet that always lay in front of his desk, no matter where his assignments took him. "We must try to keep faith, Viktor Sergeyevich. We must try to keep our faith."

For all of his earnestness, the tiny smile reappeared on the general's face. "That carpet you're standing on. I bought that in Baku. Back when I had to count my rubles carefully. You know, I was detailed to the Interior Ministry that first time—and lucky to have a job, at that. So many of my friends were put out of uniform completely. That was back before we began the post-Gorbachev rebuilding, of course."

Kozlov knew the story. He always made it a point to know everything possible about his superiors. But he gave no sign of it now.

"Thirty years ago now," Ivanov went on. "And it seems like yesterday. I'd been serving in the Western Group of Forces in Germany when that all went to hell—I can't tell you how we all felt. One moment it's all brotherhood, then, overnight, you've got half a million people in the streets of Leipzig shouting for us to get out of their country. That was in eighty-nine."

"The year of counterrevolution," Kozlov offered.

"The year of endings, anyway," Ivanov said. "I used to love to walk the streets of Leipzig in the evenings, just to look in the shop windows along with my fellow officers. And to look at the proud German women. But I'm getting off the subject. We were talking about Baku. Well, after I got shipped home from Germany, it looked as though my military career had come to a premature end. Officers were being turned out into the street by the thousands. With no jobs waiting, not even a place to sleep. You have no idea how bad it was. Fortunately, I had a sterling record. I'm afraid I was a perfect little kiss-ass of a junior officer. So I was one of the fortunate few transferred to the troops of the Ministry of the Interior. It was still quite a comedown, after serving in the real army. But it was far better than any alternative I could see. And I served for a while, trying to beat my ragbag soldiers into shape. While things got worse in the country. New problems every day, with that silly dreamer in the Kremlin. Eventually, I was sent into Azerbaijan with the reoccupation forces. After all the bloodletting and the pogroms and the attempt at secession. We worked some long hours, I can tell you. And some of the duties were as bad as they could be." Ivanov's face reflected the memory of youth and old troubles successfully overcome. "I managed to enjoy myself in Baku, though. My fellow officers were so afraid—of the knife in the back and so forth. But I was crazy. I remember I used to like to walk up to Kirov Park when I was off duty. I was young, and fit, and I just stared down anybody likely to make trouble. Sometimes I'd even go down into the old quarter. But, usually, I'd just climb up to the park and sit. Staring at the city. The call to evening prayer would ring out over the loudspeakers, and the air was full of the smells of cooking oil and shashlik, and I was never afraid. It merely seemed like a great adventure to me. I was part of a long, long tradition. When you walked through the streets at dusk, you'd catch a sudden glimpse of some dark-eyed girl, all spice and lavender, and you could not help feeling that the world was full of great possibilities. I had such confidence, such faith. I would sit in the twilight and make plans to save my country, Viktor. I was going to be a great hero." Ivanov's eyes glistened. "And now it's come to this. The Japanese in our old headquarters building. A world in ruins."

"I never cared for Baku," Kozlov said. "I always thought it was dirty."

"Oh, yes. But you're from a different generation. You have different eyes."

"I think of the heat. And dust. And the refineries."

"Yes, yes," Ivanov said. "And it's just as well. You don't feel the loss that way. In any case, lend the Americans your knowledge of the setup in Baku. Let them make their plans. I don't think it will come to very much."

"Anything else, sir?"

There was so much he would have liked to tell the younger man. Poor Kozlov, with his diseased gums and his passion for plodding staff work. Ivanov felt the old Russian need to talk, to confess, growing stronger and stronger in him. He had seen so much in his day. And it was all disappearing in the dust. He would have liked to order up a bottle of vodka and regale the younger man with all the lost possibilities, the things that might have been. But there was no time.

"No. Nothing else, Viktor Sergeyevich. Just keep your eyes open."

Kozlov snapped his heels together and raised his right hand, offering a soldier's respect. Suddenly, Ivanov lurched forward, drunk with memories. He embraced Kozlov, kissing him on both cheeks. Ivanov knew that the two of them were unlikely ever to meet again.

Kozlov had been surprised by the generosity of the gesture, and he only managed to brush his lips across the older man's jowls. Then Ivanov released him.

When Kozlov had gone, Ivanov turned his attention back to the portrait of Suvorov. It hung crookedly, when you looked at it straight on. Well, Ivanov thought, I never made it. Didn't even come close. I was going to be another Suvorov. Instead, it's my lot to preside over defeat and capitulation.

He closed his eyes. And he could hear it. The sound of the beginning of the end. Nineteen eighty-nine. That enormous, irresistible chanting of the East Germans in the streets. Even after he and his fellow officers had been restricted to barracks, they could still hear it. Every Monday night. Echoing off the glass and steel facade of the vast train station, resounding down the boulevards and alleyways of Leipzig. It seemed to him now that he had known that it was all over then, and that the remainder of his life had merely been a long rearguard action, waged more out of obstinacy than in hope. He had only understood the most rudimentary German, but he had gotten the meaning clearly enough. The hammering waves of words had been accusing him and his kind, flooding down the crumbling streets, splashing up over the barracks walls, impervious to the witless guards and barbed wire, a torrent of rage. The individual slogans did not matter. They changed. But their meaning could invariably be translated as, *"Failure, failure, failure."*

Kozlov did not mind the cold. He did not even think about it. Even the misery of his teeth, gums, and jaw seemed to have declared a truce. Soon, the aircraft would arrive to take him away. To join the Americans. He was glad he was going.

He still did not like the Americans. But he was even less comfortable with Ivanov's despair. And he was ashamed. For all their faults, the Americans had behaved honorably, had done their best. And they were still willing to carry on the fight. While his side had withheld key information, while his people were even now looking for ways to undercut the American effort instead of aiding it. Perhaps it was biological, Kozlov thought. The result of all the years of deception, of lies told to one another. Perhaps deceit had been bred into the substance of Soviet man.

And the Americans had come so close. Really, there was no substance left to oppose Soviet forces on the ground. Even in their battered condition, they could begin to sweep back to the south, through Kazakhstan. And beyond. The Americans, with their wondrous machines, had done the enemy coalition irreparable harm. The correlation of ground forces had shifted remarkably.

The only problem was the new Japanese terror weapon. Still, it was unthinkable to Kozlov that his people would let a single tool deprive them not only of victory but perhaps of their national independence. What had happened at Orsk? A terrible thing. Gruesome. But it was nothing compared to the sufferings of the Great Patriotic War. What had happened to the Russian character? To the spirit of sacrifice?

Kozlov refused to feel beaten.

The reserves of strength he found in himself surprised him a little. He had always considered himself a top-notch staff officer—but he had never cast himself in the role of a particularly brave man. Often he had been afraid to speak up in front of his superiors—even when he knew them to be dangerously wrong.

It was time to make up for those errors now.

He did not know what he would do. But, if the Americans had not yet given up hope, then he saw no reason why he should be the first to quit.

The Americans. They were simply impossible to like. He remembered when he had been a cadet in Moscow during the long twilight of the nineteen nineties. His girl of the moment had been obsessed with paying a visit to the McDonald's restaurant that had opened on Pushkin Square. He had resisted the idea, out of the sort of self-righteous patriotism only a cadet could feel—and because the prices were painfully high on his allowance. But the girl had been pretty. Irina was her name. And his teeth had not been so bad then. They had kissed, and she had nipped his tongue, accusing him of stinginess and cruelty. So they had gone. To McDonald's.

There was a line, of course. But it moved with remarkable speed. The employees behind the clean, brightly lit counter smiled, and he assumed that they must be foreigners. That led to his first shock. The salesgirl greeted him with a lilting Moscow accent, asking after his desires. He stumbled over the peculiar names—his military English classes had not included these "Bik Mecks." With startling speed, the meal appeared before him on a tray, artfully packaged. His money was taken and change returned, and the smiling little Moscow girl repeated her greeting to the next citizen in line.

It had been indescribably painful to sit in the spotless, bustling restaurant, eating the delicious sandwich with helpless appetite and watching his girl gobble and smile, with little bits of America clinging to the spaces between her teeth. They had still played staff war games against the Americans in those days, it was an old habit that died hard, and the dexterity with which this American system had maneuvered him through a restaurant, ambushing him with food and fizzy cola, controlling his every action—it was an unnerving experience. If the Americans were this

good at so trivial an endeavor as running a restaurant
. . . you had to wonder whether they might not be considerably better at military art than his superiors were willing to credit. It went back to the Marxist dialectic and the laws governing the conversion of quantitative change into qualitative.

After finishing the last seductive bite, he dragged his girl from beneath those golden arches of triumph. Out in the street they began a loud and too public argument as he vowed never to set foot in this restaurant of McDonald's again. She called him a pompous ass and a little shit. The skirmish took place in front of an extremely interested crowd, several members of which were anxious to take sides, and, in the end, the trip to McDonald's not only failed to result in a trip to Irina's bed—its outcome was his immediate and irrevocable expulsion from the beachhead he had battled to establish in her heart. She did not even return his calls, and the last time he caught a glimpse of her it was purely by chance. He was strolling through Moscow's broken heart, passing along the windows of the fateful Capitalist trojan horse. And there, imprisoned beneath those merciless golden arches, he saw his bright little Irina, driving her little white teeth into a hamburger sandwich and sharing her fried potatoes with another man.

The powerful drone of aircraft engines called Kozlov back to the present. Siberia. The razor's edge between victory and defeat. The immediacy of history in the making. And he realized that poor old Ivanov had picked the wrong man for this job.

It was impossible to like the Americans. But he had begun to suspect that they were not without honor. And courage. Overcoming his ferocious prejudice as best he could, Kozlov had decided to cast his lot on the side of the Bik Meck after all.

Valya stared at the sandwich in disgust. The protruding corners of cheese ran from yellow to brown and the bread looked dusty and withered. She did not even want to touch the food, much less eat it. Neither could she drink any more of the tea in which she had nervously and too readily indulged herself across the endless afternoon.

"Really, Citizen Babryshkina," the interrogating officer said, "you must eat something. To keep your strength up."

"I'm not hungry," Valya said.

The officer sighed. "I'm sorry we can't offer you something tastier. But, after all, this is not a luxury hotel of the sort to which you have become accustomed."

"I can't eat."

The officer threw up his hands in a motherly gesture. He was a very large man, with white indoor skin and colorless hair. Except for his size, he would have been invisible in a crowd.

"Citizen Babryshkina—Valya, may I call you Valya?" he asked, glancing at the stack of photographs that lay in slight disorder beside the plate. Valya's eyes automatically followed those of her interrogator. "After all," the big man said, "I don't think it would be too great an intimacy, under the circumstances."

Valya said nothing. She looked at the top photograph. Even in the bad light, the details were all too clear.

"Yes, Valya," the officer continued. "You're known to have quite an appetite. And you mustn't get sick on us. You're really—" he picked up a photograph, then discarded it again "—quite thin. Please do have a bite or two."

An obedient child, Valya took up half of the sandwich. But that was as much as she could manage. She could not raise it to her lips.

The officer came around the table, rushing to her assistance. He closed a big soft hand over Valya's fingers, pressing them into the staleness of the sandwich, and he helped her find her mouth.

"No," she muttered. Then she felt the stiffened edge of cheese, the sharp crust pushing against her lips. The big hand crushed it ever so gently into her face, and the stink of the cheese made her feel faint.

Abruptly, the officer gave up on her. He let go of her hand and the crumpled sandwich slipped down over her chin, leaving a trail of odor and crumbs.

The officer sighed again, a disappointed parent. "You're such a bad girl, Valya. I worry about you."

The big man moved back to his seat across the little

table. For a moment, it seemed as though he had forgotten her. He took up the top few photos, inspecting them one after the other with the expression of a stamp collector paging through an unsatisfactory catalog. There wasn't the least hint of sexuality in his features.

"Hard to fathom," he said softly, as if to himself. "Now *this*, for instance"—he suddenly remembered Valya—"do you honestly *enjoy* that sort of thing?"

He thrust the picture at Valya. It was as if the picture, too, had a foul smell to it, an odor far worse than the rancid cheese that lay broken on the plate.

"I'm just curious," the officer went on. "I'm afraid I'm not a very imaginative man. When it comes to that sort of thing." He fumbled for a moment, hunting a specific photograph. Then he smiled and shook his head, offering yet another snapshot to Valya. "This, for instance. It never even occurred to me that people did such things to each other. I'm afraid I'm not much of a man of the world."

Valya considered the photo. Herself. And Naritsky. One of Naritsky's little games. It seemed so long ago now. How had they known? How long had they been watching her?

They had photos of her with years of lovers. With every one except Yuri. Only her husband seemed to hold no interest for them.

The interrogator made a little scolding noise, then tossed the photo back on the pile with all of the others.

"Now the American," he began, "in a way, I can understand that one. They're so rich—how much did he pay you, by the way?"

Valya looked up in horror.

"I'm just curious," the officer said.

"Nothing," Valya cried. "For God's sake, what do you think I *am?"*

The officer looked at her for what seemed a terribly long time. Then he said:

"What *should* I think, little Valya? Surely, you don't expect me to believe that an attractive young woman— well, perhaps not *so* young anymore—but let's say 'an attractive *Russian* woman,' shall we?" He looked from Valya's face down to the line of her breasts and back up again. But there still was no trace of desire in his eyes. He might have been appraising an animal at a market. "Now you don't expect me to believe that you're so . . . so indiscriminate . . . that you would simply throw yourself into bed with a foreigner whom you had met hardly an hour before without receiving some sort of . . . compensation?"

Valya felt her cheeks burning. She recalled with piercing clarity the voices in the hotel night, the bellowing American beyond the thin wall, and the Russian woman cursing and demanding money.

"I am not a prostitute," Valya said quietly, as if trying to convince herself.

"Oh, now. I never used such a word." The interrogator smiled, more paternal than maternal this time. "Far from it. You're just a girl who likes to have a good time. And who, occasionally, runs a bit short of money."

"I'm not a prostitute," Valya screamed. She gripped the sides of the flimsy table, even rising slightly from her seat.

The interrogator was unruffled. "Of course not. If you say so. In any case, I'm not a stickler about terminology."

Valya collapsed back into her chair. "I'm not a prostitute," she repeated, with a noticeable catch in her voice.

"Now, Valya," her tormentor continued. "Little Valya. Let's look at the facts." He glanced back toward the litter of photographs but made no move to consult them again. "You were a married woman. Nonetheless, you carried on a virtual carnival of affairs behind your poor husband's back. Why, when he was off supposedly defending the motherland, you even had to abort your child by a notorious black marketeer. Now let's see—that was your third abortion, correct?" He took up his pencil.

"Second," Valya said icily.

He made a tick in his notebook. "No matter. You aborted the child with which you had been impregnated by a public criminal. For whom you did . . . favors. Favors of the most questionable sort." The officer looked up from his papers, bright-eyed. "I don't suppose you would be interested in reviewing any of the photographs from the abortion clinic? No? Of course not. Anyway. You were married to a Soviet Army officer. You whored all over Moscow with a black marketeer—"

Valya caught the sudden hardening in the man's voice. And there was something else, something else. He had said something wrong—what was it? She was so tired. She could not think clearly.

"—got pregnant, aborted, then dropped your carcass into bed with a foreign spy. Without remuneration, of course."

"What?"

The officer appeared genuinely surprised at her outburst.

"What foreign spy?" Valya cried. She felt a terrible chill slither over her skin. The word *spy* had been haunted into her consciousness, into the genes of her race. The lonely syllable made her instantly afraid.

"Why, what should I call your American?"

"He's . . . he's a businessman." Even now, she wondered if he was waiting for her at the hotel. They had an appointment for dinner at eight o'clock. Had she seen a way, she would have burst free and caught a bus or a trolley . . . she would have even run all the way . . . to hurl herself into Ryder's arms, and into the embrace of the hopes he represented.

The interrogator laughed. He positively shook. Reaching clumsily for his glasses, he took them off so that he could dab at his tiny eyes.

"Oh, Valya," he said. "My little Valya. Surely, you don't expect me to believe that you—that *you,* of all people—could be so naive?"

Valya looked at him in confused horror.

"Why, my little angel," he continued, "your latest customer—excuse me, your latest *lov*er—is a warrant officer in the United States Army. A reconnaissance man, no less. Oh, Valya, you have to be more careful. You need to construct better stories to cover your tracks."

Valya sat. Frozen. Oh, no. No, no, no, no, *no.*

"Now why don't you just tell me," her interrogator went on, "what sort of information you passed to him? What messages did your husband give you for the American?"

"You're mad," Valya declared in an awkward, stunned voice. "That's insane. Why Yuri . . . Yuri would *never* . . ."

"I'm just trying to keep the names straight," the officer said. "Now this particular Yuri would be your late husband?"

Valya stopped breathing. Everything stopped. The blood had gone still in her arteries and veins. Then her eyelids blinked.

"Yuri?" she said.

"Why, Valya—surely this doesn't come as a surprise? Surely you knew?"

"Yuri?"

"Oh dear. Oh, Valya. I *am* sorry. I thought you'd been informed." The officer ruffled through his file of papers. "Now where is it? Oh, I can't believe I'm so clumsy. Forgive me. Please."

"Yuri?"

The officer looked up to meet the change in her tone. He looked genuinely ill-at-ease. "Of course, one understands how such oversights occur. I mean, it was, of course, quite recent. But, even in cases of espionage, one would think . . . a basic respect for the decencies . . ."

". . . Yuri? . . ." Valya began to sway sideward in her chair. When she closed her eyes, she smelled the ghost of the cheese sandwich on the hairs above her lip.

The officer jumped up from his chair and caught her. "Now, now," he said. "This must be a terrible shock. Why, I'm almost convinced you're not mixed up in any of this."

"Water, please."

The interrogator offered her the glass of stale tea. She sipped from it, then remembered why she had refused to drink any more. Her kidneys burned.

She tried to raise herself. But the officer's hand on her shoulder held her firmly in place.

"Please," Valya said. "Let me go to the toilet."

"All in good time." The hand pushed down ever so slightly. "It's not *so* urgent, is it? Just when we've almost resolved the issue of your involvement in all this."

She needed to go to the toilet. She tightened her loins, closing her thighs in a deadlock.

"So, let me see if I understand all of this," the interrogator said. "You had no idea that your husband was a traitor? That he was shot for collaborating with the enemy?"

Valya understood nothing. He was talking to someone else now. These words bore no relation to her life whatsoever.

"Of course, you realize that the penalty for such betrayals is *always* death?"

Betrayals? Nothing but betrayals. But which sort of betrayals was he speaking of now? None of it made any sense. It was all madness, and it had begun when they came for her at the school. After all of her efforts at maintaining a positive image before her superiors, they had come for her right in front of the students, unceremoniously hustling her out of the classroom. She had felt sick, realizing that she would never be able to explain this away.

What was he talking about now? Espionage? Yuri? And he said that Yuri was dead. But it was impossible for Yuri to be dead. She had only been thinking of him the night before.

"Please," she said, "I have to go to the toilet."

An enormous hand smashed into the side of her face. She flew to the ground, leaving the toppled chair behind her. She felt her body slipping out of her control. Then a foot kicked her very hard in the small of the back.

She moaned. A heel ground her into the concrete floor. Then her tormentor kicked her in the rump. The force slid her across the cement. But the boot followed her. The officer kicked her again. And again. In the spine. In the meager fat of her buttocks. Kicking through the fabric. Wet fabric. The hard toes hunted at her sex.

Above her, the officer grunted. She recognized the sound. She had heard it before. Under the weight of so many men.

"Slut," the officer said. He was so short of breath he could barely produce single syllables. "Tramp. Whore."

Yes, Valya thought dreamily, waiting for the next blow. Yes. I'm a whore. And Yuri. Where was Yuri?

Her American was going to take her away.

She was late for dinner.

Suddenly, a big hand gathered her hair and yanked her upward. She thought her neck would break, almost wishing it would. The interrogator dragged her across the floor like a dead game animal, hurting her badly. His other hand grasped her, briefly passing over her breast. Then he had her from behind, by the hair and an upper arm.

He dragged her back to the table where the photographs lay. He ground her face into them, then lifted her by the hair. Just far enough so that her eyes might focus. He released her arm so that he would have a free hand to peel away the layers of snapshots.

"Look," he gasped. "Look. At this one. And this one. *Look at yourself."*

Valya began to cry. It was not the weeping of a grown woman. Nor even tears of physical pain. It was the helpless crying of a child. She sensed what was coming now. She sensed it in his hand.

"Please," she moaned. "Please. Please, don't."

The interrogator tossed her back to the floor as though discarding an empty wrapper.

"You piece of filth," he said. "Is that all you ever think of?" He strode over to her and spit on the side of her face. She had curled up like an infant, and she wept.

"I wouldn't dream of dirtying myself with a creature like you," the officer said.

"I'm sorry for my comrade's excesses," the beautifully groomed young officer told her. He reached across the table toward her face. She shied. But he was quick. He gentled his fingertips along her cheek. "Here. Just let me have a look."

Valya whimpered.

"Now, that doesn't look so bad. Nothing to mar our girl's beauty," the officer continued. He was handsome, obviously athletic, and Valya sat before him in great shame. She felt destroyed. As though she belonged on a heap of garbage.

"He's been overworked lately," the young man explained. "What with the war and all. Moscow hasn't been a quiet place. I'm sorry if he hurt you." The young man withdrew his easy fingertips. "I'm sorry things got out of hand."

Valya sobbed into the lateness of the hour.

"We're not fools," the young officer said brightly. "We know you're not a spy. It was ridiculous for my comrade to imply anything to the contrary. Valya, would you like a cup of tea? Or anything at all?"

"No."

"All right. I just want you to try to understand. It's a very complex situation. To the careless observer, some of your actions might take on an ambiguous meaning. And I think you'll admit that, now and then, you've been indiscreet."

Valya stared down into her sorrow. She was contrite. No Magdalene had ever felt so deep and genuine a contrition.

"If anything," the polished young man continued, "we want to help you. Now, obviously, the fact that you were married to an officer who betrayed his trust to the People—obviously, that complicates things. And then there's the brief encounter with this American spy. Well, he's not *exactly* a spy. That's a slight exaggeration. And he's gone now, anyway—left the hotel right after you did. Off to the wars," he said blithely. "But it's still a difficult situation. And, of course, there's the matter of simple criminal law. Some of your adventures with Citizen Naritsky, for example. I'm afraid that, even without the slightest hint of espionage or the like, well, I'm afraid the law demands a certain level of satisfaction."

The young man stared at Valya as though waiting for her to help him out. She sat there trying to feel a better, truer sorrow at the news of Yuri's death. But it would not come. Yuri had been nothing but a tool to her. She recognized that now. She had been bad. But she was sorry. She was sorry for all of the things she had done. She was sorry for every scrap of joy she had ever felt. But she could not feel sufficiently sorry for Yuri.

"Valya," the young man said almost tenderly, "I simply can't bear the thought of sending you to prison."

Valya looked up.

"Simply couldn't bear it," the officer went on. "Why, by the time you were done sitting out your sentence, those lovely looks would be gone. Long gone, I'm afraid. And it would be a shame to waste them on the sort of women one encounters in our prison system. I'm afraid we're a bit behind the West in prison reform. Are you sure you wouldn't like a cup of tea?"

Valya shook her head. Infinitely fatigued.

Prison?

"But don't worry," the young man continued. "I think I see a way out of this. Valya," he said gently, flattering her with his eyes, "you really are a lovely woman. Even now, like this. I'm certain that you could be very helpful to us."

Valya looked up into the young officer's eyes. They were deep and glittering. The sort of eyes with which she would have been delighted to flirt once upon a time. Now they filled her with a horror she could not confine in words.

"I just . . . I just wanted to have some sort of life," she said meekly.

The young man smiled warmly.

"You *do* want to help us, don't you?"

21

3 November 2020

NOBURU SHUT HIS EYES AND LISTENED. EVEN THROUGH the bunkered thickness of the walls and bulletproof glass, he could hear them out there in the night. The people. Gathering in defiance of the outbreak of plague that had begun to haunt the city. Tens of thousands of them, there was no way of counting them with precision. Inside the headquarters complex, his staff continued to celebrate the success of the Scramblers, undeterred. While, out in the darkness, men who answered to another god chanted their fates in an opaque desert language.

Noburu looked at his aide's neatly uniformed back. Akiro sat dutifully at the command information console, sifting, sifting. Noburu had unsettled the younger man with a remark made an hour before. He knew that Akiro was still trying to find an innocent interpretation for his general's words. But Noburu also knew that the aide would not look in the right places.

The rhythmic chanting echoed relentlessly through the walls.

"Death to Japan," they cried.

Noburu had not understood the words at first. That had required a translator. But he had understood the situation immediately. He had been waiting for it.

* * *

The demonstrators had begun to gather even as the Scramblers did their work. His staff counterintelligence officer reported that the rally began in the old quarter, in the shadow of the Virgin's Tower. A flash outbreak of Runciman's disease had begun to gnaw its way in through the city's windows and doors. Yet, the Azeris had gathered by the thousands. They came as if called by animal instinct, by scent. How would Tokyo explain it? Marginally literate roustabouts had known of the vast scale of the Iranian and rebel defeat almost as swiftly as Noburu himself. In response, they materialized out of alleyways, or descended from the tainted heights of apartment blocks where the elevator shafts were useful only for the disposal of garbage, where bad water trickled in the taps, when water came at all. The faithful came in from the vast belt of slums that ringed the official city, from homes made of pasteboard and tin, from quarters in abandoned railcars that were already in the possession of a third generation of the same family. They came under banners green and black, the colors of Allah, the colors of death. In the heart of the headquarters building, their voices had been audible before they halfway climbed the hill, and now, as they formed a great crescent around the front of the military complex, their voices reached down into the stone depths of the mountainside. To the buried operations center, where Noburu's officers were drinking victory toasts in confident oblivion.

Noburu had gone out into the dying afternoon to have a look for himself, brushing off the protests of his subordinates and the local national guards, all of whom insisted that the situation was too dangerous.

"What are they saying?" he had demanded of his escorts as they braved the pollution-scented air. "What do the words mean?"

The light had the texture of gauze. The men who spoke the local language averted their eyes in shame.

"What is it?" Noburu insisted. "What does the chanting mean?"

A local national officer in charge of security looked at Noburu like a bad child caught out. "They say, 'Death to Japan.'"

Death to Japan. Ah, yes.

Death. To Japan.

He had expected the process to take a little longer. But then he had been wrong about so many things.

Death to Japan.

Couldn't they feel it? How could they all remain so smug? Didn't they understand? The end was coming, Scramblers or not.

Death to Japan. The crowd did not speak with a human voice. The articulated passions had nothing to do with the reasoning of the individual conscience. All were subsumed in a hugeness that no extant terms could explain. The crowd had swarmed into an entity that was vast, deaf, and blind. No single element could make a difference. No counsel of logic would move them. It was as if a god had closed his mighty hands over their ears. The crowd raged, and knew no fear.

Noburu imagined the clinical language with which a Tokyo staff officer would master the event.

"Please," the local man pleaded with Noburu, "you are to go no closer."

Noburu walked onward toward the big steel gates that shut the mob out of the compound.

"Mr. General, please not to go there."

Noburu walked on. In the last weak sun. Drawn by the single voice of the crowd, as if a woman had spoken his name in the dark.

"Please."

The headquarters building was shaped like a U with short sides, forming a courtyard that opened out onto a broader space that functioned alternately as a parking area for military vehicles or as a parade ground. It was bare now, with the austerity of wartime. Beyond the cobbled and cemented space, the wall rose, defining the perimeter of the compound. The wall was built to a height greater than the tallest man and unruly coils of concertina wire stretched along its top, connecting intermittent guard towers from which automatic weapons scanned silently over the excluded crowds.

Noburu headed straight for the central gate. Closed

now, the two oversize steel doors were crowned with spikes, a number of which had been bent or broken off. Noburu had no clear plan of action. He just wanted to see the beginning of the end with his own eyes.

The first twilight mellowed in the wall's shadow. The mob called out to him, begging him to hurry.

The security chief caught up with Noburu and tugged at his sleeve, pleading.

Both men stopped.

Before their eyes, men had begun to fly through the air. Soaring above the wall. Men with invisible wings.

The first few did not fly high enough. They caught in the curls of wire atop the wall, then hung limply. One sailed out of the low sky only to land gruesomely atop the spikes of the gate, impaling himself without a sound.

Noburu was baffled. Was this some new mystery of the East?

In a matter of seconds, half a dozen of the enchanted men had snared themselves in their attempt to soar over the wall and join Noburu in the enclave. They accepted the pain of their failures with remarkable stoicism. Wordlessly entangling themselves in the midst of the razor-sharp loops, the men sprawled their arms and legs across the barrier. They did not even flinch when the wire caught at their necks and heads. They appeared immune to pain. They flew through the sky, landed short, and took their uncomfortable rest. The man whose torso had been skewered atop the gate did not make a sound.

More and more of the odd angels rose from the crowd beyond the wall. Noburu could not understand the bizarre acrobatics. His mind filled with decades of old news film. Moslem fanatics lashing themselves mercilessly for the love of God. Riots, revolutions. Burning cities. The Arabian nights—and the tormented days. Endless calls for blood. Once, he knew, the Azeris had gathered to call for death to the Armenians, later for death to the Russians. Before that, their brethren to the south had howled, "Death to America."

Now it was "Death to Japan." As he had known it would be.

Oh, pride of man, he thought, and his heart filled with sorrow for his people.

At last one of the dervishes cleared the height of the gate. He arced just above his impaled brother, twisting in his flight, and dropped with a careless thud just a few feet from Noburu and his sole remaining escort.

The security officer had his pistol at the ready. He hustled toward the intruder, barking orders.

The visitor did not stir.

Suddenly, the security officer arched backward, away from the body. It was an exaggerated gesture, and it reminded Noburu of the way a startled cat could stop abruptly, pulling back its snout from evident trouble.

The security officer turned and bolted unceremoniously past Noburu. The man gibbered, and Noburu could make out only a single word:

"Plague."

Noburu walked forward until his toes had almost touched the body. The two men stared at each other. The dead citizen of Baku gazed up at the immaculate Japanese general, and the general peered back down in still curiosity.

Runciman's disease. It was unmistakable. The marbled discoloration of the skin. The look of pain that lasted beyond death. The corpse lay broken on the ground, in a fitting posture of agony.

Tokyo needed to see this, Noburu thought, raising his eyes back up to the bodies strung along the wire. Tokyo expected gratitude, treaties, observed legalities, interest on investments. Tokyo expected the world to make sense.

Another body cleared the wall and hit the ground with a thud.

Tokyo wanted thanks. And here it was.

Wondrous gifts flew through the air in this country. The people generously gave up their dead. Such a beautiful gift. Expressive. Noburu would have liked to have wrapped up at least one of the bodies and sent it to the Tokyo General Staff.

Noburu let his attention sink back to the corpse at his feet. You were lucky, he told the dead man. You were one of our friends. Had you been one of Japan's enemies, had you passed your years in the city of Orsk, or had you been one of those American soldiers, your suffering would only be beginning.

The crowd beyond the wall erupted in a scream that had the force of a great storm compacted into a single moment. It pierced Noburu. It was impossible to assign a cataloged emotion to the scream. The common words used to define the heart did not suffice.

We are worse than any other animal, Noburu thought. And he bent down to close the corpse's eyes.

He turned back into the parade ground's lengthening shadows, to the small group of officers awaiting him in horror.

"It's all right," Noburu assured them. "My shots are up-to-date. Tokyo has taken care of everything."

He gave an order to the effect that the guards were to hold their fire unless there was an attempt to penetrate the facility. After that, he did not look back. But he continued to see everything. The dream warrior saw. The faces of the vengeful dead, the population of Orsk, quivering in wonder, and the hallucinatory Americans from Africa, who came to Noburu even in the lightest doze now. Those dead dream-Americans were the worst of all, far worse than the reality of a diseased corpse hurled over a wall. Each time they came to him they grew larger and more clear. They came ever closer. Soon they would touch him.

The dream warrior knew that it was finished.

In the controlled coolness of Noburu's office, Akiro assured the general that the disturbance was an aberration, inspired by false reports and likely provoked by the Americans as part of a devious plan.

Noburu looked at the younger man in wonder.

"Do you really believe," Noburu asked, "that the people out there would listen to the Americans?"

"Tokyo says—"

"Tokyo is far away, Akiro."

"The intelligence officer says—"

"He's lying, Akiro. He doesn't know."

It was the turn of the aide to look shocked. It was impossible for a Japanese general to say outright that another officer, however junior, had lied.

"He's afraid," Noburu went on, trying to explain to the younger man, to reach him. "He doesn't understand what's happening. His spirit is in Tokyo."

"Sir," the aide said, "it is impossible to believe that these people would turn against us without provocation. First of all, we have given them everything, and, secondly, they need us. Without us—"

"Akiro," Noburu said indulgently, "you're thinking logically." He waved his hand at the curtained window. "But the people out there . . . I'm afraid they have no respect for logic."

"It is an impossible situation," Akiro said primly.

Noburu nodded, frumping his chin. "I agree."

"We have treaties . . ."

"Yes. Treaties."

"They will have to honor their treaties, our agreements."

"Of course," Noburu said.

"They cannot betray us."

"They believe," Noburu said, "that we have betrayed them. That what the Americans did on the battlefield was our fault. When things go wrong, they don't blame their enemies, they blame their allies. It's simply the way their minds work."

"That's inconceivable."

"Yes," Noburu agreed.

"They *must* honor the agreements."

Noburu smiled gently at the younger man.

"Or they will have to be taught a lesson," Akiro concluded.

Noburu turned toward the shrouded window and raised his hands as if conducting the choir out in the dark streets. "Listen to them," he whispered. The chanting rose and fell, rose and fell. Ceaselessly. "Listen, Akiro, and tell me what you hear."

The two men listened from their different worlds. Then Akiro said:

"I hear the sound of a mob."

Noburu listened a moment longer.

"No," he told the younger man. "That is the voice of death."

President Waters had just eaten a cheeseburger, and a damned big one. He was tired of taking advice, whether it came from the secretary of state or from the First Lady. Expert advice had gotten them all into this mess, and he did not trust the advice of those same experts to get the United States back out. He did not yet know exactly what he was going to do. But he knew he was going to make up his own mind this time.

"The President," a voice announced.

Everyone in the room jumped to their feet as Waters strode in. A quick glance assured the President that the key players were on hand: the chairman of the Joint Chiefs of Staff, his face a worn-out hound-dog mask, and the secretary of state, who looked like a Harvard man in his dotage—which happened to be exactly what he was. They were all there, down to that overbred cardsharp Bouquette and his plain-Jane sidekick.

"Sit down. Everybody. Please sit down. I know you're all tired."

"We're ready when you are, Mr. President," the national security adviser said. It was almost the only thing the man had uttered since the debacle at Orsk had become known. He had been a strong proponent of the expedition in the beginning, and now he was clearly rethinking his position.

Waters sat down, swishing back a last ghost of flavor with the tip of his tongue. The cheeseburger had been a lascivious thing, thick and studded with bits of onion, topped with blue cheese and a shower of catsup. It had been, by God, an American meal, and Waters had devoured it proudly. He had almost fallen into the usual routine of reminding the chef not to let slip his transgressions to his wife. Then he decided to blow it off. What the hell. If the President of the United States could send his armed forces off to battle, he could damn well treat himself to a cheeseburger without congressional authorization. Blood pressure and cholesterol be damned too. If this unholy mess in the Soviet Union didn't drop him in his tracks, he doubted he would topple over at the ingestion of a cheeseburger. He only regretted that he had not had the audacity to have the chef cook up some french fries, as well.

"Get me Colonel Taylor," Waters demanded.

"Sir, he's standing by," the communications officer said.

"Good." He turned briefly to Bouquette. "Cliff, do you have anything further on that demonstration or whatever it is down by the Japanese headquarters?"

Bouquette rocketed to his feet. "Nothing new on the Baku situation, sir. All we have is the imagery, and from the appearance of things, I'd have to stand by our original assessment that it's an anti-American thing, whipped up by the Japanese and the Islamic Government of Azerbaijan. A response to the commitment of American forces, a demonstration of solidarity. You know how the Islamic types love to parade around the streets. And anti-Americanism is in their blood."

Taylor's face flashed onto the communications screen. The collar of his uniform looked rumpled and stained, and, despite his facial scarring, the weary lines and dark circles were clear for all to see. But the eyes were alert.

"Good afternoon, Colonel Taylor—what time of day is it where you are now?"

"Night, Mr. President."

"Yes. That's right. You're ahead of us."

Waters paused, allowing himself time to consider Taylor. Could this man be trusted? When so many others had failed him? After one of Taylor's own subordinates had accused him of dereliction of duty and impossibly bad judgment? At any other time, Waters would have dismissed such a questionable character out of hand. But he was desperate now.

"Colonel Taylor," Waters said, "I've had a look at the concept of operations you sent us. The chairman has done his best to explain to me what it means. But I'd like to hear it in your own words. Explain it to me the way you explained that weapons system of yours. Simple words for a simple man."

Taylor's eyebrows edged into his scarred forehead. "Well, Mr. President, to begin with, I can't take credit for it. While I was out with my regiment today, an old acquaintance of mine was doing some thinking for me. The concept for this operation was developed by Colonel Williams of the Tenth Cavalry, based on an intelligence breakthrough one of his young officers came up with yesterday."

Out of the corner of his eye, Waters caught Bouquette grimacing. Have to return to that, Waters thought. Then he shifted his full attention back to Taylor.

"Mr. President," Taylor continued, "I want to be as honest with you as I can be. This is a long shot. Only the potential results make it worth attempting." Taylor briefly broke eye contact, and Waters wondered to what extent this Army officer doubted himself and his capabilities at this point.

"It all started," Taylor said, "with a damned good piece of luck. The Japanese battlefield control computers have been considered impregnable. But a young warrant officer from the Tenth, working with his Soviet counterpart, cracked a key component the Russians had recovered from a downed Japanese control bird. I understand that you've been briefed on the matter, but let me explain it from the battlefield perspective. Using the knowledge we've already derived from this computer 'brain,' we've been able to electronically transliterate various offensive computer programs into the software alphabet that the Japanese computers will accept. Most importantly, we now have the means to enter anything we want into the Japanese system, and to do it very quickly. Of course, the Japanese have no idea about any of this, as far as we know. If we can just get to one of their main terminals before they realize they've been compromised, we could deliver a mortal blow to their system." Taylor was clearly excited by the concept, and the building fire in his voice was the only real enthusiasm the President had encountered for hours.

"The possibilities are incredible," the colonel continued. "We can direct their system to make fatal errors. Not only can we completely disorient the enemy's control system, we can direct his weapons to attack each other. We can direct communications nodes to commit electronic suicide. We can offset every grid and coordinate in his automated mapping system. And we can actually conjure up false worlds for enemy commanders. They'll be sitting at their monitors, imagining that they're watching the battle, when in fact everything portrayed will be an illusion. And we'll be the master magicians. At the very least, we'll destroy their faith in their electronics. We'll be altering not just the parameters of the system, but the perception of its operators." Taylor looked into the President's eyes from half a world away. "But the most beautiful part is actually the simplest. Every Japanese military system has a self-destruct mechanism built into it. It's ostensibly to prevent the gear from falling into enemy hands—but it also functions as a safeguard, in case, say, the Iranians turned against them—"

"Never happen," Bouquette muttered audibly.

"—then the Japanese could simply send out electronic signals to every system in Iranian hands, ordering the machines to self-destruct. The component the Russians captured has shown us how it's done. And it's easy. We may even be able to neutralize these new weapons."

"The Scramblers," Waters said.

"Yes, sir. The Scramblers." Taylor twisted up the side of his mouth, a half-leer in a dead face. "Unfortunately, it can only be done through a Japanese master control computer. That's the background. Here's the plan. I intend to take my command ship and a single troop of five M-100s—manned by volunteers—on a raid against the Japanese theater headquarters at Baku. We will employ all of our deception systems going in, and, as we close, we'll jam everything in the area of operations. The Tenth Cav will be able to help us out with that. Our approach to the target will also be covered by a larger scale deception operation, as the rest of my regiment pulls out to the north. My raiding party will disappear in the noise of events. And we'll move fast. We won't be going in blind, either. The Soviets are sending me an officer who knows the layout of the Baku headquarters complex."

Taylor paused, and the President sensed that the man was searching through a tired brain for any key factors he might have omitted.

"We're banking on Japanese reluctance to destroy their computer system, no matter what happens," Taylor continued. "Since they don't know we've broken their code, they'll assume we couldn't access the system even if we had a year to take it apart and play with the components. Again, this system is considered to be absolutely impregnable, a sort of futuristic fortress. We'll count on going in very fast, loading in our programs, and getting out of there." Taylor stared hard at the President. "I want to do it tomorrow."

Waters nodded noncommittally.

"It's a long shot," Taylor admitted. "We'll have no time for rehearsals. We'll have to refuel once on the way in, and the Soviets will have to help us out on that. We won't be able to afford significant casualties—it's going to be a bare-bones operation. And we'll be counting on Japanese overconfidence so that they won't destroy the control computer and stop us in our tracks. Then, coming back out, we'll be vulnerable as hell—it appears that the Japanese can detect the M-100's signature from the rear hemisphere. Mr. President, I frankly cannot give you odds on the outcome. I'd just be guessing. We may fail. But . . . as an American soldier . . . I would be ashamed not to try."

The layer of hard confidence dissolved from Taylor's features, and he simply looked like a vulnerable and very tired man. "Mr. President, we beat them today. We destroyed their finest forward-deployed systems. Their central Asian front is in a state of collapse." Taylor was obviously fumbling for the words to explain his view of the world. "The only thing that's holding them together now is the success of this new weapon."

"The Scramblers," Waters said, retasting the word.

"Yes, sir. Otherwise, we've got them licked. You see, sir, in war . . . the loser is often simply the first guy to quit. Time and again, commanders have assumed that they've been defeated when, in fact, they were in far better condition than their enemies. We *know* how badly we've been hurt. But it's always harder to gain an accurate perception of the true state of the enemy." Taylor's eyes burned and begged across the miles. "Mr. President, just give us a chance. Let's not quit. Try to remember what it was like for our country after the African intervention, when everything seemed like it was coming apart. It's been a long, hard road back. But we're almost there. Let's not quit while there's still a chance."

Waters sucked his teeth. "Colonel Taylor," he said, "do you *really* believe you have a chance to pull this off?"

"Yes, sir. A chance."

"Nobody else seems to think so. The experts here don't think you could even get halfway."

"Sir, I know what my men and my machines can do. I saw it today."

"The Soviets want to quit," Waters added, "and, while I certainly do not want to belittle our losses, the Soviets have lost a substantial urban population and a regional population they haven't even begun to count. I even understand that the city—Orsk, was it?—was crowded with refugees from the fighting to the south. I'm not certain I could convince them of the wisdom of this move, even if I liked the idea myself."

"Mr. President," Taylor said, "I can't respond to that. All I can tell you is that I do not think the time has come to surrender."

"Now"—the secretary of state jumped in—"we're not talking about a *surrender*. The options under discussion are disengagement, an open withdrawal from the zone of conflict under mutual or multilateral guarantees, or, perhaps, a transitional cease-fire in place, to be followed by international regulation of the problem."

"Whatever words you use," Taylor said coldly, "it's still a surrender."

"George," the chairman of the JCS interrupted, "you're overstepping your bounds. Considerably."

Taylor said nothing.

Waters wanted to know what this battered-looking warrior really had to offer. Was there any genuine substance behind the disguise of the uniform?

"Colonel Taylor," Waters said, "I've even had a report from one of your subordinates, a Lieutenant Colonel Reno, that suggests you may not be competent for the position you presently hold. He makes it sound as though you had a pretty bad day."

Taylor's face remained impassive. "Mr. President, if you have any doubts about my performance, you can court-martial me after this is all over. Right now, just let me fight."

Waters measured the man. For a moment, Taylor was more immediate, more absolutely present in the room, than were any of the flesh-and-blood advisers. Time suspended its rules, and Waters slipped into old visions, accompanied by the aftertaste of a cheeseburger.

"Colonel Taylor," the President said slowly, "have you ever been bitten by a police dog?"

"No, sir."

"Neither was I. But my father was. Marching down a road in Alabama, with empty hands and a head full of dreams. They sent in the dogs . . . and my father was bitten very badly. It was a long time ago. I was not born in time to see those things. But my father had a powerful command of our language. When he described the fear he felt facing those dogs, well, his listeners felt it too. The dogs chewed him until he ran with blood. Yet, the very next day, he was out there again, marching and singing. He was even more afraid than he had been before, but, as he never tired of telling me, it might have been a very different world if he and just a few other frightened young men and women had given up." Waters tapped a pencil against an empty china cup. "My father . . . did not live to see his son become President of the United States. He died of Runciman's disease while I was off giving congressional campaign speeches to dwindling audiences. But I know that he would expect me to face those dogs today." Waters laid down the pencil and considered the image of Taylor on the screen. "The only problem is that I'm not quite sure what that means in this context. Does 'facing the dogs' mean sending one Colonel Taylor and his men back into battle with their sabers drawn—or is that merely avoidance, sending other men to face the dogs for me. Perhaps . . . facing the dogs means taking responsibility for my own bad decisions and cutting our losses."

"Mr. President," Taylor said flatly, "to quit now would be cowardice."

"That's *enough*, Colonel," the chairman said.

Waters merely nodded and looked down at his empty

hands. They were smooth and unmarred by physical labor. Or by animal teeth.

"Colonel Taylor," he said, "I have to make a decision. I'm not going to keep you hanging on any longer than necessary. We're going to drop you off the network now, but I want you to be standing by in exactly thirty minutes. I'm going to go over everything one last time with the people in this room, then I'll give you my answer—oh, by the way—you didn't mention the disturbances in Baku in your plan. Have you seen the imagery?"

"Yes, sir."

"And what do you think about it? Doesn't that complicate your operation?"

"Not necessarily. In fact, the demonstrations may provide us with a very good local diversion, if they continue. The Japanese must be worried as hell about their coming over the wall."

Waters pursed his face into a quizzical expression. "What do you mean by that? What do you think those demonstrations are all about?"

"Well," Taylor said, "my S-2 thinks it's pretty clear. And I agree with him. The Japanese are learning the same lesson we had to learn the hard way. In Teheran."

Waters thought for a moment. "Then you believe those demonstrations are *anti*-Japanese?"

Taylor looked surprised by the question. "Of course. It's obvious."

Waters nodded, pondering this brand-new slant. "Thank you, Colonel Taylor. You'll be hearing from me in thirty minutes."

Taylor's image faded from the screen.

For a moment, there was a dull silence, reflecting the inertia of weary men. Then the secretary of state shook his patrician head in wonder.

"The man's crazy," he said.

"Good to see you, Tucker," Taylor said, rising to meet his old comrade. He tried to call up a smile, but an important part of him remained with the President, awaiting a decision.

"What the hell, George, you're looking ugly as ever." Colonel Williams extended his hand.

Taylor held out his bandaged paw.

Williams hesitated to accept it. "What the hell happened to you this time, George?"

Taylor went the extra distance and grasped Williams's hand, shaking it firmly.

"My own stupidity," Taylor said. "Minor stuff. I just wanted to make sure I collected another Purple Heart."

Williams laughed, but the sound was buried under the racket of the tactical operations center. The regiment had established its headquarters in a small network of field shelters near Orenburg, in Assembly Area Platinum. The facility offered good camouflage, light ballistic protection, and no defense whatsoever, should the new Japanese weapons descend through the darkness. The staff worked hectically, as was the American custom, and no one seemed bothered by the threat of a Scrambler attack. The weapons were so overpowering that men quickly blocked them out of their immediate consciousness, as soldiers from an earlier generation had done with nuclear weapons, or as men had learned to do with the plague.

Williams pulled a younger man into the circle of power defined by the two colonels. A warrant officer. Fresh-faced kid lugging a briefcase that hardly suited the field environment.

"George, this is my wonder boy, the one who broke the bank. He's all raring to go, just dying to get into the fight." Williams smiled happily at the younger man. "Chief Ryder, this is Colonel Georgie Taylor. *The* Colonel George Taylor."

"Honored to meet you, sir," the warrant officer said in an absentminded voice, as though he were thinking of things far away. He wavered about offering his hand to Taylor, eyes dwelling on the dirty bandage. But Taylor snared the boy and gave him a welcoming handshake even as he sensed that something was wrong. There was something about the kid, something uncannily familiar . . .

"Welcome to the Seventh Cav," Taylor said.

"So, George?" Williams said. "What's the word? We get the green light?"

"Still waiting," Taylor replied in disgust. "The President's making his decision right now. With the NSC."

"And all the fucking straphangers, I bet," Williams said. He made an exaggeratedly sour face. "Christ, I know one of those sonsofbitches personally, old Cliff Bouquette from the Agency. Talk about a worthless, lying, overdressed piece of shit."

"I'm worried, Tucker."

Williams folded his arms across his big chest, nodding. "Poor old Waters just doesn't have a handle on this stuff. But, what the hell can you expect, when less than five percent of the members of Congress have ever worn a uniform. They read a fucking book by another peckerhead who's never tied on a combat boot, and suddenly they're military reformers. Jesus Christ, the country needs a goddamned draft. Even if it only applies to freshmen congressmen."

Taylor nodded, used to Williams. "I almost thought I had him. I thought he was going to say yes. He seemed on the verge of it."

As he spoke Taylor could not help turning his eyes again and again to Ryder. It was as if he had known him, years before. Yet that was obviously impossible. The warrant officer was too young.

Who the hell did he resemble?

"Chief?" Williams said. "Why don't you head over to the deuce's shop and introduce yourself. Colonel Taylor and I need to talk."

"Yes, sir." Ryder ducked his head slightly in obedience, rendered a halting salute, and moved off in search of the intelligence section.

"Good boy," Williams told Taylor as soon as the warrant was out of earshot. "Computer tech. Absolutely brilliant. Not a field soldier, of course. I'm counting on you to take care of him, Georgie."

Taylor barely responded. His head moved slightly, but it was clear that his thoughts were elsewhere.

"That bad?" Williams asked.

Taylor shrugged. "I don't know." He clenched his hands into fists, bouncing them off each other, a boxer testing his gloves. The discomfort in his burned hand did not even register on him. "Damnit, I thought he was going to give me the go-ahead. Talking about his father and Alabama. Rousing stuff. Right off the campaign trail. Then he backed down at the last minute and told me he'd just made up his mind to make up his mind in a little while."

"Washington's not as crazy about all this as they were this morning, I take it?"

Taylor snorted. "That's a fucking understatement. You can hear them all running for the trees from here."

"I'll just bet that little puss Bouquette has his snout in it," Williams said. "Typical goddamned civilian hotshot. I never knew him to get a single tough intel call right. But he's got terrific connections. Never wore a uniform, unless it was at some overseas prep school. But he figures he knows your job and mine by virtue of family lineage and intuition."

Taylor did not respond. He knew of Bouquette. More than he wanted to know. Courtesy of Daisy.

He wondered if Daisy was still there, in the same room as Waters. But better not to think of all that now.

"Hard day, George?" Williams asked. His tone of voice made it very clear that he understood as only another warrior might understand.

Taylor looked at him. "I lost Dave Heifetz," he said matter-of-factly. "In the Scrambler business. And Manny Martinez. They hit us at Omsk on the way out."

Williams looked pensive. "Didn't know Martinez. But Heifetz was a hell of a soldier."

"Yes. He was that." Taylor turned his head in disgust. "And here I am talking about him as though he's dead. While the poor bastard's bundled up in a wing-in-ground, pissing all over himself and wondering what on earth happened . . . and what's going to happen." Taylor took a step to the side, as if trying to move away from himself. "God almighty. I just don't know what to do for him. And for all the rest of them. What do you do, Tucker? What on earth do you do? You know what it's like to write the letters to the wives or parents when some poor trooper buys the farm. But what the fuck do you write when Johnny's coming home as a physical vegetable with unimpaired emotions and a perfect grasp of the world around him. With memories of what women are like, with—"

"George. You're tired."

"*No*. Really. What in-the-name-of-Christ do you do? Send the folks back home a catalog for oversize cribs and disposable diapers? Oh, by the way, Mrs. Jones, your husband may prove a disappointment to you on several counts, owing to his recent unfortunate term of military service. Jesus, Tucker . . . it's a hell of a thing to find yourself wishing that your own men had died."

"Maybe we'll find a cure."

"Yeah."

"Heifetz was a damned good man."

"And a hell of a lot life gave him for it. And Manny. Martinez. Tucker, I can't tell you what a good man he was. I'm lost without him."

Williams smiled. "George, you've never been lost in your life. Why, hell. You even found your way out of Africa without so much as a credit card or a supply of condoms."

Taylor could not smile. He retreated into silence.

"You remember," Williams went on, "lying in that damned tent in the Azores? Playing poker with the grim reaper. And I lectured you for all the saints and sinners to hear about how I was going to clean up Military Intelligence. You know what I was always thinking, George? I was shooting off my mouth and thinking, Jesus Christ, I wish I had whatever the hell it is this guy Taylor's got. You used to lie on your bunk and look right through me. You didn't need me to explain the world to you. You already knew the things I was struggling to figure out." Williams smiled into his reminiscences. "Anyway, we came a hell of a lot further than either of us had much right to expect."

"Not far enough," Taylor said.

"Not yet. But maybe we're underestimating the President after all. He just may give us the green light."

"I don't know. Everybody's telling him to head for the bushes."

"Well, hope for the best."

Taylor sighed. "I gave it my best shot, Tucker. I really did. But I'm just so goddamned tired. I couldn't get the words to come out right. All I could think was how I wanted to reach out and grab him and shake the shit out of him. To bring home to him what it means if we quit now. Damn it, though," Taylor said. "All my life I've had a healthy respect for language. I read the good books. I paid attention. I always tried to write op orders in clean, clear language. I *valued* words, crazy as that sounds. But, when I really needed the right words, they wouldn't come."

"You can't do it all by yourself, George. What the hell, if the chickenshit bastards tell us to come home, it'll be on their heads. You and me can retire and go fishing."

"No," Taylor said emphatically. "It'll be on our heads. The Army will have failed. That's what the black words on the white pages are going to say."

"Fuck 'em, then."

Taylor glanced down at the dirty bandage on his hand and shook the burned paw lightly, without really thinking about it.

"You should've seen Lucky Dave," he said. "Tucker, I honestly did not think I could bear it. Maybe I don't have what it takes to be a soldier after all."

"When's the President supposed to get back to you?"

Taylor glanced at his watch. "Seven minutes."

Down the length of the central environmental shelter, the internal entrance flap pushed to the side and a man in a Soviet uniform entered the headquarters complex. As the man straightened up in the dusky light, Taylor recognized Kozlov. He was glad to see him, anxious for any help he could get. Would the Soviets come through?

As Taylor watched, Merry Meredith came out of the S-2's compartment and headed over to greet the Russian.

Merry was the only one of them left now. Of the men Taylor trusted. And loved.

Taylor looked at Tucker Williams. It was odd how relationships developed in the Army. Taylor was never completely sure whether Williams should be classed as an acquaintance or a friend. There were varying degrees of intimacy in the military. Taylor always worked well with

Williams, respected him, and willingly drank a few beers with him whenever their paths crossed at some overly laminated officer's club. Yet, a nebulous spiritual gulf remained between them. Williams was right. In the Azores Taylor had, indeed, looked right through him, his thoughts in a different world.

There had been only Meredith, Martinez, and Heifetz, a brotherhood assembled by the odd chance of a bad year, by the simple accident of change-of-station orders and discovered affinities. And now only Meredith was left.

"I'd better get back to the comms bubble," Taylor said. "Keep your fingers crossed, Tucker."

"Will do."

Taylor began to turn away, just as a lightning bolt of recognition struck right through him. He had to call up his last reserves of determination in order to keep going, telling himself that it was all just the oversensitivity that came with weariness, a matter of emotional as well as physical exhaustion. The coincidence was absolute nonsense.

He had realized of whom Williams's young warrant officer reminded him. It was uncanny, as if the Hindus were dead right about the constant cycles, the endless and inevitable returnings.

Ryder reminded him of the young warrant officer who had been his copilot and weapons officer in Zaire, the broken boy who had pleaded for water until Taylor shot him in the head.

Daisy listened. She thought she would go mad. Wanting to speak, to cry out to them all that it was time to put an end to the folly, she could not find the opportunity or the courage. Her opinion was not asked as the men in the room labored through all of the arguments against further military action one more time. Unanimously, the President's advisers shared her view that it would be insane and pointless to accede to Taylor's wishes.

The Soviets, on the other hand, were no help at all. Speaking to Waters, the Soviet president had seemed preoccupied, inexplicably removed from the matters at hand. Readily agreeing to anything Waters suggested, the

483

Soviet seemed, above all else, to want to bring the conversation to a speedy end. Moscow seemed fractured. State security had been cooperating wholeheartedly with U.S. Army Intelligence on the scheme to strike the Japanese command computer system, while the Soviet Ministry of Defense seemed ready to run up the white flag. Something disturbing was going on in the Kremlin, and it gnawed at Daisy that she could not figure it out.

In any case, the raid was a hopeless idea. It was an act of desperation, conceived by a man who could not face reality. They all agreed. Yet, not one of them stated it with sufficient clarity and emphasis for her. She wanted to be absolutely certain that the President understood the absurdity of Taylor's vision. She had begun to trust Waters's judgment. But, given all of the evidence that had been presented, she could not believe the man had allowed the deliberations to drag on this long. It was indisputably clear that Waters needed to disengage American forces as rapidly as possible and bring the troops home.

To bring Taylor home. Alive.

On the sole occasion when she legitimately might have spoken up, she had held her tongue. The President had grilled Bouquette for the third time about the massed crowds in Baku, and Bouquette had repeated his conviction that Taylor was simply an old soldier who did not understand international realities. Of course the demonstrations were pro-Japanese and anti-American. Nothing else made sense.

Daisy had known better. Bouquette was a bureaucrat, while she had worked her way up this far with no adornment other than her talent as an analyst. And upon seeing the first scan images of the crowds in downtown Baku, then the pictures of the mob ringing the Japanese headquarters compound, she had recognized instantly that the Japanese were in trouble. Taylor, in a few simple words, had summarized her views. Those crowds bore with them the unmistakable odor of hostility.

But she did not care about the truth anymore. She did not care about the fate of nations. She realized that all of it was nothing but nonsense, games for grown-up boys without the courage to accept what really mattered in life.

Had the President asked directly for her opinion, she would have stood up and lied.

All she wanted was the return of that scarred, weary, frightened man whose features had appeared so briefly on the communications monitor.

"And what about the charge of unfitness?" President Waters asked. "What do we know about this Lieutenant Colonel Reno? Why should I put any credence whatsoever in his accusations?"

The chairman of the Joint Chiefs of Staff raised his hand from the table as if freeing a small bird. "I don't know Lieutenant Colonel Reno personally, Mr. President. But I knew his father. Good family. Army since Christ was a corporal. If you'll excuse the expression, sir."

"Mr. President," Bouquette jumped in, "I can second that. I worked for General Reno when he chaired the old interagency group. Any son of his would stand for the old tried-and-true values."

"I take it," Waters said quietly, "that Colonel Taylor does not spring from a good, old family?"

Bouquette and the chairman glanced at each other, sensing that they had maneuvered themselves into a dangerous position. After a brief mental holding action, the chairman replied matter-of-factly:

"Mr. President, I know nothing of Colonel Taylor's antecedents."

"But the man has a good military record?"

"Yes, sir. Colonel Taylor has a remarkable military record. But . . . even the scrappiest street-fighter may not turn out to be Olympic boxing material. Personally, I've always been fond of George Taylor. But we have to bear in mind that we just may have taken a superb tactical soldier and elevated him beyond his competence. Certainly, if I had to go back to, say, Mexico, I'd want George Taylor in my foxhole. Fine, fine soldier. But we may have asked too much of him by putting him in so independent and sensitive a position."

Waters nodded. "All right. Next issue. From a purely military standpoint, what chance would Colonel Taylor's operation have of success?"

This time the chairman did not require a pause to analyze the situation. "Only the slightest. One in ten? One in a hundred? It's not really possible to quantify it, as Colonel Taylor himself pointed out. But, you see, Mr. President, an operation of that kind requires careful and extensive planning . . . weeks, if not months, of rehearsals. You've got to war-game every possible contingency. Ideally, you'd want to build a mock-up of the Japanese headquarters complex, for instance. And you heard what Colonel Taylor admitted—he'd have to rely on the Soviets for refueling. Now, the Soviets are trying to look cooperative, but I personally don't believe they're about to support any more grand offensive operations, in the wake of what happened at Orsk. Turning over that computer brain, for instance—I suspect they were just anxious to get rid of the damned thing. They're passing the hot potato and they just want their fingers to stop burning." The chairman looked down at the fine wood of the tabletop. "George Taylor's a good soldier, and he doesn't want to admit he's licked. I admire him for that. But we have to take the broader perspective, sir. If nothing else, you can't just run an operation like this off the cuff. I'm willing to go on record to say I am one hundred percent opposed to this endeavor."

"You don't think," Waters asked gently, "that desperate times may call for desperate actions?"

The chairman put down his hand, retrapping the invisible bird.

"Desperate? Perhaps, Mr. President. But not foolhardy."

"Any further reverses at the hands of the Japanese," the secretary of state added, "would only lessen our international stature. As it is, we may even claim a substantial achievement in the direct effects of our latest generation of weaponry. We may even be able to turn around the world's perception of the Japanese, to advertise the fact that these Scramblers are inhuman. If we go cautiously and avoid further provocations, we may be able to draw a certain—and not inconsiderable—amount of political capital from all this."

Waters nodded. "I'm anxious to hear your view, Miles,"

he said to the national security adviser, who had been working studiously on his fingernails.

Ambushed, the man looked up in surprise. "Well, Mr. President . . . I think it's all perfectly clear. The Russians want to call it a day. They're heading for the lifeboats. We'd be fools to let ourselves get caught in the middle."

Waters began tapping his pencil on his china cup again. The air in the room was very bad, despite the efforts of the ventilation system.

"Thank you," Waters said, "for your assessment. Now, Cliff," he turned to Bouquette. "Back to the intelligence front. Are you in a position yet to guarantee that there will be no new surprises?"

Bouquette looked embarrassed. He rose to his feet with considerably less alacrity than was his habit, touching the line of his tie.

"Unfortunately, Mr. President, I can't offer you such a guarantee. As you know, intelligence work is very complex. And, admittedly, we failed at least part of our test. I am, in fact, already working through a draft plan to streamline and improve the Agency's performance. I'd like to make it my personal mission to ensure that such a failure, however understandable, does not happen again."

"Thank you, Cliff."

"Mr. President?" Bouquette continued. He fingered his tie again, hand moving closer to the knot. "I feel I should add a comment about this Colonel Williams you've been hearing about. The one who came up with this cracked-brain idea in the first place, according to Colonel Taylor. You see, I've known Colonel Williams for years. The intelligence community is one big family. And, while one may have reasonable doubts about Colonel Taylor's qualifications, I can state categorically that it was a considerable error to allow Colonel Williams to deploy forward in the first place. Had he worked for me, the man would have been out of a job a long time ago. But these people sometimes slip through the system. Colonel Williams is the sort who enjoys turning over the apple cart, then leaving the mess for the more dutiful to clean up. He is exactly the sort who brings discredit upon the labors of the hard-working men and women of the intelligence community.

He is self-aggrandizing, and he is not a team player. He is definitely not to be trusted."

President Waters gave the china cup a last good tap with his pencil and asked, "You wouldn't happen to know, would you, Cliff, whether or not this Colonel Williams comes from a good, old family?"

"Mr. President," Bouquette stammered, "as you know, I would never suggest . . . as regards Lieutenant Colonel Reno, I was only commenting that his family was known to me personally. But I certainly did not mean to suggest . . . after all, we all realize that this is the United States of America . . ."

"Thank you, Cliff." If nothing else, Waters thought, even if I have failed in my office, if I lose the election by the greatest majority in history, and even if I go down in the books as the most pathetically inept of presidents, I have had the satisfaction of seeing Clifton Reynard Bouquette nonplussed.

Waters glanced at the clock on the wall.

"Well, gentlemen," he said. "The time has come for me to make my decision. I feel that each of you has made his position abundantly clear. If anyone wishes to offer a last counterview, please do so, but it appears to me that you are unanimously opposed to any further offensive military action, and that you are specifically opposed to the plan recommended by Colonel Taylor."

The required moment of silence dusted the room, then the secretary of state said:

"I think that sums it up, Mr. President."

Waters looked around the room one last time, briefly inspecting each fixed expression. The girl, now, Bouquette's sidekick, she had fire in her eyes. Waters knew the type. The smart unattractive girls who expected the Joan of Arc story to have a happy ending the next time around.

"All right," Waters said. "Connect me with Colonel Taylor."

There was no delay. In a moment, Taylor's face filled the screen. It was evident that he had been waiting, and now Waters could read explicit worry in the haggard features.

Life hasn't been very kind to that poor bastard, Waters thought.

"Colonel Taylor? Can you hear me all right?"

"Yes, Mr. President."

"Colonel Taylor, we've discussed your proposition at length, and I have to tell you that my advisers are uniformly opposed to the action."

Taylor flinched, as if punched hard in the body.

"Yes, Mr. President."

"The consensus is that this raid would have little chance of success, that it would be foolhardy, and that it could well do great harm to our negotiating position and international standing."

"Mr. President—"

"*Don't* interrupt me, Colonel. I'm not finished. As I said: all of my advisers are opposed to your plan. It appears that there are only two people involved who are not yet ready to run up the white flag. By coincidence, Colonel, those two people are you and I."

The room stiffened around Waters. But no one said a word.

"Colonel Taylor, I direct you to implement your plan as presented to me. I will take it upon myself to delay any unilateral actions by the Soviets for—how long will you need?"

"Thirty-six hours," Taylor said hastily.

"For forty-eight hours, then. To give us a margin of error. The decision will be on record as mine alone. So be it. You see, Colonel, I can be thickheaded at times, but I believe I've finally figured out who the police dogs belong to this time around. And I am not yet ready to quit marching."

Taylor opened his mouth to speak, but Daisy was quicker. She rose from her chair, taking a single step forward.

"You *can't*," she cried. "You *can't*. They don't have a chance. Everybody knows they don't have a chance. You're crazy."

The room went as silent as the interior of a glacier. On the monitor, Taylor wavered slightly, as if trying to gain a better view against the laws of physics.

Waters looked at the enraged woman.

"Thank you for your opinion, Miss Fitzgerald," he said quietly. "Please sit down now."

Daisy sat down. Her forehead had broken out with sweat and her blouse hung limply about her. She drew back into her chair as if shrinking, and her eyes stared into a personal distance.

"I will repeat myself to ensure that everything is clear to all parties concerned," Waters said. "Colonel Taylor, you are directed to strike the enemy as foreseen by your plan. The responsibility for this decision rests with the President of the United States alone." Waters looked up at the ruined face in the monitor. For a moment, he imagined that he saw a watery light in the warrior's eyes. But that was clearly an accident of lenses and technological effects.

"Yes, sir," the distant voice responded.

Waters looked for the last time into the face of this man whom he knew he would never understand. They were as different as two men could be, and only a brief spasm of history had brought them together.

"And may God be with you," Waters said.

22

4 November 2020

KOZLOV CAME BACK IN FROM THE COMMUNICATIONS cell. He was smiling broadly, and the brown wreckage of his teeth gave his mouth the appearance of a derelict cave.

"General Ivanov has said that we will help you," he announced to the assembled members of the planning group, clearly very proud that he could make this contribution. "Moscow has approved. Your president has spoken with them. The fuel will be provided."

"Good," Taylor said. He had just been working through the selection of the M-100s in the most battleworthy condition, and he felt the loss of Martinez badly. Martinez would have known best about the status of the combat systems and how to handle the details of the fuel transfer. "That's fine, Viktor. But how about the refueling site itself?"

"It is all right," Kozlov said. "We still hold a large pocket here"—he pointed to the map spread over the worktable—"to the east of the Volga estuary. It should meet the time-distance planning factors."

The men bent over the map: Taylor and Kozlov, Meredith and Parker, who was functioning as the acting S-3, Tucker Williams—and Ryder, whose presence remained unsettling to Taylor. Meredith defined the area in question with a marker, under Kozlov's direction. Reflected off the map, the Russian's breath punished the American officers.

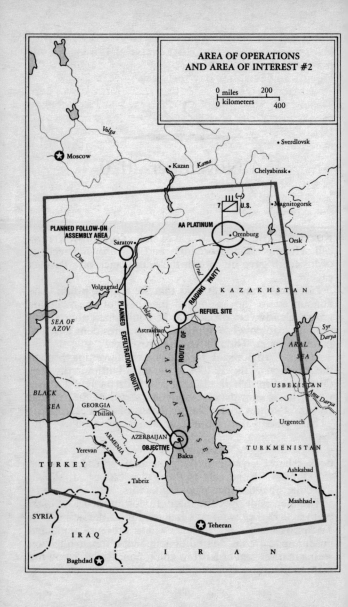

But it did not matter; Kozlov was so clearly anxious to help, to do his very best, that everyone was glad of his presence. He also appeared to be the only member of the group who had gotten any real sleep in days.

"I hate like hell to make a pit stop on the way in," Taylor said. "But putting down on the way out would be even worse. We've got a good shot at going in undetected. But, after we've hit them, they'll be looking for us with everything they've got. And our asses seem to stick out."

"The numbers work," Hank Parker said, turning from his computer workstation. "If we top off just to the east of Astrakhan, where Lieutenant Colonel Kozlov indicated, we should have adequate fuel to reach the target, conduct the action at the objective, and still make it all the way back to the follow-on assembly area."

"In the vicinity of Saratov," Meredith picked up. "In the old Volga German region."

"Not much margin of error, though," Tucker Williams said.

Taylor shrugged. "This is strictly a low-budget operation."

"This will be very good," Kozlov said, still excited. He initially had seemed to have grave doubts as to whether or not General Ivanov would be willing or able to help out, and the immediately forthcoming Soviet agreement to help apparently had surprised him more than anyone. "The area where you will take on the fuel is not a developed one, and the enemy has contented himself with the bypassing of our forces in the estuary. There is very much open space here, to the east. It will be very good."

"And General Ivanov is absolutely certain he can provide us with the fuel?" Taylor asked, still slightly skeptical of this very good luck. "At that location? On time?"

"Oh, yes," Kozlov said brightly.

"Good. That certainly makes a difference." He turned to Meredith. "Lay that map of the Baku area back down, Merry. Let's go over that again with Viktor and see what he thinks."

Meredith stretched another map across the table. After trying to squeeze in around an undersized computer screen, the planning group had returned to the use of old-fashioned tools, incidentally making the work much easier for Kozlov.

"Viktor," Taylor said, "we've looked over the terrain, and the overhead shots and the map make it look like the best approach is to come in low from the north, using the peninsula to shield us. What do you think?"

Kozlov appeared doubtful. "Yes, I think you can do that, should you wish. But perhaps another way is better. You see, there are radar sites hidden on the ridge of the peninsula. But have you thought to come in from the east? Over the water? You see, there are many oil towers—what is the English word?"

"Derricks?" Meredith asked.

"Yes. The derricks. They are of metals. You would have natural radar shielding effects. I know, because our radars were always blind in this sector."

"Fuck me," Colonel Williams said. He had been munching on a packet of dehydrated pears from the field rations. "You still can't beat firsthand knowledge of your area of operations."

"You see, this is very good," Kozlov continued. "There are many landmarks for the eye as well as for the computer. And to come in such a way over the city, there are no air defenses." He traced over the corner of the map where an outsize city plan had been inserted. "You see? Over here is the tower of television. But you will come from here. There will be the high building of the Moscow Hotel and there is Kirov Park. From there it is easy."

"That'll take us right in over the mob scene," Colonel Williams said. "If the buggers are still out there."

"I think they will not have air defense weapons," Kozlov said.

"Check," Taylor said. "Okay, Viktor. Are there any obstructions on this parade ground or whatever it is in front of the headquarters? Anything the imagery might not clearly indicate?"

"No. Unless there would be trucks that day. It is very flat. I remember clearly. In the spring, the water would not drain properly. It was terrible for the shoes."

"Okay. You've seen the M-100s. How many birds can we put down in there? In your view?"

"I think only six. Perhaps seven."

"Great. That's more space than we need. We ran the mensuration from the available imagery, but it's good to hear it from somebody who's walked the ground."

"You know," Kozlov said, "that there is also the roof here. It is not marked, but it is reinforced to act as a helipad. It is quite big. Can you land on a regular helipad?"

Taylor grew extremely interested. "Piece of cake. And that's the roof of the main headquarters building?"

"Yes. This is always for the helicopter of the general."

"Better and better. So we can access the building from up there?"

Kozlov looked up blankly. Taylor's turn of phrase had baffled him. Meredith quickly put the question into Russian.

Kozlov's expression eased. "Oh, yes. Although it may be guarded."

Taylor reached for a detailed sketch Kozlov had provided of the building's various levels.

"All right, Viktor. You're convinced that this room will still be the ops center?"

"It must be so. Only this room is of a big enough size and with so much wiring."

"All right. And this should be the computer room?"

Kozlov chewed his lip with his coffee-colored teeth. "I must think it to be. All of the specialized wiring is only to here and then to here, you see. We had great problems in the remaking of the wires in the building. It is so old."

"You don't think they might have rewired the place?"

Kozlov shrugged. "I cannot tell. But it would be very hard."

"All right. We'll just have to take our chances on that. Now, if we were to put one ship down on the helipad, say three in the central courtyard, with two flying cover for us all . . . how would the team from the helipad get down to the computer room and the ops center?"

Kozlov traced his finger along the mock blueprint. "There is perhaps a very good way. Here is the private lift for the general, but that is too dangerous, I think. Then there is a stairwell."

"Here?" Taylor asked, bending very close to the map

to read the plan that Kozlov had drawn by hand while riding in an aircraft. Taylor's finger touched a small shaded square.

"Yes. That is the stairwell. You must go down three flights of the stairs. Then you are in the main corridor. The operations center and the computer room are only here. It is very good."

"Well, that's convenient," Williams said.

Taylor nodded. "It's great. If we can get down those goddamned stairs. That stairwell's a death trap, if ever there was one."

Everyone looked at Taylor. The dead skin on his face had turned to wax. There had not even been time to splash water over the layers of oil, dirt, and exhaustion that each of the Americans wore.

Taylor snorted. "But I don't see much choice. It's too direct a route to pass up." He looked at Kozlov. "We'll try it, Viktor. The fire teams from the main raiding force can strike from the parade ground. We'll link up, if we can. If not, they'll at least provide a hell of a diversion for us." Taylor shook his head. "I hate stairwell fights, though. I lost a damned good NCO that way when we had to retake the U.S. consulate in Guadalajara."

"The classic surgical strike," Colonel Williams commented, studying the map over Taylor's shoulder.

Taylor straightened, twisting the stiffness out of his back. "Wouldn't call it that at all, Tucker. This is a classic raid. Strike unexpectedly. Take out everything that moves. Do your business. And un-ass the area. Surprise, shock, speed . . . and all the firepower you can put out." Taylor turned to Meredith and Parker. "I want to hit them at sunset. We'll be coming out of the east, riding out of the darkness. I want to strike when there's just enough twilight for us to get our bearings visually, but when it's already dark enough to fuck with their heads." Taylor broadened his gaze to include the rest of the planning team. "We're going to come out of the sky like death itself. We're going to bring them fear."

Taylor shifted his field of fire to Ryder. It was difficult for him to look at the young warrant, because it was then so difficult to look away. The resemblance to the young man who had died so miserably in Africa was the stuff of bad, bad luck.

"Chief," Taylor said, "how much time are you going to need once we boot your ass into that computer room?"

Ryder shifted his weight from one foot to the other, his expression distinctly uncertain. He was obviously out of his element.

"Fifteen minutes?" Colonel Williams prompted.

"I guess so," Ryder said. He had a flat, midwestern accent.

"Don't fucking guess," Taylor said sternly. "Tell us how much time you're going to need."

The young warrant reddened. "If everything's in working order," he said, "I think half an hour would be best. If that's all right. See, I've got to insert—"

"Thirty minutes," Taylor said. "You got it. Now. Merry. Give me what you've got on possible enemy response forces. Who are they, where are they, what's the reaction time? You know the list of questions."

"Yes, sir." Meredith began. "Within the facility itself . . ."

The men labored through schematics and figures, turning again and again to the automated support systems or to subordinate staff officers and NCOs. Neglected cups of coffee went cold. To each man, the process was as familiar as could be, and even Kozlov slipped easily into the pattern of the universal details of staff work. Warning orders went out to the volunteer crews, along with photocopies of maps and the building plans. Junior leaders gathered to listen to Hank Parker, whose stature seemed to grow by the hour, while Meredith grilled others on potential threats and contingencies, forcing them to actively remember the crucial details of his briefing. No man had any healthy energy left. They continued to function only by the grace of the wide-awake tablets and individual strength of will. The importance of each moment prodded them along, yet it was important not to hurry so much that errors or oversights occurred. The genius of good staff work was always a matter of striking exactly the right balance between speed and thoroughness—and recognizing immediately when that balance shifted as the circumstances of the battlefield changed. Right now, the paramount enemy was the clock.

In the early morning hours, Taylor and Tucker Williams found themselves alone over disposable cups of coffee that really held only heated, disinfected water with a bit of brown color added.

"George," Williams said, "you need to catch a little rest. Those dark circles are going to be getting caught under your boots."

Taylor nodded. "I just have to go back over the ammo up-load figures." He sighed as though the years had finally overtaken him. "Christ, I feel like a brand-new butterbar locked in a supply room that just failed the IG. Old Manny picked a hell of a time to get himself killed."

"I'm sure he feels bad about it too," Williams said. "Listen, George—where am I riding? With you in the command bird? Or do you want me in another ship, just in case?"

"You're not going, Tucker."

Williams blustered like a character from an old cartoon. "What do you mean, you sorry sonofabitch? Whose god-damned idea was all this, anyway?"

"You're not going."

"The hell I'm not. You're going to need me, George."

"No," Taylor said matter-of-factly, "I'm not going to need you. One more shriveled-up bird colonel won't make a lick of difference tomorrow." He glanced automatically at his watch. "Today, I mean. Nope, I don't need you, Tucker. But the Army needs you. And the Army's going to need you more than ever after all this is over. You're going to have to finish what you started. Cleaning up all the shit."

"Don't give me one of your speeches, George."

Taylor waved a hand at his old comrade. "No speeches. I just hate to think of the U.S. Army having to do without both of us. Wouldn't be a decent scandal for at least ten years."

The two men sat quietly for a moment. The words between them had not been as important as the absolutely clear but unarticulated understanding that left no room for further argument: Taylor was the mission commander, and he had decided that Williams was not going. Therefore, Williams knew that he was not going. The rest was merely a ritual.

Williams knocked back a slug of the bad water masquerading as coffee. "George," he said seriously, "you don't sound like you think this one's going to be very clean."

Taylor twisted up his dead lips as though he were chewing a cud of tobacco. "Truth be told, I don't know what the hell to expect. Too many variables." Then he grinned. "So I'm just doing what comes naturally. And we'll see what happens."

The old intelligence colonel laid a hand on his friend's forearm.

"George," he said, "you take care. I'd miss you, you know." He chuckled. "I haven't seen all that much of you over the years. But I always knew you were out there. I always said to myself, 'Tucker, they may call you crazy. But you ain't half as crazy as that sonofabitch Georgie Taylor.' It was always reassuring." He fretted his hand on the cloth of Taylor's uniform. "I'm just not ready to assume the mantle of the U.S. Army's number one damned-fool lunatic."

"Don't underestimate yourself," Taylor said with a dead man's smile.

Williams shook his head and casually withdrew his hand.

"Well, do me one favor," he told Taylor. "Just don't fuck it all up, okay?"

Taylor looked at the worn face beside him. Veteran of so many mutual disappointments, of so much trying.

"Not if I can help it," Taylor said.

For the first time in days, Noburu's dreams did not wake him. This time it was a bomb.

At first, everything was unclear. He woke from haunted sleep as if his bed had convulsed and coughed him up. Unsure of his state, he sat upright in a waking trance, gripping the darkness as if falling. Was he dreaming this too?

The last echo of the blast receded, leaving an emptiness

quickly filled by the noise of automatic weapons and the muffled but unmistakable sound of human cries from the far edge of reason.

Noburu reached toward the light just as the intercom beeped. The message began without the usual ceremonious greeting.

"They're coming over the wall," the voice warned. Volume turned down, the intercom had shrunken the voice and it sounded oddly comic: a midget in terror.

Noburu hurried into his trousers.

"—a bomb—" the voice went on.

Noburu grasped his tunic, shooting an arm down its sleeve.

"—the gate—"

Conditioned by an eternity of mornings, Noburu took up his pistol belt, strapping it on over his open uniform blouse.

Machine guns sputtered beyond the headquarters walls. Storm tides of voices swept forward. The floor pulsed underfoot as dozens of men hurried along nearby corridors.

"—local guards deserted—"

Another blast. But this one was distinctly less powerful.

Akiro burst into the room. The aide's brown eyes burned.

"Sir," Akiro barked. But the younger man could think of nothing further to say. He had been sleeping. Noburu noted that his normally precise aide had neglected to do up the fly of his trousers. It struck Noburu as odd that he still had the capacity to notice such details with death already brushing its cold fur up against him.

Noburu crossed to the wall where heavy draperies covered a window of bulletproof glass. He touched a button offset from the meaty fabric and the curtain parted.

Nothing to be seen. The fighting was around the other side of the compound, and despite the bluster of automatic weaponry, from Noburu's bedroom a man could see only the nighttime peace of the city cuddled around the bay. Beyond the moraine of buildings, the sea lay naked under voluptuous moonlight. It was a powerful and romantic view, and the background noise of combat seemed grotesquely inappropriate, as though the wrong sound track had been supplied for a film.

It occurred to Noburu that Tokyo would much prefer this view of things, but before he could smile a firebomb traced across the dark sky, tail on fire. It struck a balustrade a bit below Noburu's lookout point and flames spilled backward over a terraced roof.

"Come on," Noburu told his aide. "And pull up your zipper."

Noburu jogged out through his office and into the corridor, with Akiro close behind, trying to reason with the older man.

"Sir," Akiro pleaded, "you must stay here. You must remain where we can guarantee your safety."

Only when the closed elevator doors temporarily blocked his path did Noburu turn any serious attention to the younger man.

"Nothing is guaranteed," he said calmly. "Least of all, my safety."

The sliding doors opened with a delicate warning chime. Inside stood Colonel Piet Kloete, the senior South African representative on the staff. Two of his NCOs stood beside him. All three of the men were heavily armed. Kloete himself looked ferocious with a light machine gun cradled in his arms, while the other two soldiers had loaded themselves down with autorifles, grenade belts, a light radio, and ammunition tins for Kloete's machine gun. Noburu could not help admiring the appearance of the South Africans. He knew that he had reached an age where he would frighten no one, where a pose behind a machine gun would most likely amuse an enemy. But the South African colonel was at a perfect point in his life, his body still hard. The gray along Kloete's temples resembled reinforcing wires of steel.

"The roof," the South African said to Noburu.

"Yes," Noburu said. "The helipad. The best vantage point."

He entered the elevator. When Akiro tried to follow, Noburu barred the aide's way with a forearm.

"Go down to the operations center," Noburu commanded. "Gather information." He looked at the younger man. The perfect staff officer was out of his depth now. Akiro did not look frightened. He merely looked mortally confused. An orderly man from an orderly world, waking barefoot in a hissing jungle. "And get yourself a rifle," Noburu added.

The doors kissed shut. During the brief ascent, the muted sounds of battle surrounded them, yet the combat remained unreal, almost irrelevant. Voices bubbling down into an aquarium.

"Truck bomb," Kloete said casually. He boosted the machine gun until he had a sounder grip on it. "Fuckers took out the main gate."

The doors parted. Noburu went first, stepping gingerly through the short dark tunnel that led out onto the helipad.

"Bloody fuck-all," one of the South African NCOs spat, stumbling against something audibly metallic.

As the little group emerged from the concrete shelter of the passageway, the night wind off the sea splashed in through Noburu's unbuttoned tunic like ice water and rinsed back through his hair. Brassy flares dripped from the heavens, lighting the compound and the nearby quarter of the city. Lower down, tracer rounds wove in and out of the darkness, while the block of buildings just beyond the barracks complex burned skyward. Apparently, the first assault had been beaten off. There was little human movement in evidence at the moment. Noburu strode briskly across the helipad to gain a better look. The South Africans trotted on ahead, booted feet heavy under the burden of their weaponry.

"Machine gun," Kloete cried, "action." His voice carried the legacy of old British enemies, insinuated into Boer blood and transported now to the shore of the Caspian Sea. Kloete spoke in unmistakably British phrases, muddied by an Afrikaans accent.

The South African's long-barreled weapon began to peck at targets Noburu's aging eyes could not even begin to distinguish.

The body softened, the eyes failed. While the mind remembered youth too well.

As Noburu hunkered down behind the low wall along

the edge of the roof, blossoms of flame spread out from under one of the guard towers, a construction that housed sentinels in a bulb atop a long, narrow stalk. Now the tulip came to life. Its base uprooted by the blast, the tower shivered, then seemed to hop, struggling to keep its balance. Finally, the construction's last equilibrium failed and the tower fell over hard, slamming its high concrete compartment down onto the parade ground.

The shouting came before the sound of the guns. Screaming unintelligibly, the Azeris rushed back in through the wreckage of the main gate. The big steel doors had been blown completely off their hinges, and the masonry of the wall looked as jagged as broken bone. Black figures dashed forward, silhouetted by flames. Other shapes dropped over the wall where long stretches of wire had been torn away. The lead figures opened fire with automatic weapons as they ran.

Fresh flares arced. Inside the compound, a crossfire of machine guns opened up. A few of the remaining guard towers laid down a base of fire on the far side of the wall, but other sentry perches remained silent and dark.

Screaming. Falling.

Surely, Noburu thought, these dark men were shouting about their god. No other words would have the power to propel men into this.

The garrison's machine guns swept the invaders off their feet. As Noburu crouched forward to see, a shower of spent shell casings nipped against his cheek and chest, their temperature scalding in the night air.

"Crazy buggers," one of the South African NCOs said to his mate. The man swapped out magazines and leaned back over the low wall that ringed the roof.

"Action left," Kloete cried. His subordinates followed the swing of the machine gun with their own weapons.

Noburu peered into the darkness, trying to follow the red streaks from his companions' weapons, seeking a closer glimpse of this new enemy.

Down on the parade ground, the flares revealed tens of dozens of bodies. Some lay clustered, others sprawled apart. Here a man moved over the cobblestones like an agonized worm, while another twitched, then stilled. Snipers went to ground, then suddenly blasted at the head-quarters building, drawing concentrated fire in response.

Noburu had believed that the assault was over, when a fresh wave poured screaming through the gate. Outlined by the inferno across the road, one figure carried a banner aloft. His head had the grossly swollen look of a turbaned man at night. All around him, his followers shrilled.

Noburu thought he heard the word distinctly: "Allah." "Allah" and then a pair of ruptured syllables, repeated again and again. He knew that his hearing was not much better than his eyesight, and that he might only be imposing the word on their voices. But it felt right. He watched as rivets of machine gun fire fixed the flag bearer to a wall, then let him drop.

Another shadow scooped up the banner.

Kloete cursed and called for another tin of ammunition.

Noburu briefly considered drawing his pistol. But he knew it would only be an empty gesture at this distance, like spitting at the enemy. And he was tired of empty gestures. This was a younger man's fight.

During his career, he had been acutely aware of being a part of history, and he had possessed the gift of casting the moment into the perspective of books yet to be written. But this. This was like being part of someone else's history. When madmen with flags and a god's name on their lips swarmed into the sharp teeth of civilization. This was the stuff of bygone centuries.

The machine guns methodically built up a barrier of corpses where once the steel gates had served. But the Azeris simply climbed over the corpses of their brethren at a run, continuing on to martyrdom.

A dark form raised a hand to hurl something, then toppled too soon. The grenade's explosion rearranged the pile of corpses into which the man had fallen.

"Terrebork," Kloete shouted without taking his cheek off the side of his weapon, "bring up more ammunition."

One of the NCOs mumbled a response and scuttled off toward the elevator.

"Crazy," Kloete said loudly, his voice half-wonder, half-accusation. "They're crazy."

But the automatic weapons made in Honshu or on the

Cape of Good Hope did good work. The assault again dwindled into a sniping between a few riflemen amid the landscape of dead and wounded and the defenders of the compound's interior.

Kloete unlocked the housing of his machine gun to let the weapon cool. He rolled over against the wall. "Shit," he said. Then he noticed Noburu. The South African snorted loudly. "Long way to travel just to shoot your colored," he said. He grinned, teeth white against his powder-grimed face. "Funny, I don't remember this part in any of the briefings." He looked at Noburu with the impolite stare of someone who knew exactly how far things had gone awry, as well as who was to blame.

Noburu said nothing. He simply looked at the hard angles of the man's face. Kloete's skin was burnished by the ambient light of the fires, and he resembled a hardcase private as much as he did a colonel.

"They're all gone, you know," Kloete continued. He tapped along his tunic pockets, then drew out a crushed pack of cigarettes. In the background, desultory gunfire continued. "Your local nationals," he said, settling a bent cigarette between his lips. "All of our little security force allies. Save for a pair of shit-scared officers, who're bloody worthless anyway. Gone over to *those* crazy buggers." He tossed a spent match over the wall in the direction of the mob. "Took their bloody weapons and jumped. Good thing we had Japs in some of the towers." He narrowed his eyes at Noburu. "Japanese, I mean."

A new sound rose in the background. Singing. An Asian scale as foreign to Noburu's ears as it would have been to Kloete's. At first there were only a few voices. Then more took up the chant. Soon the volume overpowered the last gunfire, echoing off walls and rolling through the streets until the returning sound skewed the rhythm, as if several distinct groups were singing at the same time.

"Bleeding concert," the remaining NCO commented. His voice sounded distinctly on edge.

Kloete nodded to himself. "Lot of them out there," he said. He smoked and talked without once removing the cigarette from his lips. "Something to be said for numbers, from a military point of view."

"You are under no obligation to stay," Noburu said in his best staff college English. "This is now Japan's fight. You may summon one of your transports to remove your men." Noburu looked at the oversize colonel sprawled just beyond his knees. "And yourself."

Kloete laughed. It was a big laugh and it rang out clearly against the background of chanting.

"That's very generous of you, General Noburu. Extremely generous. But we'll be hanging about for now."

Nearby, the other South African chuckled wearily. But Noburu did not get the joke.

"As you wish," he said. "You are welcome to stay and fight. But I am releasing you from the provisions of your contract, given the changed cir—"

"Oh, just stuff it," Kloete said. "I'd be out of here like a gazelle, if I could. But your little wog friends took over the military airstrip while you were getting your beauty sleep. Baku's a closed city." Kloete looked up with the wet porcelain eyes of an animal. "Pity the lads at the airstrip, I do. Crowd doesn't seem in the most humanitarian of moods."

Two figures emerged from the sheltered passageway that led to the elevator and stairwell. One was large and loose-limbed even under the weight of boxes and canisters, while the other was small and exact, cradling an autorifle. Sergeant Terrebork, Kloete's ammunition hauler. And Akiro.

The South African dropped the ammo boxes one after the other.

"Bleeding last of it, sir," he told Kloete. Then he turned his nose to the wind, toward the chanting. In profile, he had the look of a dog who had scented game of unwelcome dimensions. "Gives you the willies, don't it?" he said.

A burst of fire made him duck to the level where the rest of them knelt or sat.

"*Sir*," Akiro said. Despite the fact that he was whispering, he managed to give the syllable its regulation harsh intonation. Then he began to speak in rapid Japanese, attempting to exclude the South Africans. "We have unforeseen problems."

Noburu almost laughed out loud. It seemed to him that

Akiro had acquired a marvelous new talent for under-statement.

"Yes," Noburu said, forcing himself to maintain a serious demeanor. "Go on, Akiro."

"We do not have sufficient small-arms ammunition. No one imagined . . . there seemed to be no reason to provide for such a contingency."

"No," Noburu agreed. "No reason at all. Go on."

"Should they continue to assault the headquarters . . . Colonel Takahara is not certain how much longer we will be able to return an adequate volume of fire. Another assault. Perhaps two at the most." Akiro rolled his head like a horse shaking off rainwater. "I still cannot believe," he said, "that the Americans could be so clever, that they could so efficiently manipulate our allies."

Noburu almost corrected the young man again. But he realized it was hopeless. When they were all dead, there would be an Akiro school of historians who would insist that only American subterfuge and dollars could have inspired all this. Noburu knew better. But his people were an island race in more than just a physical sense. Perhaps their worst insularity lay in their lost ability to comprehend the power of irrational faith.

"You may tell Colonel Takahara to reduce the size of the perimeter. We will defend only the headquarters complex itself and the communications pen. Abandon the out-buildings," Noburu said. "And make sure the soldiers are, as a minimum, in groups of twos. Frightened men waste more bullets."

Noburu had expected his aide to fly off with alacrity. But the younger man paused.

"There's more?" Noburu asked sadly.

"*Sir*. We have been unable to report our situation to Tokyo. Or to anyone. Something . . . is wrong. None of the communications means works. Except for the main computer link, which will not accept plain voice text. We're working to format an appropriate automated message, but . . . everything was so unforeseen."

What were the Americans up to now? Noburu shuddered. Perhaps *he* was the fool, the one who had been living in a dreamworld. Perhaps Akiro had been right all along, perhaps this insurrection *was* American-sponsored.

No. He still could not believe it.

Then what was wrong with the communications? Even at the height of yesterday's attack by the Americans, the high-end communications links had continued to function flawlessly. The only communications problems had been within or immediately adjacent to the combat zone. What was happening?

"Akiro? What does Colonel Takahara think? Is it possible that our communications have been sabotaged?"

Akiro shrugged. He knew how to operate command consoles. But he was not a signals officer, and he personally had no conception of what might be occurring. "Colonel Takahara says it is jamming."

Jamming? Then by whom? It had to be the Americans. Only they possessed strategic jammers. Yet . . . the Americans had not employed their strategic systems in the combat of the day before, and the omission had baffled Noburu. The situation made little sense to him.

Were the Americans attacking again? Despite the employment of the Scramblers?

"Akiro. Listen. Tell Colonel Takahara to transfer all automated control of military operations to the rear command post in Teheran. That can be done easily enough through the computer. But it must be done quickly, in case the enemy has found a way to jam our automation feeds, as well. Just tell Colonel Takahara to transfer control. He knows what has to be done."

"Is he to shut our computer down?" Akiro asked.

"No. No, absolutely not. The transfer of control is strictly temporary. The rear will control the battle until we get the local situation under control. But our computer will remain in full readiness. I want to be able to resume control the instant the jamming lifts and we . . . discourage this demonstration."

But he did not believe. It was all a matter of form, of the prescribed gesture. He had lost his faith. The shadow men beyond the wall had stolen the last of it and turned it to their own ends. In an instant's vision, the dark, chanting men covered the earth.

"*Sir*. Colonel Takahara says that the jamming is of such power that many of our communications sets have burned out."

"It doesn't matter. I can fight the entire battle through the computer, if need be." Noburu caught an external glimpse of himself, as if his soul had briefly left his body. How far removed he was from his ancestors who had led the way with wands of steel.

The huge background of chanting continued. His ancestors, he knew, would have understood that sound. The dream warrior understood it.

A few stray rounds pecked at the facade of the building, and Noburu just managed to hear a soft exchange between the South Africans.

"What's junior on about, sir?" the ammunition carrier asked Kloete.

Kloete snorted as though his sinuses had been ruptured. "He's telling the old man we can't talk to anybody. And that we're out of bloody bullets."

Akiro lifted off his haunches to go.

"Akiro?"

The younger man turned obediently.

Noburu held out the aide's forgotten rifle.

"*Sir,*" Akiro said. Noburu could feel his aide blushing through the dark.

"And, Akiro. Above all, Colonel Takahara is to safeguard the computer."

"*Sir.*"

Noburu watched the younger man's back as Akiro scooted across the helipad. Yes. The computer. There were some things about it that even Takahara did not know. Aspects of the machine's capabilities that were known only to full generals and a handful of technicians back in Tokyo. The main military computer system, Noburu considered, resembled a wealthy man's beautiful wife—possessed of a secret that could destroy the man whose bed she shared.

Suddenly the chanting stopped. The silence was painful. Dizzying. Then Noburu registered the aural detritus of the attack—the unmistakable sound of badly wounded men who had not had the good fortune to lose consciousness.

An enormous howl erupted from the world beyond the wall. The chanting was over—this was simply a huge, wordless wail. It was the biggest sound Noburu had ever heard.

"Here they come," Kloete screamed.

A section of the perimeter wall disappeared in fire and dust. The blast wave tipped Noburu backward with the force of a typhoon wind.

"Fire into the smoke, fire into the smoke."

A smaller blast shook the floor beneath them. Grenade launcher, Noburu realized. Either they had stolen it, or rebel regulars had joined the mob's ranks.

The first shrieking figures left the pall of smoke. Someone inside the compound ignited a crossfire of headlamps and spotlights to help the machine gunners, and more flares lit the sky. But the flares were perceptibly fewer this time, and most of the light was provided by the section of the city that had begun to burn in the background.

Waves of dark figures swarmed through the gate and rushed through the broken wall. The volume of defending fire seemed to hush under the weight of the storm, overcome by the screaming energy of the mob. More banners trailed, falling and then rising again, as the attackers clambered over the ridges of the dead.

Kloete raised himself so that he could angle the machine gun into the oncoming tide.

The South African NCO to Noburu's side crumpled and stretched himself back across the helipad. In falling, his fingertips just grazed Noburu's cheek, drawing the general's attention after them. The South African lay with his face shot away, lower jaw torn nearly all the way off. He somehow continued to give off moans that were almost words.

Kloete wheeled about, eyes demonic. He took one close, hard look at his subordinate, unceremoniously drew his pistol, and shot the man where once the bridge of his nose must have been. The NCO twitched and then lay still.

The South African colonel met Noburu's eyes and evidently mistook what he saw there for disapproval.

"It's that kind of situation," Kloete said.

Noburu nodded, then automatically took up the dead man's rifle and leaned over the ledge. As he took aim, he saw the first hint of individual features on the darting shadows. They were very close. The war was coming to him.

Noburu opened fire. The kick of the weapon was instantly familiar, even after decades of wielding only a ceremonial pistol. He aimed carefully, remaining in the single-shot mode, trying to buy value for each round spent.

The Azeris fell in waves. But each next wave splashed closer.

A ripple of close-in blasts caught the forwardmost attackers. Noburu felt a blow on the side of his head. But, whatever it was, it was of no consequence. He remained upright, sentient, firing.

"Banzai."

A wave of high-pitched Japanese shouts broke over the cries of the attackers. The sound of close automatic weapons increased to a blurred roar.

"Banzai."

In the dying firelight, Noburu saw his men charging into the oncoming mass of Azeris. The Japanese fired as they ran, and Noburu caught the glint of fixed bayonets. A miniature sun lit up in the courtyard. Noburu recognized Colonel Takahara at the forward edge of the charge, samurai sword raised overhead, its blade wielding the power of light. With his left hand, Takahara fired a sidearm.

"Banzai."

The leading tentacles of the mob began to retract at the unexpected counterattack. Noburu fired beyond the ragged line of his men, helping as best he could. He knew his days of gallant charges were behind him. But he would do what remained to him.

"Fucking Japs," he heard the surviving South African NCO say. It was half a complaint, half admiration. "They're just as crazy as the wogs."

Noburu saw a fallen Azeri rise suddenly and fire point-blank into Takahara's stomach. The staff officer fell backward, staggering. It seemed to Noburu that Takahara was less concerned with staying on his feet than he was with holding the sword aloft. Its blade shone unblooded. Then another burst punched Takahara to the ground. The sword shimmered and disappeared amid the litter of corpses. Noburu held his rifle up to fire, but another Japanese beat

him to his prey, bayoneting the man who had shot Takahara. The soldier remembered his bayonet drill well
enough, planting a foot on his victim's back and twisting
out his rifle.

The assault faded away, leaving two-dozen Japanese upright in the courtyard, firing across the parade ground toward the main gate and the breach in the wall. A last flare
helped them, and Noburu realized that he had never seen
so much death so close at hand. The broad space between
the headquarters building and the main gate writhed like
a snake pit with the wounded. But, when you looked
closely, you saw a great ragged stillness around the hurt,
waiting to accept them all. A man could have walked from
the headquarters entrance to the main gate by stepping
from corpse to corpse, without ever touching concrete or
cobbles.

A Japanese voice commanded a return to the headquarters building defenses. On the way, the men pawed
over the fallen, checking for ammunition with which to
continue the fight. The smell of gunpowder burned in Noburu's nose like dried pepper.

"Jesus Christ," a voice said. Noburu turned and saw the
ammunition handler bent over the cavity of his comrade's
skull.

Kloete lit another cigarette, then offered the open pack
to Noburu.

"I don't smoke," Noburu said.

The South African nodded as though he understood
perfectly.

"Good show, that," Kloete said. He spoke the angli-
cized phrase with his mudlike accent. "Your boys, I
mean."

"Yes."

"Christ. You're bleeding like a stuck pig."

Noburu did not understand.

"The side of your head," Kloete said, raising a hand
partway to indicate the location of the wound. The man's
fingers stank of spent cartridges.

Noburu remembered the blow on the side of his head.
And now, magically, he could feel the blood oozing warmly

512

from the wound, losing temperature as it wandered down his neck. He did not need to test the wound with his hand.

"It's of no consequence," he said.

"You'll need to have that seen to," Kloete said firmly.

But Noburu no longer cared. He realized that he had been relieved, almost overjoyed by the attack. Toward the end he had not needed to think of anything else. The dream warrior was smiling.

"It's of no consequence whatsoever," Noburu said truthfully.

Colonel Johnny Tooth, United States Air Force, was a happy man. The four big WHITE LIGHT electronic warfare birds under his immediate control were on-station and functioning perfectly, exactly twenty-four hours late.

But lateness was a relative thing. The goddamned near-sighted Army ground-pounders didn't understand that you could not risk expensive aircraft and their crews in hopelessly bad weather. Technically speaking, of course, he was a little behind schedule—but his aircraft had made it into the war after a direct supersonic flight from the States and they were performing flawlessly, jamming an enormous swathe from the Caucasus east across Soviet Central Asia and northern Iran. There wasn't going to be any chitchat down on the ground tonight.

The WHITE LIGHT aircraft had the capabilities of flying at speeds above Mach 3 or of slowing to a near hover. In either case, they were invisible to any of the air defense systems known to be deployed in-theater. A long association with the WHITE LIGHT program gave Tooth the sort of warm, safe feeling a man had when he held good investments while the economy was going to shit for everyone else. Personally, Tooth had put his money into select real estate during the plague years, and he had no retirement worries.

"Don't you think we should try to contact the Army guys?" his copilot asked over the intercom.

Tooth could hardly believe his ears. "You nuts, Chubbs?"

"Well," Chubbs said more carefully, "I just thought we ought to let them know we're on-station. You know?"

Tooth sighed. So few people understood the interrelationships. "Maybe on the way out," he said, always ready to compromise. "But first we're going to run a complete mission. Nobody's going to be able to say the U.S. Air Force didn't do its part." Tooth shuddered inwardly, picturing some rough-handed, semiliterate Army officer testifying before a congressional subcommittee, claiming that the weight of military operations had been borne by the Army alone. The Air Force didn't need that kind of heartache, with budgets as tight as they were. Tooth understood clearly that the primary mission of the U.S. Army was to siphon off funding from vital Air Force programs.

The Air Force had gone through a run of bad luck. It began in Zaire, where the South Africans had cheated and attacked the B-2 fleet on the ground—now that had been a royal mess, and a man could only be thankful that nobody in the press had ever been able to sort out the real unit cost of the stealth bomber. Then the Army had started grabbing all the glory, whether from their dirty little police duties during the plague or from their primitive roughnecking down in the Latin American mud. Why, you could have hired off-duty policemen to do the Army's job and you would have saved the country billions. And, all the while, it had been embarrassingly difficult to find appropriate missions for the state-of-the-art manned bombers, which Congress had finally come around to funding in the nineteen nineties—thanks to contractor programs that spread the wealth across congressional districts in practically every state in the Union. The minor action the Air Force had seen had shown, to widespread horror, that the oldest, slowest planes in the inventory were the best-suited to joint requirements. The underdeveloped countries simply refused to buy first-class air defense systems for stealth bombers to evade. Worse, they refused to provide clearcut high-payoff targets. Then there was the humiliation with the Military Airlift Command's transport fleet. Naturally, lift capability had been put on the back burner in the quest to acquire sufficient numbers of high-tech combat aircraft to keep fighter jocks and bomber crews in uniform

And the transport fleet had bluntly failed in its initial attempts to ferry the Army in and out of Africa and Latin America. The government had been reduced to requisitioning heavy transports and passenger aircraft from the private sector.

So the opportunity to show what the WHITE LIGHT aircraft could do was a welcome one. The birds had come in just at nine billion dollars a copy in 2015, and the program had required fall-on-your-sword efforts by congressmen whose districts included major defense contractors in order to force it through Appropriations. It would have been nice, of course, if everything could have been synchronized with the Army operation, in accordance with the original plan. But, ultimately, the thing was just to get the birds into action. His superiors had made the decision to launch the mission twenty-four hours late without consulting the other services. There was always the chance that the Army would try to block the Air Force activities with some whining to the effect that there was no further need for the jamming support, or that it would interfere with ground ops. You could never trust a grunt. They never understood the big picture, and they thought at the speed of the human foot. Absolutely no grasp of strategic imperatives. And they died broke.

"How's everything going back there, Pete?" Tooth called to his weapons officer, who was currently sending streaks of man-made lightning through the heavens, destroying billions of dollars worth of enemy electronics.

"Just fine, sir. We're putting out so much juice we'll fry pretty near every transmitter between here and the Indian Ocean. They'll be talking with tin cans and pieces of string when the sun comes up. Tokyo's going to shit."

"Well, you just keep up the good work," Tooth said. Then he called the navigator. "Jimmy-boy, you put us back in friendly airspace by dawn, understand?"

"Got it, sir."

Colonel Johnny Tooth was fully aware that stealth technology and fifth-generation electronic defenses had rendered his aircraft as invisible in the daylight hours as at night. But Tooth nonetheless preferred flying in the darkness. It might be unreasonable, but the ability to wrap himself in the ancient cloak of night just made him feel that much more secure. Besides, he wanted to be back on the ground by lunch, since he had to place a very important phone call. Supporting the Army was one thing, but a real estate transaction was serious.

23

4 November 2020

THEY CRUCIFIED THE MEN DURING THE NIGHT AND LEFT
the crosses standing just outside the gate. Akiro, who had
found it difficult enough to follow Noburu across the sea
of bodies, began to gag. The wind flapped the blood-
soaked uniforms of the Japanese officers like wet canvas.

The Azeris had not gotten it exactly right, Noburu
noted. Here a spike had been driven through the hand
instead of a wrist, while on another cross a leg dangled
free. Noburu recognized two of the three men as officers
from the airfield. Perhaps the third man was a recent ar-
rival he did not know. Noburu looked up at the lolling
faces with their expressions of torment and wonder. Behind him, Akiro finished his dry retching.

"At least they killed them," Noburu said, lowering his
eyes to look down between the ranks of burned buildings,
across the human flotsam the mob had left in its wake.

"Why?" Akiro begged. "Why did they do this?"

Noburu smiled. "They think we're Christians. All foreigners are Christians, you see. I'm afraid our allies are
not as enlightened as Tokyo might wish."

Back inside the gates, the bulldozer resumed its grunting. Moving the bodies, clearing an entryway for the relief
column that must eventually come. Otherwise, the city was
very quiet. The morning light seemed crippled, misshapen
by twisting columns of smoke and the smell of death. The
bulldozer added to the stink, disturbing the settling filth

that had been a man, its blade wrenching open another
corpse's bowels. Underneath the reek of mortality the familiar smell of the oil works came sharply up from the
coast. A thousand years after they shut down the derricks
and refineries, Baku would still stink of oil. And death.

They were waiting, Noburu realized. Down in the labyrinth of the old city. On the waterfront. Or, farther out
in the apartment blocks built to give the workers a foretaste
of paradise, and in the disease-culled slums, where families
lived under worse conditions than had their most distant
ancestors. The streets were empty now. The population
had been driven indoors by the light of day, by defeat,
plague, and exhaustion. But they were still there. Waiting.

Until the darkness returned. They would come again in
the night. Noburu could feel it.

The communications center was a ruin. The intelligence
officer speculated that the Americans had employed aircraft from their WHITE LIGHT program. But it was impossible to know with any certainty. The world was so full
of surprises. The only thing that was definite was the
burned-out stasis of the magical talking machines that directed warfare in the twenty-first century. When the interference finally stopped, only two systems remained
functional: an ancient vacuum tube radio set inherited
from the Soviets—with which the staff had been able to
contact a loyal garrison to the north—and the main computer system. The computer was Japan's pride. It had been
built to withstand any imaginable interference. The computer was the castle of the new age, wherein the modern
warrior sought his last refuge. Certainly, it was more important than any number of brave Takaharas or subordinates nailed up on crosses.

A black bird flittered down onto one of the foreign dead
in the street. Noburu feared some further atrocity. But the
bird merely twitched its head back and forth a few times,
judging the world, then settled down into the pile of rags
as if nesting.

A low humming arose in the distance. The two living,
standing men looked at each other.

"The relief column?" Akiro asked.

"Too soon."

The younger man looked back down at the street with its frozen traffic of papers, glass, and death.

The humming stopped. Another detail of events that would never be explained.

It would be hours before any relief column could arrive. Perhaps even a day or more. Everything was so unsettled. Rough, relayed messages indicated that fundamentalist elements in Iran had called for a holy war against the Japanese in the liberated territories as well as against the Russians. The Azeris were fellow Shi'as, and they had obeyed the call. Perhaps the Sunni populations of central Asia would make common cause in this, as they had in the war against the Soviets. Noburu did not know. Without communications, the world was simply a question mark. But even if they made common cause now, it would not be too long before the Shi'as and Sunnis began killing one another. It was the natural way of this world, as inevitable as the seasons.

Of course, it made no logical sense. But these people lived on a spiritual frontier where the logic of other races or religions had little value. Faith was all.

The masses had responded to the green call of their god, as had some of the rebel units and formations. But others had kept faith with Japan and her military technology. Now there was a civil war within a civil war, and a fractured world was fracturing again into ever smaller, ever more uncontrollable parts. He had known it all in advance. The dream warrior had whispered to him, smiling at Noburu's folly as he attempted to reason with Iranian generals, Arab generals, central Asian generals, each of whom was only waiting for the day when he would fight the other once again, waiting for the day when the Slavs and Japanese would be gone so that the children of God could return their attention to more exclusive massacres.

A relief column had been organized to fight its way into the city from the nearest loyal garrison, according to a message received over the old HF radio. But no one knew what obstacles and ambushes were out there waiting. Ideally, the helicopters and tilt-rotor aircraft would have provided reconnaissance as well as quicker relief, ferrying in troops and ammunition and lifting out the wounded.

But the jamming attack during the night had destroyed the electronics on virtually all of the tactical aircraft in the vicinity. The only option remaining was the dispatch of an armored relief convoy—which would have to drive blindly over mountain roads. There would be plenty of time to wait and worry.

Ammunition. Above all, they needed ammunition. If the mob returned now, they could virtually stroll into the compound.

Noburu had been forced to allow the rear command post to continue to control combat operations. His shrunken staff labored to repair at least a few of the communications systems by cannibalizing others. He could have run the war through the master computer, but he recognized that such an action would be sheer vanity. He needed a functioning headquarters around him. For the moment, the rear had a broader capacity to sort out the damage and revitalize allied efforts. Given the present state of his headquarters, Noburu would have been shooting into the darkness. As it was, he could not even communicate with the rear command post by voice. So he elected to wait. To try to think clearly. He had transmitted only one firm order through the master computer: the Scramblers were not to be employed again without his personal authorization. Beyond that, there was only an emptiness, inability.

Behind him, he heard the indestructible computer singing. A quiet song of electricity and perfection. The computer was ready to do his will. The brilliant machine *wanted* to do his bidding. It was only the man, feeble and unsure, who could not respond.

The black bird rose abruptly from its human nest and sailed up to the head of one of the crucified officers. Again, the bird made no attempt to disturb the flesh. It simply perched, fluffing its black feathers over the dead man's hair.

Akiro drew his pistol.

"No," Noburu said.

But the younger man fired. He missed the bird, which rose skyward with a baffled cry. Under the black wings the dead officer's skull exploded, coming back to life for an instant before its wreckage lolled back down on the officer's chest.

Akiro was shaking. He looked as though he had been abandoned on an ice floe. He held the pistol in his hand, struggling with its purpose.

"Organize a detail," Noburu said calmly. "It's time to cut them down."

At 12:57 A.M., Eastern Standard Time, President Jonathan Waters suffered a massive heart attack. He had slept little over the previous four days, and it had felt wonderful and a little bit strange to slip into the bedclothes beside the steady warmth of his wife. He lost consciousness quickly, descending into a tumult of dreams. His last dream was of his father. President Waters was only a boy, and red-eyed dogs chased him. Up ahead, his father receded in a mist as thick as wet concrete. The boy ran harder and harder, making ever less progress, calling out to the safe, strong man. But his father did not hear him. And the dogs were all around him. He ran as hard as he could, lifting his hands away from the relentless snouts, shouting for his father to come back.

He woke in mortal pain. He called out, "Dad," then remembered a whole life and spoke his wife's name once before he died.

The Americans came down from the meager hills that had been elevated with the name Ural Mountains. Their war machines sailed south over the wastes, registering here and there the passing of a village better-suited as a museum of poverty and premodernity than as a habitat for contemporary man. The war had not yet reached these hamlets, and smoke rose from chimneys instead of from ruins. The M-100s' on-board sensors registered defunct tractors in place of tanks. The snow had covered the last traces of the roads. The isolated settlements appeared as gray islands in an arctic sea. The sagging houses looked so thoroughly lost that it seemed certain the war would continue to pass them by as surely as had indoor plumbing.

It struck Taylor that this was no land over which to fight a war. It was merely a place of passage, through which the

great forgotten warriors of the East had passed, illiterate
geniuses whose people wove the record of their triumphs
into rugs or nicked out their chronicles in silver and brass.
Then the white-bloused Russians had marched from west
to east, for God and the Czar, bringing the tribesmen
alphabets and artillery.

Objectively speaking, this was no land over which to
fight a war. And yet, Taylor had seen enough of war to
know that a man would always love the barren plains or
hills where he was born, and that he would pass that love
on to his sons with his blood, even in captivity. Anyway,
men never really needed much of an excuse to fight.

Taylor felt weary. The excitement of planning was over,
the thrill of designing the impossible in such a way that it
came to seem inevitable. For the present, there was only
a long, dull route to fly, and he felt the big physical tiredness in his limbs, made heavier by the hard usage of a
lifetime.

Hours to fly. Until the refueling stop. Then an even
greater distance until they reached the objective. Taylor
glanced out over the frozen wastes. It was a long way from
Africa, the touchstone of his life.

He slumped back in his seat.

"Flapper," he said to his copilot, "you've got the wheel.
I need a little rest."

Vice President Maddox looked warily from face to face.
The new chair did not feel very comfortable.

"The Chief Justice is on her way, sir," the White House
Chief of Staff said. There was a totally new tone of respect
in his voice.

Maddox considered the man. Nope. He would not do.
He was irredeemably a Waters man, and he had been
carelessly inattentive of the Vice President, whom he had
rather too publicly termed a "hick with a college degree."
Nope. A new White House Chief of Staff would be one
of the first appointees.

"Martin," Maddox said to the man whose fate had just
been decided, "would you mind looking in on Mrs. Waters
one more time? See if she isn't feeling just a tad more in
possession of herself." He thought of the famous old pic-

tures of Jackie Kennedy in pink by a new president's side. "I do think the public would be reassured if she felt up to putting in an appearance at the swearing-in."

"Yes, sir." And he was gone.

Maddox looked around the table. Serious bunch. Nobody you'd want to take along to the hunting cabin for a weekend.

"About that other thing," he said.

"Yes, sir," the secretary of state jumped in. It was obvious to Maddox that the man had been waiting impatiently for an opportunity to continue his earlier tutorial.

Damned Yankees, Maddox thought. Never do learn.

"We cannot afford to waste any more time," the white-haired diplomat continued. "You must understand, sir. President Waters was ill, and probably in physical pain, when he made his decision. Why, the stress alone was enough to unbalance a man. And remember Franklin Roosevelt at Yalta. Bad health makes for bad decisions."

"I don't know," Maddox said slowly. "I'm a fighting kind of guy. I don't know whether the American people want a president"—the word had an entirely new feel on the tongue—"who's afraid to put up his dukes."

"It isn't a matter of *fighting*," the secretary of state continued. "It's a matter of *losing*. And I'm certain the American people do not want to suffer pointless, unnecessary losses. The entire affair . . . is sheer madness. God only knows what sort of retaliation it might bring. As well as making a hash out of all our diplomatic efforts."

Maddox scanned beyond the secretary of state. Didn't see a face in the room he could trust. He had nurtured a kind of liking for the chairman of the Joint Chiefs, but that was only because the man resembled an old hunting dog he'd had as a boy.

"What do you have to say there, General?"

The chairman alerted to the scent. "Mr. Vice President," he said in the bluff voice that generals like to wear in Washington, "I want to be perfectly honest with you. I'm an old soldier. I don't mind a good dustup. But, frankly, this mission has only the slightest chance of success—and it may well prove a great embarrassment."

Maddox narrowed his eyes. Sometimes a dog just got

so old and tired it couldn't hunt no more. And you had to put it down.

Maddox smiled. "Well, you all have to give me your best advice on this matter. My only experience with this sort of thing was a year in military school. My daddy sent me there to put some manners on me." His smile ripened into a grin. "Not sure it took. Anyhow, I'm afraid I'm just wandering around in the dark on all this. I do need good advice." He waved his shake-hands grin like a bright little flag. "Why, I've been out there in California, for God's sake."

"Mr. President," the secretary of state resumed, "while you were on the Coast, the President was under a great deal of pressure. He began to make—"

The door opened. Mrs. Waters stepped into the room, eyes dead. She was followed by the Chief Justice, the White House Chief of Staff, and a staff photographer.

Maddox jumped to his feet.

"Sir," the secretary of state hissed, "there's very little time. We've got to stop—"

"Just hold your horses," Maddox snapped. Then he set his face in an expression of sympathy as perfect as a black silk tie and walked open-armed toward the President's widow.

"Are you sure this is the right place?" Taylor asked. Kozlov noted that the American was trying to maintain a professional demeanor, but the undertones of impatience and disgust in his voice were unmistakable. "Is there any chance we've got the wrong coordinates?"

Kozlov looked down at the monitor displaying a visual survey of the designated refueling site. The steppe was embarrassingly empty. Where Soviet refueling vehicles should have been waiting, there was only the gray earth, naked and cold, between the Caspian Sea just to the south and the sea of snow to the north. Pressed to give the place a name, Kozlov would have called it "No-man's-land."

He looked back up. Into Taylor's disfigured, disapproving face.

"I don't understand it," Kozlov said honestly. "I spoke

with General Ivanov himself . . . with the staff . . . and they all assured me . . ."

"We've got the right grids," Meredith declared. "This is the place."

Kozlov watched the parade of expressions crossing the American commander's face: disgust, then hard concern, a brief retreat into disappointment, followed by a return to the stony look Taylor usually wore.

"Shit," Taylor said.

The operations compartment went silent, each man thinking the problem through for himself. The air turbulence rolled the deck beneath their boots, while automated systems flashed and pinged softly. The filtration system simply recycled old odors.

Kozlov felt ashamed. More and more, he felt committed to these Americans, these warriors who were ready to carry on a fight not entirely their own, despite the morbid cost. The Americans had spirit, above all, even in their black and weary moments. And spirit was a thing that had long been in short supply in his country. The spirit had been battered, tormented, starved, and dulled out of his fellow countrymen. Inheritors of failure, his people had forgotten how to hope, and hope was at least as necessary to the health of the human animal as were vitamins.

Still, he had kept his pride. Through it all. The pride of being Russian, even in the sharpest hour of adversity. But now . . . it seemed as though his country had conspired yet again to humiliate him, to shame him. The military machine to which he had given the whole of his adult life could not even deliver the fuel with which other men might carry on Great Russia's war.

So many lies, half-truths, promises forgotten as soon as they were spoken. Why hadn't General Ivanov been honest this one time?

Perhaps it was simply incompetence. Perhaps, even with the best will, the fuelers could not reach the designated site on time.

"It could be," Kozlov said hopefully, "that there has only been a delay. Because of the war. Perhaps the fuel carriers are coming soon."

Taylor turned cold eyes in Kozlov's direction. All of the other Americans crammed into the small compartment followed Taylor's gaze. Then the American colonel broke off the stare and turned to his black subordinate and the white operations captain.

"We're going to have to put down," Taylor said. "Hank, call the other birds. We'll go to ground and wait. All we're doing up here is burning fuel."

"Yes, sir," the captain said. Kozlov glanced again at the man's name tape: PARKER. They had been introduced the night before. But there were so many new names to remember. Ryder, for instance, the scared young man with the briefcase, sitting quietly at the back of the compartment. And there were so many unfamiliar details. It occurred to Kozlov that the cardinal feeling of men at war was not fear or excitement, neither cowardice nor courage, but simply weariness. It seemed to him that he had been tired for as long as he could remember. Perhaps that was why commanders were able to drive their men to achieve results at such suicidal costs: the men simply grew too tired to care what became of them.

"I want good dispersion on the ground," Taylor said. "The refuelers can shuttle around when they get here. And everybody deploys their camouflage before they so much as take a piss."

"Just the autocamouflage?" Meredith asked.

Taylor pursed his lips, then agreed. "Yeah. It's a trade-off. But we need to be ready to move fast. And let's put these babies down a few clicks to the south so we don't have those fat boys coming in right on top of us. We'll guide them to the birds after we get them under positive control."

The captain named Parker was already transmitting orders to the troop of five M-100s accompanying the American commander on his raid. They were marvelous fighting machines. Kozlov knew he should be making more of an effort to note the details of their operation so he would be able to file a complete report upon his return. But he was just so tired.

Colonel Taylor turned his back and squeezed into the passageway that led forward to the pilot's cabin. Kozlov was relieved, both because of the temporary respite from further questions and embarrassments, and because he still found it hard to look at the man. The stress of the past few days had etched the remnants of disease ever more deeply into the American's skin, further exaggerating his deformity, until Taylor reminded Kozlov of a devil.

Muffled engines shrieked beyond the walls of the control compartment and the fighting machine began its descent toward the Russian earth.

The wind blew from the south, but it was cold. Racing down from the high Iranian desert, then chilling itself as it skimmed over the Caspian Sea, the wind struck land with a force that narrowed the eyes. The M-100s were so well stablized that you did not get a proper sense of the intensity of the gusts when you were inside. But here, where the dead, colorless grass stretched from horizon to horizon, there was nothing to interfere with the wind's progress. It was a worthless, defenseless place, no matter which way you pointed yourself.

Taylor looked at his watch, then looked at the sky.

Nothing.

The afternoon continued to wither.

He could not bear the thought that it might end like this. After all the years of longing for a chance to strike back at the enemy who always lurked behind his country's enemies. After the fighting and the losses, the frantic planning and the experience of seeing a president backed against the wall, it was unbearable to think that it would all simply sputter out in a wasteland, for want of fuel.

He knew this would be the end, and he could not understand why none of the others seemed to grasp it. A failure now, on this day, in this place, would settle the order of the world for a generation. Or longer. His country would withdraw into its tattered hemisphere, and the Japanese would get what they had wanted for so long.

He tried to keep his personal prejudices out of the equation. But it was very hard. He *blamed* the Japanese. He could not help it. He wanted more than anything else in the world to face them one last time with a weapon in his hand.

He took off his helmet, and the wind pried at his matted hair. He thought of Daisy and smiled bitterly. He could not believe he had been so foolish as to imagine that there was anything real there. No woman, no matter her tarnish, was about to bind her life to his. No, he was good for one thing and one thing only: soldiering. The rest of it was an idle dream.

Surely, it could not end here. When they had come so close. He scanned the empty sky.

A voice feinted at his ear before the wind carried it off. He turned. Merry Meredith was coming toward him. Behind the intelligence officer, the M-100 merely looked like a natural blemish on the landscape. The automatic camouflage system had unfolded its fans, and the sensors read the tones of the earth, coloring the upper plates to match. The system was effective in every environment except snow. The plates could not go white and had to compromise on a mottled gray. But here, where the withered steppe remained naked to the wind, the camouflage worked magically. An enemy would have needed to know exactly where to look to find him and his men.

All this. The technology and the trying. The magic. And the sacrifice. Surely, it could not just end like this.

Meredith closed the distance. His skin was taut with cold, but his eyes had the old fire.

"Sir?" Meredith asked.

"What's up, Merry?"

"I've got an idea. Maybe you won't like it. But it's all I can come up with."

"About what?"

"The mission. There's a way we can still do it. Without the extra fuel."

"How?"

"Well, given that we don't have enough fuel to hit Baku and make it back to secure Soviet territory . . ."

"Given," Taylor agreed.

"Okay. Then where else could we go? After we hit Baku?"

Taylor looked questioningly at the younger man. Meredith's expression was that of an excited boy.

"What about Turkey?" the S-2 asked. "Okay, we don't

have the legs to get back. So we just keep going. I've calculated the distance. We can just barely make it. Head *west* out of Baku, right across Armenia, and put down inside the Turkish border. Turkey's remained neutral— the fundamentalist movement's an old nightmare there— and the Turks will obey international law. We'll have to scuttle the ships as soon as we set down. But at least we can accomplish the mission. They'll intern us until the end of hostilities—but so what? We'll at least get to strike a blow instead of going home with our tails between our legs . . ."

It was beautiful. And so simple. Taylor realized he would never have thought of it himself. He was too old, too well-conditioned. You had to bring your unit back to friendly lines. No matter what. Yet, history was full of examples of forces that had been thrust by circumstances onto neutral territory. The procedures were regulated by international codes.

And if he and his men missed the rest of the war? Well, if they didn't do it, there wouldn't be any war left to fight.

Taylor stared off to the south, imagining the sea rolling just beyond the horizon and the rest of the world beyond the sea.

"The State Department's going to hate it," Taylor said softly, as if a credentialed ambassador might be within earshot. But he was smiling. "What the hell. I've always wanted to see Turkey."

He held out his hand to the younger man.

Suddenly, a massive explosion colored the near horizon. The blast wave did not take long to reach them. Hot, rushing air pushed the southern wind aside. The noise, despite the distance of several kilometers, was deafening. The impact had been to the north, exactly where the Soviet fuelers had been designated to link up with the M-100s.

A second blast quickly followed the first.

"*Ambush*," Taylor shouted. "*It's a fucking ambush. The Russians sold us out.*"

The two men ran for the M-100.

Ryder had been standing just outside the rear ramp of the aircraft, relieving himself. As Taylor and Meredith ran toward him, the young man stood dumbfounded, watching the inferno spread across the rear horizon, penis in hand as though he intended to use it to put the fire out.

"Mount up, mount up," Taylor shouted, waving the helmet he still held in his hand.

Flapper Krebs had been quicker to grasp the situation than any of them. The M-100's engines were already whining to life.

"Merry," Taylor yelled, *"get on the horn. Get everybody up in the air."*

The large camouflage fans began to withdraw into the M-100's fuselage.

Taylor shoved Ryder up into the control compartment behind Meredith. He threw his helmet down on the floor, counting heads as he hustled toward the front of the aircraft. Behind him, Parker was already drawing up the ramp.

Taylor glanced furiously at Kozlov, whose face was utterly blank. He almost drew his pistol and shot the Russian on the spot. But he did not have the time to waste.

Taylor shoved the Soviet out of the way and ducked through the hatch that led toward the cockpit.

He jumped into his seat, grabbing his headset as he moved. He gave Krebs a thumb's up.

"Let's go."

The M-100 began to lift into the sky.

Across the horizon two big bursts colored the steppe bright orange, yellow, red. A border of black smoke began to expand above the fires. In quick succession, half a dozen more blasts erupted. Each one came closer to the ship as it struggled to gain altitude.

"Fucking Russians," Taylor growled into his headset. "Fucking goddamned Russians. They fucking set us up."

"Foxtrot one-four. Airborne. Over," the first of the other M-100s reported in. Then another ship called in, the voice of its pilot reflecting how badly shaken everyone had been by the surprise attack.

A ripple of explosions chased the M-100 into the sky.

"Rockets," the copilot reported drily. "Standoff, air-launched, looks like. Compact conventional explosives and fuel-airs. Couldn't have had too good a fix on us. We'd never have got off the ground."

The goddamned Russians, Taylor thought. They had never had the least intention of sending out refuelers. Instead, they had tipped off the Japanese or the Iranians as to the designated site. But for what? A better deal at the peace talks? For what?

Taylor thought of Kozlov and his mind whitened with anger.

"We've got a bird down." Parker's voice. Through the intercom.

"All stations, report in sequence," Taylor ordered.

"Bird down."

"It's One-five," another crew reported. *"He's gone. Fireball."*

Underneath the ship, a cushion of explosions buoyed them upward, rocking the cabin. Taylor had to clutch the sides of his seat.

"Altitude," he shouted, jamming his safety harness buckles together.

"I'm giving it all she's got," Krebs shouted back.

Merry's voice came through the intercom, struggling to remain calm. "Verify the loss of One-five. Too slow getting off the ground. She disappeared in the flames."

"All stations," Taylor barked into the mike, *"report, goddamnit."*

The other M-100s reported in sequence. Only One-five was missing. Everyone else was above the carpet of fire now.

"Merry," Taylor ordered, "start working on the new exfiltration route. Forget everything else. Hank," he called to the assistant S-3, "let's get back on the flight path. We're heading for Baku."

Krebs looked over at Taylor in doubt.

"Don't worry, Flapper. We've got a new plan."

The warrant officer shook his head.

Behind them, powerful explosions chased their tails with shock waves, bucking the speeding aircraft.

"Hank," Taylor called. "Try to call up some imagery of the spot where One-five went down. See if there's anything left."

"Roger."

Suddenly, the gray sky parted. Ahead of them a scudding green-gray sea stretched toward distant shores. The sight seemed to promise safety.

"You know," Taylor mused bitterly to Krebs, "their system must be in godawful shape. We must've really hurt them yesterday. By all rights, they should've gotten us back there." He could feel the sweat beginning to chill on his forehead. He stared out over the sea. It looked like steel mesh come to life. "The strike was too ragged. They should have hit us with everything at once."

"Imagery up," Parker's voice interrupted.

Taylor looked down at his central monitor. An X-ray radar image erased the flames and smoke to show the wreckage of an M-100 spread across several acres.

"Jesus," a voice whispered through the intercom.

Taylor touched the button that canceled the image.

"Forget it," he said in his coldest voice. "We got off lucky."

Nothing was going to stop him now. Not friendly losses. Not the Iranians or the rebels. Not the Japanese. Not even the Russians.

He slipped off his headset to rise from his seat. He wanted to talk to Kozlov. The sonofabitch had questions to answer.

The sound of Krebs's voice stopped him.

"Oh, fuck me," the old warrant said in disgust. He glanced over at Taylor. But Taylor did not need any further explanation. The flashing monitor made the situation very clear.

"I guess they wanted to make sure," Krebs said.

"*Bandits,*" Taylor called into the command net. "Nine o'clock high."

Krebs began to bank the ship upward to the left.

"I'll fly," Taylor said, grasping the manual controls. "You do the shooting."

Taylor's ops indicator showed the remaining four ships of his raiding force following his lead. But the formation was too neat, too predictable.

"One-one, One-two, this is Foxtrot one-zero. Go high. Work a sandwich on them. One-three, One-four, stay with me. Out."

Meredith's voice came over the intercom. "Good fix.

I've even got voice on them." Then he hesitated for a moment.

"What is it?" Taylor demanded.

"Japanese gunships. The latest Toshiba variant."

"Roger. Execute countermeasures program." The opposing formations were closing rapidly. Forty miles. Thirty-nine. "What else, Merry?"

Again, there was a slight hesitation.

"The voices," Meredith said, "sound like South Africans."

Taylor gripped the controls. Time playing tricks. Above the Caspian Sea.

So be it, he thought.

"Confirm activation of full countermeasures suite," Taylor said. He was determined not to let it shake him. There was nothing special about the South Africans. But he could not entirely resist the flashing images. A cocky young captain winging over the African scrub. Transformed into a terrified young captain. A pistol lifted to the head of a broken-necked boy. Ants at a man's eyes and a river journey through the heart of a dying continent.

Yes. Taylor remembered the South Africans.

Suddenly, his battle monitor fuzzed.

"The sonsofbitches," Krebs said. "They've got some new kind of shit on board."

"Merry," Taylor half-shouted, struggling to maintain control. "Hank. Hit them with full power. Jam the fuck out of them."

"Twenty-eight miles," Krebs said. "And closing."

The target-acquisition monitor distorted, multiplying and misreading images.

"Going full automatic on the weapons suite," Krebs said. "Let's hope this works."

Taylor felt sweat prickling all over his body. Frantically, he punched override buttons, trying to clear the monitors.

"Twenty-five . . ."

Taylor strained to see through the windscreen. The battle overlays were little help now. He struggled to pick out the enemy aircraft with his eyes.

"I've got them," Merry called forward. "Clear image."

"Transfer data to the weapons suite," Taylor ordered.

Other ships called in their sudden difficulties with their own electronics.

Remember, Taylor told himself, you're doing the same thing to the other guy. He's as frightened as you are. Stay cool, stay cool.

"Negative," Merry reported. "The weapons program won't accept the transfer."

"Range: twenty miles," Krebs told them all.

Abruptly, the M-100 bucked and began to pulse under Taylor's seat. The main gun was firing.

What does my enemy see? Taylor wondered. If the systems were functioning correctly, his opposite number was reading hundreds of blurred, identical targets, a swarm of ghost images in the midst of which the real M-100s were hiding. Or, depending on the parameters of his system, he might only be receiving static and fuzz.

Taylor slapped the eyeshield down from atop the headset.

"Laser alert," he said over the command net. Beside him, Krebs slid down his own shield.

The protective lenses darkened the sky, and the bucking of the M-100 as it maneuvered forward made it even harder to focus. Nonetheless, Taylor believed he could pick out the tiny black spots that marked the enemy.

He took full manual control of the aircraft and pointed it straight at the enemy.

"Full combat speed," he ordered. "Let's get them."

" 'Garry Owen,' " a voice replied from a sister ship.

"Thirteen miles," Krebs said. "We're not hitting a damned thing."

"Neither are they," Taylor said. Below the insulated cockpit, the main gun continued to pump out precious rounds, its accuracy deteriorating with every shot.

"I've still got good voice on them," Merry called. "They're going crazy. They've lost us. They're firing everything they've got."

"Ten miles."

Taylor looked out at the black dots. He counted ten. But he could not see the slightest trace of hostile action. The sky was full of high-velocity projectiles and lasers, but the M-100's rounds were far quicker than the human eye, while the enemy's current lasers were not tuned to the spectrum of visible light. Around the lethal balls and beams, the heavens pulsed with electronic violence. Yet all that was visible was the gray sky, and a line of swelling black dots on a collision course with his outnumbered element.

"Seven miles. Jesus Christ."

"Steady," Taylor said, his fear forgotten now.

Dark tubular fuselages, the blur of rotors and propellers.

It was, Taylor thought, like a battle between knights so heavily armored they did not possess the offensive technology to hurt each other. New magic shields deflected the other man's blows.

"Four miles," Krebs said. "Jesus, sir, we got to climb. We're on a collision course."

No, Taylor thought. If they haven't hit us yet at this angle, they won't. But the first man to flinch, to reveal a vulnerable angle, was going to lose.

The M-100 threw another series of rounds toward the closing enemy.

"All stations," Taylor said. *"Steady on course."*

"Two miles . . ."

The Toshiba gunships were unmistakable now. Their contours had not changed much over the years. A mongrelized forward aspect, a helicopter with turboprops on the sides. Or a plane with rotors. Take your pick.

"Hold course," Taylor shouted.

The M-100's cannon pummeled the sky. To no effect.

"One mile and closing . . ."

Where once horsemen rode at each other with sabers drawn, their descendants rode the sky in a long metal line, jousting with lightning.

Hit, goddamn it, hit, Taylor told the main gun.

He could see every detail on the enemy gunships now. The mock Iranian markings, the mottled camouflage. The low-slung laser pod.

"We're going to collide."

Taylor froze his hand on the joystick. Straight ahead.

In a buffeting wash of air and noise, the M-100 shot past the enemy's line.

"All stations," Taylor said. "Follow my lead. We've got a tighter turning radius than they do."

He felt far more confident now. The M-100's airframe was of a design over a decade fresher than the Toshiba gunships. The M-100 had all of the maneuvering advantages.

"Everybody with me?" Taylor demanded.

The other four ships reported in quick succession.

"Complete the turn. We're only vulnerable from the back."

He looked at his monitor. The fuzz cloud that marked the enemy had begun to turn too. But they were slower. He could feel it.

"Flapper," Taylor said. "Turn off the autosystems. They're just canceling each other out. Take manual control of the main gun. And use a little Kentucky windage."

"The accuracy's breaking down," Krebs said. "We're just about shot out."

"You can do it, Flapper. Come on. We didn't have all this fancy shit when you and I started out."

Krebs nodded, doubt on the lower portion of his face left visible by the laser shield.

"All stations," Taylor said. "Open order. Go to *manual* target acquisition and *manual* fire control."

The tight steepness of the turn tugged his harness. But they were almost out of it. And the enemy were still in midturn. There wouldn't be much time. But there would be a window of opportunity.

As nearly as he could remember, the Japanese gunships did not have a manual weapons override.

The sin of pride.

"Fire at will," Taylor said.

He guided the ship around as though he were reining a spirited horse. Soon he could visually track the black specks of the enemy formation describing a long arc across the sky. They looked clean. Very disciplined fliers.

Every one of his crews would be flying for themselves now. The American formation hardly existed as such. Instead, five M-100s speckled the sky, each seeking the best possible angle of attack.

Taylor applied full throttle, trying to get into his enemy's flank before the Japanese gunships could bring their weapons to bear.

"I don't know," Krebs said, hanging on the weapons control stick.

"Fuck you don't know," Taylor said. "*I* know. Take those fuckers out."

Krebs fired.

Nothing.

"Just getting a feel for the deflection," he excused himself. He sounded calmer now that he was committed to action.

Taylor flew straight for the center of the enemy formation. He watched the increasingly clear gunships coming into the last segment of their turns.

"Come on, baby," Krebs said. He fired again.

Instantaneously, a black gunship erupted in flames and left the enemy formation, its component parts hurtling through the sky in multiple directions.

Taylor howled with delight, eternally the wild young captain who had sailed dreamily into Africa.

"Well, fuck me," Krebs said in wonder. He fired again, pulsing out rounds.

Another Japanese gunship broke apart in the sky.

Remember me, Taylor told his enemy. *Remember me.*

In quick succession, two more Japanese gunships blazed and broke up. The other American ships were hitting.

There was very little time. The enemy systems defined themselves with greater clarity with each passing second. Taylor was afraid they would be able to come around at their own angle and sweep the sky with lasers in a crossfire effect.

Taylor stared hard at the enemy formation, trying to read the pattern.

"Flapper," he yelled suddenly. "Get the number three ship. That's the flight leader."

"Roger." Krebs had put his gruff old soldier voice back on. But, bubbling under the gray tones was the same unmistakable exhilaration that Taylor felt. The indescribable joy of destruction.

The old warrant officer followed the turn of the aircraft with his optics. He let go one round, then another.

The enemy's flight leader disappeared in a hot white flash. When the dazzle faded there were only black chunks of waste dropping into the sea.

Another of the enemy's aircraft exploded.

The remaining gunships began to abort their turns. Instead of trying to close with their tormentors, they were trying to escape.

Wrong decision, Taylor thought coldly. *"All stations, right wheel,"* he called, slipping unconsciously into an old cavalry command.

Two of the enemy's surviving gunships exploded in tandem, as though they had been taken out by a double-barreled shotgun.

Only two enemy ships remained. Taylor knew what they were feeling. The terror. The recognition that it was all over battling with the human tendency to hope against hope. And the frantic uncertainty that interfered with those functions it did not completely paralyze. But the knowledge did not move him.

They were on the enemy's rear hemisphere now. The attempt to flee was hopeless, since the American aircraft were faster. But the enemy pilots would not know that. At this point, the only thing they would know with any certainty was that they were still alive.

Taylor felt Krebs tense mercilessly beside him. The warrant sent off another succession of rounds.

A gunship spun around like a weathervane in a storm, breaking up even before the fire from its fuel tanks could engulf it. Then the familiar cloud of flames swelled outward, spitting odd aircraft parts.

A lone enemy survivor strained off to the southeast. Taylor could feel the pilot pushing for each last ounce of thrust, aching to go faster than physical laws allowed.

The lone black ship flared and fell away in a sputtering rain of components.

For a long moment no one spoke. The M-100s automatically slipped back into formation, conditioned by drill. But no drill had given them the language to express what they felt.

The sky was eerily clean.

"All stations," Taylor said finally. "Return to automatic flight controls. Next stop: Objective Blackjack."

Baku.

He took a deep breath.

"Flapper," he said, "I'm going back to have a little talk with our Russian friend."

"I *swear*," Kozlov said. His mouth was bleeding from Taylor's blow. "I swear I didn't know."

Taylor looked at him grimly. He wanted to open a hatch and push the Russian out into the sky. He did not know whether or not there were sharks in the Caspian Sea, but he hoped nature had not missed the opportunity to put some there.

Taylor felt another rush of fury, and he raised his fist.

"Don't," Meredith said suddenly. "I believe him."

Taylor looked at the S-2 in surprise, fist suspended in midair.

"Look at him," Meredith went on, with as little regard as if Kozlov could not hear a word that passed between them. "He's scared shitless. He's been that way since the refueling site. He didn't have a clue." Meredith made a spitting gesture with his lips. "The poor bastard's just a staff officer with a toothache, not some kind of suicide volunteer. Ivanov set him up too."

Taylor lowered his fist. But he did not unclench it. He glowered. "Goddamnit," he said to Kozlov, "I just want to know one thing. Give me one straight goddamned answer, if you fucking Russians are biologically capable of it. All that shit about the layout of the headquarters in Baku—were you telling the truth? Was that sketch accurate? Or were you just making it all up?"

Kozlov opened his mouth to speak. Two of the bad front teeth had disappeared. The mouth wavered and shut, blood streaming out onto the Russian's chin, streaking down into his uniform. He spit into his sleeve, then tried a second time to squeeze out the words. "Everything . . . everything is true. You see? I am here with you. I, too, believed."

Taylor shook his head, turning away in disgust.

"I trust him too," Ryder said. It was the first time Ryder had spoken in Taylor's presence since the flight began. Taylor almost snapped at him. But Hank Parker spoke first:

"He's straight, sir. I'd bet my bars."

Taylor suddenly felt like a big cat in a small cage. "Goddamnit," he said, turning back to Kozlov, "your country gets at least as much out of this operation as mine does."

"I understand," Kozlov said cautiously, sick gums still bleeding.

"Then *why?* Why did Ivanov do it?"

"I don't know."

"Why sell out your only friends? Christ, nobody in the world has any sympathy for you except us. Who else tried to save your asses?"

Kozlov looked down at the deck in shame. "I do not understand." He wiped his chin on his sleeve again. "Perhaps there was a mistake. I don't know."

Taylor punched his blistered hand against a side panel. It hurt. In anger, he tore off the fresh bandage that had been applied before the mission lifted off.

The pain felt right. Good. None of it made sense anymore.

"I don't know, either," Taylor said wearily.

"We need him," Meredith said. "We're going to need him on the ground."

Taylor nodded. "All right." He turned to Kozlov. "But one false step, and I'll shoot you myself."

Kozlov nodded solemnly. He was very pale and the blood smeared over the bottom of his face was very red. He seemed physically smaller now, as if shame had crumpled him, and Taylor felt almost as though he had struck a child.

"And no gun," Taylor added. "You do the guiding. We'll handle the fireworks."

Kozlov nodded again, accepting this further humiliation.

Taylor turned to Hank Parker, dismissing the Russian from his immediate concern. He leaned in over the battle control console. Then he straightened abruptly.

"Viktor," he said, facing Kozlov across the small cell. The Russian was feeling in his mouth with his fingers. "I want you to tell me one more thing honestly. Did you . . . did your people know anything about the Scramblers? Did you *choose* not to warn us?"

Kozlov wiped his bloody fingers on the side of his trousers. He coughed and his throat sounded crowded with waste. "*I* didn't know. I knew nothing personally . . ." He hesitated. Then he continued with a new resolution: "General Ivanov knew something. Honestly, I do not know how much he knew. He said nothing to me until . . . afterward."

"You people," Taylor said, shaking his head in disgust. The tone of his voice reached an odd pitch between fury and resignation. "Does *any*body in your country remember how to tell the truth?"

Kozlov shrugged slightly, drawing his shoulders together as if trying to disappear into himself. He could not meet Taylor's eyes.

Unexpectedly, the strategic communications set sparked to life: a totally unwelcome interruption. A tired voice fumbled through the call signs at the distant end. Even Washington was growing weary.

Meredith acknowledged.

"Is Colonel Taylor at your location?" the communications officer asked from the other side of the world.

"Roger. Standing by."

"Going to visual relay."

"Check."

"Hold for the President of the United States."

Oh, shit, Taylor thought, longing for the days when monarchs were weeks or months away from the soldier's camp.

To everyone's surprise, the familiar face of President Waters did not fill the monitor. Instead, the Vice President appeared, looking handsomely tanned and healthy, except for some tiredness around the eyes. When Taylor stepped in front of the monitor, the Vice President winced. The two men had never met.

Vice President Maddox recovered smoothly and leaned forward again, body language suggesting a generous intimacy.

"Colonel Taylor?" he asked.

"Yes, Mr. Vice President."

An odd expression passed across the distant man's face. Then he said: "Colonel Taylor, I'm the *President* now. As of about an hour ago, as a matter of fact. President Waters suffered a fatal heart attack in his sleep this morning."

"Yes, sir," Taylor said flatly, calculating as swiftly as he could the implications for his mission. Nothing else mattered now.

"Colonel Taylor, it sounds as though you're not alone."

"That's correct, sir. Several members of my staff are present."

The new President glanced off to the side. It seemed as though he was about to speak to another party off-camera. Then he faced the screen again and said:

"Could you clear the room or whatever it is you're in? I'd like to talk to you privately."

Bad sign. The only question was: how bad? Another time Taylor might have stated that his staff needed to continue at their posts. But he sensed it would be a fatal move at this junction.

"Merry," he said, turning from the monitor for a moment.

"Yes, sir," Meredith said. He quickly began shepherding the others into the narrow passageway that led to the cockpit. Hank Parker went first, heading for the cockpit itself, since he was flight-qualified and could reasonably lay a claim to the comfort of Taylor's forward seat.

After a few awkward seconds, the compartment was clear and the internal hatch had been shut.

"I'm alone now, Mr. President."

Maddox nodded, chewing slightly at his lower lip. It was evident that he was trying to get past the shock of Taylor's scars, to size up the total package.

"Colonel Taylor," he began in a voice that belonged on a veranda in the Deep South, "I did not want to embarrass you in front of your subordinates . . . however, it appears to me that the mission upon which you are presently embarked . . . may be ill-advised."

Taylor didn't blink. He had been preparing himself for this.

"Why, Mr. President?"

Maddox looked surprised. Taylor heard an off-camera voice say:

"You don't need to explain anything to him, Mr. President. All you have to do is tell him to turn his ass around and he'll by God do it."

"Colonel Taylor," Maddox picked up, "I'm afraid there may be insufficient time to explain all of our . . . considerations. I am directing you to terminate your mission immediately."

"Mr. President," Taylor said desperately, struggling not to sound as desperate as he felt, "we're almost at the objective area. In one hour—"

"Colonel, I don't intend to argue with you. The best minds in Washington have advised me to put a halt to whatever it is you're up to over there. So just turn yourself around and head on back to wherever it is you started from. You've done a fine job up until now, and, I can assure you, your country's grateful to you."

"No," Taylor said.

Maddox looked at him in disbelief. "What did you say?"

"No, Mr. President. I will not abort this mission. I believe you are receiving bad advice from men who do not understand the situation here in-theater. I have never before disobeyed an order, least of all from my president. But I believe my duty is clear. I intend to execute this mission, as directed by President Waters."

"By *God*, Colonel, you're going to do what—"

Taylor switched off the strategic link. Then he unlatched the encryption insert, withdrew it, swung it with all his strength against the deck, and inserted it again, doing up the latch as if nothing had happened. Farewell to Washington.

He went forward and opened the internal hatch that led to the cockpit passageway.

In the faint light, the crammed officers looked ridiculous, huddled against each other like college students playing some prank. Taylor could smell Kozlov's decayed, bloody breath bathing them all.

"Gentlemen," Taylor said, "the President of the United States died this morning, of natural causes. The Vice President has been sworn in and has assumed the presidency. There have been no difficulties with the transition process. Now," he bent to help Ryder up out of the tangle of limbs and torsos, "we've got a mission to run."

Maddox sat bolt upright. He was angry. He could not recall the last time he had been so angry, but he knew it had been a matter of years, if not decades.

"Well." He looked around the room, disgusted by the extent of the mess he had inherited. "You heard him. Now what in the hell are you all going to do about it?" He looked at the secretary of state, then at the chairman of the Joint Chiefs of Staff. The old general just shook his head in amazement. He'll definitely have to go, Maddox thought. In good time. Couldn't stage an immediate massacre of *all* Waters's appointees.

"Mr. President," the secretary of state began, "perhaps we could alert the Japanese. Make it clear to them that this is a maverick action."

Absolutely worthless, Maddox thought. How did Waters ever manage with such a hopeless bunch?

"Mr. Secretary," Maddox began, stretching out the syllables as though he were speaking on the hottest of summer afternoons, "you might talk me into a lot of things. But you are *not* about to talk me into selling out American soldiers to our enemies. And I don't care how crazy this ugly sonofabitch of a colonel is. Hasn't anybody got any sensible ideas?"

"Court-martial?" the chairman of the Joint Chiefs said meekly.

Maddox glared at him. "General"—he pronounced the title with only two syllables—"I had something a bit more immediate in mind."

The chairman shook his head. "Too late, sir. We couldn't even begin to intercept them. And I know Colonel Taylor. He'll have everybody restricted to one net, and he'll hide that with skip frequencies. From a military standpoint . . . I'm afraid there's nothing we can do but watch. And hope for the best."

Maddox was appalled. "Hellfire," he said. "You-all just

tell me one thing, and I want a straight answer. Has this sonofabitch got a chance in hell of pulling this caper off?''

"Oh, he's got a chance," the chairman said. "About one chance in hell, exactly. Maybe two chances in hell, considering that it's George Taylor."

President Maddox was unhappy. This did not strike him as an auspicious start to his presidency, and even if that presidency was only going to last until the swearing in of the other party's candidate in January, he did not intend to smear himself with any avoidable shame.

"You boys," he said disgustedly. "I swear to God, I just don't know." He faced the secretary of state, but he spoke to the room at large. "I'll tell you what we're going to do. If this fellow screws it all up and lives to tell about it, we're going to court-martial him and everybody in uniform who can so much as spell his name." Maddox sat back. For the first time all day, he felt as though he were actually in charge. "On the other hand, if the sonofabitch pulls it off and kicks him some ass, everyone in this room is going to forget that this conversation took place." He looked methodically from face to face. "You-all understand me?"

Valya entered the hotel bar alone. Clutching her purse to steady her hands, she scanned the musty interior as she made her way through the clutter of early drinkers and women for sale. The Americans were in uniform now, and they stood a bit straighter. Sudden laughter splashed out of the gloom, but it sounded formal and forced to her ears. She saw no one whom she recognized.

It was impossible. She could not do it.

She settled herself on a barstool, trying to project a graceful sexuality. But it was terribly difficult. Her buttocks ached where she had been kicked by her interrogator, and there was no comfort left in the small saddle of flesh beneath her dress.

She tried to adjust her eyes to the brown air, still searching the profiles grouped around back tables. The Russian women smoked heavily, and the dreary lighting barely penetrated the depths of the room. But that was all right. Valya touched her face anxiously. She had layered herself with far more makeup than was her custom in an attempt to disguise her bruises. Thankfully, most of the swelling had gone down. Only the discoloration remained.

She had kept herself on course with the faint hope that her American boy would be here after all, her lover of a single night, and that he would smile and wave, coming anxiously toward her, wondering only why she had been unable to meet him as promised the night before, offering salvation.

But her boy was not there. No one was going to magically rescue her. Ignored by the bartender, she leaned onto the counter, struggling to see. Her boy was not there. And neither was the man to whom her tormentors had consigned her.

Then she saw him. With his back three-quarters to her. He swung his jaw back over a heavy shoulder to bark at a waiter in English. A silver ornament and colored device decorated his shoulder strap.

She could not do it. She did not have the strength.

She rose carefully from her barstool, avoiding as much of the pain in her rump as she could. It was hard to imagine bearing the weight of a man on top of her now. She felt bruised to the bone. But, she reminded herself, there were worse things in the world, as the security officers had been glad to point out.

There were no women at the man's table. It was still early, and the man and his comrades were drinking brown bottles of beer and talking. Valya hunted her way between the tables, catching an already-sore hip on the jut of a chair. She tried to walk with dignity, while her insides sickened. The big man turned and called to the waiter again, with less patience this time.

She could not do it. She had no idea where the words would come from.

She paused for a moment, aching for an excuse not to continue. She would have been glad of an incontestable physical illness, one so fierce it would give her tormentors pause. She thought again of the darkened room, the single lamp, of questions and irresistible blows. She remembered the threats, and how it felt to lie soaking on a concrete floor.

One foot in front of the other, she told herself. Just like a soldier. It won't be anything. You've been through far worse.

She stopped behind the man's chair, waiting for him to notice her. But he was speaking rapidly to the two other men at the table. Finally one of his listeners looked up in Valya's direction. A moment later, the big man's head turned to seek out the new attraction, twisting coils of fat over his collar.

"Hello," Valya said.

The big man looked up at her with a mix of curiosity and suspicion. He said nothing.

"We have met," Valya went on.

The big man nodded. "I know that."

"The other night," Valya said, fighting to remain calm. She wanted to cry and run away. Instead, she tried to outfit her voice with the easy sexuality of a woman in a film. "I was with my friend. Her name is Tanya."

"I know," the big man said. "I never forget a woman who walks away from me with a full drink on the table."

Their eyes met fully for the first time. Valya saw hatred in the dark pupils.

I cannot do this, she told herself.

She laid a hand on the man's shoulder, resting her fingers over a cold colored shield. She felt as though she had been forced to touch a snake. But she kept her hand in place.

She smiled as richly as she could manage. "Oh," she said, laughing, "this is such a misunderstanding. But I thought you did not find me to be attractive. I thought you wanted me to go away. I believed you to be in love with Tanya."

The big American's eyes softened just a little. Then his face widened with a smile full of big white American teeth. Meant to devour their American steaks, Valya thought.

"Me?" the man laughed. *"Me?* In love with old Tanya?" His drinking companions joined in the laughter. "Wouldn't that be the day?"

"You hurt my feelings," Valya lied. "I thought you wanted for me to go away." She tried to remember a few colloquial English phrases of the sort not taught in the Soviet school system. "You made such eyes for Tanya."

"I didn't know you had the hots for old Tanya, Bill," one of the other drinkers said. "Didn't know she was your type."

The big man laughed again, but less forcefully this time. "Old Tanyer," he said. "Now that gal's been drove hard and put away wet. Wouldn't nobody but Jimbo take that mare for a ride."

The third man shook his head as if he had tasted something foul. "Old Jim's blind as a bat."

"I think Jimbo just likes a lot of bacon on his gals," the big man said. His accent made it hard to catch all of his words. He still had not moved to shake off Valya's hand, and she warmed it back and forth on the heavy shoulder. "Christ," the big man said, "I remember him way back when at Huachuca. Sonofabitch was always over in Naco or Agua Prieta jumping some big Mex gal. Almost lost his clearance."

"Those were the days," the third man agreed. "At least them Mex gals had sense enough to wash every so often." He looked up at Valya, then down along the trace of her figure, then back into her eyes. His face bore an expression of incomparable insolence.

The big man turned out from under Valya's hand. She thought he was going to send her away. She nearly panicked. She was ready to do anything, to get down on her knees. She saw the huge, soft-faced interrogator standing over her again. And the younger, handsome officer, telling her that they merely wanted her to befriend someone for them, saying it in an easy tone that threatened the end of the world.

The big man kicked a chair back from under the table. "Have a seat," he told Valya. "What are you drinking?"

Valya half-tripped down into the chair. Her backside hit with force, and her backbone shook with a presentiment of age. It took her a moment to relax into the pain.

"Anything," she said. "It does not matter. Something strong."

Suddenly the big man leaned in close to Valya, inspecting her. She cringed back into the bad light.

The big man whistled. "Jeez. Your boyfriend give you that shiner, honey-pie?"

Valya could feel her face swelling with the blood of embarrassment. "An accident," she said. "I have fallen down the stairs."

The big man smiled slightly and sat back. "Yeah, I guess I fell down them stairs a couple times myself."

He reached around behind Valya and jerked her chair next to his. He settled a big hand on her far shoulder, then trailed it down her side before halting it on the swell of her bottom.

He nodded, figuring. "You're a skinny little gal," he said, "but I guess you'll do." He leaned in close so that his friends could not hear. His lips brushed Valya's hair. He smelled like a puddle of stale beer.

"One hundred American dollars," he said, "and not a penny more."

24

4 November 2020

NOBURU DREAMED OF A YELLOW HORSE BY A SALT LAKE.
He approached the horse, but the animal paid him no
attention. Browsing over tufts of stunted grass, the animal
appeared weary beyond description, and its back was so
badly bowed that a child's weight might have broken it.
Noburu himself wore a fine English suit, but he had come
away without his cuff links. He was searching for his cuff
links on the sandy waste, and he feared that the horse
might devour them by mistake. He called out to the animal. He knew its name. And the horse raised its head,
swiveling dully in Noburu's direction. The yellow horse
was blind. Disease had whitened its eyes. It soon turned
its nose back to the dying grass.

Brown men came. Out of nowhere. Coming from all
sides. They rushed slim-legged from the sea, wailing in a
foreign language. Noburu assumed they had come to
slaughter the horse. He ran toward the uninterested
animal, determined to shield it in his arms. But the
brown men were not immediately concerned with the
horse. Noburu had been mistaken. They were coming for
him.

Countless hands slithered over him, catching his limbs
in small firm grips. They had made a cross of light from
antique headlamps, and they intended to crucify him. He
struggled, for he sensed that hanging from that cross of

light would be the most painful of tortures. But the mob had him in its power. Their hands grew in strength, clamping him. He smelled the foreign spice of their breath. He tried to reason with them, explaining that he could not possibly be crucified without his cuff links. It was impossible to think that he might end like that, badly dressed in public.

Then the dragon came out of the sky. The world burned. He could see the profile of the Imperial Palace in Tokyo, dark against the flames. He could not quite see the dragon. It was dark and shapeless. But he knew it was there. He could feel the wash of wind slapped earthward by its wings. The brown men were gone. In their place, the dead approached him, in moldering uniforms. Crippled by plague, with white skulls showing beneath old flesh, they limped hungrily toward him. And he knew them. He had known them for a long, long time. They were old acquaintances from his personal darkness. But they had never come so close before. The most terrible one of them all lunged forward, reaching for Noburu with fingers of light.

"They're coming back," Akiro said.

Noburu set his nose to the wind. The scent of death. He had tried to nap, to rest a little. But it would have been far better to remain awake. His dreams were on a collision course with reality. Hungover with visions, he had staggered back to his vantage point atop the headquarters roof.

Yes. You could hear them now. Climbing back up the hill in the retreating light. The brown men. Singing.

"I cannot understand it," Akiro said. "I cannot understand it." He was not speaking to Noburu now, but to himself, in the vacant tone of a man confronted with the collapse of all his certainties—and with the simultaneous prospect of death.

"Has the ammunition been cross-leveled?" Noburu asked. He touched the silly skullcap bandage on his head. It had loosened during his nap. His mind was still unsure of what was real. The dream warrior danced on a ragged carpet of facts. Noburu felt drugged after his healthless sleep, and the unearthly singing and chanting out in the streets seemed to weave the world of dreams into the pattern of common existence.

"*Sir,*" Akiro answered, glad to busy himself with a concrete matter. "The redistribution is complete. The men have an average of eighteen rounds per automatic rifle. We have also brought in a number of irregular weapons taken from enemy casualties. There are approximately seventy rounds per machine gun. One grenade for every two men."

Yes. So much had been unforeseen. The mob climbed steadily up through the streets, preceded by its medieval wail. The ammunition might suffice to beat off the first rush, if they were lucky.

"Still no direct communications with the rear, or with Tokyo?" Noburu asked.

Akiro hung his head. "The situation seemed to be improving. Then, an hour ago, the interference began again."

"The same parameters as last night?"

"No. Different. The communications officer says that last night's attack was barrage jamming. He calls the present effort leech-and-spike."

What could it mean? In the course of his military career, Noburu had never been so utterly cut off from information. He had come to take ease of communication for granted. Now, at too old an age, he had been transported back through the centuries, to fight his last battle in darkness.

Well, he thought, it did not make so great a difference now. Even had the communications leapt suddenly back to life, it would have been too late. The friendly forces were too far away. He had scoured the map, analyzing the undeveloped road network from the standpoint of both a relief column and an interdiction effort. And the advantage was all on the side of his enemies. In an hour, perhaps sooner, the foreign, foreign faces would come over the walls for the last time, blowing in the doors, clambering through the windows. It was finished.

He wanted to say something to cheer up Akiro, to buoy him to the last. But the words would not come. Even his language had failed him in the end.

"Come on," Noburu said. "We'll try a last broadcast. For form's sake."

They went down through the arteries of the headquarters building, stepping between the lines of wounded men lying in the hallways. Here and there, a conscious soldier tried to rise at the passage of his commanding officer. But each attempt failed. Two officers and an enlisted helper shuffled boxes of documents into the room where the paper shredder was kept. You could smell the heat of the machine as you passed by, and Noburu caught a glimpse of disembodied hands dealing papers into the device's gullet. The days of careful document control and neatly logged numbers were over.

They negotiated a stretch of hallway cluttered with bureaucratic tools but no men, and Noburu halted Akiro by grasping his arm.

"Someone," Noburu said, "has been designated to . . . look after the wounded? Just in case?"

"Sir," Akiro said sadly. "The necessary ammunition has been set aside. Two NCOs have received the task."

"Reliable men?" Noburu asked.

Akiro hesitated for a moment. In the space of little more than a day, his armor of self-assurance had been reduced to a coat of rags.

"The best we could find," the aide finally replied.

It was a terrible waste, Noburu thought. For the first time, he began to feel a measure of real affection toward the younger man. Akiro was learning to empathize with his fellow man at last. But the development had come too late.

But that was eternally true, Noburu realized. Understanding always came too late. It certainly had come too late in his own case.

They passed the room where the master computer culled through its electronic dreams, unperturbed. The computer had been left running, but its consoles were locked so that no outsider could enter it without possessing an unbreakable complex of codes. For the mob the machine would be a useless prize. But if the Azeris did not physically destroy it, the computer would be invaluable after its recapture by the relief column.

553

And the relief column would come. Eventually. It just was not going to come in time to save the defenders of the compound. Noburu could feel that much in his old soldier's bones.

He stopped, then backtracked a few steps and opened the door to the computer room. The machine glowed in the soft light, unattended. Looking in on it, Noburu felt as one of his ancestors might have felt in saying good-bye to a favorite horse in its stall. Noburu had ridden the magical horses of a new age to an unanticipated end. In the final hour there was no warm coat to stroke, no eyes asked affection, there was no wet nuzzling. The machine simply moaned to itself, ticked, and sailed off into its galaxies of numbers.

Noburu, who still imagined himself to have been hardened by the years, found it uncharacteristically bitter to reflect that this machine was worth far more to his country than any combination of men. He himself, along with all of his principal officers, down to the assistant of the helper's helper, meant nothing beside the power and splendor of this machine. The machines made war now, while the men involved simply meandered through a waking dream of bygone glories.

No. He knew that, even now, it was not true. The glib formula was as false as everything else in his life had been.

He closed the door on the bright machine, leaving its fate for other men to determine. Tokyo could still send an electronic self-destruct message, should they so choose. It was not up to him. It would have embarrassed him, even under the present circumstances, to reveal to Akiro that he, the senior officer in the theater of war, did not have sufficient personal authority to order the destruction of a master computer.

They entered the operations center. The room was astonishingly calm. The well-staffed excitement of modern warfare had given way to a watch consisting of a single officer and NCO, while the rest of the logisticians and programmers, technical advisers and fire support specialists, were up above ground, manning a thin line of final defensive positions.

"The radio set is over here," Akiro said, leading the

way. Noburu followed him to an antique Soviet-built radio, something he might reasonably have expected to see only in a military museum.

"And this . . . seems to work?" Noburu asked.

"It's the only way we were able to establish contact with anyone," Akiro answered. "It's an old VHF set. The loyal garrisons are using them. But the jamming is very bad."

How he had laughed at the ancient gear with which the Soviets had been equipped. It seemed there would be no end to his lessons in humility.

No. That was wrong. There would be an end soon enough.

"It works . . . the same way?" Noburu asked. Even as a lieutenant, he had never handled anything so crude.

"The same way. You press this, then speak into the microphone."

"But no one has answered?"

"Not for hours."

Noburu picked up the chipped microphone. He looked at the younger man to ensure he was doing everything correctly.

"We have the call sign Castle," Akiro added.

Noburu pressed the button to transmit. "Any listening station, this is Castle . . . this is Castle. We are under siege by indigenous elements . . . and require immediate support." These old sets were not secure, of course. It was impossible to enumerate the concerns he felt required to address as a professional soldier. There was as much chance now that his enemies were listening in as that his own side would monitor the broadcast. ". . . Let it be recorded that the subordinate officers and men of this command served the Emperor honorably . . . and fought to the last man." The words felt wooden in his mouth. But he owed his men at least that. The final tribute of their commander. But he could not bring himself to end on a note of false enthusiasm. "This is Castle. End of transmission."

The two men stood over the old radio in the big quiet. The operations center held the silence of a theater after a performance, when even the janitors had gone home. Each man, in his different way, hoped that the radio would crackle to life on its own, bringing them words of hope, news of an approaching relief column, or at least the acknowledgment that some distant station knew they were still alive. But there was nothing.

Noburu looked at the younger man. Despite the marks of weariness on his face, Akiro looked impossibly young. Noburu wished he could send the boy back to a safe office in the General Staff complex or to some overheated academy classroom. And to the young wife Akiro had neglected, as all ambitious young officers neglected their wives. Simply, he wished he could send Akiro back to the world where grown men played at being soldiers and still had their lives ahead of them.

Noburu took the younger man by the arm, a little surprised that Akiro was every bit as warm to the touch as were other men. This little staff tiger.

"Come," he told the younger man. "We'd better go back upstairs."

They made their way back to the helipad on the roof. Colonel Kloete was still on guard, with the stump of a cigarette in one hand and his other hand holding fast to his light machine gun. Beside him, the surviving South African NCO slumped with his eyes closed. It was impossible to tell whether the man was merely resting or deep in sleep. Noburu had to admire the arrogantly casual attitude of the South Africans toward their impending deaths. But each culture faced the inevitable in its own way.

And the inevitable was approaching. The enormous chanting of the mob had virtually surrounded the headquarters complex, although the bulk of the Azeris remained out of sight, hidden in buildings, alleyways, behind rubble, walls, and wreckage. Only a few stray figures could be seen, scuttling through the twilight. The mob was marshaling its strength, just below the crest of the hill. Beyond the no-man's-land of burned-out ruins.

Kloete sucked down a last dose of smoke and flicked the butt over the wall. His features remained hard and clear in the deserting light.

"Noisy bunch," he said. "Aren't they, General?"

Noburu nodded. Kloete had never been too anxious to

pay a full measure of military courtesy to Noburu, and he made no move to rise or salute. His attitude seemed to say, "We're all equal now and we'll be even more equal before the sun comes up again."

"You have ammunition?" Noburu asked, touching the bandage layered over his scalp. It had begun to itch.

Kloete grinned. "Enough to make the little buggers angry. After that, I can just take this thing apart"—he slapped his weapon—"and throw the bloody pieces at them."

The chanting stopped. Initially, a few ragged voices continued, but they soon faltered into the gathering darkness. In the absence of the vast wailing, the racket of a later age was clearly audible: heavy machines on the move.

"The relief column," Akiro declared, his voice sweet with wonder.

Noburu caught him by the shoulder. "No. If it were the relief column, they'd be shooting."

Above the mechanical growling, a single high voice sang out. It sounded like a Moslem call to prayer.

In reply, the crowd howled so loudly that the concrete shivered beneath Noburu's boots.

Kloete reared up, staring into the fresh pale night settling over the courtyard and the walls.

"Tanks," he shouted. *"The bastards have tanks."*

In agreement, the first main gun sounded. The round hit the far wing of the headquarters complex, sending a shock wave through the air.

"Here they come," a Japanese voice screamed from a lateral position.

With a wave of noise, the crowd surged out of the shadows. Off in the distance, on the fringe of the city, the slums were burning, cordoning off the city with fire. Why was it, Noburu wondered, that in times of disruption the poor burned themselves out first? Despair? A desire to be clean of their scavenged lives?

A single Japanese weapon opened up nearby, then stopped firing after expending a few rounds. His men were holding their fire, waiting until they could get the highest return on each bullet paid out. They did not need orders now. Every man understood.

Noburu could see three tanks crawling toward the gate and the breaches in the wall. It was hard to listen past the thunder of the crowd, but it sounded as if even more tanks were following the first machines.

That was it, then. There were no antitank weapons. No one had imagined a need for them here.

The tanks fired above the crowd, hammering the headquarters building with their guns. The shots seemed random and undisciplined. But they could not help having an effect.

The quickest members of the mob dashed through the gate and scrambled over the breaches in the wall. They stumbled across mounds of shattered masonry, firing wildly and shrieking.

The Japanese held their fire.

Kloete drew out a lean commando knife and teased it twice over the broken stucco that lipped the roof before returning it to its sheath.

"Sir," Akiro cried, "you must take cover."

Noburu turned to the younger man. Akiro stood upright beside him, unwilling to go to ground before his superior did so. But the aide's eyes glowed with fear in the dusk.

"In a moment," Noburu said. He wanted to look his death in the face.

Akiro began to speak again, then choked and staggered against Noburu, grasping the general with uncustomary rudeness. Noburu had felt the warm wet of the young man's blood peck at his own face.

The aide clutched Noburu's arm, astonished. He remained on his feet, with his insides slipping out of his ripped trousers. He looked at Noburu with the innocence of an abused pet dog.

"Akiro," Noburu said.

The aide relaxed his grip on his master and collapsed onto the cement. Freed from the constraints of muscles and tight flesh, the young man's lower internal organs flowed out of him as though fleeing his death and attempting to survive on their own.

Akiro's eyes remained open, and his head moved slightly on the intact axis of his spine. He looked at Noburu with a hopefulness the older man could not bear, as though

Akiro expected the wise old general to fix him and make everything right again.

"Akiro," Noburu said, reaching out to steady the boy's twitchings, which continued to expel the contents of his torso.

The aide's lips made a word that Noburu could not decipher.

"Akiro," Noburu repeated.

The tension went out of the boy's body, and the terrible vibrancy left his eyes.

Kloete opened up with the light machine gun, firing short bursts and cursing. The other machine guns kicked in, as did a few automatic rifles. Noburu kept waiting for the rest of his men to open fire. Then he realized that there were no others.

He picked up Akiro's automatic rifle, wiped off the wet mortality on his trousers, and knelt beside Kloete and the South African NCO. The three men fired over the edge of the roof. Noburu had stopped thinking now. He gave himself up to the trance of action, trying to fire as calmly as if he were on range.

The lead tank surged ahead of the crowd. It shot point-blank into the headquarters, following the main gun round with bright tracers from its machine gun. Tides of bodies fell to the Japanese weaponry, but there seemed to be no end to the mob. The space between the headquarters and the wall grew dense with the living and the dead.

In the blaze of the firefight, Noburu saw one of his men dash from a side door, charging without a rifle. In the last seconds before the man threw himself on top of the tank, Noburu recognized the swell of the grenade in the man's hand.

The explosion drove the nearest members of the mob to their knees. But it did not stop the tank.

"Sonofa*bitch,*" Kloete spat. The machine gun had clicked empty.

The tank fired again. The building shook beneath them.

The South African NCO fixed a bayonet to his rifle. Kloete drew out his sidearm. He stood up carelessly, cursing and leading his targets, one by one. Noburu fired and watched a dark form tumble.

The line of machine gun tracers crisscrossed down below as the remaining Japanese fired their final protective fires.

Noburu heard a noise that did not fit.

Something was wrong. There was a great hissing, a new noise for which he could not account. Up in the sky. As though enormous winged snakes were descending from the heavens. Dragons.

The lead tank disappeared in a huge white flash that dazzled Noburu's eyes. A stunning bell-like sound was followed by an explosion. His vision of the world crazed into a disorderly mosaic. But he could see the tank burning.

"I can't *see*," the South African NCO howled. "I can't *see*."

The explosion had been as bright as a sun come to earth. The tremendous force of the impact made Noburu's head throb under its disordered bandage. He tried to see into the sky.

Two more explosions drew his eyes back to the earth.

Thank God, he thought, sinking down into himself. Oh, thank God. He found the thought that he was going to live unexpectedly pleasant.

The hissing and sizzling grew louder. The drone of engines began to emerge from under the cowls of their noise suppressors.

Someone had heard. Someone had monitored one of the radio transmissions. Someone had managed to muster an air-mobile relief force.

Kloete glanced over at Noburu between shots.

"Looks like your mates came through," he said. Then he straight-armed his pistol down at the mob.

The massed attackers wavered at the destruction of their armored support. The tanks had promised them a magic victory. Now the tanks were gone. In the midst of the swarm, high voices sang out prayerlike encouragements.

Noburu still could not see the relief aircraft in the darkened sky. He tried to place them by the sound of their engines. But his ears were ringing. The blast had shocked his senses. And his hearing was half-gone at the best of times.

Nonetheless, it annoyed him that he could not identify the hissing, descending ships.

Whatever kind they were, they were welcome.

As if at an invisible signal, the mob surged forward again. In the suddenness of the rush, the lead figures gained the building. Noburu rose to his full height to spend his last bullets where they were most needed. But he could already hear the distinct echo of fighting inside the headquarters.

Perhaps the relief force would be too late after all. By minutes.

He followed a running figure through the firelight, leading him carefully with his sights. When he was certain he had the man, he squeezed the trigger.

Nothing.

He drew out his pistol. But the man he had targeted had already made his way to the shelter of the building. Down in the belly of the headquarters, something exploded.

"Your boys are fucking *slow,*" Kloete screamed. "They're too fucking *slow.*"

Noburu fired and dropped a running man. The figure rolled over, clutching his knee.

There were too many of them. The attackers were already swinging themselves up to enter the building's second floor windows, leaving no point of entry untried. The last Japanese gun had been silenced.

The noise of the aircraft loomed in heavily. A pillar of fire descended from the heavens, followed by another, then a third. Noburu recognized the accompanying noise: Gatling guns.

Heavy bullets rinsed over the packed courtyard. The rounds were so powerful that they did not merely fell their victims but shredded them and threw the remnants great distances.

Kloete ducked, hugging the roof. Noburu followed his example. The South African was laughing like a wild man, his behavior insanely inconstant.

Beyond the lip of the wall, the fury of the crowd turned to wails of despair. Noburu could feel the intruders scrambling to avoid the godlike weapons, and he could picture the oversize rounds rinsing back and forth across the courtyard. Sometimes the old weapons were the best.

Noburu went cold. Underneath him, the sounds of combat within the headquarters building punctuated his horror.

He had realized that none of the new Japanese systems in the theater of war mounted Gatling guns.

Behind him, the dream warrior laughed and laughed and laughed.

The sound of the aircraft was deafeningly close now. He could begin to make out their swollen black forms against the deep blue sky. Each time one of the ships unleashed another burst from its Gatling gun, the cone of fire was shorter, closer. The Gatling rounds made a sharp crackling sound as they split the cobblestones amid the dead and the dying.

"Americans," Noburu said to Kloete.

Perhaps the noise was too much. The South African merely stared at him in incomprehension.

"The Americans," Noburu shouted, cupping a hand beside his mouth.

Kloete looked at him as if the general had gone mad.

The rotor wash began tearing at their clothes. The big ships were settling, hunting for places to nest.

The dream warrior howled with glee, goading Noburu to laugh along.

No. He was not giving up so easily. He pushed the phantom away.

One of the descending aircraft was heading directly for the helipad.

"Come on," Noburu shouted, already moving. "We've got to let somebody know about—"

The noise was too great. He scrambled toward the passageway that led to the elevator and the stairwell. It would take too long to route a message through the computer with the system locked down. The only hope was the old radio.

It had to work. Tokyo had to be informed.

He turned his head to hurry Kloete and the NCO along. But the roof erupted in a holiday of sparks. One moment he was watching the scrambling forms of the two South Africans. An instant later, their bodies disintegrated as the approaching gunship's Gatling cleared the rooftop helipad.

Noburu threw himself into the deepest corner of the passageway until the drilling noise of the gunnery stopped. He felt as though he had been stung by dozens of wasps. Masonry splinters, he calculated, glad that he could still function. He threw himself into the shelter of the stairwell, just as an enormous black monster settled onto the roof.

"This way," Kozlov shouted. Taylor followed the Russian across the helipad, ducking under the flank rotor of the M-100. The roof was slick with the spread remains of several corpses so badly shot up they were barely recognizable as human.

Meredith moved up past Taylor, weapon at the ready, determinedly shielding the older man. Hank Parker followed, lugging a man-pack radio over his left shoulder and shepherding the young warrant officer who held the magic keys in his briefcase.

A few surviving members of the mob who had been stranded in the courtyard fired up at the spectacle on the roof, but they seemed to be too dazed or shaken to make their efforts tell. Meanwhile, other M-100s settled across the parade ground, their Gatling guns sweeping the living and the dead across their chosen landing zones. American soldiers leapt from the lowering ramps and hatches, their short automatic rifles clearing each fire team's path toward the headquarters building. Protected by lightweight body armor and face shields, here and there an American fell backward, knocked down by the force of a bullet, only to rise from the dead and follow his comrades into the fight.

Taylor scanned the scene just long enough to make sure that the three birds designated for the assault had put down safely. In the low heavens, a last M-100 patrolled above the near streets, now and then issuing a spike of fire that warned the rest of the world to keep away.

There wasn't much time. Even as the raiding force approached Baku, enemy relief columns had been shooting their way into the city from multiple directions. The lone M-100 flying cover shifted its fire from axis to axis in the ultimate economy of force effort, striking the long columns selectively, blocking as many streets as possible with burning combat vehicles. But all of the main guns desperately needed recalibration now and the Gatlings, too, were down to their last reserves of ammunition. Here and there, the combat vehicles from the relief columns snaked their way inevitably into the labyrinth of streets. Worse still, the strategic down-links feeding the M-100's on-board computers showed a fleet of enemy aircraft over the Caspian Sea, flying on an axis whose aim was unmistakable.

Taylor followed the others into a passageway littered with chipped masonry. Kozlov yanked open a steel door and was about to rush headlong into the stairwell. But Meredith caught him, knocking the unarmed man out of the way. Kozlov tripped back against a wall just as Meredith hurled a grenade into the darkness. The S-2 turned and pulled Kozlov to the ground with him.

The explosion rang so loudly from the concrete stairwell that it sounded as though the entire building would collapse.

"Let's go," Taylor shouted.

But, once again, Meredith was quicker. He took the lead, spraying short bursts into the smoke and crunching over litter splintered off the walls. Taylor threw a compact flare past him into the recesses of the stairwell.

No one fired at the light, which was little more than a pale glow in the shroud of smoke left by the grenade. It was very hard to see.

But there was no time to waste.

Standard drill, learned in L.A., perfected in Mexico. Taylor slapped Meredith on the shoulder.

"Go."

Meredith pounded down the stairs, laying down a burst as he made each corner. The bullets punched at the walls, rebounding, making quick spiderwebs of light.

"One flight clear," Meredith shouted.

Taylor turned back to Hank Parker and threw a hand in the direction of Kozlov and Ryder. "Keep those two here until I blow the whistle. Then get down those stairs as fast as you can."

The colonel hustled after Meredith.

"Three floors," Kozlov called after him. "It is three floors of stairs."

Taylor caught up with Meredith, then pushed past him, taking his turn in the two-man drill. Meredith covered him. The smoke bothered Taylor's lungs, and he felt faintly dizzy. He realized that he still had not recovered completely from the futile rescue attempt of the day before. The smoke had eaten into him.

But he kept going, holding his short-barreled automatic rifle tight against his side. He had entirely forgotten the pain in his hand.

Beyond the stairwell, the building echoed with rifle fire and shouts in three distinct languages. On the ground and upper floors, the Japanese defenders were battling the Azeris hand-to-hand, with the Americans slashing in behind, fighting everybody.

But the other American efforts were only distracters. Supporting strikes. Everything depended on getting Ryder down to the computer room before somebody blew the machine apart.

"Clear," Taylor yelled. He crouched against a wall on the next landing. Meredith's boots clambered down the concrete steps, closing on him. The younger officer slapped Taylor's shoulder and moved past him like a shadow. It was the best they could do. An emergency drill. There was no time for a careful, completely thorough clearing operation.

This time Meredith went all the way down the stairs without firing his weapon. The earlier bursts had met with no response. And the bullets had nowhere to go from the bottom of the stairwell except back up toward the firer.

Speed, speed. All risks were justified now.

"Clear to the bottom," Meredith shouted. "I'm at the door."

Taylor pulled a sports whistle from under his blouse, drawing it up by the lanyard. He blew two blasts, then scrambled down toward Meredith. From above, the rest of the party made a terrific racket stumbling down the stairs. Taylor popped another of the disposable mini-lights to guide them. It was hard to believe that the Japanese had not yet alerted to their presence. The fighting out in the corridors had not lost any of its intensity, and Taylor figured that the defenders had their hands full and probably could not do anything even if they were aware of the new threat posed by his ragged team.

He drew up beside Meredith, hacking in the dense smoke. Once, his lungs could have withstood everything. But you got old, did foolish things.

Meredith held the handle of the basement door in his left hand, autorifle ready in his right, poised off his hip. In the chemical glow of the mini-light he looked like a beautiful animal, taut and deadly.

Taylor readied another grenade. The smoke had thinned just enough so that the two men could look each other in the eyes. Both knew that this was it. If the Japanese, or anyone else, were waiting to ambush them, they would have to do it now.

Taylor had already made up his mind. He was going to be the first one through the door this time. If anything happened, Merry would know what to do.

The younger man's eyes were sharp, his nostrils flared.

Kozlov, Parker, and Ryder joined them at the bottom of the stairwell.

"To the left now," Kozlov said. "Three doors down, I think. The operations center is at the end of the hallway. The computer room is the last doorway on the left before you reach the operations center. It's very easy."

Taylor nodded, not at all certain how easy it was going to be. "We'll have to clear the ops center first." He glanced at Parker and Kozlov. "All right. I clear the ops center. Merry covers to the right down the hallway. You two get golden boy into the computer room. Then you relieve Merry. Everybody got it?"

Each man mumbled his assent.

"All right," Taylor said. "Everybody back against the wall." He pointed to where he wanted them. Then he turned to Merry. "Ready?"

Meredith's hand tensed on the door handle.

"Do it," Taylor said.

Meredith ripped open the door. Taylor lobbed the grenade out into the corridor. Then Meredith slammed the door shut again, and both men hunkered down away from the door's swing radius.

The blast tore the door right off its hinges. It popped from its frame and fell at a cant across the stairwell.

Instantly, Taylor hurled himself into the hallway, diving flat to the left and firing burst after burst. Meredith mirrored his actions, rolling to the right and shooting into the smoke.

"Come on," Taylor shouted.

A foreign automatic weapon coughed in the artificial fog. Merry fired again and again, hunting the sudden jewels of light. Taylor rolled over to help him with a burst, then rose and began to run in the direction of the operations center.

So close, he thought, so close. Please, God, no fuck-ups now.

He heard the others hurrying along behind him.

The door at the end of the corridor was shut. Taylor increased the force of his movement and struck it with all his weight, knocking it open. He rolled into a sudden clarity of light, into the coolness of an artificially controlled climate.

Behind him, the others had turned to their own mission of locating the computer room. Taylor was alone. He came up fast from the carpet, rifle ready. Everything happened in parts of seconds. A standing figure fired at him, missed, and Taylor knocked the man back over a bank of consoles with a short burst. Another man raised a pistol, but Taylor was quicker, putting a full burst into him at waist level. Then his rifle's magazine went dry.

Standing almost on the other side of the big room, a Japanese officer held a microphone in one hand and a pistol in the other. His scalp was swathed in loose, bloodstained bandages, giving him the appearance of a renegade sheik. The layout of the room was such that there was no cover between the officer and Taylor, not a single obstacle. The Japanese lowered the microphone and raised his pistol.

Taylor did not try to run. He stared at the man with a lifetime's worth of hatred. His lips curled in a snarl. He kept his eyes locked on those of his opponent, as if staring down an animal. And he methodically ejected his empty magazine and reached into his ammo pouch for another.

The Japanese officer aimed his pistol at arm's length. There was no way he could miss at such a range. Taylor felt the pistol reaching out to him with invisible lines of power, searching into him, testing the softness of his body. But he did not break the stare.

He continued to reload.

He waited. And waited. Growing hideously angry at the Japanese officer's delay, at this teasing. He almost wanted to bark a command at his opponent: Shoot. Goddamn you.

With a chill, Taylor recognized the man under the dirty bandages and bloodstains. It was General Noboru Kabata. The Japanese theater commander.

Why didn't the bastard fire?

The Japanese stared into him with a look that Taylor could not comprehend. The eyes made no sense, the facial expression did not come from Taylor's catalog. Its closest relative was fear. But that was crazy. The Japanese was the one who held the power of life and death between the two of them.

The Japanese general's eyes began to weaken, eyelids twitching. He looked beyond Taylor now, through him, as if he had seen a ghost.

Noboru's pistol began to waver. He thrust it harder in Taylor's direction, as if warning him, trying to frighten him off. Taylor could see the finger straining at the trigger. He could feel it as though the hand were his own.

Their eyes met in a perfect line.

Taylor jammed the fresh magazine into his weapon and put a burst into the Japanese without an instant's hesitation. Noboru twisted, firing his pistol into the carpet at Taylor's feet. The general stepped backward with the disjointed movements of modern dance. Taylor shot him again. And again.

"Fuck you," he told his enemy. "Fuck you, you bastard. Fuck you, fuck you, fuck you."

He was breathing as though he had just run the race of his life. Half sick, clutching his weapon against his side with the desperation of a terrified private, he walked over to where Noboru lay.

The Japanese lay absolutely still, eyes wide. Taylor stopped just short of the body, shaking with old wordless fears. As though Noburu might suddenly spring back to life, reaching for him, biting.

Taylor emptied his weapon into the torso of the corpse, then spit into Noburu's face. He kicked the body in the side, then kicked it again, harder.

"You bastard," he said. "You filthy bastard."

A burst of automatic weapons fire out in the corridor called him back to the present. He reloaded another magazine and took off at a run.

The smoke had partly cleared. He could see Merry lying at the elbow of the hallway, shielding himself behind an overturned file cabinet. As he watched, Meredith sent two shots into the distance.

Taylor scrambled down the corridor to the S-2, covering each doorway as he passed. In the last office, two Japanese lay sprawled before a shredding machine. Another lay just behind Meredith.

A grenade explosion on the upper floor shook the ceiling and sifted dust over them like a curtain of rain.

Taylor tucked himself in behind the corner where Meredith was on guard.

"Need help?" he asked, surprised at the normalcy in his voice.

"Sonofabitch," Meredith said, voice quivering. "I almost missed the sonofabitch."

Taylor noticed that the younger man was bleeding from the neck.

"Merry, you all right?"

"The sonofabitch," Meredith repeated, panting. His breathing was quick, but healthy. The wound was very light, of the sort that misses taking a life by half an inch. "I didn't see the sonofabitch. He came at me from behind. With a goddamned knife."

Taylor glanced at the dead Japanese. There was no knife in his hand, only a scissors. But, in Meredith's mind, it would always be a knife. That was how men remembered combat, part hyperreality and part imagination. That was how they remembered it when they wrote up their reports, which historians would later cite as indisputable eyewitness accounts. Taylor had learned how history was sculpted years before. He knew it could never be fully trusted. Yet he had never stopped reading it. Searching for a truth deeper than his own life could offer.

There was a noise in the hallway behind them. Taylor swung his weapon around. It was Parker. With Kozlov, who was still unarmed.

"Colonel Taylor," Parker called. His voice was agitated. "Sir, the warrant officer needs to see you."

Taylor felt on the verge of illness. What was wrong now?

"What's the matter?" Taylor demanded.

"Nothing," Parker said. Then Taylor noticed that the captain was grinning. As though he had just won a blue ribbon at the county fair. "He just needs you. You're not going to believe this. He wants you to make a decision."

Taylor got up angrily. The plan was clear. The kid, Ryder, had his instructions, and there wasn't a second to waste playing games. The relief columns could shoot their way into the compound at any time. Or some lunatic or fanatic could blow the entire headquarters to hell. Upstairs, the fighting stormed on, with screams and shouts underscored by resounding gunfire.

Taylor tossed his automatic rifle to Kozlov, who caught it awkwardly. "You might need it," Taylor said. "I want you two to take over from Major Meredith. Merry, you come with me."

Taylor did not wait to see his orders carried out. He ran down the hallway in a fury, anxious to see what kind of bullshit Ryder was up to. The mission was as clear as could be.

Taylor burst into the computer room. Ryder jumped, then calmed when he saw who it was. He sat before the central workstation of a large computer. Smiling.

"What the hell's going on here?" Taylor barked.

Ryder ignored his tone of voice, grinning like a fool. "Look at this here, sir," he said. "Just look. It's incredible."

Jesus Christ, Taylor thought. What now? He walked over to the workstation in a rage that the boy was not already putting all of his energy into destroying Japanese combat systems. Ryder gave the appearance of just playing with the great machine.

Taylor wanted to scream at him. But he was not certain that would be the best approach. The important thing, he reminded himself, was to accomplish the mission. Even if one of your key players turned out to be an incompetent nut.

"What's the problem?" Taylor asked, straining to keep his voice calm. Meredith came up beside him.

Ryder looked up brightly. "There's no problem, sir. This is *great*. Just look."

Taylor bent over the computer. But he could not read the arcane symbols of the Japanese computer language.

"All right," he said. "Tell me what it means."

"That column of numbers on the right side?" Ryder said. "See?"

Taylor mumbled. "Yes."

"Those are control nodes for the Japanese space defense system, the what-do-you-call-it? Satsee or something?"

"SAD-C," Taylor corrected automatically. "Okay, so what does it mean?" No sooner had he spoken the words than he began to realize why the warrant officer was so excited.

"Well," Ryder said happily, "we knew the Japanese had programmed all their tactical stuff so it could be ordered to self-destruct. But we never dreamed—"

Taylor put his hand on the younger man's shoulder, anchoring them both to reality.

"You're telling me," Taylor said, "that this computer can order the Japanese *space* defenses to self-destruct? The home islands shield?"

"Well," Ryder said, "they probably won't blow up or anything like that. The self-destruct order will probably just destroy the electronic circuits. The satellites will still be up there and all. They just won't be able to do anything."

Taylor tightened his grip on the boy's shoulder. "Are you absolutely certain? There's no possibility of a mistake?"

Ryder shrugged as though it were really a minor matter.

"No way," he said. "It's clear as day. Just look over here. See, I told the computer I was that Japanese general and—"

Taylor listened. Yes. General Noboru Kabata.

Meredith interrupted. *"Do* it," he begged. "Stick it to the bastards while there's still time. If we take out the space defenses, Japan won't be able to defend itself against shit. It changes everything."

Yes.

It changed everything.

"Is it hard to do?" Taylor asked Ryder.

"Piece of cake," the warrant officer said, as though he had been surprised at the question. "You want me to do it then, sir?"

Taylor listened to the sounds of battle above their heads.

"Absolutely. How long will it take?"

Ryder didn't answer. He began to punch keys. The screen changed, and the warrant officer began to sort his way through a parade of numbers. Heavy footsteps pounded overhead. The fighting intensified again.

While waiting for Ryder to set up the program, Taylor turned to Meredith. The S-2 was putting pressure on his neck with a handkerchief. There was a lot of blood.

"Merry? Are you sure you're all right?"

The intelligence officer nodded heavily. "Just messy. Slash wound. Doesn't even hurt. Christ, I thought my number was up."

"Merry, the general's dead."

The S-2 looked at him.

"General Noboru Kabata," Taylor went on. "I killed him. It was a fluke. The bastard had me cold. And he didn't fire." Taylor shook his head, still unable to understand it. A shiver passed over him at the remembrance. "He had me cold."

"You're sure? You're sure it was him?"

"Yeah. You can report it as a confirmed kill. He's in the ops center, if you want to see. Not very pretty, I'm afraid." Taylor lowered his eyes. "I got carried away. Flashing on Lucky Dave. And Manny."

Meredith lifted the handkerchief from his neck, testing. Taylor tugged at his first aid pack, letting the bandage drop into his hand. "Here. Use this. And where's *your* goddamned aid pack? I ought to give you an Article Fifteen."

"When we get out of this," Meredith said, "you're welcome to give me anything you want, sir."

"I still don't understand it," Taylor said. "All he had to do was pull the damned trigger."

Out in the hallway Parker or Kozlov fired a burst down the corridor. Then another.

Ryder slapped at the keyboard one last time, then swiveled around to face Taylor and Meredith.

"Ready to do it, Chief?" Taylor asked.

"It's already done," Ryder said nonchalantly. "No more Japanese space defenses."

Taylor looked at the warrant officer, unsure whether he was joking or not, unable to quite believe that things could be this easy, after all the years of struggle, of failure, of dreaming of a better day.

"Chief," Meredith said, speaking for Taylor, "this is no joke. Are you absolutely certain the Japanese space defense system has been . . . incapacitated?"

Ryder shrugged. "Unless the computer's lying."

"Jesus," Meredith said.

"All right," Taylor said, businesslike again. He had commanded himself not to think of anything but the matters at hand. History and greater decisions could wait.

There was more shooting out in the hallway.

"Chief," Taylor said urgently, "we've still got to take out the systems in-theater. Can you find the Scramblers?" He almost added that there was no time to waste. But Ryder was doing just fine. In his own little world. Taylor did not want to make him nervous at this point.

The warrant officer was easily the least troubled of the three men in the room. He was an expert, doing what he had been trained to do. If anything, the boy seemed blithely happy.

Ryder's fingers worked over the keyboard as though he were a master pianist playing scales and arpeggios. Taylor, who had worked with computers for so many years, who had even forced himself to study them, despite the fact that his natural interests lay far afield, admired Ryder's confidence and dexterity. Taylor knew enough to understand the complexity of the formulae with which the warrant officer was working, but the boy made it look like the easiest thing on earth.

Such a man could have made a far better living out of uniform. Taylor wondered briefly what story lay behind the warrant officer's boyish features, what had called him so irresistibly to military service. It was one of the wonders of the world that the Army always seemed to come up with the men it needed in a desperate hour.

"Chief?" Taylor said. He could not help interrupting. "Are we going to make it?"

Ryder brushed away the colonel's concern with a slight gesture. His fingers continued to dance over the keys. "The tactical stuff's in a different file. They didn't set this program up to be user friendly. I mean, it's a totally different logic system. And I guess they didn't want every Tom, Dick, and Harry destroying their aircraft and tanks and stuff."

"Chief, if you can only find one thing, find the Scramblers."

Ryder nodded. Then he paid his full attention back to his labors.

Three heavy explosions sounded in the distance. Taylor and Meredith looked at each other.

"Those were outside," Meredith said, putting their mutual knowledge into words.

A moment later, Hank Parker came into the room. His face was grimed and he was no longer smiling.

He held out the pork-chop microphone from the radio slung over his shoulder. "Sir, it's Captain Zwack up in the overwatch bird. The relief columns are all over the city. He can't hold them anymore. His main gun system's gone to shit. He's trying to slow them down with his Gatling gun, but he's almost out of ammunition."

"What's Nowak say?" Taylor asked, referencing the commander of the diversion force fighting in the building overhead and in the courtyard. "How's the situation on the ground?"

"They all say the same thing," Parker answered. "It's a matter of minutes. If that. If we don't get everybody ack up in the air, they'll be able to take us out on the round."

Taylor turned to Ryder. "Come *on*, Chief."

Suddenly, Ryder pushed back from the console. It was gesture of triumph. The boy was grinning, and the screen an from top to bottom with fields of numbers.

"Got them," Ryder cried. "We got them. We're into he program."

"Good work," Taylor said. "Let's take them out and et the hell out of here. Merry, you—"

"No," Ryder wailed. "Oh, shit."

Taylor turned. In the background, Parker's radio cracked with another message from the officer who was flying he rear guard M-100, announcing that he was out of Gating gun ammunition and begging the raiding force on the round to hurry before the enemy vanguard reached them. aylor knew the officer well, a born cavalryman who was n the Army because he loved it, who could have led a life f leisure but chose instead to serve his country in black imes. Taylor also knew that, despite the uselessness of is empty weapons, the officer would remain on-station ntil his comrades joined him in the sky. Taylor knew he vould get the same sort of performance from the hardeaded raid commander slugging it out above their heads r somewhere out in the compound. That officer was an ll-American ethnic Pole with a sense of honor beautifully ut of place in the new century. Every man would remain t his station until the job was done.

Ryder's face had turned pale. He looked up at Taylor vith an expression of helpless loss.

"What's the matter?" Taylor said calmly.

"I . . . I can't tell which system is which," Ryder said. 'I don't have the right key."

"Fuck it. Just destroy them all," Taylor said, beginning o lose his patience.

Ryder shook his head. "Sir . . . the way the program's et up . . . you have to destroy each system individually." Ie half-turned back to the console. A flashing star idenified an alphanumeric. Ryder tapped a key. The alphaumeric disappeared and the blinking star moved down to he next number.

"See?" Ryder said. "All you have to do to destroy something is tap the control key. Right here. But you might be destroying anything. Maybe a tank. Or just a radio set. Or one of the scramblers. I can't tell. But you have to hit the key for every single number. And there are thousands in the data base." Ryder tapped the key again, erasing another number, destroying another unidentified system out on the distant battlefield. "It's going to take a while," he said. And he hit the key again.

More explosions sounded from the world beyond the building. A closer blast shook the ceiling. The overhead lights blinked. But the computer had its own miniaturized power source—it was an independent world.

Ryder shifted his full attention back to the computer, striking the control key again each time the star moved down. It seemed to take two to three seconds to destroy each system. So easy. And yet.

"Give me the microphone," Taylor ordered Parker. "And get Kozlov in here."

Parker handed over the mike. Meredith dashed into the hallway to fetch the Russian.

Taylor had forgotten the day's call signs. He had forgotten everything but the business at hand. "Nowak," he called the ground force commander, "can you hear me?"

He waited. Hoping. And then the familiar voice came heavily over the comms set. "Bravo four-five. Over."

"I want you to disengage. Start pulling out. Get your men loaded up as fast as you can and get into the air. Do it now. Over."

"Wilco. You need help?"

"Negative. Just get in the air. Zwack's out of bullets. Your ships can do us more good in the air now than your men can do on the ground. We're almost done," Taylor lied. "Break. Zwack, you sonofabitch, don't do anything crazy. As soon as Nowak's in the air, I want your ass on the way to Turkey. We're going to exfiltrate individually, and you won't do anybody any good dead. The war's not over yet. You read me?"

"Lima Charlie." It was the voice of a man who had chosen hard service over the safest life money could buy.

"Don't screw around," Taylor said. "Regard my transmission as a lawful order. Out."

Ryder continued to punch the control key, deleting line after line. But his mood of playful competence was long gone.

Meredith brought Kozlov in from the hallway. Taylor tossed the mike back to Parker.

"Want me to cover the hallway again?" Parker asked.

Taylor considered this officer he had only recently gotten to know. They were all so brave, so fine. What a lucky, lucky country to have such men.

"No," Taylor said. "I want everybody to listen to me. Chief, you keep punching that keyboard with your ears open." Taylor looked at the faces. Meredith, so handsome and bright. Kozlov, with his bad teeth and naive honesty. Parker, a little bulldog of a man. And Ryder. Time had begun to collapse for Taylor. Since he and Noburu had looked into each other's eyes, Ryder blurred into another young warrant officer, a boy hardly known, suffering in a wreck in the African grasslands. It was only a moment before that Taylor had raised his pistol, with ants chewing at his hand, to shoot a boy through the forehead. Then he had blinked his eyes and found himself here.

Ryder sat at the computer, while Taylor raised an invisible hand with an invisible pistol.

No. Never again.

Taylor settled his eyes back on Meredith. A tormented boy growing up late in the streets of a diseased city. An earnest lieutenant, standing stiffly before his commander's desk, while outside combat helicopters churned the night air above Los Angeles.

Manny was there too. And Lucky Dave. But they stood apart from Meredith and the rest of the men, forming a distinctly different group. Taylor knew to which group he belonged. He was overdue for membership.

"Merry," Taylor said, "you are now acting force commander. Your mission is to extricate the raiding force and get every ship and every man across the Turkish border. I'm staying."

"*No,*" Meredith said. The word of complaint had none

577

of the pompous formality of duty perceived but unfelt. It was a cry. "No," Meredith repeated. "Sir . . . you're too valuable. *I* can stay."

Taylor briefly closed his eyes and shook his head. "God damnit," he said softly, "you're a soldier, Merry. And soldiers take orders." Outside, the thumping and sputter of battle underlined each word. "There's no more time. And there's no point in all of us . . ."

Meredith set his jaw. His facial expression had grown so serious it almost made Taylor laugh. "I'm staying with you," Meredith said adamantly. "The others can go."

Taylor dropped a hand onto Ryder's shoulder, steadying himself. He could feel the young man trembling. But the warrant's fingers never stopped working the control key.

An enormous blast shook the building. The lights went out and the only illumination in the room was the coc colored glow off the computer monitors. Then the ceiling lights flickered back on.

No one had moved. The officers in the room simply looked at him. Taylor saw his last hopes for any decency in the affair's conclusion slipping away. And he could not bear it.

"*Please,*" he said, offering them the strangest of words. He carefully chose his language to include them all. But his eyes remained on Meredith as he spoke.

"Listen to me," Taylor said. "You're all I have. I have nothing else. No children. No life. You're my children. Don't you understand that?" He stared hard at Meredith. He wanted to take the younger man in his arms, to protect him now and forever. "You're the only sons I'll ever have. And no man wants to watch his sons die." Then he narrowed his focus. "Merry. *Please.* Get out of here. Take them all with you. For Manny and Lucky Dave."

Meredith opened his mouth. His lips formed the word "No." But he never spoke it.

The sounds of battle ruptured something in the building above their heads.

The tiny voice of the radio squawked, barely audible. "*Where are you? Everybody's in the air. Your ship's exposed. Where are you?*"

"Go now," Taylor said. "It's time."

Hurriedly, Taylor reached down inside his tunic to an inner pocket. He drew out a worn cavalry guidon. The tiny flag unrolled from his fingertips. The cloth had grown very thin. The red flash was a faded pink, the white had gone yellow. The numbers were shriveled and bent like old men. He held it out to Meredith.

"There's a woman," Taylor said. "Back in Washington. You'll find her name and address in my gear." He briefly broke eye contact. "It won't mean much to her. If anything at all. But I want her to have it."

Meredith accepted the rag, his fingers briefly grazing Taylor's with a last warmth.

"Get out of here," Taylor said. He could no longer look at any of them. He roughly pulled Ryder from his chair before the computer and took his place. He turned his back to them all.

They left. In a local silence. With the lulls and sudden eruptions of combat shaking the building above their heads. They moved slowly as they exited the room. Then Taylor could hear them running down the corridor, with Meredith shouting at them to *move, move, move*. Taylor smiled. Meredith sounded like a merciless old drill sergeant. Then Taylor lost the sound of them in the clamor of battle.

He pressed the code key. Again and again.

In a little while, he imagined that he heard the sound of an aircraft lifting off. The building trembled. But it might only have been from the increasingly frequent shell impacts.

Taylor chose to believe it was his M-100, taking Meredith and the others home.

The door opened behind his back.

Taylor did not sway. He continued to press the control key at the required cadence. Fighting to the last, as best he knew how.

"Colonel Taylor, sir?"

Taylor whipped around in shock and fury.

It was Kozlov. Cradling an automatic rifle. The staff officer looked awkward and uncomfortable with the killing tool.

"I told you to go," Taylor said coldly. He turned his

attention back to the computer, immeasurably relieve
that he had not found Meredith standing in the doorway

"They're all gone," Kozlov said. "I watched them tak
off. All of your men are safe."

"I told you to go, goddamnit," Taylor said. "You're
soldier. Soldiers obey orders." He pressed the magic ke
again.

"This is *my* fight," Kozlov said to Taylor's back, hi
words competing with the racket of combat. There wasn'
much time now. Not much time at all. "This is *my* country
It's more my fight than yours."

"You're a fool," Taylor said. But his voice was not s
fierce. He wasn't sorry for this bit of company, after al
The selfishness never ends, he told himself.

"And you, too, are a fool," Kozlov said. "We are bot
fools. But sometimes . . . I think it is better to be a fool."

I should say something kind, Taylor thought. Somethin
decent. To reach out to the poor bastard. But he coul
not make the words. There was only the screen and th
key and a lengthening shadow.

"Anyway," Kozlov said, "I will guard you. Perhaps
can make some extra minutes for us."

Taylor's finger punched the wonderful key again. An
again. Hundreds more systems had been destroyed. It wa
impossible to keep count. Perhaps the Scramblers wer
already gone.

I am the destroyer, he said to himself, recalling th
disembodied quote but not its source. Poetry? An India
religious text? It was all the same.

I am the destroyer.

"I am going to the hallway now," Kozlov said. His voic
was almost feminine in its sadness. "Good-bye to yo
Colonel Taylor."

And that was the end. Kozlov never reached the co
ridor. He died in the doorway. A burst of automatic weap
ons fire sounded loud and close. The Russian made a singl
weak sound and dropped to the floor.

Taylor swiveled around in his chair. With one hand h
reached for the deadly fruit hanging from his carrying ha
ness. The other hand remained on the keyboard, tappin
away in the acquired rhythm.

Kozlov lay on the floor, his face pointed away from aylor's field of vision. Above the body, a wiry Japanese ommando stood with his legs spread, weapon at the ready. Ie looked at Taylor, then at the computer. He shouted a ngle word in Japanese.

Taylor drew the pin from the grenade without removing from his harness. In the seconds before it exploded, he ad time to appreciate his opponent, who was young, lean-featured, and obviously well-trained. The com-nando stood helplessly in the doorway, frozen by the inev-ability of the moment. Unable to fire, as long as Taylor at framed by the precious computer. The commando had ie look of a healthy, magnificent animal. Ready to kill, ut restrained by a higher authority. With his dark, hy-eralert eyes and the feel of brutally conditioned muscles eneath the fabric of his uniform, he was a perfect example f what a soldier should be. Taylor pitied him, understand-ig him as well as any man could ever understand another.

Taylor felt wonderfully peaceful as he waited and waited or the grenade to do its work. He even smiled at the ecognition that his opponent's face was, after all, identical) his own, and that it had always been his own face on ie other end of the gun.

25

5 November 2020
morning

"WE'RE NOT GOING TO MAKE IT," KREBS TOL
Meredith. The S-2 sat in Taylor's old seat in the cockpi
watching the frozen landscape scream by. The M-100 w₁
following the terrain as closely as possible on its exfiltratic
route. And the terrain of Armenia was rugged and wild

"You can do it, Flapper," Meredith said. "It's not muɕ
further." And, in truth, it was not far. The Turkish bordₑ
lay just beyond the next line of mountains.

"Major," the old warrant said, "you can kiss my ass aₙ
suck my dick, if it makes you feel good. But we ain't goiₙ
to make it. I done my best. But the sonsofbitches put ₛ
many holes in us you could run the Mississippi River
one side of this ship and out the other. We're falling apaₙ
And we're running on fumes. I can either put her doῳ
now, or we can just wait until we fall out of the sky."

They were so close. Each of the other M-100s in tℎ
raiding force had sent the code word hours before to iₙ
dicate that they had crossed the border into neutral aℹ
space and safety. But the command ship had waited tₒ
long to lift off from the rooftop helipad. Its armored sidₑ
had been battered and pierced. Barely half an hour out
Baku, Krebs had found it necessary to put down in tℎ
hills so that he could try to carry out whatever immediaₜ
repairs were possible. With Meredith trying clumsily

help and the others standing guard with their popguns in the darkness, they had struggled to slap enough mechanical Band-aids on the ship to get her back into the air before dawn brought about their inevitable discovery by the enemy. With the first light sweeping over the barren hills, Krebs had miraculously managed to get the M-100 airborne again. It sounded like a sick old used car. But it flew. And they climbed up above the snow line into high Armenia.

Meredith stared obstinately forward, across the gray and white landscape, as though he could will the ailing machine to continue over these last critical miles. The broken earth beneath them was terra incognita. The situation in Armenia was so chaotic, with so many factions and occupation forces engaged in butchering each other, that a landing would bring completely unpredictable consequences. If the Islamic Union occupation forces got to them first, they would be shot out of hand. If the wrong partisans got them, their fate might be considerably worse.

"*Ma*jor," Krebs cried in exasperation. "Look at the goddamned controls. We're fucked. I've got to land this baby. *Now.*"

Meredith refused to look at the control panel. He stared at the line of white mountains that meant freedom. And life. They had to make it now. For Taylor. So that it would not end as a bad joke after all.

"How far is it?" Meredith asked.

In response, the engines began to choke.

"So much for the decision-making process," Krebs said.

"*Mayday, mayday,*" Meredith shouted, working the radio and intercom simultaneously. "*Prepare for uncontrolled impact.*"

The engines were finished. Krebs struggled with the manual controls, trying to bully the autorotation system to perform at the top of his voice. But the threats didn't help. They were too low for the autorotation to fully activate, and before Meredith could call any further warnings or instructions to the men in the rear compartment, the M-100 began to slice its way through a stand of evergreen trees in a shallow valley.

The machine crashed through the forest, splintering tall

conifers. The armored sides and underbelly screamed as the M-100 scraped through the boughs. The ship bucked madly, tilting over on its side. Meredith could hear the sound of man-made materials wrenching apart in the last instant before the fuselage slammed into the ground, and he thought of Taylor. His wife, his parents—they all deserted him now. Only Taylor remained. With his ruined face and haunted eyes. Taylor wanted him to live.

What was left of the ship ploughed into a snow field amid the trees and came to rest on its side.

To his astonishment, Meredith found that he was still alive. The slash wound on his neck had torn open again from the strain, and his spine and joints felt as though he had made a very bad parachute landing. But his seat harness still held him in place. And he was unmistakably, incredibly, deliciously alive.

"Sonofabitch," Krebs said with spectacular emphasis. "That's it. I've had it. I'm going to retire."

"You all right, Chief?" Meredith asked. He could hear his own voice shaking.

"Sonofabitch," the warrant officer repeated. His voice, too, had begun to tremble.

Meredith moved to try the intercom. But the mike had been torn from his headset in the crash. In any case, all of the electronic systems appeared to be utterly inert.

He tested his limbs, then carefully undid his safety harness, lowering himself until his feet caught the edge of the copilot's seat. The M-100 had settled almost perfectly at ninety degrees, its right wing and rotor torn away. Awkward and stiff, Meredith clambered back through the passageway that led to the ops compartment, crawling in a sideward world, under the surreal glow of the emergency lights.

Parker and Ryder were both bloody and unconscious. The ops-and-intel NCO was awake but dazed, the lower half of his face covered in blood. At the sight of Meredith, the NCO's eyes gave a flicker of recognition, but he immediately sank back into himself.

Parker was in the worst shape. The seats in the ops cell had safety belts, but the overall ergonomics were not nearly as well developed as the cockpit seats. Parker's chair had ripped free of its pedestal, throwing him forward. His arm was badly twisted and there was blood seeping through his uniform sleeve where an unnatural jut against the cloth announced a compound fracture. His face was misshapen on one side, and it appeared as though both the jaw and cheekbone might have been broken. Parker snored blood out of his nose and mouth.

Ryder came to. The young warrant officer was bruised and stiff, but far luckier than the others. Hardly a minute after waking, he was moving tentatively about the cabin, trying to assist Meredith.

"What happened?" Ryder asked.

"We crashed."

Ryder thought for a moment. It was evident that his head was not yet completely clear. "We in Turkey?"

"No. Somewhere in Armenia. Indian country."

"Oh." The younger man thought for a moment. "So what do we do now?"

Parker groaned. Meredith had repositioned him for maximum comfort. But he had not yet managed to scavenge material for a splint. Shock, too, might be a problem.

Parker groaned again. It was the noise of a man waking after an ungodly drunk.

"First," Meredith said, "we zero out all of the electronics. Then we collect whatever we can carry and use. Then we rig the grenades in here and in the cockpit. Then we start walking."

Krebs slipped into the compartment from the canted passageway. His face looked deadly serious.

"Major," he said, "we got company."

Working frantically, the men wiped out the codes on the electronics that had not been destroyed in the crash. Krebs rigged a splint for Parker's arm with the same casual dexterity he displayed working on an engine or a control panel. Parker had an ever greater perception of the pain he was undergoing, and he bobbed just above and below the surface of consciousness. Working together, Meredith, Krebs, Ryder, and the NCO, who had largely regained his senses, carefully lowered Parker out into the snow.

Parker came up from his dreams just long enough to say:

"You can leave me, guys. Don't let me hold you up. You can leave me."

And he swooned back into his pain.

Their visitors could not see them at the rear of the M-100. Only the machine's snout and cockpit protruded from the treeline, and the dense evergreens offered good concealment with their impenetrable blankets of snow. But every man waited for the sound of movement in the deep snow. Or of gunfire.

Krebs had spotted the first intruders through the windscreen: men in ragtag winter clothing, but heavily armed. In the moments before he crawled back to inform Meredith, the old warrant had watched the entire visible rim of the little valley fill with armed men.

It was very cold outside of the shelter of the M-100.

"They make any gestures?" Meredith asked. "Did it seem like they were looking for trouble?"

Krebs threw him a bitter laugh. "I'm not sure we're in a position to be much trouble to *them,*" he said. "Anyway, they were just standing there. Probably trying to figure out who the dumb shits were who just crashed their asses out in the middle of nowhere."

Meredith nodded. "I'm going to blow the cockpit and the ops cabin."

Krebs shook his head, as if in sorrow.

"Won't they, like, think it's a hostile act or something?" Ryder asked.

Meredith answered him as honestly as he could. "Probably. But we don't have any choice. This baby's loaded with top secret gear." He shivered with the sharp mountain cold. "All I can do at this point is toss in a couple of grenades. Before these characters, whoever they are, start closing in. It may not do a hell of a lot of good. But we've got to do everything we can to make it hard for the enemy's technical intelligence boys."

Krebs raised his head sharply.

Meredith followed the turn of the old warrant's attention.

"You hear something, Flapper?"

"I don't know," Krebs whispered.

Parker moaned.

"What the hell," Meredith said. And he pulled himself back up into the belly of the M-100. "Get your asses over behind those fallen trees," he ordered. And his boots disappeared.

He had to stand on a monitor worth several million dollars to reach the compartment where the extra ammunition was stored. Despite the fact that he was about to do his best to blow the furnishings of the cabin to hell, he still felt awkward planting his boots on the state-of-the-art equipment.

Boxes of ammunition came crashing down, starting his work for him. He had to duck out of the way.

He retrieved the box of high explosive grenades from the fallen clutter, ripping open the top of what resembled a very special egg carton. He filled the blousy lower pockets of his tunic.

He didn't waste any time. Popping his head into the cockpit, he could just make out the line of armed men up on the valley's rim. There were hundreds of them now. Standing in a dark, still line.

He primed two grenades, tossed them at the control panel and scrambled back to the ops cell, banging his knees and elbows without caring a damn. He just managed to slam shut the compartment door when the twin blasts blew it open again. But the door had absorbed most of the force, and except for a huge ringing in his ears, Meredith was untouched.

Smoke.

Meredith scrambled out through the hatch. As soon as his boots hit the snow, he primed three grenades in succession, lobbing them forward into the ops compartment. Then he flattened himself on the ground along the armored side of the M-100.

The machine's belly shook and groaned under the blasts. But the armor and insulation contained the power. The design was so good that there were not even any secondary explosions from the stored ammunition. The machine had been far more reliable than its human masters. And that, Meredith figured, was that.

He hustled over to the remainder of the crew. Krebs and the NCO were rigging a litter for Parker, stripping down branches the M-100 had sheared off during its crash. Ryder knelt behind a fluff of evergreen boughs, on guard.

Krebs looked up. "I don't figure those guys just went away, by any chance?"

Meredith shook his head.

"Why don't they come for us?" Ryder asked nervously. "Why don't they make a move?"

Meredith did not know. They had crossed into a world where the best analysts found their knowledge to be spotty. Behavior and allegiances did not fit the sensible, predictable patterns that gave bureaucrats a chance to get their forecasts right. There were countless armed factions in Armenia, representing indigenous nationalists, occupiers, sectarian Moslems, obscure irredentists, and splinter groups more closely aligned with a particular family or valley than with any coherent platform. The only thing of which Meredith was reasonably certain was that the men who lined the valley's rim were not Islamic Union forces, since they would have been in uniform.

What would Taylor have done in such a situation? Meredith wondered. Would the old man have made one last valiant stand? That sounded like the obvious thing, but Meredith didn't really think so. Taylor always found a way out of spots like this—really, this was minor stuff, by the old man's standards. He remembered Taylor in Mexico, bluffing his way through situations where the odds were impossibly against him.

"I'm going out there," Meredith said suddenly. "I'm going to try to talk to them. There's a good chance they speak some Russian."

Krebs looked at him sadly, without any of his usual "grizzled old warrant" banter. The NCO simply carried on with the construction of the litter. And Parker's eye wandered ineffectually from one man to the other, propelled by misery.

Unexpectedly, Ryder spoke up. "I'll go with you, sir. You shouldn't go out there alone."

"It isn't necessary," Meredith said.

"I *want* to go," Ryder said adamantly. But he looked frightened.

Meredith shrugged. It was an hour for every man to make his own decisions. Anyway, it might be better to have a white face out there beside his own. There was no telling how these partisans or whatever they were might react.

Suddenly Parker arched from the bed of evergreen boughs where his comrades had laid him while they prepared the litter. There were beads of sweat on his forehead, and his eyes looked through Meredith.

"Get the colonel, get the colonel," he cried. "We've got to go back for the colonel."

Krebs gently pressed the captain back down on his green bed.

"It's all right," the old warrant said. "The colonel's just fine, don't you worry." The old soldier's voice managed a tenderness Meredith could hardly credit. "Don't you worry," he repeated. "The colonel can take care of himself." Meredith noticed that Krebs's eyes were glistening. "You just lay down and keep still now. The colonel said he wants you to keep still."

"No time like the present," Meredith said. He dropped his pistol belt in the snow and emptied the last grenades from his pocket. He left his rifle where Krebs had propped it against a tree trunk.

He began to trudge up through the trees.

Ryder followed, jogging through the snow with his knees high like an old-fashioned runner.

It was very beautiful to Meredith in the little strip of forest. The boughs were heavy and white, and as he moved away from the wreckage of the M-100 the world seemed a pure, clear place. It was not a bad place to finish up, if it came to that. Far better than many of the other places where he had spent time.

And he had the satisfaction of knowing that he had done good work. The strategic communications set had been on the blink, for some reason, but he had been able to relay the results of their mission by conventional means—including the brilliant surprise about the Japanese homeland space shield. If he had to die, he was going to die in a world he had already changed for the better. His nation and his people would prosper.

He thought of his wife, suddenly and luxuriously. He owed her so many debts on promises unkept. Hard to be a soldier's wife. Maureen. But she would get over him. She was a handsome, handsome woman, still young and so full of life that life would not be able to resist her. He was sorry that he would not hold her again, sorry that he had not done better by her.

"Sir," Ryder called after him, panting heavily at the burden of climbing up through the snow. "Maybe we ought to call out or something. To let them know we're coming. In case they're jumpy or something."

Yes. The kid was right.

Meredith began to whistle. Then he smiled, and it bothered the whistling, so he forcibly tightened his lips. Taylor would appreciate it, he thought. Proudly. And he marched up toward his fate, whistling "Garry Owen" and remembering the guidon in his pocket.

The trees came to an abrupt end. Up across a smooth low slope of the sort richer cultures used to teach their children to ski, a skirmish line of armed men stood silhouetted against the winter sky. The valley was very small, a matter of just a few contour lines on a map. The sort of place easily overlooked during a planning session, or perhaps noticed, then rapidly forgotten. Its only distinguishing feature was transient—the hundred or so armed warriors standing slightly hunched against the wind, many of them bearded, all of them with the hard look of men who had been fighting for a long, long time.

Meredith stopped whistling. He continued to walk up the slope until he was within easy calling distance of the line of men. The guerrillas watched without a trace of emotion.

When Meredith sensed that the distance was right, he stopped. Ryder's footsteps came to a crunching halt in the snow beside him. Cold wind rinsed down the slope.

As good a time and place as any.

"Hello," he called out in Russian. "We're service members in—"

Dozens of the men raised their weapons in unison.

"*Don't shoot,*" Ryder shouted in English. "*Don't shoot.*"

A man in a black kid hat barked an order, and the men lowered their weapons partway. Obviously a leader, he stepped forward, his bearing proud, and came a little way down the slope toward Meredith and Ryder. Another man followed, and Meredith pegged that one as a bodyguard.

The two guerrillas halted about ten yards up the slope from Meredith and Ryder. The bodyguard's trigger finger poked naked through a woolen glove, tickling the old Kalashnikov automatic rifle in his hands.

"Who *are* you guys?" the leader asked in the English of a stumped cab driver.

Meredith was so surprised that Ryder had to answer for him.

"We're Americans. From the United States Army," the warrant officer said. "Who are you?"

The guerrilla leader drew himself up to his full height.

"We are members of the Armenian Christian Liberation Front," he declared. Then he smiled broadly, revealing strong white teeth in the frame of his black beard. "Hey, maybe you know my Uncle Abel in Chicago?"

Epilogue

New Year's Day, 2021

CLIFTON REYNARD BOUQUETTE SAT ON THE EDGE OF the bed in his boxer shorts. Behind him, the woman breathed regularly and deeply, with her plain face half-buried in the pillow. She had had too much to drink, and he could smell the decaying alcohol in her body. He did not find it offensive. Had she stopped drinking at a reasonable hour, she would not have allowed him back into her bed.

The draperies were closed, but enough light filtered through to give the air the color of gray flannel. He listened to the rain. He did not need to look outside to register the appearance of the world. Northern Virginia was drearily predictable on a wet winter morning. Anyway, he did not want to admit that the morning had come. Traditionally, New Year's Day was a time of family parties with old friends, with the morning reserved for taking stock of his achievements in the year past and his prospects for the year ahead. While the rest of the family slept, he would drink black coffee with a side of cognac in his study and treat himself to a triumphal mental procession featuring Clifton Reynard Bouquette of Newport and Georgetown. But this year there would be no victory parade, and he simply wanted the morning to be over. Much better to have slept through it. Only the old trouble in his kidneys had roused him from his hiding place in the woman's bed.

It had ended as a very bad year. Against all odds, Maddox had won the election, riding the triumph of American arms abroad. And the cracker in the overly tailored suit had demoted him. Had he been fired, the situation would have been bearable. It might have been represented as the result of an important policy disagreement. In Washington important men were fired all the time. But he had not been deemed of sufficient importance to fire. Maddox had simply condemned him to a smaller office and fewer perks.

Then that little bitch from Smith had given him a Christmas present. She had come down from school with his daughter for a holiday visit, and Bouquette had merely made a few suggestions to her of the sort that had often brought a fair return in the past. The little tart had passed on the details to his daughter, who in turn shared them with her mother. Bouquette's wife had filed for divorce the day after Christmas.

Money wasn't a problem, of course. Thank God for that. But money was not really an important consideration to him, since he had always had plenty and knew he would always have enough. What mattered was the respect of men and the admiration—preferably active—of women. But he was under a cloud, both up on the Hill and between the sheets. Oh, the trend had been noticeable for some time. But he had refused to admit it. When his wife filed the papers, he had smiled, poured himself a drink, and picked up the phone. He had left messages on a vast archipelago of answering machines. But the plain, drunken girl in bed beside him was the only one who had bothered to return his call.

He had not seen her for over a month. She had quit her job at the Agency, against all logic. She was unemployed, and she drank. It couldn't go on, of course. One could not live within a reasonable commute of the District without a decent job. For a girl from her class background, the position would be financially untenable. He could help her out a bit there, of course, but he did not think he would. A part of him wished she would move to distant parts without leaving a forwarding address.

The woman moaned, as though all the alcohol was hurting her at last. She rolled to the side and the bedclothes tightened under Bouquette's shorts. In her drunken vigor she had torn at his back and called him "George." The slip had rather spoiled things.

She was inconsolable. It wounded him deeply. Perhaps he was not all that he once had been—his hair was thinning just a bit, though the effect was not undistinguished. But while his stamina had diminished ever so slightly, he believed he made up for it in art. He was rich and accomplished. He could offer a woman everything she might reasonably desire. He could not begin to fathom how the woman had talked herself into the notion of loving a man with whom no discriminating female would be seen in public.

No. He was being dishonest. He rested uncertain hands on his horseman's thighs. The woman had genuinely loved. She had loved with a depth of feeling that shamed Bouquette, for he recognized that he had never inspired such uncalculated love in another, not even in his wife, when they had both been young and utterly perfect. His loss would not have shaken the life of anyone the way her lover's death had broken this woman. He wondered what magic his competitor could have possessed. Bouquette had known something of a genius for bedding the right girls, and not a few deliciously wrong ones. Yet he had never filled another's life so fully that his loss would have left such distress in its wake. Certainly, he had left regiments of women in tears—but their expressions of grief, by and large, had been matters of style. He had made love to many, but he had reached no one as that shabby colonel had managed to reach this woman. He wondered how it was done.

Then again, it might be nothing but affectation on her part. He had been deceived before. After all, she had not bothered to attend the memorial service at Arlington, and when he tried to pass her a few off-the-record details that had not appeared in the media, she cut him off sharply. Perhaps no one loved with such literary perfection, after all. Except for the emotionally unbalanced, of course.

Bouquette stood up, rising gently so that he would not wake the woman. She began to snore. He stepped over the litter of their clothing and went back into the bathroom, turning on the light to examine his face in the mirror, trying to understand how things had managed to turn out so badly.

Lieutenant Colonel Meredith sat beside the hospital bed, listening to the hideously cheerful music piped into the ward. This was one of several wards in the Veteran's Administration hospital serving the victims of the Scramblers and, during the day, radio programs, recorded books, and the General Accounting Office's notion of appropriate music sounded nonstop over cheap speakers. The men in the beds remained as helpless as infants. They could not keep their eyes on a television screen. But they could hear, and preliminary studies indicated that they could process audible information as well as any healthy man. They simply could not act on it.

Meredith recognized many of the faces in the ward, and he had made a brief stop at each bed, offering the men the encouragement he had struggled to assemble during his drive to the hospital. Then he settled into the gray chair beside Heifetz, scooting it around so that he could look at the expressionless mask of the man's features. Christmas decorations drooped above Heifetz's bed, and a string of garland framed the little plaque of medals that hung over the headboard. Meredith had been on the verge of pointing out to the duty nurse that Christmas decorations were not quite appropriate in Heifetz's case, but the woman looked exhausted, and she had not stopped moving since Meredith entered the ward. It was a bad day to be on duty, and a very bad ward.

Meredith would have liked the hospital to be cleaner. He would have liked the treatment of his comrades, and especially of Heifetz, to be a bit handsomer, and he would have liked the hung-over clerk at the information desk to show a little more respect when giving directions. But, most of all, he would have liked an excuse not to come. He already knew he would avoid coming back for as long as his conscience would let him.

The odd thing was that Heifetz looked younger, less troubled. When they had served together, the operations officer's features had been permanently clenched, the eyes lined with tension and the chin set hard. Now Lucky Dave appeared beatifically calm. The tufts of flesh were smooth around the wandering eyes, and the mouth lay partway open in a mock smile.

Meredith reached for words. It had been hard enough with the succession of passingly familiar faces on the other pillows in the ward. But what could you say to Lucky Dave?

"I'm a lieutenant colonel now," Meredith began. "Just like you, goddamnit. Presidential promotion too." He tried to call up a manly smile. "Hell, just about everybody got one. The chief of personnel went through the roof. He said there hadn't been so many presidential promotions since the Civil War. So I'm a lieutenant colonel now. And I'll be damned if I'm going to call you 'sir.' Unless you want to get up out of that bed and whip my ass."

Meredith stared at the uninterested planes of his comrade's face. Wondering how much Heifetz could really hear and understand. The doctors said it might be a hundred percent. But the face remained that of an infant who grasped nothing.

"You know," Meredith went on, "the old man's in for a posthumous Medal of Honor. He's going to get it too. Just takes Congress a while to go through the formalities. They're already getting together a display about him out at the Cavalry Museum at Riley. You're going to be in it, and Manny. All of us. But mostly the old man."

Meredith looked at the living death of Heifetz's eyes, then looked away. "You remember that old rag of a guidon he used to carry? The one he brought out of Africa? I passed it on to them for the museum. They're going to put it with his Medal of Honor, when that goes through." Meredith let his eyes wander over the blanket, the bedframe, the floor. "The old man didn't have any family. No wife or anything. So I'm making sure that all his effects go to the museum, where they belong. Where he'll be remembered properly." He suddenly looked up, hoping Heifetz would offer some sign of agreement. "With nothing that could have embarrassed him."

Meredith realigned himself in the chair and smiled. "Those sonsofbitches," he said. "You know how they get all hepped up on appearances. They're going to use a picture of the old man from back when he was a captain. Before his face got screwed up. But . . . what can you do?"

To his surprise, Meredith took Heifetz's hand. It was soft and warm, yet utterly without human character. The fingers gave way as Meredith pressured them.

Meredith's smile widened into a terrible grin. "And that sonofabitch Reno. He's got the regiment now. Got his colonelcy out of the operation. Under the hand of the President, and all that. Of course, he's all sweetness and light for the press. He and the old man were best buddies, to hear him tell it. But the first duty day we had back at Riley, he assembles everybody in the post theater. And he comes out on the stage like a little Patton. And you know what the first words are out of his mouth, Dave? He puffs himself all up and says, 'We're going to make some big changes around here, men.' He told me to my face he intends to reshape the regiment in his own image." Meredith laughed. "The chairman of the Joint Chiefs loves him.

"Then the goddamned Russians. They sold us out, Dave. Plain as day. But nobody wants to hear that now. The war's over. And the Russians are our best buddies."

Meredith tightened his grip on his comrade's hand. He wanted a response. Anything.

"I'm bailing out," he said. "You know how the old man was. He would have told me to stay in the regiment and tough it out, to do what I could to control the damage Reno does. But I just can't, Dave. I know you understand. The old man just expected too much sometimes." The hand seemed to cower under Meredith's grip. He suddenly relaxed the pressure, afraid he was hurting Heifetz. But there was no response. It was all in his own head. "Anyway, I'm leaving the Seventh. Tucker Williams is going down to Huachuca with a mandate to try to clean up the intel school, and I'm going to be his XO. Who knows?

Maybe we'll get it right this time. If they don't close the place down again. Christ, the peace treaty hasn't even been signed, and Congress is already looking for big cuts in the defense budget."

Meredith released the other man's hand altogether. Down the ward one of the patients made a violent gargling noise, then his body began to contort like a fish tossed onto a boat deck. The duty nurse darted from behind her medicine trolley and manhandled the patient over onto his belly, burping him as if he were a baby.

"Dave? I've got to go. I've got a hell of a drive ahead of me, and I'm on a tight schedule. Tucker Williams wanted me out there yesterday. You know how it is. I want to make Knoxville tonight."

Meredith stood up. He had imagined that something dramatic might happen, that Heifetz might begin to weep or to otherwise acknowledge his presence. But the eyes just continued to flick haphazardly from right to left, up and down, and the mouth hung slackly, poised forever on the verge of speech. It was hard to believe that Heifetz understood a word.

The tinny loudspeaker broadcast a pop song about the joy of being in love.

"I've left Maureen, you know," Meredith said suddenly. "I can't explain it. I just couldn't go back." He smiled down at Heifetz. "You know, the old man was plain fucking crazy sometimes. I remember, oh, it was years ago now, the old bastard gave me a copy of *Huckleberry Finn* and told me to read it. He said it was his favorite book. I never could quite see myself in the Nigger Jim role. But I don't think that's what the old man had in mind. Anyhow, I feel a little like Huck at the end of the book. Only in a really shitty grown-up sort of way." He sat back down and hung his head. He began to cry.

"I don't know what to do, Dave," he said. "I just don't know what to do."

Snow was falling in Moscow, and Valya told herself she really had to get dressed and go to the park. It would be beautiful for a little while. But she made no move to rise from the couch. On the television, a silver-haired man read an economic report.

The Americans were gone. She had been reinstated in her teaching post, and the other members of the faculty simply pretended nothing had happened. She heard nothing further from the state security officers since the departure of the Americans. But she still imagined that they were out there, watching her.

She had gone out a few times with Tanya, and once with Naritsky. But it had not been satisfactory. For the past week, she had taken to declining all invitations, and when she was not teaching or standing in line for foodstuffs, she stayed in her apartment. She considered getting a cat, but she did not much like the idea of trying to housebreak it.

She looked into the future and saw nothing. She looked into the mirror and felt cold breath on the back of her neck. And she had not had her period since November. Soon she would have to go back to the clinic. She had flirted briefly with the idea of having this baby, but the notion lost its appeal the moment she began to consider the practicalities involved. Really, she would be far better off with a cat. And she did not want to lose her figure. While there was still any hope at all.

They did not need to put her in prison. She was already a prisoner in her life, her city, her country. She glanced from the television screen to the window again. The snow continued to fall as the day waned. For a while it would be beautiful in the park. Then the crowd would make it dirty again.

The doorbell rang. Valya surveyed the wreckage of her room in distress. She decided that she really needed to develop more regular cleaning habits. Then she shrugged and rose from her nest on the sofa. It was probably only Tanya, after all.

Running a comb of fingers through her hair, she opened the door. It took her a moment to recognize the man. There were so many men in the world. After a few awkward seconds, the quality of his clothing spurred her memory. It was the American who had bought her dinner, the pleasant-enough boy with whom she had shared a single night. He stood before her now with flowers and a brightly wrapped package in his hands, and he looked nervously happy. He held out the flowers and began his stammering speech.

"Valya," Ryder said, "will you marry me?"

Garmisch, West Germany
4 April 1990

Author's Note

This is a book about nightmares. Its central theme plays on an enduring Russian nightmare. Although the Soviet Union's short-term problems will arise primarily west of the Ural Mountains, the enduring vision of racial and religious apocalypse scorching inward from the south and east haunts the Russian mind. The plot embraces extremes, as fiction demands. A likelier scenario would describe decades of intermittent unrest, often grim enough in local consequence, but with the anger of the common man never sufficiently well organized to weld very different ethnic groups into a militant union. As a Soviet analyst, were I forced to predict the future of Soviet Central Asia, I would describe it as locally unstable, sporadically fanatical and spotted with blood, blighted by disease and economic malaise—and generally far too dull to attract more than a passing glance from the Western news media. We shall hear of occasional massacres, but far less of the hot, dreary, and limited life of the average man or woman. In short, I expect central Asia to be pretty much the same as it has been for countless centuries.

The Russians, like the Mongols, Persians, and the shadowy conquerors who preceded them, will eventually fade into the heat and dust. They will leave their traces, but they will leave. Will it be a matter of years, of decades, of a century? The clocks in Samarkand betray less anxiety than do the digital marvels of Washington—or the timepieces of Moscow, which forever seem to be rushing toward midnight.

Driven by Aristotle and an unquenchable thirst for blood, Alexander the Great crossed the Oxus—today's

Amu Darya. And what did he leave behind? Legends and sand. These poisoned deserts swallow history.

But what about the issue of Islamic fundamentalism?

I admire the perfect accuracy of Levi-Strauss's description of Islam as a "barracks religion," and I take a far less complacent view of Islamic fundamentalism than do colleagues for whom the *only* story of our time is the twilight of the Soviet Union. Nonetheless, I see the future of these varied peoples united by a common name for God as condemned to eternal mediocrity. Islamic fundamentalism is an exclusively negative phenomenon. Even more so than its Christian counterpart, it is a struggle against history, a nasty rear-guard action against time and the hard material logic that will always dominate mankind and our crippled world. The ferocious Iranian attacks upon the Great Satan America, for instance, are merely manifestations of the collective Persian inability to cope with modernity. God becomes an excuse for personal and national failure.

Only outside enemies, real or imagined, allow the Islamic world to display the odd, fleeting semblance of unity. The destruction of Israel in a nuclear exchange, for example, would be less likely to trigger Islamic unity than to utterly dissolve it. Unable to direct their frustrations at the Zionist devil, the Islamic nations of the Eurasian landmass would quickly rediscover the holy and delectable mission of slaughtering each other over trivia. Islamic fundamentalism does not offer hope for the future—it simply serves up excuses for regional impotence.

And what of the Russians themselves in this book? Several of the subplots are obviously metaphors for the Soviet Union today. Valya need not wait thirty years for her dose of misery. Her life describes the Soviet Union now. To me the Soviet Union is a land without hope. The only question of relevance to us is this: Will the USSR continue to muddle through, losing a restive republic here and there yet somehow groaning onward, or will the processes of decline and violent confrontation continue to accelerate, ultimately threatening healthier nations beyond the Soviet borders? I see no prospect whatsoever of a Soviet renaissance. Even if all the citizens of the USSR could miraculously begin to pull together and work very, very hard in spirit of sacrifice, they would, at best, take one halting step forward—while the state's relative decline would continue to accelerate as the United States and New Europe took three or four steps forward and Japan took five in the same time frame.

There is no hope. There will be no vast, prosperous market for Western goods in Greater Muscovy in my lifetime. For the short term, there may be no shortage of good-hearted believers and inept bankers in the West (the same people who brought us the cancer of Third World debt), but, in the longer term, I envision only a landscape of failure, indigence, and misery. The Russians are a doomed people. We must be careful not to let them know.

The Soviet Union needs a new revolution, but it is unlikely to come. The people are too weary. They are good only for short, brutal outbursts. Should some constellation of events trigger a revolution after all, it will be neither kind nor gentle. And, despite the exaggerated Soviet promises on disarmament, they still have many, many nuclear weapons littered throughout a land that is proving impossible to control, if only because of its sheer size.

The vastness that saved "Russia" time and again haunts her now. To become healthy and competitive, the USSR would need, among other things, a network of new roads, rail lines, and telecommunications on a scale so enormous that the United States, Japan, and Western Europe, pooling all of their assets, could not afford to construct it. Stir in a host of ecological problems that are already poisoning the last good earth and destroying the population's health, and the prospects are grim, indeed.

And yet, the Soviet Union continues to attract me like a magnet. Perhaps that has more to do with *my* nightmares.

Regarding the Japanese themes in the book, they are, obviously, take-offs on a current American nightmare. Again, I chose to exploit extremes for the purpose of metaphor. I do not envision Japan as ever again mounting a direct military challenge to the United States. It isn't necessary. The modalities of warfare have expanded, bringing economic combat increasingly to the fore: We *are* presently at war with Japan, and we have been for decades. But the formalities of warfare are also changing. Such wars not only do not require a conscious national decision and declaration, they do not even require general awareness on the part of the citizenry. I would never suggest that every Japanese businessman is party to a secret compact drawn up twenty or thirty years ago to economically defeat the United States. But I would suggest that the average Japanese executive is, however inarticulately, more deeply aware of the seriousness of the struggle.

Just another case of trendy Japan-bashing? I hope not. In any case, I find General Noboru Kabata to be far and away the most sympathetic character in the book.

The all-American theme in this book is military unpreparedness. Clearly, as an Army officer and true believer in the historical role of the United States, I am unabashedly biased. As a student of history, I cannot help feeling deep concern over the popular and legislative conviction that, with the Soviet Union in crisis, the Armed Forces of the United States can be reduced to a size that is barely ceremonial. Significant cuts *can* be made in our arsenal, but we must struggle against the American tendency to overdo everything, to view the world as black or white, either/or. Yes, the Soviet conventional threat has been reduced. But the world remains a brutal, hostile, and jealous place. We must maintain our standing military forces at a level that will allow us to avoid the sort of tragic sacrifices we were forced to make at the beginning of our wars, from 1812 on down to the great wars of this century, when our starved military establishments struggled desperately to buy time and green citizen-soldiers were thrown into battle unprepared. If we cannot afford the military the generals demand, we should nonetheless demand the best military we can afford. To make judicious cuts in our military at the present time makes economic, social, and political sense. Wanton cuts are just plain dumb.

Finally, a note on the subtheme of "Runciman's disease." I have long been fascinated by epidemiology. Had I been a man of profound courage, I might have become a doctor. Possessed of lesser bravery, I became a soldier. I am interested in the influence of disease on history, whether it be the effect of the Black Death on economic systems, or of stomach cancer, hepatitis, and parasites on the political consciousness of the residents of the Soviet territories surrounding the Aral Sea. Spurred by the phenomenon of AIDS—a disease which has had a far greater impact on social consciousness than on mortality figures in the United States—I tried to imagine what effect a really virulent and contagious disease might have today. On one hand, our level of medical care in the First World is stunningly good; on the other, the world has acquired a new porousness, thanks to technology. A disease that once took a decade to two to creep from China to the English Channel can now make the trip in a day. We have a host of new vectors. After all, it was not really homosexuality or fouled syringes that delivered AIDS to the wealthy West— it was the airplane.

This is a shamelessly American book. We are the good guys on its pages as surely as I believe we are the good guys in "real life." When this novel reaches publication, I will have lived and served abroad for almost a decade in total. Instead of becoming more worldly, I find that I only become more convinced that the United States of America is mankind's most perfect creation to date. Certainly, we Americans are not without our flaws. We have, at times, been mortally foolish. But it is only thanks to us that even a small part of the world may live peacefully and decently today. There has never been a victor more benevolent, nor an ally so generous. Our errors were committed with the best of intentions, and our sacrifices redeemed the grimmest century in the history of mankind. I can only hope that my writing, for all of its many, many failings, serves my country well.

—Ralph Peters

About the Author

RALPH PETERS is a U.S. Army Foreign Area Officer specializing in the Soviet Union and Eastern Europe—where he has traveled widely and speaks a variety of local languages. He is the author of two previous novels—*Bravo Romeo* and the *New York Times* bestseller *Red Army*.

$$\begin{array}{r} 3427.40 \\ 255.00 \\ \hline 172.40 \\ 255.00 \\ \hline 4\ 27.40 \end{array}$$